Tessa [...] editor and journa [...] many successful novels, among [...] four-part Craigallan saga (*A Sower Went Forth**, *The Stony Places**, *Harvest of Thorns** and *The Good Ground*) the Champagne trilogy (*The Wine Widow, The Champagne Girls* and *The Last Heiress*) and the Corvill Weaving saga (*A Web of Dreams**, *Broken Threads** and *The Final Pattern**), *A Professional Woman** and *Gleam of Gold**. She lives in south-west London.

* available from Headline

Praise for previous novels:

'Powerfully plotted and well-written'
Daily Mirror

'Takes up where Cookson left off'
Glasgow Herald

'Lots of intriguing detail' *The Sunday Times*

'Filled with fascinating historical detail and teeming with human passions' Marie Joseph

'Tessa Barclay always spins a fine yarn'
Wendy Craig

A Hidden Beauty

Tessa Barclay

HEADLINE

First published in 1993
by HEADLINE BOOK PUBLISHING

First published in paperback in 1993
by HEADLINE BOOK PUBLISHING

10   9   8   7   6   5   4   3   2   1

ISBN 0 7472 4172 4

Typeset by Avon Dataset Ltd, Bidford-on-Avon

Printed and bound in Great Britain by
HarperCollins Manufacturing, Glasgow

HEADLINE BOOK PUBLISHING
A division of Hodder Headline PLC
Headline House
79 Great Titchfield Street
London W1P 7FN

A Hidden Beauty

Chapter One

The restaurant staff always sat down to their own meal in the kitchens after they'd cleared up the lunchtime debris and set up for afternoon teas. Kitchen lunch was regarded as part of their wages – the phrase 'Meals supplied' was an important inducement to take a tiring and often troublesome job as a waitress.

Corie Duggan hurried through her meat-and-mostly-vegetable hotpot so as to get out to the phone box at the foot of St James's Street.

'Corie!' cried her mother when they were connected. 'What makes you ring up at this time of the day?' Then immediately, 'Heard of an audition?'

'No, Monna, at least not a stage job. There's a man who comes regularly to the restaurant, he needs someone to do a cookery demo—'

'Cookery?' cried Mrs Duggan. 'You can't boil an egg!'

'Not real cookery, it's just pix for a booklet. It's a rush job, got to be done this evening. All right by you?'

'This man's a photographer?'

'Yes.'

'Has he any theatrical connections?'

'I don't think so.'

Mrs Duggan lost interest in him at once. 'You'll miss the wireless broadcast from the Celebrity Club,' she remarked. 'I wanted you to hear it, my friend Janet gave voice lessons to the girl who sings with the band . . .'

'Sorry about that, Monna, maybe another time.'

But the truth was, she was glad to miss it. It would only have been another occasion to have her own shortcomings pointed out: she should learn to breathe like that, at the right place in a line of music; she should lighten up and put a lilt in it when the words suggested happiness; her voice was slight but here was an example of how to make the most of it.

And so had said all the teachers at stage school: try harder, with hard work you might make it.

According to her mother, Coral Duggan was 'resting'. The winter pantomime season of 1949/50 had just ended, during which Corie had been a lead dancer in a production of 'Jack and the Beanstalk' at the Hull Rialto; First Flower Fairy, The Woodland Sprite, The Spirit of Beauty in the principal girl's dream-sequence. The dressing-room painted chocolate brown was shared with ten other girls; at night she went home to digs that smelt of kippers and brown ale.

No fun at all. Corie had decided when she came back to London that it was the last time she'd dance in panto. The last time, in fact, that she'd dance in anything. She wasn't cut out for show business.

Her mother, Crystal Duggan, formerly of Crystal & Clark (Songs with a Smile), had no idea of this decision. Mrs Duggan still expected her duckling to turn into a swan.

'But Monna, I'm twenty,' Corie pointed out. 'If I were ever going to turn out to be a raving beauty, it'd have happened by now.'

'Nonsense, darling, some people just develop late.'

But Corie had no illusions. She knew she wasn't pretty. She was tallish, rather thin – coltish, her mother preferred to call it. Her hair had once been described by an unkind fellow pupil at stage school as being 'the colour of burnt oatmeal' and, worse still, it was straight. She had big hazel eyes in a squarish face, a mouth somewhat too large, and a stubborn chin. 'The Spirit of Beauty', she remarked to her reflection the first time she put on the second-act costume at Hull. 'Who are you kidding?'

Waitressing was a useful fill-in when roles in musicals or pantos were scarce. What Mrs Duggan didn't know was that her eldest daughter preferred it to show business.

Not that she intended to be a waitress for ever.

What she would do, she didn't know. Marriage and a home and children? Her experiences with men had not on the whole been encouraging. Men in the hiring and firing business tended to expect a little something extra if they were offering a part. She'd found it better not to trust them.

Paul Pierson, who was the photographer offering her an evening's work, was strictly respectable. A middle-aged bachelor, plump and quiet. Which had made it all the more startling when he'd said as she brought his after-lunch coffee, 'I suppose you wouldn't come and model for me?'

She'd drawn back so sharply that she'd spilled some of the coffee she was pouring. Modelling? How dare he!

She hid her expression as she added milk and sugar. What did he take her for − an innocent raindrop who came down in the last shower? Yet he was the last man she'd expect to nudge her towards the casting couch.

'I'm afraid that's not my line, Mr Pierson,' she said stiffly.

'Ever tried it? It's not hard work and I'd pay you—'

'No thank you, sir, I don't go in for "artistic poses".'

'Eh?' Startled, he set aside his cup. 'Where did you get that expression?'

'I've worked in the theatre, sir − some of the girls do that kind of thing to eke out their earnings but I'm not the type—'

'How right you are,' he agreed, plump features creasing in amusement. 'Too bony by far, if you don't mind me saying so. No, no, Corie − all I need is a pair of hands and a view or two of someone in an apron.'

'An apron?' Saucy French maid pix, frilly apron and fishnet tights, her suspicious mind said.

'Over a respectable dress, of course,' he added in haste. He made gestures with stubby fingers. 'Fixing little bits of preserved peel on a cake, taking the casserole out of the oven − that kind of thing.'

'What on earth for?'

'That's what I do. Commercial photography. This is for a brochure that goes with a gas cooker. Only my model hasn't turned up. That's why I was so late coming in for lunch, I've been waiting round for her all day. And if I don't get the pix done today, they can't go in the first post tomorrow morning and then they won't reach the makers' Press Office in time for them to make a selection for the printer . . .'

'Oh, I see.' The mental vision of posing with two or three pieces of gauze and a white dove faded. Instead she saw herself at a kitchen table with a few strings of onions hanging nearby. 'Cookery?'

'Yes, how-to-do-it pix.'

'But I don't know anything about cookery.'

'Neither do I,' confessed Pierson. 'But I've got a complete set of instructions from the Press Office boys, and the cake and so on are already made. I've got them on the window ledge outside my study, wrapped in a towel to keep them fresh.'

'A real cake?'

'Yes, and a tray of little buns and some cherry scones with sugared cherries. The casserole dish only has sawdust in it, I'm sorry to say.'

'Hm,' said Corie. Food was still scarce this cold winter of 1950. 'Do you get to keep the cakes?'

'Of course, that's one of the perks. And there'd be money in it, Corie. How about three pounds?'

'An hour?'

He laughed. 'Come on, be realistic. Three pounds for the evening.'

She hadn't expected to get three pounds an hour but it had been worth a try. 'I don't get off until six,' she said.

'That's OK. So long as we can work on until we're finished. I *must* get those black and whites in the post first thing tomorrow.'

'And I get some of the cakes to take home?'

'Sure thing.'

'You're on,' she said, and much to the consternation of the restaurant manager they had shaken hands on the deal.

The three pounds offered by Paul Pierson were import-ant. Corie hoped they might be spent on extra heating for their rambling home, for it was proving to be a cold March. She would even be content to see it used for a raincoat for her sister Opal because the coat she was wearing was a hand-me-down quite out of fashion now that skirts were getting longer.

Or, if she could spend it entirely to please herself, it would be nice to have a bike. Travelling to and from the restaurant in St James's by Tube was so tiring, especially in the rush hours. A bike, so that she could pedal home through the park. Or, better still, if one day she came into a fortune, a motorbike . . .

Smiling to herself at this dream, she made her way back from the phone box to the restaurant. It kept her happy through the rush of afternoon teas and the setting up for the evening diners.

At six she tidied herself up in the tiny staff washroom. Why am I bothering? she asked her reflection in the spotty mirror. A pair of hands, that's all that's wanted. She scrubbed her nails well, wishing she'd put on some nail lacquer – but she seldom bothered with cosmetics; make-up classes at stage school had given her her fill of them.

From the age of four, first Coral, then Opal, and lastly Beryl Duggan had attended the Betty Bonnar School of Dance and Drama. The Three Little Gems: Coral, Opal and Beryl – that had been why their mother gave them the names of semi-precious stones.

Coral wasn't pretty enough and had no real ambition. Opal was quite good-looking and danced quite well but never learned to sing in tune. Only with Beryl, the last of her children, did Mrs Duggan's hopes of producing the new Gertrude Lawrence look like coming to fruition.

Beryl, now aged fifteen, was with a troupe in an advertising show that went on every afternoon in connection with a big trade exhibition in Manchester. Opal, nearly eighteen, had a chorus-line job in a revue in Portsmouth. They wrote home twice a week – but they wrote to Corie, not to their mother.

All through their career at the B.B. School, all through

the dramas of wartime evacuation and parting from their parents, Corie had been the protector of her younger sisters. When their father was killed in an accident at an Army camp where he and his wife were entertaining, it was to Corie that the two younger girls looked for comfort.

Truth to tell, neither of their parents had been really close to the children. Often away on tour with their music-hall act, Crystal & Clark — even before wartime ENSA companies booked them — were distant, faintly glamorous figures. And even when they were at home, they lived lives that took them out of the house — to take voice lessons, to see costume makers, to cajole agents for work.

They didn't like to be called Mummy and Daddy. Clark Duggan was called Clicks, which had been his stage-name when he worked with a male partner (Clicks & Kicks, Tapdance Twosome). And when one day someone told Mrs Duggan that Monna was the medieval Italian for 'my lady', she decided she preferred that to Mummy.

'Other children have Mummies and Daddies,' Pal once remarked bitterly to Corie, 'but the Three Little Gems have Monna and Clicks.'

And now they had only Monna, who concentrated most of her attention on poor Beryl. The three pounds Corie was earning at the photographic studio would go towards extra tuition for Beryl.

'One day she'll be at the Palladium. You'll see,' Monna would insist, the light of prophecy in her dark eyes. 'You'll see, she'll have the whole country at her feet.'

There was no use arguing. It had become a point of faith in the Duggan household: the pretty little youngest child would fulfil all Monna's dreams. If Mrs Duggan couldn't herself be a great star, she was determined that at least one of her daughters should succeed. Beryl's name would go up in lights one day, of that she was fiercely convinced.

For Pal she had lesser hopes, and as to Corie . . . Well, thought Corie as she made her way to the address Paul Pierson had given her, she'll give up on me in time.

The studio turned out to be a basement in Bury Street,

under a fine-art dealer's. The photographer almost seized her in an embrace against his embonpoint, he was so glad to see her.

'Everything's set up,' he said, urging her through a small vestibule with a table and a couple of chairs and on into the studio. Here there was a curving sheet of what looked like simple cardboard, standing six feet high. In front of it was an enamel-topped table on which were spread various cooking implements and bowls. Around were tripods holding lights, but these weren't yet switched on.

'There you are,' Paul said with pride. 'I bought the ladle and rolling pin in Fortnum's. What d'you think?'

'I don't think you use a rolling pin for either a cake or a casserole,' she said with a chuckle.

'No, well, it's to make it look as if you're in the middle of a lot of cooking, using the stove, see? Miracle gas cooker, you can bake or grill or roast or simmer . . .'

'Where is it?'

'Next set – behind the screen. We'll do the baking bit first.' He paused. 'Changing room's here.' He showed her to a corner across which a folding screen had been placed. 'Nothing elaborate, I'm afraid, I don't generally have clients who have to change – just tidy up the hair, freshen the lipstick, that kind of thing.'

Though he was chattering, he wasn't nervous. It was part of his patter, easy chat to put people at ease. 'If you'll take your coat off and put on one of the aprons—'

'Which one?' she asked, surveying the array hanging from hooks on the wall.

'Doesn't matter, we'll change it two or three times, give a range of pix. I'll leave it to you.'

She took off her tweed coat, straightened her woollen jumper, and put the frilled band of one of the aprons over her head. It was made of printed floral cotton, brand new, the frills still stiff with dressing. She tied the strings at the back, smoothed down her hair just out of habit, and went out into the studio.

Paul was setting up an old-fashioned plate camera,

placing the tripod feet on three little circles painted on the linoleum. He looked up.

'Oh,' he said.

'What?'

'I thought you'd be wearing your black dress.'

'That's my waitress uniform. I change into it when I get there and out of it before I go home.'

'Oh dear.'

'What's wrong?'

'Well . . . a jumper and skirt . . .'

'They're not going to show much, are they? It's mostly apron,' she pointed out, indicating her front view.

'But the sleeves . . . you see . . . your hands coming out of wrinkly woollen sleeves . . .'

'I'm sorry.'

'Could you go back and borrow the black dress?'

'Well . . . I suppose I could . . . But you know, Mr Pierson, I don't think many women would do their cooking in a black dress with long sleeves . . .'

'No?'

'Well, wouldn't they get flour on the cuffs? Or splashes of milk or something?'

'How would I know?' he protested. 'I never do any cooking – that's why I eat in restaurants.' He stood in uncertainty. 'Push your sleeves up.'

She obeyed. He sighed. 'That jumper isn't new by any means, is it?'

'Afraid not.'

He shook his head. 'It would look terrible under the lights.'

'I'm sorry.' It seemed an impasse. 'Let's call the whole thing off, shall we?'

He looked about to say yes then caught himself up. 'But I can't! If those pix don't go in the post first thing tomorrow, I lose the job. They've *got* to be done tonight, I told you.'

'Hm.' Corie pulled her sleeves down and stood rubbing her arms. The studio was cold, and later she learned why – there was a stone floor under the linoleum. She looked about her. 'Have you got anything I could put on? An overall or something?'

'An overall — I have an overall, I wear it when I'm handling the chemicals. But it's not . . . I mean . . . It's tatty.'

'Nothing else?'

'No, nothing. Unless . . .' He frowned. 'I keep a couple of clean shirts in a drawer, in case I ever want to go out straight from here in the evening.'

'Shirts? Evening shirts?'

'No, just ordinary dress shirts — pin stripes — look, I'll show you.'

He led her to a door at the far side of the studio, behind the enamelled table and cardboard screen. Beyond was a little room, spartan, with a sink and a plug-in kettle and a chest of drawers and a pallet bed. It said much for the confidence she had in Pierson that she didn't even glance at the bed.

He opened a drawer and pulled out a shirt in its laundry-folded state. It was striped cotton, black and white. Beneath it lay another with a grey check.

'How about one of those?' Corie said.

'But the sleeves will be too long—'

'I'll turn the cuffs back — the way I would if I were going to do some kitchen chores — let's try it and see how it looks.'

She took the checked shirt and bore it off to the dressing area. Behind the screens she took off the apron and her woollen jumper, then put on the shirt. It came down to about hip level. When she put on the apron again, the effect from the waist up was as if she were wearing a print dress. She turned up the shirt sleeves, two folds so that her wrists were exposed.

'How's this?' she asked when she emerged, holding out her arms for inspection.

'We-ell . . . Let's have a look at it under the lights.'

He went to the wall, flicked a switch. Corie blinked. The flood of brightness was like the sun suddenly coming out from behind a thundercloud. At once the studio seemed warmer, more welcoming.

At a wave from Paul she went behind the table. As she'd expected, it came to about her waist, hiding the shirt tails and the plain serge skirt below.

Paul went under the velvet cloth covering the camera. She heard him muttering to himself. Then, louder: 'Put your hands on the table. Pick up the ladle. Lean forward a bit. Smooth out that wrinkle in the apron. Right. Push up your right sleeve a bit – no, don't fold it, push it up – right, yes, stop. Keep still.'

A pause.

He emerged from under the cloth. 'You know, I think it looks OK.'

'Oh, that's good.'

'You've got nice hands. Capable.'

'Glad to hear it.'

'I think . . . Let's give it a go. I'll develop the first plate straight away and we'll see if it's working. If it is, we'll do the whole thing. If not, it's all off and I lose the work.'

'Look on the bright side,' Corie said, leaning across the table to touch him lightly on the shoulder with the ladle.

He went to the room where he'd stored his shirts, and she heard the window being opened. A moment later he returned with a cloth-covered tray. This he set on a stool out of camera range, uncovering it to reveal cardboard boxes. The largest box contained the cake, still in its tin. Corie tipped it out, Paul set it on a plate already on the table. From the box he produced a little bag of greaseproof paper.

'Now, there's preserved peel in the bag. You're supposed to be putting it on the cake.'

'Right.' She took out two or three strips of peel, laid them by the cake, took one and began to lay it on the surface of the cake. 'Like this?'

'I imagine so. Let me have a look.'

She stood patiently under the lights, leaning slightly

towards the cake, holding the peel about half an inch from it.

'Keep still. When I tell you, take a deep breath and hold it while you count to five, like this – one and two and three and four and five. Got it?'

'You mean it takes five seconds to take a photo? I thought cameras were pretty well instantaneous these days—'

'Not this old girl. And no, it doesn't take five seconds but if you know you've got to hold your breath for five seconds you'll keep absolutely still before and after the exposure. Ready? Breath in and count!'

She did as she was bid. She held the peel and breathed. Paul pressed the valve, emerged from under his cloth, withdrew the plate and hurried off.

Corie amused herself with decorating the cake. It dawned on her that if you put the peel on the cake, it just fell off again. Obviously if you were really putting peel on a cake for decoration, you'd have a little bowl of something sticky with which to press it to the surface.

When Paul returned to say that the shirt sleeves looked rather nice, she made her suggestion.

'Haven't got a bowl. A cup, I've got tea cups and saucers – nothing fancy though.'

'I don't think a housewife would use fancy china for cookery jobs. As long as it's clean . . .'

She washed and dried a cup at the little sink, they put it on the table as if she were using it to dip the peel into.

'Let's get on with it,' Paul said, looking at his watch. 'It's nearly seven already.'

For the next hour and a half, Corie placed the peel and breathed, she pressed the peel on with the blade of a knife (her suggestion) and breathed, she tilted the cake towards the camera and breathed.

'That's enough for the cake. Let's do the buns now.' He consulted his script from the Press Office. 'You're supposed to be icing the buns.'

'I don't know how to do icing!' Corie exclaimed in alarm.

'No, no, the buns are iced already. You've just got to hold

11

the thingummy – icing-bag,' he said, reading the script.

'Oh yes. Well, this would be a different day, would it? Should I change to a different apron?'

Paul hit himself on the brow. 'Of course! And look, try a different shirt, eh?'

Newly attired, she resumed her place. The icing-bag was full of straw to bulk it out – no one was going to waste precious sugar to fill a bag needed only for photographs. While Paul loaded yet another plate into the big old mahogany camera, she experimented with pointing the icing nozzle. Clearly it would have to be on the circle of icing on the bun, as if she'd just finished doing it. How would you raise the nozzle so as not to leave a smear? Like this. She flicked her wrist. So her wrist ought to be turned slightly away when the picture was taken.

She 'iced' the buns in varying numbers – two on the plate, four on the plate, a plate full. She tilted the plate with both hands towards the camera. Paul muttered and inched his lights about. There was a shadow on the table. No, now her left cuff had slipped down. Stand closer. No, don't lean on the table, it makes a distortion in the apron.

How tiring it was! She'd never expected it. Almost as bad as auditioning for a part. And the lights, so welcome at first because they took away the chill, began to seem unbearably hot.

'We'll switch off for a bit, shift to the cooker. Why don't you make us a cup of tea while I move the screen behind the cooker and shift the lights?'

Glad to be allowed to move at will, she went to the back room. While she waited for the electric kettle to boil, she found the tea and sugar in a tin box, and a half-pint milk bottle out on the window-sill. When the tea was made she took two cups into the studio.

The new gas cooker was now revealed in all its splendour of mottled blue-grey enamel. It had thermostat knobs and dials. 'Do you get to keep the cooker too?' Corie inquired, thinking it would be a great asset.

'No fear. The local showroom gets it back tomorrow

morning. This is their latest model, there's a waiting list for it.'

'Too bad.'

'You'd have liked it?' Paul said. 'What for, to sell?'

She told him about the great old black monster at home in Bayswater. While they sipped the hot tea she told him a little about her family.

'Yes,' he said, nodding, 'you move like a dancer now I come to think of it. So waitressing's only a stop-gap?'

Corie shrugged. 'I'm not going back to the stage. It's a dog's life unless you're very pretty or very talented, and I'm neither.'

'Oh, I wouldn't say that—'

'Don't bother to be polite, I've been told often enough at auditions,' she said with complete calm. Her wide mouth curved with amusement. 'Last thing I ever expected was to be a photographic model!'

'What would you really like to do?'

'I've no idea, really. It's always been assumed because my parents were in the theatre, I would be too. That's all I'm trained for. Otherwise I had a rotten education. I can do sums when it comes to whether it's worth taking a part in Scunthorpe if the lodgings cost twenty-one shillings a week, and I'm good at geography if you ask me which seaside towns have the best end-of-the-pier theatres — but I don't know any French except what's on the restaurant menu and I don't understand how the atom bomb works.'

'Who does?' sighed Paul. He set aside his tea cup. 'Well come on, let's put this casserole in the oven.'

This proved an even more tiring pose than at the table. In the end they had to make a makeshift cushion so that she could kneel on one knee. Paul photographed the casserole going into the oven, coming out of the oven, being stirred with the lid half-tilted. Next he took pictures of the cake coming out of the oven, for which Corie had to slip it back in its cake-tin, and then some of the scones on their baking sheet.

Now and again Paul would disappear to put a plate in the

developing bath to see what he was producing. On the whole he seemed pleased with the results. 'Just a couple more and we'll be finished.'

Corie had used his absence to sneak a look through the camera lens at the cooker and cushion on which she'd been kneeling. From inside the black velvet hood she uttered a stifled exclamation.

'What's the matter?' Paul said anxiously.

She emerged, smooth brown hair ruffled. 'Everything's upside down! Has it developed a fault?'

He laughed aloud in relief. 'Of course it's upside down. Don't you know anything about optics?'

'I told you,' she reminded him. 'I had a rotten education.'

'Didn't do any science?'

'Er . . . rubbing a bar of something against a cloth so that it picked up scraps of paper. Turning water blue − or was it pink?'

'Oh, very profound.' He produced a pencil from his waistcoat pocket and began to draw a diagram on the back of an envelope. A box represented the camera, a line represented the object being photographed, lines with arrow-heads flew between them. There followed a lecture about spherical aberration, curvature of the image field, focus, and a lot more, all of which flowed past Corie like a swift stream in which she had no desire to dabble.

'Understand?' he asked when he stopped.

'No.'

'Oh. Well.' He was baffled. 'Well, a lot of people use cameras and have no idea how they work. Doesn't matter, really. The thing is to be *able* to use them, and that's largely a matter of having an eye for a picture. You see something or someone, they're in their setting, you see the light and shade and shape of the things and you choose the moment to take the picture.'

Corie made a gesture that took in the cooker in front of its cardboard background, the accoutrements lying around. 'Why d'you talk about choice? I mean, the cooker's there, just sitting, waiting to be photographed—'

'But you have to choose how to light it, where to focus. And with people, of course, you have to choose the moment when they feel at ease, get them to smile or look pensive or whatever . . . Well, let's get on. Two more shots.'

'And then we pack up?'

'Well, you do. I've got to develop and print those plates.'

'What, now?' Corie exclaimed, looking at her Timex watch. 'It's past midnight!'

'That doesn't matter. Those plates have got to go north on the mail train in the morning. Good God!' he cried, slapping himself on the forehead in the gesture that seemed to mean he condemned himself. 'How are you going to get home? You'll have missed your last Tube!'

'Don't worry. I can get an all-night bus.'

'No, look here – we'll put you in a taxi—'

'No, no, I often use the bus when I'm on the evening shift at the Cameo—'

'No, no, I insist—'

'Look, let's not stand here arguing, Mr Pierson, let's get on with it. And if you like I'll stay and help you with the developing and printing or whatever it is.'

He threw up a hand. 'No, thank you,' he said in a horrified tone. 'I don't suppose you've ever been in a darkroom in your life.'

'No-o, I haven't.'

'Very well then. You'd be like a bull in a china shop. Thanks but no thanks.'

'All right then,' Corie said, somewhat put out. 'Let's get the shots taken and I'll get out of your way.'

He could see his immediate rejection had offended her. 'I'm sorry,' he said, 'it's just that plates from this dear old girl are so precious – they give marvellous prints but they're so easily damaged or, worse still, dropped.'

'I thought cameras had rolls of film these days.'

'So they do. This camera I'm using tonight is ancient – made about 1920. But she's a darling, I'll get everything sharp and clear on the paper and the Press Office up in Doncaster won't have to do a thing to the prints they choose

— just shoot them off to the firm that's producing the brochure.'

As he spoke he was making herding gestures towards her. Corie moved to the cooker, smoothing the borrowed shirt and the apron as she went. 'What a lot you have to know,' she murmured in some admiration.

'Nothing to it. It becomes a sort of instinct. Now, this time, fold the cloth away from the cake-tin more and tilt the tin.'

Obeying, Corie took up her position. Paul dived under the hood, muttered, 'OK' and came out. 'Now, breathe and count.'

'One and two and three and four and five,' Corie said to herself. And then, aloud, 'You don't have to count with a camera that takes rolls of film.'

'Of course not.' He extracted the plate and put it in the safety case. 'Push up both your sleeves and keep your head tilted to one side — you're casting a shadow with it.'

'Right-o. How can you tell what's right and what's wrong when you see it all upside down in there?'

'I'm a genius. No, really, in time you don't even realise it's upside down — it just becomes natural to see it that way when you use this type of camera. Of course, the camera I used in the RAF, I saw things the right way up.' He put in a fresh plate.

'You were in the RAF?'

'Observation work. But I kept getting airsick so they put me in the lab. Liked that better, I prefer the technical side.' He went under the velvet cloth, came out, said, 'Breathe and count,' and pressed the valve.

'One and two and three and four and five,' murmured Corie. 'You mean you like being stuck away in a darkroom?'

'No, no — well, that's enjoyable, but what's great is seeing a print, picking out the bit that's interesting, enlarging it and getting a good commercial pic. See, if I were doing these cookery things on my own initiative, I'd take pic after pic, print them, choose the good bits, enlarge them, and send a whole range of different angles and things . . . Well, never mind, I'm paid to do it this way and we're finished at last.'

Corie got up stiffly. Her back ached. She was glad it was over. Yet it had been an interesting evening.

She shed Pierson's shirt and the apron, put on her jumper, pulled on her coat. When she emerged from the changing area he was waiting with the agreed fee in his hand, three one-pound notes. Plus two half-crowns.

'What's this?'

'It's for the taxi.'

'I told you, I can take the bus—'

'No, no, I insist—'

'I can't take this, it isn't fair, we agreed—'

'But I didn't know we'd go on so late. I'm sorry if it's worn you out and bored you . . .'

'Not a bit. It was fascinating.'

'Really?'

'Yes, it was something absolutely new. Can I borrow one of those magazines I see you reading about photography?'

He laughed. 'They wouldn't mean anything to you. They're full of technicalities.'

'I could look at the pictures,' she said, smiling at the childish phrase.

'So you could, I s'pose. OK, here you are.' He picked up a couple from the table in the vestibule. He accompanied her up the basement steps to the pavement and shook hands. 'Thanks ever so much, Corie.'

'Thank you, Mr Pierson.'

'Goodnight.'

'Goodnight.'

She walked up St James's Street to Piccadilly. Taxis cruised by and slowed but she didn't hail one. What, waste five bob on a taxi? Never mind what Eliza Doolittle might think, Corie Duggan preferred to save her money.

The tall old Bayswater house was in darkness when she let herself in. She made herself a sandwich with Spam on white bread. Eating it, she went upstairs to her bedroom. She cleaned her teeth, washed her face, brushed her hair, though not with the two hundred strokes her mother insisted upon, and got into bed. She sat up looking at the photographic magazines.

Mr Pierson had been right. She could understand only about one word in ten, and those words were usually 'and' and 'but'. However, the examples of photographic work were interesting. Two pages of pictures of machinery by a commercial cameraman, a big section of portraits – some good, some dull, but all very clear and well-defined.

Gradually the magazine slipped from her grasp. She fell asleep in the contented knowledge that she'd earned a good day's money and needn't work until eleven-thirty the next day.

Monna accepted the three pounds five shillings with pleasure, but when she heard the star of last evening's show had been a gas cooker, she returned her attention to the theatre reviews in the newspaper. Corie went to work a little late, but even so found herself looking with interest in the windows of photographic shops as she walked from the Tube station to the Cameo.

Cameras stared out at her, their lenses like eyes watching her. How strange they were. Through those eyes you could look at the world piece by piece – not overwhelmed by a thousand images but choosing what to look at. Perhaps by doing that you could make some sense out of things?

These thoughts kept her occupied through the business of laying the tables for lunch. Mr Pierson came in at his usual time and occupied his usual place.

'All right?' she asked as she brought the first course of the three-and-sixpenny set lunch.

He gave a thumbs-up sign. But his plump pale face looked tired, so she didn't bother him with conversation. Poor man, up all night at work in the darkroom and then a full day in the studio ahead of him. She managed to extract an extra spoonful of fish pie from Chef for his main course.

That was Friday. In the evening, while she was darning a hole in Pal's practice tights, the phone rang. Monna sprang to answer it. She lived in the eternal hope that one day her agent would ring and say, 'Crystal darling, I've landed you the lead in a new musical.'

'It's for you,' she called from the hall.

'Me?' said Corie, sticking her needle into the darning mushroom. She didn't expect it to be an agent saying he had landed her the lead in a musical. In fact, she expected it to be the restaurant asking her to come in for a half-shift because, being Friday, they would be rushed off their feet.

'Hello?' she said, sighing.

'Corie? This is Paul.'

'Who?'

'Paul Pierson.'

'Oh. Oh, hello, Paul.' So she was to call him Paul, was she? What was this, a come-on?

'Listen, Corie, I hope you don't mind, I looked you up in the phone-book.'

'That's all right.'

'Are you doing anything on Sunday?'

So he was going to invite her out for the day. She hesitated.

'You don't work on Sunday, do you?' he prompted.

'No, the restaurant's closed on Sundays. But I'm meeting my sister off the Manchester train—'

'What time?'

'Around lunchtime. Why?'

'Are you free in the afternoon?'

'We-ell, she and I are supposed to go to dancing class at four—'

'Supposed to? Can you get out of it?'

'Er . . . What's this about, Mr . . . er, Paul?'

'Let me explain. Tomorrow's Saturday and I've got a heck of a day in front of me, one wedding after the other all over Central London—'

'You mean,' she said, stifling a laugh, 'you lug that huge great camera round the churches?'

'Don't be silly,' he said, rather cross, 'of course I use an s.l.r. for jobs like that.'

'What's an s.l.r.?'

'Single lens reflex. Will you listen, Corie? I could do with some help and you seemed interested—'

'I thought you said was I free on Sunday.'

'Yes, yes, I'm not expecting you to come out with me taking wedding pix. I know you work on Saturdays. But it's the d-and-p—'

'What?' she said.

'Developing and printing. I've already got stuff backing up, studio portraits and things, and by the time I've got the film from six weddings—'

'Six!'

'Well, Easter's coming on, it's always the same. Anyhow if I can't get help in the darkroom it means sending the film away to be processed, and that means another time-lag and really it's something I could do without.'

A pause.

'Yes?' said Corie, quite at a loss.

'I was wondering if you could come in on Sunday and give me a hand in the darkroom.'

'Me?'

'I thought you seemed interested.'

She frowned to herself, pulling at a strand of her straight brown hair. 'You said I'd be like a bull in a china shop.'

'That was because of the plates. But this is *film*. You can't break film. And I thought if I showed you how to do the printing – it's elementary stuff, just contact prints to let the customer see what I've got, and then you see they choose the shots they like and I do proper enlargements and present them in mounts and they can send them round to their relatives and put them in an album.'

He stopped. She was still trying to catch up. 'Developing film?'

'*I* do the developing, you do the printing. I'd show you how. It's not difficult, it's just a question of exposing to the light for the required amount of time and then—'

'But would I have to count one-and-two-and-three-and . . . ?'

'No, no, of course not, it's really simple, the whole

thing's set up as a timed process. Two minutes' practice is all you need and then you're efficient. I thought maybe you'd give me a few hours, just to help me get the prints done, and then if you like I'd take you for a meal at the Corner House—'

I'm not doing it for a meal at the Corner House, Corie said to herself. It sounds deadly dull. 'Well, I ought to go to this dancing class . . .'

'But I thought you told me yesterday you didn't want to go back to the stage?'

'What's that got to do with it?'

'What's the point of dancing class if you don't want to be a dancer?'

Well, what? She didn't quite know. She kept in practice because her mother insisted that she must. She did what her mother told her. They all did. Pal would get off the Manchester train, come home, have a wash and a meal, and then obediently go to dancing class. But was there really any reason why Corie should go too?

As the silence grew between them, Paul said, 'I'd pay you of course.'

'I don't know,' she murmured. It would mean telling her mother she wouldn't be going to class, and explaining, and perhaps an argument.

'Three pounds?' urged Paul. 'Same as last time?'

Three pounds. It was an awful lot of money. It would mean that, on top of her wages, she'd have made six pounds five shillings this week. You could do an awful lot with six pounds five shillings.

But still . . . Not going to class . . .

'Couldn't I come tomorrow evening after work?' she suggested.

'No, I have to develop miles of film tomorrow evening. It wouldn't be ready for printing. In fact, I'll still be developing on Sunday morning. It's a slow process, you know – and then the film's got to be hung up to dry.'

'Really? Like washing?'

'Just like washing, on a line.' She could tell he was

smiling to himself. 'The time I need your help is Sunday afternoon and evening. Three pounds and a meal at the Corner House – what d'you say?'

'Three pounds ten shillings and I go straight home when we're finished.'

'Done!'

And that was how Corie Duggan took the first step along the path that was to make her name famous in the world of photography.

Chapter Two

That Sunday was the first of many. Through a busy Easter and on through the season of May balls, of June brides, openings of fêtes and garden parties – the social scene of the wealthy and the aristocratic.

As a background there was always the commercial work – photographs of buildings, of machinery, of equipment. There was also studio portrait work, less of that than of the other categories, but it always pleased and intrigued Corie to see human features emerging in the shallow dish of chemicals.

Almost painlessly she learned the routine of the dark-room, learned to be nimble of finger and deft of movement. The amber safe-light became pleasant to her instead of, as it had seemed at first, gloomy and depressing.

Paul never let her touch the cameras. Sometimes she helped move the lights or set out the material to be photographed. She said, 'I'd rather like to – you know – have a go at taking a picture.'

'Not on your life!'

'I'd be careful, Paul.'

'Look, ducks, these beauties represent my livelihood.' He laid a protective arm across the top of the old plate camera. 'You ever taken a photo?'

'No, but I've had my photo taken, for publicity stuff, so that my agent could show it around. And I've watched you . . .'

He shook his head. He looked at her. There was a genuine disappointment in the hazel eyes. She was a nice kid – shame to say no to her.

'Tell you what,' he suggested, 'I've an old camera, had it for years. I'll give it to you, you can take it out and about and use it, see how you get on.'

'Oh, I couldn't let you give—'

'I never use it. Too limited for the kind of work that's expected these days. You're welcome to it.'

'Let me buy it from you,' she insisted. It was important to her not to be any more in debt to him than she already was. He had taught her so much, been so patient in the face of ignorance and her uncertainty.

'Nah . . . It isn't worth anything. I'll bring it in tomorrow, you'll see, it's just about ready for the museum.'

She went home that night in a state of suppressed excitement. A camera of her own! She would take pictures of Opal and Beryl and her mother, not the vapid publicity shots that they had to accept from theatrical photographers, but showing them as real people . . . She would take pictures of Paul, with his tummy bulging over the band of his trousers, his growing bald patch and his incipient double chin . . .

Her sister Beryl was upstairs asleep when she got home; Pal was in Birmingham with a touring company. Her mother was walking about the big dusty living-room with a script in her hand, declaiming, 'You must remember who you are, my child—'

'Hello, Monna. Got a part?'

'*Maid of the Mountains* with the Maidstone Operatic Society next week — somebody's dropped out sick and I'm stepping in.' Her mother threw out an arm, palm outwards. 'Stop, my child, never turn your back on your own people.' Her tone was thrilling, commanding — and absolutely ham. 'Of course,' she added, in her normal voice, 'when I played it before, I sang the lead.'

'Yes, of course. Is there anything to eat, Monna, I'm starved?'

'If you'd come home at a reasonable hour . . .' Monna murmured, frowning, her attention still on her lines. 'I think there's some macaroni cheese in the larder.'

'Cold?'

'You must remember who you are, my child!' announced

Monna. '*You* must remember who you are, my child! You must remember *who* – I hate speaking parts. It's far easier when words are set to music.'

Corie had gone to the kitchen to find the dish of macaroni cheese. As she emerged from the larder with the remains of supper in a pie dish, her mother came in. 'By the way, Corie, Pal said you didn't go to dancing class on Sunday.'

Corie drew in a deep breath. 'I haven't been to Sunday class more than twice in the last two months.'

'Corie!'

Corie was looking uncertainly at the macaroni. 'Should I heat this up?'

'Corie, how are you ever going to do well at auditions if you don't keep in practice?' her mother demanded, her voice vibrating with concern and reproach.

'But I haven't had an audition since March.'

'That's your own fault. You could have gone after the chorus work in *Jack of Diamonds*.'

'I was busy.'

'Busy! Grubbing about in a darkroom . . .'

'Monna, it brings in real money. Going to auditions *costs* money in fares and lost wages.'

'Good gracious, which is more important – to land a part or to have two or three extra shillings in your pocket?'

'The extra two or three shillings,' Corie said, finally deciding to attack the macaroni as it was. She got a spoon and a fork from the drawer of the kitchen table, sat down, and tried to part a spoonful from the congealed mass.

Her mother snatched the dish away. 'I won't have you talking like this,' she said, and there was real indignation in her tone. 'No daughter of mine is going to put money before talent!'

'But Monna . . .' Corrie hesitated. She hated arguing with her mother. Usually when she did, it was on behalf of one of her sisters. But this time it was for herself, and for herself she was very unwilling to face the emotional outburst that was almost sure to follow.

'Monna,' she said at last, 'I think you have to face the fact that I really haven't any talent. I can sing a little and dance quite well and walk on and off a stage without falling over. But I don't bubble over with personality or knock an audience out with my good looks.'

'My dear child, you have your own special appeal.'

'Really? And what is it, exactly?'

Mrs Duggan pursed her full lips and hooded her dark eyes. She was thinking. 'Well,' she said, 'you have dignity, and a certain sort of calm.'

'Oh, great. That's just what's needed in musical comedy.'

'Not for juvenile leads, I agree. But one day you might be very much in demand for the character parts.'

Corie almost laughed. 'When I'm forty, you mean? And what do I do while I wait for that?'

'Well,' said her mother, 'there's always chorus work.'

Corie got up, filled the kettle, set it on the stove and lit the gas. She'd had her fill of chorus work. Tap steps, high kicks, costumes stained with sweat, producers and stage-managers cornering you for a kiss and a cuddle and whatever else they could get.

'Monna, darling, I'm earning more now than I ever would in the chorus.'

'Oh, if we're going to talk as if money is everything . . .'

'But it is important, Monna. It pays for our food and clothes and lessons for Pal and Beryl.'

'Everyone who ever achieved anything in the theatre has gone through hard times.'

'But that's because they wanted to do it.' Corie clenched her hands on the handle of the kettle. 'I don't really want to, you see.'

'How can you *say* that!' It was a cry of utter disbelief.

'Because it's true. I don't think I've ever wanted it.'

'But that's not so, you were so keen to go to your first dancing class, I remember so well, you could hardly wait!'

'I was five years old. Of course I thought it would be lovely,' Corie agreed sadly. 'And I ate up my crusts because it would turn my straight hair curly, and I waited to fill out and have a gorgeous figure – but none of it happened. So what we have here,' she went on, turning her head to meet her mother's startled gaze, 'is a duckling that never turned into a swan and gave up expecting it years ago. So I would be a lot happier, Monna, if you'd just let me slide out of the theatrical life. I just don't want to go on pretending about it any more.'

Monna clasped her hands together near her heart. 'I can't believe this,' she gasped. 'I never thought I'd ever hear any daughter of mine say a thing like that! What your dear father would say if he could hear you, I dread to think.'

'Look at me as if I were somebody else's daughter,' Corie suggested. 'If I were brought to you for voice-production lessons, wouldn't you say, "Don't put your daughter on the stage, Mrs Worthington"?'

'Never!' cried Monna. 'Never! You have talent, you've just never had the right chance—'

The kettle boiled. Corie turned off the gas, put tea in the smallest pot, and poured on boiling water. Through these mundane motions Mrs Duggan flowed on, explaining how Corie's abilities would one day glow before a theatre full of applauding admirers.

'I don't think so, darling,' she said when her mother paused for breath. 'I honestly don't think so. I've less talent than Pal and a lot less than Beryl.'

This was true, and even Crystal Duggan couldn't deny it. 'But even so . . .' she began.

'Look at it from my point of view. I'm at the beginning of a theatrical career that's likely to be as static as that macaroni cheese. What's the *point* of it, Monna?'

There was something in the way she said it, a sort of desperation that for a moment penetrated the cloud of dreams on which her mother lived. She said, with a little uncertainty, 'But what could you do instead, Corie?'

'Oh . . .' Her daughter shrugged, found a cup, put milk in and poured the weak tea on top.

'You wouldn't want to go on waitressing and creeping about in that basement darkroom?'

'Perhaps not. All I'm saying is, don't make me go to dance class and try for auditions.'

'Darling, I only do what I feel is best for you . . .'

'Yes, I understand, but what if you're wrong?'

'Wrong?' Her mother drew back. The idea was utterly foreign to her. 'I think I know what's best for my own daughter, for heaven's sake! And it isn't serving in a restaurant, let me tell you.'

'That's a stop-gap, we've always known that. All I'm saying is that when I look for a better job, it ought to be outside the theatre.'

Her mother whirled about. 'I can't talk about this! You've upset me dreadfully. How can you expect me to concentrate on learning lines when you say things like that to me?'

'I'm sorry, Monna . . .'

'We'll just forget we've ever had this conversation. I shall blot it from my mind!' With that she swept out, back to the living-room and her lines for a three-day semi-pro production of *The Maid of the Mountains*.

Corie, suddenly weak from reaction, sat down. She put her thin hands for comfort round the cup of hot tea. It was always so after these big encounters with Monna. Yet she knew she had won. When Monna had been made to face something she didn't want to accept, she always took refuge in these sweeping exits.

There would be no more checking-up to see if she went to Sunday class. There would be no more insistence on auditions. Something that was a version of freedom lay before her.

And tomorrow Paul Pierson was bringing his old camera for her to see.

The camera turned out to be a 3¼ × 4¼ Graflex, worn and battered. But when she looked through the viewfinder and clicked the shutter, it felt as if it had belonged to her for years.

'Like it?' asked Paul, smiling at her.

'Not bad,' she said. 'How much do you want for it?'

'Sixpence.'

'Be serious. How much?'

'A shilling?'

In the end they settled on five shillings, which was what she would have paid for a Box Brownie. Paul could supply her with endless amounts of film, surplus RAF film which one had to cut in lengths and boringly roll on the spools, but it meant you were taking pictures at only a ha'penny a click.

From then on she and the Graflex were inseparable. She took pictures of Pal at practice, of Beryl stepping off the train at Paddington, of Pal and Beryl in the garden at the back of the Bayswater house, of people waiting at bus stops, the lions in Trafalgar Square, weed-grown bomb sites, anything, everything.

Paul would laugh when he saw her negatives. 'What on earth are you trying to do?' he asked. 'Photograph the universe?'

'I don't know yet. Are any of them any good?'

'You always stay too far back. That's lack of confidence. Get in close to your subject.'

'But strangers in the street?'

'I don't do that kind of thing myself. Don't know why you want to.'

'I don't either.' She was studying a shot on a length of negative. 'Camera shake,' she sighed.

'Never mind. You're learning.'

It was on an evening in October that she took her first studio portrait. Paul had something that turned out to be flu and was staring at things through streaming eyes.

'Why don't you go home?' Corie asked, coming out of the darkroom where her prints were drying.

'Can't. I've got a late sitting, can't let them down.'

'What are you going to do, sneeze and wheeze all over them?'

'Arrgh!' he said, something between a cough and a sneeze. 'My head is thumping like a drum.'

'Go home and get to bed, Paul.'

'I can't. This is a golden wedding portrait, I can't just close up.'

Corie hesitated. 'Let me do it.'

He shook his head.

'Go on, Paul. The camera's set up, the subjects'll be sitting where you've arranged, all I've got to do is squeeze the shutter.'

It was the old camera, which she'd nicknamed Betsy. By now they were old friends. She had looked through the lens many a time and squeezed the valve when there was no plate in the slot. She felt a sudden confidence. She could take the picture, she knew it.

In the end he gave in because when it came to loading Betsy he couldn't even see to insert the plate. 'I give in,' he said. 'You'd better have a go. And if it all turns out a mess, I'll invite them back and do it all over again.'

She put him in a taxi and saw him off. Then she went down to the studio, her heart all at once beating fast. Here she was, alone, in charge. She looked about. My studio, she thought. Gaunt, uninviting. If it were really hers she'd have flowers in the vestibule, pastel paint on the walls, perhaps good china cups to offer tea or coffee.

She switched on the lights to study the arrangement that Paul had made for his golden wedding couple. There was a brocaded bench in front of a screen which could be rolled on and off the set, an expanse of parchment-coloured rough silk. Diagonally across this Paul had draped a blue velvet curtain with a gold fringe.

She ducked under the velvet hood to look. To her the background seemed distracting. But what did she know about studio portraiture? She was still feeling her way towards understanding daylight photography outdoors.

At six the bell rang. She went to admit the sitters. They were a good-looking couple: he silver-haired and in an old but well-tailored suit, she still dark but greying, very smart in a powder-blue dress and a mink coat. They were going on to a party afterwards.

'Mr Pierson is unable to be here,' she explained at once.

'He's got flu. But everything is arranged, so if you'd just like to take off your coat, Mrs Grant . . . ?'

They had no idea she was inexperienced. They obeyed her as if she'd been in the job for years. Chatting to them as she'd heard Paul do, she took three exposures, one with the couple looking straight at the camera, one with them half-turned towards each other, and one with Mr Grant's arm around his wife.

In each, as she made certain all was well before taking the shot, the draped curtain seemed to be too intrusive.

'Would you step aside for a moment while I change the background?' she asked.

Obediently they stepped out of the circle of lights. She lifted the curtain, which was on a rod, from the top of the screen. Now she had an absolutely plain background. Against it Mrs Grant's dark hair would look fine, but Mr Grant's shock of silver might be a little lost. She swung the screen round to its other side, a neutral grey. Better.

When she had them seated again she inspected the result. Yes, OK. She took the picture. Yet somehow . . . somehow . . .

'It's fifty years to the day today, is it?' she asked as she put in another plate.

'Fifty glorious years,' the husband said gallantly, picking up his wife's hand and kissing it lightly.

Corie ducked beneath the black hood. His hand was coming away, his wife's was dropping into her lap. They were both smiling fondly.

'Do that again,' Corie said, coming out to watch them.

'What?'

'Kiss Mrs Grant's hand.'

'Oh, I don't think—'

'Go on, Edward, why not?' urged his wife, laughing.

Looking embarrassed yet pleased, he did as she commanded. His wife smiled at him, he smiled back. Corie squeezed the valve.

When the pictures were printed Paul dubiously sent all of them for inspection. 'This was supposed to be a formal portrait,' he said. An order came back for six copies of the last shot, with a little note. 'My wife wants me to say that this is the best photograph we have ever had taken.'

'Well,' said Paul. 'Have I been entertaining angels unawares?'

'I'm just relieved they liked it.'

For the rest of that evening he said no more while Corie did the usual darkroom chores. When ten o'clock came and they got ready to sally forth into the November darkness, he said, 'Come and have a cup of coffee.'

'No, thanks, I ought to get home, my kid sister's been in a talent competition this evening. I want to know how she got on.'

'She won't be home yet. Spare me half an hour, Corie.'

'What for?'

'I want to talk about the future.'

'Whose future?'

'Yours.'

They went to a café in the Haymarket. There, over coffee and egg-on-toast, Paul put his proposition. 'I wondered if you'd like a full-time job, Corie.'

'In the studio?'

'Yes.'

'Not nine to six in the darkroom, Paul. I couldn't do it.'

'No, I wondered . . . Perhaps you'd like to be my assistant?'

'Assistant?'

'Photographic assistant. Some studio work, some darkroom, some accounts. What do you say?'

She gave the appearance of chewing toast thoughtfully, although her heart had leaped up at his offer. 'Would I get to use Betsy?'

'Yes, and the Anastigmatic and the flash equipment.'

'The s.l.r.?'

'If you come out on weddings and things.'

'What sort of pay would I get?'

They haggled a while, but she intended to accept whatever figure they reached. She wanted to be a full-time photographer more than anything in the world.

Her mother was not pleased. 'I can't see what you expect to gain from this, Corie,' she declared. 'I agree you couldn't stay a waitress for ever, but why on earth don't you get a pleasant job in an office, as a receptionist or something like that?'

'I like photography better.'

'But look at your hands,' Monna said. 'Chemical stains – and on your skirt too. It makes you look like a factory girl! I want you to give it up.'

'No,' said Corie.

'Now look here, Corie—'

'I've accepted the offer, and I've given in my notice at the Cameo. It's settled, Monna.'

'It's by no means settled! I forbid you to—'

'Forbid me?' Corie said. She sprang up from her chair. They had been sitting face to face in the living-room. Now she stood, tall and determined, over her mother.

'Monna,' she said, 'in three months' time I have my twenty-first birthday. If I don't have your agreement to live my life the way I want to, I walk out of this house on that day. Do you understand?'

Her mother looked up at her. After a moment she slowly rose to her feet, for she understood the stagecraft involved in being level with your antagonist. But somehow she failed to dominate as she had in the past.

A great many thoughts rushed through her head. Was it worthwhile wasting time and anxiety on Corie when she had two other daughters who might be a credit to her? Besides, the money brought in by Corie was very, very useful in an uncertain world.

'If you would just try to look more like a *lady*,' she burst out.

'Oh, I'll try, if that's all you want.'

'Photographic assistant? What does it *mean*?'

'A little more than third chorus girl at the back on the right,' Corie said with a faint smile.

'I won't have you sneering at our profession!' cried her

mother, and made one of her dramatic exits.

So that was the end of any attempt at interference. Which was just as well because, about ten months later, Paul was offered a very good job in the laboratories at Kodak.

Before he went, he sold the lease, the goodwill, and most of the equipment in his studio to Corie at a very low price.

Stand or fall, live or die – she was on her own.

Chapter Three

Beryl was home from her tour of *Call Me Madam*. Corie fetched her from the station in the sidecar of her BSA Sunbeam M33.

'Whoever does this belong to?' Beryl cried as her eldest sister helped her in and propped her suitcase behind her.

'Me, who else?'

'Monna never let you buy a thing like this!'

'I didn't ask her.'

Beryl's blue eyes grew round. 'You just went out and bought it?'

'Yes, because I needed something to transport my equipment to weddings and things. Great, isn't it?'

'We-ell,' said her sister with some doubt. 'Wouldn't a car have been better?'

'Oh, a car . . . Not so economical. Not nearly so much fun.'

'What does Monna say about it?'

'Monna says, "Coral Duggan, if your dear father could see you on that contraption he would be filled with shame".'

There was just enough mimicry to make Beryl smile and forget her alarm at the machine.

'Hold tight,' said Corie, 'here we go.'

With a muted roar they were off, and in minutes were pulling up in front of the house. Corie saw the curtains twitch. Her mother hated her to park the motorbike in front. She said it was low class.

There was a lot of catching up to do. Since Beryl had gone away with the second-tour company three months ago, Opal had taken an office job while she was 'resting', Monna had acquired two regular voice-production pupils, and Corie had been bringing in a decent income from her photographic work.

'So what's your news?' they demanded as Beryl sat, feet up on the sofa and a mug of coffee in her hand.

'Oh, we sank like a lead balloon in Cardiff. And the juvenile lead went completely out of the beat in *You're Just In Love* at Swansea and Mary Gladney was *furious*. But by the time we got to Bristol we were playing to pretty well full houses—'

'There you are!' cried Monna, glancing around in triumph. 'I've always said a good musical comedy will fill any theatre in the provinces!'

'But the big news is,' said Beryl, holding up her coffee mug for attention, 'I've got an agent!'

'You haven't!'

'I have.'

'Norman Clines? I always felt Norman Clines might take you up . . .'

'No, Monna darling, not an old has-been like Norman Clines. This is someone quite new, young and keen – oh, wait till you meet him!'

Beryl's cornflower-blue eyes were shining, her soft lips were parted in a dreamy smile. Alarm bells began ringing in Corie's head.

'So who is he then?' she asked, already wary. It was so easy for young actresses to be taken in.

'His name is Sasha Lenoir.'

'Sasha Lenoir!' chorused her mother and sisters. There was surprise in all their voices, and disbelief in Corie's. No one could really be called Sasha Lenoir, surely?

'Is he French? Lenoir sounds French,' Pal said.

'He's got French and Russian blood. His mother was a Russian countess who had to get out of Moscow during the Revolution. She was a dressmaker in Paris and married this French actor and they came to England after World War I and Sasha was born here.'

'Isn't that romantic!' breathed Pal.

Too romantic by half, thought Corie. 'You say he's new in the agency business?'

'Yes, that's why it's so super he's agreed to take me – he's only going to take a limited number of clients so he can give them a lot of individual attention—'

'Darling,' her mother interrupted, 'has he any contacts?'

'Oh yes, ever so many. He met all kinds of people while he was doing his National Service. That doesn't seem right does it, that someone from an aristocratic background like his should have to do National Service?'

'Who else is on his books?'

'He's got a jazz combo that's doing well in the clubs, and Charlie Venn – you know Charlie Venn? Compères a revue that's touring the north. I forget who else – he'll tell you when you see him.'

'I shall be delighted to see him,' Monna said in her grandest manner. 'Naturally I want to meet the man who thinks he can handle my talented daughter. And let me say at once, darling, if I have the least doubts about him, I shall put my foot down.'

'Doubts? Oh, wait till you meet him, Monna. He's got so much charm, and he's full of ideas. For instance, he says he thinks I should change my name.'

'What?' It was a concerted cry of indignation.

'And what, may I ask,' Monna said in her most magisterial manner, 'is wrong with Beryl Duggan?'

'He says it sounds too hard for someone as delicate-looking as me.' Beryl's fair skin coloured up like an Alexandra rose. 'He's got one or two new names he wants to try out on you.'

'Has he indeed. He'll have his work cut out to make me accept a new name for my own daughter. Duggan was good enough for your father and me, and so it should be for you.'

'But wait a minute, Monna, you never used Duggan,' Corie pointed out. 'Your stage name was Crystal and Clark, Songs with a Smile.'

'That has nothing to do with it,' Monna insisted, a little flustered. 'Who is this upstart to think he can foist a new name on someone from a good old theatrical family?'

'Now, darling,' pleaded Beryl, 'don't talk like that about him. Don't take against him without even seeing him. You'll like him, I know you will.'

'I rather doubt if I'll take the trouble to see him. Where is his office, exactly?'

'Well, in fact, he's been working out of Birmingham. He's just moving to London so I invited him to drop in for tea.'

'Here?'

'I was sure you'd want to meet him. I said we'd expect him about four o'clock.'

'Not today?'

'Well . . . yes.'

'Good heavens!' Mrs Duggan was thrown into consternation. She was aware that her thick mane of dark hair needed a shampoo and set, that her nylons had a run in them, and that if she made improvements it would be taken as weakening in her opposition to this upstart. All the same, he was an *agent* – who could tell what he might be able to do for her once he became aware of her talent and experience.

'I thought I'd better not invite him to lunch,' Beryl explained. 'I didn't know if there'd be enough for five.'

'Thank goodness you didn't, it's toad-in-the-hole and five into eight sausages won't go,' Corie said.

'We'd better get on with it, or it'll be dried to a crisp,' suggested Pal. 'I'll make the gravy.'

'What are we having with it? Oh, not cabbage again.'

None of the Duggans could cook. In a childhood of stage school, evacuation, dance practice, singing lessons, touring, costume-making and auditioning, there had never been time. They took what the shops allowed them on their ration books or, as extras, did something as simple as possible according to what they'd picked up in theatrical lodgings, and for the rest lived on bread and margarine.

So their lunch was quickly on the table and as quickly disposed of. Afterwards Corie and Pal washed up while

Beryl unpacked and Monna retired to her room, unable to resist the temptation to make herself more attractive for the visitor.

'The kidlet seems taken with this chap,' Pal remarked, putting plates away.

'Too taken, if you ask me.'

'Well, she's at the age,' Opal said, from the solemn heights of nineteen. 'I remember having a bit of a pash on my singing teacher when I was seventeen.'

'Sasha Lenoir,' mused Corie. 'He'll be dark, intense and want to put her in Chekhov.'

She was wrong on the last two points. Sasha Lenoir proved to be dark, hard-headed, and not at all interested in classical theatre.

'I think the future lies with television,' he said as he balanced one of Mrs Duggan's best cups and saucers on his knee. 'Theatres are going to lose their attraction.'

'How can you say such a thing!' cried Monna. 'The idea! Sitting alone at home staring at a box – how can that compare with being swept up in an audience by a great performer?'

'I know what you mean. And colleagues have told me that you yourself have shared with your audience those moments of one-ness.' Sasha sipped his tea, shaking his head in wonder. 'I wish I could have heard you sing, Mrs Duggan.'

'Oh . . . well . . . My husband and I did have a following . . .'

'Have another biscuit,' said Corie, offering the plate to their guest.

He glanced up at her. The dark, sharp eyes made a swift examination of her features. 'Thank you,' he said, and looked quickly away.

Got you, she thought. You couldn't look at me with a straight face.

'You're not in show business, Miss Duggan?'

'Oh, my goodness, you can tell that from the way she dresses,' Monna burst out. It was a favourite complaint.

'My daughter's given up any attempt at elegance.'

'Darling, you can't ride a motorbike in a silk dress.'

'But corduroys and a duffle coat — I ask you!' It was an appeal to Sasha, whom she now seemed to regard as friend and ally.

'Come on, Monna darling,' said Pal. 'What Corie wears is right for her work.'

'Indeed? If it was *my* wedding, I wonder whether I'd like someone roaring up on a motorbike, dressed like a road-mender!'

'Mrs Duggan, no daughter of yours could ever look like a road-mender,' protested Sasha.

Monna beamed. Beryl flashed a smiling glance at her sister. Isn't he wonderful, she seemed to be saying.

Well, he's clever, thought Corie. He can twist Monna round his little finger. Is that good or bad?

'What exactly do you have in mind for the youngest of the Duggans?' she inquired, putting her slender length into an armchair opposite him so she could watch him without straining. 'Beryl said something this morning about her name.'

'Oh yes. You'll think I'm presumptuous,' he took it up with a little bow towards Monna, 'but Beryl Duggan is phonetically too hard. You, Mrs Duggan, as a singer, are an expert on phonetics, of course.'

'Of course,' she agreed, delighted to hear it.

'Now, when you look at your youngest daughter, what do you see?'

'Skinny little seventeen-year-old who can't add two and two to make four?' Beryl suggested, laughing.

'Young chorus girl who has looks enough for the front line,' said Corie. Pal nodded confirmation.

'A performer!' cried Monna. 'A product of good teaching and good breeding!'

'You're looking at her background,' Sasha reproved gently, wagging a finger in admonition. 'When I looked at her for the first time I saw something gentle and sweet, something from a garden — a flower, a bird, a butterfly . . .'

There was a moment of silence. Corie let her gaze stray to her mother. To her surprise, there was a glint of tears in those dark eyes.

When she looked at Pal, her sister gave a tiny shrug of agreement. Corie studied Beryl, trying to see her as if for the first time. The slim, trim figure, the light, soft and curling hair, the blue eyes, the petal skin . . .

'So what sort of a name would you give her?' she challenged.

'I've been thinking about it ever since I saw Beryl in the show at Bristol. I've tried over a few and discarded them. But I think I've hit on exactly the right thing. How about this?' He rose, threw out an arm. 'Let me present to you the new star of stage and screen – Miss Lynette Lee!'

There were exclamations from all the Duggan family. Beryl cried, 'Lynette Lee!' and jumped up, twirling around so her flared skirt floated out. Her mother said, 'What? Lee? Lee is undistinguished . . .' Whilst Pal remarked, 'Lynette, like "linnet", the bird?' And Corie asked how you spelt it.

When they had quietened down, Sasha addressed Crystal Duggan. 'The judgement rests with you. You have so much experience, if you don't like it, I'll try and think of something else. But let me explain first.'

Monna gave him a dignified gesture of acquiescence. He said: 'The new name has to be pretty, to suggest pretty things. It has to be easy to remember. It has to have soft vocals. Compare the two names: Beryl Duggan – ' he pronounced it to give hardness to the consonants – 'and Lynette Lee, which is pronounced, as you of course know, Mrs Duggan, from the front of the tongue.'

Whether this was scientifically correct or not, Monna was nodding agreement.

'Alliteration is always good. Greta Garbo, Charlie Chaplin—'

'Yes—you're right.'

How about William Powell, Myrna Loy, thought Corie. Alliteration has nothing to do with it. But aloud she said,

'You don't think it sounds contrived?'

'Contrived?' He considered it. 'What if it does? So long as it's pleasing on the ear and summons up a good image, I can't see that it matters if people think it's contrived. I mean to say, Margot Fonteyn isn't exactly a likely name if you come to think of it.'

Nor is Sasha Lenoir . . . She saw him read the thought in her eyes. He waited for her to say it, but she couldn't quite bring herself to do so. He was, after all, a guest in their house.

'I like it,' Monna announced. 'Yes, I must say, I like it. Lynette Lee. Yes, yes, I think it would look well at the top of a placard.'

Pal was nodding too, and Beryl, now Lynette, was glowing with pleasure. There's too much approbation, thought Corie. 'Beryl mentioned—'

'Lynette! You must call me Lynette! That's my name from now on.'

'Oh, very well, then, "Lynette" – Lynette mentioned you had good contacts?'

'Of course. Well, I know Tommy Trinder, and Kenneth More, and Georges Périnal – he was the cameraman on *The Fallen Idol*, you know. And of course, again in cinema, the Boulting Brothers and in music there's Reg Calvert – you know of him? He's collecting a lot of good groups. Then there's Maurice Winnick and Sidney Black among the big bands, and—'

'Stage producers?' Corie prompted. 'Do you know any stage producers?'

'I'm like that –' he held up two fingers together – 'with the producer at the Windmill.'

'My daughter is not going to perform at—'

'No, no, of course not, it was just the first producer that came to mind. I know Ivor Novello – not well, but that will change. But what I wanted to say to you was, I have a lot of excellent friends in broadcasting. I know you disagree about the drawing power of television, but radio is an excellent way to get a singer known.'

'That's true,' Pal acknowledged. 'I mean, look at Alma Cogan and Kathy Kirby.'

'Right. And I have first-class connections among the BBC producers. I did my National Service alongside Percy Mullan, who's putting on a lot of middle-of-the-evening shows, and if I could persuade you to let me take Lynette into television I know William Tranton very well.'

'Well enough to get a part?' Monna asked quickly.

'To get an audition, certainly.'

'I don't know that I've anything really against television,' Monna murmured. 'I ought not to judge, I suppose. We don't have a set.'

'So I noticed. One thing's for sure,' he replied with a confident laugh, 'when I get Lynette into one of the TV shows, you must have a set so you can watch her.'

Everyone looked pleased at the thought. Even Corie, guarded though she was in her view of this wonder-man, caught the feeling of hopeful anticipation.

Fresh tea was made, they talked about the current state of show business. Cyril Fletcher's summer show had just ended its season, noted by the *Stage* as being the best in the six years since the war ended. The Grade Agency, headed by the brothers Lew and Leslie, had a growing list of top-rank entertainers. 'Variety Bandbox' on radio drew a huge listening audience. Max Miller was in trouble – again – for saying things he ought not to have said on stage.

As to musical comedy, Monna's first love, Ivor Novello's *King's Rhapsody* was the only British musical making money. Otherwise all the musical shows in the West End seemed to be American, a wave started when the baritone walked on stage singing 'Oh What a Beautiful Morning' in *Oklahoma*.

'I don't thing I'd care to sing in any of them,' Monna mused. 'There aren't any good songs for mature voices – they're mostly for the juvenile leads, and some of them are what I believe are called "belters" – you don't so much sing them as belt them out.'

'I think you would say, if I'm allowed to guess at your

thoughts,' said Sasha, 'that the style lacks subtlety. One day, dear lady, you must let me hear you sing.'

'Oh, of course,' Monna said, glancing towards the piano.

'But not this evening, alas,' Sasha continued, 'because I see it's almost six o'clock and I'm meeting someone for dinner at my hotel. You remember, Lynette, I mentioned to you, it's an assistant to Val Parnell.'

'Yes, I suppost you must go,' agreed 'Lynette' with a sigh. 'Shall I see you again soon?'

'I'll ring as soon as I get something firm on that television audition.'

He moved round the family, bestowing a kiss on the cheek on everyone. When he came to Corie she resisted. 'I'm going too,' she said, 'I've got negatives waiting for me at the studio.'

'Oh yes, of course, you're a photographer, so Lynette said.'

They went into the hall where Corie retrieved her duffle coat. They walked together to the door and down the stone steps to the pavement, waved off by Monna. Corie's motorbike and sidecar stood patiently at the kerb. 'Give you a lift?' she offered.

She knew he would rather be dead than seen in that kind of conveyance. And certainly in his neat, dark blue suit, pearl-grey tie and Jermyn Street shirt, he looked more the type to have a Bentley. He was about five foot ten, very dark of hair and olive-skinned – more Italian that Russian, to Corie's way of thinking. It had amused her to see him using his soulful dark eyes on her family.

He watched her as she mounted her bike and switched on. He knew that she hadn't taken to him, which troubled him, because as a rule he was a success with women. He hadn't tried to pay compliments to her because he could see she thought he'd gone a little over the top in his handling of the mother.

In fact, what was there to compliment her on? She had light brown hair of a sort of pale toast colour, and rather lovely lashes, quite untouched by mascara, fringing hazel eyes. Her figure was more like a boy's than a girl's, and she seemed quite uninterested in fashion; she didn't put herself out to please or to attract.

And yet . . . If he had allowed it, his eye would have been constantly drawn to her. She had something – a power, an aura. Even now, astride that idiotic bike with her figure thickened by a dark grey duffle coat, she didn't look absurd.

He tried to think of a way to say goodnight that would bring forth an eager response. She spoke first.

'You'd better look out,' she said, 'or Monna will be asking you to take her on your books.'

He knew she caught the flicker of alarm in his eyes. 'Oh, I'm sure she's much too loyal to leave Bicky Bemmell. Lynette tells me she's been with him for twenty years.'

'Lynette,' Corie repeated. 'You don't really want us to call her Lynette?'

'I do indeed.' He picked up one of her hands from the handlebars. 'You see, Corie dear, I'm trying to create a new personality—'

'What's wrong with the one she's got?'

'Very little. She's very sweet, very appealing, a real summer-garden girl. I want the rest of the world to see her like that – Lynette Lee, as gentle and fresh as the dew on a primrose.'

'Very poetic. Tell me really – what's behind it?'

He couldn't prevent a little frown. She was so intensely wary of him. Perhaps the way to win her over was a little frankness. 'All right, I'll let you into my plans. I'm trying to create an English Debbie Reynolds – did you see *The Daughter of Rosie O'Grady*?'

Corie shook her head.

'Well, there's a resemblance between Lynette and Debbie Reynolds, except that Lynette is softer, less vivacious and more confiding. I know for a fact that Hollywood is spending millions on building up the Reynolds girl's career – so it seems to me that an English version must have a good chance. Part of the plan is presentation – there are hundreds of girls going for auditions, Mary Joneses and

Betty Browns. A girl who's pretty and sweet and gentle, who can sing so as to melt your heart . . . I think she'll stand out from the rest, particularly if she has the right name, the right advice, and someone behind her to push her.'

To his relief Corie Duggan gave him no argument. 'She's got something special. Even when you discount my mother's grandiose ideas about her, my kid sister is something special. So all I want to know is, are you going to treat her on the square?'

'What a question!' He squeezed the hand he was holding. 'Lynette is safe with me, Corie darling, I assure you.'

'I'm glad to hear it.' She extricated herself from his grasp. 'Goodbye, Sasha. Don't take any wooden roubles.'

Before he could think of a suitable reply, she had gone.

Corie had plenty of work to occupy her for the next few hours, but most of it was by now routine. Her mind was free to worry about this stranger who seemed to have taken her family in thrall.

Corie loved her sisters dearly, but she was under no illusions. Since Opal couldn't sing, her future lay in dancing roles. She was pretty and had some talent but no personality to speak of. Beryl . . . *Lynette*, she corrected herself, could sing and dance and act and had something of the air of a character out of *A Midsummer Night's Dream* – a gentle version of Titania. What she didn't have was ambition. Perhaps Sasha was the person to instil that in her. Perhaps he could bring her some success. If he did, Monna would be in seventh heaven.

But was it right to let it happen just so Monna's ambitions would be fulfilled?

The next question was, right or wrong, could Corie prevent it? You only had to look at Lynette to see she was infatuated with Sasha. There was nothing to wonder at in that. His spare, neat body and confident manner, his dark good looks – they were enough to have helped him in an acting career if he had chosen it rather than starting an agency.

Was it any use saying to her, He's a phoney?

So many people in show business were phoney. They were always 'on', always giving a performance. Sometimes they themselves believed in their version of their personality, sometimes it was a conscious act to conceal a vulnerable soul. You learned to discount about fifty per cent of what they claimed.

How much of what Sasha claimed was to be believed? Anybody could say, 'I'm having dinner with someone from Val Parnell's organisation.' Val Parnell, head of Moss Empires, was a dream figure to most variety artistes. Get a booking with Moss Empires and you played before half of Britain.

The half, anyhow, that still went to see music hall or musical comedy.

In that, Sasha was right, Corie thought. When he'd said that television was the medium of the future, she agreed with him.

Like all households where there were actors, the Duggans took the *Stage* and the American paper *Variety*. You only had to read them to know that in the States television was booming. Before long, once the UK really recovered from the war, the same thing would happen here. Why, already, during the Festival of Britain just ending, an audience had been attracted to television because of the visual coverage of events on the South Bank.

Corie had a feeling that music hall had begun to die the moment talking pictures were invented. They had already existed when she was born in 1930, but the people around her had discussed them and the competition they offered to live theatre all through her childhood. She had once outraged her parents by making a very innocent remark. 'If I had one and sixpence,' she said, 'I'd rather go and see Fred Astaire than a juggler and a dancing dog.'

Now, it seemed, the public might prefer to remain at home on a wet December night and watch the pictures on the box. And if Sasha really could get Lynette an audition, it might be the best thing in the world for her career.

For her career, yes. For Lynette herself?

The only thing to do was play it very cool. In the first place it probably wouldn't happen – just one more disappointment on the bumpy road to recognition. If it did happen, Corie would be supportive but cautious. Don't build on it too much: there are probably thousands of girls trying out for TV variety shows; but on the other hand don't be nervous: do your best.

By the time she went home a little after midnight, she'd talked herself into believing the whole thing would die away. Sasha wouldn't land the audition for Lynette, she'd be sent for the usual chorus-line try-outs, the glamour would die away from the Russian aristocrat and everything would be back to normal.

As she went quietly upstairs, the door of her youngest sister's room opened a crack. 'Corie!' It was a whisper from inside. She went in, to find Lynette in nightdress and her old flannel dressing-gown, looking less like a TV star than it was possible to imagine.

'Corie, I wish you hadn't had to hurry off,' she murmured. 'I was dying to talk to you about him. Isn't he wonderful?'

'Well, if he can land you a part in a TV show, he certainly is.'

'Oh, you're always so dreadfully practical! I meant, don't you think he's gorgeous? You know, he reminds me of Tony Curtis. You know? In *The Prince Who Was a Thief?*'

'Good heavens, we're all alike, show-business families – we always compare acquaintances to someone in the showbiz world!'

'But don't you think so?'

Corie agreed there might be some resemblance.

'I just feel I was so lucky he picked me out. There were fifteen other girls in the chorus he could have chosen.'

'How did it happen? I gather he saw you in the show . . . ?'

'Yes, something made him drop into the theatre, though he doesn't like *Call Me Madam*. He said the minute I came on, he knew I was born to be a star.'

Corie wondered how, in the mêlée of the dance sequences in *Call Me Madam*, Sasha had been able to see star quality among the peasant girls in their mock-rustic outfits of yellow and cinnamon and pink. They weren't even colours that were very becoming to her sister's blue-eyed blondeness.

Perhaps after all he really did have the discernment, the judgement, that made a good theatre agent. Because, when Corie had watched the dress rehearsal, she herself had felt that only her sister looked as if she belonged in the make-believe kingdom of the play.

'Darling,' she began, hesitating.

'Yes?'

'Don't build too much on what he said about the audition.'

'Of course not. You and I know what it's like – a million things could go wrong . . .'

'He might not even be able to wangle it.'

'Yes, he will. He was in the Combined Services Entertainment group with this man who's now in the BBC—'

'But that doesn't mean he can get auditions—'

'It means he's got contacts, Corie. But it's not just that.' Her eyes were aglow with fondness. 'He told me – he actually said – that from the moment he decided to be an agent, he was hoping to meet someone as promising as me. Wasn't that sweet of him? To confess that to me? Because you know, some girls would take advantage – but he said he knew I wouldn't.'

I bet he knew you wouldn't, thought Corie. You're too trusting by half. 'I just want you to keep your feet on the ground, Beryl—'

'Lynette! My name's Lynette now!'

Her sister sighed. 'I've really got to call you that?'

'Yes,' she laughed. 'Otherwise I shan't answer.'

Monna appeared, splendid in a nightgown of crêpe de Chine and lace, bought in the days when she was near the top of the bill at the Alhambra.

'Corie!' she scolded. 'You ought to know better, waking your sister up at this time of night! You know an artiste needs her sleep if she's to give of her best.'

'It was my fault, Monna—'

'Lynette darling, you always want to take the blame when Corie gets you into trouble . . . Off you go to bed, dear heart, you have classes in the morning.'

'Yes, Monna. Goodnight.'

Monna waited until she'd gone in and closed her room door. Then she turned on her eldest daughter. 'If you must come in as late as this, have the goodness not to wake up the household.'

'I'm sorry, Monna.'

'You must surely know that if Lynette is summoned for audition, she won't do any good if she's suffering from lack of sleep.'

'She won't be "summoned" tomorrow.'

'How can you be so sure? Sasha was going to ring first thing, and who knows whether this man in Light Entertainment might not call her in.'

'Monna, we ought not to expect too much of Sasha . . .'

'I expect what he promised, no more and no less. I think at my stage in the profession, I can tell when an agent knows what he's doing. Now kindly go to bed and let the rest of us get some rest.'

She floated off down the landing to her room. Corie watched her go then went slowly into her own. So many hopes and expectations − and all for something that she was fairly sure would never happen.

She was quite wrong. Sasha rang two days later to say an audition was called for the following week for a band-show called 'Café Charmant'. Lynette was to present herself at Alexandra Palace where Sasha would meet her so as to introduce her to his friend, William Tranton, an assistant producer.

All the other members of the family waited in terrible anxiety for the result. Corie kept telling herself that her kid sister was as good as if not better than any other girl that might turn up. But she was sure they were all going to be disappointed.

Once again she was wrong. When the telephone rang and Monna leapt to it, her face broke out into a radiant, beaming smile.

'She got it! My angel child got the part! She's going to be on television! Oh, bless him, bless the man!'

Chapter Four

Seriously considered, Sasha Lenoir's efforts didn't quite deserve such an outburst of benediction. He'd got an audition for Lynette Lee, but in Corie's opinion, it was Lynette herself who had landed the job.

But Lynette was as delighted as her mother. 'A seven-week contract with two weeks' rehearsal! And the chance of another series if this one catches on! Don't you think it's marvellous, Corie?'

'I'm very pleased for you, sweets. What exactly is it, a revue or what?'

'Yes, sort of, under a different name. It's really a Bob Barlow band-show, but they're calling it "Café Charmant" to give it a touch of class, and the dance director is Jix Cropper — you know he did those dances for *Now You See It* that got such good reviews. I'm looking forward to working with him.'

Lynette was to be one of a dance troupe of eight, four couples. Her partner, she reported, was a handsome dark boy who would be a nice contrast to her fairness.

'Not that you'll be able to tell much about complexions on a black and white screen,' she added with a rueful smile. 'I saw a programme being broadcast in the waiting-room and honestly it was a bit murky ... Never mind, Mr Tranton says as many as half a million people may watch it.'

'Go on with you,' Pal said. 'There aren't half a million TV sets in the UK.'

'No, but Mr Tranton says they reckon about four people watch every set ...'

'Who is this Mr Tranton?' Monna inquired in a rather haughty manner. 'Someone we should know?'

'He's the producer, Monna. He's very nice, I think, but very anxious and preoccupied. He's responsible for one or two other Light Entertainment productions, I think.'

'Ah ... Do they ever do productions of musical comedies? There would be a large audience, I'm sure, for *The Desert Song* or *Rose Marie*.'

'No ... well ... when you actually see the studio, Monna, you realise how difficult it would be for them to do anything on a big scale. The camera, you know ...' Lynette made a spanning movement of her hands and arms. 'It can only take in so much. In fact, Mr Tranton was saying to Jix that getting all eight dancers in the frame at once is no easy matter.'

'I see,' Monna said. Another hope dashed.

'So when do you start?'

'Gold's Rehearsal Rooms, ten o'clock Saturday morning. Ten till five for fourteen days. We have five numbers to learn for the first show, and in Rehearsal Week Two we'll start learning the numbers for the second and third show. After that we'll have to learn the routines the day before the broadcast. My word, it's scary,' Lynette murmured, 'going in front of a camera with half a million people watching – if you make a mistake, they all see it!'

'You won't make a mistake,' her mother said. 'No daughter of mine would ever disgrace herself in front of her audience.'

'I'll certainly try not to!'

At first there was a terrible disappointment. The scheme was cancelled, because in February the King died, and the BBC was thrown into a panic about its programmes. After about three weeks, however, the dictum came down from Lord Reith that the British public couldn't go into mourning for ever, and programme planning resumed. Lynette's 'Café Charmant' was put back in the schedule.

Though it was all very strange and exciting at the outset, it soon became routine. Lynette would come home from rehearsals ready to pantomime the dance routines for her family, and they would watch and nod and offer suggestions. But by and by she fell out of that habit, simply saying, 'Watch and you'll see it,' which was true.

For the opening of the series they hired a TV set, gathering round it in apprehension to see the star of the family make her television debut. They soon saw that what William Tranton had said was true. It was difficult to keep eight dancers in the frame. And true, too, it was difficult to know who was a blond and who was a redhead.

Perhaps they were biased, but they did truly feel that Lynette had a special something that shone even through the black and white. Her soft fair hair would fly out as her partner spun her round, when he lifted her she seemed to float like a drifting feather.

But the dancing was only part of the show. Most of it was taken up with big-band numbers by the Bob Barlow Band. There were two featured singers with the orchestra, a girl and a man. There were also guest spots, sometimes a pianist or a saxophonist, sometimes a dance couple who might do a rumba or a Viennese waltz, and often a ventriloquist – Bob Barlow had a soft spot for ventriloquists. Very much a family show, it went out at eight o'clock and ended with the chimes of Big Ben for the nine o'clock news.

A little more than half-way through the series, Sasha dropped by one evening to report great news. 'They're going to do another seven,' he announced. 'I knew they would!'

The Duggan family were delighted, full of praises for him, as if somehow he alone had persuaded BBC Light Entertainment to renew the contracts of the 'Café Charmant' team. 'When is it going on again?' Monna wanted to know, already worried at the thought of her daughter *not* being on the box.

'They're scheduling the new series in three months' time.'

'Oh!'

'No problem, I've got Lynette an audition for 'On the Town'. I know it's not the same as being on a band-show – she'll just be tucked in here and there between the interviews, but it's something.'

'On the Town' was a Saturday-night magazine pro-gramme which tried to interview people who had made the headlines during the week. Naturally there were gaps between interviews because the interviewees might have to come in, for instance, after winning Wimbledon, or from an international conference, or whatever seemed fitting to the producer. In case of any 'empty space' in the programme, there were two fill-ins – a small dance troupe and a trio of close-harmony singers.

Sasha could tell Monna was displeased. She expected her daughter to step up, not down, from 'Café Charmant'. 'I would rather my daughter took a stage part in the interim,' she remarked. 'To be a time-filler hardly seems dignified to me.'

'Perhaps not. I'll see what I can arrange.'

Corie could tell he didn't want an argument with Monna, but that he had no intention of doing anything to find theatre work. He had made up his mind that televison was his métier, no matter what anyone else might say.

In fact, the appearance in 'On the Town' did Lynette's career no harm. It might even have put her before a wider audience. She actually got one or two fan letters. As soon as they began turning up, Monna's disapproval evaporated.

Corie began to benefit from Lynette's new career. Dancers and singers needed photographs to put in the various casting directories, and for their agents to send around to impresarios. As soon as Lynette's colleagues discovered her sister was a photographer who didn't charge exorbitant fees, they began to turn up at her studio.

Because in her short theatrical career she herself had suffered from stiff-looking portraits and badly lit settings, Corie took especial care with her new clients. She perhaps spent more time on them than was profitable from the monetary point of view, but the portraits she produced were seized with delight by the artistes.

'You just somehow seem to get it right,' one girl, a comedienne, commented. 'You just put your finger on it, in a way I've never seen before.'

For her, Corie had taken a provocative shot. Sally was lamenting over a hole in her fishnet tights. She was in practice kit, standing on one lovely leg, the other raised in a half-high kick while she tilted her head and studied her knee. It was funny yet graceful, showed off her legs to the best possible advantage, gave her a chance to smile yet frown; somehow it was touching as well as faintly sexy.

Much better, to Corie's mind, than a picture of the girl in some fancy costume trying to look like a star. And so it proved, because a couple of weeks after the picture was sent out, Sally landed an audition for a summer-long review in Blackpool.

Nor was she the only one. Perhaps the fact that their pictures had something different about them caused their agents to make a special effort, but four or five of Lynette's friends found jobs.

That was a busy year for the Duggan family. Corie had all the work she could handle, Lynette was constantly at Alexandra Palace, Opal had a dancing role in a production of Gounod's *Faust* and Monna acquired four regular students for voice lessons.

Sasha, too, was busy. Other clients had come to him. 'It's all beginning to happen,' he would cry, throwing out his arms and snapping his fingers. 'And next year will be even better. Next year's the Coronation, and everybody will want a TV set to watch it, and after that just you wait . . .! There'll be all kinds of programmes to entertain the foreign visitors and show off how good we are at television − jobs galore, I tell you!'

It wasn't only in the world of entertainment that Coronation Year meant a bonanza. Corie found her appointment book absolutely full. Every local bigwig, every 'somebody', was involved in some event in celebration of the crowning of Elizabeth II. Every one of them wanted a photographic record of the great moment. Those who could afford it hired Karsh of Ottawa or Cecil Beaton. Those who had thinner purses went to less expensive photographers.

Corie got a plentiful share of these – businessmen who knew her through her commercial work, stage folk who had seen her publicity portraits, private individuals who'd had her take their wedding or birthday or anniversary pictures.

And there were also some rather lofty people who left it too late to book with the top photographers and so turned to the business directory to find someone. Corie had a small group of peers and peeresses who wanted a record of the day they went in their coronets and ermine-trimmed robes to Westminster Abbey.

The day itself was dreadful. The second of June was cold and dismal. The threatening rain came down as the procession set out on the return from the Abbey. Corie, out among the crowd, had to take shelter in doorways or under awnings to take shots of the scene around her. There was no guarantee the light was good enough to get anything on film.

Then, in the early evening, the sitters began to arrive at the studio, some of them drenched and weary. She had by this time furbished the studio so that it looked welcoming, and had installed a neat little kitchen. For her damp and disheartened sitters she provided hot tea or coffee or soup. She tidied up dishevelled hair, set coronets straight, helped them put on the cumbersome robes – and somehow, because of that little interval of kindly attention, she got some beautiful shots.

After that there were the debutantes. Naturally the 'season' that year had a special glamour: there was a very full list to be presented, so there were many presentation balls and coming-out parties. Corie was hired to attend two or three of the parties and take what were called 'candid-camera' shots for the family albums.

One picture that she took became famous. It happened by chance. Lady Barrington had just said goodbye to her last guest and turned back into the hall. She sank down on the nearest chair, kicked off her satin slippers, and from around her neck unclasped her heavy diamond necklace with an expression of fatigue and distaste.

Corie put up her camera and clicked. Her ladyship said, 'Oh!' and looked put out. Corie clicked again. Lady Barrington frowned, then laughed. 'Candid, eh? It's all right to be candid with the pretty little eighteen-year-olds, but not with an old fright like me.'

Corie shook her head. 'You've got twice the character of any other person I've photographed tonight.'

'Flatterer!' All the same, Her Ladyship was pleased. 'Let me see what you get, my dear. It'll do me good to see what I look like when my feet are killing me.'

The photo that pleased her best was the one in which her great old-fashioned necklace was hanging from her fingers like so much old rope. In a fit of mischief she showed it to the gossip columnist of the *Sunday Express*. 'That's what happens in the end to all those pretty little chits you write about, Teddy.'

'Ri-ight!' said Teddy. 'May I borrow this?' And it appeared in his column next day.

No amount of paid-for advertising could have brought Corie as much attention. As the summer of the Coronation began to fade and autumn came, she was still as busy as ever. Now it was the famous, the successful, who wanted her services. To have a character study by Corie Duggan hanging in the drawing-room or the reception area of your office suite began to be the fashion.

One afternoon her telephone rang at the studio. 'Corie Duggan Photographs,' she said.

'May I speak to Miss Duggan?'

'Speaking.'

'Ah, Miss Duggan, I'm putting you through to Mr Holstead.'

'Who?' Corie asked. But the caller had gone.

There was a long humming pause during which she debated whether to put the phone down and do something useful. She'd had experience with the secretaries of businessmen before – they always wanted you to hang on for ages while they made the connection with the boss.

Who, anyhow, was Mr Holstead?

'Miss Duggan on the line, Mr Holstead,' said the secretary.

'Hello?' said Corie.

'Miss Duggan? This is Ingram Holstead. Miss Duggan, I've seen some of your portrait work and I thought it very impressive.'

'Thank you, Mr Holstead.' Who are you, she thought? Give me a clue.

'My board of directors have mentioned that they would like a portrait study of me for the boardroom. I should like you to do it.'

'Thank you, Mr Holstead,' Corie said, 'that's very kind of you. Do you want to fix a date?'

'Oh, my secretary will take care of that,' Holstead said. 'I thought I'd better have a private word to give you a hint or two. I don't want anything formal or posed − I'm not a formal sort of man, as I expect you know.'

'Of course,' said Corie, lying politely. 'Does that mean you would prefer not to have a studio portrait?'

'Certainly not! I want you to come here with whatever equipment you think necessary and take me while I'm at my desk − which is, after all, where my working life takes place.'

'I see. Does that mean people coming in and out?'

'No one will come in if I give instructions not. But business can't stop because I'm having my picture taken . . .'

'I quite understand that, but it could be distracting—'

'Look, just set up a date and time with my secretary and we'll leave details until the day, huh? Goodbye, Miss Duggan.'

There was a clunk, then a moment later the secretary's voice. 'Miss Duggan, I have Mr Holstead's diary in front of me now. When can we make this appointment?'

Corie drew a breath. Her recent experience with businessmen had shown her that they like to let someone else handle the boring bits such as dialling the telephone and making entries in diaries. But few had been as brusque as this barbarian.

'Is there any urgency in this?' she inquired.

'Urgency? Well, I suppose not.'

'How about one day next week?'

'One day next week . . . Thursday?'

'No, sorry, Thursday I have to do some work on site.'

'On site?'

'Out of the studio. If I come to Mr Holstead's office, that will be "on site".'

'Not Thursday. Friday? There's a space early Friday afternoon.'

'I'm afraid not, I have a studio appointment then.'

'Perhaps you could put that off, Miss Duggan.'

'Perhaps I couldn't, Miss—?' Corie said with some coldness. 'Let's go into the following week . . .'

'Oh, I believe Mr Holstead wanted the photos taken next week . . .'

'Very well, let's look again at next week. I have a space on Wednesday, the whole of Thursday is out, but I could manage either Friday morning or late Friday afternoon.'

'Friday morning is no good, Mr Holstead has a weekly conference on Friday morning.'

'Perhaps he could put that off?' Corie said with some irony.

'Certainly not!' The secretary was aghast at the mere thought. 'Mr Holstead always has a planning conference for the following week on Friday morning. Well, then . . . late Friday afternoon . . . But Mr Holstead is always very busy in the late afternoon.'

'I gather that was the point of coming to the office,' Corie remarked. 'I'm to portray him at his desk, where he spends most of his working life.'

'Is that so? I hadn't quite . . . Well, then, let's say late Friday afternoon . . . I'll check to see if that will be all right. Please hold.' Clunks, clicks, a moment's silence, then the brisk voice resumed. 'Mr Holstead says that will do, but you must accept the fact that he'll be very busy indeed.'

'Very well. What time?'

'Shall we say six o'clock?'

It was a little surprising. She'd expected 'late afternoon' to mean five-ish. But she hadn't anything against six o'clock. 'Very well. Now if you'll just give me the address . . .'

'The address?'

'Where you're speaking from.'

'Oh, you thought we were perhaps at the country house. No, you're to come to the office.'

'What office?'

'In Fleet Street,' the secretary said, as if she were speaking to an idiot.

Corie sighed. 'Fleet Street is a long street. Whereabouts in Fleet Street?'

'But surely you know our building? Mr Holstead's office is on the top floor, the receptionist will show—'

And at that, Corie's patience ran out. 'Listen, Miss Whoever-you-are, Mr Holstead's office might as well be in Zanzibar for all the good we're doing here. Who is Mr Holstead? I've never heard of him.'

'Never heard of Mr *Holstead*?'

'Never heard of Mr Holstead, that's right.'

'But everybody knows Mr Holstead—'

'Excuse me, can we stop wasting time? I'm expecting a sitter any minute now. What number in Fleet Street?'

'It hasn't got a number,' the secretary said, much shaken. 'It's the building of *Globe* Newspapers.'

'Right. Is that near the Strand end or Ludgate Circus?'

'It's about half-way.'

'Thank you. Is there parking?'

'Parking? Of course there's parking,' the secretary burst out, 'where do you think the editors park their cars?'

'I've no idea. All I want to know is whether I can bring my equipment in my own transport or do I need to take a taxi.'

'I see. Of course. I'm sorry. Yes, we have an underground car park in Bouverie Street. I'll tell the attendant to expect you.'

'Thank you very much,' Corie said, putting down the receiver.

She wrote the appointment into her book. Mr Holstead, *Globe* Newspapers, 6 p.m. Friday 13 November. Friday the thirteenth! Well, even arranging the appointment had gone badly; perhaps it would be a total disaster. She shrugged to herself, grimaced, and put the appointment book aside as her next client rang the bell.

On the day of ill-omen she chugged up to the entrance of the *Globe*'s car park in Bouverie Street.

''Ere,' said the car-park attendant, 'gerroutof it! You can't park here.'

'Pardon me?' said Corie, pulling off beret and goggles so as to hear him better.

'Take that contraption out of here!'

She throttled down. 'Miss Duggan,' she said. 'Mr Holstead's secretary is supposed to have told you I was coming.'

Startled, the attendant fetched a clipboard. 'Arrh . . . Yes . . . Sorry, miss. Right you are.' With his hand up to his mouth to hide a smile, he directed Corie in and helped her park her Sunbeam sidecar alongside a grey and black Rolls Royce.

Corie switched off, dismounted, and hefted her camera bag out of the sidecar.

'What you gonna do, then?' the attendant asked, openly grinning. 'Give him a massage, cut his hair?'

'I'm going to shoot him,' she replied, returning the grin.

'Good for you,' he said, 'somebody shoulda done it years ago.'

The receptionist in the hall of the *Globe* building was less surprised at Corie's appearance. Duffle coats and a certain bohemianism were allowed in reporters. She raised her eyebrows a little, though, when told the visitor wished to see Mr Holstead.

By now Corie had found out from friends in the publicity world that she'd been summoned to take portraits of Ingram Holstead, owner and managing editor of *Globe* Newspapers, and as a matter of fact had taken some care over her appearance. She was wearing new slim worsted trousers and a white silk shirt under the duffle, and her straight fawn hair was tied back with an Asher kerchief.

A trip in the lift brought her to the top floor where a young woman was awaiting her. 'Good afternoon, Miss Duggan, Miss Bryant is expecting you.'

'Who's Miss Bryant?'

'Mr Holdstead's secretary. This way, please.'

Miss Bryant was on the telephone when Corie was shown in. She proved to be young-middle-aged, wearing a wool suit and pearls. She nodded at Corie's escort, who showed her to a comfortable row of chairs in front of which stood a low table with magazines.

Corie sat, put her camera bag on the chair next to her, then gazed about. Very lush. Designed and fitted out in the early thirties, it had something of the Hollywood look – straight lines with contrast inlays on the furniture, deep smooth carpets in a zigzag black and brown, floor-to-ceiling curtains at the window in biscuit-coloured raw silk.

Miss Bryant ended her telephone conversation. She turned to Corie. 'Good evening, Miss Duggan, Mr Holstead is held up for the moment,' she said. 'I hope you don't mind waiting for a few moments.'

'That's all right.'

'Can I get you anything? Tea, coffee, sherry?'

'No, thank you.'

'Please smoke if you would like to.'

'No, thanks, I don't.' Bad for the voice, Monna had always said.

Miss Bryant turned back to her desk. She was putting sheets of paper into folders – letters to be signed at the end of the day, no doubt. There was no sign of a typewriter in the room, from which Corie had deduced that Miss Bryant was more in the nature of a personal assistant than a secretary. The donkey work was no doubt done by such as the girl who'd met her at the lift.

Time passed. As her watch ticked up a quarter past six,

Corie inquired, 'Will Mr Holstead be much longer?'

'Er . . . Just let me inquire.' Miss Bryant picked up a phone, pressed a button on an intercom manual, and spoke softly. She nodded, replaced the instrument, then said to Corie, 'He hopes to be free in a few moments. Will you change your mind about a drink?'

'No thank you,' said Corie.

Time passed. At twenty-five past six, she asked again. 'Will Mr Holstead be much longer?'

'I'll just find out.' The same performance. Miss Bryant reported to the visitor. 'Mr Holstead has a few matters to finalise and then he'll—'

'Right,' said Corie, getting to her feet. 'I have work waiting for me in my darkroom. Tell Mr Holstead that if he's serious about having me take his portrait, he must make a firm appointment for a specific day and time and then keep to it. Good evening.'

'Miss Duggan!' cried Miss Bryant, horrified. 'You can't go!'

'I certainly can,' Corie replied, heading for the door to the corridor.

'But Mr Holstead wants you to take his picture—'

'No he doesn't. He's got dozens of photographers on the paper, no doubt. Tell him to get one of those to hang round in his outer office waiting for him. I've got other things to do.'

'Miss Duggan!' gasped the secretary.

But Corie had already left her.

Angrily she strode to the lift. Luckily it was waiting at the top floor. She got in and, as the doors closed, saw the secretary flying out of the office to detain her. The lift sank downwards. Corie, with her camera bag slung over her shoulder, stalked towards the outer doors. A girl listening to a phone at the reception desk flew out to meet her.

'Miss Duggan, Miss Duggan! Please wait!'

Corie paused. 'What is it?'

'Miss Bryant wants you to go back—'

'Not on your life,' said Corie and made a move to walk on.

The receptionist took hold of her sleeve. 'But Miss Bryant says—'

Corie looked at her. 'Take your hand off my arm.'

'Oh!' The girl went red, hesitated, and took her hand away. 'But Miss Bryant says—'

'Tell her I have work waiting for me in my darkroom.'

She retrieved the Sunbeam without further ambush, and drove back through the light traffic of early evening. As she drew up in Bury Street she could hear her phone ringing in the studio. A grin creased her thin face. Miss Bryant, no doubt, hanging on the other end, waiting for her to arrive home.

Once in, she answered the phone with a sharp, 'Yes?', quite unlike her usual business manner.

'Miss Duggan, oh, I'm glad I caught you before you went into the darkroom.'

'What is it, Miss Bryant?'

'Mr Holstead asked me to say he's quite ready now if you could come straight back.'

'Certainly not,' said Corie. 'I started some processing this afternoon and once started it can't be switched off like a light. I have work to do for the rest of the evening.'

It seemed the secretary had been given a fall-back position. 'Of course, I quite understand. Could you come tomorrow then?'

'Saturday? Mr Holstead comes into the office on a Saturday?' To tell the truth Corie was surprised. She'd imagined the newspaper magnate lolling on his country estate over the weekend.

'Certainly, there's a *Sunday Globe* as well as a *Daily Globe*.'

'Is there?' returned Corie, though she well knew there was. She'd seen the placards outside newsagents advertising scandalous revelations about the private lives of the famous. But she had never read the *Globe*. Monna had strong views about newspapers. They took the *News Chronicle* and the

Telegraph on weekdays, and on Thursdays the *Stage*. For weekends they had American *Variety*, which had to be bought as and when available in a shop in Charing Cross Road.

'I have appointments tomorrow,' Corie said.

'You won't be free in the evening?'

Well, in fact, she would. Had it been a Saturday in June, she would have had weddings lined up until late in the day. But tomorrow there was one wedding, together with two studio appointments and a certain amount of bookkeeping.

'What time in the evening?' she asked, not to seem too willing.

'Six o'clock?'

'I can make it at six-thirty,' she said, 'but only if Mr Holstead really intends to give me his time.'

'That's quite understood, Miss Duggan. And I'm to tell you that you are to send in a bill for the time you spent at the *Globe* today.'

'I fully intended to,' she replied, though the thought hadn't crossed her mind. 'Good evening, Miss Bryant.'

'Until six-thirty tomorrow, Miss Duggan.'

Friday the thirteenth had turned out to be not a total disaster after all.

There was something flattering in being pursued. And having heard a little about the newspaper owner, she was quite interested to do his portrait. From everything she could learn, he seemed a frightening figure. To capture that formidable presence would be quite a challenge.

When she returned to the *Globe* car park the next evening the attendant wasn't on duty and there were far fewer cars in the spaces. The receptionist in the main hall was a uniformed concierge. He said, 'You know your way, miss?' and nodded her on.

Miss Bryant herself was waiting for her at the lift. Corie was on the verge of asking, 'Do you have to work all the time Mr Holstead works?' but thought better of it. The secretary led the way on, apologising for yesterday's fiasco: 'Running late, you know, it does happen . . .'

There was no delay this time. She was ushered straight in from the secretary's outer office into the inner sanctum. Ingram Holstead stood up behind his desk to stretch a hand across in greeting.

'Miss Duggan. You gave us quite a surprise yesterday.'

'Really? Do most people just sit around kicking their heels until you decide to see them?'

His thick eyebrows went up. 'It seemed to cause you a lot of annoyance.'

'Mr Holstead, I've been ignored by experts,' Corie said with a sigh of irritation. 'Agents, producers, casting directors – they like to keep you hanging about in the hall while they chat to Hollywood on the telephone – or so they'd like you to believe. When I left that profession, I decided I wasn't ever going to put up with that again.'

'You were an actress?'

'No,' she replied. 'Now, are you going to be actually working, or just sitting at the desk?'

He coloured. She was at once contrite. She'd come in in a fighting mood, but there was no need to lay it on so thick. 'I'm sorry,' she said, 'what I meant was, is this to be a portrait of you sitting at your desk or is it to be a character study of you actually at work?'

Holstead relaxed. 'I'm going to be working,' he said. 'I've still got to approve the leader page of tomorrow's *Globe* and one or two other things.' He waved a hand at the broadsheets lying on his desk. 'Most of the paper is in the hands of the sub-editors and the lay-out boys, but I always like to see the leader page and the main features page every day before they go to the printshop.'

'Very well. If you'd just settle down to work as you usually would, I'll have a look and see how it goes.'

She looked round for a surface on which to put her camera bag. The room had a sitting area, a sofa and armchairs at a low table. She put her camera bag on the table, got out the portable lights and looked for a power outlet.

'Behind the door,' Holstead prompted.

'Thank you. But don't watch what I'm doing, get on with your own things.'

'Right you are.'

When she'd got the portables set up, Corie got out the Leica. She moved softly about the room, looking at the desk and its occupant through the viewer.

She saw a big man, almost burly, fifty-ish, in a Savile Row suit of fine grey cloth and a silk shirt. The wiry hair was brushed back from a tanned, broad face. He wore horn-rimmed glasses which made his features even more strong and impressive. In one squarish hand he held a thick pencil with which he was making marks on the paste-up he studied.

The light in the room came mainly from two desk lamps, green shades lined with pure white – this for clarity when he was working on the lay-outs. It would have been good to take the photographs using only those lights, for they made a dramatic effect, a pool of brilliance on the edge of which sat Holstead, a presence half defined and half hinted at.

On the other hand, she'd been asked to do his portrait, not produce a mood piece. She thought about where to place her working lights and wondered whether she should bring out the portable spot to reflect off the ceiling.

When she glanced up, Holstead was watching her.

'Work!' she commanded him.

'I am working.'

'No you're not, you're wondering what I'm up to.'

'Well, that too. I'm surprised at how much preparation you're putting in. I thought it would just be a case of "Snip, snap" and it would be over.'

That shows how little you know, she thought to herself. Something of the thought must have reflected in her face for he said, 'I don't know anything about photography. I have editors to look after the illustrations in the paper.'

'I think that's the same on all the newspapers. It accounts for how bad the reproductions are.'

'What's that?'

'The photographs – they're usually very badly reproduced.'

'Not in *my* paper!' When she said nothing, he insisted: 'Photographs in the *Globe* are well-produced.'

'I don't know. I never read the *Globe*.'

'What?'

'Do you usually work with your suit jacket on?'

'What?' This time the word held bewilderment at the change of subject.

'When you're working in the evenings on lay-outs – do you generally have your jacket on?'

'Well . . . no . . .'

She hid a smile. Like almost everyone she ever met in her work, he felt impelled to be on his best behaviour for the camera.

'Take off your jacket then.'

'Yes . . . well . . . I don't think I want to.'

She left him to make up his own mind, busying herself with tilting one of her floods to bounce some glow off the ceiling. She didn't want the room too light if it was normally rather dark except for the desk itself.

Holstead, for his part, returned his attention to the leader page of the next day's paper. Something caught his attention, he began to track down the lines with his pencil. After a moment he wrote something in the margin. Muttering, he picked up another broadsheet to lay alongside the one he was working on. Corie gathered they were two version of the same page and he was trying to assimilate something from one into the other.

She looked through the viewfinder and focused. It looked dull. A big man in a good suit looking at some paper. She took the picture, however, because one must make a start somewhere.

Ten minutes later she'd made about six exposures and Holstead had forgotten she was there. He peeled a piece of text off the sheet, pasted on another in its place. His fingers were sticky with gum. He pulled his breast-pocket handkerchief out to wipe them clean. Corie took a shot.

He had a habit of running a hand through his hair when he was thinking. Soon the carefully brushed surface was in a mess. He had loosened his tie. He fished for a cigar, lit it, breathed upwards so as not to obscure his view. It all went on film.

With an angry gesture he threw away the sheet on which he'd been working. It floated down past his desk surface to land on the floor. Corie, prowling quietly behind him, saw that there were already three or four try-outs lying at his feet. She stayed behind him, watching for a profile. The lights weren't best placed but the atmosphere was there – the evening-time with the paper waiting to go to press, the uncertainty over the lay-out, the end-of-day wish to get the thing finished and yet the need to get it right . . .

As always happened, she found herself being drawn into the scene as well as observing it. For the time of taking the photograph she became part of that life, and in so doing breathed warmth, involvement, excitement into what appeared in the eventual print.

A tap at the door brought Miss Bryant. 'Sorry to interrupt, Mr Lowther's had to change the front page which means the run-on of the Ealing Studios story begins six lines further up—'

'Which column's that?'

She glanced at her notebook. 'Column five, Mr Holstead.'

'Oh, God! Is he expecting a six-line cut?'

'He says you've got two inches on the Bannhill School story that could go—'

'Where? I don't see it.'

'On Lay-out Two, sir.'

'All right, tell him to ring me if he can put it back to the way it was, it looked good at that point.' He had quite forgotten Corie's existence. As his secretary went out he got down on his knees to find a discarded paste-up. When he got up he was perspiring. He took off his jacket.

Now there was light reflected on to his features from his shirt. Corie walked quietly round from his left to his right behind him, taking shot after shot.

When she looked at her watch, it showed almost eight

o'clock. She switched off her floods. Startled, Holstead looked up. 'What—'

'It's me. I've finished.'

'Oh.' It took a moment to remember who she was. 'Get what you want?'

'Yes, thank you.'

'When do I see them?'

'Proofs the day after tomorrow.'

'Right.' He turned back to his lay-out, then waited impatiently while she dismantled her gear and stowed it away. She was sure he'd forgotten her before she even closed the door behind her.

In that she was wrong. Ingram Holstead seldom met people who refused to be over-awed. This woman photographer was something different from the kind he usually collected around him. She wasn't pretty, she wasn't glamorous, she wasn't rich or influential.

All the same, she intrigued him.

Chapter Five

There was a little ceremony at the unveiling of the photograph. After the Friday editorial conference, heads of departments and their wives, a few of the directors, even fewer of the journalistic staff, some art critics and a scattering of bigwigs from the law, Parliament and the House of Lords gathered. Corie was of course invited.

'Now at last you'll wear a dress,' suggested her mother.

'I haven't got anything suitable.'

'Well, buy something! Surely your fee from Mr Holstead will be enough to pay for a dress!'

'Just about, I'd say. But I begrudge spending any of it on a dress. What use is it going to be afterwards?'

'You can wear it the next time you're invited to a party.'

'Most parties are evening events. As I'm invited to a buffet lunch, this would have to be a day dress. You know I spend my days in slacks.'

'To my shame and disgrace,' Monna lamented. 'It's so unladylike—'

'But much more practical for the bike.'

'You're not thinking of turning up for this unveiling on that dreadful bike!'

'Why not?'

Corie was teasing her mother, but Monna was too much in earnest to discern the fact. Her daughter had actually been thinking about buying a dress, but those she saw in the shops seemed so bizarre with their nipped-in waists and bell-shaped skirts. Corie had the waist for them, no doubt of that – but the idea of having to manage the skirt, and presumably a layer of underskirts . . .

In the end she bought a pair of black velvet toreador pants and a blouse with bishop sleeves and a black bow at the collar. With these she wore flat black patent shoes with silver buckles.

'You look more like a page-boy than a businesswoman,' Opal laughed when she saw the finished result. 'And what are you going to wear over it — not the famous duffle coat?'

'No, you know that old Spanish shawl that used to be draped over the piano . . . ?'

'Good heavens, it must be filthy dirty, Corie!'

'I've had it cleaned.' She took it out of the drawer in her dressing-table, unwrapped the tissue paper, shook it out, and whirled it about herself. With its outrageous display of pink and red roses on black, it made an effect. Good or bad, she wasn't sure which.

As a sop to her mother's feelings she went to the *Globe* offices in a taxi, not on the Sunbeam.

She was expected at the *Globe*'s reception desk. When she stepped out of the lift, the sound of laughter and conversation directed her to the open door of the board-room. On her entrance one or two heads turned, then when Holstead espied her and hurried to greet her, people paused to look at her.

'Miss Duggan! Everyone's dying to meet you. Come in, come in, let me get you a drink.' He gestured with a hand, a tray of champagne glasses appeared as if by magic.

Corie allowed a waiter to relieve her of her shawl. She accepted a glass of champagne.

'Now, everyone . . . Attention, please! The great moment has arrived. I'll ask my art editor to conduct the proceedings.'

Paterson the art editor stepped forward. He had a few notes scribbled down on a scrap of paper. 'My lords, ladies and gentlemen . . . Over the past year or so the name of Corie Duggan has become well known to us. Most of you will have seen the magnificent study of Lady Barrington which appeared — I regret to say — in the Diary feature of a rival newspaper.' Muted cries of 'Shame!' and some laughter. 'If you look around you'll see it's been the custom of *Globe* Newspapers to have portrait studies of its managing editors on the boardroom walls. In the far corner by the door, there are sketches and engravings from the 1840s which used to hang in the old building. As soon as photography began to be a dependable art, the *Globe* – always being of course in the vanguard of technical change – began to commission photographic portraits. I'm happy to invite Mrs Leneuve-Brown, wife of our chief legal adviser Edward Leneuve-Brown, to unveil the study by Miss Duggan of our present chairman and managing editor, Mr Ingram Holstead.'

Mrs Leneuve-Brown, in a dress with a nipped-in waist and a bell-shaped skirt and wearing elbow-length gloves, pulled a little cord. A small curtain fell from the portrait.

Holstead had chosen one from the group Corie had taken at the end of the sitting. He was in his shirt sleeves, his hair was somewhat on end, cigar smoke wreathed up from an ashtray at his elbow. Round his feet discarded sheets of paper lay in disarray. A thick pencil in his right hand was poised to make a mark on the lay-out before him, and to judge by his expression the change he was about to make was going to improve matters one hundred per cent.

Corie had printed it to make the most of the contrast between light and dark. The face was three-quarters turned to the camera but there were shadows which lent drama to his eyes and to the bone structure of his jaw.

Applause greeted the unveiling. People gathered round Corie to ask inane questions such as, 'How does it feel to photograph such an important man?' She made brief replies, sipped her champagne, and was glad when they drifted off to sample the display on the buffet table. A handsome young woman now caught Corie's elbow.

'I'm Madge Burnaby, the fashion editor of the Sunday paper. Can I do a feature on your clothes?'

'My clothes?'

'I hear you turned up to take the pix in a pair of narrow trousers and a man's silk shirt – is that right?'

'Well, yes.'

'And today this sort of toreador look. Do you generally wear trousers?'

'Yes, it's more convenient for my work.'

'Explain that,' said Miss Burnaby in a tone which conveyed she was accustomed to being obeyed.

'Well, I still do a lot of commercial photography, which means I have to go to factories or warehouses or industrial estates. Trousers are more practical.'

'I see that. But in town – do you wear trousers all the time in town?'

'Yes.'

'You feel they express something about yourself?'

'I feel that it's easier getting on and off a motorbike in trousers.'

'So they're not part of your fashion philosophy?'

Corie laughed, and then coughed as champagne went down the wrong way. 'I haven't *got* a fashion philosophy! I don't bother much about fashion.'

The journalist looked at her with disbelief. 'That outfit you've got on is proof to the contrary. What you've got there is a "total look". That shawl you were wearing when you came in, for instance – I imagine you planned everything around that?'

She was on the verge of confessing that it came off the grand piano in the living-room. But before she could commit such a gaffe, they were joined by a thin, middle-aged man in a suit that had seen better days. 'Introduce me,' he prompted Miss Burnaby.

'Go away, Norm, we're talking fashion.'

'Be careful what you say, Miss Duggan, or she'll have you telling the world you wear Jaeger combinations under your skinny pants. I'm Norman Gibson, a writer of genius forced to work as a hack for this blighted publication.'

'Don't believe a word he says,' the fashion editor said as she moved off.

He laughed. 'I thought you seemed a bit badgered, so I came to the rescue. Not everybody shares Madge's obsession with clothes. Though, mind you, I think you know a thing or two about them, from the way you look in those togs.'

She shook her head. 'I'm being credited with a lot more expertise than I actually possess. So, Mr Gibson, what kind of things do you write?' Always ask a man about his job, Monna had impressed on her daughters from an early age.

'Oh, in-depth investigations, special features. I'm on the Sunday, not the daily. I gather we're going to publish the portrait on Sunday.'

'No!'

'Yes. Why so surprised?'

'I thought this was a character study for the boardroom.'

'Two for the price of one — that's Holstead at all times. He never misses a trick. If he can let the world know that the board of directors wanted his picture done, and he had the good taste to hire Corie Duggan, and the said Corie Duggan produced a masterpiece of photography—'

'Oh . . . A masterpiece?'

'It's very good,' Gibson said, nodding. 'You've got him to a T — absolutely sure he's right, changing something his lay-out boys have taken all afternoon to set up . . .'

Corie eyed him. 'You don't like him.'

'Who does?' He produced a cigarette case, offered it to her then, when she shook her head, lit up. Nicotine-stained fingers told how much he'd been longing for one.

'Why do you work for him, then?'

''Cos he gives me the chance to go where the action is, to think about what I write and maybe make some sort of impact. He's not *all* bad. But this rubbish about seeing the leader page and getting it right . . . There's a highly trained staff who do that when he's off visiting his missus in the USA, and no one rings up to say, "You've made a mess of it".'

'You mean he's kidding himself?'

'Well, we all do it to some extent. I'm probably kidding myself when I say my feature articles have impact. So . . . How will you feel when you're featured in the fashion page on Sunday?'

'Don't suggest such a thing!'

'But I mean it. Madge never wastes her time. And here come the staff photographers to make an imperishable record of today's great event. Your clothes will be featured in the *Sunday Globe* with commentary by Madge Burnaby.'

Corie didn't believe him but it turned out to be true. Almost word for word, her conversation with the fashion writer was reported, but somehow it was made to sound as if she was conscious of leading a fashion trend.

'Wow!' said Lynette when the family passed the paper around at Sunday breakfast. 'Never got publicity like this when you were First Flower Fairy in *Jack and the Beanstalk*.'

'She's dancing under better beanstalks these days,' Opal chimed in.

They went into gales of laughter. 'Now, now,' Monna reproved. 'You see, it's what I always say: clothes *are* important.'

'Even when you aren't wearing a dress,' said Opal.

'Don't encourage her! Think how much nicer the pictures would have been if she'd been wearing something by Hardy Amies,' Monna insisted, totally missing the point of the fashion article. She sighed, rustling the pages. 'I wish Sasha could get this kind of coverage for you, Lynette dear.'

'But Lynette herself is seen by a far bigger public every time she appears on telly, Monna.'

'But she never gets a write-up – except one or two lines in the *Stage* now and again . . .'

Corie had got hold of the paper and was looking at the portrait study, which had been printed on the Arts page of the paper. The *Sunday Globe* could hardly be said to pay much attention to 'Art'. Only if there was something shocking or otherwise newsy did it bother with exhibitions.

Today, of course, as far as the *Globe* was concerned, this photograph was news. Its managing editor and owner was always news. The art editor was happy to justify his salary by telling the readers what a wonderful portrait it was. And there was no doubt it did look good, whole-plate size across four columns at the top of the page.

She couldn't help a surge of pride as she looked at it. But the pride turned to laughter the next day.

The photograph having been put in the public domain, rival newspapers couldn't resist commenting on it. The funniest quip, to Corie's mind, was in the *Express*, where the cartoonist had portrayed the board members looking at her study of Holstead with all the discarded lay-outs round his feet. One board member was saying to another, 'Can't get good help anywhere these days.'

Corie's name was already known to some extent, and certainly readers of the *Sunday Globe* had been made to take note of it. But now, thanks to the general comment and the jokes at the expense of Ingram Holstead, the whole of Britain had heard of Corie Duggan by midday on Monday.

Holstead himself was quick to cash in on the publicity. He rang before the end of the week to invite Corie to a charity performance at the Coliseum the following Sunday.

'Oh . . . Sunday . . . I have a lot of processing to do on Sundays,' Corie told him.

'You don't mean to say you do your own?'

'Certainly I do! How do you think I got such a dramatic effect with your portrait studies? I took a lot of care over the developing and printing.'

'But surely for just ordinary—' He broke off. She was convinced he'd been going to say 'ordinary people'. He altered it to, 'Ordinary engagements – birthday portraits, weddings – surely you don't do all the developing for those?'

'Yes I do.'

A pause. 'Well, since you seem to be heading into the Big Time, don't you think you ought to hire an assistant to do the donkey work?'

Corie was about to say she wasn't 'heading into the Big Time'. But he'd think she was fishing for compliments. And besides, she sensed he was right. Public perception, public interest, had caused her phone to ring almost ceaselessly since Monday afternoon. The great and the would-be great wanted their picture taken by Corie Duggan. It was time to stop being a one-woman business.

'I think I might look around for someone,' she murmured into the phone.

'Start looking right away, so that you'll be free on Sunday to come to the show.'

'We-ell . . .'

'I've taken a box. You'll meet some interesting people.'

She accepted the invitation. Monna was thrilled when she heard about it that evening. 'The Coliseum! In a box! And I was just reading yesterday that all sorts of people are taking part. Valerie Hobson and Herbert Lom from *The King and I*, Cicely Courtneidge . . . Now, darling, you will buy a dress for this, won't you?'

'I'll think about it.'

In the end she did not. Her sister's remark about looking like a page-boy had reminded her of an item in their communal wardrobe. In the past their mother had made them enter any talent show for which they were eligible, and for these there was a small variety of costumes, now unused, in a theatrical basket in the attic. Corie bethought herself of a certain crimson satin shirt which she and Opal and Lynette had all worn at some time. It went with either black satin shorts – the page-boy look – for tap routines, or a matching net skirt and a white rose for romantic songs and dances.

Corie partnered it with her new toreador pants.

'If you want to wear the blouse, why don't you wear the skirt that goes with it?' cried her mother in despair.

'Because, Monna darling, my "fashion philosophy" is that I wear trousers. Madge Burnaby told everyone so last Sunday – I can't disappoint my public.'

'Your public? Corie, you're not letting this go to your head, are you?'

'Of course not, Monna. I'm only joking. The point is, for a do like this, a dress from Pontings wouldn't fit the bill, it'd have to be more like Harrods. And I can't afford that if I'm going to pay wages to an assistant.'

'Well, at least if someone else is going to do all that messy business in the darkroom, you won't have chemical stains under your fingernails any more.'

'Quite right,' Corie agreed, although privately she felt she would always want to do the important pieces herself in the darkroom.

The evening at the Coliseum was moderately enjoyable. Excerpts from successful shows, songs by the current recording stars, some specially written sketches for the funny men, a hardworking chorus-line who had her heartfelt sympathy as they danced their under-rehearsed way through the programme . . .

The best part was afterwards, when they all went to the Savoy for supper. Ingram Holstead had reserved a private room for his guests. They sat round a big oval table to eat a very fine meal, talking and laughing. Corie watched her fellow guests, wishing she'd brought a camera – people in their unguarded moments made such good subjects.

That was the first of a sequence of invitations from Ingram. He liked to be in the public eye; she soon gathered that he liked to have a current woman-friend whom he could escort and show off. Nobody ordinary – he had been paired with a film star, a woman playwright, a beauty-of-the-year debutante, a well-known owner of racehorses – and now a photographer.

There was nothing sexual in it. Or at least so it was with Corie – she didn't care to guess how he'd viewed the debutante or the film star. Gossip columnists usually described his partners as 'and friend, Miss Whoever . . .' and then would follow what was interesting about the 'and friend'. Corie was universally described as 'a well-known photographer'.

On one occasion, when others from the *Globe* were present, she found Norman Gibson at her elbow. 'So,' he inquired, blowing smoke-rings to one side of her head, 'how do you like the limelight?'

'Not really my kind of thing.'

'That would be my guess. Most of his chicks are out to

get something from him. Not you, I imagine.'

'What could he give me, anyhow?' Corie wondered.

'Money? Contacts?'

'Oh, well . . . I suppose I'm gathering contacts. But I don't do it on purpose. I think I really accepted his invitations in the first place because my mother was so thrilled to be connected with a newspaper tycoon.' She hesitated a moment then said, 'Can I ask you a naïve question?'

'Try me.'

'There's a Mrs Holstead, isn't there?'

'Certainly. And two young Holsteads.'

'Oh, help. I . . . I sort of knew about his wife, but not the children.'

'Don't worry about them. We're not talking about little kiddiwinks. They're in their teens, at posh American private schools.'

Corie relaxed in relief. It had troubled her a lot, the thought that she was going out with a married man, even though on a rather formal footing. 'I heard something to the effect that Mrs Holstead lives in America,' she said.

'Her choice. She went there with the children when war broke out and only comes back occasionally, for a birthday party or something like that.'

'Oh . . . So they're not on bad terms, then?'

Norm grinned. 'Depends what you mean by bad terms. If you want my opinion, I think Helen Holstead despises her husband. She comes from old American money – she thinks the *Globe* is trashy. But on the other hand, she's got a strong sense of duty, doesn't want to let Eddie and Mirabel grow up fatherless. So she does what she can to give the impression of being a family by bringing them across the Atlantic a couple of times a year. You'll probably meet her some time.'

'Good heavens!'

'Don't let it frighten you. She won't be much bothered about you. She never has been about any of the others.'

Corie felt herself go red to the roots of her hair. 'Look, all

I did was take his picture,' she said in a mixture of embarrassment and anger.

'Did I say different?' Norm patted her on her satin-covered shoulder. 'But you see what comes of being in the photography game. How did you take it up in the first place?'

'So as to earn more money than I did as a waitress.'

'You were a *waitress*?'

'What's wrong with that?'

'Very hard work and low pay, that's what's wrong with that.' Norm looked for an ashtray to dispose of his stub. 'Your family surely couldn't approve of a job like that.'

'My family are quite accustomed to taking what we can get while we're "resting".'

'Ah! Your family is a stage family!'

She laughed. 'Let's say, our family is a television family. The only one that's really doing anything worth mentioning is my kid sister. She's a dancer in "Café Charmant".'

'Really?' Then after a moment he added, 'Well, I think I heard something about that the other day.'

'About "Café Charmant"? What?'

Now he looked embarrassed. 'I shouldn't have said that,' he mumbled, running a hand through his thinning hair.

'Why not?' Corie felt a prick of alarm. 'It's something bad?'

'It's only a rumour our showbiz editor mentioned.'

'What? Come on, you can't leave it at that – what did you hear?' She laid a hand on his sleeve, to let him see her anxiety. He was a man who didn't like close contact.

'Well, I hear it's coming off.'

' "Café Charmant"? It can't be!' It was still popular. Audience research by the BBC showed it to have an enthusiastic following for its mixture of song and dance and big-band numbers.

'Sorry,' Norm muttered. 'It may not be right. I was told it's to do with the band-leader – what's his name?'

'Bob Barlow.'

'That's it, Bob Barlow. I was told he's putting on too

much weight to be a romantic link among the songs and so forth. It was a gossip item about him, really – he told Joe Mathers he didn't want to do any more Sophisticated Sam stuff, wants to change his image. So the show's going into the out-tray.'

Corie's first thought was not 'Poor Lynette' but 'Poor Monna'. Her mother's pride and ambition were bound up in her youngest daughter's success. Lynette herself wouldn't fret. She had too much faith in Sasha Lenoir to think her career was at all endangered by the closing of the show.

Ingram Holstead bore down upon them, frowning a little, 'Now, now, what's all this "heads together" business?'

'We were just talking about television, Ingram,' Norm said in haste. It was clear to Corie he knew he ought not to monopolise the boss's lady-friend. 'Corie's family is—'

'Charles Rabowitz wants to meet you, Corie, he's a merchant banker, wants a picture done for the *Economist* – come and fix things up.'

She allowed herself to be swept along, to talk appointment dates with the banker while her mind stayed on Lynette. It couldn't be true about 'Café Charmant' – but on the other hand her own experience had taught her how uncertain showbiz could be. And particularly when the star, the big name, became dissatisfied.

She kept the rumour to herself. No need to upset her family before the event, which might never take place.

A vain hope. About three weeks later Lynette came home looking subdued. 'We all got our notice this morning,' she said. 'Bob Barlow's pulling out and the BBC feel they can't replace him.'

'My darling!' Monna cried, rushing to take her youngest child into her arms. 'You mustn't let it worry you! A girl with so much talent will always find something—'

'Oh, I'm not upset for myself,' Lynette put in, patting her mother on the back as she hugged her. 'It's the other dancers – they've got to begin looking for work.'

'It's so typical of you, dear heart, to think of others,' said

Monna, stepping back to look with some irritation at Lynette. 'All the same, we don't want a setback in your career . . .'

'No, Sasha says not to worry,' her daughter replied with perfect good cheer. 'He's lining up something for me.'

'There! I knew it! The right agent, you know . . . It makes all the difference.'

'What's he lining up for you?' Opal wanted to know.

'Don't know. It's sort of hush-hush, Pal. Some of the other dancers want him to act for them and he says he'll do his best but he can't promise to get them into this thing he's working on for me.' Lynette dropped into an armchair and clasped her hands behind her fair head. 'Anyhow, *I'm* not going to worry.'

Corie, taking it all in and worrying, said nothing. And it turned out her fears were groundless because, before Lynette's week of notice was up, Sasha appeared at the Duggan home in triumph.

'Congratulate me, everybody! What d'you think? I've landed a featured part for Lynette!'

Featured! Her name near the beginning of the credit lines, not merely mentioned among the group headed 'Dancers'! All the Duggans exclaimed in delight.

'But what? What's she going to do?' Monna demanded. 'Whatever it is I know she's going to be a credit to me, but what sort of a role *have* you got for her, dear boy?'

'Yes, what am I going to do?' Lynette asked, her eyes shining.

'It's a new show, "Bob Barlow Presents". You know up till now he's always been portrayed as a bit of a heart-throb – now he's decided he wants to be a family figure.'

'To go with his girth,' suggested Corie with some dryness.

'Now, now, Corie, don't belittle a fellow artiste,' her mother scolded. 'Go on, Sasha.'

'What he wants to do is, he's going to introduce a guest star or two—'

'But that's just like "Café Charmant"—'

'No, no, there's to be a bit of acting as well — a couple of comedy sketches that are being written for him.'

'But where does Lynette come in?' Monna implored.

'She's going to be the pretty niece, playing up to Barlow as "Uncle Bob".'

To say they were rendered speechless was an understatement. This was a very big step up for Lynette. From one of a group of eight dancers, she was to be spotlighted, playing against the star of the show.

'Is that why . . . Is that why Mr Tranton had me read those lines the day before yesterday?' Lynette faltered.

'You've got it. He wanted to see if you could carry off a few joky exchanges with Bob. See, the sketches are to show Bob coming to the rescue of this innocent little sweetie who keeps falling for the wrong man, or being diddled by a salesman, or in some sort of comic trouble. Then we'll see Bob going into action, sorting out the baddie, and it ends with him and Lynette beaming with smiles and Lynette saying, "You're so wonderful, Uncle Bob".'

'Lynette is not as important as Mr Barlow?' Monna queried, with a stifled sigh.

'Now, now, I know what you're thinking, Monna dear,' Sasha said with a little bow in her direction. 'You, with your sense of stagecraft, can see Lynette is really only a foil for Barlow. But it's good money, and she's made for the part.'

'Ye-es . . . Does she get to sing or dance? I never think learning lines is as interesting as a good singing role.'

'I think so — she sings along with Barlow at least once, and I think she'll be featured as leading the chorus.'

'It's an ingénue part,' Monna decided.

'I think you could say so.'

Corie saw it more clearly than her mother. Lynette was going to benefit from this new part. Anyone who appeared close-up on British television almost automatically became a household name. It could only be a good thing, even if it meant still being under the shadow of Bob Barlow.

The show went into rehearsal so as to be put into the

programme schedules in the spring of 1954. The first episode was screened in April for the Easter Holiday. The Duggan family, now the proud possessors of a non-rental TV set, sat watching with all their fingers and toes crossed.

The programme started in a way that Monna felt inauspicious for her daughter. The opening title faded to show a beaming Bob Barlow, filling the screen. The big-band number that followed was very much the usual opening from 'Café Charmant'.

'But this is just the same old thing,' she sighed.

'Perhaps the producer wants to bring the following from "Café Charmant" into this new show by slow degrees,' Corie suggested.

'Mr Barlow seems to me to be having everything his own way,' Monna replied.

But she began to approve about five minutes later, when Lynette drifted on to sing 'By the Light of the Silvery Moon' with Barlow. She danced, Barlow did a few soft-shoe-shuffle steps and handed her to and fro. It was charming if not exactly inspiring.

Guests followed, then a dance number. Monna expressed pleasure that Lynette was well out in front of the chorus and dressed in a filmy garden-party frock, whereas the other girls were in print and the men were in dungarees.

But her total approval came in the comedy sketches. In the first, Lynette had come home from a party to say the boy who'd taken her there turned out to be engaged to somebody else. She looked ravishing in mid-calf length petticoats covered in pale, floaty organza. True, she didn't appear again until Uncle Bob had sorted out the villain who had trifled with niece Sally's affections, but when she did she was once more pretty as a picture in gingham with lace ruffles and a big white daisy in her hair.

'That costume designer knows what he's doing,' mused Corie. 'He's making our kidlet look like every father's dream of a beautiful daughter.'

'She should have had more to do,' Monna objected.

'Never mind, perhaps she'll get to recite "The quality of

mercy" in the next sketch,' Opal suggested.

'Opal, how many times have I told you not to be frivolous!'

'More times than I care to remember,' Pal said below her breath, but now the show was rolling on to its next item.

They sat through another guest appearance, another big-band number featuring the band's crooner, and then the last sketch. This one was about niece Sally losing the money collected in her office for the wedding present of a colleague. She hung on her uncle's shoulder, sighing and looking helpless but with a glint of humour that somehow conveyed no one was to take it seriously. Uncle Bob sallied forth, found the money, Sally bought a hideous vase with it for her unfortunate colleague, and the sketch ended with Barlow and his 'niece' singing 'It All Depends On You'.

Even Monna had no fault to find. 'Lovely,' she sighed. 'Just lovely. Oh, my darling girl, I always knew she had it in her.'

'Not bad for our kidlet,' Corie said, filled with pride.

'Not bad? It was gorgeous! She *must* get a mention in the reviews!'

Monna was right. Next day's television columns all mentioned Lynette especially. On the whole they were approving of 'Bob Barlow Presents' but their main pleasure was at the new format, the sketches which made the show different from other strings of variety acts that were put on in the name of Light Entertainment.

'Mention must be made of a new young charmer who pleased the eye . . .' 'Lynette Lee, a personality fresh and new . . .' 'Some may remember her as a dancer in "Café Charmant", but here she displays further talents . . .'

The family cut out the reviews for the family scrapbook. Corie felt that nothing more exciting could possibly happen to the Duggan family.

She was wrong. At the end of April Ingram Holstead asked her to come to his office for a conference.

'A conference about what?' Corie asked, surprised.

'I don't want to discuss it over the phone. Be here tomorrow, three-thirty.'

'But, Ingram, I have sitters coming—'

'Put them off. This is really important.'

He had rung off before she could protest further, but in any case it wasn't difficult to hand over the sittings to her assistant, a middle-aged man called Bertie Lulsworth, competent if uninspired.

She arrived at the *Globe* and, by now well known to the receptionist, was waved on. When the secretary showed her into the inner office, she was surprised to see Norman Gibson sitting there. He rose, shook hands, then subsided into his chair again.

'Miss Bryant's bringing tea. We'll just wait till that's done.' Ingram leaned back in his leather chair, the very picture of the powerful managing editor.

'Saw your sister on the box the other night,' Norm said. 'Jolly D.'

'Not at all bad, was she?'

'Liked her. I'm not so keen on Big Bob. He's not really much of a comic turn. I wanted the niece to turn up more — at least she's pretty to look at.'

Corie laughed. Miss Bryant came in pushing a tea-trolley bearing a silver tea service, bone china, a plate of Fortnum's biscuits. She smiled at everyone, looked an invitation at Corie, and withdrew. Corie realised she was to pour the tea for the menfolk. Sighing a little to herself, she rose to do so.

'Now,' Ingram said, raising a thick forefinger, 'you know that the prisoners-of-war from Korea were in bad shape, some of them.'

Corie concentrated on pouring tea into the fine cups. She thought the question was addressed to Norm.

'Corie!'

'Yes?'

'Did you hear what I said?'

'About the soldiers from the Korean war — yes, I heard.'

'The last of them are about to be released from hospital in Tokyo,' Ingram said. 'I want you and Norm to go there and do a big photo feature on it.'

Chapter Six

Corie almost dropped the silver teapot. She felt it waver in her hand, took a firmer grasp, then set it down.

'That was, of course, a joke.'

'I never joke about important assignments,' Ingram retorted. 'I've arranged for you and Norm to fly out of RAF Lyneham on Sunday.'

'But I've never taken news photographs!'

'Here's your chance to start.'

'You must have a dozen photographers on your staff who'd be better—'

'But their names would mean nothing to the readers. You're somebody, the pix you take will be looked at. See here, Corie,' he said, frowning at her with great earnestness, 'during the war the papers were full of news about "our boys". What have you heard about the troops who fought in Korea?'

'Well . . .'

'There was some good reporting while the fighting was going on,' Norman Gibson took it up, 'but since the ceasefire Korea's a forgotten country. And the men who served there – and some of them are still there as a garrison – who hears about them?'

Corie studied him. 'Why do you feel so strongly about it?'

'My neighbour at home has a son who served in Korea. All he has to show for it is four toes damaged by frostbite and a year and a half lost out of his career. I want people to *think* about the war. It cost something – I want them to be aware.'

She looked from one man to the other. 'It's your idea, Norm?'

'Yes.'

'Surely you'd rather have an experienced newspaperman along with you?'

'I want you to go, Corie,' Ingram said. 'Norm agreed when I suggested it.'

Norm was nodding. 'My name means nothing much to the readers. Other newsmen know my byline but I don't suppose one reader in a hundred notices who's written the feature. But if we had "Pictures by Corie Duggan" as a heading, people would look, and read, and get to thinking.'

'I really don't feel it's my kind of thing.'

There was a little pause. 'Look,' Norm said, embarrassed, 'if you don't take it on, it's no go. I put the idea up to Ingram and he didn't really think too much to it, until he got the inspiration to send you as my cameraman.'

Corie flushed. 'That's a kind of blackmail,' she said.

'Not at all. If you don't take it on, it's just another idea that goes into the discard. There have been plenty of those, believe me. But I really would like to do this.'

'I really can't. I've got appointments lined up for the next month—'

'Didn't you tell me you'd hired an assistant?' Ingram put in.

'Yes, Bertie . . . But . . .'

'Anything extra-special you could put off until you get back. It's only going to be a week or ten days.'

'To Tokyo and back?' she said, amazed.

'Of course. Fly out with RAF transport, fly back with the hospital plane. According to the War Office, the schedule finishes on 8 May — and the Army is usually efficient about dates.'

'But I can't! I haven't got a passport.'

Ingram smiled with satisfaction. 'I have friends in high places. That can all be taken care of.'

'But I've no experience — what if the pix are no good?'

'Scared of the challenge?' Ingram asked.

After that it was only a matter of time before she gave in. She could never allow it to be said that she was afraid.

But in fact she was. During the next hurried days the fear

was always there – fear that she would look silly and inexperienced to the officers who dealt with her, fear that the plane would crash on take-off, fear that it would crash on landing, fear that the cameras would be damaged as she lugged them on and off, fear that when she began to use them she'd have the wrong film loaded or the flash wouldn't work.

In between times she experienced a sense of great exhilaration. Flying, once the plane had got off the ground, was great. A floor of woolly cloud beneath you, a sense of freedom from all earthly care, of rushing towards some great adventure.

The RAF transport plane wasn't the acme of luxury but, as she had no standards of comparison, she didn't complain. The food that was served pleased her, in its dinky little containers. Norm, on the contrary, said very rude things about it. He also said very rude things about Tokyo, which was still trying to recover from World War II. Imperial Plaza had been tidied up, but there were many vacant lots, many scars. Matters weren't helped by arriving in the dusk in a drenching rainstorm.

'Rotten country,' grunted the corporal who drove them in an Army car to their hotel. 'Either it's raining, or it's hot and humid, or it's cold and snowy, or there's an earthquake.'

Corie was too tired after the plane trip to care. All she wanted was to get to the hotel, have a bath, and fall into bed.

'I don't know what's the matter with me,' she apologised to Norm.

'It's called jet lag,' he told her. 'Don't worry, it isn't fatal.'

She slept for twelve hours. When she became conscious again she found a message on the floor inside her room door: 'I'll be in the dining-room if you surface before ten a.m. If later, ask for a message at Reception.'

She looked, bleary-eyed, at her watch. Nine-sixteen. She got up, showered under hot water, then cold, until she felt more human, then cleaned her teeth for long minutes to get rid of a dreadful taste in her mouth – partly due to sitting alongside that smoking machine, Norm Gibson.

When she looked out of her window, she saw that it was a fine May day. Cheered, she put on corduroys and a Sea Island cotton shirt, stuffed a pullover into her bag in case it was cooler than she expected, checked her cameras, and went downstairs.

Norm was at a table cluttered with the remains of the full English breakfast. She found she was ravenously hungry. 'Is it too late to order the same?' she ventured.

'Good morning, Corie. No, in a Japanese hotel it's never too late to order anything. Politeness is the name of their game.' He pulled out a chair for her, but before he could complete the action a waiter was there, doing it for him.

Corie ate while Norm set out the plan for the day. They were to be escorted to the British Army Hospital on the outskirts of the city. There they would be met by an Army Press Officer who would be their guide and guardian.

'He'll probably try to stop us from asking awkward questions or prying into things they don't want known, but pay no heed. If there's an argument, leave it all to me – I've had a lot of experience at getting my own way.'

His warlike attitude was uncalled for. The Press Officer turned out to be a pretty WRAC, Captain Heighton. She disarmed Norm from the outset, so that in fact it was Corie who asked the questions, though none of them was awkward. How far to the hospital, how many patients, were all the men due to be home by 8 May?

'Yes, the British Army's winding up its hospital here. From now on, any cases will be taken by the Americans. It makes sense – while the peace negotiations go on and the ceasefire lasts, there's very little work for a hospital.'

'While the ceasefire lasts? Do you think it's likely to break down?'

'Who knows? The North Koreans are a tough bunch.'

Corie looked at Norman, waiting for him to take the opportunity. Here was a chance to get background information. Instead he said, 'Been here long, Captain?'

'Six months. I'm expecting a posting any day now.'

Corie listened to the ensuing conversation with ironic amusement. Norm was laying up material for a different article, one about what it was like to be a woman in a man's army. But she wasn't surprised. She'd realised quite early that Norm was manipulative. He'd helped Ingram Holstead bulldoze her into accepting this assignment, but only because without her his idea would be thrown out. Now he was collecting information for something in the future, something he might sell to a women's magazine.

The hospital's main building had been the house of a disgraced Japanese general. The grounds were extensive – the sign of wealth in Tokyo – so these had been used for Quonset huts to provide extra amenities.

As they walked towards the main building, Corie could see men in wheelchairs, men walking carefully with crutches, men being helped along by nursing orderlies. The sun shone, lilac scented the air, the scene was peaceful.

They were welcomed by the matron, Major Belling of Queen Alexandra's Royal Army Nursing Corps. Elevenses were offered and, though Corie hadn't any need of refreshment after her huge breakfast, at a nudge from Norman she agreed.

'We always have mid-morning drinks,' Major Belling explained. 'Another chance to get something body-building into our patients. You understand that these are the last of the men who were prisoners-of-war? They came to us needing all kinds of medical care, some with wounds that had received little or no attention when they were captured, some suffering from severe malnutrition. Before we could help them, we had to nurse them into a state where they were well enough for an operation.'

Norm nodded, got out a notebook, began to act more like a journalist on a story. Corie felt it would be awkward to ask if she could take pictures in the Matron's sitting-room. But she checked her cameras.

With her she had brought a view camera for the larger

scene, a minature for the quick-action or taken-on-the-wing shots, and a Rolleiflex, by now a comfortable friend. Her bag was full of film stock.

When at last they set off with the matron's blessing and the Press Officer as guide, she began using the Rollei. Almost at once she had shot it out. Rather than reload, she began using the miniature and soon had taken seventy-two shots.

'Hold hard,' Norman murmured. 'We haven't even got to the wards!'

She moved aside to load once more. As she did so, she came face to face with a man in khaki, walking by himself under the trees, head bent. He looked up to apologise as he stepped around her.

She knew – and was ashamed – that her face showed horror. The man's features were terribly disfigured.

'Sorry, miss,' he said as he went by, 'didn't mean to scare you.'

'No – of course not—'

But he was gone, and her apology was lost on the soft May air.

That was her introduction to the aftermath of war. In stricken silence she went round the grounds at the side of Norman Gibson, taking shot after shot. One of the orderlies was detailed to take on the task of reloading the miniature for her. She gave up the Rollei quite early – it was out of place in the wards.

Lunch-break came at one o'clock – a typical English hospital meal served in a hospital in Tokyo – Lancashire hotpot, potatoes and peas for those on normal diet, steamed fish for those on light fare. Pudding was fruit tart and custard.

Norman tucked in heartily. Corie couldn't get a bite to go down. She drank the milky coffee that came afterwards, grateful for something to ease her throat, which seemed to have seized up with the horror of what she was seeing.

In the afternoon, Norm set himself to single out three or four men whose stories would form the backbone of his feature. He sat in the day-room chatting, while Corie took photographs. She tried to get shots of every aspect of the hospital's routine – the afternoon nap on beds or chaises-longues, the card games, the sailing of model yachts on the Japanese general's pond . . .

At last the day ended. Captain Heighton ferried them back to their hotel. Norm arranged times for the next day's schedule.

'Now then,' he remarked as the Press Officer drove off, 'a shower and a clean shirt, and then it's down to the bar for a drink. What d'you say?'

'All right.'

'It's . . . let's see . . . five-forty. Shall we say six-thirty?'

'All right.'

'Tired?'

'A bit.'

'What you need is a stiff gin.'

The lift arrived, driven by a little Japanese boy in a grey uniform. They were borne upwards to their floor, at which the lift-boy insisted on carrying Corie's camera bag to her room.

'See you downstairs,' Norm called as he went into his own.

'All right.' Corie went into hers, the boy bowed himself out, Corie walked to the chair by the dressing-table, sat down.

And burst into tears.

She had never wept since she was a little girl. The storm that engulfed her took her by surprise. She felt as if she were coming apart, unglued, her personality washed away by a salt flood that had nothing to do with her.

She was saying to herself, 'Stop it, stop it, you fool!' but it had no effect. She let her head fall on the surface of the dressing-table, combs and toilet articles brushed aside by the arms with which she shielded herself. She shut out the daylight, took refuge in a darkness which quickly became peopled with the sights she'd just seen.

Shuddering, she sat up. She caught sight of herself in the

mirror. Eyes streaming and red, mouth trembling, marks on her cheeks where her fingers had pressed to stem the tears. What a mess . . . But she couldn't seem to stop, couldn't seem to get control of herself.

Time passed. At length she drew a trembling breath, wiped her eyes with the palms of her hands, and looked at her watch. Six o'clock.

She had to pull herself together, get ready to have a drink with Norm. And tell him . . . tell him . . .

She turned on the shower and while it gained heat, pulled off her clothes. When it was running fiercely hot, she stepped under it. For a long time she stood there, arms propped against the tiled wall, letting the water pour down her body. Perhaps there were still some tears mixed with the cleansing stream.

At last she turned it off, dried herself, combed back her wet hair, put on fresh clothes. Feeling empty and weak, she went downstairs.

Norman Gibson was there before her, well into his first whisky and already wreathed in cigarette smoke. He signalled to her, and she went to join him at his table in a corner graced by a handsome bonsai pine.

'What'll you have?'

'Nothing, thanks. Norm, we have to have a talk.'

'Well, drink while you talk. You look like you need it.'

'No, listen to me, Norm!' Her voice rose. He drew back in surprise.

'What's up?'

'Norm, I'm going home tomorrow.'

'You what?'

'I should never have let you and Holstead talk me into this. I'm not cut out for it.'

'What on earth's got into you?' he demanded, screwing up his face to study her.

'I can't take it. I didn't know what it would be like.' Her voice broke. 'Those poor men . . .'

'Ah!' He raised his hand, and immediately a waiter was there. 'Brandy and soda,' he ordered.

'Not for me,' Corie said.

'Yes, for you. Look here, Corie, be sensible. You can't just walk away. You signed a contract.'

'I don't care.'

'Doesn't breaking a contract mean anything to you?'

'Holstead can sue me if he likes. It won't do him any good. I haven't got much money.'

'Corie, Corie ... Nobody wants to sue you ...' The drink came, set before her gently by the waiter. 'Drink it up,' Norm ordered.

'No, I don't want it. I want to go *home*.'

The last word was uttered on a sob. She closed her lips on it, then searched wretchedly in her handbag for a handkerchief.

For a moment Norman said nothing. Then, in a much softer tone, he began again. 'Never been abroad before?'

'N-no.'

'Poor little lass ... A lot of what's wrong with you is simple homesickness.' This in a fatherly tone. 'Everything here is strange—'

'It's not that, Norm, it's not! It's just that after all, I'm a coward. I agreed to take the assignment because Ingram seemed to think I was afraid of the challenge, so I was silly and stepped into the trap; but the challenge isn't what's wrong, it's trying to do any kind of work in that hospital among those poor men ...'

'But you *have* been working, Corie—'

'No I haven't! I've been pointing the lens and clicking the shutter – do you know I've had my eyes half-closed most of the time? I just can't bear to see them! I've no idea what I've got on film – I may have taken the walls and ceiling, for all I know. I can't *do* it, Norm, it tears me apart!'

Norman drew on his cigarette, then tapped ash carefully into an ashtray.

'What you feel is quite all right,' he told her. 'I feel the same. I had to clench my teeth all day so as not to let the horror show on my face.'

For a moment she was convinced. Then she called to her

mind the man she'd watched chatting and laughing with two of the patients just before they left. 'That's a lie, Norman. You're saying it to comfort me.'

He shrugged. 'It's not entirely a lie. I feel dismay, pity, all the things you feel. But then I've been around a lot longer than you have, I've seen it before. This is new to you.' He thought about it. 'Mebbe I was wrong to throw you in at the deep end like this. I'll confess I never thought of it from that angle. My chief consideration was to get Ingram to do the feature at all, and the only way was to involve you in it. Well, hit me for it, if you want to. But I still think you can take the pictures and make this a first-rate feature.'

She shook her head in helpless denial. 'You don't know what it's like. I try to bring them into focus through the lens and there they are – wan faces, haunted eyes, damaged limbs, scars, wounds . . . I can't look at them, it's unbearable.'

'But *they* have to bear it, Corie.'

It was such a simple, genuine remark that she was taken aback. She'd thought him self-centred, tricky. But he had looked into the minds of the patients and seen something she had turned her back on.

'Listen, Corie-girl, I know it's hard,' he said, nodding as if to himself. 'I've been around a long time and one thing is certain – having to watch other people suffer makes your heart ache. But you have to see it from their point of view. You can walk away from the pain and the uncertainty of their future. They have to live with it. So it seems to me we owe them something.'

'But why me?' she cried, desperate to be let out of this obligation.

'Because you can use the camera, that's why. You can do more than show men who've been prisoners and nearly died of malnutrition or wounds. You can show what it's cost, and how they've come through, and what they'll build on. You can show that though they were prisoners they were always free in the sense that matters – men who knew their own worth.'

She sat looking at him. After a moment she found her handkerchief and blew her nose.

'Are you going to put that in the feature?' she asked.

'Something like that. But only if you provide pictures to show I'm telling the truth.'

'Norman Gibson, you're as clever as a cartload of monkeys.'

'Drink your brandy,' he said, 'and let's go and have a steak.'

The camera is a wonderful thing. Once you lose any thought of yourself and are thinking only of your subject, the camera becomes a mere extension of the photographer. A third eye, an extra sense.

Corie immersed herself in her work. She forced herself — at first it was hard — to talk to the men. But after the first hour of the following day, she began to find it easy.

They were brave without thinking about it. Patient, determined not to complain. Cheerful about their future, trying to forget the months in prison camp, the attempts at brainwashing. 'They made us write down the story of our lives,' one boy said. 'Crikey, what a yarn I spun. Dunno what good it was to 'em.'

That was Tuesday. Wednesday they were all excited, although the nurses tried to damp them down. They were being got ready for the plane journey home.

Home! Some had last seen it two years ago. Since they left for Korea, rationing had ended, their Queen had been crowned, Gordon Richards had won his first Derby.

'Bikinis, miss,' they asked Corie. 'Is that right what we hear — bikinis show off bare skin in the middle?'

The convoy on Friday to the airport was slow. Corie travelled in one of the coaches carrying the ambulant patients. She sat at the front, snapping pictures as they pointed out of the windows, struck up a song.

The air ambulances were really transport planes adapted for the purpose. Not luxurious, but there were berths for those not well enough to sit up. Corie had a seat among the nurses but, once they were airborne, she, like them, was on the move. Drinks were fetched, pillows were arranged, one or two sedatives administered.

Corie recorded it all. By now she had augmented her cameras with a Nikon bought in the hotel shop. It was an excellent miniature, the lens picking up shade and detail even in the poorest light. She found she was using very little flash – she wanted to show the scenes with an honesty that flashlight might diminish.

The flight was long. They touched down once for refuelling and supplies of milk. Those fit enough were allowed an hour to walk about in the transit lounge of Bombay Airport.

The arrival home was the most moving of all. The steps were run up to the aircraft, the attendants opened the door and stepped out, the first of the men emerged to see England at his feet.

Corie wished she could be in two places at once – at the top of the steps to record the look of wonder as they saw parked aircraft with British roundels, rose-beds, a green lawn, and on the ground to see the relief, the sense of belonging, as they walked slowly across the tarmac to the airport building.

She was quickly passed through Lyneham formalities and allowed to rush to her studio with the film and the notebook detailing the subjects. She set the developing in progress at once, warning her assistant Bertie that if he didn't write names and dates on the tags, she would hang, draw and quarter him.

A quick change of clothing and she was back at Lyneham to take part in the dispersal. Some of the men were going to a skin-graft unit, some to orthopaedic hospitals, some were to spend one night recuperating from the flight and then would be allowed home. She recorded their meetings with commanding officers who had rushed to welcome them, their farewells to one another.

She got back to her studio at midnight with eight more rolls of film. She gave them to Bertie, yawning, scarcely conscious. 'Bring in some help if you need it,' she muttered, 'but I want to see the negs when I wake up – about twenty-four hours from now!'

Norman Gibson had already gone home to get over his jet lag. He rang her on Sunday morning at home. 'How are you feeling?'

'I think I'll live,' she said.

'Looked at your pix yet?'

'No, I'm just going into the studio to have a look. How's the writing going?'

'All right, I think. When can I see what you've got?'

'I'll have the proofs tomorrow afternoon. Do you want to come to the studio?'

'Ingram wants us to take a selection to the *Globe*, to give him some idea of what's available.'

For the first time in days, it dawned on her what the pictures were for. She'd been taking them for publication in the *Globe*. She had a moment of protective ownership – they were hers, she wouldn't let anyone else tamper with them.

But they were not hers. Ingram Holstead had bought and paid for them. So he must be allowed to see them as soon as possible.

She took them the following day to a pub lunch with Norman. He leafed through them, quite silent.

'Well?' she said anxiously.

'Corie, you've done well,' he said. 'They're wonderful. But I don't know what Ingram's going to say.'

What Ingram said was, 'Couldn't you find any good-lookers?'

'Good-lookers?' The question was so unexpected that she was almost speechless.

'Look here, these pix were to illustrate a feature about what marvellous chaps we'd got in our army. Most of this lot look like ghosts.'

'They'd been in prison camp—'

'But did you have to take so many pictures of the ones who look gaunt and tired? Why didn't you concentrate on those who were better-looking?'

Corie glanced at Norman Gibson, hoping for his support. He said nothing, looking with his head on one side at the pictures spread on the desk. He wasn't going to get involved in this discussion.

'I took what was there, Ingram,' she said. 'If you wanted good-looking ex-prisoners, you should have sent some actors to play the part. But to me there's a hidden beauty here – the spirit shines through.'

'Huh,' grunted the managing editor of the *Globe*.

But when the feature appeared on the following Sunday, Corie Duggan's photographs filled the page, untouched, unclipped. There they were, the men she had come to know in those few days in Tokyo.

Ingram had even stolen her words for a caption. 'The Spirit Shines Through', said the headline.

Chapter Seven

For three weeks the Duggan family had seen almost nothing of the eldest daughter. First she'd been rushing about between government departments obtaining passports and permissions. Then she'd been in Tokyo. After her return she'd spent almost all her time in her studio, sometimes using the truckle bed there so as not to waste time getting home.

Now that the feature had appeared in the *Sunday Globe*, they could sit around after Sunday lunch catching up. Sasha had come to hear all about it. It was strange to see him again after a gap. His slender body in its Cardin suit was a pleasant change after days in the company of Norman Gibson, who seemed to like appearing crumpled and dotted with cigarette ash.

Neither of Corie's sisters had ever been abroad. Her mother had had two singing engagements before the war, one in Nice and one in Ostend. Sasha had been in Canada during his National Service.

But Tokyo! They were eager to hear all about it.

'Honestly, I've nothing to tell,' Corie confessed. 'I only saw the bits I drove through to get to the hospital, and the street with the hotel in it. Mostly it looked pretty shabby.'

'But the shops – the shops where you bought the presents?' Lynette said, looking with delight at the blue kimono spread out on the sideboard.

'I bought it all in the hotel shop. I'm sorry, everybody.'

'Well, the people – tell us about the people . . .'

'I only saw the people in the streets and the hotel staff. The hotel staff all wore European clothes except for the waitresses in the special Tea Garden restaurant. In the streets, some wore European clothes, some wore kimonos

105

and funny little blocky shoes.' She was embarrassed at having so little to tell. 'It wasn't a holiday trip, you see.'

'It certainly wasn't,' Opal agreed, with smiling gratitude for the length of Japanese silk draped over the back of her chair. 'On the usual twenty-five pound allowance for going abroad, you couldn't have bought these lovely things.'

Corie laughed. 'It was all on expenses, friends and neighbours! The *Globe* financed it all, although I think bits will be deducted from my fee.'

Sasha gave her a dark-eyed glance of appreciation. 'That's really a big-business way to do things,' he said. 'Perhaps you'll get a chance to go to the States on some fiddle like that.'

'It wasn't a fiddle!' She was indignant. 'It was a genuine business trip, and even if we did stretch a point or two—'

'Only joking, Corie,' he said. 'I know you wouldn't really get involved in any sticky-fingers operation.'

'Sasha's dying to get to the States,' Lynette put in fondly. 'But the way the government keeps foreign travel tied up, he just wouldn't be able to finance the trip on the allowance.'

'What's so marvellous about the States?' Corie wanted to know. She was lolling in her chair, her half-finished coffee getting cold in front of her. She was still suffering from fatigue after three weeks' non-stop effort.

'They tested colour television there at the end of last year,' he said. 'I'd love to see what it looks like. The report in *Variety* said it was an absolute smash.'

Corie heard the words, and the genuine enthusiasm behind them. Wary though she was of Sasha, she understood that he truly believed the future of entertainment lay with this new medium.

'So what?' Opal said with a shrug. 'This country's not likely to get it for years and years. We can't afford luxuries like that.'

'I don't know about that, Pal,' Sasha said. 'Now that we're to have Independent Television . . . I bet what you like they'll go for colour when they start broadcasting – put

BBC noses out of joint.' He smiled at the thought. It was easy to guess there were one or two old scores he'd like to see settled with producers who had been unfriendly.

'Lynette would look lovely in colour.' Monna remarked. 'If the independent companies could put her in a colour broadcast, you'd take her away from the BBC, wouldn't you, Sasha?'

'Good gracious, Monna, Lynette's under contract—'

'There's ways round that, Corie. But in fact, no — the BBC is so anxious not to lose talent to the independents, it's advantageous for us to stay where we are for the present.'

'How's it going?' Corie asked. In the three weeks that she'd been so busy, she'd lost track of Lynette's career.

'Oh, it's wonderful,' breathed her mother. 'Lynette's absolutely taken the show over! They rewrote last week's script so as to give her more to do — isn't that right, dear boy?'

'Certainly is. You missed the drama, Corie. All the critics have been saying that it's Lynette Lee who gives "Bob Barlow Presents" its charm. Poor old Bob's been elbowed out of the limelight.'

'You don't mean literally?' Corie said in alarm, for she knew from past experience how difficult it could be when a local war broke out in a show. The sniping, the traps laid for the unwary, the extreme childishness that some stars could display . . .

'No, of course not,' Lynette said, giving her agent a playful pat on his suntanned cheek. 'You're naughty to say things like that, darling. No, but it's true, Mr Tranton says he has to pay attention to the public response—'

'Letters have come pouring in,' Sasha broke in, capturing Lynette's hand and holding it. 'They absolutely love little Lynnie. So now we're building her up in the show — she gets to sing another number, she doesn't just act as a foil for the Uncle Bob role, she has more personality. Tranton agrees with me that there's a chance to exploit Lynette's special talents.'

'I always knew the British public would love my little girl,' Monna said.

Corie tried to make her woolly mind pay attention. 'Let me get this straight. Lynette's been given more to do? And Bob Barlow gets less?'

'We-ell, not really—'

'Of course he does, Lynette. It's no good being soft-hearted about it. The audience research has shown that people are bored with Bob Barlow and his band. It's Lynette they're interested in. So Tranton has had the scripts altered to give Lynette equality with him, and let me tell you this – if things go the way I plan, Lynette will have a show of her own before too long.'

'A show of her own!' Monna clasped her hands and raised them in the air in thanksgiving.

'Sasha!' gasped Lynette.

He looked round the lunch table, thin face agleam with triumph. 'Not bad, is it?'

'You really mean it, darling?'

'I certainly do. But keep it under your hat,' he said, folding Lynette's hand between both of his for emphasis. 'It's just at the planning stage.'

'Who's doing the planning?' Corie asked. 'I mean, is it just an idea of your own or—'

'Don't say it like that!' her mother reproved, quick to take offence. 'Sasha has been an absolute boon to this family. Whatever he has in mind is good enough for me.'

Sasha gave Corie a rather grim smile. 'Oh, I know it's difficult to impress our Corie. She's into the big time herself these days, she's got to know some of the good and great—'

'There's no need to take that tone,' Corie said, stung. 'I only meant, is there a show on the stocks or are you just having discussions with this producer, Mr Whatever.'

'Tranton, William Tranton,' Lynette murmured, a little apprehensive at the irritation being displayed.

'Yes, Willam Tranton – I've got him really sold on Lynette,' Sasha took it up. 'He wants her in a new show, something really using Lynette to the full. We'll portray her as sweetness personified—'

'Oh, Sasha,' Lynette protested, going prettily pink.

'Well, you are, my angel,' said her mother. 'Go on, go on, Sasha.'

'We're going to have her dressed in soft floaty things – gauzy frocks, layers of petticoat, tiny waist—'

The Debbie Reynolds look, thought Corie.

'And all the songs are going to be gentle, optimistic – a bit of nostalgia sometimes but never anything unhappy or depressing.'

'Won't that be a bit—'

'What?'

Cloying, had been the word Corie was going to use. Instead she said, 'Sugary?'

'We've got plans to give it a bit of pep, don't you worry. William and I have talked it over and over. He's going to put it to the programme planners in a few days – I'm pretty sure it's going to be accepted.'

Lynette was aglow at this news, Monna couldn't prevent a torrent of questions and congratulations. Opal and Corie looked at one another and smiled. At last, Monna would see her child as a star.

There was little more to be told. As yet the new series was in the planning stage. But it seemed certain that it was being planned around Lynette.

'What happens to Bob Barlow when his series ends?' Corie inquired.

'Who cares? Perhaps the independents will take him up, or he may go back on the variety circuit – there's still a place for a big-band show in the city theatres.'

'I can't help feeling sorry for him,' Lynette murmured. 'After all, it was through him that I got my break—'

'There! Corie, why did you have to ask about him?' Sasha was indignant. 'Bob Barlow can take care of himself, nobody needs to be sorry for him.'

'It wasn't so much that I was sorry for him, I just wondered if he was getting out of this with any dignity—'

'Dignity! What the dickens does dignity matter when it comes to contracts? Really, Corie, you say some peculiar things sometimes!'

'Sorry, sorry. I don't have your expertise on elbowing people out.'

'Who elbowed him out? The public just wasn't interested in him.'

'Now, Corie,' Monna said in her more-hurt-than-angry tone, 'that's enough. I won't have you spoiling this precious moment for Lynette. Today she's heard the best news of her life.'

'That's true. I'm sorry, Lynette.' Corie got up to plant a kiss on top of her youngest sister's head. 'What about moving into the living-room and having a pot of tea? It's after three, and I'm sick of looking at the remains of apple pie and custard.'

'Good idea.' Monna led the way, still throwing out questions about the forthcoming show. Sasha and Lynette followed. Corie went to put on the kettle while Opal cleared the lunch table.

When Opal came in with her laden tray, she dumped it on the draining board. 'What's the matter with you and Sasha?'

'What?' Corie said, surprised.

'The air crackles between the pair of you. Why do you dislike him so much?'

Corie leaned against the kitchen dresser, head against the best cups hanging on their hooks. 'Can't say,' she said. 'I just don't trust him.'

Her sister ran hot water into the sink and began dumping plates and bowls into it. 'I could understand it at first. He came on with all kinds of promises, and I felt the same as you — it'd be a marvel if half of them came true. But you see . . . She's going to have her own show.'

'Yes.'

'Aren't you pleased?'

'Of course I am.'

'Corie, you aren't jealous of her success?'

Corie straightened up abruptly. She stared at Opal. 'How can you ask such a thing, Pal? You and I have always known she's the only one of us with any real talent.'

'Then what is it?' Opal insisted.

'Something . . . I feel a sort of pricking in my thumbs when he's around.'

'He's good for Lynette,' Opal pointed out.

'Good for her career.'

'Well, that's what counts, isn't it?'

'She's so besotted by him!' Corie burst out. 'It doesn't even occur to her that he only sees her as a meal ticket.'

Opal turned off the water, began to pursue the crockery around in the soapsuds with a washing-up mop. After a moment's thought she said, 'You and I have seen a hundred agents and their clients. There are always some who rely very heavily on their agents – the insecure ones, the shy ones. Whoever took on Lynette, she was going to lean on him.'

'If it had been old Norman Clines, aged nearly sixty and with false teeth, she wouldn't have fallen in love with him.'

'Is that what bothers you? That she's in love with him?'

'What bothers me is that he doesn't really care a fig for her. He'd walk away from her tomorrow if it suited him.'

Opal pointed warningly. 'Kettle's boiling. Listen, Corie, I understand that. He worries me too. But you can see Monna thinks he's a wonder because of what he's achieved for the kidlet. Try not to cross swords with him when Monna's around.'

Corie gave her attention to warming the teapot and making the tea. She would try not to cross swords with Sasha Lenoir, simply because it made life easier for the Duggan family if Monna wasn't in a tizz about something.

Later, when the family were chatting in the living-room, Pal's words returned to her. 'The air crackles between the pair of you.'

Yes. Because – and the realisation hit her with the force of a thunderbolt – there was a strong physical attraction between them.

She didn't like Sasha. She didn't trust him. Both those confessions to her sister were true. But she *desired* him.

It was a thing of the senses only, nothing to do with the mind. There was no liking or trusting or approving, yet still she found herself hungering for him. He was so handsome, the hard charm of an Italian court portrait in his dark features, his body the epitome of masculine beauty, broad-shouldered, narrow-hipped, finely muscled.

Her former life in the theatre had taught her to understand the opportunities that came to people with good looks, but to distrust those who used them as a weapon. Sasha did this. He used his looks, and his charm, and his instinctive knowledge of the weakness of others. He understood that her mother loved to be thought of as a theatrical personage, that Lynette needed constant support and reassurance, that Pal would shrug and be glad if he brought success to the family.

And Corie herself? So far, he hadn't been able to pinpoint the gap in her defences.

It doesn't matter, she told herself behind clenched teeth. I don't care about him, I *won't* care about him, he's nothing to me.

But it wasn't true. She knew it. And, something told her, Sasha might one day know it too. So far he had shrugged off the almost sexual animosity that sometimes flared among their words to each other, because he had too many other things on his mind. After all, her only importance was that Lynette respected her. Well, he could always talk Lynette round to his own point of view. He simply didn't regard Corie as worth much thought.

She could only hope and pray that it would always be so, that he would always be too busy to pay much heed to someone as unimportant to him as Corie Duggan.

Around her, the family chatter ran on. Corie, deep in her own thoughts, was saying to herself: I'm going to have to be very, very careful where Sasha is concerned – and the easiest thing is just to steer clear of him.

The new show came on air at the beginning of

September. It was called 'You're a Sweetheart', the old song of the same name being used as the running-in music. A close-harmony trio, all men, sang the words: 'You're a sweetheart, If there ever was one, If there ever was one, It's you . . .' The signing off music was 'Sweet Annabel Lee', once again sung by the close-harmony trio but with the words altered to, 'Who's wonderful, Who's marvellous, Our sweet Lynette Lee . . .'

There were no other women in the regular cast, only Lynette. In the dance sequences, she had men as partners and as background, a perfect foil in their white tie and tails for her pale coloured gowns.

The comedy sketches with the Uncle Bob character were retained but a character actor now played the part. Usually he was rescuing Lynette from romantic entanglements. In the sketches, occasionally another woman would appear, but always as a complete contrast to Lynette's ethereal prettiness.

There were guests in the show, but no longer people from show business. Instead, each week, an engaged couple appeared. The first couple, found rather quickly, were the daughter of the commissionaire in the front hall and her fiancé. Lynette helped the girl to choose a wedding dress from a wide selection brought to the studio — there was much trying on of veils and wreaths of orange blossom by both girls. The young man was shown in two or three morning suits. At the end they were presented with the wedding dress and morning suit they had liked best.

The studio audience was enraptured.

Nor did Corie blame them. It might be marshmallow, but it was marshmallow beautifully tinted and flavoured for the public still haunted by memories of war, longing for something sweet and optimistic in their lives.

The Duggan family watched it on the monitor in the hospitality lounge, brought there as honoured guests for the first night. Sasha walked up and down, hands in pockets, unable to look at the screen but occasionally stopping and turning when a burst of laughter or applause reached him.

When it was all over and the cast had shed their make-up, champagne bottles popped. TV critics from the dailies, invited to the first night, drank up hastily then hurried off to file their views.

'Not to worry,' the producer said, going from one to the other topping up champagne glasses. 'They liked it, you could see it from the way they shook hands and patted backs before they left. If a show's a turkey, they avoid looking at you while they scurry out.'

He was right. Next day's papers had only good things to say. Several reviewers congratulated themselves for having singled out Lynette in 'Bob Barlow Presents' . . .

'What we have to do now,' Sasha said at a celebration party the following evening, 'is build on that success.'

'Isn't he just a whizz?' Lynette cried in admiration. 'We're just getting our breath back after the opening—'

'That's when to strike – while the opening's hot,' said William Tranton.

They were out in the back garden of the Bayswater house, under a late-evening sky. Monna had been inspired to give a party but, thank heaven, had made no attempt to do the catering. For this an outside firm had been brought in, while Monna manned the telephone, inviting everyone she could think of who had known Lynette in pre-stardom.

Teachers from the Betty Bonnar School of Dance and Drama, managers from suburban London theatres, a talent-show host who had once given Lynette a second prize, as well as some of Monna's own cronies from the days of Crystal & Clark. She'd told her two elder daughters to invite a friend or two. Opal had asked a colleague from the car-sales office in which she was presently working, and Corie had asked Norman Gibson.

In candlelight the shabby living-room looked welcoming. The food was buffet-style, the wine plentiful. Music trickled out from the gramophone, the records dropping down from a stack on the spindle so that at least an hour's play was guaranteed. A few people had gone out to the paved area beyond the french windows to dance, and so the party had stretched into the garden.

In the shelter of the old pear tree, Lynette and Corie, Sasha, the BBC producer and Norman Gibson were sitting on a variety of garden chairs and orange boxes, passing a bottle of vinho verde around.

'What you want to do,' Norman volunteered, 'is get one of the women's magazines interested. Big feature spread, that's what you want.'

' "Quite Unspoiled by Success",' Tranton suggested.

'That's a rotten headline. You need something that refers back to the show. More this sort of thing — "She's a Sweetheart — Really!"'

'Is this going to be a press release?'

'From the BBC? Nah, you want to let the magazine interview—'

'Oh, no,' Lynette said, quickly alarmed. 'I couldn't be interviewed. I'd be no good at that.'

'What d'you mean? All you have to do is smile and say yes or no.'

'No, Norman, that wouldn't be enough,' William Tranton objected. 'People write in to us, dying to know all about her. If it was an interview, it would have to show what Lynette's like off-screen.'

'What's wrong with that?' Sasha said, rather cross. 'She's just as nice off-screen as she is on.'

'Oh, darling,' Lynette murmured, resting her head against his shoulder.

William coughed over a sip of wine. In the dusk Corie couldn't make him out too well, but she thought there was perhaps a look of anxiety on his face. Did he too feel that Lynette's dependence on Sasha had its dangers?

Corie had seen a keen intelligence glinting behind his thick glasses. A little older than Sasha, with whom he'd become acquainted during his National Service, William Tranton had completed his university degree before applying for a post in broadcasting. Willingness to take responsibility in the whirlwind of live TV broadcasts had brought him quickly to a position of some influence in

Light Entertainment. Tallish, brown-haired, short-sighted, he looked more like a bank clerk than a show-business manager.

'The danger in interviews,' Norman said, wagging a nicotine-stained finger, 'is that once you've said a thing you can't take it back. Not that Lynette would say anything bad – I mean, she's never been in jail or stolen towels from a hotel—'

'Good gracious,' said Lynette, half shocked and half amused.

'But interviewers are always on the alert for anything to give a bit of spice to their article.' He shrugged. 'I should know, I do it myself.'

What he left unsaid, and what everyone except Lynette understood, was that she could easily come across as insipid without a script full of little jokes to help her. In front of the cameras she came alive – pretty, charming, giving a little lilt to her dialogue that made it a delight. But without a script she could easily seem just another 'dumb blonde' – a nice one, but not interesting.

Sasha had been taking in the discussion and racing on ahead in his quick way. 'The ideal thing,' he said, 'would be a lot of pix and not much text. You'd like that, Lynnie, wouldn't you – not to have to be interviewed, just to have a few things about your home life and so forth – wouldn't that be better?'

'Oh yes, if that would do,'she agreed, looking from him to Norman and then to William. Then, brightening, 'And of course Corie could take the pictures.'

'Oh, well, now,' Sasha began in objection.

'No, Sasha, it's good,' William said. 'Lynette comes from a clever family, you see? Parents a former famous stage duo—'

'Famous?' Sasha challenged.

'Look, they got medium billing in their day – and didn't they selflessly go on tour for the Forces during the war?' He looked at Corie, who nodded. 'There you are – famous stage duo, brave too, and her sister's the well-known photographer Corie Duggan who took the pix for this feature.'

'What about Pal?' Lynette said. 'We couldn't leave her out.'

'Filing clerk in a car-sales office,' Sasha said, sighing ironically.

'Making a career in business,' Norman translated. 'Not bad. Look here, why don't I put it up to the features editor of the *Globe*? We've got an interest in Corie, after all – readers are still writing in for copies of the pix she did at the Army hospital.'

'But the idea is to get Lynette right out in front of the public – not give publicity to Corie.'

'It's just a lead-in,' said Norman.

'But I thought you said we should get a women's mag?'

'Later. Here's an easy first-shot at putting Lynette across the way you want her – a sweet girl-next-door type, going to dance practice, running to catch a bus, learning her lines over a cup of cocoa—'

'No, no, that's too down-to-earth,' Sasha said. 'She's a girl like a flower – spun-sugar, gossamer—'

'Excuse me,' Corie said, unable to keep the resentment out of her voice, 'could we please include my sister in the conversation instead of talking about her as if she were some kind of dressing-up doll?'

'Oh . . . Corie . . . I don't mind, really . . . After all, it's important to get the right kind of publicity. And Sasha understands me so well . . .'

Corie thought she heard Norman give a snort of irritation. 'OK, then, Lynette, you're a forget-me-not sort of girl, is that the way we're going to do it?'

'Sasha . . . ?'

'I think that would be about right,' he replied. 'And see here, Corie – none of that gritty stuff like you did with those soldiers.'

'Oh, how can you, darling – Corie knows all about it, she's photographed dozens of debutantes and show people. Oh, it's all going to be much easier than I thought. If

Corie's doing the pictures, I shan't feel a bit nervous.'

It was left that Norman would speak to his features editor. The party drew to its close. As the last of the guests took their leave, Sasha and Corie found themselves alone after putting away the garden chairs.

'If this comes off with the *Globe* it'll be important,' he said. 'Try to forget that she's your kid sister, will you? You'll be taking pictures of a new star.'

She closed the garden-shed door on the last deck chair.

'Sasha,' she said with a sigh, 'I knew Lynette was a star long before you ever appeared on the scene.'

'Oh yes? And what did you do about it? You and that idiot mother of yours – you'd have let her throw herself away on panto audiences and summer shows. I was the one who put her where she is.'

'We know that. There's no need to get so—'

'Oh yes there's a need! I don't appreciate it when you stick your oar in, trying to make Lynette think I'm bossing her about.'

'Is that what this is about?' she said in wonder. 'You didn't like it when I pointed out you were talking over her, as if she wasn't there.'

'I know what's best for Lynette,' he said. 'I don't need the big-sister act from you.'

'And a bit less of the Svengali from you wouldn't come amiss! "A spun-sugar girl" – she's flesh and blood, Sasha!'

'Listen, keep out of it, will you?' He seized her by the wrist to pull her close so that he could speak very low. 'No more interference, do you understand?'

The diffused light from the dining-room touched his dark hair, gleamed in his dark eyes. How very handsome he is, she found herself thinking.

They stared at each other, caught in a strange moment of intimacy.

'Now, then, Sasha dear,' carolled Monna as she came out of the lighted interior, 'sorry to pack you off home, but it's almost two a.m.'

'Sorry, Monna,' he said, letting go his grasp on Corie's arm.

'What on earth are you two up to?'

'We've been putting away the garden chairs.'

'Oh, no need to have done that tonight. Come along now, dear boy. Time for dreamland.'

He allowed himself to be led away. Lynette came out of the living-room, weary but smiling. She kissed him goodnight, and he was gone.

Upstairs, when the tidying-up was finished, Corie undressed for bed. She looked at her wrist. It was still red from his angry grasp. She ran cold water over it when she washed.

Yet later, in bed, the flesh still seemed to tingle.

The *Daily Globe* accepted the feature idea. Ingram Holstead rang Corie at her studio. 'So you're going to take on another assignment for us,' he said with bluff good humour.

'You heard about that? I thought it would be just the features department.'

'Norm told me about it. He knows I'm interested in you.'

'Is Norm going to do the feature?'

'Not at all! I save him for the deeper things. No, no, I'll tell Features to send you a nice young man who'll fall in love with Lynette Lee on sight.'

Whether he actually did give any instructions, the fact remained that a young reporter arrived and fell headlong when introduced to the star of 'You're a Sweetheart'. He sat in for an evening with Sasha and the Duggans, was saved from the longest of Monna's anecdotes by Sasha's skilful management, and begged an autograph before he left.

The photographic sessions were easy. Corie went to Alexandra Palace to take pictures during rehearsals. She went with her sister out into the autumnal colours of the parkland round the buildings and there, among leafy branches, she took roll after roll of studies, colour and black and white.

As always, Lynette was excellent under direction. Asked to whirl out her gauzy skirts, she did so with a pretty tilt of the head. She was pictured tucking a flower into her hair, dabbling her fingers in the dark waters of a pool, cupping a chrysanthemum between her hands.

Later, at dance class, Corie took shots of her leaping into the air in a classical *temps de flèche*, pirouetting round and round in a whirl of soft tulle, and always with that unmistakable sparkle of her own.

Last of all, Corie had her in her studio. Here, carefully lit and with a variety of dresses, Lynette posed for study after study – thoughtful, debonair, wistful, carefree.

Corie did all the developing and printing of the film herself. She used a variety of papers and emulsions. She even printed two or three using the solarisation technique, a reversal of light and dark tones, to give a twilit Arthurian quality to some of the thoughtful poses.

Lynette was positively overawed when she saw the portfolio of finished work. 'How will they ever choose half a dozen for the feature?' she marvelled. 'They're all so good . . .'

'Well, that's the feature editor's job—'

'But Sasha must see them first!'

'Yes, of course.' That was inevitable. Lynette could never be happy until Sasha had given his approval.

He came the following evening, while Corie was making some enlargements for another client. She let him in, showed him the big cardboard boxfile with the portraits of Lynette and left him to it.

It was an evening in late October, unseasonably warm. In the darkroom her shirt was sticking to her shoulderblades. She pulled it free, shook it at the neckline and collar to let some cool air circulate against her skin. She was longing for a cool drink.

At last she had finished. She came out, switched off the safe-light, closed the door. Without looking around she made for the back of the studio where she had made a neat little flatlet, kitchenette on one side of a plasterboard partition, cell-like bedroom the other. She ran cold water into a mug, holding her sticky shirt away from her waist with one hand.

'What do you think of the pix?' she called.

There was no answer in words. A soft step behind her, and then a hand slid under her shirt to caress her moist skin.

She whirled. 'Sasha!'

She had walked straight into his arms. He pulled her against himself.

'Let go!' she gasped.

Still he said nothing. He kissed her on the lips, hard, fierce, possessive. She struggled to free herself. All that happened was that she bruised her mouth, and he caught at her tied-back hair to hold her head still.

'Don't do this—'

He took a firmer hold of the pony-tail of hair, kissed her again, but this time long and soft.

A will-o'-the-wisp fire seemed to run along her skin. Her legs seemed no longer able to hold her up. She made a sound of protest, and he let her go to a distance of a few inches.

'You know you want this as much as I do,' he whispered. 'Come on.'

'No! No, Sasha, you're wrong—'

'Wrong, am I? You mean you didn't feel anything that night after the party?'

'No, of course not—'

'What a silly little liar . . .' With one finger he traced her eyebrows. 'Don't pretend to frown. Inside you're smiling, and longing to give in.'

'No, Sasha – we can't . . .' She tried to say that it would hurt Lynette, that it would be wrong, that she would never forgive herself.

But the words were lost in the strength of his embrace. When he pulled her to the bedroom she scarcely resisted. Her body seemed on fire, her breath seemed to be caught forever in some fluttering little cave behind her ribcage.

He lay beside her, kissing first her shoulder and then her breast as he unbuttoned the cotton shirt. She tried with all her might to remember the reason why she mustn't let him do this.

But everything was lost at last as she put her arms about him and pulled his body against her own.

Chapter Eight

Triumph, exultation ... Soaring, soaring like a seabird, while below the ocean sparkled in sapphire splendour ... Wings spread, free, tilting and wheeling, the great bird flew for Corie. And then the long, slow, gliding flight back into reality.

They lay clasped to each other on the narrow pallet. Sasha let his head droop upon her shoulder then, kissing it in gratitude, rolled to lie alongside her, one hand holding hers.

She felt the warmth of his skin, the length of his limbs against her own. She could hear the rise and fall of his breathing, then its slow reversion to normality.

What was struggling to surface in her mind? Something ... She didn't want to know. She wanted to prolong this moment, this precious moment.

'Ah, Corie,' he murmured on a sigh.

She tightened the touch of her hand in his.

'I always knew it would be wonderful with you,' he said.

'Sasha ...'

'I didn't know how you felt until that night in the garden ... the way you looked at me ... the way you came alive when I touched you ...'

She made as if to sit up. He drew her back by turning and putting his other hand on her shoulder. 'Why,' he said, 'you've no flesh on those lovely bones ... You ought to take care of yourself, lovey, not work so hard ...'

'Sasha, what have we done?' she gasped, staring up at him as he leaned over her.

'It's called making love, chicken – but you know that, you've done it before, eh?'

'Oh, please – don't make fun—'

'No, I'm curious. I never heard tell of any boyfriend in your life. Who taught you all that?'

'No one − it was a long time ago − just someone who wanted payment for a job when we badly needed the money . . .'

'We?'

'Opal and I − it was for the chorus of a summer show, and we got the jobs, but I try not to think about it now.'

'And you were how old?'

'Eighteen.'

He let himself fall back on the pillow, a little gurgle of laughter escaping him. 'And in between?'

'Nobody, Sasha. Not till you.'

'My lord, you've got a good memory, then!'

'Please . . . don't joke . . . Sasha . . .'

He sat up, clasping his hands round his knees. 'Don't be so serious about it, Corie. It's no big deal.'

'No big deal!' She too sat up, and ran angry fingers into her tangled hair. 'What about Lynette?'

'What about her?'

'It would break her heart—'

'Who's going to tell her? Are you?'

'But it's wrong, Sasha—'

'Look here, what Lynette doesn't know can't harm her. All we have to do is be a bit careful.'

'But it would break her heart! She thinks the world of you, you know she does.'

'Well, right, and that's the way the partnership works. She thinks I can do no wrong and so she does what I tell her − and you can't say it's been bad for her career.'

'No, she's near the top − I see that, and of course you put her there. But there's more to it from her point of view. She loves you, Sasha.'

He shrugged expressively. 'Oh, "love" . . . What the dickens is it anyhow? I agree there's something special between Lynette and me, but that's the way it goes sometimes in an agent-client relationship. You must have seen it yourself a hundred times. Somebody comes along who knows just how to handle this particular talent – well, I was that someone for Lynette. But as to "love" . . .'

'Doesn't it bother you? That she's building her life around you?'

'Why should it? It's in my interest to keep her happy, to make her a success – Lynette isn't going to suffer if I have a little relaxation of my own now and again.'

Did she love him? Could she love such a man? But if not, why was it that when he touched her, her very bones seemed to melt?

She must put a stop to it here and now. First of all, she was betraying her own sister. And then there was the feeling that, though she had known physical ecstasy in their lovemaking, the price was too high. She couldn't let herself belong to Sasha Lenoir.

She leaned forward, reaching for discarded clothes.

'What're you doing?' he asked, tugging the cotton shirt away from her.

'I'm getting dressed. I've got to get home.'

'Nonsense. You often don't go home at night.'

'But I can't—'

'Yes, you can, my sweetheart, yes you can.' He began to drop little kisses along her shoulder-line and when she shivered at the touch he murmured, 'There you see?' His hands caressed her with instinctive skill. She tried to will herself not to respond, but there was a traitor within who made nonsense of her defences.

She wanted him, that was the truth of it. The practised lover, the giver of joy, the partner on the path to Paradise – embodied in this man, this careless, casual, self-centred man . . .

He stayed with her until almost four in the morning. At that hour they rose at last, languorous, heavy-eyed. While he dressed she pulled on an old dressing-gown and made tea. He sipped it, wincing at its heat but thirsty, as was Corie.

'That's a rotten uncomfortable bed,' he joked.

'Well . . .' She went red. 'It's only meant for one.'

'We'll use my place in future.'

'No!'

He looked at her. 'A lot more comfortable and more convenient too.'

'No, Sasha, this isn't going to happen again.'

'Says who!'

'I mean it. I never meant . . .'

'Well, I did. I always guessed there was a different Corie underneath all that practical common sense. D'you really think I'm going to let you go?'

'But we *can't*, Sasha!'

'Yes we can. Come tonight.'

She shook her head with vehemence. 'I have a business appointment – retirement banquet for a managing director.'

'Well, come after.'

'It would be late – after midnight.'

'What difference does that make? I'll be there whatever time you arrive. So that's settled, eh? See you late tonight.'

'No, Sasha, I shan't come.'

He smiled. 'Yes you will,' he said. And, setting down the half-full mug of tea, he left.

When she had drunk more of her own, she emptied both mugs and washed them up. I shan't go, she was telling herself. It would be wrong. We both know it.

All day she was fatigued, listless. She went home at six to change into more suitable clothes for the evening event – black satin trousers, velvet blouson. From seven-thirty till midnight she was busy with her cameras, threading her way among the guests of the banquet, then assembling the VIPs for a session of portrait groups at the back of the salon.

All the while she was saying to herself, I shan't go, I shan't go.

But it was like a torment in her blood, the longing to be with him. What's the matter with me, she asked herself in dismay. Am I under a spell? Have I lost my mind?

She shook hands with the organiser of the banquet, assured him he would have proofs of the pictures in two days and enlargements of any within a week for their in-house magazine. She loaded her equipment into the second-hand Citroën that had replaced the faithful old Sunbeam sidecar. She headed from the banqueting hall, west, towards Bayswater.

Then, at Park Lane, she turned left for Chelsea and Sasha's flat.

So it went. They were with each other two or three times every week – as often as it could be arranged without upsetting routines or drawing attention. They met as usual in the run of everyday life, at discussions on which pictures to use for the *Globe* feature, at get-togethers with William Tranton and the costume designer of 'You're a Sweetheart', at little parties and outings.

And when they met there was no way for anyone to know what he meant to her. She guarded her expression, spoke to him as little as ever – perhaps less. He for his part would tease her for being taciturn: 'Miss Mum's-the-Word, that's Corie! If I can get a sign of approval from her, I know I've had a brilliant idea.'

'Really, Corie, I do wish you'd at least try to be agreeable to him,' Monna scolded. 'What must he think of you, so ungrateful after all he's done for Lynette!'

'I've got other things on my mind, Monna.'

'Oh, yes, studio work, I quite understand, darling, being quite famous in your own line. But it's not like being a star, after all. Lynette's agent is a very important person in our life, so I hope you'll—'

'Yes, yes, all right, I'll smile at him if that's what you want.'

To Sasha she pleaded, 'Don't make things difficult for me. I have to work hard at not showing how I feel. It's different for you, you seem to be able to play the part quite easily.'

'I should have been an actor,' he laughed. 'Maybe that's why I took up agenting – next best thing to going on stage myself.'

She studied him. 'I wonder which is the real you?'

'What d'you mean?'

'The watchful businessman who negotiates contracts for his clients? The kind adviser who guides and encourages Lynette? The courtier who flatters my mother?'

'All of those,' he said, patting himself on the chest. 'Sasha Lenoir, man of many parts.'

'It's not your real name.'

'What's that?' He was startled.

'Sasha Lenoir — it's not your real name.'

'Yes it is!'

'Not at all. You haven't a drop of Russian aristocratic blood in you.' She could see it had shaken him to be challenged and, not averse to unsettling him, went on: 'Sasha Lenoir — I bet it's just a translation of Sandy Black.'

He gave a weak grin. 'Sidney, actually.'

'Sidney Black?'

'Of Bromsgrove. I got my mother to change her name by deed poll, couldn't bear her to be Nellie Black of Bromsgrove. My father died in the war so there was no one to argue against it. What I say is, if you don't like something, change it — don't be tied down to what other people want.'

'But you invented all the bits about the Russian grandmother and the French actor father?'

'Why not? Just like I invented Lynette Lee, and like I'll invent any other names and personalities to suit the showbiz climate.'

'You didn't invent Lynette,' Corie objected.

'Oh, for Pete's sake, don't let's get into another argument about Lynette. I never knew a girl who had such a case of the conscience.'

She was silent for a moment. Then she said, the words drawn out of her against her will, 'Have there been a lot of other girls?'

'What's the matter, jealous?'

'I don't know why you bother with me!' she broke out. 'There must be a hundred pretty, willing, would-be actresses you could have fun with—'

'Ah, but then they'd expect something back, wouldn't they? What I like so much about you, my little Corie, is that you don't ask for anything – a job, an introduction to a producer, an audition – No, the thing with you, Corie, is that it's all for love.'

'Love,' she echoed bitterly. 'Is that what it is?'

It was a question to which she didn't know the answer.

The feature spread in the *Globe* had been very effective. Hundreds of people had written to the paper saying they'd always known Lynette was just like that, sweet and unaffected, a home-girl. Could they have a signed photograph? Lynette, amazed, had signing sessions.

With every show, her audience increased. Fanmail became such a problem that Sasha had to hire an extra secretary to deal with it. Now, unbidden, the women's magazines began to clamour for interviews.

'I think we'll have to do it,' Sasha remarked. 'We'll give an interview to the biggest, and then the others will cool off.'

'Oh, Sasha!'

'It's all right, love, I'll be there to hold your hand. We'll have them come to the office.'

But the features editor of *Woman* wouldn't be satisfied with that. She wanted her readers to see Lynette in her home setting and to take her own pix. Lynette was reluctant but Sasha, abetted by Monna, persuaded her.

He chose a date in mid-August, when the garden at the old Bayswater house was looking its best. The house itself had had some smartening up: after the daily care of their charwoman, Mrs Kingsley, it wouldn't disgrace them under the cold eye of the camera.

Corie expected it to be all over by the time she got home. But the interview had been delayed by a minor crisis at Alexandra Palace, so to Corie's surprise the woman journalist and her cameraman were still there. Coffee and snacks had been produced, an easy atmosphere prevailed.

Corie, having put her head into the living-room to say hello, intended to escape upstairs. But Anne Ainsworth wasn't going to let her get away. Two for the price of one – the famous Corie Duggan as well as the more famous Lynette Lee.

She found, alas, that Corie Duggan wasn't forthcoming. Asked direct questions, she would say yes or no, or shrug.

'You'll get very little out of Corie,' Sasha said with a smile. 'For her, pictures speak louder than words.'

'Are you thinking of holding an exhibition of your work?' Miss Ainsworth inquired.

'An exhibition?'

'Well, you've reached a certain stage, haven't you? The next step would logically be an exhibition.'

'It never entered my head.'

Like a block of wood, thought the journalist. She turned back to the TV star who, though not eloquent, would at least respond to her leads.

'What about marriage, Miss Lee?'

'Aha, the sweetheart of the British public can't be married, now can she?' Sasha said.

'But one day, perhaps?'

'Oh, yes, of course, one day,' Lynette breathed, her eyes sparkling with that hope. 'That's every woman's dream, isn't it – a home and children?'

'And have you someone in mind to share all that?'

Lynette blushed and looked down.

'I'm sure I can guess,' Anne Ainsworth said. 'Someone not a million miles from here, eh?'

Lynette impulsively put out a hand. Sasha took it and pressed it. Monna beamed on them, glanced in triumph to Miss Ainsworth to make sure she got the point, and then at Corie.

What she saw in Corie's face made her almost frown. But she instantly regained her 'fond mother' expression. Later, she'd ask her eldest daughter what had been in her mind at that moment.

'So you and Mr Lenoir are . . . engaged? Can I say that?'

'No, no, that's not a term we'd want to see in print,' Sasha said.

'Can I say that you are close?'

'You can say that I don't know where I'd be without Sasha,' Lynette said with fervour. 'I owe him everything.'

'Yes, that's been a thread throughout all our chat,' the journalist said, nodding and smiling. Transparent, she was thinking to herself. Luckily her darling seemed to be as smitten with her as she was with him — look at them sitting there holding hands like a pair of lovebirds. She signalled with her eyes to the photographer to get a shot of that.

'In your show,' she began again, changing tack, 'all your songs are about happy love, or love that's going to come and brighten your life — everything optimistic.'

'Of course,' said Lynette. 'Love makes you happy.'

'But when love goes?'

'Goes?' Lynette echoed. It seemed to be a new thought to her.

'Yes, for instance, if you and Mr Lenoir ever broke up—'

'Don't say such a thing!'

'It's never going to happen?'

'Of course not,' said Sasha, pulling Lynette a little closer to him on the sofa.

'It's lovely to hear your confidence,' remarked Miss Ainsworth. 'But show business is chancy, and relationships do break up.' She hesitated before asking the question, because it was a big one. 'Has it ever occurred to you to wonder what you'd do if you were on your own?'

Lynette shook her blonde head from side to side. 'Don't!' she begged in a voice of desperation. 'If Sasha ever left me I don't know what I'd do — throw myself straight in the Thames, probably.'

From the soft, gentle Lynette, the words had extraordinary power. Even a seasoned interviewer like Miss Ainsworth drew in a breath.

Corie was shocked, the more so because she could see it was true. Trusting and unwary, Lynette had pinned all her hopes on Sasha.

The interview ended soon after. Sasha bore Lynette off to have a quiet dinner together in a country restaurant, there to restore the spirits depressed by the journalist's question. Monna settled down to give a blow-by-blow account of the interview to Opal, who came home about seven. Unable to bear it, Corie went out for a walk.

Her mind returned again to the eternal problem – what was she to do? She longed for someone to confide in, someone who would tell her how to break the shackles she had so thoughtlessly donned. But her best friends had always been her sisters, and they were the last people she could turn to now. Never a hint must reach Lynette herself, and even Pal would be angry.

And she deserved that anger. Why should anyone sympathise with her? What she was doing was wrong, she knew it was wrong, all she had to do was stop. Yes, stop – tell Sasha it was over, refuse to go near him.

It was the conclusion she reached every day. It never seemed to make any difference. She was like an addict, she couldn't give him up. It was a sexual obsession that dominated her entire being.

A week or two later she was taken to a party by Ingram Holstead. It was a big affair in honour of a song-writer who had reached his seventieth birthday, so had a full contingent of show-business people. At a moment when Corie had gone out on the terrace for a breath of air, she found William Tranton on a bench by a statue of a wood nymph.

'Ah, so you had to beat a retreat too, did you?' he greeted her, patting the bench beside him.

She took her place alongside. 'The trouble with showbiz is that everybody is always *performing* – and usually too loudly.'

'I know what you mean. But of course, hearts of gold.'

'So everybody always says.'

'Are you by any chance a little disillusioned?'

'I was disillusioned when I was still at stage school,' she confided.

'Ye-es . . . Isn't it funny that Lynette still trusts everybody to be good and honest?'

'She's always been like that,' Corie said, stifling a sigh. 'I wouldn't want her any different and yet . . .'

'And yet, how's she going to get through life without being hurt?'

'All we can hope is that it won't happen for a while yet.'

William was silent a moment, then seemed to come to a decision. 'Listen Corie, you know I think the world of Lynette.'

'Yes.'

'I don't want to see her hurt.'

'I know that.'

'But the way she feels about Sasha . . .'

'That's a fact of life. There's nothing to be done about it.'

'But look here — I mean, I know he's a very good agent, he gets great opportunities for his clients and Lynette has done tremendously well . . . I mean, I know your mother has a very high opinion of him, and you too, I expect . . . This is very difficult.' He broke off, got a handkerchief, and mopped his brow.

'What are you trying to say, William?'

'Promise you won't be angry.'

'I promise.'

'Sasha Lenoir isn't to be trusted where women are concerned.' When she made no response he rushed on: 'Even in the old days when I knew him, he always had a crowd of girls fluttering round him. He used to make out he was something very important in the Army, but we just had desk jobs alongside each other. And now of course — now that he doesn't have to *pretend* he's somebody — he only has to flick a finger . . .'

'It's common knowledge?'

'No, no, he's reasonably careful. He wouldn't want Lynette to know, you see.' He looked seriously at Corie. 'It doesn't surprise you?'

'No, because . . .' I'll tell him, she thought. Here's someone I can speak to openly. But then she reminded herself that he was more than half in love with Lynette himself, that he would perhaps be unable to keep it to himself.

William was pursuing his own train of thought. 'It would

destroy Lynette if she knew what he's really like,' he muttered. 'She worships the very ground he treads. Yet I feel someone ought to put her on her guard . . .'

'It wouldn't be worth trying,' Corie replied. 'She's always been like that, since just a kid. Thinks the best of people, wants everybody to be happy . . . Pal and I had a sort of pact to look after her. Not that she's avoided all the hard knocks, mind you. She's had her let-downs, like everybody else. But with Sasha it's different. Sasha's her knight in shining armour.'

'I can't think what the women *see* in him,' William broke out. Then added with a wry smile, 'That's just jealousy, of course.'

'You care about Lynette a lot, don't you?'

'From the minute I saw her,' he confessed. 'Sasha had pulled the Old Pals' Act to get her an audition and I thought, She'll just be another popsy, and then on she came, so fresh and innocent and sincere . . . And I knew at that moment she had something precious, unique . . . and that if she was handled right everybody would see it and love her.'

Corie gave a gasp. 'It was you!'

'What?'

'It was *you* that made her a star! It was you who moved her on, saw that she had the right designer and choreographer . . . And I thought it was Sasha.'

'What does it matter who it was that helped her?' William said. 'She was there, waiting to be discovered, and we must just make sure that nothing damages her now.'

'Amen to that,' Corie said.

'And one of the first things to do is get rid of that new secretary Sasha hired. She's fallen like a brick for Sasha, and though it may shock you to hear it, he's got his eye on her.'

She felt an inward shudder. How could she still allow herself to be involved with a man like this? She was just another in the list of conquests − perhaps a little different in that she had a career of her own, didn't need his help to get on in the world, yet just another girl he had flicked his finger at. Where was her pride? Where was her sense of honour?

Ingram appeared through the open french window. 'Corie? Oh, there you are, Corie, I'm leaving now — d'you want to come with me or stay on a bit?'

'I'll come with you, Ingram, thanks.' She rose, giving her hand to William. 'We'll look after Lynette,' she said.

'Yes we will.'

She and Ingram made their way through the rooms towards the door, thanking their host and hostess, kissing and congratulating the song-writer, making their goodbyes. The Rolls was waiting in the driveway. The chauffeur handed her in, waited to close the door after Ingram, then took the wheel to move them grandly round the semi-circle of gravel and out into the Hampstead summer night.

'What was all that about?' Ingram said.

'The birthday party?'

'You and Tranton. You had your heads very closely together.' He thought about it. 'Are you and he involved?'

'Of course not,' Corie answered on a laugh. 'We were talking about my sister Lynette.'

'Really? Why?'

'He produces her show.'

'Ah, so he does.' He nodded, satisfied. He went on to discuss one or two of his friends they'd seen at the party. After a while, sensing he didn't have her attention, he said, 'Something bothering you?'

'I don't know, Ingram,' she said, unable to keep the despondency out of her voice. 'Sometimes it all seems to get on top of you, doesn't it?'

'Not if you don't let it. What's the matter with you? I've never heard you complain before.'

Was that what she was doing? Complaining? Whining? Trying to blame some unknown fate for the problems she'd brought on herself?

'Your problem is you work too hard,' Ingram said.

'No, I like my work.'

'Well, if it isn't that, it's your family. You worry too

much about them. I often think it's a funny set-up – there's you with a career to be proud of, and your sister a TV star, and you're all living at home in each other's pockets.'

She said nothing.

'When I was your age,' Ingram said grumpily, 'I'd been out on my own for going on ten years.'

'So I've often heard you say. Selling second-hand American magazines in Walworth Road, wasn't it?'

'You can laugh! I bought them off the crews of the big liners for twenty bob a bundle, waste paper they thought – and then I sorted them out and sold them at sixpence each, a shilling for the true-crime mags . . . By the time I was twenty I was importing them from the publishers, and then I began publishing an English version of one of them . . .'

'And then you went on to newspapers.'

Ingram had quite forgotten why he'd embarked on this reminiscence. It kept him chatting happily until he set her down in Bayswater. But when he'd said goodnight and been driven away, she thought about what he'd begun to say.

He was right. It was time she left home. Not because she and her family were too involved in each other's lives although that was perhaps true. But the chief reason was that if she lived somewhere else it would be easier to avoid Sasha.

Because that was what she must do – she could see that now. It was useless to lament the power he seemed to have over her – she must put all her strength into breaking it. After all it was a power of the senses only, which absence must surely weaken. While she remained an occupant of the Bayswater house and he dropped in so often, avoidance was impossible.

For her own sake she must take action. And for Lynette's sake too. She'd said to William, 'We'll look after Lynette.' She had always done so, and now she must make even greater efforts or else her little sister might be irreparably hurt.

She must find a place of her own.

Her mother was astounded. 'Why on earth do you want to live elsewhere?' she demanded. 'You practically grew up in this house.'

'No, Monna, I grew up in Shropshire where we were evacuated during the war,' Corie said with a smile, 'or perhaps in digs here and there around the country when you were touring. But that's nothing to do with it. I'm twenty-five years old, Monna — it's time I had a place of my own.'

'But what for? I don't see the point of it.'

'Well, never mind. It's what I've decided to do.'

After some declarations that it was all foolishness, Monna took a different tack. 'Well, if you must, you must. I'll look around and see what I can find for you.'

'No need, thanks, Monna, I've got a flat picked out.'

'You have? Where, may I ask?'

'It's the top half of a house in Stamford Street, near Blackfriars Bridge.'

'But my dear *child* — that's hardly a suitable neighbourhood, is it? Why, it's practically a slum, still full of rubble left over from the Festival of Britain.'

'I like it,' Corie said. 'It's quiet and the flat is capacious and not too expensive, and the river's nearby . . .'

Monna tried to persuade her to go somewhere more respectable. Having no success in that, she then decided she would take over the matter of furnishing and decorating her daughter's new home. But no, Corie was satisfied with the decorations as they were, and would be happy with a few pieces from the Bayswater house and some things she would pick up as she felt she needed them.

Frustrated, Monna had to admit defeat. 'I think it's very strange,' she said with disapproval. 'But you always were a strange girl, Corie.'

Opal, to the contrary, didn't think it a bit strange. 'You want to be on your own,' she said. 'I've been half expecting it.'

'Really?' Corie was surprised, because she herself hadn't thought of it until a couple of weeks ago.

'I've seen a sad look on your face now and again,' her sister said. 'I've had a feeling something's wrong . . . What is it, Corie?'

'Nothing, Pal, really. Just restlessness.'

Opal nodded. 'I sometimes have little flutterings of my own,' she said. 'It would be nice to have a home where life didn't revolve around show business . . .'

'You could come and share with me, if you like.'

'What, and leave Lynette to cope with Monna on her own?'

'Lynette ought to have her own place—'

'Lynette's never going to go anywhere except to the home she'll share with Sasha when they're married.'

Corie had been collecting belongings to put into a box for removal. She stared into the box so as not to have to meet Opal's gaze. 'Do you think Lynette and Sasha will marry?' she asked.

Her sister hesitated. 'I think Lynette thinks they will,' she said carefully. 'And it might happen one day. But I wouldn't take any bets on it.'

'Nor would I,' Corie agreed.

Sasha had been in the north since the beginning of September, overseeing the début of one of his clients in a Blackpool end-of-season spectacular. He came home only briefly, before flying to New York on business. By the time he came back it was October and Corie was safely removed to her new flat. Then came the autumn schedules of the BBC, with the new series of 'You're a Sweetheart'.

Corie began to relax. Presumably Sasha was too busy to notice that she wasn't around much.

She should have known better than to believe any such thing. One evening, a little after eleven o'clock, her doorbell rang. She answered it unthinkingly, the magazine she was reading still in her hand.

'Well,' said Sasha, stepping inside. 'So this is the new love nest.'

She was so shocked that she felt herself go cold. The magazine dropped from her fingers.

Sasha slipped his arms about her. 'Lord, it seems a century or two since we were together, Corie. Missed me?'

She stiffened and tried to pull away. 'I don't want you here, Sasha,' she managed to say with trembling lips.

'What's that?' He laughed, walked her into her own living-room, then stood glancing about with a critical air. 'Not bad. High ceilings – I like high ceilings, I always think they've got class. Are the rugs real Persian?'

'I want you to go, Sasha,' she insisted. 'I don't want you here.'

'Are you kidding? What's the point of a place of your own except so that—'

'I came here for privacy. I don't want you coming here. It's over between us.'

Totally disregarding her, he strolled back to the little vestibule, opened the door of the next room, and looked in. 'Aha! Now this is something like it. Better than that little nook at the studio.' He crossed to the bed, sat down on the edge, and smiled at her as she stood irresolutely in the doorway. 'Come on in, sweetheart. After all, it's *your* place.'

'Please go,' she said.

'You keep saying that. I only just got here.'

'I didn't want you here in the first place. I purposely didn't let you know where I lived.'

'Oh, come on, Corie, I only had to ask Monna for your address. You didn't really think it could be a secret?'

'No, but I didn't think you'd come here without an invitation.'

'Between you and me there's no need to stand on ceremony. You're free to come to my flat any time you like, and I'm free to come to yours.'

'No! It's over.'

He got up, came to her, and took her by the shoulders. 'It isn't over until I say it is,' he said in a low voice.

'What you say doesn't matter.' She put up her hands to try to loosen his grip, but his fingers dug into her shoulderblades. 'Let me go, Sasha. I tell you, I've made up my mind. It was all wrong in the first place . . .'

'There you go again. I don't know what makes you keep saying that. I'm free and you're free and if we want to have a good time together, where's the wrong in that?'

'You're not free, you know you're not.'

'Listen, kiddie,' he said, and there was anger in his tone, 'don't tell me I'm not free. I do what I want to do, right? And what I want to do at the moment is go to bed with you, so let's stop the song and dance.'

'No, I've made up my mind—'

'Don't talk so silly,' he said, and stopped her words by kissing her. She tried to draw back, but felt her lips begin to part under that kiss. The old familiar spell seemed to draw around her like a net, its mesh catching at her nerve-ends, the warmth spreading through her body from the electric current that ran between them.

Because she had given in, that night was all the more feverish in its passion. She made herself think that she must love him or she wouldn't be making love with him – that it wasn't just physical desire, it was of the heart. She said little loving words against his chest, kissed him in a surge of tenderness, thought of him as her beloved, her one and only darling.

So that in the morning the awakening, the disillusion was all the greater. Sasha was cheerful and good-natured towards her, quite different from the resentful and possessive man who had arrived last night. But his very good humour jarred on her. It seemed to say, 'You see – all you have to do is give in and I'll be sweet to you.' And it reduced to its proper state any view she might have of their relationship. She was his good-time girl – let her not think too much of herself.

Christmas came, and there was a family gathering at the Duggans' house. It was timed early so that they could exchange presents and drink egg-nog before Lynette had to be at the TV studios for a special Christmas show. Sasha drove her away in the early dusk, and the rest of the family went indoors to eat Christmas cake and drink coffee.

'One thing about not being famous,' Opal remarked as she flopped back into an armchair, 'you don't have to turn out on Christmas Day.'

'One has a duty to one's public,' Monna said. Then, after a pause, she added, 'So good of Sasha to take her. The BBC would have sent a car.'

'Oh, Sasha likes to be around the studios,' Corie said. 'That's where titbits can be found.'

Monna frowned at her. By and by Opal departed to make fresh coffee, so giving her mother an opportunity to say something that had clearly been on her mind.

'I don't like the tone you take about Sasha,' she said to Corie. 'You sometimes sound downright disrespectful.'

Corie was too taken aback to answer.

'You've never really done him justice,' her mother went on. 'He's been a hundred per cent right about Lynette from the outset, and all I can suppose is you're jealous—'

'Jealous!'

'Well, you never have had anything like the same talent as Lynette, nor the looks; as long as she wasn't a success you didn't seem to mind too much. But now you seem to want to spoil things for little Lynnie by making trouble with Sasha . . .'

'Monna, that's the last thing I want—'

'Oh, really? We all know you're the clever one of the family – all right, she's got the looks, you've got the brains, but there's no need to keep trying to impress Sasha – it would take more than a few clever remarks to take him away from Lynette.'

'Oh, God,' groaned Corie. Getting up, she walked out of the room.

It seemed that nothing she did was right. And now Monna was on the watch. However wrong her first impression might have been, by constantly observing them she might well end up discovering the truth.

Disaster was looming. Help me, somebody, Corie cried inwardly.

Ingram Holstead came to her aid. He sent for her on a day in the New Year.

'How would you like to go abroad again on an assignment for the *Globe*?' he inquired.

'I'd love it,' Corie replied.

She didn't even ask what it might be. Anything, anything at all, if only she could get away from London and all its dangers.

Chapter Nine

As soon as she heard the details, Corie began trying to back out.

'You can't mean it,' she protested. 'It's a publicity stunt got up by the film company.'

'Metro-Goldwyn-Mayer? I don't know so much,' Ingram said musingly, 'I rang the press boys at MGM in Wardour Street and they were so excited about it they could hardly string words together.'

'Maybe Hollywood hasn't kept them in the know.'

'Anything's possible with Hollywood. But the Church is involved here.'

'The Church?'

'The Prince's chaplain – Father Tucker. From what we hear on the grapevine, he's been acting as marriage broker.'

Corie shook her head. 'Be sensible, Ingram,' she said, 'a European prince isn't going to marry a Hollywood film star.'

'But this isn't just *any* film star. For my money she's the most beautiful blonde in the world, she's an Oscar winner, she's a millionaire's daughter, she's a lady, and she's a devout Catholic. They say the Prince is enchanted with her.'

'But she was supposed to be going to marry that dress designer—'

'Cassini? That was last year. You don't keep up with the gossip, Corie dear.'

'True enough,' she agreed. There had been a time when she'd been a keen cinema and theatre goer. But now that she was so much in demand as a photographer, she didn't keep up with film and stage as she used to, except in the area that concerned Lynette.

Grace Kelly and her romances were in a whole different realm. Now and again her name had caught Corie's attention in the gossip columns, but she'd never been interested enough to keep informed.

Now Ingram was saying the film star had become engaged to Prince Rainier of Monaco. Unlikely, to say the least.

'But even if it's true, Ingram,' she began again, 'it's not my kind of thing.'

'That's what you said when I sent you to Tokyo.'

It silenced her for a moment. Then she said, 'I just don't want to get involved in the kind of three-ring circus that will grow up around it if it happens. Where's the wedding supposed to take place, anyhow? On a set in Hollywood?'

'Come, come, don't make jokes about what will probably be the media event of the year,' he scolded. He was grinning to himself at what was being offered to the world. His heavy-lidded eyes were aglow with eagerness. 'At the moment there's a wrangle going on – the Kellys are saying the wedding will take place in St Bridget's, Philadelphia, the Grimaldis are saying it will be in St Nicholas's Cathedral, Monte Carlo.'

'Who are the Grimaldis?' wondered Corie.

'Don't you know anything?' Ingram laughed. 'They're the princely family of Monaco. The Prince is a Grimaldi, his title is His Serene Highness, and the people he reigns over are called the Monégasques.'

'You know a lot,' Corie applauded.

'Got it all out of our "morgue". There's a thick file on Monte Carlo. You'd better have a copy to study before you leave.'

'Well, we haven't decided yet if I'm going to leave. Nor where I'm heading if I do.'

'Oh, it'll be Monte Carlo. The Prince has the Vatican behind him – the wedding will be in St Nicholas's.'

'And when, exactly, if it really is going to happen?'

'That hasn't been settled. But it'll be quite soon, I think – before June.'

'How do you work that out?'

'Well, look at it this way – the tourist season starts in June and the hotels are probably booked out from then on. So the wedding will be either earlier or later than the tourist season—'

'Ingram, that's cold-blooded!'

'Oh, come on,' he retorted, 'd'you think Buckingham Palace didn't take that sort of thing into consideration for the Queen's Coronation? Of course officials have to think about press coverage and accommodation and travel facilities. The harbour at Monte gets choc-a-bloc from June onwards with millionaire's yachts, the roads from France through Monaco into Italy teem with cars, every hotel and villa is booked up with northerners looking for the sun. In July the whole of France shuts up shop and moves to the coast until September. So you can take a bet Grace Kelly and her Prince will be married either before June or after September – and my money is on an early event because MGM probably has a film lined up for her the minute she becomes Princess Grace.'

'She's never going to go on acting if she marries Prince Rainier!'

'The press boys at MGM think she is.'

Corie found it incredible. 'I tell you, the whole thing is a take-in. There'll be no wedding and no Princess of Hollywood.'

'Want to bet?'

'How much?'

'I'll tell you what,' Ingram suggested. 'If within the next couple of weeks the whole thing dies away, I'll buy you any camera you choose to name. But if, on the contrary, the wedding day is announced, you go to Monte Carlo.'

She hesitated. 'What would be the point, Ingram? There would be news cameramen in and around the cathedral in their hundreds. You'd be far better advised to send one of your men to cover the event—'

'And so I will, a camera team that will cover it for the *Daily* and the *Sunday Globe*. But I want to do something more, something a bit different. I want you to go a bit in advance and find out what the people of Monaco think of it. I want pix of the ordinary man in the street and his wife.'

'What use would I be? I don't speak any French beyond "Bonjour" and "S'il vous plaît".'

'That's all right. I'm going to team you up with Mabel Hitherton. She not only speaks the lingo, she knows the area well because she loves to gamble and treats herself to a fling in the casino every Christmas.'

'I see.'

'And by the way, *there's* a place where you won't have to look for "hidden beauty". It's the most photogenic landscape in the world! And it's full of handsome people – so don't give me any nonsense about finding a light of the spirit or whatever it was.'

'Are you telling me you want a spread of pretty pictures with girls in bikinis? Is that it? Because if so—'

'No, no,' he said in haste. 'Don't get on your high horse, Corie. Mabel Hitherton is going to look for the man in the street and talk to him. You take the pix. I want to look behind the scenes a bit more than the other papers. Is it a bet? You get a camera if the whole thing turns out to be a publicity story, I get your view of the home life of Monte Carlo if I'm right about the marriage.'

Her earlier reluctance had waned. If she weren't after all caught up in a mad publicity event, here was the excuse she'd longed for, to get her out of London.

'It's a deal,' she said, and they shook hands on it. But she didn't really think it was going to happen.

By the end of January the news was confirmed. Miss Grace Kelly was to marry Prince Rainier of Monaco in mid-April, first in a civil ceremony at the palace in Monte Carlo, and then on the following day at a religious ceremony in the Cathedral of St Nicholas.

Mabel Hitherton rang Corie at her new flat. 'You don't know me yet, but since we're going to Monte Carlo in a week or two, I thought we ought to meet and get acquainted. Can do?'

'Of course.'

They had lunch together at the Waldorf. Corie found a plump, four-square-looking woman of about forty waiting for her in the light and airy lounge. 'How do you do?' they said to each other, and shook hands.

'I've seen your work, of course,' Mabel said. 'Admired it. I suppose you've never read a line I've written.'

'We-ell . . .'

'It's all right, why should you? I do the human-interest bit – sometimes serious, sometimes silly. Did you see that piece I wrote about the so-called "King of the Teddy-boys" last month?'

'I'm afraid I . . . er . . .'

'It wasn't bad, if I do say so myself – a strange lad, needed a psychiatrist more than a jail sentence, but there, if you go round attacking policemen . . . Well, I booked a table, let's go in, shall we?'

Mabel had somehow managed to get a timetable of the bride-to-be's movements. A wedding dress was being made for her by the chief designer of MGM, Helen Rose, and Mabel was off to Hollywood soon, not of course expecting to be allowed sight of the gown, but to speak to the women who were making it.

'It's going to cost about seven thousand dollars – absurd, isn't it?' said Mabel, chewing steak vigorously. 'But there's to be a lot of handwork on it – I want to hear what the workers think about the wedding as they make it. Then Grace is going to New York to buy her trousseau. I don't think I'll try to get in on that, I can't feel I'd get much sentimentality out of the New York garment industry.'

'Perhaps not,' Corie agreed. 'So when do we start out for Monte Carlo?'

'I thought we'd go in March. I always stay at a little hotel in the Condamine – that's down by the port – and I've spoken to them on the telephone. They're willing to take us. I haven't set any definite date for us to leave, thought we'd play it by ear, but I gather they won't want us in April – they'll have some of the Hollywood contingent there.'

'Are we going to stay right through till after the wedding?'

'Could be. You know, there's a lot of uncertainty and trouble in the air. That wedding might yet be cancelled.'

Corie didn't know whether she hoped it would happen or be cancelled. But she could see Mabel was enthralled by the prospective drama.

'So, while you're off in Hollywood and so forth, what ought I to be doing?'

'You could mug up on the background. I've brought the file for you. I know,' she put in quicky as Corie was about to protest, 'you're not going to do any of the reporting so you don't really need to know the background. Read it or not, as you like. But there's one thing you could do that I think really would be useful.'

'What's that?'

'Take a speed course in French.'

'What!'

'Look, we can't always be hand in hand all the time we'll be in France and Monaco. Since you'll have three weeks with nothing to do while I rush off to Hollywood—'

Corie laughed. 'Nothing to do? I have a business diary full of appointments! The rearranging I've had to do to clear the space for this jaunt!'

'OK, OK, that was a daft thing to say. But all the same, you do have a bit of time before we leave. I think if you went to a language laboratory and got a few phrases of everyday French, it would be useful.' Mabel put her knife and fork on her plate and pushed it aside. 'Of course, you can put it on expenses with the *Globe*.'

'Really?'

'Of course! Likewise, when you buy new clothes—'

'Why would I buy new clothes?'

Mabel wrinkled her nose. 'You're going to Monte Carlo in corduroy trousers and a sweater?'

'Well, I've got some shirts . . . quite good ones . . . Do

you set a lot of store by clothes?'

Mabel looked down at her silk suit with some approval. 'Special price from Hardy Amies,' she said. 'Don't you think you should grab chances like that when they come your way?'

Corie didn't, as a matter of fact. But she could see it would be better not to say so. They turned their minds to the serious matter of dessert, and over that and their coffee mapped out a plan of campaign.

The commission to go to Monaco had raised Corie by several notches in her mother's estimation. 'Well, after all, it seems, going into photography wasn't such a bad move. Fancy being asked to take pictures of a royal wedding!'

'I'm not going to take pictures of the wedding, Monna.'

'Well, no, I suppose there'll be official photographers for that. You'll be doing things like you did with Lynette when she had that spread in the *Globe* . . .'

'I don't think I'll even see Grace Kelly, except maybe from a distance—'

'She's a very great star, you know,' said Monna, as if it were something no one else knew. 'The eyes of the entire world will be upon her on the great day.' And then she said something that was to come back to her daughter's mind with tremendous force later. 'In a way she belongs to us, you know. The public gives its love, its loyalty, to a star of that calibre.' Beaming, she threw out a hand in a gesture of salute. 'It's a great honour to have a part in that, Corie.'

Useless to explain that she would have no part, that her assignment was with the ordinary people of Monaco.

She was kept very busy with preparations. First there was the language school, where to her own astonishment she was doing very well. Her stage-school training had given her the knack of learning words, and though it was only a superficial knowledge, she hoped all the same that she'd be able to get by in French.

Then there was the file of information Mabel had given her. She read and re-read it, charmed to discover that the Principality of Monaco was only about two miles long and less than a mile wide, that most of the inhabitants weren't in fact Monégasque but French and Italian, and that it belonged to an ancient culture called the Languedoc.

Corie had never heard of the Languedoc. When she asked her tutor at the language school, she got a long and enthusiastic lecture about poetry, song, earthy enjoyment, and shrewd business sense as epitomised by the famous casino of Monte Carlo and the Grand Prix.

Shrewd business sense was being shown by the authorities when it came to handing out permits for access to the ceremonies. Ingram became quite blasphemous in his comments.

'They say each newspaper group has to be limited to a team of one reporter and one cameraman, because *all* the American newspapers want access. I've had to agree that you and Mabel are not the *Globe*'s team—'

'What are we, then?' Mabel asked in annoyance. 'I'm not going as a private citizen, Ingram. I'm going to use my press card when I have to.'

'We're doing our best, Mabel,' he retorted. 'But depending on how things turn out, I may have to withdraw you and Corie and send in another pair.'

'All right, all right—'

'On the other hand, I don't see how they're going to keep track,' he swept on, a malicious twinkle in his eye. 'The authorities are going to be absolutely swamped with foreign pressmen. In fact, I'd take a guess that on the day of the wedding there will be twice as many reporters in Monaco as troops trying to keep the crowd in order. So you see, children . . . You can more or less do as you like, because no one is going to be able to cope with the invasion.'

Corie couldn't help feeling sorry for the people of Monaco. To be overrun by gossip-hungry reporters wasn't her idea of celebrating a royal marriage.

In the midst of all this she scarcely had a moment to think about Sasha. As it happened, he too was busy. The first modest programmes by the independent television service had opened in London the previous September, so now programme planning by both Associated Rediffusion and Associated Broadcasting was in full swing. Sasha was kept negotiating in the producers' offices or arguing on the telephone.

Three days before Corie was due to leave, he telephoned her at her Bury Street studio. 'I absolutely must see you, Corie.'

'Sasha, I don't have time for—'

'It's terribly important, lovey. Look, all I want to do is talk.'

'Talk?' She was amused that he should use a ploy like that.

'Can I come this evening?'

'No, I'll be at the language laboratory.'

'Whereabouts is that, for heaven's sake?'

'Off Oxford Street. But—'

'What time d'you finish?'

'Nine-thirty. But I've got things to do.'

'Corie, you can spare time for me, surely? I absolutely have to talk to you—'

'But what about?'

'It's about Lynette. It's very important.'

She gave in at once. They arranged to meet at the big Lyons' at Marble Arch.

Her heart was in her mouth as she hurried up Oxford Street at a little after nine-thirty that evening. Had something about their relationship come to Lynette's ears? Had their mother said something to alarm her? The last thing in the world she wanted was for Lynette to find out – even though Corie herself was trying with all her might to end the affair.

In the event, the situation was almost laughable. What Sasha thought so vitally important about Lynette was this: should he take up a very good offer from Associated Rediffusion to transfer Lynette to their company, or should he stay with the BBC who, though paying less money, nevertheless seemed more sympathetic to the kind of show Lynette excelled in.

'You see, although money's important, we have to think of the long-term effect. William Tranton has a personal stake in making Lynette look good – he helped to "discover" her. Whereas at Rediffusion we get a producer who doesn't really know her and wants to put her on without the personal touches, such as the engaged couples . . . What do you think, Corie?'

'Why are you asking me?' Corie marvelled. 'I'm no expert, for goodness sake! In any case, isn't it for Lynette to decide?'

'Oh, you know Lynette – she says she'll do whatever I think best.'

'And what do you actually think is best?'

'Damned if I know! This is a big step for Lynette. You see, her following on the BBC channel might not go with her to the independent. A lot of people haven't got sets that can receive ITV.' And on he talked, agonising over the decision.

It dawned on Corie that he really had no one else he could discuss it with. Although most people would have said he had hordes of friends, they were in general clients and theatre-chain managers and producers – people with whom he couldn't afford to seem indecisive. In a way it was flattering that from her he expected an honest, unbiased opinion.

Yet it was strange that he thought he could call on her, almost casually, for advice on the career of the sister she was deceiving.

Whether she helped or not, she parted from him in a state of mixed anger and amusement. He said to her: 'Look, I won't come back to your flat if you don't mind – I need an early night, I've got an appointment first thing tomorrow morning.' No inquiry as to whether she was longing to have him come to her, no apology for walking away from her even if she'd been expecting his company – in fact, she felt as if he saw her as some kind of secretary or general counsellor, not as a lover.

Well, that's good, she insisted to herself as she walked

home along Bayswater Road. It must mean he's cooling off. He said, didn't he: 'It's not over until I say it is.'

Mabel and Corie made the journey to Monaco by ferry and train. At Nice a car was waiting for their use. This wasn't entirely to Corie's satisfaction because Mabel insisted on driving – 'I'm used to Continental roads.' She turned out to be the world's worst driver.

But, all the same, nothing could diminish the beauty of the coastal road to Monte Carlo. To the west was Le Rocher, the Rock, where stood the palace of terracotta and white in which Grace Kelly would live with her Prince after the wedding. There was a medieval town, Monaco-Ville, huddled close to what had once been its protection, the palace and its guards. Here dwelt the small population of Monégasques.

At the foot of Le Rocher the port of the Condamine lined out along the shore. Here in a row of old houses stood the hotel where Mabel had booked rooms. It was a tall, narrow house, painted a rich ochre outside and very elegantly appointed inside. Now Corie understood why Mabel had been so perturbed about the slacks, sweater and swagger coat in which she'd travelled. The guests at La Palmette were the kind who dressed for dinner and expected everyone else to do likewise.

While Mabel unpacked her wardrobe of designer clothes with the help of a maid who made her au fait with the latest gossip, Corie went out to explore. Almost at once the sea lay before her, the Mediterranean, unbelievably blue – turquoise, aquamarine, sapphire, cobalt, the colours mixing and merging under the evening sun of mid-March.

There were palm trees at intervals along the pavement. Palm trees! Corie had never seen a palm before. Nor had she seen mimosa in bloom, nor orange trees with fruit gleaming among the glossy leaves.

She breathed in the scented air – sea-salt, flowers, smoke from the chimneys of the old houses, rope-hawsers, and even, as an old lady trotted past on her way to the casino, the rich perfume of Chanel No. 5.

The Riviera! Glamorous, fashionable, frivolous – far beyond her reach, she would have thought at one time; yet here she was.

The sun began to decline. She noticed that people began to filter out of the cafés where they had been enjoying an aperitif. Time to go back for dinner at La Palmette.

Mabel was all prettied up for the evening in a black lace gown. Corie did her best to achieve a like effect, brushing her smooth tan hair, touching up her brows with a little eyebrow pencil and her lashes with a hint of mascara. She wore a peacock-blue silk shirt belted in with a gilt chain over black trousers.

'Aha! Well! When you said you had some quite good shirts, I didn't quite understand . . .' Mabel was clearly taken aback by the svelte good looks of her colleague. Luckily, she was reflecting, trousers were very à la mode on the Riviera.

After the excellent meal, she insisted on taking Corie to the casino. The interior of red plush and gilt was pretty and gave Corie a nostalgic glimpse of the Edwardian era. But standing by while Mabel lost money on the roulette wheel struck her as a sheer waste of time. After a while she whispered goodnight and walked home under a cool, starry sky, to fall into bed and sleep like a log.

Next day they had to present letters of introduction provided by Ingram. It appeared that his wife, Helen Pittsworth Holstead, knew the Kellys of Philadelphia on a social basis. Through Mrs Holstead, contact had been made with the organisers of the wedding – those handling the guests from the American contingent, and also the public-relations people dealing with Grace Kelly's friends from the world of New York television and theatre.

The public-relations firm was working out of a suite at the hotel Sangiorgio. They were received by a pretty American girl in black, who asked them to wait. After a moment she returned to say that Mr Richter would see them.

'Mr Richter, who's he?' whispered Mabel.

'How should I know?' Corie asked.

Mr Richter proved to be a tall, fair-haired American in a light grey flannel suit. 'Good morning,' he said, 'Miss Hitherton?'

'I'm Mabel Hitherton. This is Corie Duggan, the photographer.'

'Glad to know you,' he said, shaking hands one after the other. It was plain to see he had never heard of either Mabel Hitherton (journalist of some renown) or Corie Duggan (famous portrait photographer). 'Please take a seat. Now then, can I offer you anything? Coffee? Fruit juice?'

'Nothing, thanks, we just had breakfast a few minutes ago in the hotel.'

'Oh, you're staying in Monaco?'

'Yes, at the Palmette. We just dropped in to make ourselves known and to hand over the letter of introduction from Mrs Holstead.'

'Er . . . Mrs Holstead?' the publicity man said, trying not to appear at a loss.

'Helen Pittsworth Holstead – she's a personal friend of John Brendan Kelly senior.'

It seemed to Corie that he stifled a sigh at hearing this. His was a face that had been trained to keep its own counsel, rather long and thin-lipped. His eyes watched the world with some disillusion, although laughter wrinkles around them let it be known he had a sense of humour. Corie put his age at about thirty and his normal place of residence somewhere less sunny than Monaco, for he had a pale, slightly freckled skin.

With a slight smile of apology he took a thick, loose-leaf book out of a drawer. Its printed cover announced 'Confidential File A, Pelham & Richter, Andrew Richter's copy'. He consulted it quickly then gave them a glance of apology. 'You'll have to forgive me – so many people come along with fake claims to know the family that I have to check up . . . Oh yes, Helen Pittsworth Holstead, daughter of the textiles millionaire Orvil Pittsworth, married to . . .

ah, I get it! You're from the *Globe* newspaper?'

'That's right. But rest easy, we haven't come to ask for any special favours.' Mabel flickered beringed fingers at him. 'We're not here for the wedding – at least, not for the ceremony. We're trying to get a behind-the-scenes look at the people.'

'Ah.' Mr Richter was nodding, although without much conviction.

'We don't want you to introduce us to any of the bigwigs or get us a pass to attend the wedding.'

'Right.' Still he was waiting for the punchline. Corie realised he was used to trade-offs. A publicity man, she supposed, must always be making deals with members of the press.

'I was just wondering if you had teletype facilities here?'

'We-ell . . .'

'I'm not saying we'll need to use them. My copy won't be urgent, as far as I can see – home-life of Mrs Monégasque; what she thinks about this fairy-tale wedding, and so forth.'

'In that case, what's the point?'

'There might be in-coming messages – instructions from my boss or background stuff. Mr Holstead asked me to check in with you and make sure it was all right to send from his office in Fleet Street.'

'Sure, I see nothing against that,' Richter replied. 'Anything else I can do for you?'

Mabel was shaking her head. Corie said, 'Mr Richter, can you recommend a good photographic processing firm here in Monaco or nearby? I'll have masses of film and where we are, at the Palmette, there's no possibility of a darkroom.'

For the first time he turned his attention to her. He took in the capacious camera bag slung at her rather angular shoulder. 'You look as if you're going to be busy,' he remarked with what might have been approval in his greenish-grey eyes.

'Well, that's my intention. I've got to take the pix to go with Mabel's interviews, but this is the first time I've ever been on the Riviera – I don't intend to miss the chance.

The light . . . !' She gestured at the spring sunshine pouring in at his office window. 'I've never seen anything like it before.'

'Yet more views from the Grande Corniche,' he said, but with a faint grin that took any ridicule out of the remark.

'Well, those too, but it's the roofs that fascinate me. That lovely terracotta tile . . .'

'The roofs. I see. Well, I'm sure you'll find Antoine at this address a very efficient darkroom man.' He scribbled on a pad. 'As to prints, I'm not so sure—'

'Oh, I shouldn't want him to do my prints! No, I just want to make sure I've got something on the negs that's worth keeping for more work at home.'

'Well, Antoine does our black and white publicity shots – he's been OK for that so far. Of course we're not going all out as yet. I don't know how he'll be under pressure.'

'It must be a big undertaking. You're handling the press on behalf of who? The film studios?'

'Lord, no, they've got a vanload of their own people. No, some of the New York agents and theatres hired me to deal with things for their people. Miss Kelly has invited quite a few of the actors and directors she worked with before she went to Hollywood.'

'Who, for instance?' demanded Mabel, scenting the possibility of introductions and future articles.

From a folder he produced a typed list. Mabel glanced at it. 'No Monaco addresses?'

'No, I must ask you to contact them through me. They're coming primarily as wedding guests, and they want to be very careful with the press. I'm sure you'll appreciate their point of view.'

Mabel laughed. 'Well, the press is making remarks like "Monaco is a ten cent stamp that's kidding the world it's a hundred dollar bill". So I can see your clients would want to be careful what they say.'

'It's terrible,' Corie remarked in indignation. 'How can they behave like that? If Grace Kelly wants to marry the ruler of a tiny kingdom, that's her own affair—'

Richter shrugged. 'You may think that, but most of the world thinks otherwise. American journalists have persuaded themselves she belongs to the American people, and half the time they're mourning the fact that she's marrying a foreigner, and the other half they're thrilled against their will that she's going to be a princess.'

'And what's your view?' she inquired.

'Miss Duggan, a public-relations man doesn't have a view. He just does what the client wants. Now, is there anything else I can do for you, ladies? No? Well, good luck with the roofs.'

Having been told to go, they went. Mabel glanced at the list of clients as they descended in the ornate lift. 'He must be a top-notch man,' she remarked. 'He's handling some very big names.'

Corie was sighting her camera at the odd-angled views of landings going by. 'Mm . . .'

'And he probably has personal access to the palace, since he's handling some of Grace's personal friends.'

'I suppose so.'

'You know, Corie, we could get an inside view of what the palace servants think . . .'

'You told him you just wanted to use his teletype,' Corie reminded her.

'Well, that was before I'd thought about it.'

'No wonder he's so much on his guard. Anyhow, I wouldn't bother trying it on with him. He strikes me as not being easy to persuade.'

'You know all about him, eh? After ten minutes' conversation?'

Corrie shrugged and let it go. But she felt she did know something about Andrew Richter. In some ways they were alike. They had learned not to put too much trust in the rest of the world.

She and Mabel began the work that had brought them to Monaco. They took it easy at first, because the townsfolk of

Monaco-Ville were quite willing to confide in them. Later, as they were badgered by wave after wave of pressmen, the Monégasques began to resist questioning. Particularly when the American journalists insisted on saying rude things about their little country, the people grew more and more uncooperative.

The press photographers were the worst. They tried to bribe their way into the palace, they dressed up as waiters in the hotels so as to spy on eminent guests, they climbed trees to look in at bedroom windows, they crawled along eaves, they hid in wine-cellars, and one of them risked death under the wheels of Prince Rainier's Lamborghini so as to get a shot of the shocked driver as he climbed out to inquire if he was all right.

Worst of all, and the one which turned the entire population against the invading horde, was when several male photographers put on monks' robes in an attempt to get into the royal palace. In the people's eyes, this amounted to sacrilege.

As a result, Corie found it increasingly difficult to move and work with ease. The moment the cameras slung about her neck were noticed, people froze. They refused permission to photograph, they turned their backs.

'This is no fun at all,' she muttered to Mabel at the end of a drizzly day when nothing had gone right.

'And to make matters worse, it's only two days until we get turned out.'

They had to leave the Palmette. Their rooms were required for relatives of members of the Council of State. Corie expected them to leave Monte Carlo also, but instructions came through that very day on Andrew Richter's teletype. They were to remain as back-up to the news-reporting team which, en route by car across France, had developed engine trouble.

The problem was, where could they find rooms? By now Monaco was choc-a-bloc.

Appealed to, Andrew Richter said there was nothing to be had within the Principality. 'But if you don't mind rather cramped quarters, a friend of mine has a cabin-cruiser anchored on the outskirts of Nice—'

'Oh, anything!' Mabel cried fervently.

Suppressing a smile at her eagerness, he gave directions and handed over keys.

'Thank you very much, Mr Richter,' Corie said as she took them.

'Ah . . . My name's Andrew. Friends call me Drew.'

'Thanks a million, Drew,' Mabel cried.

She was less full of gratitude when she'd had a day's experience of living on board a small cabin cruiser. Now she found herself envying Corie's slacks and sweaters. Slender skirts and elbow-length gloves weren't really ideal for clambering in and out of the dinghy by which they reached their vessel.

But at least they were still in Monaco each day, filing a report back to the *Globe* in the evening in time for the morning editions.

Three days before the wedding, the two-man team still hadn't turned up. They had insisted on pushing on with a car not properly repaired after it had broken down, and as a result got involved in an accident and were detained by the French police.

Mabel and Corie were perforce the *Globe*'s team in the Principality. Because they were having their own problems, they had asked Ingram Holstead to talk by telephone with Drew and hire proper facilities in his office suite at the Sangiorgio. So now they would call in two or three times a day to check for any messages.

On 15 April they stopped by on their way to Nice at day's end. The receptionist, Trudi, said there was an urgent message to ring Ingram Holstead at the *Globe*.

Sighing, they went downstairs again so that Mabel could put the call through the hotel switchboard. At a signal from the desk, she went into a callbox in the big marble-floored lobby and lifted the receiver.

Corie, sitting on a sofa across from the box, saw her face change as she listened to the call. She spoke into the receiver, nodded several times, held a brief conversation, then came out looking rather white under her recently acquired tan.

'What is it?' Corie asked in alarm.

'Come into the bar.' In its cool dimness Mabel ordered brandy for herself and wine for Corie. When it had been brought, she waited until the barman left them. She took a quick gulp of her brandy.

Then she said, her head bent close to Corie so that no one could overhear: 'Ingram says they've had three letters from a man who says he's going to kill Grace Kelly.'

Chapter Ten

Corie couldn't quite understand why Mabel was taking the death threat against Grace Kelly so seriously. 'It's a hoax,' she said.

Mabel shook her head. 'Ingram doesn't think so.'

'Why not? Newspapers must get hoax letters all the time.'

'This time it looks like the real thing. The first two letters came from somewhere in the Midlands. The third came from Monaco.'

Corie felt a little shiver of apprehension. It took a serious kind of hoaxer to travel to Monaco just to make his threats seem real.

'Well, we'd better pass this on to the police—'

'Ingram says not,' Mabel said, swallowing more brandy.

'I beg your pardon?'

'He wants us to find the man and interview him.'

'You're joking!'

'Not a bit of it. It would be the story of the decade if we could get him to talk.'

'Mabel! This man's clearly unhinged and he's threatening someone's life!'

'As to that, the murder threat isn't too important. I mean, how's he going to get near her?'

Corie thought of men dressing up as monks to get into the palace. 'He might find a way,' she said.

'Well, the boss says we're to keep it to ourselves. Our job is to find him and interview him – and then, if he's still talking about killing, we hand him over to the Monaco police.'

'And you seriously intend to carry out those orders?' Corie demanded, shocked. 'Your first priority is to get an interview?'

'Yes, of course.'

'But Mabel . . . Mabel, that makes you even worse than those vultures who've been hanging round the palace for the last ten days!'

Her colleague lifted unfocused eyes to her. 'Not at all. We're not trying to break into the place, we're trying to find a man who's got a grudge against Grace and prevent him from harming her.'

'But the best way to do that is to tell the police.'

'Afterwards,' said Mabel in an unsteady voice.

'Mabel, are you drunk?' Corie demanded, startled at her friend's manner.

'On one brandy? Are you serious? But − ' Mabel shook her head slowly from side to side − 'I feel awfully peculiar.'

'Oh, for heaven's sake, Mabel!' At first Corie thought it was the result of a double brandy taken too fast. But as the minutes passed and Mabel didn't steady herself, she switched on the table lamp nearby to have a good look at her.

Her friend's eyes were slightly bloodshot, her colour was high. She was breathing a little faster than usual. Corie put her hand on her brow.

'You've got a fever,' she said.

'Nothing of the kind. Something I ate. That Salade Niçoise last night . . .'

'Whatever it is, you ought to be in bed. Come on, let's go.'

She paid for the drinks, helped Mabel up, and got her into the hired car in the hotel's parking lot. She drove through heavy evening traffic to Nice Havre, and then along a quayside to the jetty where their dinghy was moored. With difficulty she got Mabel into it.

'O-oh,' said Mabel. 'O-oh, I feel rotten.'

She could barely make it up the two-step ladder to the cabin-cruiser. Once there, she floundered about until Corie directed her into the cabin, where she flopped on to a bunk. Corie got her shoes off, loosened the neck and the belt of the slim St Laurent dress, then threw a thin blanket over her.

'I'll fetch a doctor,' she said.

She inquired at the tobacco kiosk for a doctor. It took all her newly learned French to explain to the reception-nurse at the doctor's house that she had a friend aboard a boat who needed attention. At last the doctor himself came out of his consulting-room, listened to the story and, clearly intrigued by this *gamine* and her strange accent, picked up his bag and went with her.

'Ah-h-h,' he said when he had examined Mabel. '*Un petit coup de la grippe*. We have our own version here, mademoiselle – brought on by a warm day with *bruine de mer* – what do you call that in your country?'

'I don't know – drizzle from the sea?'

'Perhaps it is that. Well, no need to be perturbed, your friend will be well in two or three days. Meantime, she stays in the bed, has hot drinks, *du bouillon, du citronnade*, and also the *aspirine*. You understand?'

'Two or three days?' groaned Corie.

'*Oui, c'est ça.*' Cheerfully he doled out aspirins in a paper strip and went out on deck. Here he looked expectantly at Corie, who realised she would have to ferry him back to the jetty. He waited to be paid. She brought her wallet out of her back trouser pocket, to his surprise, and counted out what he asked for.

As he shook hands in farewell he said, 'Allow me to remark, mademoiselle, that for an English lady you are *très chic*!'

The women of the Duggan family were accustomed to looking after each other when a little under the weather. It was no trouble to make a series of hot drinks for Mabel and administer aspirin every four hours. What bothered Corie was how to manage next day, when she ought to go into Monaco-Ville to contact Ingram.

She had to let him know his news-gathering team had been reduced to one inexperienced woman. He simply must send someone to replace Mabel. And also he must give up any idea of keeping the knowledge of the death threat to himself. Even if it was a hoax, or a confused simpleton with no real plan of action, there was some possibility of danger.

Next morning she rowed herself ashore under a sun that was already hot. At the tobacco kiosk she hesitantly explained to the kindly owner that she needed someone to go aboard the cabin-cruiser *Alerte* every hour or so just to keep an eye on Mabel. Once he understood her needs, the kiosk owner produced a married daughter who undertook the task for a small fee.

Next she drove into Monaco-Ville. At the Sangiorgio she repeated the process she'd seen Mabel use − she asked the desk to place the call and when it came through, took it in one of the callboxes.

Ingram hadn't yet arrived at the *Globe*. She clutched her hair in despair. 'Give me his home number, then.'

'No one gets that,' scolded Miss Bryant. 'Besides, he's on his way to the office by now.'

'Well, please tell him Corie Duggan called from Monaco. It's urgent, I've got to talk to him, Miss Bryant. Please, he must call me as soon as he arrives.'

'Give me the number.'

'Er . . .' She looked at the number on the base of the phone. But she couldn't stand in a hotel callbox for half an hour or so. She made up her mind quickly. 'He knows it, it's the office of Pelham & Richter at the Hotel Sangiorgio.'

'Of course,' agreed the secretary, who had been responsible for putting through the teleprinter messages.

Corie went upstairs to Drew's office. Trudi was opening windows to let in some air. 'It's going to be a warm day,' she said.

'I think you're right. Trudi, I'm expecting a call in half an hour or so. I asked to have it put through here. All right if I wait?'

'Sure,' said Trudi. She studied Corie for a moment. 'You look kind of frazzled. Something wrong?'

'Mabel's gone down with some bug.'

'Oh, my, that's a shame. Do you feel all right?'

'Yes, just a bit at a loss.'

'Like some coffee?' the other girl asked. It was her remedy for every ill.

'I certainly would, I was so bothered this morning I forgot all about breakfast.'

'Oh, say, we can do something about that.' She picked up the phone, called room service, and asked to have croissants and fruit preserves brought up. The coffee she made herself in an electric percolator using American coffee. So when the call came through from London, Corie had her fingers covered in croissant crumbs and jam.

'Hello, hello – yes, this is Corie Duggan.' She waited until, after the usual short pause, Miss Bryant put her through. 'Hello, Ingram? Ingram, there's been a bit of a disaster here.'

'What's that? You mean you've let somebody else scoop that story?'

'What? Oh, no – no, it's something quite different.' She explained about Mabel. 'So you see I'm on my own – and I simply don't have the qualifications for the reporting job.'

'Hmm . . .' Ingram thought it over. 'Well, let's not get too perturbed about that. We always intended to get a lot of coverage from the American agencies because they've been given the best access. The service in the cathedral we couldn't have covered anyhow because we weren't allowed a press pass for it – and most of us will be getting views of the bride and groom from the film the Monaco government are making. No, I don't think it's too much of a disaster, Corie. Just keep going on the general public's attitude.'

'But then there's the other thing – I can't do that part of it, Ingram—'

'No, you haven't anything to go on, I understand that. It would have been the same for Mabel. But I told her – didn't she tell you? I'm sending a package of photocopies of the letters by air messenger. And what's more important, I'm sending a copy of a photograph of the man.'

'A photograph!'

'Well, he says it's of himself. He's standing turned away from the camera at a quayside, holding a gun.'

'Oh, Ingram! A gun?'

'It's probably a toy gun. This guy's cracked, don't forget. The photo was airmailed from Monaco. He's written on the back, says he got "a friend" to take it. Anyhow, I want you to look out for him. There are one or two distinguishing features that should help you to spot him, and I want pix if anything happens—'

'You mean you want me to stand there clicking my camera if he rushes the cathedral doors, brandishing a gun?'

'You bet,' he replied.

'Ingram!'

'The packet should arrive at Pelham & Richter about mid-morning. I sent it with one of the junior reporters. Since you've got no help, you'd better hang on to him and get him to share the work. What you have to do is walk around Monaco looking for this character, and if you see him, get into a conversation with him and ask him for an interview—'

'Absolutely not!'

'Corie, be quiet. Listen to what I'm saying. Once you've got his story, then you can turn him over to the cops.'

'But the man might be a murderer! You can't ask me to walk up to him and ask him for an interview!'

'It's what he wants, Corie. It's why he wrote to us in the first place. He wants publicity. If you tell him you're from the *Globe* and you'll publish his story, I bet he'll be as quiet as a lamb.'

She was trembling at the mere idea of it. 'I simply can't—'

'There's nothing to be frightened of. Anyhow, you've got plenty of time to find him before the wedding – two whole days.'

There was a sharp click as he hung up.

Trudi was watching her round-eyed. 'What on earth was *that* all about?' she asked, half disbelieving. 'You were talking about a man with a gun!'

'My editor,' groaned Corie. 'He's hoping for a scoop.'

'I believe you,' said Trudi, with a little shake of the head.

About half an hour later there was a knock on the door.

Trudi called 'Come in!' and in walked a gangly young man in an English sports jacket and worsted trousers.

'Miss Duggan?' he said into the air of the room.

'I'm Corie Duggan.'

'How d'you do.' They shook hands. He took from his inner breast pocket a manila envelope which he handed to her. It was sealed up with tapes and wax. 'Strictly confidential,' he said, grinning.

Corie sat down on the sofa of the reception office. She peeled off the wax, unwound the tape. Inside were photocopies of three typed letters.

The first said: 'This is to let you know that the wedding of Miss Grace Kelly to Prince Rainier of Monaco cannot take place. Miss Kelly is engaged to me. I won't let her marry another man even if he is a prince. Please publish this letter so the world will know a great injustice is being done.'

The second said: 'You didn't publish my letter so I'm writing again in case it went astray. Grace Kelly belongs to me. I am her true love and will never let her marry anyone else but me. Print this letter so she'll understand the mistake she's making.'

The third said: 'Why don't you print my letters? Maybe you don't think I'm important enough. You'll see, because I'm going to be important. I'm going to shoot Grace before I'll let her marry another man.'

There was something about the matter-of-fact tone that made Corie's heart give a thud of apprehension. This man actually *believed* what he was writing.

The other items in the manila envelope were two copies of a snapshot taken in bright sunlight. The snapshot had been carefully enlarged in the photographic department of the *Globe* to make full-plate black and whites. The subject was a tall young man of about twenty-six or -seven, clad in sports slacks, open-neck shirt, and brogue shoes. His upper body was turned so that his face was in only quarter-profile to the camera.

Ingram had spoken of 'distinguishing features'. The first

thing that leapt to the eye was the gun — Corie was no expert but it looked like a very old service revolver. He held it in his left hand. So perhaps another distinguishing feature was that he was left-handed. He wore a signet ring on his little finger.

He had short dark hair with rather long sideburns but cut close into the nape of the neck. The ear that was visible — his left — was rather large and had a long lobe. His chin appeared to be rounded.

'Camera-shy, isn't he?' said the messenger, looking over her shoulder. 'Who is he?'

'You weren't told?'

'All I was told was to bring the package to you as fast as I could. I flew to Marseilles last night and came by train to Nice and then by taxi. I'm Johnnie Gavin, by the way.'

Corie nodded in acknowledgement. Distinguishing features . . . ? Here was a very ordinary-looking man, in a photograph taken by a friend who hadn't insisted, 'Look at me, smile!'

A feeling of helplessness swept over her. She'd had no training in seeking out wanted men in a crowd. She didn't even want to do it — the idea scared her, and moreover she felt in her bones that it was fundamentally wrong. Putting a newspaper story above the lives of people? It couldn't be right!

Drew Richter chose that moment to come into his office from outside. He had his jacket and a briefcase under his arm. He looked in surprise at Corie and her newly arrived companion.

'Hello there,' he said on a slight note of query.

'Drew, can I talk to you in private?'

He raised his eyebrows. 'Trouble?'

'I need to talk to you about it.'

His first instinct was to shy away. 'Look, Corie, I've got troubles of my own—'

'No, honestly, Drew, this is something vital. I don't know who else to ask.'

Johnnie Gavin was making shushing movements with his

hands. 'I say, I don't know the background but I got the idea this was very hush-hush—'

'Be quiet!' Corie said in sudden anger — not so much at Gavin but at Ingram for placing her in this position. She took hold of Drew's arm. 'Come on,' she urged. 'Stop wasting time.'

Divided between surprise and amusement, Drew let himself be led into his own inner office. There Corie offered him the photocopied letters. 'Read these,' she said.

He threw jacket and briefcase on his desk, took the proffered sheets, and read. His expression changed from faint irritation to alarm.

'Who wrote these?'

'We don't know. They arrived at the *Globe* in London, as far as I can gather over the last two weeks. Two had postmarks in the Midlands — that's about a hundred miles north of London,' she explained as he looked his query. 'The third was postmarked Monaco.'

'Jeepers!'

'He sent them this photograph, also postmarked Monaco.' She handed him one of the copies. 'I think that probably got to the *Globe* yesterday. The managing editor rang Mabel with instructions to get an exclusive and saying he'd send on this material — that lad outside just brought it. But Mabel's gone down with flu or something and I'm supposed to handle it.'

'Handle what?' Drew asked.

'That's just it.' She explained the instructions Ingram had given. 'But I simply can't do it, Drew. I just don't think we have the right to put anybody at risk.'

'You're right!' he agreed at once. 'What we want is for this whole wedding thing to be perfect — the Dream Wedding, with the bride and groom looking glamorous and all the important guests enjoying it—'

'Yes, of course, that was what you were hired to do, to keep everybody happy. But more important than public relations, Drew — there's public safety. That man is here in Monaco and he's got a gun.'

Drew took another look at the picture. 'I think . . . I think this was taken on one of the quays along in Larvotto . . .'

'That's the residential area along to the east.'

'Right, and some of the houses have private jetties and you have to go around them to get back to the sea, and then there are moorings rented out by the Harbour Authority.'

'The police would be able to identify it.'

'Sure thing. But I don't know whether that'd be much help. After all, he could get a friend to take a picture anywhere that there was public access.'

Corie shrugged. 'That's up to the police to sort out. What I thought was . . . Drew, you must know somebody high up in the Monaco police. Could you make arrangements for me to hand over this stuff?'

'You've got it.' He looked in his contact file, dialled a number, and was connected after a slight pause with someone with whom he had a conversation in French. Corie heard him address the man at the other end as 'Commissaire'. '*Non, c'est très sérieux,*' she heard. '*Pas de blague.*'

No joke. It certainly was no joke.

Within five minutes he was ushering her out of his office. To Trudi he said, 'Hold the fort.' To Johnnie Gavin he said, 'Stay put.'

They walked briskly to the prefecture of police. When Drew mentioned the name he'd been told to ask for, they were shown at once past the desk in the hall and upstairs to a capacious but old-fashioned office looking out on the *place*. There were two men in it, plain-clothes officers.

'*M. l'inspecteur?*' Drew said to the man whose desk faced the door.

'*Inspecteur Lemarche. Vous êtes M. Richter?*'

They shook hands. Drew indicated Corie. 'Mlle Duggan,' he said.

Lemarche shook hands with her, indicated chairs, nodded at his sergeant to take notes. There followed a laborious conversation partly in French and partly in the inspector's few words of English. Drew acted as interpreter when Corie's vocabulary failed. She felt a fool but nothing she'd learned at the language laboratory had prepared her for trying to explain about an anonymous letter writer making threats against the life of a future princess.

'*C'est très, très grave,*' Lemarche said. 'Because, mademoiselle, already we police have too much. *Les visiteurs importants et non, les journalistes, les escrocs qui en profitent – vouz savez, j'en suis sûr, que déjà on a prit les diamants de Mme Walker . . .*'

'What?' said Corie.

'Too many important visitors and ordinary tourists, too many crooks who prey on them, he says somebody's diamonds have already gone missing.' He turned back to express sympathy. Corie was able to follow that and his suggestion that the picture showed a quay on the east side of Monaco.

'I think you are right. So perhaps this *mécréant* lives near – or perhaps on a boat – this Midlands, mademoiselle, it is a coastal area?'

She shook her head. 'You're thinking he may have come by sea into Monaco,' she guessed. 'It could be, of course, but the postmarks were from an industrial town, an inland town.'

'I think also that if there are two of them – this man and his friend – it is easy to come the two on a boat, perhaps.'

Corie was studying the picture. 'But let's stop a moment,' she said. 'Are we sure he has "a friend"?'

'Does he not say so, on the back of the photo?'

'That's what he *says*. It needn't necessarily be true. He's far more likely to be on his own, don't you think? I mean, he's living in a fantasy world. It would be difficult to get anyone else to share it, surely?'

'*Comment?*' Lemarche said, looking at Drew.

Drew translated, adding in English, 'You've got a point there, Corie.'

'*Mais non!*' protested Lemarche. '*Qui a donc pris ce photo?* Who take the picture?'

'I think,' Corie said slowly, 'he took it himself.'

The inspector looked at Drew, then at his sergeant, as if

to say, 'You see how illogical women are?' Corie said, 'I'm a photographer by trade. It's my business to know about taking pictures. And now that I come to look at this again, and think about it, I believe that Mr X took this picture of himself by delayed release.'

Lemarche looked at Drew, who began on a translation. But before he had finished, the inspector was making clicking motions with his right thumb and forefinger. He had understood about the extension release trigger.

'You see, that explains too why he's holding the gun in his left hand. If he's right-handed, as he probably is, he used the right hand to trigger the mechanism. Then he had to dash to the spot on which he'd focused the camera, and as he probably had the gun in his left hand while he set the mechanism, he didn't have time to transfer it when he posed.'

'*Dommage*,' sighed Lemarche. 'Then he is not a left-handed man. That might have helped us to find him.'

'No, but he's perhaps an amateur photographer. Most holidaymakers don't bother with extra equipment – they just have a pocket camera which they point and click.'

'Click?' queried Lemarche.

Corie demonstrated holding up a miniature and pressing the release. 'That's all that most people do. It means someone's taking a little more interest if he buys equipment to take timed release.'

'Camera shops,' suggested Drew. 'He might have bought film—'

'*Ou en fait développer—*' the sergeant put in.

'Or had it developed – right!'

'*D'accord!*' cried Lemarche. 'First we inquire with the picture in all the camera shops, if they have seen this man – *un Anglais* – and the development firms; but of course they are all very, very busy because of the large tourism.'

'Does the gun tell you anything?' Drew asked.

'*C'est un Luger*,' said the sergeant. '*Mon père, il en avait un, souvenir de la guerre première.*'

'What's that – souvenir of World War I?'

'Yes, a German Luger. Many men of the services took them home as mementoes. At the Armistice, you know, the men in the front lines – they walked over, exchanged cigarettes, bought things from each other. I myself did not buy a gun,' the inspector said, 'only a helmet. I have it still.'

The sergeant said something. Even Drew didn't catch it. The inspector said: 'Nival says if he has ammunition for it, the ammunition by now would be very . . . *comment dit-on?* – not reliable.'

'That's great! You mean the gun wouldn't fire?' cried Corie in heartfelt relief.

'*Au contraire, mademoiselle* – it might fire but the bullet might explode in the barrel – there could be *un accident affreux.*'

They talked it over from every angle for about half an hour. They were ushered out at last with the assurance that Inspecteur Lemarche would send men to the photographic outlets with copies of the self-portrait, that he would have all the boats searched in the harbour waters closest to the jetty which he identified as Netely, and that every police post would be alerted to look out for an Englishman acting suspiciously.

Meanwhile, the prefect of police would ring Ingram Holstead to ask for any further information that he might have. Corie felt her spirits tremble at the mere suggestion.

'That's put you in dutch with him, I imagine,' Drew said as they left the building.

She shrugged. 'What can he do to me? He can't sack me, I'm not on his payroll.'

They went back to the Hotel Sangiorgio, where Johnnie had struck up a friendship with Trudi. 'Now I suppose you're going to explain everything to me,' he said hopefully.

The inspector had told them to keep the trouble completely under wraps. 'No,' said Corie, 'I'm not. What I am going to do is drive you back to our quarters, where you can meet Mabel.'

'Oh, I know Mabel—'

'In that case you won't mind acting as nurse to her.'

'Nurse?'

'Come along,' she said, and led him out.

She drove him to Nice and then, learning that he didn't know how to handle an oar, rowed him out to the *Alerte*. There the plump daughter of the kiosk owner, Bettine, was sitting placidly knitting.

'*Elle dort*,' she reported. '*Tout va bien.*'

'Thank you, Bettine,' Corie said, handing over some francs. Bettine curtseyed, lowered herself into her wooden rowboat, and ferried herself ashore.

'Are you telling me you're living on this little tub?' Johnnie cried in dismay.

'Yes, and lucky to have it. Accommodation in this neighbourhood is as scarce as light in a tin of beans. Now, if you'll be so good as to make some tea—'

'Make tea?'

'There's a spirit stove in the galley and a container of fresh water. Tea in the cupboard, and some biscuits.'

'Did I make an emergency trip to France to drink tea and eat biscuits?' wondered Johnnie. But he did as he was bid, busying himself in the galley while Corie checked on Mabel. True enough, her journalist friend was restlessly asleep in her bunk, still a little feverish. There seemed nothing to be done except wait until she woke and keep her supplied with drinks.

Her mind at ease on that point, she fetched her camera bag out and began delving in it for a magnifying glass.

Through this she examined the photograph that had remained with Johnnie when she went to the police. By its help she hoped to be able to see if there was a monogram on the signet ring on the man's left little finger. But through the magnifying glass all that appeared was a grainy blob. Deciphering a monogram, if there was one, was impossible.

However, she did discover one extra piece of evidence. The subject of the photograph was wearing a leather belt round his slacks, and the buckle, although not totally in view, was distinctive. It was a stylised lion's head, perhaps in silver.

Corie jumped to her feet. As she made to lower herself into the rubber dinghy, Johnnie exclaimed, 'Where are you going?'

'I have to make a phone call.'

'But what about me?'

'You stay and look after Mabel.'

'Look here, I'm not a nurse . . .'

'Mr Holstead told me to make use of you to cover the story. Your job is to see to Mabel.'

Johnnie's expression was mutinous. 'Look here, what about lunch? It's nearly one o'clock!'

'I'll send you a sandwich from a café on the pier.'

With that she sat down and pushed off with an oar.

At the café, after ordering a sandwich for Johnnie, she asked for a jeton for the phone. She was at once connected with Inspecteur Lemarche on request. It proved more difficult to speak to him by phone than face to face. But when she had established that she wasn't talking about locks of hair but fastenings to a man's belt, they got on better.

'*Tête de lion?*'

'Yes, a lion's head. Look at the photo with a lens. You'll see the buckle is about four inches across – quite noticeable.'

'*Merci infiniment!*' cried the inspector.

But the hopes inspired by this further piece of description gradually faded. By late evening no policeman had reported sighting an Englishman in slacks banded by a leather belt buckled with a lion's head. No such man had been found on any of the boats. No photographic shop had sold film or developed any for an Englishman of that description.

'So far it's no go,' Drew said. 'Not surprising, when you come to think of it. That snap shows him in shirt sleeves. When he's got a jacket on, that belt won't be visible.'

'Time's running out,' Corie worried. 'Less than forty-eight hours now to the wedding.'

'You look beat,' he remarked. 'Come and have some dinner.'

'No, I must get back to the boat. I've left that boy in charge, with nothing to eat but biscuits—'

'Biscuits? You made him a stack of biscuits?'

'I didn't have to make them. They come in a packet.'

They established that she meant what he called cookies. He persuaded her to come and have something to eat, after which she stocked up on provisions and drove back to the *Alerte*.

She found that Johnnie had solved the nourishment problem by asking the boy who brought his sandwich to return with a three-course meal at six. Mabel had woken up, had some soup, and gone back to sleep.

Corie settled Johnnie down with an inflatable beach bed in the galley where, complaining, he nevertheless fell asleep almost at once. As for herself, she showered and got into the bunk opposite Mabel, but at first couldn't sleep.

Partly it was the emotions that had churned through her throughout the day: uncertainty, anxiety, excitement, disappointment. Partly it was the realisation that she hadn't used her camera once in twenty-four hours. It was so unusual that she felt as if some part of her life had been cut off. She hadn't even collected the negatives waiting for her at Studio Antoine.

At last she too fell asleep. It was perhaps four in the morning, the hour of the grey dawn, when she was suddenly awake and alert.

She hadn't collected the negatives that had been developed for her by Studio Antoine. She had had to take her film to Studio Antoine because in the hotel La Palmette she'd had no darkroom facilities.

Mr X had taken a snapshot of himself by controlled release. That meant he was – at least to some slight extent – a camera enthusiast. It might also mean he did his own developing and printing. Lemarche's men had found no work done for him by the Monaco photographic firms – and surely they would have remembered if they'd developed and printed a picture of a man holding a gun.

Therefore it probably meant that Mr X was staying in

some sort of accommodation where he had at least a makeshift darkroom, a place where he could develop and print that picture. Not a boat, unless the boat was at anchor some distance from Monaco, because the police had searched the boats.

Nor was it likely to be a hotel room or a villa, because it would be absurd to think he'd booked a room weeks before the wedding. On the contrary, Mr X had thought his letter would be published and Grace Kelly would cancel the ceremony.

So within the last week or so, Mr X had decided to come to Monaco. He had found himself some nook or cranny where he could live and set up a temporary darkroom. Surely, *surely*, that shouldn't be impossible for the police to find?

She pulled on slacks and sweater, rowed to the pier, hammered on the door of the café, and at last persuaded the tousle-headed proprietor to come down and open up. His reproaches in French reached her long before he got his door unlocked.

'*Pardon,*' she said, hoping it made sense. '*Il me faut le téléphone.*'

'*À cette heure?*' cried the café owner.

'*Oui, oui, la police.*' That silenced all complaints. Everyone on the Riviera knew that this was a difficult time for the police because of the wedding.

When she was put through to the prefecture in Monaco, it was to be told that *M. l'inspecteur* had gone home for a few hours rest. However, a different officer, who in fact spoke better English, volunteered to hear her out.

'A darkroom,' he repeated.

'*Chambre d'obscurité,*' she said, making a guess at a translation.

'Ah, yes, I understand. He did his own work on the photograph he sent?'

'That seems to follow, don't you agree? He wouldn't take that film to a commercial firm to develop – it would lead right back to him.'

'If he's thinking clearly enough to realise that, mademoiselle.'

'Well, yes. But you haven't had any of the firms say that they developed and printed that picture, have you?'

'No, that's true. It may of course have been processed in Nice or Cannes.'

'Oh,' groaned Corie. 'I never thought of that.'

The policeman made a chirruping sound of encouragement. 'Nevertheless, it is very well thought, mademoiselle. I will at once begin investigation for a place of that kind – a place where he might have found accommodation even in these busy weeks, and where he could do photographic work. Thank you, mademoiselle.'

Yawning from reaction and lack of sleep, Corie thanked the proprietor of the café. He, in dressing-gown and slippers, had been busy while she talked to the prefecture. A delicious aroma of coffee filled the salon. He brought a filter-pot to the bar, upturned two cups and put them on saucers.

'Coffee, mademoiselle?'

'Oh, how kind! You shouldn't have bothered. I expect you want to get back to bed . . .'

'*Ce n'est pas la peine*,' he shrugged. 'And all goes well with the police?'

'Yes, thank you. I have to report to them when I get to Monaco.'

'You have a very busy time, I observe. Always going back and forth, and Albert tells me you have a friend who suffers *la grippe.*'

'Yes, the doctor said she'd be better in a few days. I hope so, that little cruiser isn't the best place for someone who's unwell.'

'Why do you not move her ashore, mademoiselle?' he inquired, sipping gingerly at his hot coffee.

She laughed. 'Where to? There's nothing available because of the wedding.'

'Oh, I think you could find something in one of the caravan parks.'

Corie set down her coffee cup to stare at him.

A caravan park!

'Monsieur,' she said, 'may I please have another jeton for the phone?'

Inspector Lemarche had come back on duty when she got through for the second time. 'Thank you, mademoiselle,' he said when he heard her suggestion, 'we have called in the day shift and they are already making a search. However, we don't have any caravan parks in Monaco . . . I think I had better get in touch with my colleagues of Nice and Cannes.'

All that day and the following night the police of the Riviera made quiet inquiries at the caravan sites dotted around in the countryside behind the coastal resorts. The results were telephoned in. Nothing, no sign of such a man, no report of anything suspicious.

Drew sighed. 'I really thought we were on to something there.'

That was disappointing enough but, to add to Corie's unhappiness, Ingram Holstead had rung her in mid-afternoon at Pelham & Drew's suite to tell her she was fired.

'I'm not on your staff,' she retorted, too tired to care.

'Your contract with us is at an end,' he yelled. 'I had some twit from the Foreign Office asking me why I hadn't handed those letters over to the police.'

'Well, so you should have—'

'What, and miss the best story in the whole jamboree? You're out of your mind, girl!'

'Rather that than lose my sense of values—'

'You'll never work again for *Globe* newspapers,' Ingram raged, 'and let me tell you I'll see to it that the whole of Fleet Street turns its back on you!'

'I can live without Fleet Street,' Corie said, and hung up on him.

About seven o'clock on the morning of 19 April, Corie was already at the Sangiorgio. Whether or not the police had succeeded in finding Mr X, today was the day of the nuptial mass at St Nicholas, and Corie felt she must be out and about among the Monégasques with her camera. She'd checked in with Trudi and was preparing to set out on foot for the cathedral when Sergeant Nival, Lemarche's aide, burst into the room.

'Mlle Duggan!'

'Yes?' said Corie, looking up from checking her cameras.

He poured out a flood of words in Monégasque French.

'What?' asked Corie.

Drew, who had heard it all through his open door, came out with a rush. 'He says they think they've found the darkroom.'

'The darkroom!'

'He's asking for your help. Something about chemicals.'

'Yes?' she said, turning to Nival, expecting questions.

'*Venez!*' he begged, taking her by the arm.

She understood that. 'Of course I'll come. Drew – come with me, I can only understand one word in ten,'

Drew asked the sergeant if he could come. The sergeant blurted a reply, of which Corie caught only that they must all hurry.

They piled into a police car waiting with the engine running. Slowly they drove through the crowded seafront of Monaco. The whole place was en fête for the great day, despite clouds and rain. Music poured out of every café and restaurant, people in their best clothes lined the pavements, flowers were garlanded on every lamp-post.

It was difficult to have a conversation with Nival because his English was so sparse and the noise from outside was too great. After only a short drive they turned into an uphill road among some industrial buildings. This was the manufacturing district of Monaco, where furniture and perfumes were made. One of the articles Corie had read as background had mentioned that there were 'industries', although the country's income came mainly from tourism and gambling.

The police car stopped. They got out. Corie expected them to enter one of the buildings but instead Nival led the way round the side of one, to a parking lot.

There several cars and vans were standing. One of them was a motorised caravan with a uniformed man on guard.

Nival gestured. 'English number plates,' he said.

The door of the caravan had been forced open. Inside was a tidy little home all equipped in cream and cherry red, only visible by the light from the open door because the windows had been pasted over with brown paper. Immediately inside and to the right was a tiny sink.

Although it was empty, it had that indefinable smell of developing solution.

'Yes,' said Corie.

Nival opened a cupboard above. There stood a row of dark brown bottles. She nodded, picked one up, turned it to read the label, and said: 'This van has been used as a darkroom.' She touched a string stretched across from one side to the other above head height. 'Drying line for negs,' she said.

'*Comment?*'

Drew translated for Sergeant Nival. He looked pleased. 'But he says,' Drew told her, 'that they've found no pictures. Nothing to say he developed and printed *that* photograph.'

'Perhaps he's got the negs and any other prints with him. Where is he?'

Nival looked grim. It seemed that the warehouse to which the parking area belonged had a watchman, and the watchman, in view of the forthcoming wedding, had introduced a sideline whereby he leased parking space to a few people. The motorised caravan belonged, so he had confessed, to *un anglais* called John Smith, who had been parked in the parking lot for the last six days. This morning M. Smith, like everyone else, had gone out early to get a good place from which to see the bride.

'John Smith. Very helpful.'

'We are questioning the watchman at present. He has given us a good description of John Smith, particularly the clothes he was wearing when he set out this morning. A light blue cotton raincoat, striped shirt, grey trousers, and the lion's head buckle on the belt.'

'A raincoat, yes,' Drew said, with a glance at scudding clouds.

'Ah, monsieur, the raincoat is not because of the rain, it is because of the gun – to hide it.'

With these chilling words Nival dismissed them. He and his team had to make a thorough search of the vehicle. Every other man who could be spared was watching the crowds in Monaco-Ville for 'John Smith'.

Since it wasn't too far, and since in any case wheeled vehicles were almost at a standstill, Corie and Drew walked back towards the town centre. As they went, the clouds broke, the sun suddenly beaming down with rays of scintillating brightness, causing Drew to unbutton his jacket.

Seeing him, Corie said, 'He'll take off his raincoat.'

He stopped in his tracks, then shook his head. 'No, he'll keep it on – the gun must be in its pocket.'

They walked on, soon finding themselves among the crowds lining the pavements to see the notables drive to the cathedral. Corie couldn't help being on the alert for 'John Smith'. She could see it was the same with Drew, who kept glancing about. They were both looking for a tallish man whose shoulders, clad in light blue poplin, might show a little above the crowds.

When the procession of wedding guests ended, the crowd began to move in a purposeful way. Everyone wanted to be in the Place St Nicholas when the bride and groom emerged. Fathers had children on their shoulders, cardboard box-periscopes were peeking out like necks of giraffes.

Corie took shot after shot of the crowd. She found them enchanting. The plainest face was brightened by the eagerness to see the newly-weds, by hopes for their future, by the feeling of being part of their happiness. Ingram Holstead could say what he liked about the Beautiful People, but for Corie the beauty was here, among the simple folk.

The princely couple emerged into the Midi sunlight.

'There they are!' cried Drew, raising his hand to wave as did almost everyone else.

Corie didn't even catch a glimpse of Princess Grace in her fairy-tale gown of lace and satin. She was looking at the crowd, fearful that now — now, at this supreme moment — 'John Smith' would make his attempt.

But nothing happened. The Prince and Princess got into an open Rolls Royce and were driven away. The crowd, who seemed to know the plan, hurried off up side alleys. Corie and Drew went with them, to find themselves outside a little old church, the church of Ste Devote, the patron saint of Monaco.

'Why are we here?' she asked Drew. He in his turn repeated the question to an elderly lady next to him.

'*Vous verrez*,' was the reply with a knowing smile.

Sure enough, the Rolls Royce edged its way into the narrow street. It stopped. The happy couple alighted. The Princess took a few steps into the courtyard of the church and there knelt down to ask for the blessing of Monaco's own saint.

At that moment there was a sudden stir in the crowd. People swayed to and fro. Corie was already turned away from the church because her chief interest was in the people.

She saw a tall man in a striped shirt being wrestled to one side by two others. 'Drew!' she gasped.

He turned to look where she was staring. 'They've got him!'

One of the assailants was holding down the man's right arm, over which he carried a blue raincoat, folded. The coat was so arranged as to cover his wrist and hand. Corie had no doubt the gun was hidden under the folded coat.

She stood transfixed, terrified, while the two men struggled with the gunman. Then a uniformed constable shoved his way to them, pinioned the man from behind. After a moment or two of violence the man was pushed through the crowd and away.

As they went away, Corie raised her camera and looked through the lens. She saw the assailant's face. It wasn't the face of a criminal. He looked puzzled, upset, almost childlike in his bewilderment. As she clicked the shutter, the captors forced him round so that his head was in movement. She knew his features would come out a blur.

The police of the Principality had found 'John Smith'. And unaware of the tussle in the crowd outside, the Princess knelt in the courtyard, saying her prayer to Ste Devote.

Chapter Eleven

Johnnie Gavin was summoned back to London the day after the wedding on the grounds that he was an unnecessary expense. Mabel recovered enough by the following Monday to make the trip home. The two women went by easy stages, overnighting in Paris, then flying home on Tuesday morning.

They parted at the air terminal with muted good wishes. 'I don't even know whether this feature is wanted any more,' Mabel muttered. 'I'm quite scared of what Ingram's going to say when I report in.'

'It wasn't your fault you were laid low,' Corie comforted.

'I don't even know if he's going to believe that. He's got this idea that I'm a gambling addict: he'll probably accuse me of spending all my time in the casino.'

'He's only got to look at you to know you've been ill.'

'Oh, thanks a million,' Mabel said, adjusting her hat and trying to feel fashionable.

Corie gave her a hug. She felt quite protective towards Mabel. But she also felt a little apprehensive herself, for she had a large batch of film which was the property of *Globe* Newspapers and which ought to be delivered.

She decided the best thing to do was to run off prints of the negatives she thought promising, parcel it all up, and send it by messenger to the features editor. Whether he used it or not was up to him – and, presumably, Ingram.

Bertie's greeting at the studio was in much the same class as her remark to Mabel: 'You look worn out, not what I expected from a month on the Riviera.'

'I *am* worn out, Bertie,' she agreed. But she set him to work at once on the printing.

By this time it was mid-afternoon. She went home, to

unpack, have a long soapy bath, and put on some old slacks and a favourite shirt. Then, hair wrapped in a towel, she rang her mother to let her know she was back. Her mother greeted her with enthusiasm, full of questions about the wedding.

'I didn't actually see it, Monna—'

'Her dress looked fabulous. Was that guipure lace on the sleeves?'

Corie said she thought it was. She didn't add that she only thought so because she'd seen pictures of the gown. To prevent further questions she asked: 'What's the news with Lynette?'

'Oh, yes, splendid news – Sasha decided not to take her away from the BBC but negotiated a better contract with them. The series has just ended, if you remember, and then for the summer Sasha's arranged personal appearances for her in the big resorts—'

'When does she get a holiday?' Corie inquired.

'Good gracious, child,' her mother said in surprise, 'a true professional doesn't need holidays – and certainly not when her public is asking for her.'

Well, that might be true. Certainly, when Corie dropped in at her old home to hand out holiday presents, Lynette looked well and happy. She threw her arms round her sister, exclaiming, 'Where's the suntan? Where's the chic Riviera casual wear?'

'Never had time for it,' Corie laughed.

'You're hopeless. But at least tell us how you enjoyed yourself – those scrappy postcards were useless.'

'If you want to know,' said Corie, 'I was too busy to enjoy myself. And though the French are marvellous cooks, they can't make tea – so let's get into the kitchen and—'

Lynette aimed a mock punch at her. But in fact they went to the kitchen, made tea, and sat talking until Opal came home with the same set of questions: Did you enjoy yourself, why aren't you sunburnt, did you bet in the casino . . . ?

The family reunion cheered Corie. No matter how much

trouble she was in with Ingram Holstead, she still had her sisters, she still had the bulwark of family affection.

She began her usual schedule of work at the studio next day. There were sitters coming, and in between times she had to make assessments of the roughs Bertie had printed up. She couldn't help feeling it would be a pity if Ingram junked the feature, because she had some lovely shots of the ordinary people of Monaco.

In the late afternoon her phone rang. It was Mabel, sounding very agitated. 'Corie, can you come to the office?'

'What's up?'

'Ingram's sacked me. The feature's been cancelled. He says he can't be bothered with the people of Monaco and we threw away the only good story to come out of—'

'So why do you want me to come?'

'He wants to see you. I told him I thought you got a shot of the man at the little church, and he wants to see the prints. Can you bring them?'

'They aren't any good, Mabel. Besides—'

'Please come. He ordered me to get you . . .'

'Why do you care, if he's given you the push?'

'Oh, Corie, don't make things worse for me!'

'All right,' she agreed. 'I'll be free to come in a couple of hours.'

'Please come at once, Corie.'

'No, I can't, I've got an appointment due. Tell Miss Bryant to pass on a message – she knows how to handle him. I'll be there about six.'

Mabel was still protesting when she hung up.

At five-thirty she put together a selection of the best shots from the Monaco assignment. In a separate envelope she put three or four prints of the wedding day – she had a shot of the mobile caravan with the policeman on guard, one of the would-be assailant as he was led away, a couple taken immediately after his arrest showing the faces of the members of the public hard by.

She took a taxi to Fleet Street. Rush-hour traffic meant that she was a few minutes late for her appointment. She was passed on at once, as always, went up in the lift, and tapped on Miss Bryant's office door.

'Come in, Miss Duggan,' the secretary said in a neutral way. 'Just one moment, I'll let Mr Holstead know you've arrived.'

She went into the inner office, giving Corie a chance to examine herself in the mirror on the adjacent wall. She wished she'd made more of an effort with her appearance. She had on her 'working clothes' – denim trousers, cotton shirt, red bandana holding back her straight hair. All the same, quite suitable for walking into the lion's den.

Miss Bryant returned, and with a gesture invited Corie to go in. As she passed her she heard Miss Bryant whisper, 'He's in a very bad mood.'

That hardly needed to be said, because the man himself told her as she entered. 'I'm so angry with you I could hit you!'

'I'm sorry,' Corie said.

'Sorry! Is that all you have to say? You disobeyed orders, you messed up a great story, you hung about in Monaco with Hitherton instead of rushing back with the pictures—'

'I've apologised.'

'What the devil did you think I was paying you for?'

'Not to be a news reporter,' she riposted. 'As to the original assignment, I'll forgo the money due to me for the pictures I took. Mabel will have put in a claim for the expenses, I suppose, and so long as that is honoured, I won't expect—'

'Expenses? Who gives a damn about expenses? I want to salvage something usable from the wreck. Mabel says you have pix of the gunman?'

'Yes but not—'

'Let me see them.'

She opened her portfolio, handed him the special envelope. He shook out the prints with an impatient twitch, spread them on the desk.

'Good God! Is this the best you could do?'

'There was only a fraction of a second when he was

visible. That's all I could get. In any case—'

'What?'

'I don't think it would be right to publish a photo that showed his features—'

'Not right? Look here, there's going to be a big scandal, a trial in Monaco, and *we* have the only pic—'

Corie was shaking her head. Ingram broke off to stare at her with angry, astonished eyes.

'Why are you shaking your head?'

'There isn't going to be any scandal, any fuss. The Monaco police aren't going to prosecute.'

'*What?*'

' "John Smith" didn't commit any crime worth prosecuting him for.'

'He threatened their princess—'

'He wrote letters to the *Globe*, two in England and one in Monaco. The police found the typewriter in his caravan, and some photographic equipment with which he printed the photo he sent.'

'A photograph of a gun!'

'But he didn't say he was going to use it, did he, Ingram? All he said was that the snap had been taken by a friend. It's no crime to have pictures taken holding a gun.'

'But he *was* going to use it – Mabel tells me he was arrested with it in his hand.'

'He had it covered over by his folded coat, and he never pointed it at anyone. The police expert told me that, if he'd fired it, it would have exploded in his hand because the ammunition had deteriorated. So you see, all the Monaco police have against him is carrying a weapon and sending a threat from Monaco to a British newspaper. The *préfet* decided not to proceed. They've had enough trouble due to the wedding – thefts of jewellery, damage to property. They simply deported him.'

'Deported him . . .'

'They put him on a train for Paris under guard. In Paris the French police put him on a plane for London. On the plane he made a nuisance of himself by protesting and carrying on, so he was arrested at Heathrow for causing a disturbance on a British aircraft.'

'How do you know all this?'

'Inspector Lemarche told me. He sent copies of the threatening letters to Scotland Yard together with an affidavit that the typewriter in the caravan was the one used to type them. So the poor man's been charged with sending threats through the mail, and has pleaded guilty to the whole thing. Lemarche said he'd appear before a British magistrate and be sentenced leniently on condition he accepts psychiatric treatment.'

Ingram jumped to his feet, swept the prints from his desk on to the floor, and walked across the room in an angry stride. 'The whole thing is a non-story!' he exclaimed. 'We had it right in our hands and you muffed it!'

'No, I think I made a good job of it,' she replied, edging away a little, because he was towering over her like an angry bear.

'Oh you do! Took rotten pix, worked for the police instead of for me—'

'I was never hired to cover a news story, Ingram. I told you on the phone I couldn't do it – and I couldn't—'

'Because you were soft-hearted! What are you made of, cotton wool? I *told* you how to handle it—'

'And I told you I wouldn't.'

'It never occurred to me that you'd really let such a chance—'

'Do you imagine that everybody shares your ideas? That it doesn't matter who you hurt so long as you get a story?'

'Damn right I do! Anybody with any backbone—'

'You mean anybody with armour-plating! It's just too callous.'

'Look here, *Miss Duggan*,' he shouted, 'don't lecture me on newspaper ethics! That man told me he intended to kill the bride at a state wedding and *I was entitled* to run that story!'

'Even if it meant people were hurt? Perhaps even killed?'

she countered, her own voice rising as her anger mounted. 'That's monstrous—'

'Mind what you're saying!' he stormed, taking her by the shoulders and shaking her. 'You're not here to criticise me, you're here to ask forgiveness.'

'Forgiveness? For doing what I thought was decent and right? And take your hands off me!' she cried.

'Oh, too saintly to let anyone touch you? Is that it? I don't know who the hell you think you are!'

With that he dragged her forcibly against him and kissed her with savagery.

Her first reaction was total astonishment. He had never kissed her, except on the cheek as a welcome or a goodnight.

Then utter fury possessed her. How dare he! She kicked and struggled. He took his mouth away, but only to get a firmer hold of her body. She managed to get her hands up so as to beat him on the chest with her fists.

'Stop it!' she cried. 'Let go! *Let me go this minute!*'

'Damned if I will,' he gasped, and pushed her towards the sofa by the coffee table.

She staggered, they went down in a flying muddle. Corie's legs hit the coffee table, overturning it. She was screaming now, in real trouble. 'Help! Help!'

Ingram's hands were clutching at her hungrily. She thought her back was going to break as he bent her over the upturned table.

The door of the office opened. 'Did you call—' Miss Bryant broke off. 'Oh, sir!' she gasped.

Ingram scrambled to his feet. 'Get out,' he growled.

'No!' Corie cried. 'Don't go, Miss Bryant.'

'Get out, I said,' he insisted. Then with a glance of resentment at Corie. 'Don't worry, the fun's over.'

'Is it all right, Miss Duggan?' faltered the secretary.

'Yes, all right.' Corie had staggered to sit on the sofa, pushing her shirt back into her waistband, smoothing down her hair. She was trembling so much she was making a poor job of it.

Her assailant went back to sit behind his desk. Corie got

unsteadily to her feet. She collected her portfolio, stooped to pick up the scattered prints. When she straightened, she'd had just enough time to steady her breathing.

'I suppose you want an apology,' Ingram said grudgingly.

'Don't bother. Let's just call it a day.'

'Not before I sort this out. You've got to understand—'

'I'm just bewildered, that's all. There's never been anything of that kind between us.'

'Don't be coy. You must have known I've been getting more and more attracted to you.'

She shook her head in rebuttal. 'I was just one of your "companions". You have a dozen or so, don't you? Someone suitable for every occasion.'

'Don't be sarcastic! They were just to give the other newspapers something to write about. You were always a cut above them and you know it.'

'No.'

'Corie, don't make it worse for me. I'm not good at humbling myself before anyone, especially a woman.'

She felt herself grow warm with indignation. He had attacked her and now he was trying to make her feel guilty. 'Your problems with women are no business of mine. I think we can agree we've finished the matter we had in hand—'

'Don't be like that about it, Corie,' he said, and there was a different note in his voice — something that might have been genuine remorse. 'I'll say I'm sorry — there! And now everything's OK between us again.'

'You think it's as easy as that? You can't really imagine things can go back to what they were?'

'No-o,' he agreed. 'And I don't think I'd want them to. There's been a change in you, Corie — it's intriguing. And I want to be closer to the new Corie than I ever was to the old one.'

'No,' she said again.

'Oh, come on.' He held out his hands. 'You and I could mean a lot to each other, sweetie. I've done a lot for you in the past, I could do a lot more.'

'Stop talking like that, Ingram.'

'But it's true! I mean, when I said I'd see you wouldn't work in Fleet Street again – well, that was just because I was annoyed. I can open all kinds of doors for you. I've helped you a lot already, introduced you to interesting people, put your name before the public. Don't you think you owe me something for that?'

She gave a little, angry laugh. 'You should have shown me the price tag a long time ago, Ingram. I thought you were doing it out of friendship.'

'There's no such thing between a man and a woman,' he said with irritation. 'If you think there is, you're too naïve for this world. I want more than friendship, Corie.'

'I'm sorry.' She had collected all her belongings and turned now for the door. 'I don't want an emotional entanglement. I think we'd better just say goodbye.'

He got up quickly, to get between her and the door. 'Don't go,' he said. 'Look, perhaps I've let things get a bit out of hand, gone too far – but I really want us to mean a lot to each other, love, I really do.'

She gave a hopeless shrug and made to pass him.

'Why not?' he exclaimed. 'I've said I'm sorry, what more do you want?'

'From you, nothing,' she replied, and made to walk round him.

He caught her arm and pulled her back. 'There's someone else!' he gasped.

'No, Ingram—'

'That's it! There's another man! Who is it?'

She shook her arm free. 'There's no one, Ingram – and if there were, it would be none of your business.'

'Tell me! I insist you tell me—'

'Do you want me to call Miss Bryant in?' she demanded and when he frowned and drew back, she walked out.

She was lucky enough to get a taxi outside at once. Falling in exhaustion on the leather seat, she tried to come to terms with what had happened.

What she'd said was true. She had never thought of

Ingram being anything but a friendly patron for her. She had certainly never wanted anything more from him. In no way did he rouse her — not like Sasha, whose merest touch had had the power to make her heart tremble.

I never gave him any encouragement, she told herself. And he never felt anything very deep for me — not until today. What had changed him?

It wasn't until later in the evening that the answer occurred to her. It was her opposition, her rebellion, that had sparked a different interest. Until she defied him and went her own way over the Monaco story, she had been just another girl in his entourage.

But her stubborn refusal to bow to his orders had made her important, different, a challenge he must overcome. Now by his own admission he was caught in a trap of his own making — he had made himself want someone he couldn't have.

She was roused from this train of thought by the telephone. To her surprise it was Drew Richter.

'Drew! Where are you?'

'I'm in Paris, on my way home from Monaco. It's hot and stuffy here, Corie. How's London?'

'Stormy,' she said with hidden irony. 'Finished up all the chores?'

'Yep, my group of clients hung around a bit after the wedding, partying and going to the casino to throw money away. But they've left now — some of them are taking the same flight as I am. Say, Corie, what happened with your newspaper boss?'

She suppressed a smile. What if she told him she'd been physically attacked? She said, 'He wasn't pleased. We've agreed to part company.'

'Oh, that's a shame. I'm really sorry. But if you hadn't gone to the police—'

'I know, I don't regret it. Don't worry about it.'

'So what are you going to do?' he asked, with what sounded like real concern.

'Oh, I'm not too bothered. My main interest is

portraiture, you know – I only recently took up photo-journalism. I shan't starve.'

'I sure hope not. Well, see here . . . If you ever wanted to come to the States, Corie, I'm pretty certain I could put some work your way.'

'To New York?'

'Why not? It's a great city!'

'So I gather. I never thought of . . .'

'Think of it now. I mean, I don't expect you to up-stakes this very minute, but if you ever wanted to give it a try, I'd be happy to lend a hand.'

It was an interesting idea, but for the moment she'd had enough of helping hands from men friends. 'I'll think about it,' she said.

They exchanged a few more pieces of news then parted with mutual good wishes. She thought to herself, He's a very shrewd man; if he really thinks I could make it in New York perhaps I ought to consider it. But did she want to be indebted to him?

Why not? She liked him, they had got to know each other unexpectedly well over the few days of drama in Monaco. Yet when you came to think about it, he was just another hard, clever businessman. Not quite so open and ruthless in his view as Ingram Holstead, but nevertheless a man out for himself, a man with few illusions. She remembered with a wry smile that when she first told him there might be a mentally unbalanced gunman on the loose, his first thought was that it might make matters unpleasant for his public-relations clients.

She dismissed the matter from her mind. She had the usual amount of business to deal with at the studio, and out of professional interest she finished printing the negatives from Monaco. Some of them were so good that she hated to think they would never be seen.

After some thought she wrote a very business-like letter to *Globe* Newspapers asking that the rights in the photographs be returned to the photographer, in view of the fact that she had forgone any money due to her from the original contract. A few days later she received a stiff letter of agreement, signed by the chief accountant.

On the evening of the next day, her sister Opal came to see her unexpectedly. After the usual greetings and offerings of refreshments, Corie sat down to study her anxious expression.

'Something wrong?' she asked.

'I don't know. It's weird. A man came to me outside the office today when I left to go to lunch, asked if he could speak to me.'

Corie raised her eyebrows. 'A stranger?'

'Yes. He said he was a reporter. I took it for granted he wanted to talk about Lynette so I said all right, he could come and pay for my sandwich at the café.'

'Well, that's OK,' Corie encouraged.

'But he didn't want to talk about Lynette.' Opal fidgeted with her coffee spoon. 'He wanted to talk about you.'

'Me?' That startled her.

'Yes, and specifically about your love life.'

'Pal, what on earth . . . ?'

'I told him I didn't know if you even *had* a love life, and he kept on pressing me to say who you go out with, and I said nobody really, except Ingram Holstead, and *he* said, "I know all about *that*" and laughed as if it was a joke.'

The two girls sat looking at each other. 'When you said it was weird, that was an understatement,' Corie murmured.

'What do you think it's about?' Opal said.

'I've no idea.'

'I just kept saying I didn't know of anybody you were involved with. In the end he got fed up and went away.' Opal gave a little laugh. 'He didn't even pay for his sandwich and coffee – I had to pay for it for him.'

'He sounds a real charmer.'

'Should we tell the police?'

'Oh, no, I don't think that's necessary.' A strange notion had come into Corie's head. 'I'll ask around, see if I can find out what's going on.'

Relieved, Opal finished her coffee and left. Corie thought

for a moment, then looked up the home number of Norman Gibson, since it was too late in the evening to catch him at the newspaper. His wife answered, agreed he was in and not busy, then put Norman on the line.

It seemed to Corie that he was unwilling when he spoke. 'Corie?' he began. 'How goes it?'

'Not bad, thanks. You heard, I dare say, that the great pictorial feature on the people of Monaco was thrown on the scrapheap.'

'Ye-es, Mabel told me.'

'How is Mabel? Has she found another job?'

'No need. Ingram changed his mind and kept her on.'

'Oh, I *am* glad to hear that! I felt I was partly to blame in having her fired.'

'Yes,' Norman said. 'She thought so too.'

That silenced Corie for a moment. 'I'm sorry to hear that,' she said. 'I suppose I ought to have rung her to ask how things were going but . . . I don't know . . . I just wanted to make a clean break with the *Globe*.'

'It's difficult to do anything "clean" with the *Globe*,' Norman said with some bitterness. 'Scandal seems to be its chief interest these days.'

'Norman,' said Corie, 'do you happen to know if the *Globe* or any other paper has sent reporters out on my trail?'

There was a long pause.

'Norm?'

'I'm not supposed to talk about it.'

'Then there is something?'

'Look, Corie, you're a nice girl and I enjoyed working with you in Tokyo, but I really don't want to get into trouble over you.'

'Why should you get into trouble?'

'You might go marching into Ingram's office and have a stand-up fight with him — as I heard you did last week.'

'How did you hear about that?' she cried, astonished.

'Oh, for Pete's sake, Corie — it was all over the office by next morning.'

She drew in a troubled breath. 'Norm, I promise I won't

make a fuss with Ingram. But please tell me – what's going on?'

'I'm not quite sure, chickie. All I know is, Ingram kept Mabel on the staff for the sole purpose of running an investigation on you.'

'But why? I don't understand!'

'Neither does Mabel. But if it means she can keep her job, she'll do it. So she's sent out her snoopers, and the instruction is: find out the name of Corie Duggan's lover.'

Chapter Twelve

Corie felt the confirmation of that vague suspicion of a moment ago. All the same, she found it hard to take. 'Can I come and talk to you, Norm?' she requested.

'No way! If you come here and Ingram gets to hear of it, he'll know I put you wise.'

'But there's no reason he should ever know I visited . . .'

'Don't you believe it. There's probably somebody door-stepping you now.'

'Door-stepping?'

'Somebody hanging about, waiting to see if you go out tonight or, if you don't, whether anybody comes to see you.'

'Norman!'

She heard him clear his throat apologetically. 'It's common practice, Corie. Although it's usually reserved for big film stars or politicians, because it costs an awful lot in time and money.'

'I believe you! Are you telling me Ingram has sent people to spy on me night and day?'

'Oh, no, not quite that. I mean, if you went to bed about eleven o'clock and the lights in your flat went out, the guy on watch would probably take it that he could go home. He might come back in time to see you leave for the studio tomorrow morning.'

'It's outrageous!'

'And don't forget, it's quite likely someone will tail you during the day as well.' After a moment he added, 'I don't know what the quarrel was about last week, but it's got Ingram on one of his obsessive jags. He can be like that – take up a subject and run it to death. Usually, of course, it's a story for the paper.'

'Yes,' Corie agreed, remembering headlines of the past.

There had been a racing driver whom the *Globe* had pursued over his supposed drinking bouts, a pools prize winner who had taken an unwise succession of lovers . . .

'I take it,' Norman said, trying for lightness, 'that even if you do have a lover, it wouldn't make much of a scandal headline.'

'Certainly not,' she said at once. But in her mind she could see it: 'Star's Sister Steals Sweetheart' . . .

It would destroy Lynette.

'What should I do, Norman?'

'Be good,' he said, still hoping to make it seem less unkind than it was. 'And if you can't be good, be careful.'

But he knew very well how hurt she felt — that Mabel, whom she'd thought of as a friend, was prying into her private life. And that Ingram, a friend of even longer standing, was hiring Mabel to do it.

'Well, thank you, Norm,' she said. 'I won't tell anyone you told me.'

She rang Sasha at his flat. No reply. Well, he was probably out first-nighting or entertaining some contact in showbiz. She spent the evening much as she would have done in any case — doing some personal chores, making herself a snack, reading, listening to music.

At midnight she rang Sasha's number again. This time he picked up the phone. 'Hello?'

'Sasha? This is Corie—'

'Corie!' He was clearly startled. 'Well, now, Corie . . . Were you thinking of coming round? Because it's not—'

'You've just come in? I'll call again later. Or you can call me back.'

'We-ell . . .'

There was a faint sound in the background, a clinking of glass and a giggle.

'Ah,' Corie said, 'you've got company.'

'Just a friend, you know,' he said easily. 'Brought him home for a nightcap.'

The giggle had been feminine. But Corie didn't want to argue about it. 'Listen, I have something very important to tell you. I realise this isn't the time, but ring me back. Are you listening, Sasha? Ring me back — or we could end up in *big* trouble.'

'Who could?' he demanded, alarm clear in his tone. 'What's this about?'

'Ring me back and I'll tell you.'

'Give me ten minutes,' he said, and hung up.

Sure enough, about ten minutes later her phone rang. She asked, 'What did you do, show her straight out?'

'Who? I told you — it was a man.'

'Never mind, Sasha, we have more important things to discuss.' She had thought out what she wanted to convey. 'From now on you and I must stay away from each other.'

'Oh, for heaven's sake, we've been through all that . . .'

'Not like this. I've got reporters camping on my doorstep and asking my family questions about me.'

She heard him give a muffled exclamation. '*You* have?'

'Yes. I don't want to go into details about it, but Lynette might get a reporter snooping around about me, and I suppose you too — they might talk to you about me. So don't be taken by surprise.'

'What's this about?' he demanded.

'It's a personal vendetta,' she said. 'Don't let it bother you. Just keep your head and don't make the mistake of thinking the questions have anything behind them. And we certainly mustn't see each other.'

'You can say that again!' he agreed. 'How did you find out about this?'

'Never mind. Just take care, that's all.'

'I certainly will. The last thing I need is trouble, with Lynette just setting out on these personal appearances.'

'Goodnight, Sasha.'

He had never asked if she felt scared, or needed comfort.

When she was ready for bed that night, she put out the light then went to the window. There was a half-moon sailing against pearly cloud. Across on the former bombsite that had been cleared for the Festival of Britain, various builders' huts and sheds gleamed in the silvery shine, looking almost rural among the weeds. Factories and warehouses made a darker background.

At first there was nothing to be seen. Then she saw the gleam of a cigarette as the smoker dragged on it. A moment later the red tip made an arc in the air as it was tossed away. She stood, listening, and heard footsteps moving off.

The reporter had called it a day.

Next morning when she got to the studio she found Bertie moving about dusting and muttering. 'Good morning, Bertie. Got out of bed the wrong side?'

'Corie, there was a man here when I opened up − sitting on the area steps, if you please!'

Her heart sank. 'A reporter.'

'How did you know?' Bertie said. 'I thought he was someone after an urgent passport and was just telling him we didn't do them − had he been round at your flat?'

'What did he want, Bertie?'

'Said he was working on a feature about you, so I told him a bit about the studio and the work we do here—'

'And he wasn't interested.'

'Not a bit. He kept asking about your friends, and I said why didn't he ask you about that, and he said you weren't likely to tell him the juicy bits − so I told him to buzz off or I'd get the police.' He looked at her with concern. 'They been badgering you?'

'In fact, no, Bertie. This is all being done behind my back, as far as I can tell.'

'You'd think a young feller like that would have better things to do—'

'Young? How young?' Corie interrupted.

'Oh, I'd say . . . nineteen, twenty . . .'

'He didn't give you his name, I suppose?'

'No, he never, and now I come to think of it he never said what newspaper he was working for. He had a notebook and all, of course. Tall lad, too tall for his strength, I'd say − all bones and angles, and his clothes could have done with a press.'

It sounded just like Johnnie Gavin. And he was a likely

choice of newshound to put on her trail – he knew her from having worked with her a few days in Monaco and, since he was a cub reporter, probably a trainee, it kept the cost of surveillance down. After all, they weren't going to waste highly paid newsmen on somebody as unimportant as Corie Duggan.

She took off her jacket, checked that she had no appointment until ten o'clock, then rang Norman Gibson at the office of the *Globe*.

'Norm, this is Corie. Just answer yes or no, I know you can't talk much in case someone at the next desk hears you. Is Johnnie Gavin one of the team being used to look into my private life?'

'That's right, madam,' Norman said.

'Thank you. That gives me a way to challenge Ingram without dragging you into it.'

'I would advise caution there, if you don't mind my saying so.'

'Would you say this is likely to come to a stop soon?'

'Er . . . Define soon.'

'A few days? A week?'

'Oh, I think it'll run for longer than a week, madam. Depends upon what our managing editor thinks of the story – and he is intensely interested in it.'

'I see. Then I'll have to take action. You may hear of another row in the office,' she said with some grimness.

'Oh, I don't think that's likely,' Norman said at once. 'There's a security check.'

'You mean they wouldn't let me in?'

'Exactly, madam.'

Corie didn't know whether to laugh or cry. 'When you get out of his good books, it really means something,' she said. 'Well, I'll have to run across him accidentally somewhere, that's all. Is he going anywhere public in the next day or so?'

'Er . . . That's difficult to say.'

'Can you find out from Miss Bryant and ring me?'

'That might take a couple of hours, dear lady.'

'I'll be here at the studio.'

The information, when he got in touch from a public phone box, was that Ingram was to be at a charity première that evening at the Empire Leicester Square, that he was opening a May Festival near his country house on Saturday, and that on Monday he would be at Heathrow to welcome a delegation of journalists from Jordan.

She couldn't give up Saturday because she had bookings all day. She didn't feel like interfering with a welcome of Jordanians. That only left this evening.

She had no difficulty buying a ticket for the première even at this late stage. She hurried home at six to bathe and change. It was a very fine evening, so she put on a white silk suit bought in Paris in the few hours she'd spent there with Mabel – slender trousers and a safari-type jacket. She left the jacket unbuttoned to a deep cleavage, then filled in the space with a gold chain Lynette had given her for her birthday.

She tied back her soft oaten hair with a black silk handkerchief, added black court shoes and a black handbag slung on a chain handle, and was ready.

When she went out into Blackfriars Road she sensed she was being followed. She went into the Cap and Badge pub for a sandwich and a drink in lieu of an evening meal. A man in a sports jacket and flannels came in a few minutes later, to linger at the bar with a glass of lager.

She saw him again while she was waiting to hail a cab on Blackfriars Bridge. Another taxi followed behind, but then the City and West End were always full of taxis between six and eight in the evening.

When she drew up at the cinema, there was the usual little crowd watching the celebrities go in. No one rushed up to ask for her autograph. She proffered her ticket and was shown into the foyer. The bloodhound was left arguing with the commissionaire. What would he say, she wondered, if he knew she was here on purpose to confront his boss?

She was among the early arrivals, and had done it on

purpose so as to be able to watch for Ingram. He arrived about a quarter of an hour before the performance was due to begin, a little before the junior royal who was giving his patronage to the charity.

The film was enjoyable, a war film with a strong humanitarian message. Two or three speeches were made about helping humanity, the audience applauded, and then they were free for what had brought most of them there — to see and be seen.

Ingram had three guests in his loge. He now ushered them to the bar where drinks and canapés were spread out on the buffet. The guests went ahead of him; he brought up the rear.

Corie stepped up behind him, took him by the arm.

He turned. Utter amazement washed over his broad features.

'I want to speak to you,' Corie said.

'Get out of here!'

'Don't be silly, I paid for my ticket. I want to talk to you.'

'Not here—'

'Yes, here.'

'Clear off!'

'Either you come and have a little private chat, or I make a big fuss and make you look silly in front of your friends.'

'You little—'

'Sh-h,' she said and, holding his sleeve, tugged him out of the little file heading for the buffet.

He saw there was no help for it. 'Just go ahead, Natalie,' he called over the heads of the intervening people. 'I'll be with you in a minute.'

Corie had already sought out a little corner in the foyer behind the loge boxes where they could speak in private. She led him there. She felt his presence behind her, like a following thundercloud.

'How did you know you'd find me here?' he demanded.

'It was in the *Evening News*.' This was untrue but she doubted whether he'd check it. 'I've got something very important to say to you and this seemed the best way to do it. Stop sending people to spy on me.'

'Why should I? If I want to know things, I always send out investigators.'

'Do you often decide to "investigate" the lives of your former friends?'

'Quite often,' he said without any sign of guilt. 'But I'd better choose someone who's better at it, I see. How did you find out?'

'I recognised Johnnie Gavin.'

'Who's he?'

'The junior you sent to Monaco with the photocopies.'

He shrugged. 'He's not very good at door-stepping, that's evident.'

She looked at him with dismay in her hazel eyes. 'Aren't you even a little bit ashamed of your behaviour?'

'If it gets me what I want, satisfaction outweighs any finer feelings.'

'I thought you had better taste, Ingram.'

'Taste? Who the hell are you to talk about taste?' he burst out. 'To waste yourself on a creep like Lenoir . . . !'

Corie felt herself go cold. What had he found out? She controlled her expression with an effort that almost turned her to marble. When she could breathe easily she said, 'Lenoir? You mean my sister's agent?'

'The Russian émigré from Birmingham, yes, Sasha Lenoir.'

'You've got hold of a non-starter, Ingram. Sasha is my sister's boyfriend.'

'But means nothing at all to you – is that it? Not from what I've heard.'

'From whom?' she asked, surprised to hear how cool she sounded.

'Your mother, for instance,' he retorted in angry triumph.

She almost laughed in relief. Her mother had had misgivings about her elder daughter trying to draw Sasha's attention to herself. Corie would have bet her life that Monna had no idea anything serious lay between them.

'My mother,' she said lightly. 'Is that who you're relying

on for information? You've met my mother. She still thinks *Chu Chin Chow* was the height of theatrical entertainment. How can you take her seriously, Ingram?'

He shook his head like a stubborn bull. 'There's something going on,' he said. 'You were seen together late at night in a restaurant a few weeks ago, talking very seriously.'

'We were?' She searched in her memory. Yes, Sasha had said he had to speak to her, and they'd had a meal in the Lyons' Corner House at Marble Arch. That had been before she went to Monaco. So much had happened since then that she'd almost forgotten about it. All the same, the fact that Ingram's reporters were asking questions in restaurants showed how determined he was to ferret out information.

'Don't deny that you were with him,' Ingram persisted. 'The waitress who served you recognised Lenoir – she'd seen his picture in a feature article about your sister.'

'Why should I deny it? He wanted to ask whether I thought he should move Lynette to the ITV network.'

'The waitress said he held your hand.'

'The waitress has a good imagination,' Corie said. She couldn't at all remember whether Sasha had held her hand.

'There'll be more,' he said. 'I'll find out.'

'And then what, Ingram?'

'Ah! So you admit there *is* more?'

She shook her head with vigour. 'I'm not the one who has to admit or deny – you're the one, Ingram, who's behaving badly. Leave me and my family alone—'

'Not while there's something to be learnt about you and the Russian aristo.' He stared at her with angry perplexity. 'I don't know how you can even like him!'

'What has it to do with you who I like or dislike!' she cried. 'But perhaps this'll convince you you're on the wrong track. If I'm so taken with Sasha Lenoir, why am I leaving for New York in a week or two? Why am I going to spend months on the other side of the—'

'New York? You're going to New York?'

'As soon as I finish up some commissions at my studio.'

Until she'd said it, she'd had no idea she was going. But now all at once she knew it was the ideal solution. She would go away, and stay away, and the loosening of the sexual ties that bound her to Sasha would continue. Already she found herself feeling less and less involved with him.

The drama of the days in Monaco had taught her something. 'John Smith' and his obsession were like herself and Sasha, though writ larger. Giving in to her infatuation had only brought unhappiness, with more to follow if she didn't take steps to end it.

Ingram had said, 'I don't know how you can even like him!' The truth was, she didn't like him. She didn't love him. Affection didn't come into it. And that being so, it was a worthless liaison. Worthless, pointless, and dangerous.

'What the devil are you going to do in New York?' Ingram was demanding.

'Take pictures, of course.'

'You won't find it so easy as here. America's full of first-class photographers.'

'Do you think I don't know that, Ingram? But I've a friend who's promised—'

'A friend? Who?' He was jealous at once.

'No one you know, Mr Inquisitor. But you'll be interested to hear that while you were pouring out money meddling in my London friendships, you attention should have been on New York. So goodnight and goodbye.'

She brushed past him and along the corridor. She heard him call something, but it was lost in the chatter from the buffet. It had sounded like, 'Don't go, Corie.'

But all at once her mind was made up.

When she consulted Drew Richter on the transatlantic line, he was enthusiastic. 'I'll fix up a hotel room and put out a few feelers for commissions. There's work I can put your way in my own line – I've got some clients who need new portraits to put with their c.v.'s.'

'What'll I do for a portrait studio, though?'

'Oh, we can hire into one – plenty of studios to share in

New York. Leave it with me, Corie.'

'It's very kind of you.'

'I owe you one, after all. When's the date?'

'I thought . . . End of next week?'

'Let me look at the calendar . . . Can you get a flight before the twentieth? There's a parade on the twenty-first – Norwegian Day, really neat, I've got a PR client who's second-generation Norwegian, he'd probably pay you for pix of him in his national costume to send to his relatives in Bergen.'

She laughed at the idea. Suddenly America really did seem the Land of Opportunity.

When she made the announcement to her family, Sasha was present. He had brought Lynette home from a session with a new song-writer. He and Lynette sat on the sofa, his arm about her shoulders. Monna was at the piano trying over one of the new songs. Opal was leaning over her to read the notes and trying to sing them in her sharp-flat voice.

'I'm going to New York next week,' Corie said.

It was a game of giant statues. Everyone was stricken to immobility.

'On an assignment?' Lynette said. 'Oh, lucky you!'

'No, I've got one or two things on spec but nothing definite. I'm just going.'

'But why?' Monna cried in astonishment. 'If you haven't a job there—'

'I envy you,' Opal said. 'I've always thought New York must be a great place for theatre.'

'My darling child, Corie left all her theatrical interests behind her years ago,' her mother rebuked her. 'And as to going there without a definite engagement . . .'

'Oh, it'll be wonderful for her,' Lynette insisted. 'One day I hope I'll get a chance to go there.'

Sasha shook his head and pressed her shoulder. 'Your kind of English presentation wouldn't go down well there,' he said. 'But I think it's a wonderful thing for Corie.'

'You do?' said Monna in surprise.

'Oh yes. Get out and see the world – why not?'

'But so suddenly?'

'I just felt this would be a good time to go,' Corie said, catching his eye.

'Absolutely right,' he agreed. 'Spring of the year, it'll be lovely, I bet. I was in Canada when I did my National Service, you remember. Got down to New York a couple of times – it was terribly hot and airless in July, but I think it's fine in May.'

If Sasha felt it a good idea, for Monna that was the seal of approval. 'Well, darling, I suppose if you must, you must, although I still think it's strange. What will you do with your studio and the flat?'

'Bertie's going to run the studio with a friend of his – a bit down-market from what I've been doing, but still I think they'll make a living. I'm sub-letting the flat.'

'So it's all arranged,' Monna said faintly. 'How long will you be gone?'

'A while.'

Her mother fell silent. Her two sisters enthused over the idea. When she left to go home to her own flat, Sasha accompanied her out to her car.

'I think you've made a good decision,' he said.

'So do I.'

'Might have landed us all in hot water otherwise, eh?'

'Oh, quite.'

'Maybe I won't see you again before you go, so all the best.' He offered his hand, she took it, they shook.

Goodbye Sasha. What was that song by Tosti that Monna always said was so unlucky?

As Corie drove away she was humming it. 'Goodbye for ever, Goodbye for ever, Goodby-ye, Goodbye!'

Chapter Thirteen

In Greenwich Village the bar-restaurant where Corie usually ate her evening meal was called Beginner's Luck. She liked it because the theme of its decor was the Fred Astaire films, notably *Shall We Dance?* In Corie's childhood, Fred Astaire had been an example often held up by the tutors at stage-school. She liked to sit eating tuna-fish pasta with the great man himself in mid-air on the wall above her, caught by a camera as he executed a cabriole.

It was September. She was just back from a gruelling trip to Wyoming with a journalist from *Life* magazine, to photograph the present-day Indians of Yellowstone National Park. She had been driven in a jolting jeep, half-drowned when a power-boat capsized on Yellowstone Lake, and bitten by a thousand insects.

All the same she had enjoyed it. The pictures were good, she'd seen more of the United States, the cheque she'd banked that afternoon would see her through at least until Christmas.

She glanced at her watch. Drew Richter had rung to ask if she'd had a good trip, then invited her out to dinner.

'Honestly, Drew, I appreciate it,' was her reply. 'But I'm so worn out that my plan for this evening is just to toddle round to my neighbourhood pub and have a sandwich.'

'Where do you usually go?'

When she named it he said, 'I know it well. See you there – about seven?'

So, although she'd intended to go out wearing the crumpled jeans and shirt she'd pulled from her hold-all, she felt it necessary to choose instead linen slacks and a soft blue angora sweater. Her face was beyond hope, she told herself as she looked in the mirror. She'd collected a decent tan which enhanced her hazel eyes, but had lost several pounds in weight so that her cheekbones were too prominent. She also had several scars from insect bites. Ah well, scars of war, she told herself, and went out.

One of the things that always struck her about New York was how shadows engulfed the city at evening. When the sun moved westwards, the skyscrapers cast their shade over half of any roadway running north and south, and then, quite soon, all of it. So that even on the very brightest, hottest day, relief came around four o'clock, and by seven the warm September day had been replaced by a cool, hazy dusk.

She took her usual place and was recognised by the waiter. 'Miss Duggan, isn't it? You been away?'

She explained about the trip to Yellowstone.

'You don't say,' he remarked. 'Only Indian I ever saw was outside a cigar store.'

He nodded when she said she was waiting for someone, came back at once with the obligatory glass of iced water, and left her to read her newspaper. The *New York Times* was telling her there was still trouble over the Suez Canal, as there had been when she had left in August. Maria Callas was still the darling of the Metropolitan Opera after her sensational *Norma*. There was yet another outburst by a Baptist minister about the unseemly conduct of those who went to rock-and-roll concerts.

'Hi there,' Drew said, arriving with briefcase and a sheaf of magazines, looking the perfect New Yorker in his grey-flannel suit. He dropped a friendly kiss on her brow before sitting down. 'This is the outdoor-girl look, is it?'

'Don't,' she begged. 'I was eaten alive by mosquitoes on the lake. No wonder Red Indians are red – they probably got that way from insect bites.'

'Have you ordered?'

'No, I was waiting for you.'

He beckoned the waiter. 'Let's have a drink to celebrate your safe return. What'll it be?'

'I'll have a campari-soda, please.'

'Make mine a screwdriver.'

Corie was folding up her newspaper. 'What were you reading so intently when I got here?' he asked.

'A protest about the behaviour of rock-and-roll fans.'

'Oh, that! A waste of printing ink . . .'

'I went to a dance hall in Chicago on my way west. There were people outside with banners, calling it the dance of the Devil.'

'I believe they said that about the Charleston too.'

'But they didn't play the Charleston so loudly,' Corie pointed out.

'A military band is loud, Corie.'

'Military bands play in the open air. Have you ever been to a place where rock-and-roll is being played?'

He grinned and shook his head. 'I'm tolerant, but not that tolerant.'

'Well, let me tell you, the noise is deafening. And the singing . . . They don't really sing, they shout.'

'Oh yes,' he agreed. 'That's part of a long tradition.'

'You're joking.'

'Not at all. "Shouting for the Lord" – that's part of the negro revivalist tradition.'

'You seem to know a lot about it.'

'I have to. In public relations, you have to pay attention to the *Zeitgeist*.'

Their drinks came, they sipped them with appreciation. 'What's a Tight-bight?' she asked.

'Don't show your ignorance,' Drew laughed. '*Zeitgeist*, which is a classy way of saying Spirit of the Age. You have to know words like that if you want to impress the clients.'

'And you have clients who think rock-and-roll is the Spirit of the Age?'

'Not exactly. But you see, if somebody wants to . . . let's say present a new artist at a gallery . . . He might ask us to help plan a party. And we might suggest, if the painter is very much into pop-art or action-painting, we might say, "How about a rock-and-roll band".'

'I'd be sorry for anyone trying to look at art in a gallery

with a rock-and-roll band playing alongside.'

Drew looked at her in wry agreement. 'Perhaps that wasn't a good example. Maybe West Coast jazz would be better there. But everything that influences a large part of society has to be taken into account.'

'You think rock-and-roll is going to influence anybody?' she asked with scepticism.

'Sure. Already the teenagers are going after rock-and-roll fashion—'

'Teenagers,' Corie said. 'Everywhere I go in America I see that word, teenagers. Where I come from they're called schoolchildren.'

'They are? You just wait until they've got as much money as American teenagers. I tell you, Corie, any section of the public that has money to spend is worth considering where public relations is concerned. American teenagers spend money on records of Little Richard, they buy jeans and sweaters to dance in . . . You can't afford to ignore them, they're a part of the market; and rock-and-roll is what they like.'

'It's just a passing fad.'

'You may be right.'

'I'd better be right,' she said. 'If it ever caught on in the UK, it's goodbye to Lynette and "You're a Sweetheart".'

But she didn't mean it seriously, and turned without another thought to consideration of the menu.

Once their food had come, Drew said, 'I wanted to see you for a reason. Are you free this Sunday?'

'I don't know, I haven't got my diary with me. But so far as I know, nothing's happening.'

'How would you like to go for lunch at a posh family estate in Upper New York State?'

'Mm?' she said, with a forkful of fish stew on the way to her lips. 'Who in Upper New York State is offering me lunch?'

'Helen Pittsworth Holstead.'

'Who?' For a moment she was at a loss. Then she made the connection. 'Ingram's wife?'

'The very same. She lives on a big place up near New Paltz. She asked me to bring you next Sunday.'

'Oh no,' said Corie at once.

'What d'you mean, oh no?'

'I don't want to meet Helen Pittsworth Holstead.'

'Why on earth not?' he said, amazed. 'It could turn out good for you. She wants you to take portraits of herself and her children.'

'No,' said Corie, shaking her head.

He sat back from the table, looking at her in concern. 'We-ell,' he said, 'that's kind of awkward because I already accepted on your behalf.'

'Who asked you to?' she cried with irritation. 'I never gave you permission to make arrangements—'

'Corie, Corie, I thought it would be a good opportunity for you,' he soothed. 'Mrs Holstead's a woman of importance, she's got a lot of influence. Of course I thought you'd want to, she's the wife of that newspaper tycoon you were working for in Monaco.'

'And if you remember,' she returned in a sarcastic tone, 'I disregarded his instructions and lost him a story he thought was going to be a headliner. Last time I saw him we were not on friendly terms, to put it at its mildest.'

'She must surely know that, honey,' he said. 'She keeps in touch with him − it's her money that keeps his newspaper going so she likes to know what's going on. If she still wants to see you—'

'Why should she want to see me?' Corie demanded. 'There must be a hundred well-known photographers in New York that she could have . . .'

'I got the impression,' he began, then stopped.

'What? Got what impression?'

'Never mind.'

'What?' she insisted.

'Well, she said you were "a friend of her husband's". I kind of thought . . .'

'What, for heaven's sake?' she urged, exasperated.

'That you and Holstead . . . But if you say you and he

weren't on speaking terms . . . Maybe I got it wrong.'

'You certainly did! And so did Mrs Holstead! Ingram Holstead and I were never anything more than friends, and we're a lot less than that now.'

'Then if that's true, what's your objection to going to lunch with her on Sunday?'

'She'd probably put poison in my soup!'

He chuckled. 'Well, she is a formidable lady. But if you explain the real facts, she might give you the antidote.'

'There'll be no need. I'm not going.'

He looked perturbed. 'Corie, I've already told her I'll bring you.'

'Well, you'll just have to tell her you were wrong.'

'But why should you turn down a commission for a portrait? She's got so much money that if she put it under her mattress in dollar bills, she'd be sleeping on a level with Mars. I'd like it if we didn't offend her by backing out.'

Corie sighed. 'She's a client of yours?'

'From time to time. But more important, she puts work my way.'

'And if we don't go, she'll stop doing that?'

'I don't know. I'd rather not risk it, though.'

'I'm not going, Drew.'

'So you keep saying. But if what you say about you and Holstead is true, where's the problem?'

'It's what Mrs Holstead seems to think that's the problem.'

'Look, Helen can be abrasive, but she's a woman of the world. She knows her husband plays around—'

'He didn't play around with me!' Corie exclaimed. 'How often do I have to say it?'

'All right, all right, keep your cool. Helen wants to take a look at you, that's obvious, but she genuinely wants the portraits. She said she had a copy of the portrait you did of Holstead and wants one just as good of herself. The kids too – and she wouldn't be mean about money.'

'I'd rather not.'

'But she's expecting you on Sunday!'

'You'll have to ring and say I can't make it.'

'She'll only invite you for the following Sunday.'

'Tell her I'm busy at the weekends.'

'Corie, if she wants to meet you – and apparently she does – she'll arrange to come upon you accidentally.'

Since this was the method Corie had used to speak with Ingram, she knew it was only too true.

'What good does it do you to antagonise her?' Drew said, pursuing his advantage as she paused, perplexed. 'And anyhow, what can happen in a household of people?'

'There'll be others there?' she asked, a little relieved.

'Oh, sure, Sunday lunch at Gitchetak is well-known. Financiers, writers, sportsmen, a senator or two . . . You can hide among them except when you're talking business.'

'Are you manipulating me?' she wondered aloud.

A half-smile creased his narrow features. 'You're not supposed to be aware of that.'

'You mean you admit you're manipulating me?'

'That's what public relations means – manipulating people.'

'Oh, Drew . . . That's not a very pleasant thought.'

'What makes you say so? It's just a way of getting others to accept what you say—'

'But what if you're saying something wrong?'

'Me?' he said, all innocence. 'Would I do that?'

'You mean you only ever take on clients who are squeaky-clean?'

'I refuse to answer on the grounds that it might incriminate me. And, as a matter of fact, it's easier to make headway with something that's straightforward and honest than the slippery stuff.'

'Implying you've had experience of the slippery stuff.'

'Look, Corie, I'm in business to make money. I can't afford to look behind my clients' ears to see if they've washed them. And that's not the point. Can I take it you'll come to Gitchetak on Sunday?'

'If I don't, I make it awkward for you.'

'Right. So I'll pick you up at ten a.m., OK?'

Until the last minute, Corie thought she was going to back out. But when Drew drove up in his Pontiac, she went down from her third-floor apartment to meet him.

He was standing by the open door of the car as she crossed the sidewalk. She saw him inspecting her. 'Will I do?' she asked as she got in.

'You certainly don't look like any *femme fatale*.'

'Is that a compliment or not?'

'It's a statement of fact. But if you want to know, I always think you look good in your own special way.'

They drove out of New York by way of Yonkers and White Plains. The skyscrapers were left behind, and as they sped along Route 87 it struck Corie yet again how wrong Europeans were about their transatlantic cousins. They thought of them as city-dwellers, led into that mistake by gangster movies and newspaper stories. But a large part of America lived its life in rural quietude, among these autumnal fields, inside these white-painted houses, going to the church whose steeple rose above the brilliant leaves of maple, gingko and redwood.

Drew had said the home of Helen Pittsworth Holstead lay near New Paltz. They drove through without stopping, though Corie had time to notice traffic directions to State University College, and a collection of fine old stone houses in Huguenot Street signposted as 'Open Wed-Sat, Entrance 50c.'

Now they were driving along a road into the 'highlands', where notices invited the traveller to put up at lake resort hotels. 'Fishing, swimming, archery,' they offered. 'Skiing, snowmobiles.'

'This is vacation country,' Corie suggested.

'To some extent. Lots of big estates too. Hyde Park is in the Hudson Valley.'

'Hyde Park?'

'Former home of President Roosevelt. A strong Democratic tendency hereabouts − Roosevelt was a Democrat.'

'Ah,' she said, for she found American politics very confusing. It was easy to make a big mistake in conversation

by saying something complimentary about President Eisenhower. Corie had been brought up by Monna to think
President Eisenhower was a wonderful man because he had
applauded at a wartime concert in which Monna and her
husband had appeared.

Drew turned in between stone pillars. A short paved
drive brought them to wrought-iron gates. There was a
glass-fronted box with a telephone on the left-hand post.
Drew got out, opened the glass front, lifted the telephone,
and spoke. He nodded and returned to the car. The gates
opened for them.

'What is this, Bluebeard's Castle?' Corie exclaimed.

'When you're as rich as Mrs Holstead you can afford to
be a little Blue-Beardish. Her grandfather built the place
somewhere about 1870 – that's old and blue-blooded for
this part of the world.'

They drove on uphill between butternut and sycamore
turning a bitter-lemon yellow. The house, when it came
into view, was squarish with turrets, gold and scarlet with
Virginia creeper. Several cars were already parked in the
courtyard in front. A manservant was waiting to open the
door and usher them in.

'If you and the lady would like to go upstairs first,
Mr Richter, you'll find the guests out by the pool afterwards.'

Corie was shown into an upstairs powder-room all
furnished in grey-blue. She washed her hands, put a little
mascara on her eyelashes, took off the jacket of her white
safari suit, then put it on again.

Why should she be nervous? What did it matter what she
looked like? She was here to arrange a photographic session,
nothing more.

Drew was hovering in the hall. He led her to open double
doors, beyond which lay the dining-room. Beyond that
again, french windows gave on to a wide paved area sloping
down to a big oval pool.

One or two swimmers were in the pool. The other guests
were scattered around it, some in cushioned wrought-iron

chairs enjoying the September sun, some strolling with glasses in their hands.

Corie walked at Drew's side to a canopied swing-seat. Here, with a terrier squatting by her feet, was Helen Pittsworth Holstead.

She was handsome rather than beautiful. She had a Roman nose, narrow dark eyes, a wide firm mouth and, overall, an authoritative air. Her gown was a thought too formal for sitting in a swing-seat. She was in conversation but turned as they approached.

'Mrs Holstead, here's Miss Duggan.'

'How do you do, Miss Duggan? I'm glad you could come.'

'Thank you for asking me,' Corie said, wondering why she was expressing gratitude when what she felt was apprehension.

Mrs Holstead introduced the man to whom she'd been speaking, who turned out to be the manager of a baseball team. The conversation picked up, incomprehensible to Corie with its examination of last season's triumphs and failures.

'Now, Chuck,' Mrs Holstead said after a few minutes, 'this is all very dull for our English friend. And I'm sure Drew would like a drink. Why don't you take him to get what he wants?'

Drew, with the hint of a shrug to Corie, rose. 'Shall I bring you something, Corie?'

'Er . . . some juice?'

He nodded and left with the team manager. It was all Corie could do not to jump up and run after them.

'Corie,' repeated Mrs Holstead. 'That's a curious name.'

'It's short for Coral. All the women in my family have names of semi-precious stones − Coral, Opal and Beryl, and my mother's Crystal.'

'Charming,' said her hostess, in a tone that belied the words. 'I was in London during the summer . . . I think I was told you had stage ambitions?'

'Not in the least. My sister, Lynette−'

'I thought you said you all had names to do with semi-precious stones?'

'My sister is known as Lynette Lee—'

'That is supposed to be an improvement, I take it?'

'It's supposed to be a name the public will remember,' Corie said, refusing to be nettled, 'and they do.'

Mrs Holstead leaned down to pat the terrier's head. The little dog made a snuffling sound of appreciation. 'My dog's called Snuffy,' she said. 'People remember that, too.'

'But I hardly think he gets reviews in the London papers,' Corie said with a smile.

'Talking of papers, I saw the feature you did about your wounded men coming home from the Korean War. Quite impressive.'

'Thank you.'

'Photography interests me. Your style is odd, don't you think? Rather gritty, yet refusing to be sombre. You seem to sympathise with your subjects.'

'Yes, on the whole.'

'Do you think you'll sympathise with me if you take my photograph?'

'Why should that matter?'

'Because the portrait won't be so good if you don't.'

'I shall do my best as a professional, Mrs Holstead.'

'I gather you've been doing your best,' Mrs Holstead said on a rising note, 'but your tactics have failed so far.'

Corie frowned. 'What tactics?'

'Playing hard to get. It won't work, Miss Duggan. Ingram's not the kind of man for whom absence makes the heart grow fonder. If you wanted to land that catch you should have stayed in London.'

'Mrs Holstead, I assure you—'

'You'll never get my husband, Miss Duggan! He'll never divorce me because it's my money that keeps his press empire going!'

'What makes you imagine,' Corie retorted evenly, 'that I want your husband?'

'Oh, come, I have the London papers flown here every

day. It's been in all the gossip columns, how you and he were seen everywhere together and now he's eating his heart out since you left—'

Corie got to her feet. 'I'd have thought that the great Helen Pittsworth Holstead would have more sense than to believe gossip columns. Not that it's any of your business, but I didn't leave London to make Ingram yearn for me. I left to get someone out of my system – someone you haven't heard of, and certainly not your husband.' She made a little bow. 'And now, if you've satisfied yourself on what was bothering you, perhaps you'll allow me to say goodbye.'

The other woman stared up at her through those narrowed dark eyes. 'You haven't had any lunch, Miss Duggan.'

'If I was feeling hungry, you've taken away my appetite.'

'I can't allow you to leave without having had something to eat. It offends my sense of hospitality—'

'Hospitality!'

'And besides,' she sailed on, 'we haven't fixed a date for the portrait studies.'

'But that was—' Corie broke off.

'That was what?'

'Just a pretext to get me here so you could take a hack at me.'

Helen laughed, a rolling, hearty sound. 'You're quite a girl,' she said. 'If Ingram really was interested in you, I can see why. Sit down, Miss Duggan, sit down. I think we might say we're in a state of truce.'

'I'm not in a state of truce,' Corie said, making no attempt to sit down. 'Not if you imagine I had designs of any kind on your husband. I assure you I hadn't.'

'But he had, on you. Oh, it's all right, my dear, I've been through it all before. Generally I don't get a chance to warn off "the other women", but since you were in New York it seemed only decent to tell you you were wasting your time – as all the others were. Sit down, Miss Duggan, I accept that you're not interested in Ingram. Wouldn't he be wild if he knew!' She gave a gleeful grin.

And Corie, captivated, sat down.

Helen Holstead toyed with an earring. 'Do tell, dear – who's the man who made you chicken out of London?'

'No, no. That's a secret,' Corie said, half-laughing and half-sighing.

'It's not Drew obviously.'

'Of course not! He and I are just—'

'Just good friends,' said Helen, in chorus with her.

They laughed. 'Well, it's true,' Corie insisted.

'Maybe it is. In any case, I wonder if he's husband material? He's got one failed attempt behind him.'

'Really?'

'You didn't know?'

'No reason why I should. Honestly, most of our conversation is about business. He's been very helpful to me in getting work over here.'

'I must see what I can do for you, my dear,' said the older woman, patting her hand. 'I'm known as very helpful when I feel it's worth my trouble.'

Drew arrived bearing in his left hand a tall glass crammed with ice. 'Cranberry juice,' he said, handing it to Corie. He sipped his own, which was clearly something stronger. 'What were you two giggling about a moment ago?'

'You, of course, dear,' said his hostess, aiming a playful slap at him. 'You knew that, of course. Men always think women talk about them.'

'You mean you don't? Another illusion shattered.'

'You haven't any illusions, Drew. Don't try to kid us.' Mrs Holstead then leapt to her feet. Surprisingly, even in high heels, she was much shorter than Corie. Yet for a tiny figure she was surprisingly impressive.

'Eddie!' she called through cupped hands. 'Stop chasing those girls in the water – I want you here.'

One of the youngsters came to the side of the pool in a lazy crawl. He hauled himself up and out. He was about middle height, broad-shouldered, his body that of an athlete.

'Oh, *Mother*,' he protested, 'I wasn't chasing the girls, we were racing.'

A manservant appeared out of nowhere to hand him a towel and help him into a beach-robe. 'Miss Duggan, my son Eddie,' Helen Holstead said.

'How do you do?' he said, holding out a hand still slightly damp. 'You're the photographer?'

'Yes.'

'I'm sorry for you. Mother hates having her picture taken. And Mirrie always begs to be made to look beautiful – an impossible task, I keep telling her.'

'That's enough. Go indoors, make yourself decent, and bring your sister out to lunch.'

'Yes, Mother dear.'

When he came back with his sister, Corie felt that it wouldn't be an impossible task to make the girl look beautiful. Still very young, her features as yet unformed, she had good bones and a tip-tilted nose. Her hair, like her mother's, was a rich brown. The son was rather plain and darker, yet his thick brows and air of self-containment made him interesting.

The two children were directed to take Corie to the buffet and to introduce her to the other guests. She met a member of the House of Representatives, a woman lawyer, a skiing champion, two ladies who ran a charity committee. Helen Holdstead moved about chatting, then at around four o'clock sought Corie out.

'You'll want to be on your way soon, so let's you and I set up a date for this photographic session. Do you want us to come to your studio or would you rather come here?'

'I'd rather come here. I only have shared studio facilities.'

Mrs Holstead raised her hand and beckoned, apparently at no one. A secretary appeared as if by magic. 'Donna, bring my diary out, will you?'

When it had come she leafed through its pages. 'Not this week . . . Not next, unless you want to take pictures in the evening? You could come to dinner.'

'That would mean bringing lamps and other equipment.

I'd rather use "available light", take the shots in daylight and perhaps outdoors.'

'Then that takes us into October. Oka-ay . . . What do you say to the third? I'm free that day.'

'And your children? Won't they be at school or college?'

'Oh, that.' She waved a hand. 'No problem, Eddie's at Yale, he can come home for the day, Mirabel's at a nearby day school, she won't be leaving home till she goes to college.'

Corie wrote the date into her pocket diary, thanked her hostess for an interesting day, and went with Drew through the house and out to the car.

'Well, what do you think?' he asked as they turned out of the gates into the valley road.

'She's *formidable*!'

'Oh yeah, a power in the land. And not such a harpie as you expected, I take it.'

Corie laughed. 'Luckily.'

'She liked you, I'm relieved to say.'

'Yes, I'm pretty relieved myself. Let me ask you something, Drew — if she and I had ended up having a big row, what would you have done?'

'I'd have beaten a strategic retreat and taken you home.'

'But you couldn't tell beforehand how things were going to work out?'

He shook his head.

'So you were ready to throw me to the lions.'

He understood what she was saying. 'I more or less had to take you, Corie. She made a big point of it. But if things had turned out badly I would have come to the rescue.'

'Even if it meant offending the great Helen Pittsworth Holstead?'

'Come on, lighten up,' he said in a vexed tone. 'I have to handle people all day long, seven days a week. I'd have found a way to soothe our Helen. But as it turns out, I don't have to. So why make a psychological study of it?'

She accepted that. When she thought about it, she was pretty sure he could have handled it no matter what happened. As he had said, manipulating people was his business. He couldn't be blamed if a certain cynicism had built up over the years when he saw how easy it was to do.

A few days later he invited her to dinner at his parents' home in Scarsdale. She had already met them in her first few days in New York when they had shown her great kindness.

Themselves refugees from the Nazis in 1933, Emil and Senta Richter had understood her loneliness and confusion. 'Europe seems so far away, of course. I understand,' Mrs Richter had said. 'For me it was the same. Worse, too. It took me many months to learn the language.'

'Aha,' her husband said, smiling at his wife through thick glasses, 'and even worse because she thought she spoke English. And it was true, that was what she spoke. It took her all those months to realise she had to speak American.'

'You can laugh. You at least had had American students in your classes.'

Emil Richter had been a professor of botany in Leipzig, now in the Russian zone of Germany. 'An ironic thing, don't you agree? We left because of the Fascists and now we stay away because of the Communists. Andreas visits. I couldn't bear to go now.'

'Visits? You still have family there?'

'Oh, yes, uncles and aunts and cousins,' Drew said. 'Notably one cousin, Werner . . .'

'Poor Werner . . .'

'What's so special about Werner?' Corie wanted to know.

'He wants to come to the West. But of course he can't get permission – it's very difficult to get permission to emigrate.'

'I didn't know that,' she confessed. Politics for Corie were simply the headlines in the newspapers – she seldom read beyond them.

'When I see Werner, he keeps saying that if Uncle Emil could do it, so can he. But he forgets it took my father years to get his visas and so on. And moreover Papa wasn't a troublemaking student, he was a sedate and respected professor at the university.'

Now Emil Richter ran a laboratory specialising in the diseases of plants. Their house in a quiet, tree-lined road in Scarsdale was littered with learned magazines in half a dozen languages, and every ledge was lined with plants in pots. It was a commercial undertaking, quite unlike the academc life he had left.

Senta, an excellent cook, laid on a superb meal for Corie's visit. 'You are too thin,' she scolded. 'That month in Montana or Wyoming or whatever state it was, it wore you out. Why do you allow this, Andreas?'

'I don't have any influence over her,' Drew laughed.

'Now there's a change of heart!' Corie said. 'Last week you were telling me how you earned your living by influencing other people.'

'A strange career, eh?' his father said. 'Sometimes I say to him, "Andreas", I say, "why don't you do something really useful with your life?" And do you know, Corie, he never can give me a reasonable answer.'

'Show me something where I can make the same money, and I might consider it.'

'Ach, we didn't bring you up to believe money was the most important thing,' his mother protested.

'No, that's true, Mutti. I didn't say I thought it was . . .'

Over the ensuing months, Corie found her life very fulfilling. She took the portraits of Helen Holstead and her family, to their great satisfaction. She even made the nervous Mirabel look beautiful.

'But that isn't me!' the girl cried when she saw the roughs. 'When I look in the mirror, she's not what I see!'

'Well, that's because you worry about whether you're developing a spot on your nose, and things like that,' Corie explained. 'But when I look . . . I try to look not just at the outside, but what's inside. And I try to show that hidden self – I think of it as a hidden beauty in everyone, a certain glow that comes from within.'

Mirabel's mother was so pleased that she recommended

Corie to her friends. Among those friends was a certain Democratic senator, John F. Kennedy, a young man who was said to have presidential ambitions.

'Do something special for him, Corie,' Helen instructed.

'What on earth d'you mean? What can I do for him? He's a millionaire in his own right and a Pulitzer Prize winner.'

'Yes, but everyone sees him as the handsome son of a rich man. Look at him through your camera and show him to the world as something more than that.'

The pictures when they appeared were praised, although Corie hardly knew if she had done anything more than reveal the strong mind that lay behind the handsome features. He was not an easy man to read, even through the camera lens.

Because she'd taken a liking to Corie and Corie was Drew's friend, Helen involved Drew in work for some of the charities in which she took an interest. Thus Corie and Drew saw each other often in the course of both the social and the commercial round.

But Corie liked Drew best when he was being 'Andreas', the son of his kindly parents. At their home he was a gentler, simpler person. He let more of his inner self show. She learned that he was by no means the cynic he liked to appear – the cynicism was a protective shell he had grown. He was a complex man, she felt. Perhaps he had been scarred by the break-up of a youthful and unwise marriage. No one ever spoke of that at his home: she gathered his parents had disapproved strongly at the time and didn't like to remember how right they'd been.

The months flowed by. Corie flew home a couple of times to see her family but never had the urge to stay long. Her sister Opal seemed to be growing fond of a colleague in the Mayfair car-hire firm, Barton Davis. Lynette was still among the big attractions on British television. Monna had occasional engagements to sing at evening parties and weddings and seemed delighted with life. She saw nothing of Sasha on her visits.

When she returned from one such trip in the late autumn

of 1958, she found Helen Holstead in a state of great indignation. 'I don't know what that fool of a President thinks he's doing,' she cried, thumping the table so that her dinner plate jumped a little. 'I've got money invested in that crummy island!'

They were at dinner in the splendid dining-room at Gitchetak. 'What's she talking about?' Corie murmured in the ear of her neighbour at table.

'Cuba, what else?' he sighed.

'What's wrong with Cuba?'

'My *dear* angel, where have you been?' he asked. 'The whole place is coming to pieces.'

'Really? In what way?'

'Castro. You've heard of Castro?'

'Er . . . I think I've seen the name in the papers.'

'I think you probably have,' he said with dryness. 'Fidel Castro looks like knocking President Batistá off his perch. Such a pity, I *love* Cuba, all those decadent casinos and nightclubs . . .'

He took it more lightly than Mrs Holstead, as Corie, who was staying the weekend, was to learn next morning. Her hostess was still in a rage about the political situation. 'Eisenhower is a fool, an incompetent fool,' she declared over breakfast. 'If he doesn't do something soon, the situation will be past repairing.'

'Momma, you know very well it's not as easy as you make out. He can't get Congress to approve—' her son tried to say.

'And meanwhile my money is going down the tubes. If that man Batistá doesn't keep his head, I tell you, Eddie . . .'

'But nobody really knows what's happening, Momma.'

'Do you think I don't know that? Newspapermen go over there and fall under the spell of the buxom revolutionary girls in bandanas and camouflage jackets—'

'Oh goodness, Momma,' Mirabel chimed in, 'if you're not satisfied with what the newsmen send back, it's easy enough to remedy. You know enough people in the newspaper world, heaven knows. All you have to do is have them send someone you have confidence in.'

Helen looked at her daughter as if she had suddenly acquired a halo.

'Mirrie, that's a very wise remark.'

'It is?' said Mirabelle, unused to being taken seriously on such matters.

'It certainly is.' There was a pause while Helen sat with her grapefruit glass in her hand, gazing out over the covered swimming pool as if in deep thought. Then she set the glass down.

'Corie,' she said, 'how would you like to go to Cuba?'

Chapter Fourteen

Corie was keen to go. Each time her work had taken her to a different terrain, she'd learned something new – about herself, about her craft. In Tokyo she'd learned to look at suffering and not shrink from it. In Monaco she'd been under pressure for several days and found she could endure it. Even in Wyoming, she'd lived rough and for the first time known physical danger when she'd almost drowned in Yellowstone Lake – and from that had learned that you could be afraid and not give in to your fear.

There was one snag now. 'I don't speak any Spanish,' she confessed.

'That's no problem. I'll send Eddie with you,' said Helen Holstead. 'He speaks good Spanish.'

'Gee, Mother, that's *keen*,' breathed Eddie.

Helen spent an hour on the telephone. She then said with a little smile, 'All arranged. You'll be accredited to *News Now* as a photo-journalist. Eddie's your assistant. You understand the Cuban government is a bit edgy at the moment with guerrillas coming out of the mountains at night to make their lives miserable. You have to have identity papers – but *News Now* will provide that.'

At once Corie was thrown into a state of urgent activity. She had to have inoculations, she had to buy clothes for the climate. Cuba, she found to her astonishment, was practically the tropics. She had to lay in a stock of suitable film, although Eddie assured her she'd be able to buy plenty there.

'It's very Americanised,' he told her. 'I've got Cuban friends at Yale – they're very American in every way: in outlook, in manners, in language even, because they speak both Spanish and English.'

But the background reading that Mrs Holstead's secretary supplied showed that only the rich of Cuba would be like that. The poor, the ordinary workers, were a mixture of Spanish, African and Chinese. Almost fifty per cent of the population were descended from slaves and labourers imported to work the sugar plantations in the nineteenth century. Corie very much doubted if they would speak Spanish and English, or have an American outlook.

These were the people Helen wanted her to interview. 'I don't want to hear what the politicians say, Corie. They're so used to lying they'd have difficulty remembering their own names. It's no use trying to base any kind of financial judgement on them because they want American money to stay in the island.' Helen tapped the table with a finger. 'I want to know whether it's true the people support the President or whether, if push came to shove, they'd welcome Castro and his bunch.'

'I can only take pictures,' Corie said. 'I can't do interviews.'

'That's all right, Eddie will ask the questions.' She darted a glance at her son, half-proud and half-mystified. 'Behind that college-boy exterior lies a businessman ... He'll find out what I want to know so long as he has an excuse to get in among the ordinary folk. Which he wouldn't have if he went on my behalf − that way he'd have some cute little official tagging along to make sure he only saw what they wanted him to see,'

'But as assistant to Corie Duggan, photographer, I'm just a gofer,' Eddie said. 'Like a caddie to a golfer, or a porter to a mountaineer. It's a great idea.'

Drew Richter didn't think it was a great idea at all. 'What the devil are you thinking of, Helen?' he said when he rang her to protest. 'Havana's a dangerous place these days. It's just not fair to send Corie−'

'She'll be all right,' Helen replied calmly. 'She handled herself well in Monaco over that weirdo at Gracie's wedding−'

'That was different! There she had a police force backing

her up. From what I hear, I wouldn't count on the Havana police coming to the aid of anybody trying to tell the truth about the regime.'

'Now, now, don't fuss. Eddie'll be with her—'

'Eddie's a twenty-one-year-old Yalie who's never encountered anything more dangerous than a Harvard hockey ace . . .'

'You think that's not dangerous?' Helen laughed.

'I'm serious, Helen! He's a spoiled kid and she's a well-brought-up English girl. If they get in trouble in Cuba, the Batisteros will chew them up and spit them out.'

'They're not going to get into trouble. They're only going to take some glamorous pictures of sunset over the canefields, and listen to a few old cane-cutters talking about life. Nobody'll even notice them.'

'Helen, Helen . . .'

He was just as unsuccessful when he tried to dissuade Corie. 'You'll be out of your league down there,' he insisted. 'The government is nothing but a bunch of cut-throats. What's more, there could be a real war any day.'

'That wouldn't involve me even if it happened,' she replied. 'I'm not a newscameraman, I'd just be an observer. Don't worry about it, Drew.'

'But I do worry. I want you to give up the idea.'

'No, I want to go.'

'For heaven's sake, why?'

'Because . . . I don't know . . . Because I've never been to Cuba. Because I'd regret it for ever if I passed up this chance. Because I think I might take some good pictures there.'

'Good lord, hundreds of people have been to Cuba to take pictures.'

'Not like the pictures I'll take,' she said with a faraway look in her eyes.

'That's pure vanity,' he grunted.

'Oh, thanks very much,' she said.

So they parted in irritation and resentment.

She and Eddie Holstead flew to Cuba in the November of

1958. It was extraordinary to exchange the frosty ground of La Guardia for a balmy evening in Havana. The arrivals lounge was small and stuffy, crowded with travellers coming to the island to spend a luxurious Christmas in the sun. Bright coloured dresses were everywhere; men wore white suits and panamas.

Corie had her first taste of Cuban inefficiency. Their luggage took an hour to appear on the creaking carousel. Outside, where a chauffeur-driven car should have been awaiting them, there was no one.

'Relax, relax,' Eddie said, 'I'll deal with it.' He went off, leaving her feeling very vulnerable in the midst of a throng chattering at each other in Spanish as swift and unstoppable as a mountain stream. But he came back in ten minutes with a small man driving a battered Chevrolet.

Their hotel was in Vedado, the modern part of Havana. It was a surprise – marble lobby, reception desk like an island in a green sea, a fountain surrounded with ferns, cool air-conditioning. Their rooms were like any rooms in a good hotel in New York – built-in furniture, square-shaded lamps, bathroom en suite with gilt taps shaped like dolphins. Only the hot water for the bath was tepid, and one of the two lamps by Corie's bedside needed a new bulb.

She threw wide the shutters at the windows to gaze out. She saw palm trees, buildings shining under a three-quarter moon, and beyond them the silvery blue of water – the Gulf of Mexico! Delighted, she fell into bed and into dreams full of galleons surging through waves tipped with lacy foam, and beaches where girls danced to the rhythm of drum and guitar.

Next morning breakfast proved to be a buffet served in a sort of shaded patio. The choice was excellent, except that some of the dishes, once emptied, were not refilled in time for Corie to sample them. She and Eddie went out after a quick meal to explore Havana. Corie found more than enough to bring her camera up to her eye.

Whitewashed Spanish-colonial houses with fluted columns. Mini-skyscrapers built by American money in the

Art-deco period. Theatres big enough to be a home for opera. A railway station needing paint and redecoration but with a train service to any part of the island. Modern hotels to attract monied tourists. Casinos, night clubs, restaurants with canopies over the pavement and waiters rushing to and fro.

But behind the façade lay city canyons of squalor and despair. Drunks sleeping in the gutter, naked children splashing in rain puddles, faded washing hanging out on lines strung from upper storeys, a canary singing shrilly from a cage outside a smashed window, broken staircases leading up into darkness . . .

Here there were no waiters scurrying about with prettily decorated drinks. And yet, from many of the alleys, Corie heard the strum of a guitar, a voice singing '*Cielito lindo*'.

'I guess it's somewhere in around here that Momma wants us to ask questions,' Eddie hazarded.

'Go ahead,' Corie said, focusing on two children playing some sort of hopping game.

'We-ell . . . How do I start?'

Corie spared a moment to look at him. He seemed suddenly younger, less sure of himself.

'Come on,' she said, 'I'll get a foot in the door for you.'

She went closer to the two children. The two little boys stopped their game to watch her approach. They called a few cheerful words.

'What do they say?' she asked.

'They want to know if you'll pay them.'

'Tell them yes. Then ask if I can take a picture of their mother.'

Delighted, the boys leapt up. They acted for the camera, screwing up their faces, sticking out their tongues. Patiently Corie clicked the shutter, then once again asked through Eddie to take a picture of their mother.

'They say she's upstairs sewing.'

'Come on then.' The two boys ran ahead to show the way. Corie and Eddie picked their way after them, up a staircase without a banister, up two flights of unlighted stone steps.

Here there was a gallery facing over a courtyard, once part perhaps of a fine townhouse, but now a slum. At an open door the boys called, 'Mama, Mama!' A young woman appeared at their call, her hands full of fine scarlet silk net.

This was Señora Manatero, mother of Rodrigo, Alberto, Dolores and Rosita, wife to Jago Manatero, dock-worker. She embroidered for one of the fine dressmaker shops in Calle Medio. The work in her hands was the skirt of a gown which must be ready for Christmas. They must excuse her but she must get back to work. When Corie asked if she might take photographs she said yes, but she must be allowed to work while it was done. She didn't ask for money, as her sons had. She sat down by an open window, picked her needle out of a pin-cushion, and began to pick out a flower pattern on the net.

Corie quietly got on with her task. Eddie began a conversation in which she couldn't join. About half an hour later he gave her a nudge. She packed up her cameras, said, '*Muchas gracias*', and went out with Eddie.

'Aren't you going to give her anything?' she reminded him.

'It would offend her.' Instead he gave bills to the two boys, who pocketed them and rushed indoors amid whoops of pleasure.

With a break for lunch and a rest in the afternoon (siesta time), they spent ten hours in Old Havana. Corie had shot yards of film, Eddie had had dozens of casual conversations while she took her shots. Of revolution they'd heard not a whisper and seen not a sign except for a slogan chalked up on a wall: 'Batistá is a murderer'. When they passed the same wall three hours later, the words had been washed off.

They called it a day. At nine-thirty, bathed and changed into evening clothes, for the Hotel Primario wasn't the place for informal diners, they met for a pre-dinner drink. Eddie told her he had written down all he could recall as notable in what people had said.

'Some are very disillusioned with the regime, some say

it's always been like this and always will be, some want a change but not as drastic as the guerrilla propaganda suggests.'

'Well, early days yet, Eddie. We can't expect to learn much in ten hours.'

Next day they started up again, this time going along the Malecon, the wide highway which ran parallel with the sea. The beaches, most of them belonging to the fine new hotels, were dotted with striped umbrellas and recumbent figures. More than half of the sun-lovers were tourists, but there were many Cubans too.

'My word, they are a handsome race!' Corie said, looking at the bronzed figures playing tag or splashing at the verge of the sea.

'You can say that again,' Eddie agreed, eyeing with pleasure a lovely girl in a scanty bikini who was wandering gracefully past.

The Cuban girls on the beach were of all skin shades – some creamy and fair, some a bronzed beige, some chocolate, some as dark as a rich walnut. They had all given a lot of thought to their appearance. These, of course, were the daughters of rich families or perhaps the mistresses of rich men, or show girls. But even among the poor women whom they'd seen on the previous day, personal appearance was very important – spotlessly clean clothes, a flower tucked into the hair.

The men were on the whole less tall than Europeans, but made up for it in masculine swagger. The rich men wore immaculate white or cream linen suits and panamas. The poor wore loose shirts called *gayaberos* and thin black trousers.

Both rich and poor were on the beach, but the poor were the waiters who brought iced drinks, the attendants who put up parasols and lounge chairs, who collected up discarded cigarette packets and chocolate wrappers. It was these whom Corie began to photograph as they hurried about their tasks. Eddie dropped into conversation, but the conversation never lasted long because there was always a beckoning hand from under the sunshade or a languid beauty wanting a drink.

That day they covered less ground and felt they had achieved little. The heat slowed them down. The winter temperature was somewhere in the high seventies, by no means unbearable, but the humidity made the air sluggish and it was hard to breathe.

When they returned to the hotel, rather earlier than on the previous day, each found a stack of messages in the pigeon hole from which the reception clerk took their keys.

'Good heavens, who *are* all these people?' Corie exclaimed as she leafed through the flimsies. 'They've left telephone numbers, asked me to ring back . . .'

'Me too. Karen Allison, Chris Leifheit, R.R. Waite, Castelmar, Binnie Lockhart . . . Do the names mean anything to you?'

'Not a thing. And mine seem to be almost a duplicate of yours.'

'Well, one thing's certain, I'm not going to return any of these calls until I've had a shower and a drink.'

'Right!'

'So let's say we meet in the bar when we're ready. First one there orders two whisky sours, OK?'

Corie changed into pale pink linen slacks and a checked silk shirt. The maid came with fresh towels as she was pinning up her hair on top of her head for coolness.

'Ah, *como hermosa la señorita!*' the girl said with a little sweeping gesture to indicate Corie's appearance.

'What's that?' Corie asked.

'Very pretty,' translated the maid.

Corie laughed and shook her head. '*You're* pretty,' she countered. And indeed the girl was lovely, her skin a gentle amber, her hair rich and lustrous, her eyes like pools of dark water in moonlight, typical of the *criollas* Corie had seen everywhere in the city.

'You think? My *novio*, he too think.'

'Who's that? Your husband? Boyfriend?'

The girl blushed, putting out her left hand to show a

cheap engagement ring. She pointed to it. 'Ernesto, my *novio*.' She pointed to herself. 'Mercedes.'

'I see. When are you to be married?'

'*El matrimonio*?' She held up her two hands, fingers spread wide. '*Quince*,' she said.

At a guess, Corie took this to mean a fortnight. She said, making another guess at the words, '*Buena fortuna*, Mercedes.'

'*Gracias, señorita*,' the girl said, and went out to distribute more clean towels.

When Corie got down to the shaded bar, Eddie was already seated at a table by the louvred window, drinking his whisky sour. At his gesture the waiter hurried over with a second, for Corie.

'You look nice,' Eddie said. 'I forgive you for taking so long.'

'I wasn't gawking at myself in the mirror, if that's what you mean. I was having an interesting conversation with the maid. She's getting married in two weeks' time.'

'Hot news,' he observed, sipping his drink.

'No, I was thinking – you ought to interview her. She's planning her future, isn't she? She must have a view about whether her life is going to be better if the government changes.'

'Might have. On the other hand, she's probably too busy thinking about her wedding dress.'

'Oh.' Corie laughed. She took from her handbag the sheaf of message slips. 'Are we going to do something about these?'

'I thought we'd ask the barman to bring us a telephone and—'

But he was spared the trouble, because at that moment an elderly man came into the bar. He was thick-set, tanned, and clearly not a Cubano. He came directly towards them. 'Miss Duggan? Mr Holstead?'

'Yes?' Eddie said, raising his eyebrows.

'I hope you don't think this is an intrusion. But you didn't return any of our calls so I thought I'd drop by, and they told me you were in the bar . . .' He held out his hand. 'R.R. Waites, of United Press.'

'How do you do?' murmured Corie, while Eddie said 'Please sit down.'

Mr Waite subsided into a chair, fanning himself with his panama. 'It'll get cooler soon,' he remarked. 'How are you finding things here?'

'Interesting,' Eddie said. 'Can I offer you a drink?'

'Oh sure, thanks, I'll have a *dulce de leche*. But really I should be offering *you* a drink. It's the custom to welcome newcomers.'

'How did you know we were here?' Eddie inquired with muted resentment for, although not exactly a secret, their trip was supposed to be confidential.

'Oh, nothing can remain unknown in Havana. The grapevine sees to that.'

'But I don't see why you should take so much interest, Mr Waite—'

'Call me R.R., everybody does. See, we're a close community here in Havana. The ABC – that stands for Americans, British and Canadians. It's kind of like an unofficial club. Whenever a new American arrives, we always put out a welcome mat. So the hotel let us know you were here, all the more because you're members of the press and the newsmen in Cuba stick together.'

He smiled knowingly at Corie and Eddie. He waited for a response.

'We're just here to do a picture feature,' Corie said.

'Yeah, my cameraman recognised your name like a shot. He's real keen to meet you, Miss Duggan. But he said you're famous on the whole for portraiture, not news photography.'

'This isn't a news project, it's a human-interest feature.'

'That why you've been interviewing the work force?'

Eddie exchanged a glance with Corie. 'When you said you had a grapevine, you weren't joking,' he said.

'No, in fact, it isn't a joke . . .' R.R.'s drink came, he took a grateful sip, then leaned towards them. 'The SIM have been taking an interest in you.'

'Who's the SIM?'

'Military Intelligence.'

Corie gave a gasp. Eddie flushed. 'What the devil's our visit got to do with Military Intelligence?'

'Everything in Cuba has to do with Military Intelligence,' R.R. replied. 'From what my source tells me, you're causing a certain uneasiness in higher circles.'

'But why?'

'Look, it'll be easier to put you straight if you come to dinner with me. We've got a kind of informal dinner club – different evenings we go to different houses or apartments. Tonight the party's at Karen Allison's. She told me to invite you along.'

'On such short notice?'

'Oh, it's open house for anyone working for the press. Drink up and I'll take you.'

There seemed more reason to accept than to refuse, so they obediently finished their drinks and went out with him to his car. As they went through the lobby he said, 'Just being with me will allay anxiety about you. What's been bothering Colonel Armadias is that you've been hoofing it around Havana on your own, which to him means you're spying on something or other.'

'What absolute nonsense—'

'Not in Cuba,' R.R. said.

He drove them out to the suburb of Miramar, where he drew up in front of a fine old Spanish Colonial house. 'Who lives here?' Corie asked in surprise.

'Karen Allison, the doyenne of the press corps. She's lived in Havana for over twenty years, was married to an engineer who ran the machinery on the Centrales Sugar Estate, educated her two kids at local schools. A personal friend of President Batistá . . . so far as President Batistá can be said to have any friends,' he ended in irony.

An elderly manservant opened the door to them. They could hear laughter and conversation from a room towards the back. R.R. led them on into a big room with glass doors opening into a paved garden surrounded by banyan trees.

'Karen? Here they are.'

A tall grey-haired woman turned to greet them. 'Good evening. So glad you could come. I'm Karen Allison, but you must call me Karen, that's the custom with us. And you're Corie and this is Eddie – just make yourselves at home. Drinks are on that table, and the food will come in about an hour.'

Others clustered round to offer their names and shake hands. Most of those present were men, but there was one other woman who introduced herself as Binnie Lockhart. 'I'm from Reuters,' she said in a rich Scots accent. 'Comparative new girl, compared with most of the people here. So, how do you like Havana?'

'Very Americanised,' Corie said.

'Is it?' Eddie asked in surprise.

'You hadn't noticed? Maryland chicken and pie à la mode in the hotel dining-room, more Cadillacs than I've seen even in New York, and the only ice-cream available at the beach stalls is Howard Johnson's! Yes, I think it is Americanised.'

After a while Karen came up to them again, frowning at Eddie through big horn-rimmed glasses. 'I've just had a thought,' she said. 'Holstead? Are you any relation to the textile family?'

Eddie move uncomfortably. 'I suppose you could say so.'

'We did an interview with Helen Pittsworth Holstead last year,' R.R. put in. 'Is she a relative?'

'We-ell . . . She's my mother.'

There was an outburst of laughter. Karen Allison said, 'That certainly is being related to the Holsteads. So what are you doing in Havana?'

'That's right,' R.R. put in, 'you're supposed to be taking a degree at Yale.'

'So I am, only this is a little side trip.'

'But why?' Binnie Lockhart insisted. 'Are you going to take up journalism when you leave university?'

'No, I . . . er . . .'

'It's quite simple,' Corie said, seeing there was no help for it. 'Mrs Holstead wasn't satisfied with the information that's coming out of Cuba about the trouble with the dissident groups, so she sent us to get a first-hand look—'

'There! You see?' cried one of the pressmen. 'I keep telling my editor the readership isn't a bunch of morons! But will he print the stories I send?'

'And that's when you can get to send them,' put in Binnie. She turned to Corie and Eddie. 'We're under censorship here, you know. If we write up a story that *el Presidente* doesn't like, he tries to suppress it. And if it does get out to our home office he makes sure the newspapers don't get distributed in Cuba. He just doesn't want the Cuban population to know what's really going on.'

'But what is really going on?' Corie put in. 'We've only been here two days, but so far we haven't come across anybody who wants a change in the government—'

'Oh, it's no use asking the city people.'

'Havana doesn't want a change—'

'No, it might frighten off the tourists.'

'You can't judge Cuba by Havana, Corie.'

'Hush, now hush,' begged Karen. 'You'll bewilder them. First of all, Eddie, why does your mother take such an interest in Cuba?'

He went slightly red. 'She's got a lot of money tied up here.'

'Ah.' Karen's guests looked at one another. 'In that case, I'd advise her to take it out and put it somewhere else,' Karen said, 'because there's trouble looming.'

'But in the newspapers back home they keep on saying President Batistá has it all under control—'

'Simply because they don't want to frighten investors, of course. And the US government is shoring up Batistá because so much US money is invested here in sugar, real estate, fruit exports . . .'

'It would make a lot more sense if they were to back Castro,' someone said. 'Almost anything would be better than this bunch of brigands.'

'Talk sense, Arnulf, the US thinks Castro is a Communist—'

'He's no more a Communist than I am,' Binnie said angrily.

'But he's a good deal to the left of Batistá. The State Department is scared of anybody left of Winston Churchill, it seems to me. So they'll go on backing Batistá—'

'They're making a big mistake. Whether Castro comes down from the Sierra Maestra and chases him out, or whether one of the little dissident groups in the university takes a pot shot at him, in the end Batistá's days are numbered.'

'So what?' R.R. said with cynicism. 'Some other tinpot dictator will take over and run it to line his pockets. I agree Batistá's in trouble, but it doesn't necessarily mean there'll be any real change.'

The food was brought by two servants and set on a long table indoors. By now the mosquitos were beginning to make a nuisance of themselves. The gathering drifted indoors, to help themselves to salads and seafood and cold meats.

Corie listened intently to the conversation. The press corps were almost entirely against the present government of Cuba, but were divided on what ought to take its place. One thing became clear to her. It was no use chatting with the ordinary people of the city of Havana. Everyone agreed that the protest movement had its roots among the rural population.

'If you want to talk to some of the country folk, why don't you come along the day after tomorrow?' Karen invited.

'What's happening then?'

'The government's laid on a press trip to Oriente Province. This is to prove to us that everything is completely peaceful—'

'Oh yes, completely peaceful!' echoed Chris Leifheit with his booming laugh. 'Communiqués keep announcing that government troops have stormed another rebel stronghold and killed all the defenders. But if the situation is completely peaceful in the first place, how come there's all these rebel strongholds to storm?'

'Well, it *will* be completely peaceful where we're going,' Karen insisted, 'because it's on the Juvero sugar estate, and you can bet your bottom dollar no guerillas ever got a foothold on Juvero land.'

'Shall we go?' murmured Eddie in Corie's ear.

'Oh, of course – it's a great chance to get some first-hand information.'

But it proved to be nothing of the kind. They reported as instructed at seven a.m. to Jose Marti airport, where a private plane belonging to the sugar estate was waiting to take the press party to its own landing field. They flew over miles and miles of level country, all of it a bright featureless green – sugar cane, they were told. Where they touched down there was a factory for turning sugar into molasses, but this wasn't in operation because the cane wasn't ready to cut until January.

There was a village nearby, with vegetable gardens and a few pigs rooting about. Women were at work among the plants, or doing the washing in the open air in a tin tub. Few men were to be seen, except some soldiers lounging at a crossroads.

Immediately around the factory were various outbuildings. It was to one of these that the press party were led. This turned out to be a kind of club house or community centre, funded by the estate. As they approached Corie could hear the sound of music – a local band? But no, when they were ushered in, the sound proved to be from a radio tuned to one of the commercial stations which broadcast Cuban music.

Dancing to the music were about six elderly couples. They were rigged out in their best clothes – print dresses with flounced skirts for the women, sparkling white starched cotton trousers and shirts for the men. The odd thing was that they didn't seem to be the least bit pleased to be having a party. They seemed, on the contrary, quite glum while their feet moved in the simple two-sidestep of the country dance.

'As the song says, "Ain't we got fun?"' remarked Karen Allison, making a quick entry in her notebook.

'You see how we give the workers every amenity,' said their escort from the sugar company. 'This party is to celebrate the silver wedding of Julio.' He nodded and called. 'Julio!'

One of the men detached himself from his partner. He came towards them. '*Buenas dias*,' he said, bowing.

Those of the party who could speak Spanish began an interview. Corie contented herself with taking pictures – of the couples dancing to the music but with their eyes on Julio talking with the strangers, of the sandwiches laid out on the table under attack from flies, of the opened rum bottles, of the sad little coloured-paper streamers tacked to the wooden walls of the hut.

'What do they say?' she asked Eddie when she rejoined the group.

'Oh, they say they love working for the Juvero Company, that the management looks after them beautifully, and that they have no problems.'

'You surprise me,' Corie said. 'Did you ask about Castro?'

'Chris tried, but Julio froze solid at the name. Señor Domaldo says thay have no interest in politics, know nothing about the rebels in the Sierra Maestra.'

'So where are all the men of the village?' asked Corie. 'As we walked from the airfield I counted about a dozen women and three old men, and there are six or seven more elderly men here – where are the youngsters?'

She had addressed this question to Señor Domaldo, who looked vexed for a moment then smiled. 'Of course, when the sugar is not being harvested or processed, there's no work here for the young men. So they go to Santiago de Cuba or Havana to work. But they always come back to us when the season starts,' he ended in some triumph. 'They are faithful.'

They were shown around the factory, which was largely

silent for the moment. Corie, who had had plenty of commercial assignments, surprised everyone by taking pictures of the machinery. Señor Domaldo was pleased. 'Everything modern and of the best kind,' he pointed out. 'Juvero invests heavily in its machinery.'

'Couldn't you invest a little in making that club house a bit brighter?' she asked.

'Brighter? But why? It's hardly ever—' Domaldo broke off. Corie was almost certain he'd been going to say, 'It's hardly ever used.'

They were given a fine lunch in the manager's suite at the factory. There were the usual hand-outs — brochures about the company's financial soundness, signed photographs of the directors; a box of Havana cigars for the men and, for the ladies, a cube of cardboard containing a swan made of spun sugar.

They trooped out into the late afternoon sunshine. Corie, at the back of the party, heard a shout of laughter. When she got to the front and stood on the steps of the office block, she understood why. While they'd been having lunch, someone had been up on the roof of the building and had replaced the company flag with the rebel black and red.

Domaldo was furious, stamping about, ordering people hither and thither. The soldiers from the crossroads ran up to start a search of the out-buildings. In the commotion Corie took several shots — the flag flapping in a fitful breeze, the manager stamping his foot in fury, the soldiers scurrying about like startled chickens.

'So there's no support for the rebels in this area?' Karen remarked on the homeward flight. 'Tell it to the Marines.'

Eddie telephoned his mother that evening. He told her that, although he couldn't speak with certainty, there certainly seemed to be something going on in the countryside of Cuba which had not been correctly reported abroad. Whether it meant the Batistá government would fall, he had no way of knowing.

'Mother says to keep at it,' he reported to Corie. 'Do you feel up to more of the same?'

'Why not?' she cried. She was enjoying herself. Her camera had never given her so much pleasure. Everything she saw interested and stimulated her.

At the beginning of December the hotel maid, Mercedes, timidly invited Corie to her wedding. A friendship had sprung up between them as they chatted when Mercedes made her evening rounds of the bedrooms. 'I know it is presumptuous, señorita, but you have seemed so interested . . .'

'I'd love to come, Mercedes!'

'Truly? Then it is at the Church of the Holy Mother, in Calle Persepe, at four in the afternoon next Saturday.'

'I'll be there, my dear. Thank you for asking me.' She paused, thinking of what to wear and of wedding presents. The second thought brought her an idea. 'Mercedes, you know I'm a professional photographer?'

'Of course, señorita.'

'Would you like me to take your wedding photos?'

'Oh, señorita, we couldn't possibly afford—'

'No, no, as a present.'

Mercedes stared at her, lips parted, eyes aglow. 'You would do this?'

'I'd be glad to. You'd like colour, of course.'

'Yes, if you please . . . But it is so much . . .'

'Not at all, leave it all to me.'

It was an extraordinary afternoon. To Corie's surprise, the priest made no objections to her taking pictures during the actual ceremony – in fact, he seemed over-awed that an *Americana* should be in his church at all. Outside, in the bright hot sunshine, she took dozens of shots of the bride and groom, the in-laws, the two little bridesmaids and two little bridesmen all in wedding finery, the hired Cadillac that came to take the newly-weds from the church, and the ramshackle cars into which the others piled.

Corie was taken in charge by the bride's mother. She hadn't intended to go to the wedding party, but found it was obligatory. Señora Barrera talked at her non-stop in incomprehensible Spanish while holding her firmly by the elbow.

They decanted from the twenty-year-old Chevy in front of a fairly large one-storey wooden house on the outskirts of Havana. The wedding feast was laid out in all the rooms, including two which were clearly bedrooms. There was plenty to drink, and a horde of guests had already been celebrating.

Corie accepted a plate of rice and black beans with some shreds of pork among it. She was offered the sweet Cuban wine but opted for pineapple juice – tinned juice: strange to say no fresh juice could be obtained in Cuba except in the best hotels.

Extraordinarily enough, the bride and groom didn't appear. The wedding cake was ready to be cut, but nothing could happen until Mercedes and Ernesto turned up.

'Where are they?' Corie ventured, half-expecting some bawdy reply.

'They've gone to have their fortune told.'

'I beg your pardon?' she said, thinking she'd mistaken the words spoken in rapid but broken English.

'Gone to consult the *orishas*. It's the custom with Ernesto's family.'

'I'm sorry, I don't understand.'

She'd been speaking to a pleasant, fat old lady who seemed to be Mercedes' Aunt Gabriela. She now beckoned another lady, better dressed than herself, and whose skin was a shade or two nearer to chocolate. 'Maria, come and tell the *Americana* about the *orishas*.'

Looking none too pleased, the other approached. 'This is Ernesto's Aunt Maria. She goes to the *cabildo*, she can tell you about it,' said Gabriela.

She waited expectantly. Aunt Maria said with a shrug, 'The *cabildo* is our church. Ernesto has taken Mercedes to ask Odudua if their marriage will be happy and to ask for Odudua's blessing.'

'Odudua? I'm sorry, I don't think I know . . . ?'

'Odudua is Our Lady – that's right, isn't it, Maria?'

Aunt Maria grunted in reply. Clearly she didn't want to talk about it to a stranger.

'You like to make a secret,' said Aunt Gabriela, with a wink at Corie, 'but it's all African mumbo-jumbo.'

'It's not mumbo-jumbo!' cried the other, stung into speech as Gabriela had intended. 'Odudua is Our lady and Ogun is John the Baptist, revealed to our forefathers under those names—'

'Yes, and brought long ago from the Congo or wherever it was. Funny place to find the Virgin Mary, if you ask me . . .'

'Show respect!' cried Maria. 'Our family has done well under the hand of Odudua.' A toss of the head seemed to indicate her superior appearance, her gold earrings. 'The President himself belongs to Ernesto's church.'

'The *President*? President Batistá?' Corie said, astounded.

'Oh yes. Didn't you know?' rejoined Gabriela in a softer tone. 'He's a man of the people, you see, descended from mixed blood – he's just like one of us, really. Maria's right, I shouldn't make fun.'

The two women, reconciled, now went off in search of another drink. By and by, the bride and groom appeared amid cheers and shouts of good wishes. They drank some punch, ate some food, and the cake was cut and distributed.

Corie's camera was at work almost non-stop. Presently Ernesto came to her carrying a glass of wine. 'Special toast,' he said, 'in French wine. To you, for being so kind to us.'

'Oh, thank you, Ernesto.' She sipped the wine, which turned out to be Chablis, too warm. 'Did you get good omens from the priest?'

He was startled. 'You know about that?'

'Aunt Gabriela told me. I'm very interested. Have you always belonged to this special church?'

'Of course,' he said in a tone of great seriousness. 'It is my family church. Mercedes now also belongs. And our children, when they come.'

'Does your church have services, like the Catholic and Protestant? What happens?'

'Oh . . . there are songs and dances . . . drums . . . Sometimes sacrifices . . .' He let the words die away.

'I'm sorry, perhaps I shouldn't ask. But your Aunt Maria mentioned that the President is a member so of course I took notice—'

'She told you that?' He considered, and seemed to decide she was a fit person to speak to. 'Our religion is called "*Santeria*" which means "the cult of the saints". It is really a form of the Catholic religion but – ' he hesitated – 'adapted to suit the needs of those of us with African traditions. It is true, our honourable President is a member and patron of the sect I belong to. Only last month, he gave money for a great celebration in Guanabacoa – that is what you call the headquarters of our church, it's a town on the north coast . . .'

'Did you go?' Corie asked as he paused, picturing the great ceremony.

'Alas, no, I wasn't able to get time off from my work,' he said with longing in his voice. 'I work for the electricity company and there was trouble with the generator that weekend. But I hear it was a very great event.'

'Perhaps there will be another,' Corie said, touched.

'It is likely. The President is seeking omens about the future.'

Mercedes came up to claim her husband. 'You have been so busy, señorita,' she said to Corie. 'I see you everywhere, snap-snap, you take no time to eat and drink. Please come and sit down, I've put a piece of cake ready for you.'

Corie allowed herself to be shepherded out into the tangled back garden. Night had fallen, lamps and candles were dotted about on rickety tables, moths fluttered in the light, groups of people were singing to the beat of maracas and the thrum of a guitar. There was dancing, the couples shadowy among the uncared-for bushes.

The wedding cake was very sweet and sticky. Corie took a bite or two, washed it down with the remains of the Chablis. A strange mixture. She toasted the couple in the last mouthful of the wine.

'Long life and good fortune,' she said.

'Ah, we shall have good fortune; the priest looked into the

future for us,' Mercedes cried happily.

'How does he do that?' Corie inquired. 'Does he have a crystal? Does he read your palms?'

'A *nango* would never do that,' Ernesto said with scorn.

'If you want to see,' Mercedes took it up, 'you should come to the Christmas Eve service—'

'Mercedes!'

She broke off at the rebuke in her husband's voice. But she was too high on happiness and wine to pay much heed. 'Shouldn't I have said that? I thought I could speak of it now, *mi amor*, now that I'm married to a devotee of Odudua.'

It was clear to Corie that he couldn't be cross with her, he was too much in love. '*Querida*, these are sacred things, but you meant no harm.' To Corie he said, 'It is true, there is a special service on Christmas Eve, and this one is to be here in Havana.'

'And I shall go to it,' Mercedes put in, 'and so will the President! Isn't that strange, that I should be in the same room with the President of Cuba?'

'Could I come?' Corie asked.

She held her breath.

'No-o . . .'

'Oh, let's take her with us, Ernesto! White Cubanos come, you told me so yourself. Why shouldn't Señorita Corie come?'

'It's a matter of respect—'

'But Señorita Corie is respectful – you are respectful, señorita, aren't you?'

'I'm respectful to all religions,' Corie said, although, until that moment, she'd never given the matter much thought. 'And I'm very much interested.'

'Say we can take her,' Mercedes coaxed. It wasn't that she particularly cared about Corie's wish to attend. It was that she wanted to show off Ernesto's affection for her.

After a long pause he said, 'Very well. But please, señorita – not the cameras.'

The approach of Christmas in Havana was the chance for

lavish display. Christmas trees, yet another idea adopted from the Americans, were everywhere, and more beautifully decorated than any Corie had ever seen. There were parties in every home, the hotels laid on exuberant balls and dinner-dances, the casinos had special Christmas shows advertised as 'with Blonde Showgirls!'

Corie and Eddie were out of Havana on several days, sometimes driving in a hired car to towns such as Santa Clara or Viñales. In Santa Clara there were signs of sabotage by the rebel groups but, in the west, in Viñales, everything was completely normal.

On Christmas Eve Corie was picked up outside the Hotel Primario by Ernesto and Mercedes and two of his male relatives. They drove in a very old jeep out of Varadero and to the south, into the flat countryside. Sugar cane and tobacco grew here; the cane was now almost ready for cutting. The rapid Cuban dusk fell, the landscape faded; it would have been almost pitch dark except for the brilliance of the stars.

It seemed a lengthy drive. They drew up before a long, low, black shape, a building scarcely more than a shed. Already there was the throb of drums from within.

'Now, Señorita Corie,' Ernesto said, 'you must be very respectful, and you must cover your head.' He produced a cotton bandana. 'A woman may not have her hair uncovered unless she dances.'

'I understand,' she said, tying the bandana round her head.

'Some things may surprise you. The followers of Odudua are often inspired.'

It was easy to see that he wished he hadn't brought her. He would have backed out of his promise to Mercedes if he could. But Corie had had all the wedding film developed and printed, and out of the batch she'd enlarged two beautiful studies: one, a traditional photograph of the bride and groom on the church steps; the other of the pair kneeling devoutly at the altar.

He felt indebted to her. That was why she was here. But

he was afraid she would embarrass him somehow.

She could guess that the service she was about to witness wouldn't be anything like the staid occasions when she'd accompanied Monna to St James's, Bayswater Road. She touched Ernesto's hand in reassurance, and followed him into the building.

There was a small outer room where raincoats and outer shoes had been left, for the night was intermittently rainy. Then there was a curtained doorway, from behind which the noise of the drums rolled out like a throbbing pulse.

Ernesto moved the curtain aside just enough to let them enter. The sound of the drums hit Corie's ears like pounding surf. The heat surged at her body as strongly as if an oven door had been opened.

The lighting was from candles, but there were many of them. The room was about thirty feet long and perhaps twenty wide. The walls were covered in strange decorations – figurines decked out in ribbons and paper flowers, frames with altars on which lay little boxes, cosmetics, mirrors and combs.

At the far end stood a table with a statuette of a woman. The statuette was swathed in brightly coloured cloth. In front of it on the table were heaps of pesetas, a ring or two, a string of pearls.

People of all kinds stood around the walls. There were all shades of skin colour and even, as Mercedes had hinted, several white Cubanos. All of them were moving to the rhythm of the drums, some merely swaying, some shifting from foot to foot.

The centre of the room was left almost clear. On the floor of beaten earth, white feathers were scattered. There were patches of blood. Clearly a sacrifice had taken place. A man was circling the area, in his hands a bunch of white feathers tipped with red. He shook the handful, sometimes directly into the face of one of the onlookers. Some drew back, others gazed straight past the bloodied feathers at the priest.

The priest was bare-chested, wearing loose black trousers belted at the waist with a sash of dark red satin, heavily embroidered in gold and silver. On his head he wore a crown of gilt in which palm fronds had been set. As he circled and swayed, the palm leaves swayed, as if a tree moved in the room. It was hypnotic.

Corie stood at the back of the row of watchers. She felt the power of the drumbeat, found herself moving to its rhythm. Mercedes stood beside her, almost dancing, her eyes wide in wonder at what she saw. Ernesto and his men friends had disappeared.

Some moments later the drums rolled to a crescendo, the priest gave a cry and fell to a crouch in the centre. Six men in loose white robes came into the open area and began to sing. Their voices rose and fell in harmony. It was almost Cuban, yet there was more of Africa than of Spain in their song.

The priest began to speak as they sang. His speech quickened, became a tirade, as if a dozen voices were trying to make themselves heard through him. He threw up his arms and shouted. The singers ceased. Then the priest, alone, began to chant. Everyone listened, intent.

'What's he singing?' Corie whispered to Mercedes.

'He's prophesying. A great storm is coming. Clouds fly across our skies . . .' Mercedes looked troubled, listened and ceased to translate.

Now the drums began again, and now members of the congregation began to move out on to the dance floor. They swayed and circled, but these weren't the simple steps of the country dance on the sugar estate, nor the sinuous *paso doble* of the wedding party. This was serious, ruled by the pounding of the drums, and as the noise increased the dancers became entranced. They danced wildly, throwing themselves into the air, spinning like tops. The women who danced had let their hair loose. It flew about their heads like a thousand snakes.

Some fell to the ground in a faint. They were gently lifted by white-robed men and carried to the shelter of the altar, where they lay as if asleep. Corie noticed that one of these white-clad attendants was Ernesto.

Some dancers suddenly stood rigid and began to speak in a babble. Friends crouched in front of them, looking up, listening eagerly. 'Do they understand what's being said?' Corie asked Mercedes.

'Ernesto says that sometimes they speak great truths. They must always be listened to.'

The drums began to decrease both in tempo and volume. In a moment all was normal, the drummers leaning back to laugh and receive congratulations. Some drank eagerly from bottles brought to them by attendants.

A small, very dark woman stepped to the centre of the floor. She wore a black flounced skirt, a white blouse, and over this a long tunic of red and gold striped cotton. Her feet were bare, her wiry hair hung down her back. She carried a long white stick.

At once the room became silent. The woman closed her eyes, folded her hands around the staff, and began to pray. All heads bent in reverence. Corie caught occasional words: *'Maria Santisima'* and *'perdon'*. Mercedes whispered, 'She's praying to Lady Odudua.'

Ernesto, still in his white robe, rejoined them. His dark face above the white looked exalted. 'I didn't realise you were a church elder,' Corie remarked softly.

'We take it in turns to help the priest. I shall not have the honour again for six months. But to be an attendant at the *Nochebuena* brings much luck.'

The priestess ended her prayers. Now she turned, looking expectantly towards the congregation. From it stepped a short, square, plump man in a white *gayabero* and black trousers. Like the priestess, he was barefoot.

Ernesto bent his head towards Corie. 'Our President is with us tonight,' he murmured.

Batistá! Corie had glimpsed him at public events in grandiose uniforms of pale blue or tan, weighed down with orders and medals. She'd also seen him enter the Havana Riviera for a grand dinner, in white tie and tails and patent-leather shoes.

This seemed another man. His yellowish-brown face was

pale, his narrow black eyes were almost closed. He was carrying in his arms a cockerel, a fine bird, its feathers golden-brown, its coxcomb a brilliant red against his white shirt.

He came slowly across the beaten earth floor to face the priestess. She asked him a question, he bowed his head and said, '*Si, ama respeta.*'

She pointed to the floor. He knelt, putting the cock down between them.

With a dramatic gesture the priestess brought from a pocket in her skirt a long-bladed knife. She held it above her head. It glinted in the flickering candle-flames. She gave a cry of salutation, a cry that summoned the goddess.

As the knife flashed downwards, Corie guessed what was happening and turned her head away. There was a sudden cry from the cock, a flurry of struggle, then silence.

All the congregation gave a sighing sound. It was like the wind in the palm trees.

When Corie looked again, the priestess was daubing blood on the shirt of the kneeling man. He held out his hands, palms up. On these she placed her own bloodstained hands. Then slowly she knelt so that they were face to face.

She whispered something to him. They both looked down at the body of the sacrificed cock. She began to speak to Batistá, softly, so that no one else could hear. The congregation began to croon in unison: '*Odudua, madre poderosa, señora de vital y muerte . . .*'

How long a time went by, Corie couldn't have said. At last the priestess rose stiffly to her feet, nodded firmly at Batistá as if to say, 'That is all I have to say' and raised her arms towards the ceiling. '*Gracias, Odudua, por vuestro favor*', she called out. The congregation echoed her words.

Corie's eyes were on the President. He too rose to his feet. His glance was still downcast on the body of the cockerel. He stood for a long moment looking down at it. Then his gaze lifted.

On his face Corie read despair. Then next moment it had

gone and he was walking in among the other supplicants, soon lost to her view.

The evening wore on. Others came to ask the priestess for prophecies, but none had such a magnificent gift for Odudua as a cockerel. Some offered sweets, some lengths of cloth or garments fresh in their wrappings, some held out envelopes clearly containing money. The priestess laid the offering on the earth, made the inquirer kneel, whispered to him or to her what the goddess had told her in gratitude for the gift.

Some looked pleased, some anxious. Not one was as stricken as Fulgencio Batistá.

In the early hours of the morning, Ernesto drove Corie back to her hotel. She was so tired she could hardly walk to the lift. She fell into bed, slept as if she were drugged.

When, about ten-thirty next morning, she joined Eddie for the Christmas Day breakfast, he asked her if she'd enjoyed last night. She had told him she would be going to a religious service, and he'd taken it for granted it had been at the Protestant Church. He himself had been to a dance with one of the Cuban beauties he so much admired.

They had presents for each other – Eddie gave her a special colour filter for one of her cameras; in return he received a very gaudy beach shirt. They dawdled over their coffee. There was nothing urgent to do today, Havana was on holiday for Christmas. But they had a lunch engagement with Karen Allison and some of her friends.

'You're kind of quiet,' Eddie said. 'Tired after midnight service?'

She shook her head. 'Eddie, I've something important to say to you. You should telephone your mother and tell her to move her funds out of Cuba.'

'What makes you say that?' he asked, immediately alert. 'Somebody give you a political tip-off?'

'No, but President Batistá doesn't think he's going to win this struggle.'

'How can you possibly know that?'

'He consulted a priestess of the *Santeria* cult last

night and she gave him bad news.'

Eddie grinned. 'Oh yeah, and I'm Billy Graham.'

'I mean it, Eddie. He doesn't believe he can stay in power any longer. He's been told his reign is at an end.'

He was irritated. 'What is this? You been at the rum or what? Even if this story about consulting a fortune-teller is true, why should he believe it?'

'He believed it,' Corie said with conviction. 'I saw his face.'

'You saw him?'

She told him about the *Santeria* service. He whistled beneath his breath. 'That was a rash thing to do, wasn't it? It might have got quite violent—'

'It was just a religious service, Eddie. Strange, quite different, but the people there were concentrating on their faith, not on violence or anything else.'

'And Batistá got bad news?'

'It shattered him.'

'But so what? It won't come true. After all, there's really nothing in this fortune-telling business.'

'But that's not what matters. Batistá believes it. When I saw him get up and walk away, he was a man who'd accepted failure.'

'Look, I can't call Mother and tell her a story like that—'

'If you don't, I will,' she said. 'I think it's important, Eddie.'

He protested and grumbled, but in the end he made the call. They went out to their lunch party.

There the talk was all about news which had just come through of a strong attack by an alliance of rebel forces in Las Villas province. Las Villas included Santa Clara, one of the towns Eddie and Corie had visited – not far off compared with where the revolt had started, seven hundred miles away in the Sierre Maestra.

It was said the President tried to send reinforcements in armoured trains, but the first train had been wrecked on a burning bridge at Santo Domingo, so that further reinforcements couldn't get through.

'All the clubs have cancelled their big Christmas parties,' Karen said. 'A lot of the rich Cubans have hurried away to their country estates because they expect trouble here in the city. The grapevine says the guerrillas are about thirty miles out.'

'Should we be doing anything?' R.R. Waite wondered.

'What, exactly?'

'Well, anyone who's not actually needed could catch a plane and fly out.'

'You try it,' Karen said. 'Jose Marti airport is like a madhouse.'

The tension in the city was almost palpable during the next few days. From the point of view of the government, the news went from bad to worse. The general in command in Oriente Province, the region where the rebels were strongest, flew to Havana to tell his President that they were demanding the surrender of its main city, Santiago de Cuba.

What was more, it was said that the government troops were refusing to defend the town. It was only a matter of time before the rebel army took it and then marched on Havana.

On New Year's Eve, a significant fact became known. President Batistá was not giving his traditional New Year party at the big main barracks, Camp Columbia, just outside Havana.

'Things must be going super-badly,' remarked Chris Leifheit. 'If there's one thing Batistá always loved, it's the New Year party where everybody gives him expensive presents.'

'What should we do?' asked Karen Allison.

In former years the press corps had always shown up at the party with a gift paid for by their combined news services. This year, as usual, they had bought a gift – a gold pen-and-pencil set for his desk.

'Well, I'm not leaving my office,' R.R. said. 'Something might come in on the teletype or by radio – I don't want to be hanging about at Camp Columbia.'

'Somebody ought to go,' said Karen. 'Suppose all this hoo-ha dies down and things go back to the status quo – how's it going to look if we didn't give him his New Year's present?'

'I don't mind going,' Corie said. 'I haven't got a teletype machine to watch.'

'Neither you have,' Karen agreed.

'That's not a bad idea,' R.R. said.

After some discussion it was agreed that Corie and Eddie should go to Camp Columbia with a New Year card bearing the signatures of all the members of the press corps, together with the velvet-lined box in which lay the pen-and-pencil set.

At ten o'clock on New Year's Eve, 1958, they set off in their hired car for the camp. The word camp implies something temporary, but Camp Columbia was one of the most impressive collections of buildings in or near Havana. It had been constructed to show Batistá's pride in his army. It had modern quarters for both officers and men, excellent restaurants, a swimming pool, a dance hall, a conference hall, a training college, a weapons range, and a runway for military planes.

The intention was to arrive not long before midnight and to present the gift as soon after the chimes of New Year as they could. But the journey proved much more difficult than they could ever have imagined. Troops were being moved both in and out of the barracks, staff cars were dashing about. The military police kept bringing everything to a standstill while important staff officers went rushing by.

'It must be a council of war,' Eddie said. 'Maybe they're planning a counter-offensive in Las Villas?'

'Maybe we should turn around and go back,' Corie suggested.

But it was impossible to turn around. They were jammed in a convoy of traffic which held them fast.

Slowly they drove on, headlights picking up the tail-lights of the vehicle in front. At almost midnight they reached the gates and sentry-posts of the camp. Here military police made them get out while the car was searched. Their press cards were carefully examined. The parcel, gift-wrapped, was torn apart and the gold pen and pencil scrutinised before they were waved on.

At the entrance to the officers' compound, within which the President's quarters lay, they were told that the President was seeing no one that evening except his junior officers.

'No party?' inquired Eddie.

The sentries took that as a joke. They waved them away.

'Well, we have to go back after all,' Eddie sighed. 'At least we can tell the others that the President and his officers are still planning to fight the rebels. So much for your soothsayer's prophecy, Corie.'

There were several roadways within the barrack's perimeter by which they could return to the main gate and the road back to Havana. In an effort to avoid the traffic congestion of their inward drive, Eddie took a route around the perimeter of the officers' compound. This took them along the wire-mesh fence that bounded the airstrip.

As they were driving along, lights came on in the airfield.

'Look!' said Corie.

Eddie pulled up. They sat looking at the lights.

'That's a runway,' Eddie said.

'And there's a plane warming up.' They could hear the rumble of engines as they sat. 'Several planes.'

Corie opened the car door and got out. At the wire fence she stopped, leaning against it and staring at the airfield. To the right, double doors opened, light streamed out.

Several men came hurrying out carrying boxes. There was the gleam of polished leather belts, cap peaks.

'Military setting out for duties in Oriente Province?' wondered Eddie.

Corie unslung her camera bag. She'd brought her cameras in hopes of getting a shot of Fulgencio Batistá receiving his New Year present.

She got out her camera with the telephoto lens. She

squinted through it. At once the men coming and going at the wide doorway became clear to her.

'They're not particularly senior officers,' she said. 'Would junior officers be sent by special plane?'

Then a feathered hat went past. Corie gasped, drew back in disbelief, then looked again through the lens.

A woman! A woman in a fur coat and a feathered hat! At the moment she went past Corie's line of vision, her face was clear in the light from the doors.

She was in a state of panic.

What was more, she was the wife of Fulgencio Batistá.

'Eddie!' she cried. 'It's the President's family! They're getting out!'

'Getting out? What does that mean—?'

'They're running!'

'Oh, Corie, don't be silly!'

'I tell you, they're going — look for yourself!'

He took the camera, looked through the lens. Corie heard him give a gasp. 'What?' she asked.

'That's Batistá's son! Corie, I think you're right, they're pulling out!'

She grabbed back the camera. She focused on the doorway and, as each person came out, she clicked the shutter.

Among the last to emerge was a little square, plump figure in a lounge suit and trilby hat. He scurried out of the building clutching a briefcase to his chest. His features were contorted in a mask of fear and bitterness.

Corie Duggan was the only person in Cuba to get a picture of the President of the country fleeing for his life on the morning of 1 January 1959.

Chapter Fifteen

The drive back to the hotel was just as bad as the outward run. But this time, instead of viewing the activity as a sign of a future offensive, they saw it as the running-about of a headless chicken. No one knew what was really going on, that was clear. The President's departure hadn't yet been made known to his troops.

When, at about four in the morning, they drew up at the Primario, Eddie rushed inside to telephone New York State – if the phone system was still in action. Corie took over the wheel. She drove at once to Karen Allison's office, where she knew a twenty-four-hour news-watch had been in force since the fighting in Las Villas province.

She ran up the stairs and into the brightly lit office, panting. 'The government's giving in,' she gasped out.

'We know,' said Karen from behind one of the little cheroots she favoured.

'You know?'

Karen nodded to her assistant, who was sitting with earphones at a radio. 'We've been tuned in to the short-wave military broadcasts. The government hasn't been telling the truth about the rebels' position for weeks.'

'Did you know that Batistá's gone?'

'In what way, gone?'

'He boarded a plane at Camp Columbia airfield at about one a.m.'

'You know that for sure?'

'I've got pictures to prove it,' Corie cried, holding up her camera.

'My *God*!' Karen crowed. She dived at the telephone. It was still working. She asked for a number, was put through, and said in excitement, 'Billy, get your body round here this minute! Somebody's got pix of Batistá boarding a plane to fly out . . . Yes, this morning . . . Come on, Bill, we need your darkroom . . . Billy, this is the beat of the decade, get round here and develop this film for us.'

When she'd hung up Karen swung round to her assistant. 'Anything about Batistá?' When she shook her head she went on: 'They're keeping it quiet until General Zamora can announce he's taken over. If he succeeds, it means more of the same but under a different president.'

Billy arrived, a fat young man whom Corie had seen at gatherings in one house or another. He took the film roll eagerly. 'If this is what you say it is, Corie, you're up for the Pulitzer!' He promised to have prints by later that day.

Corie drove back to the Primario. The streets were silent, although it was now six o'clock and time for the city to be stirring. Still, this was New Year's Day – even transport workers and cleaning staff might be expected to be late to work.

Eddie had got through to his mother. 'She says we're to pack up and come home at once. She seems to think the city will go up in flames, though I told her it wasn't likely.'

'How can we go home? The airport is jammed up already, and when news gets out—'

'That's what I said, but she took it in her stride. She's sending a boat.'

'A boat!'

'Yeah, she'll get someone in Miami to hire a cabin cruiser and run it out here to collect us. She says the boat captain will collect us, all we have to do is wait.'

'We'll see,' said Corie with some scepticism.

And it seemed she was justified, because when after a few hours' sleep she went downstairs, it was to find the hotel strangely silent.

'Fidel Castro's called for a general strike and everybody's obeying him,' explained Eddie, who was sitting at a table in the dining-room drinking coffee. 'There's almost no staff except those that live in, and they're not lifting a finger. It's OK, though, all you have to do is stroll into the

268

kitchens and take what you want.'

This proved to be true. There were no cooks in the kitchens, only other guests opening the big American refrigerators and making toast in the American toasters.

'We must just make the best of it,' remarked a hearty British type as he spooned coffee into the coffee-maker. 'Quite like the Blitz again, you know.'

In the late afternoon Corie went to Karen's office to check on the news, the official broadcasts having said nothing about the departure of the President, nor about the general strike.

'Some of the rebel troops from Las Villas are coming into the city to keep order,' Karen reported. 'The government troops seem to be staying stubbornly in their barracks, which I think is very sensible of them. They know the entire population is backing this general strike, which seems to mean Castro's nominee will take over as President. Besides, the army is very unpopular, after the terrible things they've done in the past.'

She produced a big envelope. 'Your pix – and boy, have you got a winner!'

Corie opened the envelope and let the black and white roughs slide out.

Some of course were very obscure, because the light had been from one side only, from the open doorway. But half-way through the pile Corie stopped and stared.

There he was, the man who had ruled Cuba with a rod of iron for over twenty years. Small, pudgy, clutching his briefcase to his chest in a beam of light against the darkness – he looked like a scared insurance salesman being chased off the premises by an irate householder.

'Yeah, isn't it great?' Karen said over her shoulder. 'Your name will live on in history, chickie. I think, if you want a caption, you might try "Not with a bang but a whimper".' Then she sighed. 'Of course it's no use at the moment. With the strike, no newspapers can be printed – even if we could get a Cuban paper to use this pic. And we can't get it out because we can't get it on a plane, since of course the airport isn't in action either.'

'Eddie and I are supposed to be getting out soon – perhaps tomorrow.'

'How come?'

'Helen Holstead is arranging for a boat to come for us.'

Karen burst out laughing. 'No half-measures for millionaires? Right, as soon as you get to a United States port, get that pic to my paper—'

'Sorry, Karen. Don't forget I'm working for *News Now*.'

'By heaven, so you are – I'd quite forgotten that.' Karen looked wistful as Corie put the prints back in the envelope. 'You couldn't just leave that behind accidentally?'

'What good would that do? By the time you could use it, it would be old news.'

That night the streets of Havana were dark. There was no electricity. The Hotel Primario was lit by candles. The coffee-maker had ceased to work, so had the refrigerators, the freezers, the lifts. The cheerful man who had lived through the Blitz complained just as much as everybody else.

Next morning, rebel convoys began to appear on the outskirts of Havana. A group of jeeps roared into the parking lot of the Primario, bulging with young men in battle fatigues and a lot of hair – these lads were known as '*barbudos*', bearded ones, but they also had long flowing locks after the style of an ancient prophet. These were the visible signs of long months fighting on jungle-clad mountainsides.

A young man with an armband began directing the others into the hotel. It seemed they were taking over such of the rooms as were empty, also the ballroom and the conference room, as sleeping quarters. Two of the men immediately set up in the kitchen, producing hot food on camp stoves – but only for their fellow-soldiers.

The officer summoned the hotel guests together in the lobby. He made a speech in Spanish. 'He says he's Lieutenant Orfero, that foreign visitors to Havana are in no danger, but he'd like to see our papers and to search our rooms.'

'Can we refuse?' Corie inquired, raising her eyebrows.

'Don't let's try,' said Eddie.

Papers were examined, and then each visitor was escorted to his or her room. Corie stood by while two young soldiers opened the wardrobe, the drawers of the dressing-table, the bedside cabinets, the writing bureau, and finally her suitcases.

One looked up when he opened the camera bag and saw the collection of cameras. '*Fotografa*?' he asked.

'*Si.*'

He came to the centre of the room, shouldering his rifle, asking her for something. She understood he wanted her to take his picture. She picked up her miniature, attached the flash, and took two shots of him and then two of his companion. While she took the pictures the other continued the search. Suddenly the elder of the two gave a shout of laughter. He'd found her portfolio and in it the envelope with photographs of the scurrying departure from Camp Columbia. The two had an enthusiastic discussion, then one ran out with the picture. After a pause, Lieutenant Orfero came in holding the picture. He was smiling broadly.

He asked a question in Spanish. She said helplessly, '*No hablo espanol.*'

The lieutenant thought for a moment. 'You—?' He mimed clicking the shutter.

'Yes.'

'Very good.' He nodded in laughing approval and turned to go, the picture still in his hand.

'Hey, that's mine,' Corie protested.

'*Propriedad de la Republica de Cuba,*' he said, and walked out.

And, reflecting that she still had the negative, Corie thought it best not to argue.

People had come on to the streets to welcome the rebel army, so there was nothing remarkable in the arrival of a young man in soiled duck trousers and a T-shirt early next morning. He sauntered into the lobby, where the hotel guests were sharing out a scratch meal of stale bread, processed cheese, and water from the kitchen tap – the hotel's roof-tank still supplying a mild trickle due to the force of gravity.

'Mr Holstead?' said the young man, looking about.

Eddie stood up. 'Yes?'

'Er . . . I'm here with a message from your mother.'

The other guests listened with interest. Eddie, his mouth full of hard bread, mumbled, 'Let's just go outside in the fresh air,' which evoked nods of sympathy. The hotel's air-conditioning had of course broken down.

Outside, the newcomer introduced himself as Joe Stanislas. 'I'm anchored about a mile out, in a cove to the west. The docks are on strike, but there are a lot of fishing boats still going out, so we're not too conspicuous. If you could . . . er . . . dress a bit low-class . . . And bring just one bag – we can't be seen loading suitcases into the dinghy.'

'You mean we'd be stopped?' Corie asked, surprised.

'From what I gather, there's an embargo on arriving or leaving for the moment. Maybe it won't last long, but on the other hand maybe it will. My instructions are to take you out straightaway.'

'Give us ten minutes,' Eddie said.

They climbed the stairs to their rooms. Corie looked at the clothes she'd bought especially for this trip. Some she'd become very attached to. But if only one bag was allowed, it had to be the camera bag.

They walked out of the hotel not a quarter of an hour later, got into the hired car, and under Joe's direction drove out to a little fishing port called Buengengita. Here a motorised dinghy was moored among the boats at the jetty. They clambered aboard, Joe pulled the starter on the outboard, and they were off.

'And so we say farewell to Romantic Havana,' intoned Eddie in the manner of a film travelogue.

Contrary to Mrs Holstead's expectations, the city didn't

become enveloped in flames when, seven days later, Fidel Castro drove in. By that time Corie's precious picture had been printed in *News Now*. She was famous.

Only the fact that she wasn't an American citizen prevented a nomination for the Pulitzer prize. But she received quite a different accolade. Some weeks later a letter with a Cuban postmark arrived at her Greenwich Village apartment. With great curiosity she opened the envelope.

'Dear Miss Corie Duggan,' she read, 'We were unable to keep track of your movements after the Glorious Revolution but believe you left with other Americans when flights from José Martí airport resumed.

'Please forgive us for our failure to thank you for the wonderful news-picture of ex-President Fulgencio Batistá hurriedly leaving Camp Columbia. It has proved of enormous propaganda value to us.

'We offer you our sincere gratitude for the picture and also for the sympathy with our Revolution which so clearly underlies this truthful portrait of a contemptible ex-dictator.

'Long live the Republic of Cuba!

'Assuring you of our continuing interest in your career, in which we wish you every success.

'Yours sincerely, Rinaldo Despuentera, Chief Press Officer, Department of Information, Republic of Cuba.'

Corie laughed aloud. Because she happened to be in the right place at the right time, she had taken a photograph. Had she come upon Fulgencio Batistá honourably defending his family with a sword, her camera would have come just as quickly to her eye. That was always her aim – to seize the moment of truth, when the real character showed itself through the veneer.

Neither Helen Holstead nor Drew Richter were altogether pleased with her over the photograph. 'That man was America's friend,' Helen rebuked her.

'Helen, I didn't take the picture to make trouble for America. I took it because . . . because it would have been wrong not to take it. There was a truth there that had to be recorded.'

'Huh,' said Helen.

They were at Gitchetak. Helen had invited both Corie and Drew to the famous Sunday lunch. Corie noticed that more than half the guests were politicians, which was unusual – Helen usually aimed for a mix of politics, the arts and sport.

The reason became clear when the time came to leave. Corie was asked to stay on. Drew apparently had already been asked, as had about half a dozen wheeler-dealers of the Democratic party. Corie knew that Helen was a devoted supporter of the Democrats.

About five o'clock, when everyone else except this inner coterie had gone, tea was served in the drawing-room.

'Now, fellows and gals,' said Helen when they were all settled with tea and English sandwiches, 'you all know why we're here. All except Miss Duggan, and if you'll all just bear with me I'll explain the game to her.'

Game? What game, Corie wondered. Clearly it was something to do with politics, but why include her? Where politics were concerned, she was an innocent.

'These here guys and gals,' Helen said jokily, waving a red-tipped hand to take in the gathering, 'are what we call a ginger group. We're into spring now, and by the fall Senator Kennedy will be making his moves more open—'

'Senator Kennedy?'

'You remember him, I'm sure?'

'Certainly,' She'd done a portrait study of him – well received, praised by Helen, but not what Corie thought of as one of her great portraits. But an interesting man, for all that she had been uncertain how much she'd learned through the camera lens.

'This is in confidence, dear. The rest of us already know and we're pledged to keep it dark until Kennedy himself chooses to reveal it.' She paused, drew a breath. 'The Senator is going after the Democratic nomination.'

The nomination . . . That meant that he would campaign up and down the country and, at the Democratic Convention, would hope his party would choose him as their presidential candidate.

Was it possible? Compared with Eisenhower, he seemed so young, almost boyish – although in fact he was a World War II veteran. But more importantly, he was a Catholic. Could a Catholic senator hope to be chosen by his party to run for President? And if chosen, could he possibly be elected?

Corie's face must have reflected her doubt because others took up the story from Helen.

'The United States needs fresh blood. Too many old men get into the White House.'

'The women's vote is becoming important. Women would vote for Kennedy.'

'His father's a hundred per cent behind him. He's going to put all his money into the campaign.'

'It's time for a new look.'

Corie sat listening, nodding acceptance. She still couldn't imagine what it had to do with her.

'Now, it's early days yet, dear,' Helen resumed, 'but I'm putting up money for a public-relations campaign for the Kennedy faction. We're going to try to get good press attention for everyone who supports Jack Kennedy between now and the election, so that people will feel that they're electing not only a President, but a group of men and women they can feel confidence in. And Drew here is going to head it up for us.'

Corie was startled. She turned her glance on Drew, who shrugged and made a face.

'And Drew has suggested,' said Helen, 'that you would be an ideal choice to take the pictures for such a campaign.'

'Good Lord! Why me?' Corie exclaimed.

'Because your work is excellent. Those pix that were run in *News Now—*'

'I thought you disapproved of making Batistá look scared—'

'Not that one, the others: the studies of the citizens and rural workers; the people on Havana Beach; the whole thing was first class. And Drew says he feels he could work with you.'

'Thank you, that's very flattering.' Corie's tone was full of doubt.

'Of course it wouldn't be a full-time assignment. There would be occasions when we'd want you to be on call, and other times when you'd be completely free to carry on your own projects.'

'I don't think so, Helen,' she said after a moment.

'What?'

'I don't think I'd like it.'

'Why on earth not?' Drew demanded. 'It could bring you a lot of useful contacts . . .'

She was shaking her head. 'Suppose I didn't like someone you asked me to photograph? Suppose I showed them up somehow, as I did with Batistá?'

'Oh, now, that's not going to happen,' someone protested.

'No? Can you assure me that everyone who supports your party is brave and good?'

Helen was vexed. 'This is very disappointing, Corie. I thought you'd jump at it.'

'I'm sorry. I just don't think it's my kind of thing.'

'I think you'd like it if you gave it a try,' Drew encouraged. 'Let me introduce you to a few of the politicians—'

'No, honestly, I'd rather not.' She set aside her tea cup and got to her feet. 'And now, as I suppose what you want to talk about is confidential, I think I'd better make myself scarce.'

'No, wait,' Drew began as she walked to the door.

But she merely paused at the threshold to say, 'When you're ready to go, Drew, you'll find me down by the lake.'

More than an hour later, when the spring twilight had fallen, he came to collect her. They had driven up to Gitchetak in his car, as they usually did. She couldn't leave without him.

He seemed preoccupied as they drove away. Finally she

said, 'Are you annoyed with me?'

'Disappointed. I was looking forward to working with you.'

'You must have dozens of photographers on call for your PR firm—'

'You don't understand,' he interrupted. 'I'm giving up the firm. I'm going to devote myself full-time from now on to helping get John F. Kennedy elected President of the United States.'

That silenced her. After a pause she said, 'Are you sure about this, Drew? Suppose you've ditched your career and then he doesn't get elected.'

'That's a chance I'm willing to take.'

She hesitated. What she was going to say next was not entirely tactful. 'Is there some advantage in this for you, something that I can't perceive?'

He smiled, and in the light from a passing car she saw there was bitterness in it. 'You'd imagine so, I see that. Always out for Number One, that's been Drew Richter up till now. But I'm sick of it, Corie, I've had it up to here. I'm sick of helping no-goods to look good. It's time I did something to stop this country becoming nothing more than a sick merry-go-round!'

His words were forced out by a real passion. She laid a hand on his arm, then after a moment said, with a trace of humour in her voice, 'Is this idealism, Drew?'

He half-laughed, took a hand off the wheel to pat hers. 'Damned if I know. Let's give it a chance and see if it turns into idealism. All I know is that I've heard Kennedy discussing his ideas and they seem to have a lot more in them than anything else on offer.'

'Well, well. Your mother and father will be pleased. Your father once told me he couldn't understand why you should waste your life on the kind of work you were doing.'

'Maybe they've influenced me more than I know. Mutti is a clever lady, she doesn't use a sledge-hammer but she usually taps the nail home all the same . . .'

They parted at her door in Greenwich Village with a

promise on her side that she'd think about Helen's offer. And for a day or two she was half-tempted. Not because of the prestige she might gain, the important political contacts. Not for the money, which might prove to be considerable. Not because it would please Helen Holstead, although that was a good reason.

No, what tempted her was the idea of watching Drew in action where something more than money was involved. The side of this man that she liked most, the side she saw when he was at home and his mother called him Andreas – that was what attracted her. It might be worth going along with the plan just to see Andreas in action.

Yet there was another claim on her attention. Letters from home had begun to worry her. Her sister Opal was the best correspondent, generally writing a lot about her outings with Barton Davis, the man in her life. Recently, though, there had been remarks that seemed to show things weren't going too well with Lynette.

About ten days after Corie's lunch at Gitchetak, a letter from Pal caused her so much uneasiness that she made a note in her appointments book to ring home at two-thirty the next afternoon. That would mean the phone would ring in the Bayswater house at about seven-thirty, when Pal was almost sure to be back from the office.

Somewhat to her dismay, it was Monna who answered the call. 'Corie! What a surprise! Have you some special news for us?'

'No, Monna, I just wanted a chat.'

'Darling, I do understand. You're lonely for home – I used to feel the same thing when I was on tour. Well, you'll be happy to hear everything's fine here. Lynette's out at a rehearsal, as it happens – they're trying a new item in the show, a big dance number: with colour coming along, they're thinking about special costumes and so forth.'

'How is Pal?' Corie managed to ask.

'Very well, darling, I'm glad to say. And I'm having some success these days with my popular song recitals – I have a Masonic dinner and a wedding later this month. Have you seen these "trapeze" dresses, Corie? Are they being worn much in New York? I'm thinking of buying one for afternoon appearances, but I don't really know if it's quite *me*.'

'I'm sure you'll look very nice, Monna,' Corie said. 'Can I speak to Pal, please?'

'Just a minute, I'll call her.' She heard the summons, her mother's 'operatic' voice, a rising and falling note. 'Op-al!'

'Here she comes. Lots of love, darling, I must rush now, I'm giving myself a conditioning shampoo.'

Her sister came on the line. 'How're you, Corie?' she asked.

'I'm OK but a bit worried. What's actually going on about Lynette?'

'It's hard to say. You know the showbiz scene here has changed a lot. It's all teenage boys with guitars these days. Sasha's signed up about a dozen of them—'

'A dozen!'

'Well, not really, but he's got a very full list and somehow Lynette seems to be left out.'

'But Pal, how can that be? She's one of his top clients.'

'I wonder if that's true . . . ?'

Corie felt her heart sink. 'What does Lynette say?'

'Oh, you know Lynette, anything Sasha arranges is bound to be good. But I'm not so sure. I've tried to talk to him about it but he just waves me off. And of course Monna's certain all this business with rock-and-roll will pass.' Pal gave an excellent imitation of their mother. ' "Half-educated youths who can't even read music – I give it another six months at most" . . .'

Corie made a sound, half-amusement and half-concern. 'The rock-and-roll scene's been big in the States for a couple of years now, Pal.'

'There you are. I don't know what to make of it. I wish you were here, Corie,' she said with a sigh that came clearly over the transatlantic line. 'I miss having someone to talk to.'

'I'll come,' Corie said, making up her mind all at once.

'Oh, don't be silly – just because I'm at a bit of a loss—'

'No, I'll come. I've been away too long. I'll start making arrangements right away. I'll ring you again in a few days, Pal.'

'Do you really think . . . ? Well, it would be nice to see you. And I'd like you to get to know Barton.'

'I look forward to that,' Corie rejoined, and they hung up.

Her American friends were astonished at her decision. 'It's madness to go, Corie! Now that you've made your name with your Cuban pictures . . . !'

'Don't go, dear. I believe I'd miss you if you left.'

But Drew was the most reluctant to see her leave. 'I thought you'd be settling here, Corie. I pretty well took it for granted you'd take out US citizenship.'

She shook her head. 'I'm needed at home, Drew. I can feel it in my bones. Things aren't going well with my sister Lynette.'

'Why do you have to go rushing back? Can't she look after herself?'

'It's difficult to explain,' she sighed. 'I have a feeling of responsibility where Lynette's concerned.'

'But why? She's not a baby, is she?'

'She's twenty-four now. But somehow she always seems vulnerable . . . I have to go, Drew. She needs me.'

He saw it was useless to argue and instead helped her tie up loose ends so that she could leave. He saw her off at La Guardia. 'When will you be back?' he asked.

'Who knows?'

'Corie, this isn't a final goodbye, is it?' A sudden anxiety had come into his voice.

'Of course not. We'll keep in touch. I'll call you when I've settled back into the London routine.'

The public-address system announced the boarding gate for her flight. She slung her camera bag on her shoulder.

Drew put his arms around her and kissed her with unexpected fervour. '*I'll* call *you*,' he said. 'I don't trust you to remember your promise once that family of yours engulfs you again.'

She returned his kiss, conscious of things she might have said. But it was too late to start a discussion of their feelings. The boarding call was resounding through the airport. She went up the walkway, looked back, waved, and then turned to make her way to the gate.

London looked its best when she arrived. It was early morning, there had been rain but now the city sparkled under the rising sun. Lilac bloomed in the gardens she passed on her way home, magnolia held up ivory blossoms to the blue of the sky. After the skyscrapers and the hurried tempo of New York, London seemed leisurely, sedate.

Her mother and sisters were at breakfast when she rang the bell. Opal opened the door with a piece of toast in one hand. 'Corie dear!' she cried, hugging her. Lynette ran out to greet her. Behind her came Monna, splendid in a blue taffeta dressing-gown.

When her luggage had been brought in and the taxi paid, she was plied with offers of tea, coffee, toast, scrambled eggs, fruit juice.

'No thank you, I had breakfast on the plane. How are you all? Pal, you've had your hair tinted! I like it. Have you lost weight, Lynette?'

She sat down at the breakfast table, accepting coffee so as to give them a chance to fuss over her. Pal said she had to finish her food and get going, she was expected at the office. 'But I'll get an hour off and be home early. We must have a celebration, a welcome home! How about we go out for dinner?'

'I can't, I have a recording session, Pal—'

'Can't you put it off? After all, it's Corie's homecoming party.'

'No, no, don't bother,' Corie put in. 'By this evening I'll probably be laid low with jet lag anyway. We'll celebrate some other time.'

Opal was reluctant to let her celebration be pushed aside, but had to leave to catch her bus. Monna went to let in the daily help and give her her instructions. Lynette volunteered to help Corie unpack.

Nothing could have suited Corie better. She wanted to get her younger sister alone. After a certain amount of chat about her New York clothes and answering questions about Cuba, she worked the conversation around to Lynette's career.

'Everything still on the dazzle for you, love?' she asked.

'Oh yes, can't complain, though of course the fashion at the moment is for these guitar-players with names like Tommy Havoc and Johnny Tempest – they make me laugh, those names, they sound as if they're disasters about to happen.'

Lynette was smiling as she said it. Corie's anxiety lessened. 'The BBC still giving you prime time?' she went on.

'Yes. That was in the contract. Although . . .'

'What?' Corie prompted, the anxiety stirring again.

'There's a new contract coming up. For the series due to start in the autumn.'

'Of course.' Corie had got out of the habit of thinking in terms of TV seasons. 'No problems with that, I suppose?'

'We may have to make changes. For instance, we're thinking of including a big dance number—'

'Oh, yes, Monna mentioned that.'

'Yes, it's anticipating the coming of colour TV – lots of swirling orange skirts and pink spangled bodices . . .' Lynette paused. 'I don't know if it's my style,' she ended.

'But you're a good dancer, Lynette.'

'Oh yes, the routines are no problem. But the costumes, you know . . . They seem very melodramatic to me. Not my kind of thing, Corie. I've always had a softer image.'

'The costumes are settled, are they?'

'Oh no, it's only sketches. It may all be scrapped. You know, only one house in a hundred will have a colour TV set – I can't really see that it's all that important.'

'What does Sasha say?' Corie inquired, and waited with bated breath for the reply.

'Oh, Sasha's doing wonderfully well, didn't I tell you in my letters? He promoted Danny Vulcan, you know – heard him playing in a coffee bar in Bradford, groomed him up to stardom. His last record was in the Top Ten for three weeks.'

'I'm delighted to hear it,' Corie said drily. She had never heard of Danny Vulcan. 'And your record? The one you're doing this evening?'

'It's part of an LP I'm doing. It's called "Sing Me a Happy Song". The idea is to get it out for Christmas and family get-togethers.' Lynette looked pleased but added, 'Of course I don't expect that to get into the Top Ten.'

'Sasha doesn't think so?'

'I don't know,' Lynette said, with a frown between her fair brows. 'It's a while since we signed the contract – he worked ever so hard to get it for me but of course since then he's been frantically busy with Danny and one or two other boys he's promoting.'

'Aren't there *any* girl singers these days?'

'Well yes, one or two, but it's funny how the boys have taken over,' Lynette remarked. She put one of Corie's silk shirts on a hanger. 'When do you get your flat back?'

'It's sub-let until the end of June. The studio of course is different – I must ring Bertie and let him know I've landed. I must start there the day after tomorrow.' She stowed underwear in a drawer. 'If you can get hold of an advance sample of the costume for this big number, I'll do a portrait of you, Lynette. It'll give you a chance to see how you look.'

Lynette smiled and nodded.

'Lynette, is everything all right?'

'Of course,' her sister said.

But it wasn't so. Something was wrong, Corie could sense it.

Next day, recovered from her flight, Corie got out the clippings book which her mother had kept religiously ever since her youngest daughter became a star. She read the most recent entries, turned back, read the previous page, and so back to the beginning of last autumn's TV series.

Everything seemed fine. All the reviews were favourable. Yet it didn't quite add up.

She began to leaf forward again. Then something dawned on her. There were far fewer reviews and pictures the closer you came to the present day.

She sat in the living-room, thinking about it. She had a thought, and it was something to be worried about.

Her mother being as she was, she would only clip favourable reviews. Certainly there was nothing derogatory among those Corie had just read. But there were fewer — did that mean that others had been discarded because they were critical of Lynette's show?

She went out, called a taxi, and drove to the offices of the *Stage*. There, after introducing herself, she was allowed to look at the back-numbers file.

By the time she'd read back to Christmas, she understood why it was she'd had forebodings.

' "You're a Sweetheart" made its autumn debut with the usual mix of song and sentiment. Hard to say what's happened to this show — nothing, perhaps! Maybe it's the rest of the world that's moved on.'

'Ratings for "You're a Sweetheart" have suffered in comparison with two new shows which hit the airways this month. "Peaktime Pop" is a new idea, bringing hit recording stars to the TV audience. "Rocking Tonight" is a down-market show to introduce rock-singers as yet unknown to London.'

'The special Christmas number of "You're a Sweetheart" raised the show above its recent level, but why did the director feel obliged to include "White Christmas"? Even Lynette Lee's sweet tones couldn't make this number anything but trite.'

Corie closed the file, thanking the girl who had shown her the way to the library. She had learned something of what she needed to know. Now she tried a different tack. She rang Norman Gibson at the *Globe*.

'Who's that? Corie? Corie, I didn't know you were back!' he cried.

'Just arrived yesterday morning. Norm, can I ask a favour?'

'What is it?' he countered warily. 'Nothing to do with our lord and master?'

Corie had hardly given Ingram Holstead a thought for months, and then only in conjunction with his wife Helen. She said now, 'It's about my sister.'

'Lynette?'

'Yes, I'm a bit worried.'

'Um,' said Norman.

'Could you have a drink with me? Put me in the picture a bit?'

'Corie, I'm not the showbiz column. I don't keep up with Lynette.'

'But you've got a clippings file on her? In the basement?'

'Well . . . yes . . . sure to . . .'

'Could you bring the clippings for the last month or so? I'll buy the drinks.'

'Oho, now that's different. Glenmorangie?'

'Whatever you like.'

'You're on.'

They arranged to meet at two in the Dragon. By that time the lunchtime crowd would be leaving. Corie arrived a little late, having detoured to put an advertisement in the more respectable papers announcing that she was back and about to give personal attention to patrons of her studio.

Norman waved to her from the bar. 'I thought we'd go outside and sit in the sun,' he said. He led the way out to the back garden, having ordered their drinks.

'You look different,' he said to her.

'Is that good or bad?'

'I'm not sure. Partly it's the clothes – Bergdorf, are they? And partly it's . . . I don't know, New York has changed you somehow.'

'Well, you look just the same to me, Norm. I think you're even wearing the same old jacket.'

'That's an insult. This is this year's model. And let me tell you, I even have a suede waistcoat.' He sat back to let the barman put down their drinks. 'That was a great snap you took of the President of Cuba. "Exit dictator pursued by bear", as Shakespeare almost said.'

'Glad you liked it.'

'I hear the rest of the Cuban pix were good. You ought to do an exhibition, Corie.'

'Me?'

'Why not? You've done some good work.'

'Norman, I didn't get you here to talk about myself. I want to hear if you've got any idea what's happening to my sister's career.'

He shrugged. 'I asked Ken Gladwin, the TV critic. He didn't sound enthusiastic.'

'Did you bring clippings?'

'Ye-es . . .' He brought an envelope out of his inside pocket. 'Look, Corie, you must understand Ken isn't in the business of being good-natured. He makes his mark by being a bit scathing.'

'Let me see them.'

Rather unwillingly he handed over the envelope. Corie drew out the contents.

The first was a half-column in which Norman had marked an item in pencil. 'Among the offerings for Easter Bank Holiday was "You're a Sweetheart". I expect there was an Easter Bunny hiding amongst all those flowers.'

The next was a line-up of music shows on BBC television. 'It must be said that "You're a Sweetheart" still has an audience, but whether they're awake or asleep remains in doubt. If I were a less kind-hearted reviewer I might remark that the interview with an engaged couple begins to seem downright soppy.'

The last was the worst. 'A little bird tells me that there are doubts about bringing back "You're a Sweetheart" in the autumn. Seems the slot could be used for a sock-it-to-'em show that would draw the younger viewers.'

Corie put them back in the envelope.

'Bad, eh?' Norman said sympathetically.

Corie took a sip of her campari.

'You don't want to pay too much attention,' he insisted. 'Ken always writes knocking copy.'

'But there's something there to knock,' she replied.

'Ah, it's always easy to find fault.'

'Do you watch the show, Norman?'

'What, me? I'm an opera fan.'

She smiled. 'I never cared for it much myself,' she confessed. 'Even before I went away, I thought it was . . . backward-looking, you know? Yet the public seemed to love it.'

'It's true the public taste has changed,' he said. 'I don't know whether it's improved or regressed, but you can't go by what I say – to me nothing more recent than *Pagliacci* is worth listening to.'

'It says in that last clipping that Lynette's show may be cancelled.'

'What does her agent say?'

'Not much, as far as I can gather. He's busy with Danny Vulcan—'

'Oh, him. Well, he's hot stuff, all right – always in the gossip columns. I don't blame Lenoir for concentrating on him.'

I do, thought Corie, I certainly do. But commercially speaking Sasha was right to think more of this new star than of the one that was fading.

Fading? Was that what was happening to her sister? Her first instinct was to reject the thought. Yet there had been a change in Lynette – the glow, the happy certainty, they were gone. In its place was something else – not yet defeat, but a puzzled uncertainty.

She changed the subject by asking how things were going at the *Globe*. 'Pretty good. Mabel got the boot, though – seems whatever she'd been trying to ferret out about you, she got it wrong. His Wonderfulness was very peeved. A bear with a sore head for weeks.'

'But that's all over now.'

'I wonder . . . ? He was more than averagely interested in that picture you took of Batistá. I don't think he's quite got over whatever it was he felt about you.'

How very strange . . . She looked back at the parting between herself and Ingram Holstead as if through the wrong end of a telescope. Very small and far away.

Norman had to get back to the paper. He kissed her lightly on the top of the head as he left. 'Great to see you again. Don't forget what I said about holding an exhibition. I know a few people with galleries, might pull a few strings for you.'

'Thank you, Norm.'

'Any time.'

After he'd gone she bought a sandwich and a glass of wine at the bar. As she ate she tried to think what to do next. Eventually she went to the Dragon's phone booth, dialled BBC Television. The extension she used to call for William Tranton went through to someone else now. She was put back to the switchboard, requested him by name, and was put through to a secretary.

'Whom shall I say?'

'Corie Duggan.'

'If it's about "Up in the Clouds", we're not researching yet for the next series.'

'No, this is a personal call. Mr Tranton knows me.'

After a longish pause, William came on the line. 'Corie! You're back!'

'Didn't Lynette tell you?'

'Lynette,' he said, his voice dropping a tone or two. 'I haven't seen Lynette for a while – not since before Christmas.'

'Oh, William . . . I'm sorry, I thought you were still producing—'

'No, I was moved on to something else. Sort of documentary stuff – I felt it was time to try something new.'

'It's going well?'

'I think so. I've got a couple of programmes I'm running, the main one is interviews, mostly, about what has made certain people very happy – "Up in the Clouds", you see.

If you'd like to see it being done, I'll arrange—'

'What I really wanted, William, was to talk to you about Lynette.'

'Oh.'

'I've just got back. I'm a bit puzzled.'

'I see.'

'Could we meet?'

'Listen, Corie,' he said with vehemence, 'I've nothing to do with Lynette's show any more. I was taken off it, I can't tell you anything that would help—'

'If you could just fill me in a bit, about how it's got to where it is at the present time.'

'I'm pretty busy, Corie.'

She could tell he simply didn't want to meet her. 'All right,' she said, 'I'm sorry to have bothered you. It was just that I thought you took an interest—'

'Of course I did! She had something *special* . . .'

'She had it. You put it in the past.'

'Oh, it's still there. But the problem is—'

'I know. It's not what the public wants any more.'

A silence developed. 'All right,' he said with a sigh, 'I can be free later today – mid-evening – would that do?'

'Of course. Where shall we meet?'

'Savoy Grill, eightish. I'll buy you a steak.'

'I'll be there, William. And thank you.'

There were several matters of business to deal with: a visit to the studio in Bury Street, and to the estate agent to make sure the tenant of her flat knew she was due to leave in a month. She got home with only time to change.

'You're not going out again?' her mother said in vexation. 'I bought a bottle of wine, I thought we could have a little celebration at home instead of a restaurant.'

'Keep it till tomorrow night, perhaps Lynette will be home too.'

'Oh well, yes, that would be better, I suppose.'

She took a taxi to the Savoy through quiet London streets shining damp after a May shower. I must buy another second-hand car, she thought, can't keep throwing money away on taxis. Although she'd made a reasonable income in the States, she'd been able to save very little. Helen Holstead had wanted to give her a big bonus but that she had refused — she felt she would rather be on terms of friendship than those of employer-employee.

William came into the hotel lobby almost simultaneously with her. He had a table booked. They sat across it from each other in the famous lofty room with its gleaming cloths and sparkling crystal. William looked uneasy.

'So,' he said, 'you covered yourself with glory in Havana. They used a still of your picture in the nine o'clock news. Mentioned how you came to take it.'

'They did?' She was inordinately pleased. That to her was real success.

'I didn't expect you to come back, from the way things seemed to be going for you.'

'I came back because when I talked to my sister Opal I got the impression something had gone wrong for Lynette.'

He busied himself calling a waiter and ordering the steaks.

'What's the matter, William?' she asked.

'Let's choose the wine,' he said, avoiding her eye.

'Oh, hang the wine! Tell me what's the matter.'

He threw down the wine list. 'Lynette's show is being dropped.'

She was too stricken to speak. He picked up the wine list, ordered claret, sat back in his chair, and glared at her through his thick glasses.

'Well, you insisted on knowing,' he said.

'I was shown a clipping from the *Globe* but I thought it was just malicious innuendo—'

'Ken Gladwin? He likes to get the knife in when he can, right or not. But this time he was right. They're not going to renew the contract.'

'Does Sasha know?'

He shook his head. 'Not definitely, but he's been given enough hints, I gather. And he's not fighting back very hard.'

'If he did,' Corie asked with a stirring of hope, 'would it do any good?'

'Not at this stage. I'm sorry, Corie, her ratings have been slipping for a long time now, and unless the show was given a shake-up the writing was there on the wall. And I wasn't there to give it a new twist — I'm doing something quite different these days. Light Entertainment isn't my department any more.'

'Do you think Sasha can sell her to the commercial channels?'

He shook his head. 'They wanted her a couple of years ago but it's different now. Of course they're negotiating with him over other clients — he's got Danny Vulcan on his books, you know.'

'So I hear.'

'He might be able to do a deal for Lynette as part of a package: "OK, you can have a series with Vulcan if you give me something for Lynette Lee".'

'Oh no!' Corie said at once. From early experience she knew how bad it was for a performer to get work on what was called a 'drag-in': I'll let you have a big star if you let me drag in some old has-been.

Their steaks came. Corie was hungry. She'd had nothing to eat all day except a sandwich. After a mouthful or two, when she'd taken the edge off her hunger, she said, 'I gather Lynette's making an LP.'

'She is?'

'Yes, a collection for Christmas. Called something like "Happy Songs".'

'It might do all right,' he said, pushing angrily at his food.

'But you don't think so.'

'Heavens, you know what it's like at Christmas, Corie. A hundred collections of party songs come out. Hers will get left in the racks while people buy Bing Crosby or the Black and White Minstrels.'

'Her name wouldn't attract the buyers?'

William said, 'I told you already. The viewing public is losing interest. The record-buying public has hardly heard of her.'

He gave a sudden thump on the table with his fist. 'I don't know what you expect me to say,' he said, in a voice tinged with accusation. 'Sasha should have been thinking ahead. When hard rock came across the Atlantic it took this country by storm.'

'But Sasha understood that. He's collected a list of rock-singers—'

'Oh yes, he was thinking ahead for *himself*.'

'Couldn't you have given him a nudge, William?'

'Me? What influence do you think I have on Sasha?'

'But you've known him a long time.'

'We did our National Service together. That doesn't make us friends. He thinks I'm a twit, I think he's a pushy schemer. Of *course* we've done each other a bit of good from time to time, we're in the same business to some extent; but as to taking advice from me, that's a myth.'

Corie had completely lost her appetite. She put her fork and knife together on her plate, sipped some claret. The rich red wine soothed her enough to help her to go on.

'So what does Lynette do now, William?'

He sighed. 'The best she can, I suppose.'

'Any ideas?'

'No.'

'It's over, is that the message? Twenty-four, and she's washed up?'

'Don't be angry with me about it, Corie. Blame the Great British Public. She's not what they're looking for just now.'

This was the phrase so often used by dance directors at an audition: Very nice, dear, but it's not what we're looking for just now. Corie winced.

All that sweetness, all that lightness and gaiety – the public didn't want it any more. And it was useless to expect Lynette to change. She was what she was – not a great dancer, not a great singer, not a great comedienne, just a very pretty, genuine, lovable girl with a lot of charm.

The waiter came hurrying up, consternation in his manner. 'Is something wrong with the steak, madam?'

'What? Oh no – thank you – I'm just not hungry.'

'Can we offer you something else?'

'No thanks, really . . .'

William indicated that he too had finished and ordered coffee. While they waited he said moodily, 'I could kill him.'

'The thing is, she still thinks he's wonderful.'

'You think I don't know that? Why d'you imagine I accepted the move to Features? My God, it broke my heart to see the way he mishandled her . . .'

'What would you have done, William?'

'Dunno. Perhaps tried to get her into situation comedy.'

'Oh, she's not much of an actress—'

'She used to do those niece-and-uncle bits very nicely. It could have worked, something along the lines of "I Love Lucy" but not so zany . . .' He shook his head. 'Too late now.'

'It's too late?'

'There's an old-fashioned feel to her now. I don't think anyone would let her read for a part. I'm sorry, I really am, Corie.'

She reached across the table to press his hand. 'Yes, I know you are, love.'

They drank their coffee while they went over the ground yet again. Now that it was out in the open, it was easier to talk about the dying of Lynette's career. But they came up with nothing constructive.

When at last they parted, Corie said, 'If you think of anything, get in touch, won't you, William?'

'You know I will.'

She thought as she walked home under the soft lamplight, He's a good friend. He's more than a friend for Lynette, if only she had sense enough to know it. But what could you do with a girl who obstinately remained entranced by a man like Sasha?

Lynette was home from her recording session when she got indoors. She was with Monna in the big drawing-room, going over a song while her mother played the accompaniment at half-pedal. 'Silver bell, silver bells,

It's Christmas-time in the city—'

'No, darling, the opening should be *mezzo-voce*.'

'But the tubular bells will drown it . . .'

'Darling, listen to your mother. I've been singing for half a century now, I ought to know—'

Lynette turned away as her sister came in. 'Where have you been off to, Miss Gadabout?' she demanded, smiling. 'I expected you to be here when I got back.'

'I was having a chat with an old friend. How did the recording go?'

'Oh, well, we got another one on tape . . . Day after tomorrow I have to record "Silver Bells", I don't know if I can make it work with the orchestration . . .'

'What does Sasha say?' Corie asked.

'He hasn't heard it. He's very busy at the moment, you know.'

'With Sammy Vulcan.'

'Danny Vulcan.' Lynette laughed. 'He's Charles Tugwell, really. But never mind, he's all the rage at the moment so that's what matters.'

Monna rose from the piano. 'Raucous, unpleasant young man,' she remarked. 'I can't imagine the British public accepting *him* as a performer. I think he only knows four chords on that guitar.'

'That's not what matters, Monna – it's all to do with personality.'

'Humph.'

Corie guessed from her sister's serene manner that she'd no idea 'You're a Sweetheart' was to be cancelled. What would happen when she found out?

The following week showed her. Lynette came home from what was supposed to have been a choreographic session for the new dance number, with her eyes red and her make-up smudged.

'My darling!' cried her mother at the sight of her. 'Has there been an accident?'

'No – nothing – don't ask—' gasped Lynette, and ran past her upstairs to her room.

Corie, Opal and their mother, together at the door of the drawing-room, heard her bedroom door slam. Monna made as if to rush after her. Corie grabbed her arm.

'No, don't,' she warned.

'But I must—'

'Don't' said Opal. 'Leave her alone.'

'But—'

'She's had bad news,' Corie said.

'But what? What's happened?' And then, bemused, 'How do you know?'

'I was told last week. They've dropped "You're a Sweetheart".'

Opal gave a deep sigh, in which there was immediate understanding.

'Dropped? What can you possibly mean?' Monna cried.

'It's been chopped — wiped off — put an end to. What do you think I mean?' Corie retorted, suddenly angry at the obtuseness of her mother.

'You're imagining things! They couldn't possibly cancel "You're a Sweetheart"!'

'Why not? Because it fits so perfectly with your dated ideas of what a show should be? The whole thing is passé, outmoded, extinct.'

'Corie!' Opal gasped, startled.

'That's not true! Everyone loves it! You only have to hear what my friends say—'

'Yes,' Corie said cruelly, 'and they belong in the same time-scale as the show — back in the forties. Get it into your head, Monna, the show has been put back in the cupboard.'

'No,' protested Monna.

'Yes,' said Corie.

To her horror, her mother collapsed on the big sofa and began to cry. 'No,' she wailed, 'no, they can't do that to my little girl! They can't turn their back on my angel! I won't let them! Sasha won't let them!'

Corie looked at her, then at her sister. Opal shook her head helplessly, went to the door and hurried out.

Hesitating, Corie sat down beside her mother on the sofa

and tried to put her arms round her. 'Don't, Monna,' she soothed, 'don't, it's no use—'

'Don't touch me! You want it to be true! You've always been jealous of her success!'

'No, no, you're wrong—'

'You're absolutely heartless to say it's old-fashioned. It's full of decent values and—'

'Monna, Monna, it had its value, I accept that, but it's not right for the times, that's all that can be said.'

'I won't let it be true! I'll make them withdraw—'

'No, Monna darling, honestly—'

'Sasha will consult his lawyer.'

'I don't think so, dear . . .'

'They can't close her down! The whole world loves her!'

Against so much partisanship there was no argument. Corie sat beside her, trying as best she could to give comfort though it was stubbornly refused.

At long last her mother sat up, searched for a handkerchief, and blotted the tears from her cheeks. 'It's all a stupid mistake,' she said with an attempt at briskness.

'No, it's true.'

'You think you know, do you, Miss Know-it-all?'

'William Tranton told me last week.'

Monna gaped at her. Then her colour flew up into her face. 'You've known for a week, and you didn't tell *me*?'

'I didn't think it right to say anything until Lynette had had the news herself.'

'You should have told me! I would have protected her!'

'Darling,' cried Corie, wracked with pity for her, 'you couldn't have done anything. You have to accept it.'

'No! Never!'

'William says—'

'What does it matter what William says? It's Sasha who matters, it's Sasha who'll put right this monstrous mistake.'

'When Lynette was told she must have heard it from Sasha. Does it look as if he's been able to prevent it?'

'Oh, you don't understand how these things work! Your heart was never really in the theatre: you never sensed the under-currents. I'll ring Sasha and he and I between us—'

'Please don't, Monna. Please, please don't.' She knew nothing but disappointment would come of it.

But her mother refused to hear her. She went to the telephone, dialled Sasha's home number, and waited.

But the phone rang and rang. 'Of course he's at his office, sorting this out—'

'It's ten o'clock at night, Monna.'

Disregarding her, Monna redialled. Once more the phone rang without response.

Only at a little after midnight did she give up and let herself be persuaded to go to bed. To Corie it was quite clear that, if Sasha was at either of those numbers, he simply wasn't going to answer.

Next day, despite argument from both Opal and Corie, Mrs Duggan went to see him. What exactly happened was never quite clear, but she came home in the afternoon somewhat brighter.

'Sasha says he's got his own way of dealing with it,' she reported. 'Don't worry, my darling, it'll be all right.'

Lynette, who had emerged from her room at about lunchtime, smiled and nodded. To Corie she seemed only half-aware of what was going on. The shock had numbed her. Perhaps it was a blessing.

The days went by and they survived the blow. Lynette said little, Monna remained convinced it was all going to be sorted out, Corie and Opal watched it all and didn't know whether to make them face facts or leave them in their dream world.

The two older sisters had their own world to attend to. Opal had to go to the office, Corie had to go to the studio. There was an influx now that it had become known she was back in action. The studio was busy.

About two weeks had gone by when William Tranton showed up there. 'Can you spare me a minute, Corie?' he asked when she met him at the reception desk.

'Why, yes, we're just setting up for a sitter who's not due until six.' She led him through to the little cubicle of an office. 'What is it, William?'

'You remember you said to me to get in touch if I had an idea?'

'Of course.'

'I thought of something. The only thing is, I really don't want to talk to Sasha about it. I'm more likely to strangle him than offer him suggestions.' And from the stress in his thin, plain face, she could tell that was true.

'I'm with you on that,' she said grimly.

'All the same, this is a way to bring Lynette in front of an audience.'

'Go on.'

'First of all, let's agree that her appeal is the unsophisticated, girl-in-a-garden kind of thing.'

'Yes, that's always been so.'

'Nobody wants it in the UK any more. But I was thinking . . . There are other audiences. Abroad.'

'You don't mean the States?' Corie countered. 'I just can't see her—'

'No, I was thinking . . . Australia, New Zealand, South Africa . . . Scandinavia, Italy . . . They're still more inclined to like big-band music, ballads – they don't seem to have taken to rock-and-roll yet. To them, Lynette Lee is still a big name. If she were to go on tour, I think she'd find a big public still ready to pay money to see her.'

'On tour . . .'

'I don't think it's even occurred to Lenoir. He's too busy with big recording contracts for Danny Vulcan and the other sex-symbols on his books.'

'You might be right.'

'So I thought . . . Corie . . . If you were to go and see him, put the idea to him as if it were your own . . .'

'Oh, William, I don't really think—' She desperately didn't want to do that. To see Sasha again, to stir up old passions . . .

'Who else is there? I don't feel it would work if I did it, and your mother—'

'No, not my mother,' Corie said quickly. Monna would

resist any idea that came from herself or from William.

'I feel we ought to try the idea on him. It's not that I want Lynette to go overseas . . .'

'I know, William.' She understood perfectly. He hated the thought of not having a glimpse of Lynette for months at a time.

'Can I leave it with you, Corie? You've always been the one to look out for Lynette.'

'Yes . . .'

When he'd gone she knew that she would take up his idea. She would do what she'd vowed not to – she would go to see Sasha Lenoir, from whom she'd dragged herself away with so much pain and heartache.

Chapter Sixteen

Sasha was in new offices these days, tucked in behind the Queen's Theatre off Shaftesbury Avenue. The building was old but handsome, the interior refurbished with marbled floors and a lift.

A brushed steel plate exhibited, in stylish cursive lettering, the legend: 'Sasha Lenoir Artistes, First Floor.'

But in the outer office, the same old batch of hopefuls were sitting waiting for interview. They glared at Corie when she appeared, willed the receptionist to refuse when she asked for her name to be taken in to Mr Lenoir.

Their astonishment was complete when Sasha himself came to the door of his room to welcome her.

'Corie! Long time no see!' he cried, using what was the present trendy greeting.

Corie offered her hand, but he put an arm around her shoulders to urge her in. She let herself be ushered to a set of low, cushioned, tapestry chairs. On the other side of the room a vast desk took up most of the space, a plain matt black oak panel on tubular steel legs. Pictures of performers hung on the walls.

'Lynette told me you were back. My, it's good to see you! Easy to tell you've been a success in the US of A.'

'Thank you, I've done all right. I see from the suite of offices you're a success too.'

'Success? I'm a smash! Practically every one of my artistes is getting top billing—'

'But not Lynette,' she said.

Sasha leaned back in his chair, threw out his arms as if stretching. 'Win some, lose some,' he said. 'You know how it is in show business.'

He was dressed in American jeans and a shirt modelled

after the Gene Autry style. A thick gold identity bracelet hung from his right wrist. He was wearing his black hair longer than he used to. Either he'd recently had a holiday in sunny climes or he was using a sun-lamp, for he had a very fine tan.

Everything about him spoke of success. He was alight with his own well-being. The contrast with her sister, cowering at home with tearstained cheeks, lit a spark of anger in Corie.

'You don't seem to be suffering any loss,' she remarked. 'Lynette's the one who's suffering.'

'Corie, old love, that's the luck of the game. Fashion makes you, fashion breaks you—' He broke off. 'Can I offer you anything? A drink?'

'Eleven in the morning is a little early for drinks, thank you.'

'Coffee, then.' He leapt up, was switching on his intercom when Corie said, 'No, thank you, nothing.' He shrugged, put his hands in his trouser pockets, perched himself on the edge of the black desk.

'So,' he said, 'you've come looking me up. Didn't take you long to see that the field's clear for us – but then you were always quick on the uptake.'

'I beg your pardon?' Corie said. 'I don't quite follow.'

'Oh, come off it, when you packed up and left we agreed it was a good idea – we couldn't have Lynette finding out about us once the newspaper boys began snooping, now could we? But the way things are turning out it's not going to matter any more what Lynette thinks, so you and I—'

Corie turned on her low chair to stare at him. Could he really be saying what he seemed to be saying?

To test it out, she said, 'But that was all a long time ago, Sasha.'

'Sure, but you and I, chickie . . . We had something special, didn't we? And you wouldn't be here now if you didn't want to revive old memories.'

'But there's still my sister's feelings to consider.'

'I say what I always said – what Lynette doesn't know

can't harm her. And anyhow, who cares now what she knows? What could she do to us?'

'She'd be very hurt.'

'Hurt, hurt! Show business is full of people who've had to be hurt. You either get over it or you go under.'

'From what I hear, Lynette is on her way under already, Sasha.'

'We-ell . . . It's a fact her career has taken a nosedive. So you see, even if by any chance she got upset about you and me, it wouldn't matter. So she walks out on me, so what? I've got a dozen girls waiting to fill the space she'll leave on my books.'

He slipped off the edge of the desk, came to Corie, and raised her to her feet by taking her by the shoulders. He looked deep into her hazel eyes with his own dark gaze.

'What is it about you?' he murmured. 'You just *send* me, that's all.' He bent his head to kiss her.

But she turned her face away.

'Hey!' he said, surprised.

She wrenched herself free of his grasp. 'You really are the most selfish, self-centred creature I ever met,' she said.

'What?'

'Did you really imagine I came winging here to say, "Let's go to bed together"?'

'Now look here—'

'Listen to me, Sidney Black of Bromsgrove. If I ever let you touch me, it must have been while I was out of my mind.'

'What's this you're giving me?' he protested. 'More of the "It's not right" routine you kept going through? Save it, chickie, it's just a bore.'

'Heaven forbid that I should bore you! I'll get on with what I came here to say. Surprise, surprise, what I came to say concerns Lynette.'

'What now?' he groaned. 'I thought we agreed – she's on the skids.'

'She is if you don't do anything about it. But—'

'Jesus!' he said. 'First the mother, now the sister. Why

303

can't you just accept that Lynette's style of performance belongs up in the attic with all the other old-fashioned stuff?'

'Is that your considered judgement? As her agent, her man of business, you're consigning her to the rubbish tip?'

'Everything's moved on, Corie, your sister just stood still.'

'And where were you while it was happening?' Corie cried. 'What were you doing, besides raking in your ten per cent?'

'What was I supposed to do? Lynette's talent was always a limited thing—'

'You know our family is a theatre family,' Corie interrupted. 'I've known a lot of agents and heard talk of a lot more. A good agent looks out for his artiste. A good agent plans for change. A good agent doesn't let a star go into oblivion if he can help it – he guides and helps her. But you – you were too busy coining money with a bunch of ignorant kids who only know how to strum a guitar and shout.'

Sasha's eyes flashed with anger. 'Don't knock what you don't understand. Those boys are going to make big money—'

'For how long? All they do is mime to their records, and the records are worked up by the recording studio – don't try to kid me, Sasha, I saw it all in America, hordes of youngsters with no talent, a hit record in the chart today and Skid Row tomorrow.'

'You don't know everything, even if you did see a few bite the dust in the States! Danny Vulcan—'

'Oh yes, Danny Vulcan, I'm sure he's wonderful. But is that what you're saying? You're so incompetent that you can only look after a rising star? You can't do anything for someone whose career has hit a snag?'

'And we're back to Lynette! Why do you have to come here and nag at me about Lynette?' he cried, in what seemed like genuine bewilderment. 'I can't do anything with her. I can't see why you even expect me to – you're too bright to imagine there's anything for her now except maybe principal girl in a panto or two, a few fêtes to open, stuff like that.'

Corie threw her hands out in a gesture of dismissal. 'You appal me, Sasha, you really appal me! Lynette loves you, she depends on you, she's trusted you with her life all these years—'

'Well, she should have had a bit more of the old iron in her.'

'Really? She should have argued with you, disagreed with you? You know very well she's too in love with you to think you could ever be wrong – and that was the way you wanted it! You exploited her, you manipulated her, and now you're saying you're going to let her dwindle away to a nobody.'

'OK, that's what I'm going to do!' he shouted. 'Because that's all she is – a nobody! A one-time wonder, a sweetheart that the world's outgrown . . .'

'Not all the world, Sasha.'

'Oh yes, don't think I haven't had the word. They don't want her on commercial TV, they don't want her on what's left of the variety circuit, they don't want her in the holiday shows except the bath-chair resorts—'

'That's in the UK.'

'Huh? You're not suggesting the States? They'd chew her up and spit her out!'

Corie got a grip on herself. She mustn't let his ugly words make her too angry to negotiate. She was trying to save what was left of her sister's career.

She took a deep breath. 'Sasha,' she said, 'there's a world beyond London's West End and New York's Broadway. There are parts of the world where they still listen to music that puts melody before rhythm, singers who make the words audible, lyrics that have charm and wit. They haven't fallen under the spell of rock-and-roll – at least not yet.'

'You mean out in the boondocks,' he sneered.

'Yes, right, out in the boondocks by your standards. But

there's money to be made in theatres overseas. There are audiences to whom Lynette Lee is still a big name. If you don't waste time, you can get bookings for her while they still want to hear her.'

'Abroad? It's such a nuisance: fixing up transport, booking hotels—'

'Oh, don't by any means put yourself out!' Corie cried. 'Don't let yourself be distracted from promoting Danny Vulcan or Tommy Tremor! Only it seems odd to me that you'd turn your back on what's probably good money, even with expenses for travel and hotels . . .'

'I've never been into that,' Sasha said, shrugging and in a tone of doubt. 'I've never wanted the trouble.'

'There are firms who'll do the transport and accommodation — all you have to do is get the bookings.'

'But bookings for what?' he objected. 'Don't suggest I send out the equivalent of the TV show — the cost would be phenomenal.'

'No, no, it's Lynette they'd want to see. It could be a one-girl show. Something like "An Evening with Lynette Lee". She'd be good at it. She's always been at her best with simplicity, with naturalness.'

' "An Evening with Lynette Lee" . . . What would she do for a band?'

'You could hire local talent.'

'I suppose so . . . We could buy the musical arrangements — I'm sure they'd be available.'

'Her costumes too — they won't be using them any more and some of them were really pretty.'

'So they were.' He began to pace up and down, striking one palm against the other as he thought it out. 'It might work. There are a couple of booking agents I know — never did any business with them because they handle Commonwealth countries and it never seemed worth the trouble . . . I wonder what kind of money they'd offer?'

'You could put out feelers.'

'Yes . . .'

'Only I wouldn't leave it too long, Sasha, because once

the word gets round that the BBC have dropped the show,
the fees would begin to drop too.' And the longer Lynette
was left in limbo, the more demoralised she would become
– but that wouldn't be a big point with Sasha.

'I could get on to it this afternoon. I've a lunch with a
circuit manager but after that . . .'

'Perhaps you could get your secretary to ring the overseas
agents and say you want to have a chat later.'

'Why not?' He switched on his intercom and said,
'Barbie, look in my personal directory – Wally Miles, and
Herb Weissmann – that's with a W, love – yes, contact
them, would you, and ask if it'd be convenient for me to
ring for a chat later. Say, three-ish.'

He switched off, made a note on his own appointments
pad, nodding to himself. The top-notch agent was showing
his mettle – instant action, shrewd bargaining . . .

'It's really good that you have these contacts, Sasha,'
Corie murmured. 'You know so many people, don't you?
That's why it's nice to be able to do something for Lynette.
Folk would perhaps have thought less of you if you'd let her
drop.'

He looked up, startled. 'Think so?'

'Well, she's very well liked, isn't she? As a person, I
mean. Might have been a bit of a black mark against your
name.'

'I never thought of that,' he said, so worried about his
reputation it didn't occur to him he was condemning
himself as totally callous. 'Lucky thing you came in full of
fire and brimstone about her then. To tell the truth, I didn't
see anything but headaches where Lynette was concerned.'
Belatedly he remembered whom he was speaking to. 'I
mean, she's a sweet kid, she and I have meant a lot to each
other in the past . . . I'd always want to do the best I could
for her . . .'

'I know you would, Sasha,' Corie lied. 'Well, you've a
lunch engagement and time's getting on . . .'

'No hard feelings, Corie?' he said, offering his hand. 'I
mean, you understand that I really think a lot of you, which

is why I − you know − hoped you and I could get together in the old way.'

'No hard feelings at all.'

'And say, listen, better not mention any of my plans to Lynette. I don't know yet how it's going to work out.'

'Certainly not, Sasha. I'll leave it to you to mention it to her when you think the time's right.'

When they parted, an onlooker would have thought they were the best of friends. Only someone who looked closely could have seen that Corie was gritting her teeth.

That evening she dropped in at her old home. Monna was giving a voice lesson, Lynette was sitting out in the back garden with a book she wasn't reading, and Opal was fussing about in the kitchen with pots and pans and wooden spoons.

'Are you studying for a part in "Chicken Soup with Barley"?' Corie inquired.

'I'm trying to learn to cook. If Bart and I really are going to get married, I want to know how to make something other than scrambled eggs.'

'Such as what?' Corie asked, coming to peer over her shoulder at the saucepan.

'This is béchamel sauce. Don't breathe down my neck, you're putting me off.'

Corie filled the kettle to make tea. 'I'm glad you're on your own in here, Pal. I've something important to say to you.'

'Yes?' Her sister tasted the sauce on the end of the wooden spoon and made a face.

'It's about Lynette.'

'Oh.' She put the spoon in the saucepan and turned off the heat. 'Something good, I hope. She's dragging about the house − it's heartbreaking.'

'I think something's going to turn up for her.'

'A contract?'

'We-ell . . . Sasha's chatting up some of the agents who deal with overseas bookings. I think it's hopeful.'

'Overseas? Overseas like where?'

'Remains to be seen . . . Spain, Italy . . . Perhaps even South Africa.'

'Sasha's setting it up? How do you know?'

'I . . . er . . . I went to see him this morning.'

'Ah.' Opal nodded. 'You put it into his head.'

'It was William Tranton's idea, really. But he didn't want to go to Sasha with it, so I did.'

Opal gave a grunt of agreement. She began to tip the lumpy sauce into the sink. The kettle boiled, Corie made the tea. Opal untied her apron.

'So Sasha is going to fix up a tour,' she remarked as she folded the apron and put it away. 'I don't exactly see why we have to go into a huddle over that, duckie?'

'I'm thinking about Monna. I'm not sure how she'll take it. When Sasha announces that he's got contracts coming, she'll jump to the conclusion it's for a TV show. You know her dearest wish is that everything should go back to how it was – Lynette the darling of the viewing public, people writing in for signed photos . . .'

'I see what you mean,' said Opal. 'This may seem a big come-down to Monna.'

'So when the word comes, I want you to be terrifically enthusiastic. Fresh worlds to conquer, working in live theatre again as opposed to the Box . . . that kind of thing.'

'Sure thing.' She got cups and saucers from the dresser, fetched milk from the fridge. They sat down at the kitchen table to drink their tea.

'I can be genuinely enthusiastic,' Opal observed. 'Anything is better than having the kidlet moping about indoors all the time. If Sasha fixes her up with a booking in Timbuktu, I'll raise a cheer even for that.' She sipped, decided her tea was too hot, and set it down. 'But what comes after the tour, Corie?'

'I don't know.'

'Another tour, I suppose – to the places she didn't cover the first time. And then a gentle winding-down . . .' She shook her head sadly. 'This was the time I thought she and Sasha might get married. But when he shied away so

thoroughly after the TV show was dropped, I realised it was
no use hoping for that.'

'It never was, Pal.'

'No, I suppose not.'

The days went by, and nothing emerged from Sasha
Lenoir, Artistes Agent. Corie began to think he had either
decided not to bother, or that he'd entered negotiations only
to find the money wasn't attractive enough.

Then, on a June evening, when she was in the darkroom
deeply engaged with a colour distortion she was encouraging in the Agfa developing process, her studio phone rang.
She paid no heed – it was outside office hours and if it
was anyone trying to make an appointment they'd soon give
up.

But the caller didn't give up. With reluctance she let the
transparency slip back into the dish, took off her rubber
gloves, switched on the safe-light and went to the desk.

It was Opal. 'Corie please come over. I need you.'

'What's happened?' she demanded, at once alarmed.

'Nothing much as yet. But Sasha rang to say he'd drop in
"after dinner" and since then everything's been like a ride
on a helter-skelter.'

'What did he say?'

'He said he had "good news". If it's what we discussed,
then Monna and Lynette are getting their hopes far too
high.'

'Didn't he say what he'd be talking about?'

'Not a hint. Monna's persuading herself he's made the
Director of Light Entertainment change his mind—'

'About "You're a Sweetheart"? Oh lord!'

'Please come, Corie.'

'But I'm in the middle of something . . .'

'It's going to be an awful let-down. I don't think I can
cope alone.'

'Give me half an hour,' Corie said, and put the receiver
back.

When she got to the house in a taxi, Sasha's car was
parked outside. Her heart sinking, she went up to the door.

Opal, who'd been watching for her out of the window, let her in.

'What's happening?' Corie whispered.

'Not much so far. Come on.'

Sasha was sitting on the sofa with his arm along its back so that his fingers rested lightly on Lynette's shoulder. Lynette was leaning slightly against him, not looking at him but listening intently to his voice. Monna was in her usual Edwardian armchair near the fireplace. From her expression it was clear she was waiting for the great news.

'Hello, Corie!' Sasha exclaimed. 'What a lucky thing! Now you can hear everything too – and there's quite a lot to tell.'

'You've brought off something useful for Lynette?' she asked, giving him a cue. 'Useful' was a word that could lead into whatever he had to report.

'Useful – yes – and profitable! Let me explain my thinking to you. It seemed to me – and I'm sure you, with all your experience, Monna, will agree – that Light Entertainment had jumped in too fast with their decision about the show—'

'Absolutely disgraceful!' she returned, spots of colour coming into her cheeks. 'To treat my daughter like that . . .'

'Yes, and you can bet they're regretting it by now,' he took it up.

Corie, from where she was standing, couldn't give him any sign that wouldn't be seen by everyone else. She was thinking, What are you up to? Don't pretend more than you can produce, you idiot.

'So I thought it over very thoroughly – took my time over it, because this wasn't a matter to rush into, you know.'

'Of course not,' Monna agreed.

'But it seemed such a long time, Sasha,' Lynette murmured. 'You never rang . . .'

'I know, angel, I know – it's been on my conscience, but my work load is punishing at the moment.'

'Of course,' Lynette agreed, with a suppressed sigh.

'I felt we ought to give them time to see their mistake,' Sasha said. 'At the moment they're absolutely besotted with the pop scene, and I don't blame them because you know, my new clients, especially Danny Vulcan, they're absolutely coining money. The girls swoon over them—'

'Very distasteful,' Monna said. 'I don't know what their parents can be thinking of.'

'Oh, I'm with you on that, Monna. But you've always said, haven't you, that it's a passing phase—'

'I give it six months,' she stated. She'd been saying this for two years now.

'There you have it!' Sasha said. 'You're so shrewd, Monna! Six months, perhaps a year — I thought, Light Entertainment needs six months or so to come to its senses and then of course they'll come back asking for Lynette.'

'Oh, Sasha!' Lynette cried. 'Do you really think so?'

'Sure thing, sweetheart. Absolutely.'

You rat, thought Corie. He knew as well as she did that Lynette's kind of appeal was over, gone to join music hall and light operettas such as *The Lilac Domino* or *Bitter Sweet*.

'But then, you know,' Monna said rather worriedly, 'there's the problem of what my girlie is going to do while the BBC comes to its senses. It isn't good for an artiste to be out of the limelight too long.'

'Right, right! I knew you'd catch on! You're so quick, Monna! Of course we're not going to let Lynette be out of the limelight. We're going to send her on tour.'

Now he'd got to it. Corie exchanged a glance with her sister Opal. They both looked anxiously at Monna.

'On tour,' she repeated dubiously. 'You mean guest-starring in Manchester and Glasgow . . .'

'I mean a grand tour,' Sasha said, throwing out one arm in a gesture to show how grand it would be. 'A world tour.'

'A world tour?'

'Yes, that's what I've been working on. After all, Monna, our little girl has never been abroad except for a couple of shopping trips to Paris and a holiday in Majorca. She's never *worked* abroad. Now you, from your own knowledge, could tell her what a *deepening* experience—'

'Oh . . . as to that . . . I never actually worked abroad except in Ostend and—'

'But you liked it, I'm sure. Reaching a new audience, refining your talent to suit the tastes of other nations . . .'

'Abroad where?' Opal asked, feeling it was time to get down to hard facts.

'You name it, we can do it,' Sasha said, and gave Lynette a triumphant hug to show how pleased he was. 'I've been hard at it for the last ten days, finalising venues. I thought we'd run in easily – I've lined up Geneva, Lausanne, Nice . . . that's for the winter. And then in the spring we're going to Hong Kong, Singapore—'

'Singapore!'

'Yes, sweetheart, there's big money to be made in the Far East.'

'Singapore!' she repeated, going pale. 'It . . . it seems such a long way away.'

'Then of course, after that, there's South Africa, but I'm just listening to what they say so far, I haven't said we're interested. My thinking is, you'll spread your name right round the world and it's sure to echo back to the TV boys at home, so that probably next year . . .'

'But Sasha,' Lynette said, with surprising practicality, 'what would I be doing? Would I be taking a company? Because if that's the idea, I wonder if it would cost—'

'No, no, that's the beauty of it,' he broke in. 'No, this is something completely new—'

'Sasha,' Monna said, 'I must tell you that if you're suggesting my daughter go abroad with a fit-up company . . .'

'As if I would, Monna.' His tone was so full of reproach that Lynette took one of his hands and pressed it. He smiled at her. 'No, love, of course it's nothing second-rate. I thought what you should do is a one-woman show.'

'What?'

' "An Evening with Lynette Lee" – how does that sound?'

At last, it was out. Corie waited for Monna's reaction. Everything hinged on it. If she didn't like it, Lynette was unlikely to have enough confidence to go through with it even if Sasha urged her.

' "An Evening with Lynette Lee",' Monna said, as if she were sampling wine.

'Just me?' Lynette said.

'A band, of course. You'd take your arrangements with you but there'd be a local orchestra – I've checked it all out, and there's plenty of musical talent at all the venues.'

'But what would I *do*?'

'Well, you'd sing, and dance, and chat about your career, and tell a few jokes—'

'Improvise? Oh, I was never any good at that in stage school . . .'

'No, no, you'd have a script – I've talked to a couple of writers who do scripts for cabaret . . .'

Lynette fell silent.

'So what do you think, Monna?' Sasha asked. 'The money's fine, and it puts Lynette on the world stage, and once things go back to normal here, the TV planning won't be dominated by rock-and-roll lads.'

'What happens about costumes?' Opal asked, to fill the gap that followed although she already knew the answer.

'We can do a deal for some of those she wore in "You're a Sweetheart". That's for starters. Once we get going we can commission . . .'

'It sounds as if I'd be doing it for a long time, Sasha.'

'That depends. As soon as we get offers here in London—'

'And of course those would follow,' Monna said.

To Corie, the sigh of relief she gave must have been audible to everyone. Opal smiled at her and gave the faintest of winks.

'Oh yes,' Monna went on, 'it would show those ridiculous programme-planners how they'd misread public taste.'

'But Monna—' Lynette began.

'It would be so good for you, darling! I myself never went abroad often, but of course I remember how much I learned from the tours I did even in this country. Touring turns you into a *trouper*, Lynette.'

'But Hong Kong . . . Singapore . . .'

'You know, Larry went to Australia on tour,' Monna said.

'Larry who?'

'Olivier, of course, Opal – don't be silly, you knew who I meant. Is there any thought of an engagement in Australia, Sasha?'

'That's on the books. I certainly wouldn't turn it down if I got a suitable offer.'

'Australia?' Lynette said faintly.

'But at the moment we're just going to concentrate on the opening tour,' Monna reproved her, seeing her nervousness. 'What was it again, Sasha darling?'

'Geneva, Lausanne, Nice.'

'What language do they speak in Geneva?' asked Lynette.

'Everybody in Switzerland speaks English, sweetie,' he laughed.

'But I'd be on my own . . .'

'Darling, a star is never alone – there are always people to do the donkey work.'

'But not people I know, Monna.' Lynette shrank into herself. 'I couldn't do it.'

Corie could see that the rejection she'd undergone had sapped her self-confidence. She said encouragingly, 'You used to go out to the provinces on your own, Lynette. That was when you were just a kid. You'll be OK—'

'This is different. There'd be no one to talk to . . .'

'I could come with you, darling, if you like?' Monna suggested, her face lighting up at the thought.

Corie gave Sasha a warning glance. Once let Monna take on the role of duenna, and Lynette's life on tour would be almost impossible, with consequences upon her performance that didn't bear thinking of.

'No, no, you've got it all wrong,' he said at once. 'I thought it was clear. Of course I'll be going with you to Geneva and Lausanne, pet.'

315

'You will?'

'Sure thing. I wouldn't let my little linnet-bird fly off on her own to start a new career.'

'Oh, Sasha, you're *such* a darling,' she cried, and buried her face in his shoulder.

Corie left her mother, Lynette and Sasha in eager discussion. Opal came to the door with her. 'So far so good,' Opal murmured.

'A near thing, though.'

'Never mind "Don't put your daughter on the stage, Mrs Worthington" — there ought to be a song about leaving your mother at home.'

'Pal,' Corie said with a little shiver, 'I hope we're doing the right thing . . .'

When she got home she felt so much in need of reassurance she put in a long-distance call to New York. She and Drew had got into the habit of ringing each other about once every week or ten days. He would tell her how his friends-of-Kennedy campaign was going, she would tell him about the London scene.

Tonight she wanted him to say that he thought her sister would benefit from a world tour. But he refused to speak such comforting words.

'If she enjoys it,' he said, 'if it keeps her from feeling her career is over, it serves its purpose. But when American stars go overseas, the gossip usually goes that they can't hack it any more at home.'

'Couldn't you say that you think it's a great idea?'

'Sure, I could say that. But would you believe me?'

'Drew,' she sighed, 'say something to cheer me up.'

'I miss you. Will that do?'

'Better than nothing, I suppose.'

'Oh, don't overwhelm me with your enthusiasm. Couldn't you say you miss me too?'

'I do miss you, Drew,' she said, and when they'd rung off realised how true it was.

Chapter Seventeen

The Genevois had come to the Theatre Bijou with the intention of being pleased. They'd had a good dinner helped along with the excellent local wine, they were in their evening clothes to see and be seen, and now they were to be entertained by a pretty, sweet girl who sang the songs they'd known and loved when they were in their teens – the songs of Gershwin, Cole Porter, Noel Coward.

They knew of Lynette Lee from records made in the heyday of her career. They'd read articles about her in the lightweight magazines. Recently they'd been able to see her television show of the previous season thanks to the wonders of the new television recording tape. She was just the kind of performer they liked.

She opened the show by saying 'Good evening and welcome' in school-girl French. It made them feel immediately superior – for they could say 'good evening' in excellent English, also in German and Italian and Romansch. Anyone who makes you feel good about yourself is lovable. They were inclined to love Lynette Lee.

Corie, Opal and their mother were in the audience, having flown over in secret earlier in the day. Their presence had been kept from Lynette for fear it would make her even more nervous. Corie could sense the goodwill of those around her flowing out to her pretty sister.

The weeks of writing, rewriting, inventing dance routines, rehearsing, rehearsing, rehearsing – they paid off tonight. From her opening chat, in clear, slow, gentle English so that her clever audience could feel even cleverer, to her final Harold Arlen number, 'Let's Take the Long Way Home', she beguiled them. They loved her drifting, gossamer dancing, they loved her really funny rendering of that old favourite of Jean Sablon's, '*Le Fiacre*'.

At the end of Part One she took four curtain calls before they'd let her go. At the finale she took nine curtain calls and was engulfed in flowers – a bouquet each from Corie, Opal and Mrs Duggan, one from Sasha, and one from the management. She endeared herself to the audience by throwing single carnations among them so that the women could take one home and think that they could be like her, and the men could take one home and wish they could get to know her.

In the dressing-room later, her family hugged and kissed her with unfeigned delight.

'You were gorgeous, absolutely gorgeous!' Opal cried.

'You did us proud, darling,' said her mother.

'Not bad, kid sister,' Corie agreed.

Sasha was almost as alight with pleasure as the Duggans. Corie could tell that, mixed in with his satisfaction, there was relief. He really hadn't quite known how this would go.

He needn't have worried. When, after a celebration party and too little sleep, the Duggans surfaced at about eleven o'clock, they were able to see in the *Dépêche de Genève* that the theatre critic had been charmed. He called her '*aimable*' and '*douée*' which Corie, with a few weeks in Monte Carlo to guide her, translated as 'talented'.

The star of the show came down to the hotel dining-room in time for lunch. All her old sparkle had come back. She kissed everyone – her family, her agent, she might even have kissed the head waiter if he had asked her.

'I feel wonderful,' she confessd. 'As if I'd come out of hibernation or something.'

'That's it – the butterfly has re-emerged to dance among the flowers,' Sasha said. 'And think how many flower-gardens all over the world are waiting for you, Lynette.'

It was nicely said. Corie had a feeling it had been rehearsed, but that didn't matter. Lynette glowed, people came up in the restaurant to say they'd seen her opening night and enjoyed it, everything was *couleur de rose*.

Monna in particular revelled in it. This was more like it!

Star treatment from an educated public, compliments and hand-kissing – not like the anonymous approval of the TV audience, the ill-written requests for a signed photo.

'My darling,' she beamed, 'this is just the beginning! I always knew you'd be at your best in a real theatre with a real audience.'

'I must confess it scared me at first,' Lynette replied, blushing at the confession. 'It was so long since I'd actually been in a live theatre – why, I think it might have been that time in Bristol when you first saw me, Sasha.'

'Lucky day for me,' he said.

She smiled at him, a smile full of love and gratitude. To Lynette it was Sasha who had performed the miracle, who had given her back her world.

They lingered over lunch until it was almost time for the visitors to go to Cornaval for the flight. Opal had only been able to get two days off, Corie had photographic appointments for early the next day. Much though they wanted to, they couldn't stay to see another performance, another triumph. Besides, it had already cost them a small fortune to make the trip – they couldn't really afford another night in the hotel.

Lynette came to the airport to wave them goodbye. 'It was absolutely super of you to come,' she cried as she hugged them. 'It meant more to me than all the applause—'

'What a fib,' Corie said. She patted her youngest sister on the shoulder. 'Look after yourself, little 'un. You're on a high of excitement – get a good night's sleep tonight, take some vitamin pills, and practise that *demi contretemps* – your heel nearly tangled in your skirt last night.'

'Oh, you!' Lynette laughed. 'You always think you know best!'

Sasha hadn't come to the airport. He was having a little word with the lighting engineer at the theatre about a muddle over the spots in 'Dancing with My Shadow'. He was staying on another day but then had to be back in London.

'I was really scared about that,' Lynette confessed, 'but

now I've actually done it I don't need my hand held any more.'

'But he'll be back for the opening in Lausanne?' Monna queried, keeping a check on her daughter's career.

'Oh yes, and for Nice — he's putting himself to no end of trouble, dashing back and forth on planes . . .'

Once in flight, the previous night's lack of sleep and the too leisurely lunch caught up with Monna. She dozed off. Opal, who'd been sitting alongside her, removed herself to go into the seat behind with her sister.

'It really went well,' she sighed, settling back in her place.

'Yes, so far so good.'

'Sasha was really delighted, wasn't he?'

'Oh yes, Sasha likes success.'

'Oh, come on, Corie, he's really put in a lot of work. And a lot of air travel — back and forth for three openings . . .'

'What you say is true, Pal, but he's loving it. The cosmopolitan man of the theatre — I bet he brags about his travels to all his contacts in showbiz.'

'I bet he does,' Opal agreed with a laugh. 'But so long as our Lynette is happy, that's all that matters.'

Lynette's next tour abroad was a much bigger undertaking. She was to go to Hong Kong, Singapore, a newly opened European theatre in Bangkok. She would then come home for a rest before touring the big cities of India. This would take her well into 1960.

On these long-distance tours it was obviously unreasonable to expect Sasha to be present for her openings.

'It would be unfair to his other clients,' Monna remarked. 'And in any case, my darling, I'm sure that by now you've found your feet in the touring game.'

'Oh yes, of course,' Lynette agreed, yet she sounded, to Corie's ear, very uncertain. 'Though what if anything goes wrong?'

'What can go wrong, my angel? Everything's been arranged in advance by cable and telephone, the hotels are booked, the bands are all hired, you have the lighting plan and the prompt script for the stage manager. Your father and I used to do this very thing month after month, up and down the length of Great Britain.'

'The Far East isn't quite the same as Manchester and Huddersfield, Monna,' Corie pointed out with some dryness.

'I wonder if perhaps you should take a personal dresser instead of relying on hiring someone on the spot? It might be more in keeping with your status as a star.'

'But who?' Lynette rejoined. 'It's a bit late to find anyone – what if I didn't like her?'

To Corie's mind it was far more important to have someone to deal with the local theatre managers. From her own recollections, Corie could imagine how often they'd contrive to lose sets of instructions or scripts.

'Wouldn't it be a good idea for Lynette to have a tour manager?' She asked. 'It's usual for a company to have—'

'Oh, but a one-woman show?' Monna interrupted, her lip curling a little. She clearly felt that she herself could have handled any problems that might arise if she were to set out on a one-woman tour.

'It would be nice, though,' Lynette murmured.

In the end Sasha saw the wisdom of hiring a tour manager. His name was Oliver Hawkesburn, he was in his late forties, and he certainly had the personality for the job. Each time Corie met him, he dominated the room. She felt sure he would handle the local press and any recalcitrant stage managers with ease.

So they saw the little sister off on her long trip divided between pleasure at her success and anxiety over her comfort and well-being in a strange environment.

'Don't forget to take your vitamins,' Corie warned, 'and don't get dehydrated, drink plenty—'

'You know I always do.'

'And if you do get bitten by anything, even if it's not a mosquito, take anti-malaria tablets . . .'

'Oh, Corie, do stop!' her mother cried in exasperation. 'No daughter of mine would ever be so silly as to neglect her health. Just be sensible, Lynette, and give the kind of performance that would make me proud.'

'I'll do my best,' Lynette promised, and allowed Oliver Hawkesburn to escort her to the departure gate.

Airmail letters and occasional cables let them know the tour was going well. Hong Kong in particular seemed to love Lynette Lee. 'It's because they think she's got Chinese blood,' teased Drew when Corie told him during a phone conversation.

'How do you come to – Oh, because her stage name's Lee. Oh, Drew, that's really *feeble*.'

'I don't feel strong enough to make good jokes.'

'Poor soul. Still slogging away in the Kennedy Cause?'

'Still at it,' he agreed.

John F. Kennedy had begun his presidential campaign in the early months of the year. Pressed by Helen Pittsworth Holstead, Drew had joined the campaign organisation. The work was very hard, the hours very long, and the financial rewards very poor despite the money being poured in by supporters such as Helen and by the Kennedy family itself.

He had given up his partnership in a flourishing public-relations firm to devote himself full time to politics, of which the outcome was uncertain. He could end up an aide in the Press Office of the President of the United States – or he could end up unemployed and poor.

Nevertheless, he seemed happy.

'How's it going?' Corie asked.

'Well, the primaries are showing support for Kennedy. We think he's pretty sure to get the nomination at the Convention.'

Whether this was true, or whether Drew was just saying this to convince himself, Corie couldn't tell. British politics were enough of a mystery to her; American politics even more so. But she understood that it was a help to Drew to chat freely about his work with someone completely unbiased. So she listened to his descriptions of city meetings, regional gatherings, cook-outs, long arguments in smoke-filled rooms. Her comments were limited to 'What happened then?' or 'Did that really matter?' – but they seemed to be what Drew needed.

They often murmured to each other that it would be nice to meet. Time was slipping by and they never saw each other. But America was a long way, and neither of them had money to waste.

'All the same, something's hovering in the air,' he said. 'Helen's talking about a trip to Europe in a couple of months.'

'How does that help us?' Corie asked in mournful tones.

'In this way, my little chickadee. She's going to Zurich for some skulduggery over finance – and she's telling me she needs someone who can speak good German to help with negotiations but keep it under his hat. I *think* she means yours truly.'

'Oh, Drew – you don't mean it!'

'I do – but don't count on it, because it's still something she's muttering to herself. I think she feels guilty about taking me away from the electioneering. But what the hell . . . If somebody who's put in as much money as Helen can't borrow a campaign assistant, who can?'

'Oh, Drew, it would be marvellous! Could you come to London? Or shall I come to Zurich?'

'Well, it gets even better. Eddie wants to go to Europe with her and take in the Olympics. A college friend of his is running in the marathon. Naturally Mirrie doesn't want to be left out. So it looks like a kind of European tour, taking in Rome for part of the Olympics – and if you can't land an assignment to do some work in Rome while I'm there, you're not the girl I think you are.'

'Rome!' breathed Corie.

'Wouldn't be bad, would it? *Three Coins in the Fountain*, and all that.'

'I'll see what I can do,' she promised.

She spent all her spare time for the next two weeks ringing around and dropping in on friends in the newspaper world. By now she had a fairly large circle of such contacts. To her pleasure, it was *News Now* who came up with the deal. 'Human interest pix of the people of Rome,' the head of the London office said to her. 'And if you could just possibly come up with another scoop like Batistá scampering out of Havana, so much the better.'

'That's not likely, Harry . . .'

'Of course not. That was a chance in a million. All we're asking for is some pix of how the Romans are reacting to the invasion of Olympics fans. How does that grab you?'

'Sounds great.'

When she told her mother and her sister Opal, Opal was impressed but Monna merely nodded. To her, athletic feats were not important. However, when Sasha began to show an interest, Monna paid attention.

'Exactly how could the Olympics affect Lynette?' she asked when he said it would be a good idea to put out feelers.

'Well, you see, with such a huge tourist population this summer, Rome is putting on all kinds of shows. And there's a thing called "Summer Celebration" – something along the lines of a revue.'

'A revue,' Monna echoed, charmed. Revue had almost died out of the British theatre, but to her it had always seemed the height of sophistication. 'And there could be an opening there for Lynette?'

'Could well be. I gather it's a mix of Italian and other artistes – to suit the tastes of all the different nationalities visiting Rome because of the Games. Yes, yes . . . just let me see what I can find out . . .'

Corie couldn't help joining the discussion. 'It would be better for Lynette if you could get this engagement and put off her Indian tour,' she suggested. 'I know she's scheduled to go to the hill resorts first and then on to Delhi, but I bet it's as hot as blazes in Delhi even in September.'

'Oh, the Indian tour,' Sasha said with a lordly wave of the hand. 'That can be rearranged in any way we like. It's far more important to land a first-class date like Rome.'

Anxieties over Lynette were never far from Corie's mind, and surfaced again and again. Reading between the lines of her sister's letters from her Far East venues, it began to be clear that Oliver Hawkesburn wasn't the ideal escort. True, he dealt with the press and the theatre management at each new city. But thereafter he seemed to leave Lynette pretty much on her own. In Singapore there were hints about his being with friends at Raffles Hotel. In Hong Kong he seemed to be at the Peninsular with 'some of the fellows'.

When they get back, thought Corie, I'm going to have a word with that gentleman.

Lynette's return from Hong Kong was delayed a few days because, it seemed, her luggage went astray between the hotel and the airport. Oliver Hawkesburn arrived back without her. Corie was incensed.

'How could you just leave her there on her own?' she berated him.

'My dear girl, she wanted to stay,' he replied, looking down at her in the super-aristocratic manner he affected. 'And it seemed good sense – I mean, if I'd stayed too, it would have meant an extra hotel bill. And anyhow, like every other woman in Hong Kong, she'd got some dresses being made and if she went back to the Mandarin and stayed on for a day or two, she could bring them home instead of having them sent.'

It sounded so unlike Lynette that Corie was convinced he was making excuses. Not so, however. When Lynette arrived three days later, she confirmed it all. 'Don't fuss about it, Corie,' she said in a cool tone when her sister asked questions. 'It was just one of those things – my luggage was left at the hotel by mistake, by the time it could be sent to the airport I'd have missed the flight anyhow, so I sent Oliver on ahead and just went back to the Mandarin.'

'But the whole reason he's with you is to prevent mishaps like that . . .'

Lynette shrugged. 'Nobody can prevent mishaps all the time. Anyway, I quite enjoyed having a few days to myself to go shopping and lounge about.'

'All by yourself?' Corie asked, amazed. For one thing had always been certain about her sister – she didn't much enjoy her own company.

'Yes, all by myself,' Lynette replied, almost snappishly. And then, seeing the astonishment on her sister's face, she smiled and put her hands together in a gesture of asking for forgiveness. 'Sorry, sorry, it's jet lag . . .'

'Of course, sweetheart, what a pig I am to bother you.'

'You wouldn't be Corie if you weren't bothering yourself about me. But now you've got to stop, otherwise I won't give you the beautiful Chinese trousers I bought for you in Hong Kong.'

Everything else was forgotten in the usual excitement of distributing presents. Lynette slept for almost fourteen hours, seemed her old self again next day, and began dance practice and rehearsals of new songs the day after that.

Three weeks later she was off to Italy. Sasha was incandescent with pride over the engagement. 'A fifteen-minute spot in both the first and second half,' he crowed. 'And a four-week season, and the money's half as much again as we were getting for "An Evening with".'

'My dear boy,' Monna approved, 'you've done wonders.' And then, after a day or two of consideration, she dropped her bombshell. She made a surprise trip to Corie's flat one evening to deliver it.

'I think, darling,' she said, 'I'll come with you when you fly to Rome next week. I really would like to see my little star shining there – the Eternal City, you know, the centre of the civilised world . . .'

'I thought you had voice students lined up—'

'I put them off,' her mother said. 'After all, others take holidays in the summer, why shouldn't I?'

'Well, that's true . . .'

'And as to the cost,' Mrs Duggan went on, 'I'm sure your news magazine wouldn't mind if I shared your hotel room.'

Corie was aghast. She had hoped to spend some time with Drew if it could be arranged discreetly. With her mother there, any such opportunity would be wrecked.

But there was nothing to be done, short of saying that Monna wouldn't be welcome – and though there were often times when Corie had wanted to say something of the sort, in the end she seldom did. Something like pity held her back. Monna's dream world could so easily come to pieces and, if it did, it was hard to see how Monna could survive.

When they reached Rome, the Holsteads were already there, settled into the Gran Colonna in the Via Veneto. Invited to dinner on their first evening, Monna was for once reduced almost to silence. The hotel was so splendiferous in its Italian style – acres of creamy marble, vast flower arrangements in gilt baskets, a little waterfall with ferns in a shaded patio, doves in an aviary, porters and bellboys in white livery, a bar in dark blue with a star-sprinkled ceiling, a dining-room as big as a football pitch.

'We had the pleasure of seeing your daughter's show last night,' Mrs Holstead said kindly to Monna. 'A pretty girl.'

'Neat,' agreed her son.

'The Italians adored her,' Mirabel added. 'Of course they go nuts over blondes.'

Mrs Duggan glowed. Drew, catching Corie's eye, gave a grin. He held up his hand and made a circle with his thumb and forefinger, meaning, 'Everything's going fine.'

'Of course, strictly speaking it isn't my daughter's show,' Monna said with surprising modesty. 'What are the other performers like?'

'The German comedian I couldn't make anything of,' Helen said. 'Drew said he was very funny – political satire, I think. There were a pair of flamenco dancers. What else, Mirrie?'

'A black tap-dance team – straight out of Harlem, I'd say.'

'Let's order, Mother, I'm starving,' Eddie begged.

Monna buried her face in her menu, but Corie could see she was pleased. The programme described held nothing that sounded dangerous in comparison with her daughter's gentle English style.

It was a strange meal. Two different sets of conversation went on. Helen and Monna talked about the difficulties of bringing up a family, the rest talked about Rome and the

Olympics. When at length it was time to leave, Drew only had a moment to murmur, 'I'll call you.'

But she had work to do. She missed his first call because she was out at the street market near the mainline station almost at dawn, and didn't get back until midday. In the afternoon she had to take Monna to see Lynette at Lynette's hotel, the Belfiore. It was necessary to accompany Monna, for she displayed a suprising lack of confidence if she had to deal with people who couldn't speak her language.

The afternoon was extremely hot. Even the Romans were complaining – but then had it not been for the Olympics, they'd have been enjoying their siesta.

When Monna and Corie went up to Lynette's room they had to wait quite a few moments before she opened the door to them. She was clad in a loose cotton dressing-gown, looking groggy with sleep.

'My angel!' cried Monna, taking her by the shoulders and surveying her. 'Is something wrong?'

Lynette rubbed her eyes. 'Wha-at?' she sighed. 'No, I was just catching forty winks. You should have rung to say you were here – I'd have come down.'

'But dearest, you *never* sleep in the afternoon!'

'I do when the temperature reaches ninety,' her daughter said, turning away in irritation.

Monna looked as if she were about to say yes, the temperature was in the nineties, yet here she was, Crystal Duggan properly dressed in a silk suit and court shoes. Corie quickly forestalled her by suggesting it would be nice to have tea.

'Tea!' said Lynette. 'I don't recommend the Italian idea of tea.'

'Well, coffee then – may I order it?'

'Do as you like,' Lynette said over her shoulder as she went into the bathroom and closed the door. A moment later they could hear the shower running.

'Well, really,' said Mrs Duggan, sitting down in a padded cane armchair by the shaded window, 'that's not how I trained my daughters to behave to their guests!'

'It's hot, Monna. And we woke her up.'

'Sleeping in the afternoon,' her mother muttered, as if mentioning some deadly crime. 'I toured the whole of Great Britain and did two shows a night month after month, and I never slept in the afternoon.'

When Lynette reappeared in a towel and with her hair wringing wet, her normal good manners had returned. She asked for ten minutes to get ready, took her clothes into the bathroom, to emerge well within her time limit looking cool and sweet. A little lipstick and some eye shadow, and she was ready.

'There's a nice little café a few turnings away with a garden – I'll treat you to ice-cream,' she suggested.

Corie and her mother sat in the shade of a walnut tree and ate the best ice-cream in the world, while Lynette drank iced coffee. Though she willingly interpreted for them, it was clear to Corie that she would have been glad not to have to act hostess to them. They parted about five o'clock, Monna promising to be at the theatre backstage to help her daughter dress.

'Thank you, Monna,' Lynette said through tight lips.

The Teatro dell'Estiva wasn't the largest in Rome but it had a very charming old interior, gilt and bedecked with cupids. Corie and her mother had seats booked in the best part of the auditorium. Rather unwillingly, Corie put Monna in a taxi, gave the driver instructions, and then had dinner with Drew. They made a date to go out dancing after the theatre.

'I'll pick you up,' he said.

'We may go backstage to talk to Lynette.'

'I'll wait,' he promised.

The show was what the Holsteads had described – a mixture of all nations and all styles, not entirely a successful mix but with enough good things to make it work. What Mirrie Holstead had said was true – the Italian males adored Lynette. They stamped and shouted, '*Da capo, da capo*', at the end of each of her numbers, throwing roses and lilies at her feet.

Backstage afterwards, Monna hugged her daughter in triumph. 'Oh, it was even better than in Geneva, darling – a warmer, more responsive audience!'

'Yes, it went well,' Lynette said.

She began to peel off the sweat-soaked silk-muslin dress with its many petticoats. The plump little Italian maid came to help her. 'No, no, let me,' Monna cried, elbowing her out of the way.

The maid looked resigned. Apparently this had happened before the show also. '*Ah, la mamma,*' she murmured, and took herself off.

Cards and flowers were brought in, mainly from Italian gentlemen who hoped to be allowed to take the beautiful English star to supper. 'How very flattering,' Monna said with a little laugh.

'Not entirely, Monna, because their intentions are strictly dishonourable.'

'Lynette! What a thing to say!'

'Just you wait until we leave. There'll be a gang of them waiting outside – and they catch at you as you try to walk past.'

'Catch at you? Well, I suppose they want autographs, dear.'

'That's not what they want,' Lynette said in tones of disgust. 'I have to get the stage doorkeeper to clear the path for me.'

Later, when her mother had gone out to try to find a vase for some splendid gardenias, her younger sister turned to Corie in appeal. 'Get her out of my hair, Corie,' she pleaded. 'I'm too tired to cope with her.'

It was so unlike Lynette to say anything in the least critical of her mother that Corie was utterly taken aback.

'What's the matter, Lynnie?'

'I'm just tired. I find the heat very trying. If I can get a good sleep in the afternoon and keep in the cool, I'm OK. But to have her barge in – no, I didn't mean that, of course she wanted to see me, she came all this way to see me–' She broke off, distressed and flustered. 'It's just that I need to keep quiet, and she wants to fuss around me . . .'

'I'll take her away as soon as I can, love. Relax, I'll deal with it.'

So when her mother came back with the vase of water, Corie was on her feet with her handbag over her arm. 'Come on, Monna, we've got someone waiting for us outside.'

'*We* have?'

'Drew is taking us out to supper.'

'But . . . But I thought I'd stay with Lynette.'

'Lynette needs to get back to the hotel and into bed. You know you've always said that a performer needs her sleep.'

'Well, that's true—'

'And poor Drew is standing around outside waiting for us.'

'Well, dear, it's not what I was planning . . .'

Nor I, thought Corie.

'Just let me arrange these flowers.'

'All right. I'll just go out and tell Drew you'll be five minutes. Five minutes, Monna – all right?'

'I suppose so, if you insist,' her mother said with ill-grace.

Drew was pacing up and down in the narrow alley outside the stage door. He turned at the little surge of excitement among the crowd of men as Corie came out.

'*Signorina, signorina* . . .'

What Lynette had said was quite true. They made grabs at her as she moved forward, and were very little discouraged when they found it wasn't the pretty little blonde but a different girl.

'Drew!' Corie called over their heads.

He came to her rescue. 'Is that what you call an admiring throng?' he asked with a laugh.

'I'm sure there's a word for it,' Corie said. 'Drew, I have something awful to tell you.'

'What?'

'My mother's coming with us.'

'When? You mean, now?'

'I'm afraid so.'

'You're joking.'

'No, I'm not. It was the only way I could think of to get her out of my sister's dressing-room. The poor kid's at the end of her tether. I'm sorry, Drew.'

'But we're going dancing! I got a recommendation to a great discotheque—'

'Could we go to some quiet restaurant? And just have a meal?'

'Corie, what do you take me for? I don't want to go to a restaurant in a threesome with your *mother*!'

'Neither do I,' she said wearily, 'neither do I.'

She sounded so depressed that he threw his arms around her and gave a snort of laughter. 'OK, here's what we do. We take Mom out and give her supper, then we deliver her to the hotel and *then* we go dancing. OK?'

'Oh, Drew, you're an angel.'

'Not at all. I had ideas that were quite unlike those of an angel. Never mind, let's play it by ear.'

When Monna joined them, he found them a taxi and at the recommendation of the driver took them to a sedate pasta restaurant in the Piazza del Popolo. Though it was by now very late by British standards, the restaurant was doing good business. Monna experimented with *pasta ai funghi*, announced with some disdain that it was simply macaroni with mushrooms, and on the whole was quite willing to be deposited at the Hotel Giulietta at about a quarter to one.

'Aren't you coming in?' she said in astonishment as her daughter turned back to the taxi.

'Drew and I are going dancing,' Corie said.

'At this hour?'

'See you in the morning, Monna.'

'My dear child, I shall still be awake when you come in. You don't expect me to sleep if I know very well I'm going to be disturbed?'

'I shan't disturb you, Monna.'

'We shall see,' her mother said huffily, and went indoors.

Drew looked at Corie as she climbed in. 'Do I gather you're in disgrace?'

'I'm used to it,' she replied.

For answer he leaned forward to speak to the taxi-man. 'Where do lovers go when they want to be alone?'

The driver made some reply.

'Take us there.'

So that was how it came about that in the warm August night, they were in each other's arms on a bench beneath a tree on the banks of the Tiber.

The trip to Rome proved to them that they were on the verge of being very much in love. Had things been easier they might have become lovers but, even without that final act, they gave and took comfort from each other in stolen moments. For Corie it was a strange, unsettling experience. All her life she'd been wary of men, and when she'd given in to Sasha there had been self-disgust rather than happiness.

Now she found herself letting her defences crumble because someone seemed to care for her unselfishly, generously. She would warn herself: It's Rome, it's the magic of the Coins in the Fountain, it's a fairy tale – don't be fooled, you've been around too long to be fooled.

All the same, the few hours of the few days they could share were tinged with magic.

Drew had to leave with the Holsteads. Eddie cheered his friend home (somewhere about fifth from the back). Mirabel had bought six dresses and had her hair cut by the best hairdresser in Rome – a significant improvement. Helen Holstead said it was time to go.

'And what she says goes,' Drew sighed. 'But we'll fix something up. I'll get to London somehow—'

'Or I'll come to Washington—'

'Washington! I'm all over the place at the moment, Corie – Chicago, San Francisco – wherever Jack's speaking, I'm there. But we'll get together as soon as we can fix it.'

'Yes, darling.'

She held on to him strongly as they said goodbye. She wanted never to let him go.

Back in London life seemed strange – dull and drained of

colour if she couldn't count on seeing Drew for an hour or so. He rang soon after he got back to the States to tell her he'd begun to miss her the moment the plane left the ground. She took comfort in his words, yet within two or three weeks he was talking chiefly about politics once more. She had a depressing conviction that when she wasn't actually with him, her power was growing less.

Lynette came back from Rome, had two weeks to rest and have replacements made for dresses ruined by too many visits to the dry cleaners, and was off to India.

'It's too much for her,' Corie said in anxiety to Opal. 'You should have seen her in Rome – really exhausted. I wanted her to cancel this Indian tour but she wouldn't.'

'Sasha would have gone through the roof at the mere suggestion. He had some problems when he put it off so she could take the Rome booking, I think – there was a penalty clause in the contract.'

'Luckily it's a short tour, Pal. We'll have to start a campaign about getting her a long rest before she goes anywhere else.'

Her sister nodded agreement. But they both knew that Lynette would do what Sasha decreed and what her mother expected.

Corie herself was busy. She was at last arranging the exhibition that Norman Gibson had urged upon her. The show was to go on in a Mayfair gallery at the beginning of November.

Because she was hard at work making perfect prints of the photographs she wanted to exhibit, she didn't see as much of Lynette as she might have when her younger sister came home from Delhi. Her conscience smote her, all the more so as Opal said she thought Lynette seemed very tired and edgy.

'I tried to insist that she should have a proper rest,' Opal said on the phone. 'But Sasha looked at me as if I'd lost my mind, and Monna got cross. There was this great opportunity that came up, you see – at the Exaion Teater in Copenhagen. Someone else had let them down at almost the last minute. So she's off tomorrow.'

'Oh, lord . . .'

'I did my best, Corie, honestly I did.'

'I know, Pal. It's difficult to do anything to help Lynette because she doesn't seem to know she needs help . . .'

In the last week of October all the work for the exhibition was done and a little lull occurred in Corie's life. She had been paid by *News Now* for her Olympics pictures, even though nothing particularly spectacular had occurred within her viewfinder. She felt she could indulge herself by dropping in on her little sister in Copenhagen.

She arrived unheralded on a foggy, chilly October afternoon. She'd booked into a hotel recently opened, on the banks of a canal where swans glided in the mist. She washed, changed, had dinner, bought flowers at the hotel shop then took a taxi to the theatre.

The doorkeeper was doubtful about letting her in to see Miss Lee. 'She told me she liked quiet and relaxful before the show,' he said in stilted English.

'But I'm her sister,' she said. 'Look.' She took her wallet out of her handbag, opened it to a family photo she herself had taken last Christmas – mother and the three daughters in front of the fireplace in the Bayswater house.

'Oh, ja, I see it,' he said, grinning with pleasure. 'OK then, you go in.'

The backstage area was just as unglamorous in Denmark as anywhere else. There was the usual smell of dust, size, scenery paint, and hot lamps. A passing workman pointed her to the right door. She tapped lightly and walked in with the flowers held out, saying: 'Surprise!'

And then at that moment she found the explanation for the moods, the edginess, the fits of being tired out. It rushed upon her with horror when she looked at Lynette.

Her sister was standing in a cotton wrapper, one foot up on a stool so that her leg was bent. And she was injecting something from a syringe into her thigh.

Chapter Eighteen

Corie didn't hesitate. In two strides she was across the room. Her arm went out in a sideways arc. Her fist hit Lynette's hand just as she was pressing the plunger.

Lynette gave a scream of pain and fright. The syringe flew away towards the dressing-table. There was a little crash and the tinkle of breaking glass.

'Corie!' Lynette exclaimed. Her voice broke, she burst into tears.

'Darling,' her sister faltered, putting her arms round her, 'I'm sorry, I'm sorry. Don't cry. I didn't mean to hurt you . . .'

'What have you *done*?' wept Lynette.

'I had to, Lynette, I couldn't let you do that to yourself—'

'You stupid, *stupid*, interfering fool!' Lynette fought free of Corie's embrace. She darted to the dressing-table, picked up the shards of the syringe. 'It's broken, oh, it's broken – oh, God, what am I going to do now?'

'Don't cry, darling, I'll help you, we'll get treatment for you . . .'

'Treatment for me?' Lynette got to her feet, staring at Corie with blazing eyes. 'What do you think that was, you madwoman!'

'Don't be ashamed, Lynette, it's something that can be cured—'

'Shut up!' commanded her little sister. 'Shut up, you chattering idiot! Look at the label!'

She pointed at a little plastic case lying on the dressing-table. Almost scared at her tone, Corie drew near enough to examine it.

It lay open. On a bed of foam rubber lay five medical ampoules. There was a groove for a sixth but that was

337

empty, the home for the ampoule now lying on the lid of the case, its neck filed off.

Corie bent over. She read: Insulin Zinc Suspension (IZS) Actetate Buffered (BP) 80 units per ml. Six prescribed injections by ampoule. Please check colour code.

Below that was the maker's name. Below that again was the reminder: Blue or green Clinitest result. If any other consult doctor at once.

Insulin?

'Lynette,' Corie whispered.

'Yes, now it's too late, ask me – ask what I was injecting!'

'You've got diabetes?'

'Oh, no, I'm a raving drug addict – you said so yourself . . .'

'Lynette, forgive me. I had no idea! When I opened the door and saw—'

'Yes, saw me, getting myself high on – what – heroin, was it? Ready to go on stage stoned out of my mind – is that it? My God, you've got a poor opinion of me, Corie!'

'No, no, darling – you know that's not true – I'm sorry, I just reacted without stopping to think . . . Oh, for pity's sake, Lynette, what else was I to think?'

Lynette sank down on the dressing-stool in front of the mirror. 'What am I going to do now?' she lamented. 'The syringe is useless – and I'm supposed to be on stage in a little over an hour, and I have to have the injection and then half an hour later some food, otherwise I can't stay in balance.'

'In balance?'

'Never mind, never mind, it's nothing to do with you—'

'But it is to do with me, Lynette! It's all my fault about the syringe – haven't you another one?'

'Of course, yes, but it's at the hotel, and by the time I dress again and get there and get back—'

'I'll go! I'll bring the syringe! What's your room number?'

'Would you?' Lynette said, seeming to calm a little. 'You'll have to be quick . . .'

'Yes, yes, I'll grab a taxi – where's the syringe?'

'In a cosmetics bag locked in my suitcase, and that's in the wardrobe.'

'Right. The room number?'

'Eight-o-six.'

'And give me a note – permission to get your key . . .' Corie remembered how the doorkeeper had stopped her at the theatre.

Lynette scrambled in her handbag, brought out an old envelope, wrote with an eyebrow pencil in her big school-girl scrawl: 'OK, Lynette Lee.' She handed it to her sister together with the little bunch of keys for her luggage.

Corie was out of the door at a run. She whisked through the backstage passages, out into the street to flag down a taxi. Within five minutes she was at the Kronen, had flourished the note and got the key, and was inside the hotel room.

The cosmetics bag was, predictably, of forget-me-not blue silk trimmed with lace. Inside Corie could feel the hard outline of a flat metal case. She ran downstairs, not waiting for the lift. The taxi was at the kerb according to instructions. She fell into it again and was driven round the side of Kongens Nytorv to the theatre.

The doorkeeper looked at her in astonishment as she ran back past him. He made no attempt to detain her however. Within twelve minutes of leaving Lynette, Corie was back.

There was no doubt that her young sister was under stress. She was pacing about the dressing-room in a nervous hustle, the flowers Corie had brought strewn about and trampled on the floor. She sprang at Corie as she came in, snatched the cosmetics bag, unzipped it to tip out the syringe case.

Then she paused, straightened, and breathed in deeply. 'Go outside and wait,' she said to Corie.

'But sweetheart, can't I help?'

'Go outside!' Lynette commanded. 'I can't do it with anyone watching!'

Humbled, Corie obeyed.

A minute or two went by while she leaned against the passage, herself trembling with nervous reaction. At last she heard her sister call, 'Come in.'

Lynette was sitting in front of the dressing-table. The insulin and equipment had all been tidied away. She was smoothing her hair back from her cheeks, her breathing consciously controlled.

'Now,' she said, not looking at Corie, 'in about half an hour I'll have a meal on a tray. It's ordered and will be brought to me here. Half an hour after that, I've got to be on stage.'

'Will you be all right?'

'I think so. I was a little late with the injection but in fact I don't have a dance routine until about half-way through the first part of the show, so I had a bit of leeway.'

'Lynette, I'm so terribly sorry—'

'Save it,' Lynette said. 'I haven't the energy to spare at the moment. No doubt you've got a thousand questions you want to ask but I can't deal with it now, Corie – do you understand?'

'Yes, of course.'

'After the show, all right?'

'Yes.'

'So clear off now, if you don't mind.'

'Lynette, don't be angry with me—'

'I'm not angry. When I need insulin I get edgy – it's one of the drawbacks of the condition. I'll explain it all later.'

'Of course,' Corie agreed and, after dropping a butterfly kiss on her sister's hair, went out.

There was an hour to go before curtain-up. Corie went to the nearest café, sank down in a booth, and ordered a brandy. She needed it, after one of the worst experiences of her life.

As its restorative powers began to take effect, she leaned back into the corner of the booth and closed her eyes.

How could she have been so utterly, completely wrong? How could she have so misjudged her own sister?

She would never forgive herself, never. To fly to such a

stupid conclusion . . . And about Lynette, too – Lynette who was so sweet, so untouched by the harshness of life . . .

And yet that couldn't be true. Lynette had diabetes – from all the evidence had had it for some time – and had been handling it without needing help from anyone. That wasn't the sweet, innocent child-woman of Corie's recollection. That was the behaviour of a fully mature adult.

I don't think I ever really knew her, Corie told herself. I just put her into a particular picture-frame when she was twelve or thirteen and in my thoughts I've never let her step out of it since then.

She was ashamed. She and Opal, trying to handle Lynette's life for her, planning behind her back to make Sasha do this or that for her, trying to shield her from hurt.

And all the time . . . All the time . . .

Tears began to trickle down her cheeks. She fished in her handbag for a handkerchief, wiped them away, blew her nose, then summoned the waiter to order black coffee. She must get herself into a respectable state so as to go to the theatre and watch her gallant, tough little sister go through her paces for her audience.

To Corie's watchful eye, the performance seemed as good as ever. There was the carefully uttered 'Good evening and welcome!' in Danish, which evoked cheers and laughter, and then the clear, robin-on-a-branch voice singing Richard Rodgers' classic 'This Can't Be Love'.

> 'This can't be love, because I feel so well,
> No sobs, no sorrows, no sighs,
> This can't be love, I get no dizzy spells . . .'

Corie glanced at the people next to her on either side. They could have no idea of the irony of the words. Without the precious insulin in her bloodstream, the pretty girl on the stage might have a dizzy spell that could take her straight into hospital.

When the time came for the dance routine, Corie felt herself go tense. But when the footlights dimmed and the spot came for 'Dancing with My Shadow' there wasn't the slightest hint of anything wrong. Lynette drifted across the stage, her every graceful move mirrored by the shadow image, her body weaving and twirling, rising and falling, featherlike in its lightness.

The first-half finale was 'Blue Skies'. Lynette sang it as if every word were the literal truth: 'Blue skies, smiling at me, Nothing but blue skies do I see . . .'

She's wonderful, thought Corie. Better than I ever dreamed.

In the interval she mingled with the crowd loitering about in the vestibule, trying to gauge their reaction. She was hampered by a total ignorance of Danish but, from the tone, she thought they approved of what they'd seen.

It seemed to Corie that the second half was even better than the first – perhaps because Lynette had recovered more fully from the emotional upset in her dressing-room. She chatted with her audience and with the band leader, the simple, clear jokes in English that everyone present could follow. She sang 'All I Do Is Dream of You'; she sang 'Round the Bend of the River'; she sang 'A Nightingale Sang in Berkeley Square'. She did a soft-shoe number to 'Tea for Two'; she floated and swerved through 'Come Rain or Come Shine'.

The curtain finale was 'Wonderful, Wonderful Copenhagen'. Corie wondered how often the audience had heard it. Yet they cheered and clapped and demanded an encore. Lynette took six curtains, curtseyed and blew kisses, accepted bouquets of flowers – all with that young-girl glow which won the hearts of both men and women in the theatre.

After it was over, Corie went backstage to the dressing-room. Here there were no cards asking for supper dates as in Rome, but there were flowers, boxes of sweets, requests for signed photographs. Most of the flowers and all the sweets were sent to the nearest hospital, the requests for photographs were handed to the manager who had a supply ready to distribute.

By eleven-thirty they were in a taxi on their way to Lynette's hotel. The night porter supplied her key while asking, 'Shall I tell room service to bring your meal?'

'If you would, please.'

'Certainly, Miss Lee.' He picked up the phone to give the instruction.

'You see, with this condition,' Lynette explained, 'I have to eat regularly. I use up so much energy in practice and rehearsal and performance, I've always got to make sure my blood sugar is OK.'

They were in the lift. The hotel was silent about them. It was like being in a little cocoon. Corie said, 'You'll have to explain it all to me in words of one syllable, duckie. I'm not good on scientific things.'

'Neither am I,' her sister said with a little nervous laugh. 'I just had to learn from experience.'

They reached the right floor, went into her room. Lynette threw her shoulder bag on the bed, pulled off her jacket, and made for the bathroom. 'Make yourself at home,' she said. 'I like to take a shower when I get in. I'll be with you in a minute.'

While she was showering, the food arrived. To the casual glance it seemed just the kind of meal Lynette would ordinarily order – a fish dish, a large salad, a roll and butter. With it came a glass of milk. Perhaps in days past Lynette would have followed it with a large piece of cake or a helping of ice-cream, because dancers use up a lot of calories. There was, however, no dessert.

Corie asked the waiter if he would be so good as to bring coffee. By the time it came, Lynette had emerged, wrapped in her bath-robe and with a towel turban for her blonde hair.

She sat down in the chair by the low table and began to eat. 'Perhaps the best way to do this is for you to ask questions, Corie. But – ' she glanced at the clock radio by the bed – 'we can't take long. I have to get some sleep soon.'

'Of course. I don't want to – I don't want to interrupt

your routine – I feel at such a loss, Lynette!'

'I know, it's a shock,' her sister said, gathering up a forkful of salad.

'How did it start? Were you feeling ill?'

Lynette chewed, trying to look back at the experience. 'I had felt sort of up and down for a while. But I put that down to nerves, you know? I'd done the European venues and they went off all right, but I was a bag of nerves . . .'

'Yes,' Corie encouraged.

'I was terribly frightened about going to the Far East. I mean, really frightened, Corie.' She stopped, set down her knife and fork, and put her hands up to her cheeks. 'I realised later that that's part of the condition – because your body isn't functioning properly your brain gets a bit out of focus, you get things out of proportion. I couldn't sleep for thinking about Singapore and Bangkok. Then Sasha hired Oliver, and I relaxed a bit, and everything seemed more or less normal, although I noticed I always seemed to have a raging thirst.'

'But you always were one to take a lot of fluids. I remember when we used to go to dance practice together, the first thing you did when we got out was to buy a bottle of pop.'

'Yes, but this was a lot more – I'd stop in the middle of class to go and get a drink. And then there was the other tell-tale symptom – I kept running to the bathroom. But I didn't think anything of it, because I didn't recognise either of those things as symptoms.'

'No,' Corie agreed, 'neither would I.'

'In Singapore I sometimes felt quite woozy. I tried to tell Oliver but he just waved it away – "The heat, my dear girl" – he's ever so lofty, is Oliver, I'm glad he's not with me when I do European engagements . . .'

She addressed herself once more to the food. Corie sipped her coffee, silently damning Oliver Hawkesburn for a useless fool.

'You felt woozy,' she prompted.

'Yes, and I thought it was the heat. Singapore *is* hot,

despite the air-conditioning in the modern hotels. And Bangkok was worse. I've never liked the heat, you know, Corie, so I didn't take too much heed. I thought I'd be better in Hong Kong. The climate's cooler at that time of year.'

'But you didn't feel better.'

'No, I felt worse. I got stupidly cross with the band leader at the theatre − well, that was partly Oliver's fault because he went off to see some friends from his old days − he was in the R.A.F. out there, you see, he has friends dotted all over. Anyhow − where was I? Well, I went home from rehearsal on the Sunday afternoon and felt really dreadful − really, Corie, I felt as if some other person was in my body . . .' she shivered.

Corie got up to put an arm about her. 'Take your time, sweetie, don't upset yourself.'

'No, I'm all right. It's just . . . it scared me so much at the time.' She smiled up at her sister, tremulous but determined to finish her explanation. 'Well, I seem to have collapsed going up the stairs − I don't know why I was going up the stairs instead of waiting for the lift. Anyway, a chambermaid found me, the hotel doctor was called, and he brought me round and sorted me out and put me to bed. Dr Chang . . . I owe him an awful lot.'

'And did he tell you about the diabetes?'

'He came next morning. He sat there holding my hand and looking perturbed. It's not true, you know, that the Chinese are inscrutable,' Lynette put in, smiling and shaking her head. 'He looked jolly upset. He said he thought I had a rather serious condition and he'd like me to go into hospital for tests.'

'Hospital?'

'I of course said that was impossible, I had a show to do. We had a great long argument and in the end he said he'd do his best to keep me going for the two weeks of the engagement but after that I *must* go in for tests because he was sure I had some degree of diabetes. Well . . .' Lynette sighed and stopped.

'Poor love,' murmured her sister, holding her close. 'Poor love, all alone at the other side of the world . .'

'Yes, that's just how I felt,' said Lynette with surprising briskness. 'Poor little me, all alone with only toffee-nosed Oliver Hawkesburn to turn to – I'd as soon turn to a lamp-post.'

Taken by surprise, Corie gave a gurgle of laughter. She let her sister go and went back to her seat. As she sat down, she was struck by a thought. 'You were late home from Hong Kong. So it was because—'

'Yes, nothing to do with luggage going astray, although it did – I arranged that on purpose to get rid of Oliver. I went back to the hotel and from the hotel into hospital. I was there four days. The tests showed I had diabetes mellitus. I got a long explanation about the Islets of Langerhans and glucose production and why my muscles couldn't get at the energy supplies and why blood wasn't getting to my brain—'

'Islands of Langerhans? Do people there have—?'

'There, you're just as ignorant as me,' Lynette said with a giggle. 'They're in the pancreas, the Islets of Langerhans – they're what produce the natural insulin. I tell you, Corie, it's a real problem coming to terms with it if you're like me, not very bright to begin with. At any rate, I was told that from now on I'd have to take insulin every day and a nurse showed me how to inject myself, and that was that.'

'Every day for ever . . .'

'That's right.'

'But why didn't you tell me?' Corie cried, appalled that little Lynette had chosen to carry this burden alone.

'I didn't want anyone to know. I felt . . . it would make me seem . . . I don't know . . . damaged . . .' Lynette faltered into silence.

The sisters sat for a moment in thought. Then Lynette said with forced cheerfulness, 'Any of that coffee left? I'll have some just to keep me awake long enough to finish this dramatic story.'

'Oh, Lynette, how can you joke about it?'

'It's the only thing to do. You either face it and come to terms with it, or you never live a decent normal life again because you're always twitching with anxiety. I was scared and anxious at first, Corie, of course I was. But then I went to see this specialist at St Mary's in Praed Street – Dr Chang had given me a letter and everything and I went the day after I got back from Hong Kong. I skipped a dance class to do it, so nobody would be asking where I was – and he – that's Dr Usborne – he told me I wasn't by any means the only member of the acting profession to be in the same boat, and gave me a long lecture, and the long and short of it is I know you can live a normal life and carry on with your career so long as you learn to handle yourself. And that's what I've done,' Lynette ended with a little businesslike nod of the head.

'Well, I just can't take it in . . .'

Lynette drank some coffee. 'Takes a while,' she agreed.

'But . . . but . . . Wouldn't it be better not to keep it a secret?' Corie asked. 'It must make life more difficult—' She broke off. 'In Rome? Now I understand! Monna and I disturbed you when you were at a low point and that's why you went into the bathroom – to give yourself an insulin injection.'

'Yes, but in fact I do take a lot of showers now,' Lynette said, with a shrug and a smile. 'You have to be careful of your skin. It's awfully easy to catch infections, they say. And you know, because of the dancing, I sweat an awful lot so I have to be extra careful. And I have to time my meals and my insulin intake to keep myself in balance. But the thing is to do it so that no one suspects.'

'But why? Why can't you just say you've got diabetes?' Corie protested. 'It's not a sin or a crime – it's just a state of health.'

'Oh yes? And can you imagine Monna's reaction?'

Corie stared at her sister, and Lynette met her gaze squarely. After a long pause Corie said, 'I see.'

'It saves a lot of trouble, Corie. I don't quite know what Monna's reaction would be – she'd be shocked to the roots at first and it would be all molly-coddling and "Have you taken your insulin, darling?" and sending me upstairs to rest. But after a bit . . . you know how she always thinks you should pull yourself together and "be a trouper" . . . I just think it's better if she doesn't know.'

Corie said hesitantly, 'And Sasha?'

Lynette set her cup down squarely in the centre of the saucer. Then she sat back, folding her hands. 'Well, as to Sasha,' she said in a voice that trembled a little, 'I know I have a lot of competition there. He sees so many pretty talented girls . . . I feel I'm lucky he still loves me when he might have anyone he wants.'

'Oh, Lynette, you always undervalue yourself—'

'Don't be silly. Monna may think I'm the most wonderful thing since pancake make-up, but I look around and I see girls with as much ability as I have, and of course younger – I'm not really a teenager any more, now am I, even though with the right lighting and make-up I can play tricks on an audience . . .'

'But he ought to know. He asks so much of you, with this touring regime . . .'

'I can handle it,' Lynette said, her mouth taking on a firm, almost stubborn line. 'I finish here in Copenhagen at the weekend and then I relax until December.'

'December – you're scheduled to go to Sydney!'

'Yes, it's OK.'

'But Lynette, it'll be hot in Sydney in December. It's high summer there.'

'It's Christmas,' Lynette objected.

'Yes, but their seasons are different from ours – don't you remember our geography books?'

'Don't be silly, it can't be all that hot at *Christmas*.'

'Lynette, they have their Christmas dinners on the beach! I've seen it in old newsreels. Look here, you'll have to get Sasha to cancel.'

'And what reason shall I give?'

'Well, tell him that . . . Tell him you don't feel up to it . . . Tell him the heat makes you feel poorly.'

'And Monna? How do you think she'll react at one of her daughters being such a slacker? "Afraid of a little sunshine, good heavens, what next"?'

'Look here, Lynette, you've got to tell them. I don't see how you're ever going to manage—'

'I managed in India. I'll manage in Australia.'

'*Please* tell them, Lynette!'

'No! And don't you tell, Corie.' Lynette sprang to her feet, came to stare down at her elder sister. 'Promise me you won't tell.'

'But it's so unfair to you.'

'Promise me, Corie.'

Corie tried to wrest her gaze from her sister's but it was impossible. She gave a deep sigh of surrender. 'I promise.'

'Cross your heart and spit?'

'Yes, cross my heart and spit.' The old childhood vow with its chain of childhood secrets and schemes had a special magic for them both. They slowly relaxed.

Lynette walked to the door. 'It's time for me to get to bed,' she said, opening it to show her sister out. 'Goodnight Corie.'

'Goodnight, Lynette. Ring me in the morning?'

'Yes, some time around ten.'

They hugged and kissed. As Corie walked to the lift, she felt as if she were in a cloud compounded of doubt, remorse, anxiety, and a strange triumph. The doubts and anxieties were over Lynette's future, the remorse for her own lack of attention in the past. But the triumph was for the courage her sister was showing.

Next day they checked in with each other by telephone. Lynette had her dance class in the morning but they met for lunch, and then in the afternoon Lynette saw Corie off on the plane to London.

Their conversation had mainly been about Lynette's ailment. Corie was so ignorant that she was continually going back over what she'd been told, and she wasn't always sure that Lynette got it right. She asked for, and obtained, the name of the specialist at St Mary's so that she could go to him for more information. The first thing she did when she got to her flat was to ring and ask for an appointment, which was arranged for two days later at his Harley Street rooms.

Dr Usborne was younger than Corie expected, stringy, sandy and, judging by the array of photographs, much-married – there were at least ten pictures of his family on the black mantelpiece. He shook hands with Corie, asked what her problem was, and was a little taken aback when he discovered she was there to ask about Lynette Lee.

'Your sister, you say? But your name is Duggan?' He glanced at Corie's left hand for a wedding ring.

'Lynette Lee is a stage name. She's really Beryl Duggan.'

'Indeed . . . In any case, I don't know that I can discuss Miss Lee's medical history with you, Miss Duggan.'

'Look, it's very important. She kept her diabetes a secret from everyone, and has been under a lot of stress on tours to the Orient—'

'I'm aware of all that, Miss Duggan. Dr Chang—'

'But there's another tour coming up,' Corie swept on, 'she's supposed to go to Sydney at Christmas, and I just think it's too much for her.'

'Are you an expert on the handling of diabetes, may I ask?'

'Well, no . . . Of course not.'

'Let's speak generally. I have under my care more than one performer who suffers from diabetes. It's perfectly possible to deal with it even in the circumstances of stage or concert work. Several of my patients haven't let it be known to the general public because it would spoil what I believe is referred to as their "image". That's their choice and I don't argue against it. But all of those patients have told their family – a wife, a husband, a parent – on the whole their families know and are supportive.'

'But not Lynette.'

'You say *you* know about your sister.'

'But no one else does.'

'Your mother?'

'No. I'm sure she must have told you she wouldn't tell our mother.'

'I'm not prepared to say what I was told by Miss Lee or anyone else. However . . .' He paused, then tapped his desk as he spoke again. 'It's extremely helpful to a diabetic to have someone to look to for support. I can't myself approve of absolute secrecy, purely on medical grounds. A diabetic must pay close attention to proper diet, regular hours, weighed carbohydrates, urine tests, and so on and so on. In special cases medical science can help by providing insulin in measured doses so that there's no danger of imprecise injection, but it's helpful to have another person not far off who would notice any signs of, for instance, hypoglycaemia and be ready to administer glucose.'

'Glucose? But I thought sweet things were forbidden . . .'

'Let's not go into that for the moment. What I'm saying is that an actress such as Miss Lee would be well advised to have someone with her, especially on tour when she might encounter extra fatigue. That person could take steps to bring her back from coma.'

'Oh, God!' cried Corie at the dread word.

Dr Usborne almost smiled. 'Well,' he said, 'that convinces me you really are Miss Lee's sister. All the same, I can't go into details about her medical story. What I will do is supply you with a copy of the typed regime I give to all my patients and to their relatives. If you study that it will give you the information you so clearly need.'

'And the trip to Sydney?'

He nodded. 'Sydney is certainly a long way off if anything were to go wrong. I'm not saying she shouldn't go – after all there are excellent doctors in Sydney if she needed one—'

'You're not reassuring me at all, doctor!'

'Miss Lee is carrying a card that gives details of her condition and her insulin dose, I'm sure. But it would be better if someone in her entourage were aware of the situation.'

'Her entourage! Lynette doesn't have an entourage. She has a tall snooty PR man who's as much help as the lamp in the next street.'

'I can just see him,' laughed the specialist, to Corie's surprise. 'Well, replace him, Miss Duggan. Find someone more sympathetic. Otherwise, I don't think you need to worry too much about your sister. She's young and strong and has come to terms with her ailment. Just give her all the help you can.'

Corie left, with the typed instructions which ran to several pages, and no very clear idea what to do next.

In the end it all came back to Sasha. If she could get Sasha to reschedule the tour, life would be easier all round. So she had to talk to Sasha.

This time she didn't walk in unannounced. She rang him, was put through, and invited him out to lunch.

'What's this all about?' he asked in a voice in which there was interest mixed with suspicion.

'I'll tell you when I see you.'

'I thought we were scarcely on speaking terms.'

'That's still the case,' she said coolly.

'So this is strictly business?'

'Yes.'

'About Lynette, of course.'

'Yes. What day shall we say? Tomorrow?'

'I'm busy tomorrow.'

'Saturday, then.'

'Saturday isn't a business day.'

'Aren't you the man who's always at work for his clients, day and night?'

He made a little sound, half-amused and half-annoyed.

'Come on, Sasha. I'll even give you a conducted tour of my exhibition.'

'You've got an exhibition?'

'The Salkwitz Gallery in Grosvenor Street. Come and have a look and then I'll buy you lunch in Claridge's.'

'Why not?' he said. 'You'll only nag me till I give in anyway. All right, Saturday, what time?'

'Twelve o'clock at the gallery. Tell your secretary to make a note of it, Sasha.'

He arrived looking very man-about-town in a John Stephen suit and suede shoes. Corie saw him pause to look at the exhibits in the window before coming into the gallery.

'You're actually wearing a dress!' he said in amazement when he joined her.

'They won't let me into Claridge's in trousers.'

'Hm . . . Well, I like it.'

She was dressed so as to make a good impression: a black and white dress with the new higher hemline, black patent-leather knee-high boots to show off her long dancer's legs. Her hair, as usual, was tied back from her brow with a bandana – a red silk kerchief, the only note of colour. She'd taken trouble to accentuate the hazel eyes, the long lashes.

He came close to give her a kiss, which from the view of the receptionist looked like the usual effusive greeting. But he tried to make something more of it, and seemed put out when she moved away.

'It's a shame things have cooled off between us,' he murmured, 'I still think you're special.'

'It's a waste of time, da-arling,' she drawled stagily, 'that part of the show is over and done with.'

'Too bad,' said he, but there were no more moves to make claims on her.

Acting the hostess, she took him round the exhibition. It was the first time he had seen a greater body of her work than could be held by one page of newsprint, and she could tell he was somewhat taken aback.

'Are these for sale?' he inquired.

'Some.'

'I wouldn't mind having that one of the girls dancing on the dockside.'

'That's Havana.'

'You know, you've been around, haven't you?'

'A bit. I'll arrange for you to have a copy of the dancing girls. Ready for lunch?'

They walked the short distance to the hotel in a bluster of wind and light rain. As they walked in, everything was warm and welcoming. She let Sasha choose the food and show off over the wine list. She rather despised herself, but she wanted to get the conversation off to a good start.

He told her about his latest clients, a group this time, destined to zoom to the top, or so he insisted.

'How's Danny Vulcan?'

'Second from the top in the charts – don't you ever look?'

Smiling apology, she shook her head.

'He's got an album coming out in December. All the kids will use their Christmas record tokens to buy it.'

'Did that LP of Lynette's ever do any good?' she asked.

'What, last Christmas? Ah, it was a break-even thing, I always knew that.' He gave her a wary glance, for Lynette's name had been mentioned. He knew very well that they were here in this famous restaurant simply to talk about Lynette.

'Let's go into the lounge for coffee and brandy,' Corie suggested.

'Suits me.'

She gave the order to the waiter, they were escorted to a quiet corner with two comfortable tapestry armchairs. Despite himself, Sasha was feeling cosseted.

'Whatever it is you want about Lynette,' he said, half serious and half in jest, 'the answer's probably no.'

'Sasha, I want you to put off her Australian tour.'

'What?' He certainly hadn't expected anything so radical. 'Absolutely not!'

'You put off the Indian tour—'

'That's different. Australian theatre circuits insist on hard and fast contracts. They've booked Lynette Lee for the Christmas period and that's what they expect to get.'

'It'll be too much for her, Sasha. The heat gets her down.'

'Good lord, the buildings are air-conditioned—'

'She doesn't spend all her time indoors. She—'

'She doesn't have to walk about in the streets; she can take taxis wherever she wants to go. There's no need for Lynette to feel the heat at all, and for Pete's sake, it's only for a few weeks.'

'Put it off, Sasha.'

'Did she ask you to put this up to me?'

'No, she knows nothing about it.'

'Then why the devil are you interfering?'

'Because I went to see her show in Copenhagen, and I thought she was under a lot of strain.' If only she could tell him the truth, that Lynette's health wasn't perfect any longer . . .

'It's not hot in Copenhagen.'

'No,' Corie agreed with a sigh, 'I just don't think touring agrees with her.'

'But for the love of heaven, it was *your* idea in the first place!'

'Maybe it wasn't such a good idea, Sasha.'

The waiter came with Courvoisier for Sasha and the coffee. After he had bowed himself away, Sasha said, 'If she doesn't tour, she's finished. Is that what you want?'

'No . . . Of course not . . . I want it to be less hard on her, that's all.'

'What's so hard? There's almost nothing to bother about except the lighting and the band parts, and Oliver—'

'That's another thing. Find her someone else to go with her on the long-haul trips. Oliver Hawkesburn is a dead loss.'

'Oh?' Sasha said angrily. 'And what makes you say so?'

'Lynette told me.'

'Lynette's never uttered a word of complaint to me about Oliver.'

'Ask her, that's all. She doesn't like him and he's not the least bit interested in her. Find someone else.'

'No.'

'But why not, for goodness sake? There must be dozens of people—'

'I owe him, that's why.'

'Well, pay him off.'

'He's not the kind of chap you can offer money to. He likes the touring assignment, it means he can do commissions overseas for people . . .'

'He's supposed to be there to look after my sister.'

'Oh, come on, Corie, you know damn well that's nothing like a full-time job. If it were a complete company – actors, singers, dancers, then yes, a full-time PR man would be justified, but with a one-woman show . . .'

'Lynette needs someone she can relate to. Find someone else for her, please, Sasha.'

'Look here, if you want it straight out, Oliver Hawkesburn walked Danny Vulcan into my office and talked him into signing up with me. There's no way to put the money through my accounts except by hiring him for a cop-out sort of job.'

'Oh, great! My sister's got to pay off the debt you owe on another of your clients!'

'That's the way it is. Lynette asked for somebody, Oliver happened to be the one. I'm certainly not going to pay anyone else to take his place, it would knock the profit down a hell of a lot.'

'Do you ever think of anything except pounds, shillings and pence?'

'What other way is there of measuring success?' he asked with a lift of the eyebrows. 'The going rate, that's what tells me what's worthwhile.'

'But Lynette doesn't see things that way, Sasha! She only takes on these foreign tours because she wants to please you! But you never even take the trouble to spend time with her. She gets back from long trips, it takes her four or five days to recover, and then all you want to talk about is business!'

Sasha shrugged. 'We *do* have business to discuss: which numbers to keep in the show, which to take out, a new arrangement for a special venue like Copenhagen, new dance routines – things keep changing, I have to have arrangers and choreographers at the ready . . .'

'But anyone could do that, and you know it. What Lynette needs is the personal touch, but you don't even bother with her. Well,' Corie said angrily, 'perhaps it's all for the best. She'll begin to wonder why she's going through these long tours if it's merely a profit-and-loss thing with you, and maybe she'll give up the famous career. After all, it's Monna who gets all the pleasure out of it. Maybe Lynette will just back out.'

'She'd better not! I've got contracts lined up—'

'I don't care. It would be a whole lot better for her if she could learn to live without you!'

Their voices had risen. Others in the peaceful hotel lounge turned their heads to stare.

'Listen, chickie,' hissed Sasha, 'aren't you a bit obsessive about that sister of yours? You ought to listen to yourself some time; you sound more like her grannie than her sister. Lynette's a grown woman—'

'Then treat her like one! Don't foist a PR man that she doesn't like on her!'

'If she's so full of dislike for Oliver let her say so.'

'What good would that do?' Corie said wearily. 'You'd only talk her round.'

She let the matter drop. She could see she wasn't going to win through persuading Sasha of the need for a change.

Instead, that evening, she dropped in at the Bayswater house to seek out Opal, who was in the kitchen making use of the new washing machine.

'It's great,' Opal said, 'you shove everything in, add washing powder and, hey presto, half an hour later it's all done. Do you remember, Corie, when we were evacuated, the problem of getting clean tights for dance class: we all had to queue up in Mrs Lewis's kitchen to do them by hand?'

' "The happiest days of your life",' Corie quoted.

'Ha-ha.'

They watched the things going round in the washing machine for a few minutes. Then Opal put on the kettle for the obligatory coffee. Now there was powdered coffee instead of Camp in a bottle as in their touring days. Corie watched as Opal spooned it in liberally. Despite all her efforts to learn cookery, her sister never bothered to measure anything accurately.

'Is this just a social call, or do you have an ulterior motive?' Opal inquired.

'I'm very ulterior, as usual. Pal, when I saw Lynette in Copenhagen, it seemed to me she was a bit ragged round the edges.'

'What, a poor performance?' Opal said, aghast.

'No, no, she went over well with the crowd. No, I thought in herself, offstage . . .'

'She doesn't like touring,' her sister opined.

'No, maybe that wasn't such a clever suggestion after all.'

'Oh, duckie, don't start blaming yourself,' Opal said, patting her on the shoulder. 'What else was there for her to do?'

The kettle boiled, she made the coffee. She sloshed milk into her own, handed the black brew to Corie.

'This Australian tour that's coming up,' Corie went on.

'Yes. First Christmas for a long time we won't be together. I was just thinking . . . The last time was when you were in a panto in Hull, apart from Havana, of course.'

'Oh, lord, that was years ago . . . I think that was when I decided it wasn't for me any more.'

Opal nodded. Then she said, 'What about this Australian tour?'

'I talked to Lynette about it. She really doesn't like Oliver Hawkesburn—'

'What, has he turned into Hot-Handed Hawkesburn, then?' There had been a Hot-Handed Henderson in their joint past.

'No, no, he's very distant and stand-offish. No help at all. And Pal — Australia's so far away!'

The last sentence came out as more of a wail than she'd intended. She thought, Pal will think I'm mental. And then, she thought, Is Sasha right? Am I obsessive about Lynette?

'It's a long way, that's true.' Opal bent to examine her

wash. 'I think that red scarf is running – now I'll have pink underwear.'

'Switch off and take it out.'

'If I do, water will slop out all over the kitchen floor. No, I'll just make do with pink underwear.' She went back to her coffee. 'So what's the next point, after the distance between here and Australia?'

'I think someone ought to go with Lynette. Someone to replace Oliver Hawkesburn.'

'You'd have to ask Sasha about that.'

'I did, over lunch. He says he's not going to pay anyone other than Hawkesburn.'

'That seems to settle that.'

'I wondered, Pal . . .'

'What?'

'If you would go?'

Opal let her coffee cup go. It fell to the table top, bounced without breaking, and sent milky coffee all over the place.

'Oh, now look what you've made me do!' she cried.

She darted to the sink for a cloth, mopped up the spillage, found another for the floor, put both cloths in the sink and then turned in a flurry to Corie.

'Why should I go to Australia with Lynette?'

'Well, she really needs someone, Pal.'

'But why me?'

'It couldn't be Monna. She'd send the poor kid round the bend.' And besides, there was a chance that she'd insist on sharing a hotel room with her daughter, in which case Lynette's secret would be almost certain to come out.

'Well, it can't be me. I can't get a month off from my job.'

'If you asked to have next year's holiday in advance?'

Opal drew in a big breath and let it out. 'Why should I?' she said, with unexpected indignation. 'Bart and I are saving up to get married and buy a house. Why should I spend money on a fare to Sydney?'

'I'd pay the fare,' Corie interposed.

'And why should I give up next year's holidays? I'm hoping to use them for my honeymoon!'

TESSA BARCLAY

'Oh,' said Corie.

Opal made fresh coffee to replace the cup she'd lost. Her movements were a little ragged. She was upset because she was having what amounted to a disagreement with her elder sister.

'I don't know what's behind this,' she said. 'Something's wrong that you don't want to tell me about. I'm sorry, love, I really am, but I can't afford to give away any more of my life to Lynette. I'm going to get married and settle down in a home of my own and have babies. And Lynette's going to have to manage without me.'

'Yes. I'm sorry, Pal.'

'I don't see why you have to have such a *conscience* about her! You couldn't possibly know that she'd be unhappy going abroad! You meant it for the best.'

Yes, but, Corie wanted to say, I didn't know then that she was going to contract diabetes.

Just then Monna came home from a recital of popular songs in a suburban concert. She breezed in, full of tales of the applause, the appreciation . . .

There was no further chance of a talk with Pal; and indeed Corie couldn't think of anything to say in face of her sister's stated opinion.

One thing became clear. If anyone was to go with Lynette to help keep her safe on the long journey to the other side of the world, it would have to be Corie herself.

Chapter Nineteen

Sasha seemed to take a new interest in Lynette. When Corie went next day to the airport to meet her on her homeward flight from Copenhagen, she found him in the arrivals lounge with a bouquet of hothouse roses.

'Good heavens! What a surprise!' she greeted him with some irony.

'Well,' he said, a little frown between his black brows, 'I thought about what you said. It's true Lynette and I haven't been seeing much of each other recently . . .'

'So you thought you'd better show a bit more interest for the sake of keeping the business healthy,' she rejoined. 'At least until she's safely off to Sydney where there's money to be made.'

'You know, Corie,' said he, 'you're cynical, that's your problem.'

The arrival was announced, they made their way to the barrier to watch for her. To Corie's anxious eye she seemed well – a little thinner perhaps than she used to be, but in her pastel-blue coat and long white boots, a fashion plate.

Her face lit up at the sight of Sasha. From that moment Corie scarcely existed. When her luggage had been collected, it was with Sasha she decided to go; it was arm in arm with Sasha that she left the airport.

Corie sighed to herself. When would Lynette stop being hopelessly in love, hopelessly dependent on this man? Until that day came, there seemed no way of getting her life on an even keel.

Corie waved them off in Sasha's car, then went home, as she'd come, by public transport. Monna rang her later to announce the safe homecoming of the star of the family.

'And so Sasha had gone to meet her and bring her home

in his Jaguar? So thoughtful. What a lovely couple they looked as they drove up! You know, Corie, I do really think there might be something brewing between those two.'

'Such as what?' Corie asked, alarmed. Her mother jumped to such odd conclusions.

'Well, he was telling us how tremendously he'd missed her all this summer, and the way he looked at her . . . And of course, she thinks the world of him, we all know that!'

'Monna, you're not thinking of marriage?'

'Well, it was always because of her TV persona that they didn't tie the knot. That's not so important now, is it? I really do have my hopes on that.'

But it was Opal who got married.

Perhaps urged into it by the conversation about being Lynette's companion on tour, Opal had a serious talk with Barton Davis. Their long unofficial engagement became official, they arranged a mortgage on a house in Surrey, and announced the date: they were to be married in November.

'November!' wailed Monna. 'The weather's always so terrible in November! And a registry wedding! I just think it's so *unromantic*!'

Corie had even more objections, but didn't utter them. It meant that she had to cancel a trip to Washington to watch the presidential election campaign reach its climax. More importantly, it meant she wouldn't see Drew Richter.

He was almost angry when she rang to tell him the news. 'Why did your sister have to choose November?' he demanded. 'Didn't you tell her you were going to be abroad?'

'Yes, of course, Drew, but she and Bart have waited a long time and I think they just felt . . . Well, they felt time was slipping by and they made a snap decision.'

She didn't say what she sometimes thought – that Opal had decided to get married to break herself off from any responsibility for her younger sister. She never actually said this to Opal, yet it lay between them like a little divide.

But she didn't want to waste expensive telephone time explaining the complexities of the Duggan family to Drew.

'I'll come for the Inauguration if Kennedy wins,' she offered, laughing.

'You'd better mean that,' he said, 'because Jack *will* win.'

'I'm sorry I've had to back out of the November visit, Drew. I was really looking forward to it.'

'We-ell, perhaps it's all for the best,' he admitted. 'I'll be so damned busy I might not have been able to give you ten minutes' company.' He paused. 'You wouldn't care to come for Christmas? My mother and father would love to see you.'

'I can't, Drew. I'll be in Sydney.'

'Sydney? Australia?'

'I'm going with my sister Lynette − the one whose show you saw in—'

'I remember, I remember,' he said with renewed irritation. 'Why the devil do you have to go to Australia with her?'

Corie tried to think how to explain. 'She needs me,' she said in the end.

'I don't understand that.'

'Well, she's been having health problems.'

'You mean you're going as a nurse?'

She could hear his impatience over the transatlantic connection. 'It's too difficult to explain,' she said. 'I only discovered about it recently. I just feel that I can't let her go so far all on her own.'

'Seems to me, Corie, you're too wrapped up in your family.'

'Perhaps,' she agreed. She couldn't tell him that it had come to be so over long years stretching back into her girlhood, a habit too deeply ingrained to be broken now. Her sisters were very dear to her. It was difficult to explain this to Drew, an only child.

They ended the conversation in a rather guarded mood. She was very depressed as she put down the phone. Was she losing him? Was she deluding herself in thinking Lynette needed her?

That latter question remained with her over the next

week or two, until the day of Opal's wedding.

Opal looked charming in a trapeze-line dress of rose-pink corded silk. Bart had an Italian-line suit with a velvet coat collar. Corie was bridesmaid in unobtrusive dark blue. Barton's parents were sedate in their best clothes, Mrs Davis in a rather elderly but fine sable coat.

But when they left the register office, all the cameramen focused on Lynette, who was undoubtedly the most beautiful of the wedding party in her butter-yellow suit and brown fur hat. Sasha was her escort, looking smarter than the groom.

It's the job of local papers to keep track of weddings. Some watchful eye had noticed as they went in that one of the group was Lynette Lee, the former TV star. The reporter rang up the national papers to see if they were interested. One or two thought it intriguing enough to send a man and a photographer. The result was a surprising crowd on the pavement.

The trouble was, some of them had the wrong idea. They thought Lynette was the bride.

'Miss Lee, Miss Lee, are you and your husband planning a large family?'

'Where are you going on your honeymoon, Lynette?'

'Are you retiring from the stage to be a wife and mother, Miss Lee?'

'I'm not the bride,' Lynette tried to explain. 'My sister . . .'

Opal and Bart were rather put out, the Davis parents were indignant. Finally it was the ringing tones of Crystal Duggan, formerly of Crystal and Clark, that brought order to the situation.

'Just listen to me a minute, boys!' she called. Even above the hubbub, she made herself heard.

Order was restored.

'My daughter Opal is the bride, gentlemen,' she announced, laying her hand on Opal's arm. 'She's now Mrs Barton Davis.'

Bart made an awkward little bow.

'You planning on following in your sister's footsteps?' a reporter called to Lynette.

'We all hope for that quite soon,' Monna assured him with a beaming smile, and led the way to the waiting cars.

The wedding reception was at the Bayswater house. The friends of Opal and Bart weren't showbiz people. In Monna's view it was all terribly un-chic, but this was how Opal had wanted it, so it must be endured. Only Lynette and Sasha came from the world of theatre which, in her opinion, knew how to celebrate.

'To you, dear,' she said, lifting her glass to Lynette. 'And may the thoughts we heard this morning about your future soon be reality.'

Corie would have prevented it if she could. Too late she tried to intervene. She saw Lynette's eyes fill with tears, but her sister blinked them away. Instead of indulging in tears Lynette on the contrary seemed to put herself out to have a good time.

When the bride and groom had driven off for a honeymoon in Torquay, the guests began to drift away. The caterers came to clear up. Sasha kissed everybody goodbye and took himself off.

It was then that Corie saw Lynette going languidly upstairs. Something in her manner warned her. She hurried after her, put an arm about her, and escorted her into her room.

'What's wrong, Lynette?'

'Been a bad girl,' Lynette said vaguely. 'Too much champagne, too much wedding cake . . . I feel very funny.'

'Lynette, did you take your insulin?'

' 'f course, always do . . . But I should have thought . . . Party-going . . . Silly me!' She began to sink down on her bed.

'Lynette! Lynette!'

Her sister lay back and wagged a hand at her. 'Don't make a noise . . . I want to have a nap . . .'

'No, darling, please – sit up . . .' She put an arm round her, held her up. 'You need your insulin. Where is it?'

'Wha'? Inna make-up bag, 's usual. Corie . . . I don't think I can do it . . .'

Corie found the equipment, propped her sister up with pillows on the bed, and with her wavering help gave her the injection. She was very frightened. It was much earlier than the usual timetable – Lynette usually took her second dose of insulin between six and seven in the evening. She had no idea whether she was doing the right thing by giving it to her three hours early.

But after about ten minutes Lynette began to improve. She sat up straight without support, rubbed her forehead, then began to cry.

'What a fool,' she whispered.

'What happened, Lynette?'

'I was upset . . . by what those men said at the registry . . . So I had quite a lot of champagne . . . Drowning my sorrows, I suppose you could call it.'

'And that's bad for you,' Corie said, summoning up memories of the instructions from Dr Usborne.

'And I *knew* it was, but I just went on.'

If Corie had had doubts about being needed, they were banished at that moment. But for her watchfulness, something terrible might have happened.

She sat on the bed and took her sister's hand. 'Do you want so much to be married to Sasha, darling?'

'Oh, more than anything! And one day, you know, it *will* happen.'

'Yes, perhaps it will,' Corie agreed with an aching heart.

Later she went downstairs to make coffee, but found her mother sitting forlornly in the newly tidied dining-room.

'You know, Corie,' Monna said with a glance around her, 'I didn't realise until now that Opal won't be here any more.'

Corie hesitated. What could she say? She took refuge in the commonplace. 'It was a lovely reception.'

'Did you think so? I thought they were a dull crew. Bart's father kept talking to me about insurance.'

'I was just going to make a hot drink. Would you like something. Tea? Coffee?'

'When your father and I were married,' Monna went on, unheeding, 'we only had the weekend for our honeymoon. We held our reception in the green room of the Sovereign Theatre – absolutely everybody came, every artiste in Southport at the time, all the theatre managers, all the stage hands . . .'

Corie could see that her mother, like Lynette, had had a little too much champagne. She was in that state where old times seem the best and tears are very near.

'I'm sure it was lovely . . .' she ventured.

'Very Bohemian. We danced until dawn. Nobody talked about insurance.'

'Well, Mr Davis is a businessman—'

'When Lynette marries, we'll have a proper reception. We'll hold it at the Savoy or the Ritz—'

'Money no object?' said Corie with a smile.

'Where is Lynette?' her mother said, coming out of the world of memories and dreams. 'I need her now, to comfort me.'

'Monna, Lynette's got a bit of a headache. That's why I'm making coffee. Would you like some?'

'Oh, Corie, you're always so *practical*,' cried Monna, and swept out of the dining-room in a flurry of floral silk skirts. A moment later she could be heard at the piano in the drawing-room thumping out 'We'll Gather Lilacs' loud enough to drown out the voices of memory.

It fell to Corie to comfort her mother through the first week or two of living without Opal. This was easier because Lynette was home; though she was seldom in the house – there was the usual regime of practice, rehearsal, costume-fitting. Moreover, she spent quite a lot of time with Sasha.

'She'll marry too,' sighed Monna, 'and I shall be left alone in this big house . . .'

Corie said nothing. She didn't want to think about what might happen if Lynette ever did leave home. Monna had spent so much of her life ordering her daughters about that she would be left without an occupation.

Corie was busy. Her photographic exhibition had wound up, bringing her many commissions. She had to arrange these for either immediate dates or for 1961, after the Australian trip she was now planning.

She tried to keep track of the American elections. The British press reported the campaign much more fully than on previous occasions, intrigued by the battle between two men who seemed so equally qualified. One, of course, was handsome, and had a beautiful wife; from the point of view of newspapermen, that couldn't be bad.

The results when they came showed it had been a closer contest than anyone could have imagined; there was a lead of only about a hundred thousand for John F. Kennedy out of a total of about seventy million votes.

Corie tried to ring Drew to congratulate him. But for the next few days he was never available. 'He's in a meeting.' 'He's with the press.' 'He's gone to Hyannis.' She left messages for him, telling him she was proud of him.

In the end, in the latter half of November, she received a wire. 'Your ticket reserved for Inauguration, 20 January. Be here!'

She understood he was simply inundated with tasks concerned with the entry of the next President into the White House.

She sent a reply: 'That's a date!'

When she told Lynette her intention of going with her to Sydney, Lynette herself was ecstatic with relief. Sasha appeared pleased, but came to Corie's studio next day to ask what she was up to. 'What is it?' he demanded. 'You don't trust Oliver? You're going along to spy on him?'

'Nothing of the kind. Oliver Hawkesburn can spend his time in the bar of Australia Hotel in Sydney for all I care. I'm going because I can do some pictures there.'

'Somebody's hired you?'

'No,' she admitted, 'but I can fix something up—'

'I don't get it. If you think *I'm* going to stand the expense, you're mistaken.'

'I'll pay my own way, Sasha. Please yourself what you do about Hawkesburn. It seems to me it would be better sense to give him something to do at home rather than have him tag along when we don't need him.'

He was totally at a loss. 'You mean you're really just going to keep Lynette company?'

'Yes.'

'You're crazy, you know that?' he said, and stamped out.

He simply couldn't make sense of it, but he raised no objections. He let Lynette know a few days later that her former escort, Mr Hawkesburn, would not be going on this trip.

'Thank goodness,' she breathed.

Monna was less easy to satisfy. 'I can't imagine why you want to go,' she said to her eldest daughter. 'You do realise you'll be leaving me absolutely alone here?'

'It's only for a month, Monna. We'll be back by the second week in January.'

'But Christmas . . . The house will be empty!' A theatrical gesture with open arms demonstrated how empty it would be.

Opal came to the rescue by inviting her mother to spend the first Christmas of her married life with herself and Bart. What Bart thought about it, Corie preferred not to guess. Monna agreed, although with murmurings that she didn't think Christmas in the Surrey suburbs was her kind of thing.

Corie and Lynette were seen off at the airport by Sasha and Monna, Sasha with another bouquet of roses and Monna beaming with pleasure at the press photographer laid on by him. It was much less attention than Lynette had attracted when her show was on television, but Monna preferred to ignore that fact.

They left on 12 December, taking the trip with stop-overs so as to minimise jet lag on arrival. They would then have two days in Sydney before the opening at the New Garden Theatre on 20 December. They were met at Sydney Airport by a representative of the theatre chain, whisked through

the formalities, and driven in a limousine to Castlereagh
Street and their hotel.

To the new arrivals, the weather seemed hot. 'Ah, this is
nothing,' said Mr Frankin from Allotts Theatres. 'Only
eighty today. You should have been here on Sunday – went
up to close on ninety.'

But the limousine was air-conditioned, and so was the
Watson Hotel. There were flowers from the management in
Lynette's room, cards with greetings from the band-leader
and the dance teacher whose class she would attend, and a
message sent in advance by Sasha, the traditional 'Break a
leg!'

After seeing her sister settled in, Corie went off to find
her own hotel. Since she was paying her own expenses she
couldn't afford the Watson, booked by Sasha as being in
keeping with Lynette's status as a star. Relying on the travel
agent, Corie had taken a room at the Silvester which turned
out to be in a turning not far off; a respectable, rather dark
little place frequented by businessmen.

Lynette had wanted Corie to share with her. 'After all,
there's sure to be two beds, there always are—'

'No, no, sweetie, I want to be out and about early to get
pix. You need a good night's sleep after a show.'

This had always been one of Monna's maxims, so Lynette
gave in. But their agreement was that they'd always have
brunch together at eleven. By eleven Lynette would have
taken her dance class and be in need of her second snack of
the day.

'But I want you to get around and enjoy yourself,'
Lynette insisted. 'This trip is costing you a *fortune*!'

'Don't worry, I'll earn it back with the pix I take,' Corie
rejoined with a confidence she didn't entirely feel.

Since Oliver Hawkesburn wasn't there, there were chores
to be done. It was Corie who fielded questions from the
press next day when Lynette looked at a loss. 'You're
taking lessons from one of our ballet teachers,' said the
reporter from the *Bulletin*. 'What do you think of Australian
ballet?'

Lynette barely knew that there *was* any Australian ballet. It was Corie who said, 'Of course Robert Helpmann's name is famous in Britain, we admire his work greatly.' Other queries about Lynette's opinion on Australian fashion, Australian men, and Australian cooking were laughingly turned aside with, 'Miss Lee hasn't any experience of any of those as yet – especially Australian men.'

There were few problems at the theatre. The lighting plan and the band parts had been sent in advance. The stage manager was calm and friendly. The band had had four rehearsals and only needed one run-through with Lynette to get the timings perfect. The new costumes – dresses without the multi-petticoat effect which had quite gone out of fashion – looked pretty.

Yet Corie was worried. Her sister seemed under a strain although everything seemed to be going well.

'Is something bothering you, Lynette?'

Lynette shook her head. 'Everything's fine.'

'Your tests showing everything OK?'

'Yes, of course.'

Yet there was something. Watching Lynette, she wondered if it was merely stage fright. This was, after all, a completely new audience. Sasha had had the script-writer do some alterations to make the lines fit the Sydney venue, but all at once Corie began to wonder if that was enough.

But it was too late to do anything about it, for the first night was upon them.

The theatre was full. The Sydney crowd were in pre-holiday mood. Christmas was five days away, they had only enjoyment to look forward to, and here was a pretty girl from all the way across the world to entertain them. They greeted her opening theme, 'You're a Sweetheart', with applause. From the wings, Corie watched her sister drift on-stage in the new gown of blue organza, sensed the audience smiling at the sight and settling to listen.

'Good evening, and welcome. Or as I believe you say here, g'day.'

Another patter of applause.

'Now came the little stories, about her career up to now.
'Auditions . . . You've heard of auditions . . . It comes from
the word "odd" meaning peculiar . . .'

Faint amusement.

She told an anecdote, perfectly true, about how she and
her sister Opal had gone to an audition without tap shoes.
They'd borrowed a pair from a girl with big feet. Somehow
it all seemed to go on too long. Corie realised the audience
hadn't understood the point, or else they didn't find it
interesting.

Now some little jokes that Arthur Baynes had written in
especially for Sydney. 'You know we just left London
where they're getting ready for Christmas. In London the
Christmas problem is pine needles on the carpet. Here I
gather it's sand in the sandwiches . . .' Then there was the
possibility of the Queen's Christmas message being
drowned out by the surf. And Hyde Park – there were a
couple of little comments about how different Hyde Park in
Sydney was from the one in London.

Lynette's jokes were never very sharp. They were merely
a way of chatting to the audience until she introduced a
song. But on this important first night, Corie sensed she
was losing them. If she were going to tell jokes, they wanted
them to be really funny. If she couldn't be funny, let her get
on to the next thing.

The next thing was a rendering of 'Along Came Bill',
which the audience liked. Then came 'Round the Bend of
the River' and a very beautiful dance routine which swayed
and twirled to the lilt of the tune. Then came 'Dancing with
My Shadow', which always went down well because of the
idea of partnering yourself in the spotlight. Next a band
number while Lynette came off for a quick change into a
costume suited to 'Button Up Your Overcoat', a Ginger
Rogers-type tap number.

The audience were happy enough now. Unfortunately
the approach to the finale for the first half consisted of a
medley of songs with the word 'sun' in the titles: 'The
Sunny Side of the Street', 'The Sun Has Got His Hat On',

'Let's Bake a Sunshine Cake' and 'Keep Your Sunny Side Up'.

The people of Sydney weren't as interested in sunshine as European audiences – they saw the sun almost every day, and tiresome it could be, especially with Christmas coming on and so much to do, shopping and cooking and travelling . . .

Their response was tepid. They called Lynette back for only one curtain call at the end of Part One.

When she came off, Corie in the wings could see that she was bathed in sweat. 'Sweetie, what a state you're in—'

'Hard work,' Lynette said, taking the wrap Corie was holding for her.

'Come on, let's get you to the dressing-room and you can have a sponge down.'

The New Garden Theatre was 'new' only in the sense that it had been built to replace the old Garden Theatre. It certainly couldn't offer amenities such as a shower. So when the dresser and Corie had peeled off the sweat-soaked dress, the only recourse was to fill the wash-basin with tepid water so that Lynette could dab at herself with a sponge. The dresser tactfully withdrew to allow some privacy, but Corie stayed.

'Should you have a little something sweet to drink?' she asked. She knew her sister usually took four small meals a day, but she saw weariness in her face and she'd certainly lost a lot of moisture that ought to be replaced.

'Some tea would be nice.'

Corie put her head out the door to ask the dresser for tea. 'Coming right up,' said Marie, who like all Australians considered strong tea to be the staff of life.

When Corie turned back into the room she found Lynette, wrapped in a towel, staring at herself in the mirror.

'What is it?' Corie asked, somehow perturbed at the minute scrutiny Lynette was giving her reflection.

'I was just wondering why they don't like me,' Lynette said.

'Lynette!'

'Well, they don't. I can feel it.'

Corie almost said, 'Then whose fault is it?' That was an iron rule – the fault is never with the audience.

People come to a theatre in hopes of being entertained, but often they've no idea what exactly to expect. The performer – actor, singer, dancer – must take them by the hand and lead them to an understanding, an enjoyment, of what's on offer.

This had been drummed into all the Duggan girls, both by their parents and by the teachers at stage school. But this wasn't the moment to bring that back to Lynette's mind. She was discouraged by a lack of rapport – it was up to Corie to build up confidence for the second half.

But as she watched the audience from the wings, she could tell they were restless. This is often the case after people have been to the bar in the interval, but tonight it seemed more marked than usual. They rustled, they murmured to each other, one or two left the auditorium, after 'A Room With a View'.

In the end Corie came to the conclusion that Lynette simply couldn't charm them. To the families in that audience, Lynette's 'girl in a garden' image simply didn't apply. The girl in an Australian garden would be sturdier than Lynette, more sun-kissed, likely to play tennis and ride the waves at Surfers' Paradise. They felt she was a stranger from a cloudy landscape.

The finale, which consisted of what was called 'A European Tour', went better than the rest. There were men in the audience who'd been in Europe during the war, who warmed to reminders of places they knew: '*Sous les Ponts de Paris*', the nightingale in Berkeley Square, Rome's Trevi Fountain . . . When the curtain came down, they were pleased enough to call her back three times.

But Corie was worried. Next morning, instead of going out as she usually did to take photographs of the citizens hurrying to their offices, pouring off the ferries at Circular Quay, loading and unloading freighters at Bankstown, she went to her sister's hotel to wait for the morning papers. The *Morning Herald* and the *Daily Telegraph* were kind enough. 'Miss Lee gave us familiar songs but it was her dancing that pleased the audience last night . . .' 'This star from British television was of course new to the theatre-goers of Sydney who gave her a warm welcome . . .'

Soon after nine o'clock, Mr Frankin of the theatre chain walked into the lounge to find her sitting with the newspapers folded to the reviews. 'You've already seen 'em,' he remarked. He took a seat alongside, waving his hat to cool himself.

'Yes,' Corie said. 'They don't exactly leap about with enthusiasm.'

'We-ell, at least they didn't say she was dull.'

'Dull!'

'I thought she was dull,' Frankin said, nodding calmly.

'She hasn't got over the time-change—'

'Yeh, yeh, I've heard all that before. Is that the act she's used on other tours?'

'Well,' said Corie, making a big effort not to lose her temper, 'there were some changes to the script . . .'

'You mean those terrible jokes about Hyde Park and so on. Look, Corie, I don't want to be hard on her, but she didn't even try to make them work.'

'She's not really a comedienne, you know . . .'

'You can say *that* again.' He paused a moment. 'She up and about yet?'

'No, she doesn't usually get going until about ten.'

'I can't hang about for that, I've got things to do. You're representing her, are you?'

'Well, not really . . . I suppose, perhaps . . . yes.'

'Tell her,' Frankin said, bringing bushy grey brows together, 'tell her I expect something better tonight. And Christmas Eve . . . Christmas Eve the theatre's full of block bookings – coach parties, clubs from out of Sydney who've come in for a day's shopping and want to top it off with something special. I don't want them going home and saying, "That show at the New Garden is dead boring, we'll never book in there again". You get me?'

'But Mr Frankin—'

'She's got to get some new jokes. I'll send a feller – he'll write her a few new ones. And all that stuff at the end of Part One. "Sunny Side of the Street" and so forth – can she replace it with something else?'

'Of course not! We haven't got band parts for anything else!'

'Well, tell her to cut it short, will you? And if she has to fill in by doing something with just a piano accompaniment, that's easy enough, Tommy can do an arrangement of a couple of numbers. Just buy the sheet music and let him have it by midday—'

'You're not seriously suggesting that my sister should put new numbers in the show at a moment's notice?'

'New numbers? Come off it, everything she sings is twenty years old if not older. All she's got to do is go into Cramer's and get the music for something she's already used on the TV show, and Tommy will work it up to sound good on the joanna —'

'Certainly not!' Corie said. It would shake Lynette's confidence to the roots if she were asked to substitute numbers at a moment's notice.

'Are we going to have an argument?' Frankin said, staring at her. 'Because if we are, I want Lynette here to listen to what I'm saying. I've been in show business in Sydney since the thirties, and I know when an audience is being bored. That show last night only just made it to curtain-fall. If Lynette doesn't know that herself, then she's in the wrong business.'

Corie was silent. She couldn't deny what he was saying.

'OK, so she's a bit at sea after the air trip and the time-change and all that. And as a matter of fact, her show isn't exactly what I thought it was – it's too English, if you get me. But she's our Christmas attraction and I've got folk coming in expecting something fancy. So it's got to be tightened up, see what I mean? She's got to grab the audience more.'

Corie wanted to say, But she usually does, it's different here, she's not well. But that was too dangerous. Besides, excuses weren't going to help.

'We can't make changes in the musical numbers—'

'Yes, it's got to be—'

'No, really, it's impossible. I agree about the jokes. If you send us a writer, we'll work with him today and again tomorrow if need be. We'll make the Sunshine Medley work: if he can write Lynette an intro, explain that in England we hardly see the sun – Australia's got the edge on us in that, same as in cricket – that sort of thing.'

'Ah . . .' He was unconvinced.

'The dance routines – if we had to have new numbers to end the first half, the dance routines would have to be altered too. It's too much to try at such short notice. But if you send us a good gag man, we can jolly it up.'

Frankin nodded. 'That's it – you've put your finger on it – it needs to be jollier!' His rather grim expression relaxed. 'Yeh, I see you're on the problem. Righto then, I'll send Charlie round – what time?'

'Eleven-ish. We have a snack about then.'

'No worries, he'll be here.' Frankin arose, made as if to go, then said almost wonderingly, 'That kind of thing goes over all right in England, does it?'

'Yes, and in the rest of Europe, and the Far East.'

'There y'are, takes all kinds, doesn't it? We'll give it another go, but I have to say, Corie, if she doesn't warm up tonight we'll have to have another think. Eh?'

She nodded, stifling a sigh. He waved his hat at her in farewell and left.

Lynette was shattered when she heard the management had asked for alterations. 'What am I supposed to do? Pluck something out of thin air?'

'They're sending a writer. We think if the linkage is improved, it would be better.'

'New jokes?' She hesitated. 'Well, they didn't like the old ones, that's true.'

'They were written by someone who didn't know

anything about Sydney, after all, duckie. Mr Frankin says it's got to be jollier. So this afternoon we'll get some new material and tonight it'll have more pep.'

'Jollier . . .'

Charlie Vickers had been a straightman to dozens of comedians in his day. 'Seen it all, dearie,' he soothed Lynette. 'Custard pie, crazy comedy, quick come-back – you name it, I've done it. But I got fed up with clambering into the soup-and-fish every night so now I just write for other fellers. Rely on me, we'll have 'em rolling in the aisles.'

'That's not my style, Charlie,' Lynette said.

'No, OK, more lady-like, I get you. No worries, we'll sort out a few funnies for you.'

They spent all afternoon working. The first hour was a dead loss, he couldn't understand that Lynette didn't tell jokes based on current affairs or politics or sex. But in the end light dawned. 'I get you – it's all got to come from your own background. Right, right, I get it now. So let's see – you know we don't have TV here, we'll make jokes about British television . . .'

And about travelling in the East, where Charlie invented disasters with rickshaws and Siamese cats, and about amorous Italians and the Olympics in Rome, and about every aspect that he could find to work on. By six they had far more material than they could possibly use. Charlie threw out two-thirds of what he had written. The rest he gave to Lynette. 'Learn those.'

'But the band cues—'

'I'll type those up, don't worry, the band will know when to come in.'

It was really frightening, even to someone who, like Lynette, had worked in live television. Corie could see she was shaking like a leaf that night when the curtain went up and she made her entrance.

But the show worked better. The audience laughed at the jokes, enjoyed the songs, and seemed really delighted with the dances. All the same, it was a different show – no longer 'An Evening with Lynette Lee', more an evening with a larky showgirl. But if that was what they wanted, Lynette was prepared to give it to them.

Frankin came to her dressing-room after the curtain. 'There, I knew you could do it,' he enthused. 'Now, if we can just get Charlie to work up something for the European thing—'

'What's wrong with the "European Tour"?' Corie interrupted, startled.

'Well, a lot of the audience have never been to Europe and never expect to go there. It's a bit unconnected, you know? If Charlie can write up a funny intro—'

'No!' Lynette cried.

'Look, love, I know what the audience wants . . .'

'The finale is supposed to be romantic, sentimental—'

'Yeh, and that's what's wrong with it! Who ever heard of a finale that doesn't end with a bang? Still, we can improve it.'

'No.'

'I'm telling you, Lynette—'

'I'm telling *you* – there will be no more changes. Already I feel the first half isn't really me.'

'I'm only trying to get you a better effect . . .'

'No, I won't even discuss it,' Lynette said, and burst into tears.

Corie took Frankin by the sleeve and dragged him out into the passage. 'Good for you,' she said. 'That's just what she needed – to have you totally undermine her confidence.'

'Dammit, girl, I'm just trying to help her!'

'Some help you've been! Let's get this straight, Mr Frankin – my sister's here to do a Christmas season of 'An Evening with Lynette Lee' and that's what she's going to do. If you don't like it, cancel.'

'Hey,' Frankin said.

'You don't want to? Then back off and stop badgering her. The audience likes the European songs the way they are.'

'But it's got no *bounce*—'

'Bounce? Who do you think you've booked, the Tiller Girls? Go away, Mr Frankin, and let my sister do her show the way that's been a success everywhere else.'

'But Christmas Eve . . .'

'Christmas Eve will be like tonight. That's *it* – no more changes.'

'I don't know if my coach-trip bookings—'

'Leave it alone, Mr Frankin. You've done enough harm.' With that she turned on her heel and went back to comfort her sobbing little sister.

All next day was spent shoring up Lynette's self-confidence. They went over and over the new lines until she could bring them off in something more like her own diffident style, so that they seemed to belong to her more than on the previous night. Charlie came back to take out a word here, polish a line there, and seemed on the whole happy with the effect. 'Sounds different than I expected,' he admitted, 'but it's OK.'

'Hear you had an up-and-a-down with Frankin,' he murmured in confidence to Corie as she went down to the lobby with him.

'You could say that.'

'He worries, you know. He's always been a worrier.'

'He ought to keep his worries to himself. He's put my sister under a lot of strain.'

'Yeh. Is she all right? Seems a bit off colour to me.'

'Isn't that just what I've been saying?'

'No, I meant . . . Well, never mind, all the best for tonight.'

Corie went to the theatre with Lynette as usual. The usual little meal was brought in for her, and while she was eating, Corie tidied up her dressing-table. It was then she noticed there was some insulin left in the measured ampoule that her sister had used for her recent injection.

'Lynette?'

'What?'

'Didn't you inject the full dose?'

'No, I knew yesterday that I wasn't properly balanced.'

'Is that all right? To reduce the dose? I thought the ampoules had been specially made up.'

'Yes, but then they don't apply in special circumstances . . .'

'I'm not sure I understand, duckie. Except for the fact that we've had a bit of a row with the management, this tour is like the others, surely?'

Lynette turned upon her sister a radiant face. 'No, Corie, it's not. Everything's different today.'

'Different?' Corie was alarmed. The change in Lynette was like a miracle – and therefore not to be trusted.

'I wasn't going to tell you, but since you've asked . . . And I'm so happy . . .'

'Lynette, what is it?'

'I think I'm going to have a baby.'

Whatever Corie had expected, it wasn't this. She felt for a stool and sat down.

'Isn't it wonderful?' cried Lynette. 'I was hoping it might happen, but—'

'A baby . . .'

'You see, it would mean Sasha and I would get married, and I could settle down at home and look after him and our baby, and I wouldn't have to keep wandering round the world pretending to be a star.'

'Oh, Lynette!'

'But when I left home I didn't really think it was so, and I've been wondering and hoping – and yesterday I knew for sure – and so everything's changed, and I'm so, so happy!'

'Lynette, darling . . .'

'Are you happy too, Corie?' Lynette asked anxiously.

'Of course I am. If it's what you want—'

'Oh, I do, you don't know how much I want it! It makes all the difference in the world! My baby, mine – and Sasha and I will be married and be like ordinary people – it'll be so *nice*, Corie: no more dreary theatre dressing-rooms and big crowds of people I don't know on the other side of the footlights . . .'

'You've never liked it?' Corie asked, stunned.

'Of course not! It was only because Monna said it was what I was meant for . . . But now I don't think that's true. I think I was meant to be an ordinary mother with a baby and a husband; so that's the future, Corie, that's the future!'

Corie got up and put her arms about her sister. They held each other tight. Corie was thinking, Is that the future? Can it really be as simple as that?

Presently it was time for Lynette to get changed. The dresser came in, took away the supper tray, and Corie went out to take up her place in the wings. It was only when the audience was settled and the opening music was playing that she had a mental image – the supper tray being carried out by Marie the dresser.

The food on it had been practically untouched. Lynette had been so carried away by the news she was giving that she'd forgotten to eat.

Corie didn't know what to do. When the band went into its special number and Lynette came off to change, there was no time to do more than say a word.

'How do you feel, Lynette?'

'Strange, unreal,' her sister said laughingly. 'It's because of the baby, Corie dear – don't worry, I'm fine.'

She was not. She only got half-way through the dance routine in 'Button Up Your Overcoat' before she suddenly swayed, threw out her arms in a wavering gesture, staggered a few steps, and collapsed in the middle of the stage.

Chapter Twenty

Although it was the early hours of the morning, there were five people in the waiting-room anxious for news of relatives or friends. The white-coated doctor came a few paces in to say the name into the air. 'Miss Duggan?'

Corie rose and hurried to him. 'Is she all right?'

He glanced at the admission card in his hand. 'You're her sister?'

'That's right. Please, how is she?'

'We've dealt with the insulin problem. She's stable now. But—' He glanced at the others in the room, all suffering their own anxieties and to be spared bad news, even the bad news of others. He took Corie a little aside. 'I'm sorry to say she lost the baby.'

'Oh no.'

'I haven't been able to talk to her, she's been given a sedative now. I suppose her blood-sugar levels seemed normal?'

'I'm afraid I . . .' She was at a loss. 'She seemed to be taking a little less insulin . . .'

'Yes, that might be indicated. You see, in pregnancy the hormones go into a bit of a spin and in the early months there is less need – she was probably right in that. But the foetus was at about three months . . . ?'

'I think that's right. She said she only found out for certain yesterday. And she only told me about it a few hours ago. So you see, I wasn't on the look-out . . .'

'Well, I don't know if anything could have been done in the circumstances. She would have needed medical super-vision from the moment she first suspected she was pregnant. Surely she knew that . . . ?'

He broke off. He was a young man, with a clever, unlined

face – probably a good doctor but without much sympathy as yet for patients.

After the briefest pause he went on, 'How long has Miss Lee had diabetes?'

'About a year.'

'I see. So perhaps she hasn't much experience yet in handling it.'

'She's been doing well,' Corie said, springing to her sister's defence. 'She's been on tour all over the world, managing her condition—'

'Not this time, I'm afraid,' he said. 'Well, she's had a big shock, both physical and emotional. Ideally we ought to keep her a week or two to run a new series of tests. But we don't have her case history. She's under someone at home?'

'Dr Usborne at St Mary's, Paddington.'

'Ah.' The name clearly meant something to him. 'In that case, it would probably be best for her to go home and see him for any tests and reappraisal.'

'Will she be fit to travel?' Corie asked, her mind filled by the picture of her sister's crumpled body on the empty stage, a broken butterfly.

'Two or three days. We'll keep her stable, supervise her intake, she'll get lots of rest and quiet.'

'Rest in bed?'

'She'll be allowed up for a little while tomorrow, probably in the afternoon. Then more the next day, and by Day Three she'll be ambulant. It'll be something like that.'

'It means she'll spend Christmas in hospital,' Corie said in distress.

'That's not so bad,' the doctor replied rather impatiently. 'Carols and turkey and all that. Probably better than a hotel Christmas.'

'Yes,' she agreed. If it must be, it must be.

'Give her a day or two to find her feet in the real world, and she can fly home. I'll give you a letter for Dr Usborne – results of our tests, things like that.'

'Thank you.'

'If you ring tomorrow about ten, we can tell you what sort of a night she's had.'

'I'll come. I'll be able to see her, won't I?' she begged, suddenly alarmed in case her sister's condition was too serious for visitors.

'Of course, no worries. She's not critical, you know. You could say it's just a very big knock to her system, and she'll take some time to get over it, if you understand me.'

'Yes. Thank you.'

She went to the Watson Hotel to use its facilities in the sending of cables. She tried to word the one to her mother so as not to alarm her unduly, but it was hard. To Sasha she sent a very business-like message: 'Lynette ill, tour ended, home next week.' Let him make what he could out of that.

Using Lynette's room, she tried to sleep, but it was hopeless. Some time before six she rang room service for tea and toast. She went out with her camera, using it as a comfort symbol for herself. But she knew she wasn't paying enough attention to get good shots.

Back at the hotel she had breakfast and was just finishing when Frankin came in. He joined her at her table, waving to the waiter for tea. 'I rang the hospital. They say she's not in any danger.'

'That's right.'

'Terrible thing,' he mused, playing with the salt cellar. 'You should have told me she was under the weather. I wouldn't have . . . you know . . .'

She might have said, You didn't help matters. But that was all in the past now. 'I'm going to see her later,' she said. 'Take her toothbrush, things like that.'

'I've sent flowers.'

'Thank you.'

'How long'll she be in?'

'Two or three days.'

'Back in time for the New Year show?'

Corie almost gaped at him.

'New Year's Eve — a big night with us,' he prompted.

'She won't be going on with the tour,' she said.

'Come again?'

'I'm taking her home as soon as she's able to travel.'

'You can't do that!'

The waiter brought his pot of tea. They sat in silence until he had gone. Frankin said, 'What's all this? She's got a contract to fulfil!'

'She's going home.'

'But what for? Exhaustion, you said last night. What's that, eh – two or three days in hospital, a day or two at the beach to put the roses back—'

'No, she needs to see her own doctor as soon as possible.'

He frowned in anger. 'What's up with her then? She was ill before she got here, is that it?'

'When you qualify as a doctor, I'll discuss my sister's health with you, Mr Frankin.'

'Don't get clever with me, girlie! I booked a class act for the holiday season and I'm not going to be left with an empty theatre. Do you realise the loss I'm facing already over refunds for today and tomorrow?'

'You've been in the business since the thirties, you told me. You'll find a replacement.'

'You're serious!' He sat back on his chair, aghast. 'You're actually telling me I've got to cancel for New Year as well as Christmas Eve!'

Corie leaned over to pour his tea for him. 'Drink up, Mr Frankin,' she said, 'it'll help steady your nerves. I'm very sorry indeed, it's the first time anyone in my family has ever had to let anyone down. But Lynette can't appear again in Sydney. The doctor says she'll probably be fit to travel by next Wednesday, and that's when we leave.'

'You're taking a hell of a lot on yourself, missie! You're not her agent!'

'Take it up with him, then.'

'You bet I will! Our lawyers will be on to him like a shot . . .'

They both knew that insurance would recoup the loss on the tickets. But it was his prestige he was worried about.

The theatre chain had relied on him to find a star for the holiday season at the New Garden. Instead he had given them an empty stage.

While his cup of tea grew cold, he argued and threatened. Corie understood that he felt he had to do it. She'd crossed swords with many a man in show business in her career in theatre and knew there was no defence but a continual 'no'. She bore his tirade with stubborn calm, feeling that in a way she was being unfair. She couldn't tell him about Lynette's diabetes and nothing else would make it comprehensible to him.

In the end he got up and stamped out without saying goodbye. The waiter came up to remove the cold tea. 'Mr Frankin lost his rag?' he inquired.

She shrugged. Frankin was well known to the hotel staff. Within an hour, the story of the row over the breakfast table would be known throughout the building. The result was an inquiry from the manager as she passed through the foyer on her way out.

'Miss Duggan, a word?'

'Yes?'

'Am I to take it that Allotts Theatres will still be paying the bill for Miss Lee's accommodation?'

She said shortly, 'Take that up with Mr Frankin. I'm in a hurry.'

Lynette was propped up on pillows when Corie was shown into her room. Her face was almost as white as the pillow-case. The soft blonde hair was pulled back carelessly in a clasp.

'How are you, darling?'

'I'm all right.' Her voice was unsteady. 'Did they tell you . . . about my baby?'

'Yes, love.'

'It was my fault. I should never have come on this tour.'

'No, now, you couldn't have known this was going to happen—'

'I should have talked to Dr Usborne. I didn't know there was any danger but I should have asked . . .'

'Lynette, don't blame yourself. You have to put it behind you.'

'I'll never be able to put it behind me. *I lost my baby.*'

Corie sat down at the bedside, took her sister's hand, and held it in silence. The scent of the flowers which almost filled the room was all about them. A girl in a garden . . . Poor little sister.

By and by she told Lynette they would be going home as soon as she was fit. Lynette's eyes filled with tears. 'What will Monna say when she sees me? I've let her down.'

'No you haven't.'

'And the theatre, and all the people Mr Frankin talked about – their Christmas outing–'

'It doesn't matter, Lynette. It can't be helped. We'll go home and you'll be able to tell Dr Usborne what's happened and he'll sort it out.'

'He'll be cross. He told me always to consult him if anything changed.'

'He won't be cross. If he is, I'll give him a piece of my mind.'

'Oh, Corie!' Lynette brought her sister's hand up to her face and held it there. 'Corie, I don't know what to do any more!'

There were tasks awaiting Corie. She had to deal with a few press inquiries, she had to book a flight for Wednesday, she had to speak to Frankin about the hotel bill.

He was angry when she telephoned her inquiry. 'What do you think we are, a bunch of Scrooges?' he barked. 'I've never welshed on anybody – of course Allotts will meet the bill!'

'Thank you, Mr Frankin. I just thought I'd better make sure because the manager–'

'Yeh, he was on to me earlier. I gave him a flea in his ear. Sick girl, miles from home – he wants to know if we're going to pay her bill. How is the kid, anyhow?'

'Not good,' Corie sighed. 'Depressed.'

'Don't wonder at it. Well, I hope she gets on all right. And in case you were wondering, I've got Al Somerville to fill the gap – you wouldn't know him, he's a popular Aussie comedian.' Something in his tone implied that Al Somerville would be a better act for his audiences than Lynette Lee.

'I'm glad. By the way, Lynette says thank you for the flowers.'

'Huh.'

Corie spent Christmas Eve and Christmas Day at the hospital with Lynette. As the doctor had foretold, there were carols and there was turkey. It all seemed incongruous in the hot sunshine. They sat outdoors, under a shady tree, listening to the Queen's speech on radio. They walked ever so gently along the shaded verandahs.

On Boxing Day Lynette was discharged. In her hotel room there were flowers and cards as there had been when she first arrived. This time they were get-well cards. She sat down on the edge of the bed and wept at it all.

Emotionally she seemed on a knife-edge. The slightest thing could bring on a weeping fit. Corie acted as a buffer between her sister and the rest of the world but it was impossible to shield her from every hurtful sight or sound. A picture of a baby in a magazine, a tune played on the radio reminding her of her repertoire – these and a hundred other little things could upset her fragile equanimity.

Lynette's name was well enough known to ensure VIP treatment at the airport. The stewardess was eager to be helpful, even asked for Lynette's autograph. 'I used to adore your show on TV,' she said with a nostalgia that made it sound as if it had been a hundred years ago.

Their first stop-over was Hong Kong. Corie loved the city, a beguiling mixture of the old and the new, set in a bay where islands floated like jade jewels on a sea of blue silk. The fresh clean air was in welcome contrast to Sydney's summer heat.

But there was scarcely time to enjoy it. It was a rest stop of only twenty-four hours. Corie didn't even go out with her camera. Somehow it would have been utterly wrong to leave Lynette, and since Lynette didn't want to go out, Corie stayed indoors with her.

As they flew on towards Europe, she seemed to grow even more depressed. 'Not long now, lovey,' Corie murmured soothingly. 'Karachi this evening, and then tomorrow we'll be on our way to London.'

'I know,' Lynette muttered, 'I dread it.'

'Lynette, darling!'

'Think what Monna's going to say. And Sasha – he'll be so disappointed.'

'Because you lost the baby?' Corie asked, stifling her surprise. She wouldn't have thought Sasha would want a baby.

'No, no, he knows nothing about that, and you mustn't tell him!'

'Sweetie, we've got to talk about that. All this secrecy—'

'No,' Lynette said, closing her eyes and letting her head fall against the back of the plane seat, 'I don't want to talk about it.'

The drive to the Indus Hotel in Karachi seemed to upset Lynette. Certainly there was tremendous poverty among the people, who thronged its streets so thickly that the car could scarcely makes its way.

'Those poor children,' mourned Lynette as they passed a group of ten-year-olds carrying broken stones to make a pavement.

What could Corie say? That it was dreadful, but Lynette must pay no heed? That the death of her own baby mustn't make her vulnerable to the woes of every child who survived?

Instead she tried to talk about the hotel, its swimming pool, its beauty parlour. 'I feel I need its attentions,' she said, passing a hand over her beige-blonde hair. 'And a swim – all that talk about the marvellous beaches in Sydney, and we never once had a swim.'

'That was all my fault,' Lynette said tearfully.

'Don't talk about it like that. Having diabetes isn't a sin, you know. You're not to *blame*.'

'But I am; I should have been more careful!'

Soon they'd passed the road gangs, and had come to the more imposing parts of Pakistan's capital. Corie pointed out the university, the government buildings. Lynette said, 'Oh yes,' without the least interest.

Luckily once they'd settled into the hotel, she went sensibly about the regime of checking her tests and having a snack. Corie went out to do twenty laps in the pool. Palms shaded it from the late afternoon sun, tired businessmen lounged in deck chairs, white-clad attendants ran about with trays of drinks. It was a glorious sensation to be alone in the tepid blue water, to drive through it in a lazy crawl, letting travel fatigue be washed away from her aching body.

She gave herself the luxury of a hair-cut and a manicure. When she got back to their room, it was time to go to dinner. What time of day it was in Sydney, or in London, Corie couldn't imagine, but as far as she could tell, Lynette was sticking to her timetable of insulin injections.

When they'd eaten a dessert of tropical fruits and were lazily watching the stars through the great open windows, Corie took the plunge.

'Lynette dear, we must decide what we're going to tell Monna when we get back.'

'I don't want to talk about it.'

'But we must. You see, I think it's time you told the family about the diabetes.'

'No!'

'But sweetheart, what else are we to say? You wouldn't have had to come home unless it was something serious.'

'We'll say it was what you told Mr Frankin – just exhaustion.'

'But he didn't really believe that.'

'I'm not going to tell them, so don't go on—'

'Lynette, if you won't tell them, I shall have to.'

'Don't you dare! Don't you dare!'

Her voice had risen like a child in panic. Others in the dining-room looked at them with curiosity.

'Shh, darling, shh . . .'

The waiter came up, anxious in case something about the meal had displeased the lady. Corie assured him all was well and ordered coffee. They sat in silence until it came. It was served in a silver pot, with tiny cups in silver holders. The coffee itself was very strong. After a mouthful Corie decided against it for fear it would keep her awake when, after all, the break in the journey was to allow them a good night's rest.

'We could say I got food poisoning,' Lynette suggested, tracing the design on the side of her cup with a finger.

'Don't let's lie about it, Lynette.'

'Oh, why not?' she replied with a shrug. 'Everything's a lie, really, isn't it? My career as a great TV star — it was all a sham, a sort of echo of the way things used to be, not real at all.'

'It *was* real, Lynette. People really enjoyed it. It's just that something else came along . . .'

'Yes, something more real, more exciting. You know, I feel as if I'm fading away to a shadow.'

'Oh, please, Lynette—'

'You know that dance I do — "Dancing with My Shadow"? I think that now I'm the shadow, and there isn't a Lynette Lee to dance the other part any more.'

'Stop this at once,' Corie said sharply. 'You're talking yourself into another weeping fit.'

'Why not? Who was it who said, "I'm in mourning for my life"?'

'I don't know and I don't care, because it doesn't apply to you in the least. You've got years and years ahead of you . . .'

'And what am I going to do with them?'

'Sasha will arrange some new engagements when you feel better.'

'I suppose so,' Lynette said, closing her eyes and shaking her head. 'And that's why I'm in mourning for my life.'

It was beyond Corie. And it was so unlike the sunny, cheerful girl who'd been her little sister for over twenty years. Trying to handle her was like talking to a stranger.

They went up to bed, and in the morning travelled on with the problem still unresolved – what were they to tell Monna?

On the plane over France, Lynette turned unexpectedly to her sister. 'All right,' she said, as if they'd been in the middle of a conversation, 'we'll tell Monna and Opal. But not about the baby. Promise, Corie – not about my baby.'

'Very well.' She was so relieved to have won the main point that she didn't try to argue on the other.

At the airport a certain amount of VIP treatment got them through Customs with little delay. They walked through into the arrivals lounge to be greeted by Monna and, to Corie's surprise, William Tranton.

Monna surged forward intending to enfold her daughter in her arms. But Lynette's pallor took her so much by surprise that she stopped in mid-stride. A hand went up to her mouth in a perfectly genuine gesture of dismay.

'My darling child! What on earth has happened to you?'

During the momentary hesitation, William stepped up to give Corie a brotherly kiss on the cheek. 'How on earth do you come to be here?' she murmured in his ear.

'I saw a little item in the papers about Lynette, and rang your mother. She was in a bit of a state so I . . . er . . .'

'Rallied round? Thank you, William.'

Monna was now embracing Lynette. The porter stood patiently by. 'Where to with the bags, ladies?' he inquired.

'If you'll bring them to the exit . . . I'll fetch my car . . . shan't be two ticks.'

William hurried off. Monna turned to Corie. 'You're not much better!' she cried. 'How thin you are! Good God, what have you two been up to?'

'Not now, Monna. We're longing to get home and relax.'

'Of course, I do so understand, it was the same with me at the end of the tour, I used to tell your father, "Click, darling, the old saying is true, East, West, Home's best".'

Urging them ahead, and with the porter bringing up the rear in stolid nonchalance, they went out into the dreary cold. It was the day after New Year's Day. William pulled up in an Austin Cambridge, the luggage was loaded in the boot, Lynette was carefully handed in to the back seat.

Her mother made as if to follow her.

'No, Monna, I want Corie to sit with me.'

'But darling!'

'I want Corie.'

'Please sit in the front with William, Monna. Let's just get on.'

Mortally offended, Mrs Duggan allowed herself to be helped into the front alongside William. With a faint grimace at Corie, he took off the brake and moved away.

Until they were out of the airport precincts Lynette sat in silence. Then she asked in a low voice, 'Where is Sasha?'

'Ah, he wanted so much to come!' Monna burst out. 'But he's so busy — overwhelmed — there are people over from Nashville at the moment, he has to squire them around, they're in the middle of an important negotiation . . .'

'Nashville?'

'Tennessee,' William said over his shoulder. 'Sasha is going to handle some of their country singers on a European tour. It really is a big-money deal.'

'I see,' said Lynette.

'He told me to tell you he'll come to the house the minute he can get away,' Monna swept on. 'And he's sent flowers — wait till you see them, Lynette, orchids! But he said that if you were too tired for visitors, just to ring and leave a message — he'll quite understand.'

'Oh yes.'

Corie said quietly, 'Perhaps you ought to put off seeing him until after you've been to the doctor, Lynette.'

Catching the word doctor, their mother took it up. 'Who was your doctor in Sydney? I hope it was someone who knew his job. It looks to me as if you had some kind of bug, dear — some sort of flu, was it?'

'We'll talk about that later, Monna.'

'I rang Dr Bennard to ask him to drop by and give you a once-over. All you have to do is fix up a time, darling.'

Lynette was going to make an impatient response, but

Corie covered her hand with one of hers and said, 'Let's leave all that until we're home, Monna. How's Pal?'

'Quite the little housewife,' her mother replied with kindly scorn. 'I can't really believe there's enough to do in that little house of theirs, but she seems to keep busy — making loose covers and curtains, planting things in the garden . . .'

'That must be nice,' Lynette said in a tone of wonder. 'Nothing to worry about but mowing the lawn . . .'

'Well, it seems to suit Opal. But I can't imagine you'd like it, darling, not after your experience of playing to a world-wide public.'

Lynette murmured, very low, 'That's not as much fun as you seem to think,' but the roar of a passing lorry meant that, perhaps fortunately, Monna didn't hear.

When they got to Bayswater, William brought in the luggage but refused to stay for tea. 'I can see you want to be on your own with your family,' he said to Lynette as he pressed her hand in leave-taking. To Corie he said, 'Please come and talk to me when you can.'

'You can be sure of it,' she said.

Lynette went up to her room, her steps slow on the stairs. Her mother stared upwards at her vanishing figure. 'She really looks very poorly,' she said in perplexity. 'What on earth happened?'

'She collapsed on stage.'

'How dreadful! And the curtain had to be rung down?' To Monna the scene was present before her eyes as she spoke of it — like an Act One curtain in a play.

'Sit down, Monna. I have something very serious to tell you.'

'What? What is it? Is something really wrong with my darling?'

'She has diabetes.'

This wasn't how she'd planned to make the announcement. She meant to lead up to it softly, to say it without giving her mother a shock. But it was better perhaps to get it over with, to prevent any summoning of dear old Dr

Bennard who might have a very limited understanding of the diabetic condition.

Monna had been holding her coat and scarf and hat to take them upstairs. She paused now, and slowly the garments fell from her arms.

'Diabetes?'

'She's had it for some time. That muddle over her home-coming from Hong Kong? That was done on purpose so that she could have tests run at a hospital.'

'But that – that was *last year*–'

'She's kept it secret because for some strange reason she's ashamed.'

'Did you know?'

'I found out by accident – when she was in Copenhagen.'

'You've known all these months and you didn't tell me?'

'No.'

'*You* knew? How dare you keep it secret?'

'Lynette wanted it that way.'

'Don't talk nonsense. My own daughter? Lynette would never have kept it from me . . .'

'Monna, please don't get into a state about it.'

'Get into a state! What do you expect me to do? I'm furious with you! To take it upon yourself to keep me in the dark–'

'I tell you, Monna, Lynette wanted it to be secret. She made me promise.'

Monna's face flushed with anger and distress. She shook her head from side to side. 'You can't tell me that my little Lynette would keep this terrible thing–'

'It *isn't* a terrible thing, Monna, it's an illness like any other except that it can be controlled by–'

'Oh, God!' cried her mother, sitting down and covering her face with both hands. 'Does she have to have injections? How dreadful, my poor, poor little girl – she's always been so fit and well, to think of her reduced to–'

'Mother!' exclaimed Corie.

It was so unusual for any of them to use the term when addressing her that it startled her into abrupt silence. She took her hands away from her face, looked at her eldest daughter in something verging on alarm.

'Mother, stop working yourself up into a scene. What Lynette needs at this moment is calm support. She doesn't want dramatic declarations about how much you love and cherish her, how much you feel for her. She needs quiet and orderliness and a relaxed acceptance of the situation. After all, she's managed the condition for a year without causing you the least anxiety – until now. And the only reason you're finding out now is because we had to break off the tour and come back to see Dr Usborne.'

'Dr Usborne?'

'The specialist dealing with her case at St Mary's.'

'A specialist. *He* knows more about my child than I do myself.'

Corie decided to go on the attack. 'And why not?' she riposted. 'Lynette's a grown woman. Her body is her own, to handle as she thinks best. She doesn't have to tell you how she feels or what she's suffering.'

'How can you say that? She's my *daughter*!'

'I'm your daughter. So is Pal. You look on us as grown-up women. For Lynette's sake, try to see her the same way.'

'It's not the same and you know it! Lynette's always been special. Between Lynette and me there's always been a special bond.'

'That's because she's done as you told her. More than that, she's a success. Oh, I know – ' Corie raised her voice as her mother tried to interrupt – 'you don't think Pal and I have done you credit. Lynette is what you wanted us to be – a star.'

'Are you daring to say that I only love my poor little girl because she's made a name for herself? How dare you! You'll soon see how wrong you are! Lynette will be even more to me now, when she's sick and needs me. I'll make her well again, you'll see! I'll give her back to the public who've always loved her.'

'Well again? Monna, for heaven's sake—'

'Of course she looks poorly now. She's been under a strain – perhaps touring has been too much for her – I ought to have gone with her myself, *I* would never have let her get so exhausted—'

'Monna, Monna, please.' Corie clasped her hands and held them out in a gesture of pleading. 'You must realise that there isn't anything anyone can do about her condition. More than that, you've got something very difficult to face: her success is fading, her health isn't perfect, she's had a big shock and it may take her a long time to recover. Monna, you must, you absolutely must think of her as a person – think of Lynette, not Lynette's career or her duty to her profession or to her public. Give her time to sort things out in her own way. Don't crowd her, don't reproach her—'

'Reproach her? As if I would! Corie, sometimes you can be terribly cruel. I shall forget what you've just said because I understand it was done out of a mistaken desire to help your sister, but I tell you plainly that I know what's best for my little girl—'

'No, you don't, Monna!'

'Be silent! Who helped her to become a star? Who recognised her talent from the time she was a tiny tot?'

'There you are – you're talking about her work, not her life . . .'

'Her work is her life, and that's what you've never understood, Corie. Just because you had no talent yourself, you don't understand what a compulsion it places upon you. Lynette can never turn her back on her career – and as to being ill, that can be seen to, I'm sure it can, I've read things in the papers about break-throughs—'

'Monna, I beg you – let Lynette sort this out for herself.'

'Oh, you just don't understand,' her mother said, 'there's a special bond between a mother and a daughter with our background – a bond of dedication.'

A thousand angry words boiled up in Corie. She wanted to take her mother by her plump shoulders and shake her until her bones hurt. But experience had taught her it was useless. Years of seeing herself as the guiding light in her youngest daughter's career had made Crystal Duggan impregnable to argument.

Since there seemed nothing else to do, Corie walked out of the room.

When she tapped on Lynette's door it opened immediately. 'I heard you arguing,' her sister said with a wince. 'Did you tell her?'

'Yes.'

'How did she take it?'

'She's going to help you get the better of it.'

Lynette turned back into her room and sank on the stool by her dressing-table. Her head was bent. 'I'll ask Dr Usborne to talk to her.'

'Perhaps that's best.'

'I can't go back on tour, Corie. I can't face it.'

Corie came to her and stroked her fair hair. 'You don't have to do anything you don't want to, love.'

'But Monna will argue . . . And Sasha . . .'

'Just keep saying no.'

Lynette drew in a sobbing breath. 'If only it were that easy . . .'

The inexorable routine took over. It became necessary for Lynette to eat, and together with Corie she went downstairs to the kitchen. Monna, who had been pacing about the living-room, immediately came to join them.

'How are you, darling?' she asked, going to Lynette and touching her too fondly on the cheek.

'I'm all right. Just tired.'

'And depressed, I can see that. I understand, Lynette, I understand completely. I remember once when I was in Grantham I got laryngitis—'

'This isn't laryngitis, Monna,' said Lynette. 'And if you'll excuse me, I've got to get a sandwich . . .'

'But dearest, I've planned a gorgeous dinner . . . I've got a bottle of champagne in the fridge – Pal and Bart are coming—'

'I have to eat now,' her daughter said. 'It's something

you'll have to get used to. Four small meals a day, carefully controlled.'

'But this is a special occasion, Lynette – your homecoming.'

'All right,' was the sharp response, 'you have a party, I'll eat crispbread.'

'Lynette!'

Lynette coloured up. 'I'm sorry,' she said, 'but you really have to understand . . . I can't do silly things like eat big meals and drink wine . . .'

'I understand, my love, I do, I understand,' her mother hastened to say. 'I'll learn all about it, I'll see to it that you get the right things to eat. Tomorrow I'll have a chat with this Dr Osborne—'

'Usborne.'

'Yes, Usborne, I'll get him to put me fully in the picture so that I can make things easy for you. After all, as Corie was explaining, you learned how to look after yourself. I can do it too, and from now on you need never worry your head—'

Lynette turned away. Corie saw her face. It looked as if she were facing a trap closing in on her.

Quickly Corie said, 'What do you want on this sandwich?'

'Oh, let me show you what's in the larder,' Monna offered with great good cheer, opening cupboard doors and pointing. 'There's cheese, of course, and some salmon mayonnaise, and cold roast beef – and of course lettuce and things in the fridge.' She paused. 'We were going to have roast lamb this evening. Can you eat roast lamb?'

Lynette had responded to Corie's question and was now taking items out of the fridge while Corie sliced the bread. Her mother talked on about the menu for that evening. By and by the moment of irritation had passed for Lynette. She said at length, 'I can eat whatever you put on the table, but only up to a certain calorie level.'

'Calorie?'

'I'll show you,' Corie offered. 'I have a typed list from Dr

Usborne giving an outline of what and what not to eat.'

'*You* have a list?'

'Monna,' said Lynette, 'don't make a big thing of it. Corie found out and she helped me. Now you've found out and you want to help me. Just let's try to take it bit by bit, shall we?'

'Oh, yes darling, yes,' cried her mother, and threw her arms around her.

Corie left them soon afterwards, to rush home in a taxi with her luggage. She went straight to the phone when she got indoors, and dialled Pal's number. 'Pal? This is Corie.'

'Corie! What a surprise – why are you ringing?' Then with added anxiety, 'Is something wrong – is this evening cancelled?'

'No, love, but I thought I better prepare you. And you'd better tell Bart to be ready for high drama. The thing is, Pal . . .' To her own surprise her voice broke. 'Pal, Lynette's really ill.'

'Really ill? How d'you mean? Pneumonia? Something she picked up?'

'I didn't mean to tell you this on the phone. But if I don't, and Monna breaks the news . . . Pal, our little sister's got diabetes.'

There was a long, long silence.

'Hello?' Corie said. 'Are you still there?'

'Corie, is it true?'

'Yes, for about a year or so . . . She kept it a secret. I'll tell you some other time. It's just . . . We had to tell Monna . . . I mean, after what happened in Sydney . . . We had to come home and . . . and . . . It just couldn't *be* a secret, and now Monna . . .'

'Oh, God, I can just imagine,' breathed Pal.

'We've got to do all we can to help Lynette,' Corie said. 'She's had a terrible shock – you just don't know – Pal, I can count on you, can't I?'

'Sure thing,' Pal said with an attempt at a laugh. 'The Little Gems, three who sparkle together – that's us.'

The evening was a trial for everyone. Corie felt sorry

for Pal's husband, who manfully tried to cope with the emotion that seemed to fly about in the very air around Monna. Lynette was quiet, Pal and Corie tried to talk with calmness and good sense about the new situation that had arisen.

When by and by they were settled in the living-room with coffee and after-dinner mints, Pal said with some hesitation, 'What's Sasha going to say?'

'I don't think he should know,' Monna said immediately.

'But surely,' Bart said, a furrow on his brow, 'it would make a difference to how he handled her bookings—'

'Exactly! And there's no need for that, when you come to think of it. After all, my clever little girl handled herself so well that it made no difference at all for a whole year—'

'But now you've had this upset in Sydney, Lynette . . .'

'Bart, no offence, but you don't understand theatre people, after all. Lynette is a *trouper* − she can face the world from behind the footlights and no one need ever know that she . . . that she . . .'

'That I've got something wrong with me,' Lynette supplied.

'Well, as Corie pointed out to me when she first told me, it's not such a terrible thing. You know you said yourself, dear, when we were chatting, people lead normal lives. And she's not by any means the only person in the public eye who manages the whole thing without anyone knowing,' Monna added as if she were very much au fait with the problem, 'or so Dr Usborne says.'

'Really? I'd no idea,' said Bart.

'But wouldn't it be better just to acknowledge the fact—'

'What fact, Opal? What fact that is any business of anyone else's? Outside these four walls,' cried Monna, throwing out her arms to demonstrate the confines, 'it need never be mentioned.'

'What would you prefer, Lynette?' Opal asked.

Corie wanted to say, that was a mistake, Pal, you're giving her a chance to take cover in Monna's family pride.

But it was too late. Lynette said in a subdued voice, 'Of course I'd rather not tell people. I know it would make them look at me differently.'

'But Sasha has to make decisions on your behalf, Lynette.' Bart's view was the businessman's view — contracts and negotiations could only take place if the negotiator was well-briefed.

'He made them all through last year without ever suspecting there was anything amiss. I don't see that anything's changed. And besides . . .'

'What?'

Lynette fell silent. But Corie could guess what she might have been about to say. It was difficult enough for Lynette to compete for Sasha's interest when he thought of her as hale and hearty. If he once knew that she was less than fit, he could easily relegate her to the less important ranks of his clients.

The conclusion was to keep the state of Lynette's health as a confidential matter within the family. Corie doubted the wisdom of the decision, but hadn't enough confidence in herself to hold out.

Sasha didn't come that evening, but sent flowers again next day with a message that he would be in touch. Lynette went to see Dr Usborne. Despite all Corie could do, their mother insisted on accompanying Lynette. Since three would certainly be too much of a crowd, Corie went to her studio to remind herself of the appointments for January and to chat to Bertie.

'Fancy you whizzing back home so quickly,' he said. 'Thought you were due back next week.'

Corie explained her sister had been unwell. 'But I'm quite glad to be back. There are things I want to get on with — some work in the darkroom.'

'So as to be right up to date when you whizz off again to America,' Bertie said rather huffily.

'I'm not absolutely sure I'll be going,' Corie replied.

'Not going?' Although he'd been annoyed that she should be absent so much, he was now annoyed that she was changing her mind. 'Why ever not? I thought it was all arranged.'

'Well, my sister's health is a bit unpredictable—'

'Oh yes? Well, save you the cost of the air fare if you don't go.'

Opal was aghast when she heard Corie was thinking of calling it off.

'Go!' she commanded. 'What possible good can it do for you to hang around here?'

'But Lynette—'

'I'll see to Lynette,' Opal said, colouring up. 'I owe you that.'

'Owe me?' Corie was astonished. 'In what way?'

'I feel badly about how I reacted when you asked me to take on the touring with her. I pushed it all off on to you. Well, in a way I don't regret it, because now Bart and I are a pair. But don't you throw away your chances with this fellow you think so much about in Washington. You go, Corie, go! I'll look after our kid sister.'

Corie wanted very much to go to Washington for the presidential Inauguration. She kept assuring herself it would be all right to go. Yet things weren't as they should be at home.

Lynette's mood of depression didn't seem to lift. Of course matters weren't helped when eventually Sasha showed up and, as far as Corie could gather, began talking about dates in Vancouver and Toronto. Lynette said she didn't feel up to it, her mother assured her she'd be fine by the time the dates came round, and Sasha went away sayng he'd be signing the contract in a few days.

'Lynette, just tell him you don't want to.'

'He'll ask why.'

'Just say you're feeling under the weather, if you don't want to tell him the whole bit.'

'I *told* him that.'

'Tell him again.'

Lynette's shoulders drooped. 'I hate it when he gets cross with me,' she said.

Corie suppressed a sigh. 'I'll talk to him, shall I?'

'Oh, Corie, would you? You've always been able to handle things like this.'

'Lynette, can't you just—'

'What?'

'Never mind,' her sister said, stifling the irritation that had almost welled up. 'I'll see Sasha, make him put off the Vancouver thing.'

Sasha didn't want to see her. He had his secretary say he was in a meeting or was out with a client, until at last Corie said in exasperation, 'Tell him Miss Duggan wants to prevent him from signing a contract that is sure to be broken.'

That had the desired result. He rang fifteen minutes later. 'What d'you mean, the contract is sure to be broken? What kind of message is that to leave?'

'I don't want to talk about it over the phone, Sasha. Can we meet for a drink?'

'I don't see why we have to meet at all! Why are you interfering?'

'I was with Lynette in Sydney when she collapsed, that's why.'

'But she'll be fit by June, for God's sake!'

'Sasha, can we talk about this over a drink like civilised human beings?'

'Oh very well then – the Ritz Bar this evening about seven.'

She got there before him, and though the place was well-patronised was able to settle herself in a corner with a campari-soda. She was wearing an oyster-satin shirt over dark red silk trousers so as not to look too workaday in these glamorous surroundings. Her hair was on top of her head in a soft beige coil; she'd taken trouble with eye-shadow to heighten the hazel eyes.

When Sasha came in and glanced about for her, she raised a hand. She saw his brows rise in appreciation.

'Well,' he said, sliding into the bench beside her, 'there's always something special about you, Corie.'

'Thank you.' She caught the barman's eye and he came over. 'What will you have, Sasha?'

'Oh, um . . . Mustn't drink much, I've got a business dinner later. A clear head, you know. I'll have a spritzer, please, waiter.'

He picked up a few cocktail biscuits and crunched for a moment. 'Now, let's get straight to the point. What's this nonsense about breaking contracts?'

'Don't make any deals for Lynette until and unless she says she wants them. She's not well enough.'

'But for Pete's sake, we're talking about six months' time!'

'I know that. But what happened in Sydney is more important than you think. She had a big shock there. The audience didn't care for her, she had to have overnight rewrites on the gags—'

'Well, we can have a new writer for Vancouver—'

'It's not just that. Emotionally she's all at sea.'

'Look, Corie, I can do without temperaments. I'm in the middle of negotiations with the Americans that will bring in—'

'Lynette's not throwing a temperament. She's struggling with an emotional upset that's left her very depressed.'

'Because she didn't go over big in Sydney? Have a heart Corie, she's lucky to have an audience at all, with that fifties material—'

'It's so wonderful to have an agent who has confidence in you,' Corie remarked tartly.

'Well, darling, you know I think the world of Lynette, but her material isn't exactly new, now is it? If she starts getting difficult about the bookings I can land for her, she'll soon find she won't get bookings at all.'

'And what then, Sasha?'

'What d'you mean, what then?'

'You strike her off your books, do you?'

He shrugged. 'My business is expanding, I can't give personal attention to every client. I would have my assistant keep on the lookout for work for her, I wouldn't leave her without representation. But if you're asking me if she'd get my personal attention in the old way, the answer's no. I'm running a business here, Corie, not a benefit society.'

His drink came, he took a sip or two. 'What are you asking me?' he inquired, studying Corie's face. 'Can I go on for ever finding dates for Lynette? No I can't.'

'And then it's over.'

'Oh, she'll get by.'

'Not without you. She loves you, Sasha.'

He drew back a little, made a little gesture of waving that away with his hand. 'A lot of my clients are a bit too fond – you must have seen it often enough in your days as a dancer, Corie. People get dependent. And that's OK if it works. And Lynette's always been a romantic.'

'Romantic! Was that what you and she had during the autumn? A romance?'

'Well, you nagged me because I didn't spend enough time with her . . .'

'So you took her to bed and thought that solved the problem?'

'Where was the harm? She was happy, I was happy. What's your problem?'

'My problem,' Corie said in a tone of ice, 'is that my sister is suffering post-natal depression after losing your baby, that's my problem.'

Sasha's dark, narrow face went blank. Then, after a moment, he lifted his drink and took a swallow. 'A baby?'

'She had a miscarriage.'

'You sure it was *my* baby?'

Corie clenched her fist. 'Take care, Sasha,' she said in a low voice.

'OK, OK, so it was my baby.' He was flustered. 'She never told me.'

'She wasn't sure, not until we were in Sydney. And then she had an upset one way and the other and the baby was lost.'

He paused. Then he said, 'Well, all for the best, if you look at it sensibly. Wouldn't look too good, would it, the sweetheart of the world with a little by-blow pulling at her skirts?'

'By-blow . . . ? But Sasha . . . Sasha . . . Surely you and Lynette would have married?'

Under her incredulous gaze he went slowly red. 'Well . . . yes . . . of course . . . sure . . .'

It was clear to Corie that the idea of marriage had never entered his head. The hopes and plans Lynette had confided to her had been based on nothing but wishes.

So much for dreams.

'Sasha,' Corie said, 'let's forget I ever mentioned anything to you about a baby. I shouldn't have told you – I promised Lynette I wouldn't.'

'Well . . . sure . . . I think Lynette's wishes have got to be respected.' He was greatly relieved.

'Certainly. And the same goes for any touring engagements. Lynette has to agree before you sign any contracts.'

'Yes, yes, I naturally wouldn't want to push her into anything.'

'Then in that case, perhaps you'd better hurry along to your business dinner, Sasha.'

He rose. He stood looking down at her. 'I wish I understood you,' he said in perplexity. 'You and I could make such a great team.'

'Goodnight, Sasha. Good luck with the business deal.'

She went home upset and angry with herself. Had she accomplished anything?

Well, at least Lynette wouldn't be pushed into agreements for which she wasn't ready. It wasn't much to have achieved, but it was something. She could leave for Washington with an easier mind.

Chapter Twenty-one

The arrangements for Corie's visit had been taken over by Helen Pittsworth Holstead. There had been a phone call late on the evening of 15 January.

'Poor Drew is being run off his feet,' Helen explained. 'They all are − Jack thinks everybody else has the same stamina as he has. Well, dear, that's neither here nor there. I want you to travel on the seventeenth−'

'But I've booked for the nineteenth, Helen−'

'I've rebooked you. Well, it's truer to say I've started over from scratch. You're on a flight arriving seven a.m. our time on Wednesday morning. You'll be met at La Guardia, and fly straight on here−'

'Where's here, Helen? Where are you speaking from?'

'Washington, where else? I've an apartment on the Alexandra side, just a rental, you know. I don't like Washington, wouldn't live here if you paid me. But the last few months it's been necessary to be on the spot so . . . You'll come to me and stay − how long are you staying, honey?'

'We-ell . . . Not long . . . I have business appointments in the week starting the twenty-third . . .'

She heard Helen make a harrumphing sound. 'I'm sorry,' she said. 'This is a difficult time for me, as it happens.'

'It's difficult for all of us,' said Helen. 'Maybe it's just as well, after all, for if you were thinking you'd see much of Drew, forget it. He's up to his ears in work for the President.'

'I quite understand,' Corie replied.

'So, is that understood? Pick up your tickets at the TWA departure desk on Tuesday evening. Oh, hang on a minute . . .' There was a muffled conversation. 'Mirrie reminds me to say, Bring a ball gown.'

'A ball gown!'

'Sure, a ball gown – we have the Inauguration and then we have a ball – what d'you expect?'

'But, Helen, I haven't got a ball gown—'

'Go out and buy one. And you need evening gloves and dancing shoes.'

'Dancing shoes I've got.'

'OK, out you go and buy the rest. See you Wednesday.'

Corie had never owned a ball gown in her life. Once it became necessary for her to attend evening occasions, her 'style' had been established: she always wore trousers and a striking top. But she could understand that these would seem inappropriate for the ball celebrating the inauguration of the United States' President.

The next day was Sunday. She went to the Houndsditch Warehouse, which was always open on Sundays, but found nothing there that seemed remotely suitable. Next day was Monday, and on Tuesday she would be flying to America.

The January sales were on. In her Sunday paper she saw an elegantly phrased advertisement by a Mayfair dress designer: Model gowns and suits for a limited period at advantageous prices. On Monday morning she was on the doorstep waiting for them to open. The sales assistant took one look at her long slender figure and said, 'I've got just the thing!'

It was a narrow gown of blue-grey satin, with a boat neck and cap sleeves. Corie, trying it on, was about to ask how one was supposed to dance in this when she discovered that, on taking a step, cunningly hidden godets allowed perfect freedom of movement.

'How much?' she asked.

If what she paid was sale price, heaven help those who bought at normal rates.

Matching elbow-length gloves were supplied by Monna from a vast store gathered over a forty-year career. Opal insisted on lending the evening bag Bart had given her as a wedding present. Lynette, coming momentarily out of her trance of self-absorption, produced a string of smoky-grey pearls.

When she collected her ticket from the departure desk she found to her astonishment and delight that Helen had booked a first-class seat. The long flight was almost a pleasure in such circumstances – champagne with dinner, pillows on the reclining seat-back to give almost perfect comfort, plenty of room to stretch her long legs.

She was met at New York by Eddie Holstead. He whisked her through Customs and then off to a further part of the airport where an executive jet was waiting.

'Good heavens!' Corie cried. 'Whose is this?'

'It belongs to one of Mother's companies, if you come right down to it. But we've had the use of it for the election campaign. Come on, we want to get home for breakfast.' They had hardly taken their seats in the bright little cabin when the pilot took off.

The weather was very cold, clear enough to see the morning stars. As the jet descended over the Potomac River, Washington lay beneath them like a model city, beautiful buildings amidst patches of greenery, lawns and trees; stretches of water that reflected the dawn sky.

The drive along the Airport Road and through Arlington hardly gave her time to get her bearings in the early morning light. They crossed a bridge and a freeway, then they were turning off a main highway into a narrower street lined with handsome houses and apartment blocks, none of them very high by American standards.

A portly black porter in a beige brass-buttoned uniform opened the car door to help her descend. They went across a wide lobby, the carpet in which seemed to Corie to be ankle-deep. A lift attendant in a mini-version of the porter's uniform bore them up to the second floor. Eddie opened a door directly across from the lift onto a vestibule with a Chinese vase on a pedestal. An arch with curtains held back in festoons led into a long living-room lit by enormous shaded table lamps. Eddie led on, through a door into a corridor from which a short flight of stairs went up. He ushered her up to a room on the floor above.

'You'd like to freshen up and so on,' he said. 'Your luggage will be up in a minute if you want to change. Breakfast's in the sun room – that's back downstairs and then at the end of the passage. See you there?'

'In a few minutes.'

When the door closed behind him, she took a little tour around the room. The bed had a canopy of dotted muslin tied back with blue silk bows, the dressing-table was stocked with paper tissues, hand lotion, a cloisonné brush-and-comb set, perfumes in crystal bottles; and in the built-in wardrobe there were hangers enough for the clothes of the entire Duggan family complete with see-through covers to keep the dust out. Compared with any bedroom in the Bayswater house, it was like a palace.

She showered, wrapped herself in the soft bath-robe she found hanging in the bathroom, and when she came back into the bedroom found a uniformed maid taking her clothes out of her suitcase.

'Which of these shall I lay out for you, ma'am?' she inquired pausing.

'I . . . er . . . I'll have the black trousers and the white sweater, please.'

'Sure thing. I'll take these to be cleaned, shall I?' She was holding up the slacks and shirt in which Corie had travelled.

'Er . . . yes . . thank you.' She discovered later that the minute she took anything off, it was whisked away to be washed or cleaned. She had never had service on this scale in her entire life.

In the sun room she found Helen, Mirabel and Eddie. They made a rather handsome family. Helen's keen face crowned with its rich brunette hair; Mirabel, whose childish features had fined down to something akin to beauty; Eddie with his athlete's body and alert air – the effect was of health and intelligence and energy.

The room lived up to its name: the morning sun was pouring in. Helen beckoned her over and, when she came, held up her cheek to be kissed. 'Sit down, dear, have some coffee. What do you eat at breakfast? Eggs and bacon? Those things – kippers?'

'No, no, thank you! Just toast and coffee.'

'Huh,' said Helen, studying her. 'You ought to eat more. You've lost weight since I last saw you.'

'She looks great,' Mirabel countered. 'How are you, Corie? I hear you've been in Australia.'

'Briefly.' She sat down, coffee and toast was brought for her, they caught up with each other's news. The news, for the Holsteads, was mostly about the election.

'It was the grandest fun,' Eddie said. 'You can have no idea – we dashed about like a racoon with a can on its tail.'

'I didn't dash about,' his mother corrected.

'No, you sat near the centre of the web, spinning away like a spider. You should have seen our house in New Palz, Corie. We had politicians going in and out like those little men in the weather boxes.'

'I think we should put up a plaque,' suggested Mirabel. ' "Plans for the election of J.F. Kennedy brewed here" . . .'

'You make it sound as if the Holstead family managed the whole thing single-handed,' Helen scolded. 'We just did what we could, like a thousand others.'

Corie was looking from one to the other with pleasure and surprise. 'I never thought of politics as being enjoyable,' she said. 'Back home it always seems very dull – not that I pay much attention.'

'It starts to get dull now,' Eddie said, with regret. 'Now the President has to plan his cabinet, and put laws before Congress, and fight to get them through . . .'

'What? Why should he have to fight? He won the election, his party must be in the majority?'

Helen smiled. 'In fact it is, but only just. But that's almost accidental. There's been many a President who didn't have a majority in Congress, so you see it can be very difficult, governing the country when you can't get an important bill through. And Jack's going to take his knocks now, I'm afraid. A lot of the Senate just doesn't want to try anything new.'

It was all beyond Corie. She asked instead about Drew.

'Well now, our boy's making good,' was Helen's reply, delivered with a satisfied tilt of her dark head. 'He's going to be a presidential aide, in the private office. At this very moment – ' she looked at her wrist – 'he's probably hanging on a telephone on Jack's behalf, contacting men all over the country. One drawback about being so big, Corie – time-zones mean you have to schedule calls at all hours of the day or night.'

Mirabel had gone out during the conversation but now came back looking somewhat troubled. 'What d'you think?' she said. 'I've just been watching TV and the weatherman says that snow is really going to fall.'

'Oh no!'

'He says it's coming from North Carolina and Virginia.'

'Oh, trust the southern states to foul up the works!' cried Eddie.

'Will it matter?' Corie asked, rather taken aback.

'Will it matter! The schedule for today is absolutely jam-packed. All we need is a traffic snarl-up. Oh, lord,' mourned Mrs Holstead, 'I hope it holds off . . .'

'Nope. It's expected by lunchtime, so Hopely had better take Snuffy out now for his walk.'

Snuffy, Corie remembered, was the brown Sealyham. She said, 'May I go with Hopely? I'd like some fresh air.'

'We'll take him,' Mirabel said. 'We'll go for a walk by the Washington Channel.'

'Have you got a good thick coat, Corie? If it comes on to snow . . .'

Corie couldn't quite take it seriously. She'd always thought of Washington as being 'in the south', so how could it suffer from bad winter weather? She was proved wrong quite soon, because as she and Mirabel came in at lunchtime after a long walk with a frisky terrier, the first snowflakes were drifting down from a sky the colour of pewter.

Mrs Holstead was out at some charity luncheon; Eddie was at his athletics club. Mirabel and Corie settled down to a cosy meal together, interrupted only by the appearance of Donna the social secretary with some typed papers in her hand.

'This is today's schedule, Miss Holstead,' she said, offering it to her. 'And I made an extra copy for Miss Duggan.'

With a straight face Corie thanked her and accepted the sheet. It was the first time she'd ever been in a household where a typed timetable was needed. But when she looked at it she could see the necessity.

'Twelve-thirty, Mrs Holstead attends Columbia Music Society Lunch. Two p.m., Mrs Holstead attends Smithsonian Reception. Three-thirty p.m., Mr Holstead acts as usher at Ladies' Campaign Celebration Tea Party. Three-thirty, Miss Holstead attends shower for Miss Adelaide Dumott. Four p.m., Mrs Holstead opens Inauguration Bazaar in aid of Veterans' Clinic . . .'

And so on, detailing the actions of the individual members of the family until: 'Eight p.m. Dinner. Nine p.m., Inauguration Gala Concert – entire family and guest attend. Midnight, Punch Party at Swannee's. One a.m., refreshments available at home. All family members are asked to be home and in bed by one-thirty in preparation for Inauguration Day. Schedule for Inauguration Day will be available at eight a.m. on the twentieth.

Attached was a list of visitors expected at the apartment during the afternoon and whom they would be expecting to see.

'Do you always have a routine typed out?' Corie asked in dismay.

'Not always. When we're at Gitchetak there isn't so much going on, but while we were helping with the election it was the only way we could keep track of where we were supposed to be at what time. However . . .' Mirabel tossed the paper on a table. 'Hey Donna, none of this is going to work.' She nodded at the window. A thick lace curtain of snow was already blotting off the view of the bare trees across the way.

Donna said, 'I only type it out, Miss Holstead, I'm not expected to make it work.'

That was just as well, for at about three-thirty Helen Holstead returned home somewhat dishevelled. Her limousine had stalled in a snow drift in Folger Square, a complicated series of taxis had brought her home, and she would have to miss her engagement at the Veterans' Clinic Bazaar. 'I take it you decided to cut out Addie's shower?' she said to her daughter.

'I rang and said I'd send her present,' Mirabel said. 'I'm fond of Addie, but not fond enough to want a St Bernard looking for me in the snow.'

On the evening news, pictures showed the havoc the snow had caused to Washington's traffic. The link-man remarked that the Inauguration Eve programme was likely to suffer.

The Gala Concert organised by Frank Sinatra started two hours late. That hardly mattered because the audience were even later. Skids and stalls and traffic jams made driving a nightmare. The President-elect and his wife were late but were greeted with tremendous applause, the more so as Mrs Kennedy looked absolutely radiant in a gown of silvery satin.

Corie stood with the rest of the audience watching them take their places. She had done a portrait study of this man. She remembered that she had been dissatisfied with it. Now, perhaps, she could have done a portrait that would please her own high standards. For what she'd been unable to convey in his photograph was revealed now: he had been destined to rule his country.

By midnight, when the Duggans should have been at a Punch Party at the Swannee Restaurant, the concert was still going on. To Corie it seemed interminable but then, show business held few charms for her these days.

'Should we leave for the party, Mother?' Eddie asked.

'I don't feel it's right to leave before the President, Eddie.'

'Well, we could switch. There's a thing at Paul Young's Restaurant for after the concert.'

'We'll see.'

The Gala Concert drew to an end at about one-thirty. The party at Paul Young's was being given by the President's father, an open-house affair for all who had helped elect John F. Kennedy; but after one glance at the road outside the theatre, Helen gave her chauffeur orders to go home.

'Enough is enough,' she said.

It was two in the morning when they got indoors from the white wilderness of Washington. They fell ravenously upon the food awaiting them in the dining-room. Hot coffee and chocolate took some of the chill out of their bones.

'I'm sorry, Corie,' her hostess said, patting her hand kindly. 'To my mind Washington isn't much fun at the best of times, but you've seen it at its worst tonight.'

Mirabel said goodnight and staggered off to bed. Eddie went to ring a girlfriend he should have met at the Gala Concert.

'And that reminds me,' Helen said, 'I ought perhaps to have tried to make it to Pa Kennedy's party – you'd have had a chance to talk to Drew there.'

'He'd have been there?' Corie said, sitting up.

'The President's there, you can bet on it. So it's likely Drew would have been. I'm sorry, Corie, I didn't think of it until Eddie said he was going to ring Joan.'

Perhaps through weariness, Corie failed to hide her disappointment. Helen studied her a moment with her shrewd eyes then said, 'It matters, does it?'

Corie shrugged.

'Hm . . . I did think something serious was in the wind when Drew allotted you one of the tickets for the Inauguration. They're like corn in Egypt . . . And you came winging across the Atlantic . . . Well, in that case, perhaps you won't mind if I say something to you, Corie.'

'And what's that?'

'If he means a lot to you, I'd make stronger efforts to hang on to Drew. There's a heck of a lot of ocean between the two of you, and there's a parcel of ambitious girls here in Washington only too eager to catch a man who's in the private office of the President.'

Wearily Corie rose to her feet to put her empty coffee cup on a table. 'What do you expect me to do about it, Helen? I can't make the Atlantic any narrower.'

'You could come and live here for a spell. You did it before . . .'

'Things are different now. My family's going through a bit of a crisis.'

'If it's money, I could—'

'No, no, nothing like that.' She was tempted to confide in Helen, but bit back the words. After all, what could Helen do? Nothing could alter the fact that Lynette had a malady which couldn't be cured and a heart in thrall to a worthless man. No one could help Lynette, not even a sister who had been her defender all her life.

Her hostess nodded in acceptance. She could tell that something was seriously wrong in the Duggan household. She herself had enough experience of family troubles to know outsiders were seldom of any use. Married to a man with whom she couldn't live in harmony but from whom she refused to part, she knew better than most that some problems just can't be solved.

She followed this train of thought. 'Do you see Ingram these days?' she asked.

'Never. We're not on friendly terms any more, I'm afraid.'

'Oh, you don't want to pay any attention if he gets in a miff with you. He's got the manners of a Kodiak bear.'

Corie said, 'It's just happened that other things have taken me away from London and the newspaper world.'

'If you wanted a grub-stake for a visit over here, I could maybe hint to him to commission something for you. He doesn't always listen to me, but on the other hand, if it suits him, he might.'

'I don't think so, Helen.'

'How about a few pix of Jackie Kennedy? She's going to be good value to the newspapers from now on. A couple of months spent following her around—'

'I can't, really, Helen. I can't spend too long away from home.'

'You know best, I suppose.' Helen sighed. 'Let's go to bed. Tomorrow's schedule will be catching up with us any minute now.'

By the time Corie had prepared for bed, it was three in the morning. Calculation told her that it would be eight o'clock at home, and her sister Pal would be sending Bart off to catch the commuter train. She wrapped her dressing-gown around her, picked up the phone on the little French bureau, and asked for a transatlantic call.

'Corie! Are you speaking from Washington? You sound as if you're in the next room!'

'It's the wee small hours of the morning here. In a few hours we'll be so busy I shan't have time to ring, so I thought I'd do it now.'

'Why are you awake so late?'

'We just got back from a Gala Concert. Everything is eight inches deep in snow. Pal, how are things?'

She heard her sister change the phone to her other hand and sensed her hesitation.

'Is anything wrong?'

'We-ell . . . When I dropped in yesterday afternoon there had been a bit of an upset. Monna arranged for Lynette to go to dancing class without telling her, and she refused to go. I know it sounds silly, but they got really heated about it.'

Oh lord, thought Corie. How could her mother be so obtuse? You can't make arrangements for a grown woman without her consent.

'How did it end?'

'It hasn't, really. Monna's saying that Lynette needs to get back into practice, Lynette's saying she'll go back to class when she feels like it, and the atmosphere at home is very sticky. I had to leave, I was meeting Bart to come home with him. Corie, I wish you were here—' She broke off. 'No, I don't mean that, the whole thing is silly, it'll sort itself out. You go ahead and enjoy yourself.'

'How about you? You OK?'

'Of course. I'm going to sign on for evening classes in upholstery so I can learn to make tailored covers. The term starts next week.' A pause. 'You'll be back by then?'

'Of course. I've got work waiting for me at the studio, you know.'

'So you have.' There was relief in Pal's tone. 'Have a lovely Inauguration, duckie.'

'We may have to go to the Capitol by dog sleigh!' They laughed and hung up.

Although it took her some time to get to sleep, in the end she dropped into its restoring depths. She was roused by the maidservant Aurelia, who came in at eight o'clock to draw back the curtains. She helped Corie sit up, piled pillows behind her, and brought a breakfast tray. Standing against the coffee pot was a typed sheet headed, 'Schedule for Inauguration Day'.

'Oh-oh,' groaned Corie, reading it. They had to be in their places at the Capitol an hour before the ceremony. That meant leaving the apartment at ten forty-five. Between then and now the Holsteads were to rise and dress and attend a communion service at St James's Church. Soon after one o'clock, the Inaugural Parade would begin. The Holsteads would watch with friends for an hour but could certainly not stay until its end. They must come home so that the hairdresser could style the hair of Miss Holstead and Mrs Holstead for the Inauguration Ball. Mr Holstead would provide transport for Mr and Mrs Richter as required. Refreshments would be served as necessary until the pre-ball dinner, which would be at eight o'clock precisely. And so on and so on.

For the first time Corie was rather sorry she'd let Helen take charge of the arrangements. It would have been much more fun to get out with her camera – because of course she'd brought one – and mingle with the ordinary

Washingtonians. It would also be nice to get free so as to visit Drew's parents, wherever they might be in this busy city.

But she was accepting the hospitality of the Holsteads so she must fall in with their plans. And in fact she received her reward, because at St James's she found Drew Richter waiting in the porch.

'Corie!' he cried, engulfing her in a hug and kissing her heartily. 'Where were you last night? I got to the Gala Concert just as it was ending but I couldn't find you.'

'Drew! Oh, I wondered when I was ever . . .'

The Holsteads tactfully withdrew to chat with friends. Drew said, 'I can't stay for the service, I'm here on an errand, but I knew the Holsteads would be here so I . . . Oh, it's great to see you, Corie! How long are you staying?'

'Only until Sunday.'

'What!'

'It's all I could manage, Drew. Things are a bit hair-raising at home . . .'

An elderly man came to his elbow. 'I can't find Hendrickson, Drew, I'm sorry. If I run across him, should I tell him you want to see him?'

'Would you? Ask him to call me. McCormack needs to speak to him about the order of business but we're having problems finding time-slots.' He turned away from Corie to scribble a telephone number on a pad. Church attenders were filing through the porch. Corie found herself separated from him by the press of people.

The Holsteads came to collect her. She was unwilling to move but luckily Drew elbowed his way back to her. 'Listen, this is impossible, honey, but I'll see you at the Capitol.' With a wave of farewell he was gone.

'You weren't exaggerating when you said he was run off his feet,' she said to Helen as they moved to their places in the church.

'A three-ring circus! And I don't think it's going to get any better.'

'Eddie said it was going to start getting dull,' she

reminded her, with a glance at Eddie.

'Dull, but not less busy,' he said with a grin.

When they came out of church the day had turned very fine and clear. Pure blue sky made a background for the spires and cupolas of Washington. On the lawns and pleasure grounds the snow lay like a white silk spread, unsullied, although sometimes whipped by a little breeze. It was very cold, yet somehow not harsh to the skin.

Workmen and machines had been out all night clearing the roads. Traffic was heavy but running normally. They were home in ten minutes. There was a dash for upstairs, to change into thick coats and footwear suitable for the conditions underfoot.

Luckily Corie had her knee-high boots and a good tweed-lined mackintosh. Mirabel insisted on lending her a fur hat. Thus equipped, she joined the family in the vestibule. Eddie surveyed his womenfolk. 'Not bad, considering it's about ten below zero,' he said. 'Anyone bringing a hip flask?'

'Behave yourself,' his mother said, and led the way to the lift.

There were already many eminent people in their places on the steps of the Capitol building. The dome, its galleries ornamented with a border of snow, soared up behind them into the blue. Somewhere a military band was playing a march by Sousa. Drew Richter smiled a greeting from the row in which they must sit, and stood while they filed into their allotted spaces.

Though it was very cold, there was something almost spring-like in the atmosphere. Every face was eager and hopeful. Corie looked around. 'I wish I could have brought my camera with me,' she whispered to Drew.

He grinned. 'That would hardly be etiquette . . .'

She studied the people around her. Here were faces worth recording – elderly men with the weight of the government upon their shoulders, young men like Drew, alight with ambition and hope, women whose influence as Washington hostesses had helped bring the new President to power . . .

By and by Corie could hear cheering some way off along Massachusetts Avenue. 'The President's car,' Drew murmured.

It came into view. Eisenhower and Kennedy emerged and walked up the steps. They were greeted by a man in a black robe. Senator John J. Sparkman began: 'We are here today to inaugurate the thirty-fifth President of this great Union . . .'

The thirty-fifth President, the youngest, the first Catholic . . . In that moment it came home to Corie for the first time that this was more than a mere ceremony, it was an historic moment, a moment that those present would never forget.

The new President took the centre of the stage to deliver his Inauguration Address. He was without an overcoat, hatless, his hair blowing a little in the vagrant breeze. His Boston accent rang out over the silent scene.

'My fellow Americans . . .'

To tell the truth Corie had expected to find the speeches dull. She couldn't have been more mistaken. Kennedy wanted to arouse in his listeners the pride in country that he felt had been fading. ' . . . The torch has been passed to a new generation of Americans . . . Let us begin anew . . . Ask not what your country can do for you – ask what you can do for your country . . .'

Afterwards she realised the speech had taken only a quarter of an hour. Yet it transformed the lives of half the nation.

Afterwards came the march-past of the American Armed Forces. According to the schedule, Helen Holstead was due to remain to watch for an hour or so, but there was a certain amount of movement among the crowds, people greeted people, paused to exchange opinions.

'What do you have to do now?' Corie asked Drew.

'I'm going to have lunch with my parents at the Waldemanns' apartment. You?'

'I think the Holstead ladies have appointments with a beauty consultant. Eddie is supposed to be looking after your father and mother, I gather?'

'Yeah, why don't you come with us? It's across town a ways, and it may not be too easy to get there on a day like this, but the Waldemanns have promised us *Wienerschnitzel* and beer – if that would suit you.'

'Sounds splendid.'

After some difficulty they extracted themselves from the parade watchers. Helen saw them go and waved a farewell.

At the Waldemanns', everyone was alight with pleasure. 'Close-up we saw him as he drove by!' cried Mrs Richter. 'And now on the radio I hear the record of his speech. Now at last, Andreas, you're working for someone I can feel enthusiasm about!'

The Waldemanns proved to be about the same age as the Richters, but childless. They had thrown their apartment open today for friends and relatives. Their living-room was crowded with people eating German food from paper plates. Both television and radio were switched on so that every scrap of news would be heard. Any hope of a quiet conversation with Drew was quickly dismissed.

But Corie enjoyed herself all the same. Discussion of the meaning of the President's call to action was brisk and sharp. 'Did you see the Russian ambassador's face at that bit about human rights?' 'President Eisenhower didn't find much to smile at either.' 'Who's he decided on for the Treasury?' 'Oh, he's tryng to persuade Lovett . . .'

Corie could see why Drew had thrown in his lot with the Kennedy faction. They were quick and alive, right at the heart of the machine that made America tick. Although she didn't know enough to take part in the conversation, she listened with eagerness until Eddie shepherded her to the foyer. 'I've got to take you home now. We'd better get going before the crowds from the parade gum up the works. You ready?'

'Whatever you say.'

Seeing them move to the door, Drew detached himself from an argument with a magazine journalist to see them off. 'I'm sorry it's such a muddle at the moment, Corie. But

I'll see you at the Inauguration Ball.'

'Perhaps I'll get a chance to talk to your mother and father there—'

'Oh, they won't be at the same one, Corie.'

'Come again?'

'There are at least five of them – Mother and Father are going to the one at the Hilton.'

'And we're going to the one at the Hay-Adams,' Eddie supplied.

'So,' Corie said, dismayed, 'I shan't see you?'

'You certainly will. I have to tag along with the President, and he'll visit every one of the balls before the night is out, you can take a bet on it!'

Where did they all get the energy from, Corie wondered? Perhaps they were simply high on triumph and enthusiasm.

A middle-aged lady, with wing-tipped spectacles and wearing a smock with the name Jocasta embroidered on the breast, was reigning over the Holstead ladies when they got to the apartment. She took a long look at Corie.

'Well, darling, if I'm to do anything with your hair, we've left it rather late . . .'

'No, indeed, I'm not one of your clients,' she replied in haste.

Helen appeared from the dining-room, her hair a work of art. She nodded acknowledgement to the newcomers. 'Anybody who can manage it should have a nap. Eddie, you checked with the Richters, right?'

'Sure did. They want to leave for the Hilton at eight-thirty . . .'

'But dinner's not till eight.'

'Mother, I spent the last two hours gorging on *Bierwurst und Sauerkraut*, I haven't any room for dinner.'

'I shall be glad when this is over,' his mother muttered.

The beautician packed up and left; quiet descended on the household. Weariness compounded with jet lag suddenly engulfed Corie. She fell on her bed fully clad, to sleep until the maid roused her to bathe and change for dinner.

'Flowers, ma'am.' She was holding out a transparent box.

Within was a single dark red orchid. The card said: 'Thanks for coming, Drew.'

The orchid looked just right on the shimmering grey satin of her dress. But with the orchid the smoky pearls around her throat looked too much. She took them off and dropped them on the dressing-table. It made her sad. Lynette had lent her them.

'Would you allow me, ma'am?' ventured Aurelia.

'Go ahead.'

The girl scooped up Corie's pale brown hair from the back of her neck, twisted it and pinned it in a loop on the top of her head, then coiled the pearls around the loop. 'How's that?'

'But that looks . . . Why, it's better than Miss Jocasta's work on Mrs Holstead.'

'Yeah,' said Aurelia with a grin, 'but don't tell the madam so.'

When she went downstairs the others were assembled. Any notion that she herself looked good was entirely banished. Compared with the splendour of the Holstead women her own appearance was only adequate. Helen was in crimson faille silk, Mirabel in flamingo shades of tulle. Both wore diamonds, Helen in a great necklace with matching drop earrings, Mirabel in a slender river of light around her throat.

'Thought you said you didn't have a ball gown?' Helen challenged, surveying her with approval.

'Neither I had. I rushed out to buy this on Monday.' On Monday! Only five days ago, through the dreary office-going streets of London. It seemed a whole lifetime away.

Eddie nodded a farewell, then went out to ferry the Richters to the Hilton. The womenfolk went in to dinner. Corie found herself amazingly hungry despite the *Wienerschnitzel* of lunchtime. 'It's the cold weather,' Helen remarked when Corie commented on it. 'And by the way, what are you doing about a wrap for this evening? Even in and out of a car, it's going to feel cold.'

'Well . . . er . . . I've the coat I wore this afternoon.'

'Now, honey, don't be offended if we lend you a wrap,' Helen said. 'The Hay-Adams is kind of a snooty place and there might be an eyebrow raised if you turn up in a raincoat.'

'Oh, it's awfully kind of you but—'

'Nonsense, the both of us have more clothes than we know what to do with, isn't that right, Mirrie?'

'And besides, this is only a fun fur, Corie,' Mirabel added.

The fun fur turned out to be a three-quarter-length jacket in a rough, upstanding pelt. 'What is it?' Corie marvelled as she tried it on in Mirabel's room.

'Wolf.'

'Wolf?' Corie burst out laughing. Somehow it all seemed to fit — bound for the ball to celebrate the coming to office of the new President, she was wearing a ball gown she would never normally have thought of buying, an orchid from a man who had invited her from across the ocean, and a coat of wolf-skin to cover it all, as in a fairy tale.

The Hay-Adams was, as Helen had remarked, 'a snooty place'. From its prime position on Lafayette Square, it looked over Lafayette Park to the White House, whose classical dome gleamed floodlit against the night sky. In the panelled lobby the cloakroom girl took Corie's wolf-fur wrap without any sign of thinking it inferior. There was a glimpse of a Tudor-style dining-room, more like an English aristocratic home than a hotel. The ballroom was resplendent with crystal chandeliers and gilt mirrors, something after the Louis Quinze style.

As the Holstead party entered, the band was playing 'Hi Lili Hi Lo' as a waltz, and a mass of people were twirling to its strains. They had hardly set foot in the room when each was claimed by a partner — Helen went off with a portly politician, Mirabel was seized by a young man with curly fair hair, and his friend, introduced as Beau, swung Corie away.

'Nice to meet you,' he remarked as they danced off. 'Did

you watch the Inaugural on TV?'

'Well, actually, I was there.'

'No! Got friends at court, huh?'

'I rather think I have,' Corie said with a mixture of amusement and gratitude.

Throughout the evening there wasn't a moment when both Mirabel and Corie didn't dance. Helen excused herself after a while on the grounds that, firstly she was getting too old for non-stop gyration, and secondly she needed a drink, but Corie could guess there would be political chat to take her attention.

Somewhere around eleven the band broke off the tune it was playing to replace it with 'The Star-Spangled Banner'. Everyone stopped dancing, the men stood with a hand across their hearts. The women craned to look. The President had arrived.

He came sweeping into the ballroom with undiminished energy. With him came his wife and a group of companions. Among them Corie was delighted to see Drew, looking very handsome in white tie and tails. He was gazing about among the dancers and failing to spot her. She stood on tiptoe, waved, and her partner said in surprise, 'You waving to the Boss?'

'Not quite,' she replied. 'One of the men with him is someone I know.'

'OK, let's go get him,' her partner said, and without more ado began to shove his way through the crowd.

Corie couldn't help contrasting his behaviour with what would have greeted the arrival of the Queen at a ball. Everyone would have stood respectfully still until perhaps luck brought them a view of royalty and a chance to curtsey. But here, this young man who'd been doing the bossa nova with her shouldered his way unselfconsciously to the presence.

'Corie!' Drew exclaimed as she was dragged up to him.

'You're the one, are you? You're a lucky man, she's a great dancer. My pleasure, ma'am,' he added, bowing himself away.

'You heard what the man said,' a voice remarked. 'Go and dance with her, Richter.'

'Yes, Mr President.'

Next moment his arm was around her and they were leading off to 'Peggy Sue'.

'Enjoying yourself?' Drew asked.

'Oh, I'm having a great time — and all the greater now you're here.'

He hugged her and swung her round. 'Shan't be staying long. This is only the second stop, there are at least three more to go. But — ' as Corie made a sound of protest — 'I'll be back. Wait for me.' He looked down at her. 'Will you?'

She didn't need to reply in words; she knew her smile gave him his answer.

Presently he had to leave her to dance with others. She couldn't help noticing, after what Helen had said in the early hours of the morning, that there were a number of very pretty girls greeting him by name and eager to take the floor with him. She was fox-trotting to 'Fly Me to the Moon' with Eddie, who had arrived from his duties elsewhere, when Drew disappeared once more in the President's wake.

Time went on, and she began to worry in case Helen might suggest going home. But Helen was having too good a time at a table with a group of Washington lobbyists to want to leave. All the same, it was well after one when Drew came back.

The band was playing a waltz medley intended as a tribute to all the states of the Union. It had reached 'Beautiful Ohio' when Drew took her in his arms again. For a time they circled the floor, lost in each other, enfolded in the moment and the lilt of the music.

'You're looking very beautiful tonight,' he murmured.

'Do you think so?' She never thought of herself as beautiful.

'And you're a great dancer,' he added with a smile.

The band was playing 'Carolina Moon' now. They had gone around the outer perimeter of the dance floor and were opposite the exit. 'Come on,' Drew whispered, and urged her through it.

He reclaimed their coats. Outdoors there was a sparkle of early morning frost, yet the street was not quiet. People in evening dress were walking, cars were drawing up to leave passengers. Drew caught a taxi after it decanted a fare.

'Where are we going?' she asked softly as they settled into it.

'Not far. My apartment.'

The street lamps glinted on the remains of the snow. The Capitol soared in its white beauty. She glimpsed bare trees, a statue or two, some government buildings, and then they were turning into a residential road where merry-makers were still spilling in and out of the houses, music was playing, street doors were standing wide open.

'*Chez Richter*,' said Drew, leading the way up a short stone stairway to an ivy-clad Colonial house. He opened a door off the ground-floor hallway. One lamp was burning in a large, sparsely furnished room. 'Sorry it's kind of bare,' he said. 'I just moved in a few weeks ago and there's only been time to buy the essentials.'

One day it would be a beautiful room, with its tall windows and moulded ceiling. Now all it contained was a sofa, two armchairs, a desk and a few rugs. Drew delved into a big cardboard carton. 'Like a drink?'

'What are you offering?'

He picked bottles out of the carton. 'Gin? Sherry? Asti Spumante?'

'Let's have some of that — what about glasses?'

'Now those I have. In the kitchen.' She followed his gesture, to find on a counter-top a box of assorted glasses.

There was something festive about the pop of the cork, the fizzing of the wine into the glasses. They sipped, Corie strolling about looking at piles of books while Drew turned up the heating. By and by they settled on the sofa.

'Lord, it's nice to see you again,' he said, leaning forward to kiss her lightly on the lips. 'I apologise for not being at the airport.'

'Don't apologise. It gave me the chance to fly in a private jet.'

'Ah yes, the Holsteads don't do things by half. You comfortable there?'

'Fine, they've been awfully kind to me. I don't know why they're taking so much trouble.'

'It's because you're my girl and I'm a guy who's now on the President's private staff.'

'Oh, you don't mean it! They're not like that . . .'

'Yes they are, and I don't think the less of them for it. Helen's family have always had influence and have known how to keep it and use it. And why are we talking about the Holsteads?'

'I don't know,' Corie said with a chuckle, 'why are we?'

'Because we're stupid, that's why. Or at least I am, because I've been looking forward to this moment for weeks and I certainly never planned to spend it talking about the Holsteads.'

'Oh, you had plans, did you? Could I hear what they were?'

'I could give you a demonstration.' He took her wine glass from her hand, set it on the floor nearby, then put both his arms about her to press her into the corner of the sofa. He kissed her on the mouth. He paused. 'That was how I intended to open the demonstration,' he said.

Her breath caught in her throat. 'I'm paying attention,' she whispered.

'Good. Because next I thought I might do this.' He bent his head to kiss the curve of her collarbone. 'And then this.' His lips travelled to her throat. She could feel them touch the spot where her pulse was beating.

She wound her arms about him to draw him down to her. A joyous warmth enfolded her. She returned his kiss with others of her own – on his mouth, on the line of his chin, then on his hair and the nape of his neck.

His mouth was seeking the depths between her breasts. She gloried in the sensual pleasure of that quest, felt her whole body relax beneath him.

Now his fingers were travelling up the back of her dress seeking the top of the fastener. She felt the tug as he began to draw it down. She thought, In a few moments we'll be lovers, it had to come, it's why I travelled so far to see him again . . .

The phone rang.

'Oh, God,' he groaned.

'Ignore it,' she said quickly, her lips against his cheek. 'It'll stop.'

The phone didn't stop. Its summons cut through the air, tearing them apart.

'Don't, Drew,' she begged as he began to straighten up.

'I have to,' he said. 'It might be the President's office. Almost nobody else has this number.'

He dragged himself to his feet, found the telephone on a stack of books. Corie sat up, pulled the shoulder of her dress into place, brushed back her hair.

'No,' Drew was saying into the receiver. 'No, he wasn't at St James's. I left messages but he didn't . . . No . . . He's probably in some twenty-four hour poker game . . . Yes. Yes, sir, I understand.'

She had only to look at his face as he replaced the handset to know that the moment of intimacy was past. 'What is it?'

'Hendrickson – I was looking for him this morning but never found him. The Press Secretary says the President wants him in his office tomorrow morning at eight o'clock.'

'But tomorrow's Saturday!'

Drew gave a grim little laugh. 'There aren't any Saturdays off in politics, Corie. I have to go out now and scour the town for Tibbald Hendrickson.'

'Now?'

'Yes, now. I'm sorry, darling, I just don't know . . .' The words dwindled into silence.

'I'll wait here for you, shall I?' she suggested, knowing as she said it that she was being a fool.

He shook his head. 'God knows when I'll be back, if at all – I may have to tidy up Hendrickson and take him in a cab to the White House.'

'I understand.'

'I'm sorry, I would give the world not to—'

'It's all right, really, I understand.' She went to pick up the wolf-fur coat from over a chair back. 'I'd better get a taxi and—'

'We'll get one, I'll drop you off at the Holsteads'.'

'No don't bother . . .'

'Come on, Corie, don't be angry with me. I've *got* to go.'

She put her arms around his neck, kissed him, and laid her head on his shoulder. 'I know,' she said in a tone of mourning, 'I know, dear.'

He set her down at the door of the apartment block at about two in the morning. The night porter let her in, the lift was on automatic and took her up to the second floor when she pressed the button. At the apartment door she hesitated, wondering how to get in without a key, but the door opened at her footfall. The maid Aurelia was there, still in her uniform.

'So there you are, Miss Duggan! You had a good time?' she said with a bright, gentle smile.

'You still up, Aurelia?'

'Jest waitin' for you, Miss Duggan. C'n I get you anything? Hot chocolate? A nightcap?'

'No, thanks, Aurelia. Goodnight.' All she wanted was to get away from everyone to the privacy of her room.

Once there she threw the fur coat on a chair, unzipped her dress and stepped out of it, unwound the pearls from her hair. Then she went to stand under the bathroom shower for ten minutes to let the drumming water ease the tension that gripped her body.

She leaned against the glass wall of the shower, head bent. She felt as if she were in a kind of limbo. Unsatisfied longing had her in its toils. She could still sense Drew's touch on her skin, still feel his kisses on her flesh.

She had wanted him as much as he had wanted her. It would have been the reaching of a goal, the meeting at the summit of the mountain they had climbed. Before now they had moved towards each other, and each time fate or

433

ill-fortune or simple bad timing had pulled them apart. But tonight had been bitterest of all.

Perhaps it was never meant to be. Perhaps she should give up this fool's dream. They lived too far apart, in worlds that were too different. Once there might have been a chance; but now he was one of the President's men, who must put his duties before everything else. What could she matter, when compared to the work he was called on to do now? A nobody, an English girl who didn't even understand American politics, who had family troubles of her own that would prevent her from paying attention to his needs.

When at last she came out of the bathroom in her robe, she automatically picked up her clothes to tidy the room. She took up the ball gown to put it on a hanger. Only then did she notice that the dark red orchid was gone from its shoulder.

It had been pulled off in the midst of their embraces. Now she remembered – she had trampled it underfoot as she left Drew's apartment.

She went to bed and cried herself to sleep.

Chapter Twenty-two

The rest of Corie's stay was just as frustrating. The Holsteads all arose late next day, lounged around until evening, and then took her to a theatre. Drew was supposed to join them but sent apologies. Sunday she spent with Drew's parents and went with them to the airport when it came time to leave: the Richters were flying to New York, Corie to London.

Drew arrived at La Guardia in time to kiss his mother goodbye before his parents boarded their plane. He and Corie had a drink together until her flight was called. He related his adventures while trying to track down the missing Hendrickson – he worked hard to make it amusing, she laughed in the right places, but neither of them was having any fun.

'I'll call you,' he said when it was time to part from her at the departure gate.

'I'll look forward to that,' she replied.

'No, I really mean it, Corie. I'll call you, and you'll call me—'

'What would be the point? You're never available.'

'But that's only while the President's taking over. Things will quieten down . . .'

'Do you think they will?'

That made him pause. 'No, perhaps not . . . But that doesn't mean we allow ourselves to drift out of touch, Corie.'

'I must go, Drew, that's the final call.'

'Wait, Corie, at least promise to write to me . . .'

She laughed. 'Yes, of course, I'll write – and perhaps you'll reply.'

'I will, darling – I mean it.'

'Goodbye, Drew. Thanks for inviting me to the Inauguration . . .'

He seized her and kissed her while she was still speaking, their mouths bruising against each other. 'I know you won't give up on me, Corie. You're not a quitter.'

His words echoed in her mind as she boarded her plane and was borne away to the problems that awaited her in London. No, she wasn't a quitter. But sometimes you had to acknowledge you were out of your class.

Matters at home had not improved. After she'd dropped her luggage at her flat, she took a taxi to Bayswater. She found her mother doing voice exercises in preparation for an evening concert and looking rather pleased with herself.

'Where's Lynette?' she asked in the first interval between sets of scales.

'At Muriel Burford's dance class.'

'But I understood from Pal—'

'Oh, you've spoken to Pal, have you? And I suppose she told you some nonsense about Lynette feeling disinclined? I never heard such nonsense! No daughter of mine is going to shirk lessons.'

'But Monna, Lynette's ill . . .'

'Dr Usborne told me that there was no reason why she shouldn't resume all her physical activities so long as her insulin level is correct. Now you made a big point, didn't you, about how she'd gone on performing and rehearsing and taking class—'

'But that was before she collapsed in Sydney.'

'The doctor says she'll soon be quite herself again physically. So don't you try to tell me she's got any reason to stay away from class. She's got to get into trim again.'

'Not if she doesn't feel like it . . .'

'Good heavens, Corie, how can you say such a thing! I never missed class in all the years I was on the stage. And look at me now – I loosen up my voice every day – I know very well Lynette needs to—'

'Monna, you mustn't keep expecting Lynette to live a life that's an exact replica of yours! She's had a lot of unhappiness in this past year.'

'Who hasn't?' her mother cried, leaping up from the piano stool in a flash of hooped gold earrings. 'How do you think I felt when my own daughter came back from abroad and told me she'd let her public down?' She pointed an accusing finger at her eldest daughter. 'But we have to surmount disappointments, Corie, that's what you've never really understood. Theatre people owe it to the world and to *themselves* to put their own troubles behind them. So I absolutely insisted that she go back to dance class because you know, once muscles get rusty—'

Corie, who hadn't taken off her outdoor coat yet, simply turned round and walked out. When she got to the dance school in the Charing Cross Road, she found the dancers coming out, pulling up coat collars against the sharp January wind.

Lynette wasn't among them.

It threw Corie into a panic. She ran in to ask Muriel Burford if her sister was still dressing.

'Lynette? She hasn't been here. Your mother rang a couple of days ago to say she was resuming class, but she's never showed up.'

'Oh, lord . . . Can I borrow your phone?'

She rang Pal in Surrey but Lynette wasn't there. 'What made you think she was?' Opal asked.

'According to Monna, she's supposed to be at class.'

'Oh, don't tell me she actually kept on about that? I thought I'd persuaded her to give it a rest.'

'No, Lynette's supposed to be at Muriel's, but she isn't. Where can she be, Pal?'

'Heaven knows . . .'

Next she tried Sasha's office, but Sasha had gone home. She rang him there. He answered expecting it to be someone else. 'I'm just getting ready, Betty—'

'Sasha, this is Corie. Have you seen Lynette?'

'What?' From the sheer surprise in his voice she could tell he hadn't given a thought to Lynette in weeks. 'No, I haven't seen her, no reason to. Look, excuse me, Corie, I'm late for an appointment, OK?' And he hung up.

Corie felt she couldn't monopolise the dance studio's telephone any longer. She thanked the teacher then walked along to her photographic studio in St James's, intending to telephone a few showbiz acquaintances. Bertie appeared from the darkroom when he heard her come in. 'Oh, so there you are! How was America?'

'Very cold and very high-powered. Everything here OK?'

'Absolutely. I've taken a couple of bookings for next week – is that all right?'

'Yes, I suppose so, Bertie.' She sighed. 'You haven't seen my sister Lynette, I suppose?'

'As a matter of fact I have,' Bertie said, astounding her. 'She's here.'

The relief was like a life-saving wave carrying her homeward. 'Oh, Bertie! Thank God! Where is she?'

'Having a little nap on that old overnight bed of yours. Really tired out, she seemed.'

Corie went to the tiny curtained area where the bed still stood, although these days she generally managed to get home to her flat for a night's sleep. Soundlessly drawing back the heavy velvet, she saw Lynette, in sweater and slacks, curled up on the blanket with one hand under the cheek, like a child. And childlike she looked – vulnerable, fragile, innocent.

With a sign to Bertie to keep his voice down, she turned to him. 'When did she turn up?'

'About six o'clock. She seemed to expect you to be here. I said you weren't due to start work again till tomorrow morning, said you'd more likely be at your flat, but she just seemed to want to hang about . . . Lost, like, you know? So I asked her if she'd like a cuppa, and then she looked a bit poorly so I said, would she like to lie down a bit, and next thing I knew, she was off to dreamland. So I just left her. Was that all right?'

'You did just right,' Corie said gratefully.

There was correspondence to look at. She occupied herself with this, and with some discussion over tomorrow's work, until in the end she heard a stirring from behind the velvet curtain. She put her head round. 'Hello, sleepyhead.'

'Corie!' Her sister sprang from the bed to throw her arms around her. 'Oh, Corie, thank heavens you're back!'

'Here, here . . . you'll strangle me . . . What's been happening?'

'Oh, Monna's been absolutely *impossible*! Always on at me: "Be a trouper, be professional . . ." I know I'm slacking, Corie, she doesn't have to tell me, but I don't *feel* like practising, and besides, what's the point? I'm not going on stage again.'

'But in June, Lynette . . . Vancouver . . .'

'I'm not going,' her sister said. 'What in the world do I know about Vancouver? And what does Vancouver care about me? It'd be like Sydney all over again . . . people who don't know me, can't see what I'm trying to do . . .'

'But you could work out a new—'

'No, Corie. I'm not going.'

'But Lynette, dearest, you're not just going to let your career totally slide—'

'Why not? You did, you just walked away from the theatre – why can't I?'

'But I was a failure, Lynette.'

'And so am I – in the biggest possible way!'

'No, darling, no, you mustn't say that.'

'It's true, and you know it. And so does Pal. The only person who doesn't seem to know it is Monna, and she just won't . . . Oh, Corie, you don't know what I've been through! "Pull yourself together, it's brightness not laziness that makes a star, your father and I had a practice session every day of our lives while we were performing" . . . She just can't seem to *understand* . . .'

Corie had her arm around her sister. She pulled her down to sit with her on the truckle bed. 'Be fair, Lynette, you haven't told her everything.'

'No, and I never will! Can you imagine what life would be like? "No child of mine ought ever to have been in that condition . . . I brought you up to know better than that" . . .' Lynette shook her blonde head violently. 'No, Corie, I've enough to bear as it is.'

'But sweetie, putting that to one side, what good does it do to agree to go to class and then play truant? What does that get you?'

'It gets me some peace and quiet, that's what!'

'But Monna's going to find out you don't go to dance class . . .'

'You're not going to tell her?'

'Well, I'm not going to lie!'

Lynette was clasping and unclasping her hands in dismay. 'Don't tell her, Corie, please don't, it'll only mean another lecture, and I'm so tired . . . so *tired* . . .' Her words fell away into sobs.

Corie put her arms around her little sister as she'd done a thousand times before in her life, and uttered soothing words. 'It's all right, don't worry, I'll sort it out, don't cry, Lynette . . .'

When at last Lynette dried her tears, she asked, 'How are you going to sort it out?' There was absolute trust in her manner. Corie would see to it. She always did.

'I think . . . Perhaps you'd better stay with me for a bit. How would you like that?'

'At your flat in Stamford Street?'

'Yes, if you'd like to.'

'Oh, it would be heaven! Not to have Monna waiting for me in the morning, asking me if I've done my tests, and then going on all day; have I taken my insulin, have I eaten the right calories, picking out a new set of songs for Vancouver, sorting out costumes to send to the cleaner, phoning and leaving messages for Sasha, and on and on . . .'

'All right, all right, you can stay with me until you feel better about it—'

'That's never going to happen! I hate living in that house with Monna! I hate it, I hate it!'

'No you don't dear, don't talk like that, you're just upset, that's all . . .' Soothing and comforting, patting her shoulder, brushing back her tangled hair from her brow. I don't think I'm the right person for this, she was saying to herself, it's gone beyond what I can deal with.

She took Lynette home to her flat. She switched on the heating, got together a scratch meal, sorted out some night things for Lynette. Then, at ten-thirty, she went to her mother's house to fetch Lynette's insulin. She packed a few clothes for her. Then she came downstairs to wait for Monna.

Mrs Duggan came home in a taxi about eleven, splendid in a dark green satin gown and a great deal of stage jewellery. She called as she entered: 'Lynette? I'm ho-ome!'

Corie went out into the hall in her coat, carrying the case with Lynette's belongings.

'What's this?' Monna said in surprise. 'Have you come to stay?'

'Quite the reverse. I've been waiting for you before I leave with some things for Lynette. She's staying with me for a few days.'

'I don't understand. Staying with you?'

'Yes, I think it would be better—'

'Just a moment. *You* think it would be better? What has it to do with you?'

'I went to find Lynette at Muriel Burford's studio. She's not been there since she got back from Sydney.'

'What?'

'She never went to class.'

'But we agreed — we talked about it and she saw it was wrong to be a slacker—'

'She never went,' Corie said, spacing the words out so that her mother could understand them. 'She agreed with you to prevent a lecture but she's never been to class.'

'That's a wicked lie! Lynette would never go against my advice.'

'I don't know where she's gone on other occasions, but tonight I found her at my studio in Bury Street. And she got so upset at the thought of coming back here that I thought it best to take her—'

'You have no right to interfere! That child needs a

mother's guidance to get back into harness.'

'She needs peace and quiet. I told you that before. It seems she can't get any here so she's going to stay with me.'

'I won't permit it!' cried her mother, throwing off the paisley shawl she used as an evening wrap and almost stamping on it in indignation. 'Lynette must get back to work or—'

'Monna!'

'I know what's best for her! I've come to terms with her ailment and I see that it means she has to work all the harder, to be *better* than anyone else — and with my experience to help her—'

'Monna!' This time her mother checked for more than a breath, and stood looking at Corie in anger and impatience.

'Monna, how old is Lynette?'

'What?'

'How old is she?'

'Twenty-six next birthday, of course.'

'Then stop treating her like a child. She doesn't want to go to dance class, she doesn't want to work up a fresh act for Vancouver, she doesn't want advice and encouragement about her career. She wants to be left alone. Do you understand? She wants to be given a chance to sort herself out.'

'But good heavens, Corie, you know as well as I do, the longer an artiste is away from her public, the harder it is for her to hold her place . . .'

'I can't stop here to discuss that now. I've got Lynette's insulin here and she must have it before she can get to bed. Goodnight, Monna.'

'Wait a minute! You stalked off earlier this evening in the most high-handed fashion, and now you're trying to do it again! I won't be treated like this!'

Corie met her gaze. 'What would you prefer, that we stand here and argue or that I go home with Lynette's kit so she can look after herself?'

'Oh, of course, put me in the wrong, that's typical!'

'Right,' Corie said, 'I'm being discourteous and you've told me so. Now can I go?'

'I really don't know how you came to be like this, I really don't! No daughter of mine ever learned such bad manners, not from me, not from my darling husband . . .'

'Monna, we were hardly ever with you and Clicks, how could we have learned anything from you? But that's not the point. Lynette's staying with me. She'll be in touch when she feels better. In the meantime please don't try to push her into things she's not ready for.'

'I hope you're not saying that I can't drop in on my own daughter.'

'I hope you won't. I think it would be better not.'

'Better not? Not to see Lynette when you're telling me she's under the weather? Who else should be there but—'

'I know, I know, you think you could do more for her than anyone else. In this case you're wrong. Is that clear, Monna?'

'You're telling me not to come to your flat?'

'That's right.'

For once in her life Mrs Duggan was left without words. She stood staring in utter disbelief at Corie. Taking advantage of the break in the argument, Corie made for the door.

'I shall ring Lynette,' declared Monna, heading for the telephone.

'Just as you please,' said Corie over her shoulder as she went out.

When she got home she found Lynette in front of the electric fire in her borrowed dressing-gown. 'Monna rang,' her sister said.

'What did she say?'

'She says she's coming round tomorrow morning to talk some sense into me.'

'And what did you say?'

'I said she could if she wanted to.'

'Lynette, the whole point of having you here is to—'

'It's all right,' Lynette said, 'I'll go to the studio with

you. You won't mind, will you?'

'Oh, Lynette, why don't you just tell her that you don't want—'

'I can't,' her sister said. 'I never can.'

She looked so wan and wearied that Corie hadn't the heart to continue the discussion. Moreover Corie's own head was beginning to reel with fatigue and jet lag. She made Lynette comfortable in the spare room then fell into bed.

Lynette spent the next day at the studio, trying to be helpful, reading magazines, dozing in a chair. In the evening their mother arrived at the flat to explain to them that this was no way to go on. 'One must remember one's obligation to the profession, Lynette.' But Lynette kept saying she would rather stay a while with Corie, and Corie kept saying she was welcome to stay as long as she wished. Short of dragging her off bodily, Monna was thwarted.

At least it meant Lynette needn't hang about at the studio. Corie often left her still in her dressing-gown, and wondered how she spent her time during the day. 'Oh, I went to a cinema . . . I watched the Horseguards . . . I had a walk round Harrods . . .' Aimless, pointless — it worried Corie.

To make matters even more complicated, she received a startling phone call one day at the studio. A voice she recognised at once asked her to hold the line and then said, 'I'm putting you through to Mr Holstead.'

And there he was, the same ringing, confident tones. 'Is that you, Corie Duggan?'

'Yes it is. And that's you, Ingram Holstead. What a surprise!'

'Just thought I'd ask if you enjoyed the Inauguration.'

She drew in a breath of surprise. 'How on earth did you know about that?'

'I'm a newspaperman,' he said with a chuckle. 'I had reporters there — remember Mabel?'

'Shall I ever forget her!'

'Oh, Mabel's all right. She's got too accustomed to living

on an expense account, that's her trouble. But she did a good piece for us about Jackie Kennedy.'

'I didn't see it, I'm afraid.'

'No need, when you actually saw her yourself . . .' He paused. 'I rang Helen, just out of curiosity. She said you'd been staying with her.'

'Yes.'

'She said I ought to use your talents.'

'Did she?'

'Look, Corie, I'm sorry for the way I behaved . . .'

'I accept your apology.'

'Oh, don't sound so delighted! Are you going to hold it against me for ever?'

'What a strange thing to say. I hardly give it a thought.'

'Oh.' That hit home. 'You make it awfully hard for me to carry out my wife's suggestion.'

'Look, Ingram, I have a client coming in about a quarter of an hour and I've got to set up—'

'It was about your photographs that I'm ringing you. Have you seen that the *Globe* is putting on an exhibition of its outstanding photographic work?'

'No, really? I get the technical journals, there's been no mention—'

'No, no, we only made up our minds a couple of weeks ago. Tell the truth,' he added in a confidential tone, 'another exhibition that we'd got booked for the main hall simply fell through. So the picture boys said they could put on something at short notice.'

'Good for them.'

'Some of your pix are among the exhibits, Corie.'

'Thank you. Please tell the photographic department—'

'Tell them yourself. The opening's in three days' time. I'd like you to be there.'

'Oh . . .'

'Six-thirty for drinks and little speeches, seven o'clock for the show to be open to the preview crowd – critics and magazine editors and such. It'd be a good chance for contacts, Corie. Why not come?'

'I might be busy.'

'Look in your diary.'

'Well . . . just a minute . . .' She did as she was bidden but all the time her mind was trying to invent an excuse should she find a blank space on Thursday evening. She didn't particularly want to be brought back into the orbit of that turbulent man. 'Thursday,' she murmured into the phone, to let him know she was looking.

'Don't bother to claim you've an appointment if it isn't true,' he said. 'Just say you don't want to come. But I think it's silly to let mistakes of the past cloud opportunities for the present.'

'Is that out of one of your leaders for the paper?' she inquired, smiling.

'As a matter of fact, yes. Last month, when the Queen went on a tour of India and Pakistan.'

All at once she felt a kinship with him. He might be selfish and ruthless, but he had a quick mind and an easy humour – when he was in a good mood.

'Come on, Corie, say you'll come.'

What harm could it do? A cocktail party to open an exhibition of pictures in the hall of a newspaper building. There would be scores of people present. And, as he'd just said, lots of them influential in the world where she made her living.

'All right,' she said. 'Thursday at six-thirty.'

'Well done. The triumph of common sense over resentment.'

'Is that from a leader too?'

'Well, you did feel resentful, didn't you?'

'Indignant is the word, Ingram.'

'Uh-huh. I'll admit you had cause.'

'What's got into you?' she inquired, laughing a little. 'All this humility – it's not like you at all.'

'I made a New Year resolution, make friends again with all the people I'd offended. It's going to take me until 1962, I think.'

'So long, Ingram.'

'Bye for now.'

When she'd put the phone down she wasn't sure if she'd done the right thing. He might say he had decided to turn over a new leaf, but he was so used to lying when it suited his purpose that there was no way of knowing whether to believe him.

Lynette was quite interested and pleased when she reported the conversation. 'You hardly ever go out,' she remarked. 'I think it's a good thing for you to be at a party like that.'

'Well, I shan't stay long, Lynette.'

'Now you mustn't feel you have to rush home. You'll make me feel guilty.'

'All right.' Corie was relieved. Lynette had been inclined to cling to her since she left her mother's house. Sometimes it seemed to Corie that her sister had exchanged one dependence for another. The last thing Corie wanted was to take charge of Lynette's life – on the contrary, she wanted her to understand that she herself must make her decisions.

Any step in that direction was to be welcomed. When they went to bed that night, Corie for the first time felt that some slight progress was being made. She was leaving Lynette alone in the evening for the first time since she came to stay.

But on the actual day, things were different. 'You're going straight from the studio?'

'I thought I would.'

'You won't be very late, will you?'

'No, no, I'll be home by about nine.'

'It's only I thought I'd get you a meal. At things like that they only give you awful little nibbles.'

'All right,' Corie said, 'we'll have supper about nine.'

Lynette's cooking was on a par with that of all the other members of the Duggan family – she was limited to dishes that they'd learned in touring digs or during the war. But if she wanted to prepare shepherd's pie or liver and bacon, so much the better.

All the same, Corie recognised it for what it was – an

unspoken claim on her, a reminder to hurry home.

She took her evening things to the studio. As she changed at six she reflected that the silk shirt was one she'd had for two years and the velvet trousers even longer. Now she regretted the money she'd thrown away on the ball gown – but then, she'd been expecting to dance all night in Drew Richter's arms.

That's over, she said to herself as she brushed back her pale brown hair. I might as well admit it to myself. Nothing's going to come of being in love with Drew. There's just too much against it.

Since she got back three weeks ago, there had been no phone calls. She'd written, as she'd promised, to say that she'd arrived home safely and to repeat her thanks for being allowed to witness the historic ceremony.

In reply she'd received an air letter full of Drew's hasty scribble: 'Wish you'd stayed longer. Things very hectic here. I've got an official title, Assistant Press Aide – means I've got to keep contacts going with people the Pres. might need as advisers on difficult issues.' And so on for the whole of one side of the page. On the reverse he told her about his parents in the same telegraphic language, signed off by saying he thought of her often and would try to ring within a few days.

But he didn't.

She'd tried to ring him instead. His secretary said he was in Iowa. She left a message, just to say she'd had his letter and sent good wishes for his career. The next few days she'd lingered near her telephone both at the studio and in the flat, but though it rang often it was never a transatlantic call.

Helen Holstead had the right of it. She ought to be on the scene in Washington. In earlier days she could have sorted out a few commissions, packed up and taken off. Not now. Now there was Lynette to think of. If she were to go abroad to live, Lynette would either have to go back to living with her mother or survive on her own – and it was still too early to know whether she could do that. Besides, Monna wouldn't give her a chance to try on her own. She would be at the flat the moment Corie's back was turned, lecturing Lynette and telling her she needed her mother.

Corie finished preparations for the evening. She looked at herself in the mirror. She saw a tall, slender girl with a narrow, rather tired face. 'What makes you think you could get Drew all to yourself even if you were there?' she asked her reflection. 'As Helen said, there's a parcel of ambitious girls in Washington who'd like to capture him – and a lot better-looking than you.'

The mirror image regarded her solemnly. She wanted it to say that Drew didn't care if she were only average when it came to looks. He loved her; or at least he was on the verge of loving her; or at least he had wanted her, physically, that night after the Inauguration Ball. Was it love, this attraction that had seemed for a while so important?

Whatever it was, it was dying – dying from lack of nourishment, like any other plant denied food and drink. The thought made her sad. She'd wanted to belong to Drew, to be one with him and perhaps to share his life for a time. But his career was pulling them further and further apart.

So what's new, she thought to herself. Thousands of women have had to stand back so as not to be a hindrance to the man they love. Yet somehow she'd thought – she'd hoped – that Drew loved her enough to put her before his career. No, that was absurd: why should he put her first? But she'd hoped he'd think of her in the midst of all his frantic activity, long enough to put through a call.

Well, it wasn't going to happen.

'You know your trouble,' she said to the girl in the mirror. 'You just aren't any good when it comes to choosing who you'll fall in love with.'

First Sasha – the worst choice she could possibly have made. Then Drew – whom she respected and liked besides finding physically attractive.

But had she chosen to be in love with either? Sasha had

attracted her as a magnet attracts steel, as if by some supernatural power. She'd known all along he was wrong for her. She'd simply been powerless until by exerting all her strength she'd dragged herself free.

For Drew there had been friendship, partnership. She'd never expected it to grow into physical desire. It had happened imperceptibly.

'The more fool you!' she told the mirror, and went out.

The hall of *Globe* Newspapers Limited had been cleared of all non-essentials except the receptionist's desk and the porter's lodge. Handsome screens had been placed in good viewing positions and carefully lit by indirect spots. When Corie had given her name to the girl at the desk and been checked in, she was given a printed catalogue – very well produced at short notice, but then the firm behind the exhibition had printing presses always at the ready.

There were already about thirty people in the hall. She could hear Ingram's tones although he was hidden from view somewhere in the interior. ' . . . News cameramen who in a way are the heroes of modern times,' he was saying. 'Sent into danger for the purpose of playing no part except observer . . . Oh yes, of course, some of the pictures were taken in a studio . . . No danger in a studio, how right you are, Your Grace . . .' Laughter at the quip from the nobleman, then the crowd parted to reveal Ingram with the Duke of Blythe at his elbow.

His gaze lighted on Corie. He smiled a welcome, gave her a wink, then continued to escort his guest around the display. A voice in her ear said, 'Howdy, pardner.' She turned to find Norman Gibson at her elbow.

'Norman!'

They hugged and kissed. 'You're in the good books again, I see,' he remarked as he picked two glasses from the tray of a passing waiter.

'He just rang me out of the blue. I was very surprised.'

'Ye-es,' Norman agreed. He looked just the same as ever, his suit rumpled, his shirt in need of a good press, his tie askew. 'Tell you something, Corie my lass. He really took it hard when you disappeared from his ken.'

'From his ken,' Corie repeated, laughing. 'Have you been drinking?'

'One or two, or three, or four,' he acknowledged. 'But I'm sober enough to know what I'm saying. Mabel told me. When she pointed out that you were sitting among the nobs in the tier of seats behind the President, she says he leapt out of his chair and walked about the office like a wildcat.'

'He's not the least bit like a wildcat. He's like a bear.'

'All right, he walked about like a bear. Then he asked Mabel what paper had sent you, and she said she didn't think you were there for a paper because you were sitting with the President's friends, and then he looked at the photo again and saw his missus alongside you.'

'Did that start him walking about again?' Corie inquired, refusing to take it seriously.

'Mabel says he was puzzled to the soles of his shoes. Simply didn't understand how you and Helen could have got so palsy-walsy that she'd invite you there. But he put through a call and it seems it was true enough – you'd been staying with her. Is that right?'

She nodded, taking a sip of the excellent red wine.

'It's got him really intrigued. He thinks a lot of Helen, you know—'

'So he ought, since it's her money he keeps pouring into the business.'

'That's true, but even apart from that, he knows Helen's shrewd. She made him take up a pro-Kennedy line on the paper, said Kennedy was the Man of the Future – and she was right, as it turned out.'

'Well, Norm, I don't know if that helps me to work out why I was invited tonight.'

'Some of your pix are in the show – didn't he tell you?'

'Oh yes, but—'

'But you don't think that's really the reason? Well, you could be right, young Corie. Oh, here he comes, monarch of all he surveys.' Norman produced a smile and a slight bow. 'Evening, boss. Quite a slap-up do.'

'Considering how well you write, it's strange how badly you talk,' Ingram said. He held out a hand to Corie. 'Welcome back, Corie Duggan.'

'Thank you. Nice to be here.'

'Come and let me show you your pix. They've got a good spot on the stands.'

Corie kept hold of Norman Gibson so that he came too. The pictures by Corie Duggan did indeed make a good show. There was the famous portrait of the *Globe*'s proprietor, the one which had been captioned, 'Can't get good help anywhere these days', and had been used as the basis for many a cartoon since then. There were the sombre but beautiful pictures from the military hospital in Tokyo, the much more readily appealing shots from Monaco.

She studied them. They weren't bad. She could do better now. She knew more, had had more experience, had more confidence in herself. But they weren't bad, even when compared with some of the superb work by the *Globe*'s newscameramen. Theirs had drama, immediacy. Hers had some special depths, as if she'd reached out in friendship to the people in the pictures and found something extra to show.

'Hidden beauty, that was what you said you were after, wasn't it?' Ingram recalled.

'Something like that.'

'Got a bit of that yourself – hasn't she, Norm?'

'Looks a treat, if that's what you mean.'

She smiled to hide her embarrassment. She knew full well she was no beauty.

'Let me introduce you to a few people,' Ingram said. 'Hi, Tom, over here!' He towed her along behind him to meet a burly man in a dinner jacket. 'Corie, this is Tom Vanderschorn of *Virtuoso*, the music magazine. Tom, meet Corie Duggan. Oh, and this is Mary Crowhurst, she edits *Europe Day* . . .'

There wasn't any doubt that from the point of view of making contacts, it was a success. The editor of *Virtuoso* told her that he was planning a photo-feature on some of the world's great opera singers — would she be interested in doing some of the work? Of course she would. He said he would ring her and actually seemed to mean it.

The time flew by. When Ingram sought her again, she glanced at her watch to find it was well after eight-thirty.

'Well, the next item on the agenda is dinner,' Ingram said. 'I've a table for twelve at the Savoy—'

'I was just thinking I must go,' Corie said.

'Go? Why on earth must you go?'

'Because it's almost nine o'clock—'

'And you've a handsome young man waiting for you,' he said rather petulantly.

'As a matter of fact, it's my sister.'

'Your sister.' He looked at a loss for a moment. 'Oh yes . . . Do you mean that one . . . ? Lily Lee . . . ?'

'Lynette Lee.'

'Of course, that's right. Whatever happened to her? I don't seem to have seen her around for a long time.'

'She hasn't been too well. That's why I've got to get home.'

'Not well? Nothing serious, I hope?' It was mere politeness. He couldn't have cared less what was the matter with Lynette.

'As a matter of fact, yes, it is rather serious and I don't want her upset because I'm late back. Thank you for a lovely evening, Ingram, I've met some awfully interesting people—'

'Hang on, can't you just ring your sister and say—'

'No, she's expecting me.'

'But I was counting on your coming with us to the Savoy.'

'I really can't, Ingram. Thank you for the thought, but I must get back.'

'No, wait — don't rush off like Cinderella on the stroke of twelve.'

'I must go, I'm afraid. Lynette's waiting for me . . .'

'It can't be vital. She knows you're likely to go on

somewhere after a cocktail party, surely?'

'She gets edgy,' Corie said. 'Really, I must go. Thank you for inviting me, I've had a great time.'

'Dammit, Corie, I've scarcely had the chance to say two words to you—'

'I'm sorry,' she said, although she couldn't help wondering what words he had wanted to say. 'I must fly!'

She hurried off, but to her surprise he followed her out through the big double doors into the lamplit chill of Fleet Street. He hailed a cruising taxi for her, opened its door. 'I'd really like to talk to you some time,' he urged, his square body leaning down so that he could look in on her. 'There are one or two ideas floating around . . . You might like to take them on . . .'

'Thank you, Ingram, it's very good of you. Driver, Stamford Street, please.' With a wave he stood back to let her go. She looked back at him. He was visible under the street lamp, staring after her in puzzlement.

Lynette opened the door for her before she even got out her key. 'You said you'd be back by nine,' she reproached her.

'It isn't much after, is it?'

'It's nearly half past! I wondered where on earth you'd got to.'

'Lynette, I couldn't just walk out without saying goodbyes—'

'Well, anyhow, here you are now,' Lynette put in quickly, to forestall the irritation she'd sensed in her sister's response. 'Everything's ready.'

As they sat down to the meal, Corie couldn't help contrasting it with what she might have been served at the Savoy. Lynette had bought some cooked meat and made a big salad — that was more or less the extent of her catering abilities while she had to take into account her limitations as a diabetic. Corie tried to enliven the moment by talking about the people she'd met, but she could see her sister's attention drifting away.

Where did she go, in these moments of abstraction? She

seemed to be looking inward, but at what?

'So what did you do today?' Corie asked, to jog her into taking notice of the present.

'I went to the cinema.'

'Again?' It was out before Corie could prevent it. She hadn't meant to sound disapproving but all the same — today was Thursday and as far as she could make out, her sister had been to the cinema four times this week.

'I like the cinema,' Lynette said, looking down at her food to avoid Corie's gaze.

'What film did you see, love?'

'Er . . . It was an Italian film.'

'*La Dolce Vita?*'

'I think it was that.'

'Don't you remember, darling?'

'I wasn't paying much attention. It was all in Italian.'

'Yes, of course, but you must have known it would be.'

'I suppose so. I didn't bother about that.'

'Lynette, if it doesn't matter whether it's in English or a foreign language, why do you go at all?' Corie asked, utterly bewildered.

Her sister hesitated. 'It's dark in the cinema,' she ventured, uncertainty in her tone. 'Nobody can see me.'

'Lynette!'

'And the time goes by. When you come out, it's two hours later, three hours later . . . And nothing bad has happened.'

Corie was shaken by the words, by the tone. She's really ill, she thought. She's frightened and lost, and I don't know how to help her.

The truth was, Lynette was heading straight for a nervous breakdown.

Chapter Twenty-three

Next morning, from the studio, Corie rang William Tranton. She'd promised to keep him up to date with news of Lynette but, more important to her at that moment, she needed to talk to someone. To someone outside the family but who loved Lynette.

His assistant said he hadn't yet come in, but that she would tell him the moment he arrived. 'He has to come up from Brighton, you know,' she explained by way of apology.

Around half past ten, he rang back.

'Is something wrong, Corie?' he asked at once.

'I think so. Perhaps not urgently, but I'm . . . well, I'm sort of at a loss.'

'Tell me about it.'

'Lynette's staying with me these days. Last night, I went out to a little party. I was home soon, about nine-thirty, but I was later than I promised. Lynette seemed upset about that but put it aside. I don't really think it had anything to do with the fact that I'd gone out for the evening. But then . . . but then . . . while we were having a meal . . .' To Corie's own surprise, her voice broke.

'What? What, Corie?'

'Just a moment. I'm sorry. I just feel . . . Hold on, William.' She found a handkerchief, blew her nose, swallowed once or twice, then picked up the phone to tell him about Lynette and the cinema.

'Oh, help,' he said.

'It really shook me, William.'

'She's hiding.'

'But from what?'

'Has something bad happened?'

457

'Well . . . There's something you don't know. I can't discuss it on the phone.'

There was a long pause. 'We could meet? I've one or two things to see to, but I could be free about noon.'

Corie would have to do some rearranging of her own schedule, but she felt she had to see William. 'Where are we meeting?'

'You know that pub in Cavendish Square?'

'On the corner? Yes . . .'

'There's a quiet booth at the back . . .'

'I'll be there.'

He was before her, sitting with an untouched tankard in front of him. Corie asked for a Negroni on her way to join him, and it was brought at once. But, like William, she disregarded her drink.

'Lynette made me promise not to tell but I had to let my mother know when we came home from Sydney. Lynette thought we ought to say that she'd caught some bug but I . . . Well, I thought it was time to tell Monna otherwise she would have made life impossible for her.'

'What's the secret?'

'My little sister is a diabetic.'

'Corie!' He looked stricken. 'Since when?'

She told him about it. He listened in silence.

'After Monna had thought about it she decided nobody outside the family needed to know.'

'Sasha doesn't know?'

'No.'

'How did your mother take it?'

'At first it was a terrible tragedy, the death of all her hopes. Then she saw Lynette's specialist and was persuaded she could live a normal life. So she took that completely to heart and began nagging at her to go back to class and get into trim "for her public".' Unconsciously Corie mimicked her mother's voice as she said the words, and despite himself William smiled.

'I can just imagine it,' he said.

'It got so bad that I asked Lynette to stay with me for a

bit. I thought it was the right thing to do but now I wonder . . . There's been talk of an engagement in Vancouver in June, but Lynette just isn't going to go. I didn't think too much about that — after all, she's kept her nose to the grindstone for years, she's got a right to say no if she wants to. But you see . . . It's not just that she's saying no to a tour abroad, she seems to be saying no to life itself.'

He took off his glasses and began to polish them on the handkerchief from his breast pocket. 'She wants time to go by and leave her untouched. She hides herself in a cinema—'

'In the dark — when it's still light outside.'

He tucked away his handkerchief. 'What does it mean?'

'I don't know.'

'What does her doctor say?'

Corie shrugged. 'He looks after her diabetic condition. I don't suppose he has any notion what's going on inside her head.'

'Could you persuade her to . . . to see a psychiatrist?'

'I don't think so. Everything scares her. She wouldn't talk to a stranger.'

'Would she talk to me?' he wondered. Then added at once, 'Not that I have any idea what to do. It's just that . . . I don't know . . . I'm someone she knows, someone from outside her family—'

'That's important,' Corie said at once. 'I want to help her but I'm too close. And in a way she knows how to manipulate me.'

'Corie!'

'I don't mean that unkindly, but she's always had me to turn to, ever since she was a kid and we were all evacuated during the war. I think she knows instinctively how to make me weaken. I *know* she ought to be facing up to things, making decisions for herself, but of course when she looks scared and unhappy I . . . well, I take over . . . Oh, lord, I think I'm as bad as Monna in my own way!'

'Don't say that. You've been marvellous.'

She shook her head. 'I may have been bad for her. But if

you would just try to help her, William . . .'

'I'll tell you what. Are you free on Sunday?'

'I can be.'

'Bring her down to Brighton for the day. I'll give you lunch at my flat, take you for a drive on the Downs or something . . . I know a February day doesn't sound like an ideal time, but at least it gets her out and about, and you never know . . . She might talk to me a bit.'

To Corie it was like a lifeline. Only when she was on her way back to Bury Street did she realise how helpless she'd felt about Lynette. William was certainly no expert, but he loved Lynette, of that she was sure. He would do all he could. And at least Corie was no longer completely alone in her efforts to care for her sister.

During the afternoon she remembered to ring and thank Ingram Holstead for the previous evening. She meant merely to leave a message with Miss Bryant, but the secretary put her straight through.

'Corie!' cried Ingram. 'Nice to hear from you! Did you get home all right?'

'Yes, thank you, and I just wanted—'

'Your sister OK?'

'Yes, thanks. I'm just ringing to thank you—'

'Quite all right, quite all right.' She could picture his square hand, waving that aside. 'You missed a lovely party at the Savoy.'

'Too bad. But I really did have to get home. My sister had a meal ready.' She recalled the cooked ham and salad and couldn't help smiling.

He caught the smile in her voice. 'Rotten, was it? Tell you what, let me give you a better meal to make up for what you missed at the Savoy. How about lunch one day?'

'Oh, thank you, Ingram, but as a matter of fact I've got a lot of work . . .'

'You have to eat, don't you?'

'Well, yes, but—'

'One day next week. Let me see.' She heard him calling for Miss Bryant. There was a break during which Corie was saying, 'No really, I couldn't make it,' and Miss Bryant was murmuring 'Not Tuesday . . . Wednesday you've got the French group . . .'

'How about a week today?' Ingram said at last, totally disregarding her protests.

'I've got clients until two.'

'All right, two-fifteen at the Ritz.'

'Ingram, I—'

'Come on, it's handy to that studio of yours, just round the corner.'

'All right,' she said, suddenly giving in to laughter. It was like trying to have a battle with a tidal wave.

On Sunday Lynette allowed herself to be taken to Brighton for the day. After a first stare of surprise at Corie's announcement of a day out, she accepted it almost without comment. The day was very cold and bright, a sky of eggshell blue with a pale sun reigning. Lynette looked fragile as a flower, wrapped in the fur-trimmed coat and hat she'd worn to Opal's wedding. Corie, as ever, was in slacks and a duffle coat.

William met them at the station. His flat proved to be one floor of a very elegant house in a Georgian square tucked behind the buildings of the promenade. Lunch was a bubbling hot bouillabaisse which, he said, had been made for him by a neighbour, a cookery writer. There was wine and French bread to go with it.

Lynette smiled prettily as she accepted her helping. But the others noticed that though she ate, she didn't seem to take any enjoyment in it. 'Don't you like it?' William asked with concern. She only shrugged and dutifully took another mouthful.

The pudding was a kind of glorified fruit pancake. Corie mentally gave William full marks. He'd consulted someone on what to offer to a diabetic that was festive without being harmful. She just wished that Lynette would relish it more.

After lunch they went for a stroll, to shake down the meal as William said. They skiffed flat stones along the surface of the sea. At least, Corie and William played this childish game. Lynette looked on, smiling but fundamentally uninterested.

Later they went for a drive. They had tea in a pretty little shop in a village. They were delivered to the station by six o'clock.

'Thank you for a lovely day,' Corie said. 'We enjoyed it. Didn't we Lynette?'

'Oh yes,' said Lynette.

'Come back on a weekday. It's great fun in the Lanes.'

'That would be lovely.' Corie looked at Lynette, hoping to hear her say, 'Yes, let's do that.'

'We could go to the cinema,' her sister said.

The next day, William rang Corie at the studio. 'I think it's serious, Corie,' he said.

'So do I.'

'It chilled me right through when she said we could go to the cinema.'

'Yes.'

'What ought we to do?'

'I don't know, love. I wish I did.'

'She needs proper help.'

'But I think I read somewhere that the patient has to ask for help − it's no good forcing it on her.'

He sighed. 'No,' he agreed, 'but will she ask?'

'Perhaps we can put it into her head.'

'Yes . . . Well, we can at least try.'

Nevertheless, there was a ray of hope. Lynette mentioned the day in Brighton once or twice, and although she gave no tremendous sign of approval, it seemed she'd liked it. When Corie proposed they should go again in the following week, she agreed with some faint show of interest.

Before that came Corie's lunch with Ingram. She wasn't quite sure why she'd let herself be talked into it. For fear that the Ritz was a hotel which wouldn't allow women in trousers within its hallowed walls, she was wearing a skirt today − eight years old and rather longer than the present fashion, but then, she'd never been one to care much about fashion. With a black silk shirt and a red scarf tucked in, she'd done what she could to make a good effect. For topcoat she had the faithful raincoat she'd taken with her to Washington. As she slipped into it, she remembered how Mirrie had lent her a wolf-fur jacket to replace it, and recalled the events of that night.

But it was no good looking back at what had happened in Washington.

Ingram was already at the table when she arrived. He rose to meet her and, to her surprise, took both her hands and kissed her on the cheek. She couldn't help but stiffen under his touch. He chose to disregard it. He stood smiling until the waiter had settled her at the table, spread a napkin on her lap, and handed her a menu.

'Lord, Corie, I've missed you,' he said.

She raised an eyebrow. 'And what about the women you've been linked with since you and I had our little argument?'

'Aha! You've been keeping track!'

'I could hardly help it. You keep appearing in the gossip columns.'

'Well, you'll be pleased to hear that none of them were as nice to be with as you, Corie.'

This was embarrassing. Luckily the waiter was hovering. He gave off no sense of urgency but by his very presence was reminding them that it was well past two o'clock and if they hoped to get the chef to prepare what they wanted, they'd better order it soon.

Ingram took it for granted he would order for them both. He then said he'd like the wine list. While waiting for that he said, 'You said something about a man who was important to you, in America. What happened? I mean, you're here and not in America, and not married or anything.'

She gazed out at the view of Green Park. 'Nothing came out of that,' she said.

The wine waiter arrived, taking Ingram's attention. He mused over Lafite-Rothschild and Château-Latour. That settled, he dismissed the waiter and said in a hearty tone, 'Well, let's get down to business, shall we?'

'I beg your pardon?'

'Did Vanderschorn get in touch?'

'As a matter of fact, yes. He's got a list of a dozen or fifteen singers he wants to—'

'Good Lord, fifteen?'

'Oh, I'm not photographing them all, just those that come to England. Two are going to appear at Covent Garden, then there's one singing in the *Messiah* in Manchester at Easter, and so on.'

'Sounds good. One thing about Vanderschorn – I hear he's a bit mean.'

'I've already found that out. He doesn't seem to want to pay my expenses if I go to Manchester or Edinburgh. But we'll work something out.'

'*Europe Day* rang me from the Hague to get your number. Mary Crowhurst had lost the card you gave her.'

'I haven't heard from them.'

'They'll get around to it. Now, what I was going to suggest for the *Globe* is this. You know all this hoo-ha about computers?'

She shook her head.

'You don't? Well, there's a lot of fuss about how they're going to take over all the donkey-work of keeping records and doing accounts and so forth – all nonsense, if you ask me, but there are two or three young men in Britain who seem to be important. They've taken part in the work on the Atlas computer, the one that's going into Harwell for atomic research.'

He paused. Corie was waiting attentively, although she was still at a loss.

'I want you to take pix of these three chaps at work – you know the kind of thing. We're going to do a two-parter, mechanical brains, stuff like that, and since our readers won't be able to understand one word in ten about the technology I want some really good pix of these lads to humanise the thing. See what I mean?'

'When is this for?'

'We're running it at the end of March. Here are the names and addresses and phone numbers. I've told them you'll be in touch.'

She saw that he'd taken it for granted she'd be accepting the commission. She was wondering whether to take issue with him about it when their first course arrived. Ingram went off at a tangent almost at once.

'I've often been on the verge of writing you a long letter of apology about the way I behaved,' he said with a shamefaced expression.

'But you restrained yourself,' Corie said, smiling.

'Well, I'm no good at eating humble pie. You know, I've taken it for granted for years that people would do as I told them. Couldn't understand it when you told me to get lost. It was only afterwards that I realised how much your *friendship* meant to me – and I'd thrown it away just because I wanted to get you into bed.'

'That's all in the past, Ingram.'

The wine arrived. Ingram watched as a little was poured, tasted it, pronounced it fit to drink, and waved the waiter away. 'Can't stand folk dithering round me,' he told Corie. 'Especially when I'm trying to say something important.'

'I don't think we need to talk about what's gone by,' she said with a little shrug of embarrassment. 'In any case I thought you said we were getting down to business.'

'Ha, we just did, didn't we? Let's say you send in a folio of pix on these three guys. You've got the details of how to get in touch with them. The contract will be at your studio by tomorrow's post – the fee is the usual standard fee plus fifteen per cent for your standing as a portraitist. OK?'

'Sounds all right.'

'I can ring Helen, then, and tell her you're working for the *Globe*.'

'Is that what this is about? Your wife's been giving you instructions?'

'Well, she did, but if I didn't like 'em I'd pay no attention.' He waited while the plates were removed and the *boeuf aux truffes et aux champignons* was served. Then he said, 'Helen's got a lot of sense. I know people think we're at daggers drawn because we live on opposite sides of the Atlantic, but I put a lot of store by what she says. When she was telling me about your visit last month and how she'd got fond of you, I thought to myself: She's right, as usual, and I was a fool to spoil things with Corie. So that's how it is. I've already told you I regret the past. So here's to a future of friendship.'

He picked up his glass of Bordeaux, held it up in toast. Corie did the same. 'To friendship,' she said.

When she was back once more in her studio she was pleased and relieved at the outcome. She made the telephone calls to arrange the photographic sessions with the computer scientists. One was in Lancaster, one was at Imperial College in London, one was about to take a post in Aberdeen. It looked as if there would be a lot of travelling in the near future. That was all right, she never minded travelling.

But of course there was Lynette to think of.

'Don't worry about Lynette,' Opal said when she mentioned the problem. 'I'll have her to stay any time you have to be away from home.'

'It might be quite often, Pal. I've got to go to Cambridge, and Manchester, and Scotland . . .'

'Stop worrying, it's no bother, duckie.'

'What will Bart say?'

'He doesn't mind Lynette – it's Monna who gets him down.'

Monna had been rather quiet ever since Lynette moved out. Now and again she would ring to ask if everything was all right. Twice she'd come to a meal. She made reproachful murmurs about how lonely it was at home in an empty house, which made both Lynette and Corie uncomfortable. But at least she didn't begin on a lecture about getting back to work.

William Tranton also promised to be around when Corie had to go travelling. 'Of course I can't offer to have her staying with me,' he said with a grin. 'Pal can do that, I can't. But I can certainly take her out to a meal or something like that, just to help things along.'

'You're a darling,' Corie told him. And added internally: I only wish Lynette understood how much he cares about her.

William was as good as his word. Now and again Corie went out in the evenings, because Ingram had included her once more in the group he invited to gatherings and events. On these occasions she was secure in the knowledge that William was with her sister − perhaps taking her out to dine or sitting with her to watch television.

He began to seem like an extra member of the family. Corie couldn't help being glad of it but on William's account she wondered if it was a good idea. She knew he didn't want to be a brother to Lynette: he had a quite different ambition. Yet for the present he was content to lay it aside.

Corie found she was glad of the opportunities to get out and about. For the last year or two, she'd been much too close to her family, had let its emergencies and dramas control her life. Because of her family she'd given up her friendship with Drew. But perhaps one day Lynette would feel whole again, and able to manage by herself. Perhaps *then* Corie could live her life for herself . . .

Until that day she was glad of the limited freedom that came to her through William's kindness and the work that took her about the country.

While she was on her travels she usually did more than the single project that had been the mainspring of the journey. She walked along the streets of the industrial towns, her camera at the ready, finding scenes of unexpected beauty − children making a slide on a snow-clad hillside, the joyous face of a young father as his little boy ran towards him, an old woman picking leaf vegetables on her frosty allotment.

As Ingram had warned, the editor of *Virtuoso* was inclined to haggle over expenses. Any time the word 'taxi' appeared on her bill, he clucked his tongue and shook his head. Corie had given up her old car when she went on tour with her sister, but now it occurred to her that she needed transport. She solved this in a manner which seemed to her eminently practical, although her mother was vexed.

She bought a second-hand motor caravan.

'Good heavens,' groaned Monna when she saw it, 'why can't you be like everybody else and have a saloon car?'

'Because a saloon car isn't quite what I need. This is nice and roomy for all my equipment, and Bertie's offered to fit it up with extra cupboards and things so I can use part of it as a mobile darkroom.'

'But why do you need a mobile darkroom? You've got a perfectly good studio.'

'But it's not always convenient to wait until I get back to do the processing. Last week in Lancaster I had the chance to do some pix of the local bigwig handing out prizes at a literary festival, and shaking hands with a couple of well-known authors. If I could have got them developed I could have sold them to the local papers.'

'So really this is about making money. No thought of what it looks like, driving about the country like a gypsy . . .'

Corie laughed. 'Monna, I'm allowed to be bohemian. I'm an artist, aren't I?'

'Humph,' said Monna, who hadn't yet brought herself to think of photography as a branch of art. 'At least promise me you won't actually *sleep* in it.'

'No no. As long as *Virtuoso* will pay my hotel bill, I don't think I'll be spending any nights in the van.'

That year, Easter was at the beginning of April. Corie went off through a blossoming countryside to Manchester, where one of the singers on Vanderschorn's list was singing in the *Messiah*. While she was there a great storm roared across England. When she got home it was to find her mother at her flat, actually staying there.

'The roof was practically ripped off the house, Corie! The

rain comes in upstairs. I simply couldn't stay there.'

'No, of course not,' Corie said helplessly.

It was terribly inconvenient. Lynette was in the spare room, her mother was in Corie's room, so Corie had the choice of sleeping either at the studio or in the motor caravan. As it happened, the motor caravan turned out to be much the more comfortable.

'It won't be for long,' Monna said when this fact came home to her. 'You can well understand – I want to be back in my own home, my dear old house which has meant so much to me. But it's cold and wet in all the bedrooms and even downstairs it's difficult to keep warm.'

'Do you mean the place is open to the elements?' Corie asked in alarm. For she too had a fondness for the tall old house in Bayswater.

'No, no, the workmen put a tarpaulin over it. It flaps about, and the draughts are absolutely dreadful. But I'm getting estimates for an immediate repair.'

They turned out to be very high. 'I simply don't have that kind of money,' Monna cried, the papers spread out on the table in the living-room of Corie's flat. 'And you know, Corie, nothing's coming in any more, now that Lynette isn't taking engagements.'

Lynette looked up in distress at the words. 'I . . . I can't,' she said.

'I know, dear, it's all been explained to me and even if I don't really understand, I accept. I have to accept, of course – what else can I do?' Monna's voice took on a tinge of tragedy. 'My children have grown away from me. I suppose I should have known it would happen. But it's hard, after I've devoted so much of my life to others, to find I'm simply not wanted any more.'

'Monna,' Corie said in warning.

'What? What have I said that isn't the truth? It's not just the money – I'm used to managing on very little: believe me, your father and I saw some hard times before we reached top billing. What hurts is to be made to feel a nuisance here. What hurts is to be disregarded. What hurts is to have to stand by and watch while years of devotion are set aside—'

'Monna, be quiet,' Corie said.

Lynette rose from her place on the sofa, to run out of the living-room to the safety of her bedroom.

'Great,' said Corie. 'Was that what you wanted to do? Reduce her to tears?'

'She's right to weep!' cried Monna in the tones of high drama. 'She's throwing her life away, she's turning her back on the one person who cares about it . . .'

'Monna, if you don't behave yourself I'm going to have to ask you to move back to Bayswater, draughts or no draughts. I cannot allow you to upset Lynette like this.'

'Oh, you are a *hard* girl, Corie! I think you have a heart of stone!'

With that Monna stalked into Corie's bedroom and closed the door on her.

Corie stood for a moment in the living-room, clenching and unclenching her hands as if to fight off the verdict her mother had delivered. When she had control of herself she went to Lynette's door, tapped, and went in without waiting for permission.

Lynette was sitting on a chair by the window, her forehead against the glass. Outside the spring dusk was gathering. From the river came the sound of a boat's siren.

'Lynette, please don't pay attention to what Monna says.'

'No, I won't.'

'You mustn't think you owe her anything. If you did, you repaid the debt long ago. But in any case it seems to me that parents ought to do things for their children without always asking for repayment.'

'I expect that's right.'

'Pal thinks the same, Lynette. She feels you ought to live your life to please yourself.'

'Yes, she told me.'

'But she means it, Lynette. So do I.'

Lynette nodded, her brow moving against the glass of the window, strands of hair catching between.

Corie knew she wasn't getting through to her. Recently this had happened more and more frequently. Lynette just seemed to switch off, almost as if she were a mechanical toy.

'Monna will be going back to Bayswater as soon as the roof is—'

'But there's no money to repair the roof,' her sister said. 'That's what she said.'

'We'll manage somehow. I've got quite a lot of work at the moment.'

'You've got work, and Pal's got a home, but what have I got?'

Corie came close to her, putting a hand on her shoulder. 'You've got yourself, love. You're Lynette Lee.'

'And who is she?' Lynette said in a whisper. 'Tell me, who is she?'

After that she seemed to withdraw again. Nothing Corie said seemed to make any difference. At length Corie gave up and, since she felt she couldn't face her mother again this evening, she went to the studio where there was always something to do to take her mind off things.

She was struggling with a problem negative when the phone at her desk rang. She left the darkroom wondering who on earth would be ringing at eight o'clock on a Saturday evening.

'Corie, that you?' said Ingram. 'I was just leaving the office when Mary Crowhurst rang from the Hague. I don't know what's wrong with that girl, she'd lost your number again. Anyhow, I've got a message here for you, all written down – can you drop by some time and collect it?'

'Of course. Thank you, Ingram.'

'What's the matter with you? You sound very down.'

'I'm all right, thanks.'

'You don't *sound* all right. What's up?'

'Oh, just a funny neg. that won't perk up.'

'Is that all? Why are you bothering about that on a Saturday night? You ought to be out enjoying yourself.'

'Any minute now,' she said.

'You're going out? Where? Somewhere nice?'

'No. No . . . I'm not going out. I just said that.'

'Corie, what on earth is wrong with you? You don't sound a bit like yourself.' There was genuine concern in his voice.

'It's nothing. Just a bit of trouble at home, that's all.'

'Corie Duggan, you wait right there,' he ordered. 'I'm coming round to collect you, and we're going out to dinner and I'm going to cheer you up.'

'No, really, Ingram, it's all right, it's just one of those things . . .'

'Stay there. I'll be ten minutes.'

In fact it was a quarter of an hour later when he came breezing into the reception area of the studio. By that time Corie had sorted out things in the darkroom, washed her hands and face, and put on her coat. She had no real intention of going out with Ingram. All the same, she knew he was right – she ought not to be in her studio alone while she felt so miserable.

Ingram arrived in his Rolls. Corie drew back when she saw it. 'Listen, let's forget it. I'm not dressed for a Rolls Royce.'

'Oh, that!' He turned back to the car, spoke to the driver, and the Rolls quietly slipped away. 'Now,' he said, taking Corie's hand to tuck under his arm, 'where shall we go? The Savoy? Julio's?'

'Ingram, honestly . . .' She made a little gesture that took in her corduroys, her duffle coat. 'Dressed like this?'

'You look great to me,' he said. 'But then you always do. But OK, you don't want to go among the top-hat crowd – so how about this? I know a great little place in Soho.'

'But haven't you got an engagement?'

'Tut, tut, stop being difficult. Come along.'

Obediently she walked at his side, up St James's, across Piccadilly, through the Mayfair alleys to that more relaxed and genial quarter where small restaurants vied for attention alongside delicatessens, violin-makers, milliners, and leather-workers.

As they walked, Ingram chatted about his day. 'I was

going down to the country for the weekend,' he confided, 'but we had to rewrite the editorial after the United Nations announced it was officially condemning *apartheid* – so you see, I had nothing planned for this evening. In fact, I'm quite glad to have the excuse to take you out. Couple of lonely people, aren't we?'

It touched her. She felt her throat tighten with tears. She was lonely – yes, so very lonely, with no one to turn to for comfort.

The great little place in Soho turned out to be an Italian restaurant with a plump proprietor who welcomed Ingram by name. 'Ah, Signor 'Olstead, nice to see you again! Lucky, lucky – tonight we have *osso bucco*, I know you like. And the young lady, *buona sera, buona sera*, this way, please, a nice table, just right, Marietta, Marietta, bring the menu!'

Corie sat down. Ingram spoke quietly to the owner, who silenced his outburst of welcome and withdrew. Almost at once a bottle of Valpolicella and two glasses appeared. Ingram poured the wine and offered it to Corie. 'Drink up, you look as if you need it.'

The wine was reviving. She sat back after a mouthful or two, unfastened her coat. A waitress came at once to take it, and Ingram's topcoat.

'Now,' said Ingram, 'tell me what's wrong.'

She shook her head.

'Come on, anyone can see you're feeling blue.' He was searching in his mind for clues. He didn't on the whole pay much attention to the affairs of other people, but he recalled something Corie had once said. 'Something to do with your sister?'

'It's nothing,' she said. 'Every family has its problems, I suppose, but ours is a theatrical family so our problems tend to be a bit dramatic.'

'Tell me about it.'

'No, I don't want to. I promised my sister not to talk about it. And then it's so boring, blaming things on other people.'

'You're never boring, Corie. If someone's making you unhappy, I want to hear about it.'

'But why should I bother you?'

'Because I'm your friend. I meant what I said, Corie – your friendship means a lot to me, and I hope mine means something to you.'

'Oh, it does,' she burst out, overwhelmed with gratitude for a kind word. 'You don't know what it's like – so many things going wrong and no one to turn to . . .'

'You can turn to me, my dear. Always. You know that.'

They were sitting side by side in a candlelit booth. He put an arm about her shoulders. She turned her head towards him so that she was leaning against his chest. He spoke gently to her, telling her he would always be there to help her, that he wanted her to be happy, that he cared for her.

The food was brought, but she couldn't eat. After a while Ingram beckoned to the waitress, paid the bill and got their coats. They went out again, Corie obedient at his side, not asking where they were going, content to let him make all the decisions.

She was so deeply tired of making decisions.

In Mayfair he led the way into a small building with a uniformed porter on duty. Ingram nodded to him, went on to press the button for a small lift. They went up in it to the first floor.

'Where is this?' Corie asked, the elegance of the surroundings sinking in.

'It's a little pied-à-terre I keep, in case I can't get home at nights.'

'Ingram . . .'

'Come along, it's quiet, we can talk.'

The flat was clearly a bachelor apartment. A tiny hall, a dark-panelled study with desk, easy chairs. He took her coat, urged her towards a chair, opened a cabinet for drinks. 'Scotch? Gin and tonic?'

'No, thanks, Ingram. I really don't—'

'Don't want anything except a little comfort – that's it, isn't it? Poor little girl.' He took her in his arms.

'Sometimes it all just gets too much, doesn't it? But I'm here, I want to help, I'm listening, Corie.'

'Oh, talking isn't going to help!' She looked up at him, and with a sudden wildness took his head between her hands to bring his lips down on hers.

Words were no use, kind thoughts were no use. She needed human warmth, physical contact, a rush of feeling that would sweep away all her unhappiness.

His response was immediate. He held her so close their two bodies seemed for a moment to merge. Then he murmured, 'Come with me.'

Beyond a doorway was the bedroom. Light from a street lamp gave enough guidance. They crossed to the bed and their hands were quick to free themselves from the hindrance of clothes.

Closing everything out of her mind, she gave herself to the healing pleasures of the body. For this moment nothing else mattered except the sturdy limbs that bound her to her lover, the wave of desire that swept them along.

Love, if it was love, that brought oblivion.

Chapter Twenty-four

Nearby there was a church tower whose clock marked the hours with a sweet, faint chime. At first, in the tempest of need and gratitude in which she was tumbled this way and that, Corie was unaware of it.

But there came a moment when all was silent in the room, except for the steady breathing of the man at her side. Then from the skies came this echoing note, four times repeated.

The darkest hour of the night, the hour of deepest self-examination.

She sat up in the bed. The street lamp sent a yellowish glow over it. She saw Ingram's dark head on the pillow, an arm outflung towards the bedhead.

He had given her release from her sadness, had brought her joy. A strong, careless lover, carried along by the tide of his own pleasure – but that was what she had wanted: a partner, a mere partner, who would let her find escape from misery.

But now there was no flicker of that response he had aroused through the first hours of their lovemaking. She felt lost, estranged. Later would come remorse, yes, and shame – because she should have known, from bitter experience, that without love she could find no real happiness. Her affair with Sasha had taught her that. But like a greedy child she'd snatched at what seemed sweet – only to find the after-taste bitter as gall.

She leaned her head down to hide her face against her knees. The question rose up in the darkness behind her eyelids – what's the matter with me? I'm not a fool, I run my life well enough – except that I let myself be betrayed, sometimes, by the feeling of being so terribly alone.

But everyone feels that, she rebuked herself. Everyone in

the final analysis is alone. It's no excuse. You're silly, weak, and selfish, and there's no real excuse, so stop trying to find one.

Ingram stirred. He put out a hand to touch her. Instead he found an empty pillow. He pulled himself up on an elbow.

'Darling? What's the matter?' After a moment he touched the switch on a bedside lamp and a soft light illumined the room. He sat up, laughing. 'I know what's the matter – you're hungry! I know I am, I'm famished! Of course we never did eat, did we?'

She raised her head, tried to find her voice.

He was picking up the bedside phone. 'I'll get them to send up—'

'Ingram—'

'It's all right, they're used to sending out for food, it's no problem. What's the time? Four-ten . . . Time for breakfast, perhaps. Hello? Russell, is that you? Send out for . . . write this down . . . coffee and rolls . . . scrambled eggs with smoked salmon, I think . . . Juice? yes, juice – Corie, orange or grapefruit?'

She was lost to words, caught up in the horror of the farce being played out. She had been telling herself she was silly and worthless, and her lover was ordering orange juice.

He smiled at her and winked. 'It'll take them maybe a quarter of an hour – I expect you'd like a robe – the bathroom, over there.' Into the phone he said, 'Orange juice, freshly squeezed, mind. And tell them not to forget the butter, they did last time.'

Corie rose, fled to the bathroom. It was a narrow room, tiled in maroon. Matching towels and bath-robes were folded on shelves of brass-edged mahogany. She pulled on a robe, ran the tap, plunged her face into the cold water again and again.

Clear-headed, she went back into the bedroom. Ingram was stretched luxuriously. 'I feel great,' he said. Still stretching and yawning, he got up to wander into the bathroom. She heard the shower running.

Her clothes were on the floor at the bedside. She picked them up and, by the time Ingram returned in a towelling robe, she was clad in her shirt and trousers, was putting on her shoes.

'What the hell . . . ?'

She stood up. 'I'm going, Ingram.'

'But the food'll be here in a minute—'

She shook her head. 'I'm going now. I'm sorry, it was all a mistake.'

'A . . . a mistake? How can you say that . . . ? Corie, what the devil's wrong with you?'

'I don't know,' she said in a low voice. 'All I know is, it should never have happened. I'm sorry.'

'But it was great – we were marvellous together – what do you mean, a mistake? For God's sake, *you* were the one who—'

'I know. I was wrong to do it. I'm sorry, I'm truly sorry . . .'

'Sorry? Oh, fine! You throw yourself into my arms, we have a wonderful night, and then you say it was wrong? What was wrong with it? We make a wonderful pair.'

'But we're not in love, Ingram.'

The torrent of angry words abated. He frowned. 'Well . . . we're not going to pledge undying love, if that's what you mean. That was never in question, was it?'

'Of course not.'

'But we do mean something to each other.'

'We were friends – or we were trying to be. And I spoiled it all, just as you did the first time.'

'That's not true! Nothing was spoiled! We haven't stopped being friends, it's just that . . . that . . .'

'That now we're lovers.'

'Well, what's wrong with that? I've always wanted you, that's the truth of it, and you can say what you like but I'm damned glad it happened.'

She shook her head.

'Oh, for Pete's sake, why can't you just accept it, Corie?

Why can't we just get what we like out of it? You were happy, I know you were—'

'That's true, I was. But not now.'

'But what's different now?'

'It's the morning after, that's what's different. And now I realise I was grabbing for something that wasn't really there.'

'I was there, Corie. You needed someone and I was there.'

'But we don't love each other, Ingram. There's nothing to hold us together except momentary need.'

'Well, that's enough, surely? What more do you expect?'

She sighed. She didn't know how to explain herself. She knew she was unfair, unreasonable.

'Ingram,' she said, taking refuge in an argument that might make sense to him, 'you're a married man.'

'Oh!' He gave a little explosive laugh. 'Oh, if that's all, you know as well as I do that there's no strong tie between Helen and me.'

She saw in her mind's eye that moment when she'd first met Helen Pittsworth Holstead. She saw the proud anger in Helen's eyes, and heard her voice: 'Don't think you'll ever get my husband, Miss Duggan!' That had not been the voice of a woman who didn't care for her man.

'Helen's a friend of mine,' she went on. 'I know her quite well, I know the children. I *can't* have an affair with their father . . . it's just . . . somehow . . .'

He looked confused, a little embarrassed. At that moment there came a tap on the door of the flat. He stormed out of the bedroom. She heard him open the door, heard him growl at the porter. When she followed him into the outer room a little later, the tray was sitting on the desk – covered dishes, tasteful crockery and silver, a carnation in a slender holder.

It was a silent witness to the fact that this had happened before, perhaps more than once. Corie saw herself as just one more in the sequence of Ingram Holstead's women. She blushed and turned away, seeking her coat.

'Wait,' Ingram said. 'I know how it looks – well, I never pretended I was a saint. But it's different with you, Corie, I mean it. I really feel something special for you.'

She nodded and shrugged. 'Perhaps that's true.'

'Stay. Let's talk it through. I'll make you see—'

'No, I think I ought to go now. I don't want to talk because I don't know how to explain myself. I just feel I'm terribly to blame for what happened, and I know it's unfair and cowardly to run away but I can't help it.'

'I'm not going to give up,' he said angrily. 'You can say what you like but you can't turn your back on me. Damn it, you *belonged* to me – for six hours, seven, you were mine completely – I'm *not* going to give you up!'

She was buttoning up her coat. He stood watching her, baffled, furious.

There was nothing more to say. She let herself out, pulled the door closed behind her, paused for a moment to ascertain which way to go for the lift.

From behind her she heard a tremendous crash.

Ingram had thrown the breakfast tray at the closed door.

Outside, the dawn sky was tinged with primrose and peach. London was still asleep so early on a Sunday morning. As she walked down Regent Street, the only sound was her footsteps. Pigeons flew up in alarm when she reached Trafalgar Square. A policeman watched her approach, asked quietly, 'Everything all right, miss?' When she nodded and smiled, she was thinking that everything was far from all right.

The air was fresh and chill. She pulled up the collar of her coat. She was glad to walk, to exert herself. The river brimmed full as she crossed Waterloo Bridge, the surface a grey silk shot with yellow, reflection of the sunrise. A barge went by, the helmsman looking up in surprise at her presence on the bridge. He waved, she waved back, a small, hesitant greeting. Did she deserve to be treated with kindness by the rest of the human race? Hadn't she just put herself outside the pale?

The clear morning light made the untended ground at

Stamford Street seem like a deserted plain. She put her key in the door of the flat and at once sensed that someone was up and about. She tensed, wondering if it might be her mother. She most earnestly didn't want to meet her mother at this moment – she wasn't ready for battle after what she'd just gone through with Ingram.

Lynette was in the kitchenette, sitting by the little table, a mug of tea in her hands. As Corie came in she looked up. Corie thought: She's stopped bothering about her appearance. Hair in a tangle, her dressing-gown buttoned unevenly . . .

'You're up early, Lynette.'

'Is it very early?'

'Have you had enough sleep?'

'Oh, I'm all right.' She looked vaguely about her. 'There's some tea . . . I think it's still fresh.'

Corie took a mug from the shelf, put in milk, and poured the tea. It looked dark and strong – by her estimation it had been brewing for at least half an hour. But she drank it and was glad of its harsh, stimulating touch on her tongue.

'You know what Monna said last night?' Lynette said. 'About no money coming in?'

'Don't worry about that. We'll manage, we always have.'

'But that was in the old days, when all of us would get work – now Pal's staying at home hoping to start a family and I'm doing nothing. You're the one who's keeping the family going, Corie.'

'Don't let it bother you, sweetie.'

Her sister pulled her dressing-gown collar more closely against her throat. 'I've been thinking . . . It's time I made some kind of an effort.'

'Only if you're ready, Lynette.'

'But that's the point. When am I going to be ready? I feel sort of . . . all in pieces. I can't get myself together. I thought about it a lot last night after you left and I began to think . . . Perhaps I need help.'

Corie felt herself go tense, but tried to hide it. Was it possible that Lynette had come to understand what had been happening, the slow disintegration of a once-lively character?

'I met someone, one evening when I was out with William. I mean, he brought her with him, she was in London for the day. You know William's doing ground-work for a new television series?'

'He is?'

'Yes, it's quite a new thing, called "Background Story". This man called Dennis Borderman − I've never heard of him but it seems he's quite well-known − he's going to interview people live, in front of the camera. William's been consulting Dr Vantoni about it − whether it's OK to ask this or that, what if the person gets angry or upset, that kind of thing.'

Lynette paused. Corie hadn't been able to follow. 'This Borderman − is that the person you met with William?'

'No, no, that was Dr Vantoni. She's nice. William met her in Brighton at some party or other. He's getting what's called "psychological guidelines" from her. She runs a private clinic in a place up on the Downs. She knows a lot about helping people who've sort of lost their way.'

'She specialises in that?'

'I think she's a psychiatrist. Or is it a psychologist?'

'I don't know, dear. I'm never quite sure what the difference is.'

'Anyhow, William offered to take me to see her place, if I wanted to.'

She fell silent. Corie didn't want to speak for fear of scaring her away from the subject. She sipped her strong tea, waiting and hoping.

'I think I'll ask him to take me to look at it when he can spare the time,' Lynette said. She looked with great seriousness at her sister. 'Do you think that would be a good idea?'

'I don't see why not.'

'You see, if it seems a nice place, I thought . . . maybe . . . I might go there. To stay for a bit, I mean.'

'Yes?'

'To see if Dr Vantoni can help put the pieces together again.'

Corie nodded. 'That sounds sensible.'

'The only thing is, Corie, I don't think it could be done quickly. I'm in such a muddle, I think even Dr Vantoni would have a problem sorting me out.'

'That doesn't matter, does it?'

'Not from the point of view of how long it takes. I've definitely decided not to go to Vancouver. In fact . . .' She stopped, and the silence went on so long that Corie thought she'd decided not to pursue the matter. But then she said with decision, 'I'm never going back on the stage.'

'Never ever?'

'Never ever. That's over. But I was thinking last night, I can't just stop dead and do nothing. I have to have some sort of a job, or something, I can't cadge off you for ever—'

'Oh, Lynette, there's no question of that . . .'

'But it's true, I have been living off you, and really until last night I suppose I was going to go on doing it. But I've realised I have to sort myself out, start on a new tack – goodness knows what, for I'm not trained for anything except the stage and I'm absolutely certain I don't want to do that any more.' She looked at Corie for comment.

'You don't have to do anything you don't want to, duckie. If you want to give up the stage, that's all right.'

'It's more like the stage has given me up,' Lynette said, with the first gleam of humour Corie had heard from her in ages. 'And what to do instead, I haven't a clue. But perhaps Dr Vantoni would put me on some sort of track . . . Oh, yes, Dr Vantoni: what I wanted to say was, it might cost quite a bit, Corie.'

'We'll manage.'

'Once I'm back in the world again I can get some sort of a job and pay you back.'

'Lynette love, don't worry about it—'

'But I want to worry about it. I want to start thinking about somebody other than myself. I've been thinking about myself almost the whole time for weeks and weeks.

Have I always been so selfish, Corie?'

'You're not selfish! Don't dare say such a thing! What you have to do is tell William you want to see the clinic—'

'Bresling Park, it's called. It's up on the Downs – did I tell you that?'

'Yes, you mentioned it.'

'I should think William might drop in to see me there, if he wouldn't find it a bore.'

'I'm sure he'd be glad to, Lynette.'

'Shall I tell him, then . . . ? That I want to talk to Dr Vantoni and be taken round the place?'

'Yes, why not?'

'I'll ring him,' Lynette said, rising from the table.

'Not now, Lynette!'

'Why not?'

'It isn't six o'clock yet, and it's Sunday!'

'Sunday?' For a moment Lynette looked dismayed, but then something seemed to happen inside her. Her lips curved up in a smile, and for the first time in many, many months, she began to laugh. 'Oh, just imagine! Six o'clock on a Sunday morning and I want to chat to William on the phone! My hat! He'd think I'd gone round the bend!'

In sheer relief Corie began to laugh too. So they sat together in the little kitchenette giggling like two school girls, while hope for her little sister began to grow within Corie's heart.

Nothing could have been better designed to put self-reproach over Ingram into proper perspective. So she'd slept with a man she didn't truly love, and had regretted it, and they'd had a blazing row about it – she would survive, and so would Ingram once he'd got over the anger of being rejected.

Corie's problems seemed so small when compared with Lynette's. She had work waiting for her that she loved and enjoyed. She was fit and well. She had courage enough to face up to life. What more could she ask?

William Tranton, when consulted by telephone at a decent hour, at once invited Lynette to come to lunch. After that he would take her to see Dr Vantoni. 'She won't mind?' Lynette queried. 'It's Sunday, you know.'

'She won't mind,' he assured her.

Corie put her on the Brighton train at eleven. Her mother took it to be a simple lunch engagement with William. 'It's nice that she has a contact with someone like that,' she said to Corie. 'He's still with the BBC, he might be able to put in a word for her.'

'He's not with Light Entertainment any more, Monna.'

'All the same, he probably still has friends there.'

Corie let it pass. She didn't feel she needed to say that Lynette had given up show business.

At about six in the evening the phone rang. Monna reached it first. 'Lynette? About to set out for home, are you?' There was a pause while Monna listened. Corie, watching, saw her face go pale. 'What do you mean?' her mother demanded, her voice going shrill. 'Staying? For how long? Lynette, you can't be serious—'

'Let me,' Corie said, and took the phone from her wavering hand. 'Lynette, it's Corie. What's happening?'

'I've decided to stay at the clinic,' came Lynette's voice, faltering, scared, but decisive. 'Dr Vantoni says she can take me and, you know, Corie, if I'm going to do it, I might as well get on with it, mightn't I?'

Corie was almost as surprised as her mother. She couldn't think what to reply.

'Corie? Corie?'

'I'm . . . I'm thinking. It's come as a bit of a surprise. Lynette, could I speak to Dr Vantoni?'

'Of course, she's right here.'

A little delay while the receiver was handed over. 'Miss Duggan?' The voice was cool and lightly tinged with some kind of foreign accent. The speaker wasn't young by any means. 'This is Dr Vantoni. I want you to know that Mr Tranton brought your sister here at about three o'clock. She has spent all afternoon with us and we've had several conversations – not long ones but they have been enough to make me think I can be of use.'

'It's just that I'm a bit taken aback, doctor . . .'

'I understand. You thought she would simply look at my clinic and then take time to make up her mind. But she wants to stay, and you know, the patient often has an instinct . . .'

'If you think . . . if you think it's all right . . . How about her clothes and things?'

'Perhaps you could bring them? I could supply necessities for overnight, but the insulin is a different matter – in due course the dosage may have to be adjusted but for the moment she needs her normal prescription.'

'I'll bring it straight away.'

'That's very good of you.'

'Not at all.'

'See you later, then.'

Corie hung up. Her mother exclaimed, 'Don't break the connection, child! I want to talk to that woman—'

'Dr Vantoni.'

'What right has she to take my daughter?'

'She didn't "take" her, Monna. Lynette wants to stay.'

'She must be out of her mind!' her mother cried. 'How can she—'

'That's just it,' Corie cut in. 'You didn't mean it, but the fact is that Lynette has been going out of her mind. Did you really not notice it?'

'What?'

'She's been heading straight for a nervous breakdown for the last three months.'

'That's utter nonsense! Lynette is a very sensible, well-balanced—'

'Sensible and well-balanced if you discount the fact that she was under the spell of a totally selfish, uncaring man, that she tried to keep going when she was very ill, that she couldn't bring herself to confide her troubles to anyone – all that apart, she was quite well-balanced. But—'

'I don't know what you're implying. Lynette behaved like a trouper—'

'Oh, for God's sake, don't start talking about being a

trouper and going on with the show! Lynette's duty is to herself now, if she's to preserve anything of her life. She's decided to put herself under a psychiatrist . . .'

'That's ridiculous! A psychiatrist? She's not a mental case!'

'But she *is*! It's nothing to be ashamed of, Monna. She's sick – sick in the mind—'

'She is not! She's only got to pull herself together—'

'Well, she can't, not without help. And she's chosen to get help, and since she's fully grown and legally entitled to make her own decisions, I think you're going to have to put up with it.'

'I will not! No daughter of mine—'

'I've heard you say that so often, Monna,' Corie said, walking into the spare room to pack Lynette's things. 'What does it mean? It always seems to stake out a claim of some kind, a right to dictate what ought to be done. But in this case you're outclassed. Someone who really knows how to help her is taking over.'

Monna followed her into the bedroom, getting in her way as she collected a few clothes and toilet articles. 'If you imagine I'm going to allow some stranger to wheedle her way into my little girl's confidence when she's a bit under the weather . . .'

'You've no say in the matter.'

'I certainly have! I shall go with you and tell this woman to her face—'

'You're not going anywhere. I don't want you making a scene at the clinic.'

'I have every right to protest!'

'Nothing of the kind. You have no right at all to come between a doctor and her patient.'

'Corie, I insist on coming with you.'

By now Corie had an overnight bag filled with the items her sister would need for at least the first few days. She now added the insulin kit. 'I simply won't go if you try to tag along with me. Which means that Lynette won't get her insulin. Is that what you want?'

'Oh, that's right – it's always the way! That dreadful ailment of Lynette's is your weapon against me any time I try to come to her aid—'

'Monna, I don't want weapons to use against you. I just want you to leave Lynette *alone*.'

'But I'm worried about her, Corie! I'm worried to death at handing her over to someone she's known five minutes!'

There was no dramatic technique in her manner, for once she was speaking with real emotion. Corie paused, studying her. After all, it was true. Monna knew nothing about Dr Vantoni and had a right to be anxious.

'All right, put your coat on, we have a train to catch.'

Two hours later they were at Brighton Station, where William was waiting to drive them to Bresling Park. 'I think you'll like the place,' he said to Monna, instinctively recognising the need to placate her. 'I was a bit staggered when Lynette said she thought she would stay if Dr Vantoni could take her, but . . . Perhaps it's for the best.'

'I must say, William, I think you might have consulted me before you let her make such a suggestion.'

'Wait till you've had a chat with Dr Vantoni. I think you'll find it very reassuring.'

Dr Vantoni proved to be small, plump and about sixty. She had abundant white hair done up in a bun at the back, snapping black eyes, a wide mouth and a strong jaw. She herself opened the door of the clinic, holding out a hand to greet the relatives of her new patient.

'Corie? And this must be Mrs Duggan? How do you do?'

Monna shook hands with evident reluctance. She'd had a little speech ready, explaining that her youngest daughter would be better off at home, even though perhaps at this moment she seemed inclined to stay. However, the doctor had an air of authority. Moreover, she was very smartly dressed in dark fine wool of a cut which, to Monna, proclaimed its Parisian origins. And around her neck there was a necklace of plain but very fine pearls. Clearly Dr Vantoni was a lady. One couldn't make speeches implying sharp practice to a lady.

Lynette was sitting in a little reception room, looking pale but serene. She smiled at them all. 'Thanks, William,' she said, taking the suitcase from him. 'And thank you, Corie for rushing here with my things,' Her glance shifted to her mother. Her voice lost some of its calmness. 'I hope you don't think I've been too impulsive, Monna, but you know . . .'

'I'm here to have it explained to me,' Monna said, 'although I must confess I think the whole idea is very strange.'

'I told Corie this morning. I think I'm at the end of my tether. I need help, Monna—'

'But my dear child, who else should you turn to but to *me*? Where is the need to go to an outsider?'

Lynette glanced anxiously at Dr Vantoni. The doctor answered the look with a faint smile of encouragement.

'You don't know how to help me, Monna,' Lynette said.

'Lynette, if you'd ever taken the trouble to sit down with me and tell me you were upset—'

'I told you. I kept telling you.'

'That's not so! You've never said a word to me about being over-anxious—'

'I didn't put it into words . . .' Lynette hesitated. 'Corie understood, though. And you think I'm right, don't you?'

'If it's what you want to do, duckie, it's all right with me.'

'Corie, how can you say such a thing! And so lightly!' Monna clasped her hands together in entreaty. 'You've always been ready to stand against me, and for the most part I've just put up with it because it's part of your nature. But this time, Corie, this time – it's Lynette's welfare that's at stake!'

'Do you think I don't know that?'

'Then tell her we must all go home and talk this through. Don't encourage her to take this step without even consulting her best and oldest friend, her mother!'

'Mrs Duggan,' said the doctor.

'Please don't interfere in this. It's a family matter . . .'

'Mrs Duggan, I was only going to say, being theatrical does not help anyone.'

Mrs Duggan's hands were still joined as if for pleading. She seemed to become aware that it looked contrived and let them fall into her lap. 'I may express myself rather . . . forcefully . . . But I mean every word!'

'No doubt. It's the thinking behind the words that we have to examine. You say you are your daughter's best friend—'

'I think she would tell you that herself.'

'From what I have heard from Lynette this afternoon, the best friend is her sister Corie.'

Monna flashed a glance of resentment at her eldest daughter. 'It's just that Corie has always had a strong influence—'

'Forgive me. *You* have influence. Corie has concern. Perhaps we shouldn't go too deeply into that. For the moment, I think we must ask a simple question. What does Lynette want to do?'

'But she's not capable of thinking straight at the moment . . .'

'Ah, you agree that she has a problem, then?'

'Well, I . . . I . . .'

'Lynette is free to walk out of the clinic any time she wishes. In the meantime the evening is going by and I believe Lynette would like to go to her room?' She looked inquiringly at Lynette.

'Yes, I must,' she agreed. 'I must get my injection, I'm beginning to feel a bit woozy. So I'll go up, if you don't mind. Goodnight, Monna. Goodnight, Corie. Goodnight, William.'

'Goodnight, Lynette,' William said. 'I'll drop by in a day or two, shall I?'

'Oh yes, that would be lovely.'

And she was gone.

There was a hiatus. Dr Vantoni merely waited it out. Monna said in the end, 'Well, it seems we have to accept that my daughter is staying here at least for tonight. I'll come back tomorrow, by which time I feel sure she'll have—'

'There is no way to be certain of what she will think tomorrow. But I must think for her and I therefore have to say, Mrs Duggan, you should not visit tomorrow.'

'Visit? I expect to take her home tomorrow.'

Dr Vantoni was shaking her head. 'She will not want to go home. The truth is, she has no home to go to.'

'Of course she has − well, at least, I'm staying with Corie for the present but very soon our house will be repaired—'

'I was not speaking of a particular place. I meant that Lynette doesn't know where she belongs. She needs time and peace to talk it over, to find out what she wants to do.'

'Excuse me, you don't know anything about her. Her whole life has been in the theatre and *that's* where she belongs.'

'She tells me no,' the doctor said. 'It is one of her greatest anxieties. She is unwilling to go back in front of the public. However, there is no question of that at the moment. What we have to do now is to let her have a space in which to stand back and look at her life. I think that she will be able to do this better if you do not come—'

'Not come and see my own daughter?' Monna cried.

'You will ring, I will tell you if she wishes to see you. If she says no, you don't come. Do we understand each other?'

'But I—'

'If you come unannounced you will get no further than the hall. I am sorry, but my patients need to be protected from over-anxious relatives.'

'It's outrageous! I shall go to the law—'

'Others have said the same. But if the patient has agreed to put herself under my care, the anxious relatives must accept it. Please Mrs Duggan, accept. Your daughter is quite ill. We both want to make her better, no?'

'Well of course . . . but I feel . . . you don't even know her . . .'

'I shall know her very well as time goes by. That is my work. It is not yours, Mrs Duggan. Leave her to me and I will try to make her whole again. It is hard for you, this I understand. But if you truly love Lynette, give her this chance. Agree with her decision. Let us both contribute to her cure. Yes?'

Corie watched with incredulity as Monna crumbled before this gentle onslaught. Her anger dwindled away, she looked uncertain, troubled.

'I don't know what to say . . .'

'Say goodnight and go home. Telephone me tomorrow for news. Don't expect to come visiting, however, this is most unlikely and perhaps remains so for some weeks.'

'Weeks?'

'It is not easy, to repair a damaged life. It is not a watch in which a new spring can be put – we must work with the parts we already have, make them function better. So it will be weeks and you must be patient, for your child's sake.' She took Monna's hand, made her rise and go with her to the hall. 'Goodnight, Mrs Duggan.'

'Goodnight,' Monna mumbled, and went out to get into William's car.

'Me too?' William asked. 'Do I have to ring first to ask if I can visit?'

'Oh yes, this is a rule with new patients. But I think Lynette would want to see you – and also you, Corie. Goodnight now, drive safely.'

William saw them on to the empty London train. Mrs Duggan sat in deep silence for most of the journey. As the train was running past East Croydon, she said: 'I'll never forgive William Tranton.'

'Good heavens, what's William done?'

'He introduced Lynette to that woman!'

'He did her a big favour. You'll see in the end, Monna. It's for the best.'

Monna gave an angry shake of the head and fell back into silence.

At the flat, Corie went into her own room, gathered up her mother's belongings, and went with them into the spare room.

'What are you doing?' Monna cried, aghast.

'I'm moving you into the spare room. I have to make an early start in the morning – I'm off to the North, on a job. I must get a decent night's sleep.'

'You might at least ask my permission before you push me out of—'

'Permission? Monna, I'm too exhausted to make an issue of it, but this is *my* home.'

'Corie Duggan, don't try to pretend you're too tired to talk. I want an explanation . . .'

Corie went into the bathroom, shut the door, and in a haze of fatigue washed her face and brushed her teeth. When she came out her mother was waiting for her. 'I insist on being told how this happened. Did you know Lynette was going to see that woman when she went to Brighton this morning?'

'I had no idea it would happen today.'

'But you knew she was contemplating it?'

'Yes, she told me early this morning.'

'I want to hear what she said, word for word.'

'Some other time, Monna.'

'Now, this minute! I will not be kept in the dark about my daughter's welfare!'

'One day, if Lynette wants you to know, she'll tell you. Until then, you'll just have to wait. And while you're waiting, Monna, think about what's happened. Lynette developed diabetes, but she couldn't discuss it with you. Lynette began to go into a mental fog, but she couldn't discuss it with you. Doesn't it strike you at all that you might be at fault?'

With that, Corie walked into her bedroom, fell on the bed still wearing her slacks and sweater, and went straight into the sleep of exhaustion.

Next morning Corie set out early to drive to Scotland. She left a note for her mother on the kitchen table: 'Back probably Friday'. It was all she could think of to say. It seemed cold and unfilial, but it was no use pretending there was a warm relationship between them.

En route, she stopped at a café for breakfast. She rang Opal from its callbox, to tell her what had happened.

'A private clinic? Corie, what does that mean? A loony bin?'

'No, no, it's a nice place, I saw a bit of it last night and William says it's OK.'

'What about Monna?'

'She's all at sea. If she rings you, Pal, and wants you to join up with her in trying to get Lynette home, just say no.'

'Bet on it. If it will really help Lynette, I'll say no till next Christmas.' Opal paused. 'You really think it's going to be good for the kid?'

'I really do, Pal. For the first time in over a year, I really feel things might improve for our little sister.'

As she drove on towards the North, she recalled Lynette sitting in the reception room at the clinic – pale, scared, but making an attempt to get her life together.

Please make it work, she prayed inwardly as she drove; please, please make it work.

Chapter Twenty-five

She was later getting home than she expected. First of all the soprano whose portrait she was to take in Edinburgh was unwell and had to be followed to her next venue in Glasgow. There Corie was asked to do some work at a conference of Gaelic-speakers, some of whom were wealthy land-owners and so paid well. This unexpected bonus made her a little late in attending to a commercial job at a weaving factory in the Borders.

Meanwhile she kept in touch with things at home by ringing her sister Opal. Everything seemed to be going quite well. Lynette had settled in, and chatted with Opal on the telephone as if she were content.

When she rang her studio to check on business matters, Bertie told her not to worry. He was dealing with the clients already booked, had taken several bookings for when she returned. 'What else . . . ? Oh, some feller has rung two or three times.'

'What feller?'

'I don't exactly remember. I wrote it down somewhere. Wait a minute.' Extensive rustling of papers. She didn't expect him to find the note. Every time she was away she found the darkroom in perfect condition and her desk in a shambles.

'Nope, can't lay my hands on it, but anyhow he wants you to ring him back as soon as you can. I made a note of the number, you'll see it when you get back.'

'Thank you, Bertie.'

She drove back to London overnight, going straight to the studio to check all was well. Bertie was busy with clients. She spent an hour or so tidying the desk. Under a pile of bills and scribbled messages she found one that made her gasp.

'Drew Richter. Please ring him a.s.a.p.' The number of his parents' house in New York was added.

She looked at the clock. Nine o'clock in the morning. In New York it was four a.m.

She found she was shaking. Drew had tried to ring her!

'You said this man rang two or three times?'

Bertie nodded. 'Of course if I'd had your number to give him I'd have done that but you were moving around. He said he was too, but if you ring that number he'll know 'cause he checks back from time to time.'

'Thank you, Bertie.'

She went home to bath and change. At the flat she found her mother making her elevenses. 'You said you'd only be gone a few days,' she reproached her. 'You've been gone a week!'

'So I have. Good morning, Monna.'

'Ah . . . Well . . . Good morning . . . Did you have a good trip?' Monna busied herself with setting out cups and saucers and a plate of biscuits.

'I think I did well financially, thank you. How are you?'

She asked the question not out of mere politeness, for her mother did seem less ebullient than usual.

'How do you think I am?' she mourned. 'I'm out of my mind with worry about Lynette! That doctor won't let me even speak to her on the phone!'

Corie was a little taken aback. Opal could speak to her sister, yet Monna was forbidden.

She realised that Dr Vantoni must have good reason for the restriction. In the sessions between doctor and patient, fears and anxieties to do with Monna must have been revealed, even more serious than she herself had sensed. Perhaps Corie should have done more and done it sooner. Perhaps Monna had damaged Lynette to a greater extent than she had suspected.

She made no reply to her mother's complaint. Monna thumped the kitchen table with her fist so that the tray of crockery jumped. 'My daughter's been stolen from me!' she declared.

'Not at all. She's in Sussex in a nursing home. When she's well enough you'll be able to ring her, and later visit her, I'm sure.'

'All they say when I ask is that she's quite well. What does that mean, quite well?'

'It means she's having treatment—'

'But who's checking that it's the right treatment? I bet they give her tranquillisers, they always do from what I hear, and you know there's her insulin—'

'That's all been checked with Dr Usborne.'

'How do you know that?' Monna demanded.

'Well . . . of course . . . Pal told me.'

'You rang Pal?'

'A couple of times . . .'

'You never rang *me*!'

It was only too true. She had shirked it. She simply hadn't wanted to be engaged in a long wrangle by telephone. She could think of nothing to say.

'That's the last straw. You never cared for me, Corie, and I'm not staying in this flat a moment longer—'

'Monna!'

'You left me all alone here to agonise over my little girl—' Monna was stamping off towards the spare room.

'But where will you go?'

'Back to Bayswater – the men have nearly finished the repairs.'

'I thought you couldn't afford it?'

'I forgot the house was insured – the insurance company is going to pay – but don't pretend you care how it's to be paid for!'

A moment later her mother was opening and closing drawers in the spare room, noisily collecting articles from the bathroom. Corie did nothing to stop her. She would be glad to have her flat to herself. Nevertheless she didn't want them to part on bad terms.

'Monna, at the moment things are in a bit of a turmoil—'

'Please ring for a taxi for me,' her mother said.

'There's no need, Monna, I'll drive you back.'

'If you think I'm going to get into that caravan contraption of yours you're sadly mistaken! Please phone for a taxi.'

'Very well.' After she'd done so there was an awkward silence. Monna sat like a stone with her suitcase at her side. Corie felt obliged to make some move to paper over the cracks. 'Monna, I apologise for not ringing you while I was away. It was a bit difficult: I had to use callboxes and it meant having lots of change . . .'

'Good heavens, couldn't you call from your hotel room?'

'I didn't have a hotel room. I was staying in my camper.'

'Good God, Corie, you have no *dignity*!'

At that moment the doorbell rang to let them know the taxi was outside. Corie carried down her mother's suitcase. 'Monna . . .'

'Goodbye, Corie. I hope when you think things over you'll have the grace to make a full apology.'

'For what?' Corie asked, baffled.

'For . . . for . . . Oh, what's the use of expecting any filial affection from you!' Next moment she was inside the taxi and being borne away.

Corie knew that in due course family ties would prove stronger than indignation and her mother would relent a little. But she was always going to be in some sort of disgrace: it had been so since she was in her early teens, and she couldn't see how to alter it.

But she had better and more important things to think about. Drew wanted her to ring him!'

The earliest she could make the call, she felt, was after lunch. By that time it would be between eight and nine in the morning in America. By then Drew's parents could be expected to be up and about.

She bathed, changed, and had something to eat by way of breakfast, then went back to the studio to attack the pile of paperwork.

The call, when she made it, proved to be quite short. Drew's mother answered the phone. 'Corie! At last! Drew has been trying to talk to you since last Tuesday! Where have you been?'

'In Scotland on business, Mrs Richter, but never mind that – can I speak to Drew?'

'Ach, Drew isn't here, no, no, he's in Washington—'

'I have a number for his apartment there and one for the office but—'

'I know, he's never there. I have the same problem, my dear! No, what must happen is this. Drew rings me this evening, I tell him you have been in touch, and then *he* rings you.'

'This evening!' 'This evening' was about ten hours away, American time.

'A long time, no? I'm sorry, Corie, Drew is kept travelling by his President. At the moment something very important is being prepared, and so it is more difficult than ever to be in touch. I assure you, *Liebling*, I don't enjoy it either. But he will ring me this evening perhaps about six o'clock – that means, what, eleven o'clock with you?'

'Yes.'

'Don't sound so sad,' soothed Mrs Richter. 'For Drew it has been worse – all week he's been hoping to speak to you and no, nothing! So now, we make an arrangement. You will be where this evening at eleven?'

'I'll be at my flat. He has the number.'

'Give it to me once more, just for fear he loses it. Wait, I'm writing it down.' Corie dictated slowly and clearly; Drew's mother wrote. 'Now I have it. I will tell my son. And Corie – he will be very, very glad.'

'Thank you, Mrs Richter,' she said, her voice breaking with smiles and tears. When she had put the phone down she sat for a long time staring at the wall of her studio. Her photographic portraits stared back, uninterested in the struggle she was having to control her emotions.

Corie had always found the best antidote to anxiety was to work. She had the commercial pictures from her Scottish trip to print up. She spent some time looking at them, deciding how to crop them to maximise the drama of the building against the cloudscape. By and by Bertie tapped on the door of the darkroom to say he was going home, and wasn't it time she had a break?

True enough, when she emerged it was seven. She took herself to dinner, knowing from previous examination that there was almost nothing in the fridge at home. She stretched the meal out until eight thirty, then went home. There she tried to watch Shirley Bassey on the television, but her mind kept wandering. In the end she switched off to set about some housekeeping – the spare room needed a good turn out and her own room had a film of dust. By ten minutes to eleven she could find nothing left to do. She sat down, poured herself a stiff brandy, and told herself to stop being a fool.

At three minutes after eleven, her phone rang.

'Corie? Corie, thank God! I thought you'd disappeared for ever!'

'Drew, it's ages since—'

'I know, I know, you must have thought I wasn't bothering. But it's so difficult, darling, I've been scurrying around the country for weeks now, and the difference in the time-zones gets worse the further west you get.'

'I understand. But I thought – I thought you'd write?'

'Yes, so did I. Turns out I'm no good at letters, I start one and don't have time to finish. I'm sorry, Corie, say you forgive me.'

'I do,' she said. 'But don't let it happen again.'

'It might. I can't promise. But that's not what I wanted to talk to you about. What d'you think, love? The President is arranging a trip to Europe!'

'What?'

'It's supposed to be hush-hush until the official announcement, so don't breathe a word of it to anyone, but there's going to be a "summit meeting".'

'In London?'

'No, not in London, though he's going to touch base there – from the way things are shaping up, it looks like an overnight stop—'

'Drew! Is that all?' All the joyful anticipation vanished. She felt as if she'd been given a physical blow.

'Wait, wait, it gets better. The summit's to be in Vienna. We'll be there for several days. Vienna, Corie! Can you get to Vienna?'

Hope sprang up again, only to waver. 'Well, I . . . No, I don't think so. Wait a minute.' Her head was spinning, but some vestige of an idea had surfaced. 'I've got to take pictures of opera stars for *Virtuoso* . . . And I'm almost sure two of them are singing in Vienna at the moment.'

'At the moment?' Now it was Drew who sounded anxious.

'When is this visit, Drew?'

'End of May, beginning of June. Will your opera singers still be there?'

'I think so. They're there for the "summer festival", whatever that is — I think it's till the end of June.'

'That sounds right. The Viennese tend to leave the city in July so the season would end just before. Corie, you've *got* to be there.'

'I believe I can manage it, Drew! I'll get *Virtuoso* to send me—' She broke off.

'What's the matter?'

'The editor's terribly mean. I don't want to take up time explaining.' Her head was whirling with money problems. She mustn't waste her own money on this trip because she had to pay the bills for Lynette's treatment. Somehow she had to get Vanderschorn to finance at least part of the trip. 'Don't worry about it, Drew, I'll get the commission and I'll be there. But I'll see you first in London?'

'Fleetingly,' he said in a voice full of regret. 'The way it's shaping up, there's going to be a banquet and that kind of thing, and we'll be off to Paris next day—'

'Paris?'

'Oh, yes, it's a hell of a programme. Never mind. The main thing is, we'll be in Vienna from about 3 June for perhaps a week. I'm going because I speak German, of course. But I'm going to make sure I get some time off if I have to hit the Press Officer over the head. Corie, promise you'll be there!'

'I promise!'

'That's what I wanted to hear. Now I must go because I've got a dinner engagement with a wheeler-dealer, but I'll ring again tomorrow. Will you know by then if you've landed the commission for Vienna?'

'I hope so. What time?'

'Let's see, I've got to go to St Louis and it'll be six-ish, seven-ish before I'm free. I'll ring you at seven – that's about two in the afternoon for you, right?'

'Right.'

'Where will you be?'

'At the studio.'

'OK, I have the number right here in front of me. About two o'clock tomorrow afternoon, Corie. Have good news for me.'

'I will, Drew.'

'Goodnight, darling.'

'Goodnight.'

When she'd replaced the receiver she sprang up and did an involuntary waltz around the room. After a few minutes she calmed down, sat on the sofa, and gave herself up to day-dreams. She would see Drew again. Vienna at the beginning of June . . . Music, wine, blue skies, the Danube . . . It was all based on old musicals from which her mother had been wont to sing excerpts, a picture of a world dominated by Johann Strauss and romance. Perhaps it would really be like that.

She rose, tipped the glass of brandy back into the bottle, and put it away. She didn't need brandy now to give her courage. She felt full of optimism and energy. So much so that she scarcely slept a wink all night.

In the morning, as soon as it was acceptable, she rang Vanderschorn at the offices of *Virtuoso*. He agreed to see her when she made it clear she didn't expect him to take her to lunch.

'You remember that Annette Rosenthal and Bayer

504

Gurnitz are on your list of singers you want to use in the series?'

'Certainly I remember,' he said, tugging at his bushy sideburns, 'it's my business to know which singers are in vogue. But at the moment they're both in Vienna, and neither is coming to London in the foreseeable—'

'I thought of going to Vienna . . .'

'No, no, it's not necessary to go after them. The cost—'

'It wouldn't cost you much,' she said coaxingly. 'I'd pay my own expenses.'

'Really?'

'Yes, I have reasons of my own for wanting to go, as long as I can cover—'

'I'd only commission the photographs on the same terms as if they were taken in London,' Vanderschorn objected.

'I'll accept that. We have an agreement, then?'

He hesitated. 'It's none of my business, of course, but have you any idea how expensive it is in Vienna?'

'I'll manage,' she said.

When Drew rang she was able to tell him she had a photographic project in Vienna which would meet her main costs. 'But that's great!' he cried. 'You managed all this since last night?'

'Miracles by return of post,' she laughed.

About a week later he was able to ring her with definite dates. The touch-down in London had been rescheduled for the return trip. The President with his wife and entourage would fly to Paris on 30 May. Next day they would arrive in Vienna for a stay of four days. They would fly home by way of London but that needn't concern Drew or Corie because he'd managed to arrange to stay on for a few days 'to tie up loose ends' at the Embassy there. 'So we could have at least a week, Corie.'

'Then I'll meet you in Vienna,' she said with delight.

'How about Paris? I know the airlines will be busy but—'

'No, I'm driving, Drew.'

'Driving? To Vienna?'

'Yes, why not?'

'You're right, why not? OK, that's a date. I'll ring again to let you know which hotel I'll be in.'

'You won't be at the Embassy?'

'That's only for the big guns. Us minions get put into nearby hotels. All the better though − it'd be difficult for us to meet if I were having to check in and out of the Embassy.'

Corie had matters to attend to in the five weeks before she set out on the trip. Ever since she began in photography, she had accepted commissions or marketed her own work. She had made a more than adequate living. But now she knew more money would be needed. Her mother had pointed out that Lynette had been earning nothing for some months. Sad to say, Lynette's savings had never been large, nor had she ever had good advice about investment.

Opal had given up her job on her marriage. Monna's earnings were really little more than pocket money. So there had to be a reliable income, and this Corie ensured by taking her freelance work to the Wilkinson photographic agency at Bertie's suggestion.

'Of course, glad to have you on my books,' Ralph Wilkinson said. 'I saw your exhibition last year, some good stuff there. I have to warn you, though, that the income from reproduction rights isn't on the same scale as what you're probably getting in your studio. Still, once I've put the word around, you'll find there'll be a steady trickle of reproduction fees, and of course if your name comes before the public − if you win a photographic prize or something of that kind, the demand will go up.'

'I'm not likely to be in the public eye,' she sighed.

In that she was wrong, for events were shaping up on the Continent that were to rivet attention there.

She went to see Lynette a couple of times. She found her sister calm, quiet, but not by any means tranquillised as Monna had suggested.

'What gave you that idea?' Dr Vantoni asked in some indignation when she mentioned it. 'Your sister doesn't need tranquillisers, quite the reverse. She needs to be encouraged to come out of her retreat, to face the world again.'

'And will she?' Corie asked, her heart aching for her.

'I think she will. The problem is that the only world she knows is the theatre.'

'That was true of all of us. We're the children of theatrical parents, we were brought up to the idea that the only possible career was in the theatre.'

'Yet you and Mrs Davis escaped.'

'Well you see, Pal didn't have any talent and I lacked ambition. Lynette was the only one of us to have them both.'

'There lies the trap,' sighed Dr Vantoni, her plump face creasing in concern. 'For Lynette, her life is bound up in the theatre. Yet now she knows she doesn't belong there. I thought perhaps if I reverted to calling her by her real name it might make her feel she had an existence outside of it. But she won't let me call her Beryl – Beryl Duggan, she says, was a nobody, she only began to exist when she became Lynette Lee, and it's as Lynette Lee that she has to go on.'

'At least she knows she does have to go on,' Corie murmured. 'There was a time when I was afraid she would just . . . let go.'

'That at least is over,' the doctor reassured her. 'And she doesn't feel the need to hide any more. She knows she has to go back into the world – but which world? The world of her mother, or some other that she can't yet imagine?'

'Does she ever mention Sasha?'

An angry shrug. 'I think he no longer has any hold on her. Thank heaven, for he did her great harm.'

'We none of us were much good for her,' Corie said.

'Don't reproach yourself. Without you she would have had no chance at all.'

'Well,' said Corie, rising to her feet and holding out her hand, 'I'm off to Austria on Monday. I've told her I won't be visiting her for a week or so.'

'Don't worry. Mr Tranton is a loyal visitor.'

'So I gather. Dr Vantoni, do you think—?'

'Hush,' said the doctor. 'One thing at a time.'

Corie set out on Monday 29 May. With the help of a travel agency she'd booked on the ferry and engaged a place for her mobile caravan in a camping site on the outskirts of Vienna. She'd made reservations for overnight stays at Metz and at Augsburg: since it was early in the tourist season, she had no problems.

She had traveller's cheques and photographic supplies. Because she'd been warned that Vienna was formal and conservative, she packed her most glamorous clothes – well-tailored trousers, shirts of cambric, silk and satin, a lightweight coat from Burberry's, and a skirt or two for fear trousered women were frowned upon.

The sky was blue, the weather was warm for late May, the route she chose kept her away from motorways. She drove along with a light heart, stopped to buy bread and pâté when she felt like it, made coffee or tea on the little stove in the caravan, and slept like a top all night. Coming into Vienna on the appointed day, she stopped to buy a street map, then orienteered her way to the camping site where she installed herself with the help of an English-speaking and efficient manageress.

Vienna!

In fact, it did seem romantic. The camping site was on a side road on the way to Grinzing, among wooded hills on whose slopes church towers reached up among clouds that had gathered since early morning. When Corie went in search of lunch at one of the inns in the village, she found a group of musicians practising for the evening's fun. There was an accordian, a violin, a guitar: they played waltzes and *Ländler*. She was almost sorry to have to leave. Even in the phone box in the inn's entrance, she could hear the lilt of the music.

Drew's hotel was the Steiermark, on Vienna's main street, the Ring. When she asked to be put through to Herr Richter she was told he was not in the hotel but had left a message: 'Sacher's at nine.'

'Where is Sacher's, please?' she asked the receptionist.

'Where are you now, Fräulein?'

'I'm speaking from Grinzing.'

'*Doch* . . . The best thing is to come to the Ring and find the Opera House. The Opera House is a very large building in brown stone with many statues—'

'Yes, I've seen photographs and in fact . . .' She stopped herself from offering a long and unnecessary explanation. 'Sacher's is close?'

'Ask anyone, Fräulein. It is a very famous café.'

She drove into the city in the camper, parked in a public parking lot, locked up, put on her Burberry against the now quite steady rain, shouldered her camera bag, and set out for the Opera House. Annette Rosenthal, the soprano, was at the theatre, expecting her.

'Mr Vanderschorn tells me you will take very good portraits of me. Please, come in, sit down. Hang up your coat to dry. What weather, eh? For Mr Khrushchev yesterday, Vienna has sunshine. Today, for the American President, we have rain. Would you like tea? Coffee?'

'No, thank you, I lunched rather late.' She was glancing around the dressing-room with interest. This was a much more comfortable room than anything she'd ever seen backstage in England. She remarked on it, Fräulein Rosenthal began on a list of complaints about opera-house dressing-rooms throughout the world, and before long they were on easy terms.

They drew up a schedule of photo-opportunities. Fräulein Rosenthal would be singing in *The Magic Flute* this evening, but it was forbidden to take photographs during a performance. However, some shots could be taken in the dressing-room or in other backstage areas. The following evening she would be in Hallstatt giving a recital. In between she would have a voice lesson, a costume fitting for *Così Fan Tutte*, attend the opening of a charity fair, and have lunch with a conductor from Milan.

It was the same with Bayer Gurnitz, except that to a busy schedule he added sessions at the gym. 'I sing *Siegfried* soon. You know *Siegfried*? It needs a lot of strength.'

'Could I photograph you in the gym?' Corie asked eagerly.

'What? Covered in sweat? This isn't very glamorous!' But he was laughing. 'Please photograph when I am lifting five hundred kilos, *ja*?'

Somehow the sessions must be fitted into the singers' busy life. But already she could feel ideas flashing about in her head. Of course she must take 'glamour shots' of the opera stars, that was absolutely understood. But there was plenty of scope for character studies, and the building itself was fascinating – old, rather pompous, full of corners where chorus-singers and stage-hands were sitting about waiting to be needed, playing cards, knitting, writing letters. She could hear vocal practice, a voice running up and down scales. The lighting engineer was bent over a faulty junction. Her camera found plenty of targets.

The opera was in progress as she left. From behind her she could hear the attendants of the wicked Queen of the Night scheming to capture the hero. It was an enchanting sound, making her smile with delight as she went out. Not exactly a Strauss waltz, but just as magically Viennese.

She had no trouble finding Sacher's. Drew was sheltering under its canopy as she walked up. Without a word she raised her face for his kiss.

A long moment later they surveyed each other. 'Well, you look gorgeous,' he said, 'even in a raincoat.'

'And you look about ten pounds thinner!'

'Oh, yeah, working on the President's staff is no meal ticket. Which brings me to the point – I'm starved.'

Their table was awaiting them. Corie looked at the menu and then at Drew for help.

'We could start with the asparagus – is that OK? Then we could have blue trout – if you would like that? And after that—'

'I leave it to you, darling.' It crossed her mind how different this was from having a meal with Ingram, who seemed to take it for granted he knew exactly what you wanted.

When at last the food and the wine had been ordered, they sat back to study each other again. She truly thought he was thinner. The bones of his angular features were more prominent, his grey eyes seemed deeper in his head. But he was smiling, and his smile lit up his entire face.

'I'm so glad to see you,' said Drew, 'I can't begin to tell you!'

'Don't pretend – you've been too busy to think about me.'

He took it more seriously than she intended. 'That's not true, Corie. I've thought about you with one part of my mind almost all the time. Even when I'm listening to some tedious congressman making a speech in Michigan, somewhere or other a voice is saying, "I wonder what Corie's doing".'

'Corie hasn't been doing much except worrying about her family, which isn't the least bit interesting. Tell me about Paris.'

'Oh, gee, yes – Paris? General de Gaulle is twice as tall as you imagine him to be and just as grand. Guess what he said when the President stepped off the plane? "I hope you have had a good aerial voyage".'

'You're joking!'

'No, that's the kind of English he speaks – if he speaks it at all. He doesn't like the English – nor the Americans, if it comes to that. I think he was really miffed because the crowds only wanted Jackie.'

'Jackie? Mrs Kennedy?'

'Sure, they went wild over her. The only criticism we heard from the press boys was that her clothes were designed in New York, not in Paris.'

'What did she wear?'

'You can see for yourself. I bought the Paris papers before I caught the plane at midnight last night.'

'Have you got them with you?'

'No, they're at my hotel.'

Their eyes met. But neither followed up the thought for the moment. Instead Corie asked about the talks which had taken place that day. Drew shook his head. 'That's under wraps, Corie. Premier Khrushchev had things he wanted to put to the President and the President had things he wanted to put to Khrushchev. We had a hard time with the press corps this afternoon – they're reading an awful lot into how the pair of them looked as they said goodbye.'

'Do you have to go back to the Embassy?'

'I'm off-duty until tomorrow morning. There's a group of women journalists who want to talk about Jackie – one of her secretaries is to answer questions but she doesn't speak German, so I have to interpret.'

The meal was ending. The waiter inquired if they would like dessert, tried to tempt them with the famous *Torte*, looked sad when they elected to have only coffee. When at last they left the restaurant, the ornate street lamps were alight, haloed by moisture, and the audiences emerging from the theatres and concert halls were desperately trying to hail cabs.

'It looks pretty hopeless. Shall we walk?'

She nodded.

It was chilly as well as wet. He helped her into the Burberry, put an arm around her to keep her warm. She didn't ask where they were going, nor did she check her step when they came to the big glass doors of the Hotel Steiermark.

As Drew took his key from the desk-clerk he asked for a bottle of Tokay to be sent up to his room. Side by side they crossed the carpeted hall, went up in the panelled lift.

His room looked down on a paved courtyard with tubs of flowers softly lit by an old lantern. Corie hung her wet coat over a chairback, went into the bathroom to dry her hair. When she came back, the waiter was setting down a tray with wine-glasses and the Tokay.

'*Das geht*,' Drew said, waving him away as he began to open the bottle. '*Wir werden selbst einschenken.*' The waiter bowed in acknowledgement and went out.

As the door closed behind him, Drew turned to Corie.

In a movement as free and light as a bird's, she was in his arms.

She felt his shuddering breath. Her own heart was thudding like a drum. They gave each other a thousand little kisses, quick, darting, to taste the savour of lips and skin. His fingers combed through her hair, he grasped strands to pull her closer.

Then there was demand and delay. Troublesome clothes were shed, they twined into each other, fell on the bed, wrapped their arms around shoulders and spine, and lost themselves in the first eager moments.

Her body turned and yielded under his. His murmurs of passion were a chorus of joy in her ears. Her breathing seemed to be suspended, her being's whole design concentrated on the welcoming of this invasion. She had no thoughts, no purposes, no wishes except to be at one with him.

When the moment came she heard herself cry out. It was ice and fire, desire and fulfilment, longing and love. The world went away, there was nothing but this golden haven.

Her voice was a mere rustle of sound. 'My darling . . .'

'Corie, Corie . . .'

They lay in each other's arms, heads close, lips almost touching lips, speaking in the faintest of tones, knowing each other's meaning without the need of words. A haze of gratitude and contentment enfolded them. Their universe was each other.

When at length they returned to their separate bodies, Drew pulled himself up on his elbow to regard her.

'When I think of what I missed in January . . . !'

A gurgle of laughter welled up. 'What if the phone rang now?'

'God forbid!' He dragged himself across the room entangled in a sheet, took the phone off the hook. He saw the wine in its silver container. 'Sweetheart I don't think we ought to waste this. How about a toast?' He picked up the bottle, examined the label. 'Smorodni,' he reported. '*Vierter Putt* – it'll make you drunk.'

'I'm drunk already,' she sighed in great contentment.

'Here we go.' He came back to her, watched her struggle up against the pillows. 'Here's to you, Corie Duggan.'

'Here's to us, Drew Richter.'

He sat on the edge of the bed, sipping. 'Not bad. Never tried it before. I ordered it because it's a favourite thing here, I gather.'

'No wonder.' The golden wine seemed to glide down her throat, leaving a piquancy to tease her.

'Corie . . . I've never asked you if you've other men in your life. I've never had the right.' He was looking down at the bedspread. She saw the strong profile, the straight nose, the long, hard jaw.

'Go on, Drew.' She could see that words were hard for him to find.

'We never made any promises to each other. I couldn't be certain, even for myself, if promises were worth making. But now . . .'

'Yes?'

'Could we say we belong? Just to each other? Because we can't be together all the time, and I need to know . . .'

'From now on, Drew.'

'You promise?'

'With all my heart.'

'I do too, Corie. I've played around – I don't want to lie to you, there have been others. But not like this, angel, not like this.'

'I say the same, Drew. All the rest seem such foolishness now that . . .'

'Now we've really found each other.'

'That's it.'

They finished the wine in little sips, sometimes drinking from each other's glass, talking of the past, allowing themselves a little regret for times when they might have learned the treasured lesson of this hour. 'But perhaps in a way it made us understand what we've found,' she said in fond mitigation. 'Like waiting to open a birthday present.'

'Or saving up for the trip to Hawaii.'

'Hawaii . . . That's supposed to be an earthly paradise.'

'Who cares about Hawaii when we've got Vienna?'

She gave him her empty glass, he took it with his own to the table. When he returned to her waiting arms they made love again, this time slowly, without haste, learning the ways of each other in a long, languorous exploration that reached its triumphant end in a careering course to a total loss of self.

They slept then, Corie sheltered in his arms, her hands holding his close against her breast. She could feel his breath warm against her neck as she slipped into dreams.

They were roused by the mundane sound of the morning paper delivered outside the door. Drew said drowsily, '*Wer da?*' then grunted as he sat up to look at the bedside clock. 'Five-thirty a.m., for God's sake!'

'When are you supposed to report at the Embassy?'

'Around eight, unless I'm summoned earlier.'

'Drew, you'd better put that phone back!'

'Oh, yeah, maybe they've been trying to ring me all night, huh?'

'Not really?'

'No, they'd have asked the desk to contact me if they'd really wanted me. Well, good morning, *meines Herzes Schöne*.'

'What does that mean?'

'The beauty of my heart.'

'Oh, Drew,' she murmured in protest. 'I'm no beauty.'

'Beauty is in the eye of the beholder and this beholder tells you you're something else. One of the things that's so special about you is that you don't *think* you're special.'

'You're only saying that so that I'll say you're special too,' she teased.

'So I am. I'm the man you're promised to.'

'What is this? Some deeply laid plot to make me blush and fall into your arms.'

'I hope it's going to work!'

As he pulled her up against him she was laughing. Their lovemaking in the soft light of the Viennese morning was playful, full of shared amusement until the moment when the only emotion was joy. When at last they thought about time and the outside world, it was going on for seven. 'Shouldn't you be getting ready to go and help with the German ladies' press corps?' she asked with regret.

'Oh, let someone else explain Mrs Kennedy's plans to refurbish the White House! I'd rather stay here.'

'That's all very well for you, but I have an Austrian baritone waiting for me in the gym.'

'Where? In the gym? Are you kidding?' Now Drew was wide awake and paying attention.

'He's in training to sing Wagner.'

'Poor guy. Well, if we must, we must. And to tell the truth, I'm starving.'

'Me too.'

'I thought you were supposed to lose your appetite when you're in love?'

'It's one of those myths,' she said. 'What do you get for breakfast in a Viennese hotel?'

It turned out to be a fine selection of rolls and croissants, a pot of splendid Viennese coffee accompanied by a jug of rich cream, and a silver basket of fruit. Drew bathed and shaved while Corie ate and drank. When he emerged, looking somehow unfamiliar in his day-time self, she dashed into the bathroom. She scarcely had time to appreciate the fine shower gel, the scented soap.

'Pour me another cup of coffee, darling,' she called as she cleaned her teeth with Drew's toothpaste spread on a finger. 'I have to collect my transport and drive to Neustift — where is Neustift?'

'I'll put you on your way. I'll have to get a cab to the Embassy so I'll drop you off en route.'

When they got outside the cab was waiting. 'Which hotel?' Drew asked her.

'It's the parking place in the Herbergerstrasse.'

'It's what?'

'In Herbergerstrasse — isn't that how you pronounce it?'

'Herbergerstrasse,' said the cab-driver, and set the car in motion.

When they reached it Drew got out beside her. 'But where's the hotel?'

'I haven't got one. I'm camping in a place near Grinzing.'

'What?'

'Come on, I'll show you.' They threaded their way through cars already parked by morning arrivals. At the mobile caravan Corie got out her keys, opened up, and said with an air, 'Welcome to my humble home.'

'You don't mean you're *living* in this?'

'Yes I am. Very handy for doing photographic work so that I can tell what I've got on the film.'

'Dear heaven!'

'Don't you like it?'

'I think it's swell! But I don't know any other woman in the world who'd come to Vienna for a meeting with her lover in a *mobile caravan*!'

'My mother says I've got no dignity,' she admitted.

'What you've got is style,' he said in admiration, and hugged her. And then, as he let her go, 'Besides, you won't be spending much time in this, will you?'

'Not at nights, no,' she agreed.

'Oh, Corie,' Drew said, 'I wish we could turn around this minute and go back to the hotel . . .'

'Later.'

'Yeah, later. Look, I think I'll be there around six-ish. I'll leave word at the desk that you're to be given my key. OK?'

'OK, darling. Now, how do I get to Neustift?'

'Where's your map?' He traced the route for her, they kissed, then Drew sprinted off to the cab whose driver was growing impatient.

The rest of the day went well. So did all those that followed. To Corie everything seemed bathed in a golden glow. Yet the glow began to fade as their week together neared its end.

On Saturday evening Corie was the first at the hotel. Drew was late. When he arrived about eight, she was in a state of alarm immediately set at rest by the grin with which he greeted her.

'Guess what?'

'Tell me.'

'I've volunteered to stay on in Vienna for a couple of months.'

'Drew!'

'Great, isn't it? I'll have to travel about a bit – I've got jobs to do for the Boss. But every week or so I ought to be able to get to London.'

'That's wonderful, that's marvellous! Oh, if you knew how I've been dreading tomorrow and the distance that was going to come between us . . .'

'Me too, honey, me too. So when they said. "Who'd like to hang around this burg and go visiting some folk for the President", I jumped at it.'

They sat down on the edge of the bed, arms about each other. She laid her cheek against his. 'So you'll be staying on when I drive away tomorrow . . .' The image conjured up made her heart contract. 'I wish I didn't have to go, darling.'

'I know, I feel the same. If only you could stay too – there's a guy in the Commercial Department who's just gone home to Vermont on leave and I'm taking over his apartment. Just think, Corie . . . A place of our own . . .'

'Just a minute,' she said, giving her head a little shake to try to clear it. 'Let me think.'

'Are you thinking you could stay on too?' he asked, without really hoping for an answering yes.

'We-ell . . . It might be possible . . . You see, I do absolutely have to get back, to deliver the pix of the opera stars to Vanderschorn . . . But once that's done, you know . . . I don't see why I couldn't come back.'

'You could?' He dragged her to her feet and swung her around. 'Corie, that would be great!' Then he sobered. 'But what about other work? You were saying the other day . . . some portraits for an actress . . .'

'Yes, but then I could do those on Wednesday. I was

going to drive home, arriving Tuesday night, and my first bookings are for Wednesday. But you know, the aeroplane's a great invention, darling. I could fly over Tuesday evening, do a day's work, send Vanderschorn's pix by messenger, tidy up any loose ends, and fly back Wednesday night.'

'So you could. It'd mean a busy couple of days, though.'

'So what? I've worked harder than that before now – doing commercial work in the Midlands, driving home to London, setting out again next day for Southampton . . .' Her mind was busy on the scheme. 'I could fly home every couple of weeks – I'd get Bertie to make bookings for specific days if the client insisted on having me do the pix personally. Then I'd spend a day taking the pix and leave Bertie to do the processing.'

'D'you think it would work?'

'I'll make it work.' She paused. 'There's only one problem.'

'Your sister?' Drew had listened to her talk about Lynette's state of health. He knew how deeply concerned she was. He made no attempt now to persuade her one way or the other, and she was deeply grateful for his reticence.

'Let me try it out,' she said. 'I'll fly over earlier on Tuesday, go down to Sussex to see Lynette, and after that I'll have some idea whether it would be right to be so far away from her.'

On Sunday they went together to look at the flat being lent to them. It was in a big, rather formidable building not far from Mariahilferstrasse, one of the main shopping streets. Inside, though, it was charming – high ceilings, polished wooden floors, tall windows opening on to a narrow balcony with the inevitable pots of geraniums. As they said goodbye to the caretaker, Corie knew in her heart she would regret it for ever if she couldn't have the joy of living here with Drew.

Lynette was pleased to see her, yet there was no especial fervour in her welcome. She talked about herself, her relationship with Dr Vantoni and with other patients; she was only marginally interested to hear about Vienna. When

Corie asked the doctor's advice, she heard what she'd half-expected.

'I think you must realise that at the moment the most important person in Lynette's life is myself,' Dr Vantoni said, with a smile and a nod of her silvery head. 'That is not conceit on my part. This state is called "transference" – the patient looks upon the doctor, to whom she's confided herself, as a mother- or father-figure.'

'So at the moment I'm not by any means necessary to my sister.'

'Not at the moment, no. She loves you still, but she knows that you are not the one who must help her.'

'I see. But all the same . . . if anything should go wrong . . .'

'Nothing will go wrong. And in any case, you leave me your telephone number, no? I can ring you if there is a crisis. But I don't think that will happen.'

Opal, when consulted, said the same. 'She likes to see me, but I never get the impression she's exactly living for my visits. Don't worry about it, Corie. Go back to Vienna.'

'What about Monna?'

'What about her? Just drop her a line saying you're staying on in Vienna. Good lord, Corie, she's not an invalid or a doddering old lady – she's perfectly capable of living on her own in the way she used—'

'But she doesn't get to see Lynette.'

'Whose fault is that?' her sister demanded in a cool tone. 'If she's lonely now, who's to blame? Certainly not you. No, no, big sister, off you go to the Blue Danube and all that.'

Bertie was equally encouraging. 'I can manage the studio, never fear, and any clients that want you special, well, all right, I'll book 'em for whatever day you say, and you ought to be able to deal with the lot in one fell swoop.'

'I feel I'm always asking you to shoulder—'

'Gerraway with you! I get paid for it, don't I? And tell the truth, I love it! Never worked in such a posh area before I came here, it's a treat.'

Corie took a folio of work to her agent. 'I'm going to be

staying in Vienna for the summer,' she said. 'This is what I've done over the past week — there're character studies, Vienna's everyday people, a few architectural shots. If you can sell any of them I'd be grateful.'

'Not bad, not bad,' mused Ralph Wilkinson as he turned over the small prints she'd made in her caravan-studio. 'Can I have enlargements?'

'My assistant is going to do them. He'll send them to you in a day or two.'

'Fair enough. I think I could dispose of a few to holiday firms — for their brochures, you know. I'll tell you something you could do — am I right in thinking there's a famous fairground in Vienna?'

'The Prater, yes.'

'Thought so, I remember it from the Harry Lime film. Do me some shots of the Prater. There's a new magazine starting up, for people in the fairground and amusement-park industry. You might do well there.'

They discussed projects. He asked her to ring him now and again. 'Openings occur, you know. It pays to be in touch.'

She was heartened by the conversation because the air fares were going to be a consideration and there was always the nagging anxiety about payment for Lynette's treatment. But she felt she was doing all she could. She refused to feel guilty because she wanted to be with Drew while she had the chance.

She went to see her mother late on Wednesday afternoon. Opal had suggested that she should write, but she felt that would be cowardly. When Monna opened the door to her, she was glad she hadn't shirked the duty. She was looking bored and frustrated. Even the flamboyance of her clothes seemed muted. Instead of the rich colours and heavy jewellery she usually wore, she was clad in a green print dress which had seen better days.

'You got back last night, did you?' she asked, thinking the original plan was still in being. 'You might at least have dropped in *before* you went to the studio this morning.'

'I flew back yesterday, Monna. I'm going back this evening.'

'Going back? To Vienna?' Her mother was startled. 'What on earth for?'

'Because I want to.' Corie had no wish to make long explanations which would be greeted in any case with disapproval. 'I just dropped in to let you know, and to give you a telephone number so you can reach me in case of emergency.' She handed over a slip of paper.

Her mother looked at the long-distance number. 'At least you have a telephone. I take it you've given up living in that disgusting van like a gypsy?'

'Well yes, I have, but that's merely accidental. I'll be staying in a flat for the rest of the summer.'

Monna's eyes narrowed. For a moment Corie could see the question trembling on her lips: Who with? But by now her mother had learned to let well enough alone where her eldest daughter was concerned. One last prick she couldn't resist. 'So much for your concern about Lynette,' she said. 'You won't be seeing her for months, it seems . . .'

'Yes I shall. I'll fly over from time to time.'

'You're keeping on your flat, I hope. Because if you're thinking of coming here for an overnight stay, you may as well know I've decided to let the upstairs rooms.'

It was Corie's turn to be surprised. 'What a good idea! When did you think of that?'

'A few days ago, if you must know. I tried to get Dr Vantoni to let me visit my poor little girl and she said no for the hundredth time and I just felt, well, if Lynette's turning her back on me, why should I sit there in her empty room grieving for her? So I decided to let the room, and the others too, and I've put an advertisement in the papers, and you can be sure there will be dozens of theatre people who'll be only too glad of a decent place to stay with someone who shares their devotion to the profession.'

This long speech made even Monna breathless. Corie seized the chance to say, 'Good for you! Let me know how it goes. 'Bye, I must rush to the airport.' And with a brief kiss on the cheek, she made her escape.

Life in Vienna was all she hoped it would be. Some days Drew had to drive out of town, some days he spent at a desk lent to him in the Embassy. She had a feeling he was doing personal intelligence work for President Kennedy, but she had the sense never to ask. Once or twice he had visitors. One visitor brought a note from his cousin Werner in East Berlin which seemed to trouble him.

'Damn fool,' he muttered to himself. 'It's great that he's all for freedom, but does he have to bring the spotlight on himself?'

'What's been happening?' Corie asked.

'Oh, the usual kind of thing – the students have been campaigning to be allowed to travel—'

'He's still a student?' There had been talk of his cousin while she was in New York some time ago, but by now she felt he must have finished his studies.

'He's doing post-graduate work. "Historical Perspectives on the Influences of Commerce" or something equally gripping. Some colleague of his wanted to go to Paris to do some research but the authorities refused a permit. So they took to the streets with banners.' He waved the note. 'The way he writes about it, it was all great fun, but Josef – that's the guy who just left – he says they nearly ended up in jail. Josef got out because he knew his name was on a blacklist.'

'That could be bad, from what I've heard.'

'You don't know the half of it . . .' He dropped a kiss on her brow. 'Never mind, Werner's been in trouble and got out of it before now.' And nothing more was said on the subject.

With Drew's help Corie had rented space in a studio over a camera shop. When he was away she spent time there, developing, printing and enlarging the shots she took in and around Vienna. The Wilkinson Agency placed several within days of receiving them, especially those of the Prater Amusement Park with its shrieking children on the switchback and its hidden lovers on the Ferris wheel.

One day in August she got home after long hours of photography in the grounds of Schönbrunn. She was very hot, very thirsty, very dusty, and very tired. She had not seen a newspaper nor heard a radio all day and, moreover, they would have meant nothing to her if she had because she never got past learning a few polite words in German.

She was in the bath, revelling in the soothing charms of hot water. She heard the door of the flat close after Drew's entrance. Instead of going into the living-room as he usually did, he went into the bedroom. She could hear him opening and closing drawers in a busy, rapid manner.

'Drew?' she called. 'What's going on?'

'I'm packing.'

She clambered out of the bath, threw on a bath-robe, and hurried barefoot into the bedroom.

'You're going home?' she asked in dismay.

'I'm going to Berlin.'

'What on earth for?' His grim expression alarmed her.

'The East Germans have put up a wall between themselves and the West. It's so weird the President has sent word I'm to go there and send him a personal report.' He paused with his hands full of articles for his travel bag. 'I'm sorry, angel, but I have to hit the road at once.'

'Wait,' said Corie, 'I'm coming with you.'

Chapter Twenty-six

West Berlin was in turmoil. And with good reason.

On the morning of 13 August 1961, the citizens had arisen to find that the Communists in the Eastern sector of the divided city were setting up a wall. Some Berliners had become aware of activity in the very early hours – the trundle of earth-moving equipment, of heavy lorries, the setting up of lights. A few had got out of bed to see what was going on. With perplexity they saw an army of workmen scurrying about.

Dawn comes early in August. Soon after first light the news was spreading. It was greeted with utter disbelief, a stunned amazement.

A wall? Around the city?

People rushed to look. It was only too true. Posts had been driven into the ground, barbed wire had been strung between the posts, rolls of barbed wire rested against the first strands to make an impenetrable fence. West Berlin, a little island of democracy in Communist East Germany, was encircled.

Behind the barbed wire, heavy excavators were digging out trenches. Armed guards were stationed every few yards.

'What are you doing?' the West Berliners shouted. 'What's the idea?'

No reply.

Dazed disbelief gave way to anxiety. Officials from the mayor's office, from the headquarters of the troops stationed in the city – British, French, American – Embassy staff, functionaries from the Bonn government: they rushed to the scene, they sent requests for explanations, they went to the usual crossing points where Communist overseers were generally to be found.

At first, no answer to their queries could be obtained. The newspapers brought out special editions, radio and television flashed the news round the world. Still there was no response from the East German government.

At some time during the day came a prepared statement from Walter Ulbricht, Communist leader of East Germany. It observed that West Berlin contained many groups carrying out propaganda against East Germany, that a tremendous amount of smuggling and currency fraud went on across the frontier between the separated parts of the country, that West Berlin was the home of large numbers of spies from the United States and other so-called democracies, and so on through a long list of complaints.

Almost all of them were true: there were large numbers of spies in West Berlin, a lot of East German goods such as cameras and fine china were brought very cheaply in East Berlin and carried across to be sold at a profit in West Berlin. The East German statement concluded that, in order to save their citizens from such corruption, it had been necessary to put up a physical barrier.

Everyone at once understood the true reason. The Berlin Wall had been put up to keep its citizens inside the Eastern zone.

Since the war, Germany had been divided between two regimes, the Communist and the German Federal Republic. Berlin, once the capital of the whole country, was under occupation by the four armies which had won the war – the British, the French, the American and the Soviet. Unfortunately, Berlin was situated within the Communist, the Eastern half of the country.

One of the great ambitions of the East German Government was to have the whole of Berlin under its control. There had in fact been an attempt to achieve that by a blockade of the city in 1948.

Corie remembered it well: the Berlin Airlift. She'd just been in the early stages of her theatre career and had for a time longed to enlist in the Women's Royal Air Force to help load the planes. Monna had told her not to be absurd.

'By the time you enlist and get trained it'll all be over.' For once Monna was right – in May of the following year the blockade was lifted. The Communist plan had failed.

All the same, it stayed in Corie's mind, that long, quietly courageous battle to bring food, fuel and medical supplies to a beleaguered city. The aircrews by their stubborn refusal to give up had ensured that West Berlin remained a little outpost of democracy in the Eastern Zone of Germany. That was the big problem – Berlin, the former capital, was right inside the Communist Zone, holding out only because the Allied troops had headquarters there.

Now once again it was a target for diplomatic attack by the East Germans – or, as most people believed, the Russians. 'You have to hand it to the Russkies,' said a reporter at the bar of Corie's hotel, 'they're always thinking up some new gag!'

'But why have they done it?' Corie demanded, baffled.

The answer was supplied at once by another of the reporters at the bar. 'Because despite the fact we're always being told that East Germany is a workers' paradise, three and a quarter million people have got out of it one way or another since it was set up – that's why. Ulbricht can't afford to let any more people go—'

'No, because the people who leave are the best, you see – the skilled workmen, the scientists, the teachers, the artists—'

'The research students,' Corie prompted, thinking of Werner. But Werner hadn't been able to get out.

'You got it,' agreed the first speaker. He finished his drink, stretched, and yawned. 'Well, got to get out there again and see what they're doing . . .'

'But it's dark—'

'That doesn't faze 'em! They set up Klieg lights. You should see it – it's like something out of Dante's *Inferno*.'

'Would you let me come with you?' she asked. She had her camera bag with her; she was ready to go.

Drew had brought her to the Hotel Schwartzwald straight from Tempelhof Airport. It appeared to be a hangout of the foreign contingent in Berlin. 'I have to report in at the American Consulate,' he explained, 'they're expecting me. Maybe you'd like to freshen up and have a meal? I'll be back as soon as I can, or I'll call.'

She'd followed his suggestions, but now it was well past midnight and he still hadn't called or returned. She quite understood he was probably tied up with worried American officials wondering what on earth to report back to the State Department and President Kennedy.

Rather than sit kicking her heels, she wanted to be out looking at what was happening.

'Glad to have you along,' said her new acquaintance. He held out a hand. 'Hank Berzinski, of the *Chicago Record*. Which paper do you represent?' He had noticed her camera bag at once.

'*Europe Day*,' she said.

She'd telephoned their Brussels office as soon as she got to the hotel, to say she was on the spot in West Berlin. The night editor was only too delighted to hear it: like most newsmen he'd been caught completely on the hop by the events in this city of drama. They had a local office, scarcely more than a pied-à-terre, in Berlin. The staff consisted of two reporters and a tele-typist. They hired local cameramen as and when they needed them, but the senior correspondent would be delighted to buy anything she cared to offer. It was an arrangement that suited her – access to a darkroom to process her film, but no strings attached about where she should go or what she should do.

She went out with Hank Berzinski and a French reporter. The Hotel Schwartzwald was near the Tiergarten, within walking distance of a section of the newly erected wall. Before they reached it Corie could hear the activity – the crowd of spectators talking to each other and occasionally trying to enter into a shouted conversation with the workmen, the throb of lorry engines, the grinding and roaring of a concrete mixer.

Berzinski was right – it was like a scene out of hell. The eerie lighting, the figures moving about with shovels and picks like demons in an old painting tending a furnace, the coils of wire like sharp-scaled serpents . . .

And to add to the sense of horror was the silence from the men on the East German side. They seemed to mutter to each other in low tones, but said no word in reply to the shouts and jeers of the West Berliners. It was as if they were a group of convicted criminals working on a road gang: in fact they were convicted, held prisoner by their government, although it was they who were building their own prison.

Corie's cameras were seldom at rest. She soon used up all the film she had with her, though the light was very poor. For a while she went with the others from place to place – Oranienstrasse, Skalitzerstrasse, and finally the Brandenburger Tor.

Everywhere it was the same: barbed wire, fence posts, tall barricades of board, bricked-up windows, concrete blocks beginning to form thicker walls behind the temporary fortifications. On one side, the bewildered and angry citizens of West Berlin. On the other, the sullen workmen of the Communist regime and the armed guards – armed guards, she began to think, who were there to make sure the workmen built the wall as well as to prevent the West Berliners tearing it down.

At about two in the morning she went back to the hotel. Drew had just come home. 'I got your message,' he said as he opened the room door to her knock. 'Sorry I took so long – I got taken off on an inspection tour.'

'Me too.' She collapsed into the chair by the desk. 'I've shot every roll of film I had. I want to do more tomorrow as soon as it's light.'

Drew nodded. He looked gaunt and tired. 'It's gruesome isn't it? Hardly believable.'

She went to him and put her arms around him. 'It scared me, Drew . . .'

'I know.'

All the romantic glamour of Vienna was gone. The rose-coloured spectacles had been left behind there. In this city there was no golden glow, only the cold, steely light of the arc lamps; here there was no lilting waltz played on a zither, only the dull throb of brutal machines.

Yet they had each other. In a hostile world they could be safe in each other's arms for a time. That night they were very close to each other, not only in body but in spirit, taking comfort in their shared belief that the evil they had seen could not possibly survive for long.

They scarcely slept, and with the dawn they were both stirring. Drew ordered coffee and rolls brought to the room. At Corie's request he asked the waiter where she could buy a supply of film. As they ate and drank he was trying to trace the outline of the new wall on a street map. Corie was putting the exposed film in an envelope to drop into the office of *Europe Day* for processing. Everything was businesslike – almost as if the spiritual unity of the night must be put behind them.

'Corie, I need a series of good shots of the Wall to take to the President with my report,' said Drew as they got ready to go out. 'Will you let me have a set of whatever you take?'

'Of course,' she said. But her heart sank at his words. He'd said, 'To take to the President' – it meant he'd be going back to Washington from Berlin.

They spent all day surveying the perimeter of the new barricade, visiting again in daylight the scenes they'd already witnessed in the night, going by taxi to new sites. The view didn't improve by light of day. Police were on duty on the Western side to prevent foolish actions, but the groups of stunned citizens seemed even more pathetic.

Some people were in tears, making protests and explanations to those next to them in the crowd. Drew translated for Corie: 'She says her son is over there – they won't let her go through to see him. This man says his sister was to be married on Sunday but the bridegroom is on the other side . . .'

When they got to the Western boundary between West Berlin and East Germany they found not a wall but a vast expanse of tangled barbed wire. Beyond the wire a bulldozer was levelling out a space about as wide as a football pitch. Beyond that again, a tall spidery construction was going up.

'What on earth is *that*?' Corie asked.

'A watchtower.'

'Oh, Drew!'

She put her viewfinder up to her eye to get a shot of the half-constructed tower. As she did so she saw a flicker of movement. At once she dropped her gaze, to focus on it.

A young man in overalls had thrown down his spade. He was running across the newly-cleared space.

A shout rang out from below the watchtower. '*Halt!*'

The youngster paid no heed. He was running fast in his heavy boots, like a rugby player out of the pack.

The guard on the other side shouted again, a longer phrase, startled, angry.

'What's he saying?' Corie asked, her eye still on the running man, her camera clicking.

'He says "Halt or I fire"!'

'But he wouldn't – not an unarmed man—' She paused, for a moment distracted by his words.

Her protest was cut off by the rifle shot.

She put her finger on the camera mechanism and pressed. Frame after frame. The workman running. Swerving from side to side. Diving in among the barbed wire. Stooping low, scuttling sideways. Now she could make out his features – fresh, smooth-skinned, fair hair damp with sweat. Very young, a faint fuzz on his chin because he hadn't shaved this morning. Dark blue eyes full of terror, full of determination.

More of the guards had taken aim. Other voices were shouting now – some from the soldiers ordering him to stop, some from the West Berliners urging him to safety.

'Run!' Drew was begging aloud. 'This way, this way! Keep low, for God's sake!'

As if the camera were a living part of her, Corie registered the scene. She saw the boy's navy-blue overalls catching in the barbed wire. She saw him tug himself free only to be caught again. She saw him claw at the wire with his hands, saw the blood welling out to cover them like crimson gloves.

He was ensnared. His dark blue eyes grew desperate. He stood almost helpless, the wire around his thighs, his arms threshing to release himself.

Corie saw his body jerk stiff. His arms flew out. Over his face came an expression of dismay, of disbelief.

Drew was shouting in German. 'Get down, get down!'

The boy fell to his knees on the wire, shielded his face with an arm as he tumbled sideways. A rose of red blood was blossoming on the blue of his work shirt.

'They've shot him!' It was a howl of rage from the crowd.

The boy got up, tried to thrust his way forward towards the wire fence which formed the final edge of the barrier. It was some thirty yards from him. He threw out his arms towards it in an agony of longing.

Another shot rang out. He toppled over on to the cruel coils of wire, lying along them on one side. His face was turned in pleading towards the West, towards the people who held out their hands to him, begging him to succeed, to come to freedom.

Corie's camera whirred, whirred. In the viewfinder she saw the boy, dying. His childlike dark blue eyes were still open, his gaze was fixed on her — it seemed as if he were staring straight into her face. His mouth gaped as he tried to draw in air. Bubbles of blood appeared on his lips.

Someone grasped at her arm. She was pulled aside. Angry words assailed her. An elderly man was protesting in a loud and tearful voice. Drew put himself between him and Corie, shielding her from his angry fist.

'What does he say?' she asked Drew.

'He says the boy needs a priest, not a photographer.'

For one second she lowered the camera. 'Tell him,' she said, 'I want the world to know what it's really like to die for freedom.'

And as Drew translated her words her camera was already back up to her eye.

The boy died. For a time he lay there, alone in the sea of wire. The crowd shouted, implored, raged. On the far side of the frontier the boy's fellow-workmen stood, staring, their features almost impossible to make out – but their bodies were stiff with horror and dismay. Uniformed figures scurried about, there was the gleam of gold braid as an officer appeared.

By and by a bulldozer began to grind towards the body. It pushed the barbed wire into a mountainous wave in front of it, so high that in a few yards the machine was hidden from view. Its progress could be measured by the moving crest of wire.

The West Berliners yelled and screamed – whether in protest or accusation Corie couldn't tell. At last the clumsy yellow vehicle had cleared enough space for the two soldiers it carried to get down near the dead boy. They glanced nervously at the crowd, then kept their heads averted. They were wearing heavy gauntlets, carried wire cutters.

Corie had reloaded. She focused on them. Her shutter clicked as they worked. They cut a rough square in the sea of wire, beckoned to the driver, and to the horror of the bystanders this dreadful funeral pyre was scooped up and borne away by the bulldozer.

And after that there was nothing – nothing but a bloodstain, a muddled heap of barbed wire, and people on either side of the divide staring at each other unspeaking.

Corie was shaking with reaction. Drew put his arm around her and, with his help, she made her way through the crowd. A hovering taxi came to them at Drew's signal.

'Where?' he asked her, holding her close. 'The hotel?'

'The offices of *Europe Day* – Gneisenaustrasse . . .'

It was then about nine in the morning. By midday, through the strange jungle telegraph that exists in the world of news-gathering, everyone knew that Corie Duggan had some extraordinary pictures of the attempted escape at the far side of the Havel. The telephone in the office of *Europe Day* never stopped ringing. The answer was always the same: 'Miss Duggan is in the darkroom and can't be disturbed.'

The darkroom belonged to a freelance journalist often employed by the paper. He and his assistant spoke no English, but it didn't matter – the chemicals, the dishes, the equipment, were all the same as those Corie used at home. They worked as a team. By the end of the afternoon they had a pile of full-plate pictures ready for examination.

The chief Berlin correspondent of *Europe Day* was a middle-aged man called Mollstret. He cleared everything off his desk with a sweep of his arm to allow her to spread out the photographs.

One after another she laid them down. The boy running. The boy caught up in the wire. The boy as the first bullet hit him, arms thrown wide, head back, eyes full of disbelief. The boy falling, his features blurred in the motion. The boy dying, mouth agape, hands outstretched towards the photographer.

Then – the bulldozer. The soldiers cutting the wire around him. The bed of tangled wire in mid-air as it was lifted, the boy's body dangling like a broken toy. A view of the bulldozer from the back, trundling away towards the Eastern Zone, with a limp arm just visible hanging from the front as if from the mouth of some prehistoric monster.

'*Du lieber Gott!*' breathed Mollstret. 'Fräulein Duggan, for this set of prints, I pay you any price you ask!' He took one of her hands in both of his. 'You have done a marvel.'

She shook her head. 'I don't want money. Take the prints. But I want everyone else to have them too – no charge.'

'Fräulein Duggan! You can't do that!'

'Why not? I couldn't make money out of the death of that boy.'

'But . . . but . . . Fräulein Duggan, you used facilities that I made available. You owe it to me to give me exclusive—'

She shuffled the pictures together in a heap and began to pick them up. 'I'm going out with these and I'm going to give them to every editor who—'

'Wait! Wait, Fräulein Duggan.' Mollstret had realised he couldn't get an exclusive, and understood her reasons. All the same, he wanted his paper to get *some* benefit from having helped her. He could at least let it be known that *Europe Day*, out of its sense of duty, was making the pictures available to all without charge and without a time embargo.

'You agree?' she said in a quiet, determined voice.

He looked into the weary hazel eyes and saw there was no alternative.

'Of course. You are right. This is a historic event. We must let everyone have the pictures.'

'Right. I leave it to you to get more copies done. I'm taking three or four sets to my hotel to give out.' She heaved her camera bag on to her shoulder. She was almost too tired to walk out.

At the hotel she was set upon at once by waiting pressmen. They shouted questions at her, demands for news of her photos.

Finally, to get their silent attention, she held her hands up in the air, holding aloft the envelope that held the pictures.

'I've made a set of eight prints,' she said. 'It shows the whole sequence of events. There are about four lots. Anyone can have them—'

Before she'd finished saying it, the envelope was snatched from her hands by those nearest. Those at the back let out a wail of protest.

'It's all right! It's all right!' she shouted, to make herself heard. 'Go to the office of *Europe Day* – they're making more sets now. Anyone can get a set just by going—'

Within ten seconds the hall of the Schwarztwald Hotel was clear. Those with copies were rushing to their newspaper offices, those without were scurrying to get a set.

The desk-clerk smiled wonderingly at Corie. 'Fräulein Duggan,' he said. 'I have messages for you.'

He took the room key from the niche, and with it six or

seven pieces of paper. One was from Drew saying he'd gone to the American Consulate to telephone an account of the escape attempt to the President's office. The rest, except one, were messages begging her to call this number or that.

The exception was a telegram. She tore it open. It was from Ingram Holstead. 'Highest offer for Wall pix. Ring me.'

If she hadn't been so tired, she would have laughed. No hesitations on account of their last parting, it seemed – everything must give way to the chance of a scoop.

'You wish to send a reply, Fräulein?' asked the desk-clerk.

'No. I won't bother,' She turned towards the lift, then changed her mind. 'On second thoughts, I will.'

He pushed a pad towards her. She wrote: 'No charge for pix, contact your Berlin man.'

That done, she went upstairs, threw her camera bag on the nearest chair, fell on the bed, and went straight to sleep.

She was awakened by being gently picked up and cradled in someone's arms. She opened her eyes. It was growing dark outside but the room was softly lit by a bedside lamp. Drew was smiling down at her.

'Well,' he said, 'you're famous.'

'Mmm?'

'The Berlin evening papers are out. Your pictures take up two pages. The headlines are about the boy – but part of the story is about you: Corie Duggan, who gave the pictures to the world.'

'Oh . . .'

'Have you been asleep long?'

'Mmm . . .' She tried to focus sleep-filled eyes on the bedside clock. 'Four hours, I think.'

'I rang, but I didn't get an answer. The desk told me they'd put several calls through but you weren't picking up the phone.'

She shook her head. 'I never heard it ring.'

As if in reply, the phone shrilled. Drew picked it up and handed it to her.

'Hello?'

'Corie? Is that you? Where the hell have you been?'

It was Ingram, sounding very angry.

'And good evening to you, Ingram.'

'What on earth did you mean by that absurd reply to my wire?'

'I meant what I said. The pix aren't for sale, they're free to anyone.'

'Don't talk nonsense. I'll give you any price you care to name for exclusive rights—'

'Ingram,' she interrupted, raising her voice so that he'd pay attention, 'Ingram, they're out on the street now in Berlin.'

'They're in print?' He sounded utterly incredulous.

'Yes.'

The phone was slammed down at the other end.

Corie gave the phone back to Drew. He replaced it. 'I gather you've thrown away a fortune,' he remarked.

'So it seems. By the way, I saved a set for you – in the camera bag. And a copy of everything else I've taken since we got here.'

He went to the chair, undid the zip, and took out a thick collection of prints held together by an elastic band. He stood looking through them in silence, shaking his head from time to time.

'Drew?'

'Yes?'

'What is it?' she asked. She could tell by the firm, sad line of his mouth that there was something he had to tell her.

He came back to sit on the edge of the bed, took one of her hands.

'I'm flying home on the next plane,' he said.

Chapter Twenty-seven

On the drive home, Corie was filled with sadness: seeing Drew off at Tempelhof, her lonesome flight to Vienna to retrieve the motor caravan, the long drive through northern Europe – these totally obliterated the memories of the happy time. On the roads she saw army trucks on the move; the Western Allies were so alarmed at what had happened in East Berlin that they were moving troops into the city and to the border areas. Surely there couldn't really be a threat of war?

When she reached London, she found everyone viewed events with much less alarm. There was much more interest in the weird new concrete fly-over bridges for traffic, or the audacious theft of Goya's *Duke of Wellington* portrait from the National Gallery.

Certainly her own family was thinking about more pleasant matters. Opal was pregnant, to her great joy. Monna was delighted with her new role as landlady: her boarders, it appeared, were well-bred and well-educated, so that she was able to regard their presence in the house as contributing to a sort of theatre *salon*.

But to Corie the best news of all was that Lynette was well enough to leave the clinic.

'I would like,' remarked Dr Vantoni in a private discussion , 'that your sister should after a while live on her own.'

'On her own? But she's never done that . . .'

'Exactly. Here is a grown woman who has had quite a big career with plenty of money, yet always she has been like a child, in someone else's house. But it's too soon to speak of living alone. When she leaves me, can she live with you again?'

'Of course!'

'Ah,' said the doctor, smiling, 'and when the time comes for her to leave, will you say "Of course!"?'

Corie hesitated. 'You mean I've been too protective towards her?'

'It has had to be so. To defend her from the circumstances brought about by the ambitions of her mother, you have been a shield. But now, not. She must fight her own battles, she must go out alone.'

Lynette came back to the Stamford Street flat looking cheerful yet anxious. 'Dr Vantoni explained it to me,' she said. 'I've spent the last year or so looking inward – in fact, ever since my career took a nosedive I've only been thinking of myself . . .'

'No, no—'

'Oh yes, that's how it's been, I know that now. Me, me, me – nobody else.'

'You thought about Sasha,' Corie said with a suppressed smile.

'Yes, but only because at the time I thought he was absolutely essential to me.'

'But now, not, as Dr Vantoni would say.'

'But now, not.' Lynette caught her sister's eye and they both chuckled. 'And the same goes for my stage career. That's over, and I'm going to make a fresh start.'

Corie didn't say, Doing what? One problem at a time. Lynette had first to learn to live in the outside world without wanting to hide from everyone in the darkness of a cinema.

As for Corie herself, she was very busy indeed. As Drew had said, she was famous. The photographs of the boy trying to escape through the wire would have been enough to make her notable in the newspaper world, but the fact that she had refused to keep the photographs exclusive, that she had refused money for them, made her something of a heroine.

Work flooded in. Certain famous people who had been indignant that she left an assistant in charge of her studio now changed their mind about cancelled appointments. Vanderschorn asked to buy any photographs concerning the Vienna Opera House at whatever fee she liked to name. *Europe Day* suddenly remembered that they'd tried to get in touch with her through Ingram Holstead with a specific project in mind which they would now like to finalise. *News Now* rang up, so did several American magazines.

There was a pile of correspondence awaiting her on her desk. Two were air letters from Drew, bearing only the message: 'Don't forget me!' To these she replied with the yet shorter message: 'Not likely!'

One letter over which she hesitated for a long time came from the London Embassy of the German Democratic Republic – in other words, from the government of East Germany. The Press Attaché, in a tone of reproach, begged to inform her that the youth she had photographed in no way deserved the sympathy poured out on him. His name, it seemed, was Hermann Belger, and he was a thief awaiting sentencing for a serious robbery. He was at the Wall as part of a work party from the remand prison, the Press Attaché assured her.

'My government wishes me to say that it is greatly distressed to see you associate your work with a misjudged campaign of abuse. We had always thought of you as a friend of democracy; your famous photographs of the dictator Batistá cravenly fleeing from Cuba seemed to show that you were on the side of the people's revolution against decadent capitalist regimes.

'My government sincerely wishes to give you the opportunity to view life in the German Democratic Republic at close quarters. You would soon see that our democracy offers freedom, equality, and justice for all. We invite you to tour our country at any time convenient to yourself, to correct any wrong impression brought about by the unfortunate episode of 16 August.'

She wasn't in the least tempted to accept. But she felt she ought to reply. She made several attempts but each time politeness was driven away as she remembered the dying boy. In the end she decided to ignore the letter.

Helen Holstead rang from upstate New York. 'I hear my husband's cross with you again,' she remarked with amusement in her voice.

'I'm afraid so.'

'You'll never be a good businesswoman, Corie, if you give away the copyright of a photographic scoop.'

'You're right.'

'Drew showed me the pix—'

'You've seen him?'

'Sure. Couple of days after he'd reported to Jack, I had him here — I wanted to know whether there was going to be anyone else firing guns, besides that sentry.'

'What does he think?'

'It was touch and go, I gather. The President has been pretty hard-nosed about it. He got the impression Khrushchev thought he was just a rich man's son playing at politics, so he's going to show him he's wrong — that's the feeling at the moment. So maybe you'll be seeing Drew again soon — Jack's thinking of sending him on a fact-finding mission.'

'Oh,' breathed Corie, 'that would be lovely.'

'Poor girl, you do sound lovelorn,' teased Helen. 'If it's any consolation, Drew's mind isn't on his job at the moment.'

'How is he, Helen?'

'Busy. All the President's personal staff are whizzing about like fireworks. You see, if things get worse over there, Jack's got to convince Congress to get tough with the East Germans, so he's sending out his personal ambassador . . . Say, you don't want to hear about American politics! That's not why I rang. I wanted to tell you I ordered that foolish husband of mine to stop being spiteful and make use of your talents . . .'

'That wasn't necessary, Helen.'

Helen laughed. 'Not from your side, maybe, but from his. When I talked to him on the phone a couple of days ago, he was breathing fire about how you'd deprived him of a marvellous scoop from some crackbrained notion of decency, and how he's telling everybody you were crazy. He shouldn't behave like that. He's his own worst enemy, I often think.'

'He certainly lets his temper run away with him sometimes.'

'Tell me about it,' Helen said ironically. 'It's one of the reasons I choose to live apart from him − I just got bored with his tantrums. And yet . . .'

'And yet you can't stop taking an interest in everything he does,' Corie suggested as Helen hesitated. 'Especially his women friends − remember how you faced up to me when we met for the first time?'

'Oh, that . . . You know, Corie, he's not as young as he was; if he could just behave more like a normal man we could have quite a nice comfortable old age together . . .'

Corie was surprised. She'd always taken it for granted that Helen Holstead preferred to live her own kind of life − something of a power-behind-the-scenes in American politics, something of an influence in such things as museums and art collections. But of course her children were grown up now; perhaps loneliness was beginning to loom.

'Men!' Helen sighed. 'If only they cared as much about feelings as women do . . . But that's wishing for the moon, I know. So long, Corie. I'll be in touch again.'

In late October, William Tranton dropped in at Corie's studio. She was pleased to see him but could tell he had come for a special purpose. 'I've something to tell you,' he said, 'and it needs a bit of explanation.'

'About Lynette?'

'Yes, and Lynette knows all about it − but she wants me to break it to you.'

Corie led him to the little kitchen, where she'd been making afternoon tea for herself and her assistant. She'd thought at first that William was going to say he and Lynette were to be married − yet the remark about 'breaking it to her' hardly sounded as if it could be about that.

She busied herself pouring tea, opening a packet of biscuits, carrying a tray to Bertie in the darkroom. That done, she perched herself on the edge of the sink, while William sat on a chair she brought from the studio.

'You know this new programme I've been working on, "Background Story"?' he began.

'With Dennis Borderman, yes,' she agreed, surprised. She certainly hadn't expected him to talk about his work.

'Lynette tells me you didn't see the first one—'

'No, I had to be in Cardiff that evening. Lynette watched, though. She said it was awfully good. And the critics like it, I gather.'

'Yes, it seems to have hit some chord with everyone. Life's a bit hectic these days: it's nice to see a programme where other people admit things can go wrong but you can start again even so.'

'I suppose so.'

'Well . . .'

'What, William?'

'I've asked Lynette to go on the show.'

'*What!*'

William forged ahead despite her explosion of concern. 'And Lynette's said yes.'

'No, she mustn't!'

'We talked it over and she—'

'It would set her right back! She's been doing so well . . .'

'You shouldn't leap to the conclusion it would harm—'

'Of course it would! As I understand it, Borderman delves into your private life and—'

'Yes, he does, but not in any prurient way.'

'Just think how Lynette would crumple if—'

'I don't think she would.'

'I don't think it would be right to let her take the risk. I absolutely forbid it.'

There was a pause, a silence. And then William said in a very gentle voice, 'But you haven't the right to forbid it.

And in any case, Lynette has agreed.'

She felt herself go hot with embarrassment. Here she was, trying to rule her sister's life for her. She had no right to make rules, that was true, but nevertheless she had a right to be concerned.

'I'm sorry,' she said, 'I shouldn't have said that. But all the same I don't think it would be a good thing. I don't think Lynette is strong enough to come out and talk about her problems in public.'

'But that's for her to say, Corie.'

'Yes . . . Yes, I suppose it is, but she could be making a big mistake . . .'

'Dr Vantoni thinks not.'

'You've asked her?'

'Yes, before ever I spoke to Lynette about it.' He adjusted the side-pieces of his glasses as he always did when he was nervous. 'It seemed to me that Lynette's life is a good example of letting other people take control. That happens a lot. It would come home to the audience in a big way, perhaps help them − and that's partly the object of the series, to teach people how to tackle their problems . . . Well, I asked Dr Vantoni if she thought Lynette was strong enough, and she said yes.'

'But . . .'

'But you think it would cause grief to Lynette?'

'Yes.'

'Dr Vantoni says that would be good. Lynette's talked it through with her many times, of course, but that was in a closed environment − a sort of magic circle where only two people existed: herself and her psychiatrist. Dr Vantoni says if she's strong enough to talk it through publicly, it would purge it from her system once and for all.'

'But afterwards . . . ?'

'Afterwards she goes on to something else. You know, it's like jumping a chasm − once you're across, you can go on. But if you keep hesitating on the far side, you're never going to move forward.'

Corie got up to move about the tiny kitchen as if to ease

tension. She thrust her hands into her trouser pockets, turned to face William. 'Lynette wants to do this?'

'Yes.'

'Did you talk her into it?'

'Well . . . I may have used a bit of persuasion, I suppose. But only because she didn't close up and say no to the idea. And now she's keen to do it.'

'Oh, is she? So keen that she couldn't tell me about it herself. She left it to you to do that.'

He shrugged. 'She knew you'd be worried and upset. She feels she's caused you enough anxiety, Corie. She thought it would come better from me.'

'Hmm . . .' said Corie.

She could see the validity of his arguments. He might be right. But she was sure that when it came to the point the TV interview would be an ordeal for her little sister and her first instinct was to fight against it.

Yet, after all, if Lynette wanted to face the ordeal, it was her right to do so. Some benefit that Corie couldn't quite understand might come from it.

'When is this to be?' she asked, signalling that she'd given up opposing the idea.

'In two weeks' time. We had Stuart Lorris the cricketer scheduled for that slot, but he's had to cry off so we've got a gap in the schedule. And you see, we don't have to do hours and hours of research on Lynette's background, we already know it, so we can supply a brief to Borderman at once.'

Corie was shaking her head. She said, 'I wouldn't like to have my mistakes held up to the public – and heaven knows I'm a tougher character than my kid sister.'

'I know. But she wants to do it. Dr Vantoni says it's like sailing away to a new land and leaving everything behind you – you have a completely fresh start.'

'If you don't get shipwrecked on the way,' Corie said drily.

'Well yes – if you don't get shipwrecked on the way,' William agreed, and adjusted his heavy spectacles with a less than steady touch.

When she got home that evening, her sister had a meal ready. This had happened several times before − Lynette trying to make some payment for the privilege of living in Corie's flat. But she could see Lynette had made a special effort with the food − not just the old familiar dishes they'd cooked on gas rings in theatrical digs, but a good vegetable soup and a succulent casserole.

'Pal gave me the recipes,' Lynette said with a flush of embarrassment. 'I hope they've turned out all right.'

'This soup's great,' Corie said. 'Just what you want on a raw November night.'

They finished the meal. Lynette brought the coffee. She was preoccupied, nervy. 'Did . . . Did William speak to you today?'

'Yes, love, he did − and I'm a bit worried that you didn't tell me about all this yourself.'

Her sister sat down across the little dining table. The room was quiet. No traffic went by in Stamford Street. From somewhere on the river came the mournful note of a tug's siren.

'I was afraid—'

'Afraid of me?' Corie broke in, startled and dismayed.

'Not of you, no, of course not, Corie . . .' Lynette's eyes were bright with unshed tears. 'You've always been the best friend I have in the world. But I sensed that you might not agree, and I was afraid you'd argue me out of it. And one of the things I've got to work at is holding to my own decisions.'

'I understand that. You've got to take control of your own life. All the same, during the interview you could make mistakes . . .'

'But they'd be my own mistakes, Corie. That's the point.'

'This seems such a big thing, Lynette. I can sort of understand that you want to make a clean break − but why do you have to do it in public?'

'Because it might help someone else. It's time for me to *give* something instead of taking all the time.'

'Oh, Lynette, you've *given* the world so much pleasure in the past—'

'Only because I was told to. Only because it made money for Sasha. Only because I liked being admired. Those aren't good reasons, Corie, and I want to try to balance them by doing something helpful. And Dr Vantoni says I should do it if I want to.'

With that there was no arguing.

The day of the interview rushed towards them with extraordinary speed. All the Duggan family were nervous about it. Corie and Opal were afraid it would prove to be too much for Lynette. Monna on the other hand was afraid her daughter might muff this chance to re-launch her career. 'I've never watched it but I gather it's a very popular show,' she murmured. 'Just think who might be watching – impresarios, film-makers – it could lead to almost anything.'

Sasha Lenoir tried to prevent Lynette from appearing. He approached William Tranton with the challenge that he was still Lynette's agent and the contract for the broadcast hadn't gone through his office. But as Lynette had arranged for the fee to go to charity, he had to back down. It's always been well understood in show business that actors and actresses can give their services to charity without having to consult their agents, and to interfere would only make him look like a Scrooge.

Corie understood his anxiety very well. If Lynette told the naked truth about her career, Sasha couldn't show up well.

But in fact his name was never mentioned in the broadcast with Dennis Borderman.

Corie went to her home in Bayswater to watch it. Her mother insisted on making a social event of the evening, despite all that her other daughters could do to dissuade her. She invited one or two old theatrical cronies, and of course her lodgers. There were drinks and nibbles, some nostalgic chat about the old days of music hall, and then they ranged themselves on chairs and sofas to watch.

The programme was introduced as usual by its signature music, an excerpt from a Mozart symphony. Dennis Borderman was revealed sitting in a leather armchair of the kind used by a managing director in his office. He was a rather heavy-set man in his mid-forties, a former editor of an arts magazine, a former university professor. Television had discovered his talent for interview in a lucky moment and had built him up to stardom.

From behind him grew the sound of yet another piece of music, utterly different from the introduction. Gently it swelled up, just loud enough to be recognised as 'You're a Sweetheart', the song by which Lynette's show used to be introduced.

'There!' cried Monna in rapture. 'That will make everybody remember how famous my daughter was!'

'You'll recall that tune,' Borderman said with a smile. 'If you enjoyed watching the Light Entertainment shows of a few years ago, you'll know it heralded a star, who is with me now.' The camera drew back to reveal Lynette sitting in a similar chair a few feet away.

'Ladies and gentlemen, my guest tonight on "Background Story" is Lynette Lee.'

The music grew until for a few moments anyone who used to watch the show could recognise it and perhaps sing the words – 'You're a sweetheart, If there ever was one . . .' Then it died, and Borderman leaned forward.

'Do you think you'll ever hear that signature tune played on the air again, Miss Lee?'

Lynette shook her head. 'Those days are over,' she said.

She was wearing a pale blue dress that looked dove grey on the black and white screen. She looked thinner – the girlish curves were gone. Her blonde hair was pulled back in soft curls behind her ears. Faint lines were visible on the once flawless skin.

'You say they're over. Is that because your style, the kind of material you use, no longer appeals?'

'Tastes have changed. Unfortunately, I never changed with them.'

'That seems strange. Usually an artiste develops all the time, has something new to offer when it's needed. But this wasn't so for you?'

'No. I got stuck in a rut.'

'Didn't you have anyone to advise you on such matters?'

'Oh, of course, I had my family, which was what you might call a show-business family. And I had an agent.'

'I would have thought your agent would be planning for the future − it would be his duty to foresee changes in taste. Do you feel you were badly handled?'

Lynette sighed. 'I was a silly girl,' she said. 'I should have had more sense than believe things could go on and on in the same way for ever. But I wanted to live in my own fairy tale, I think. I let the world leave me behind.'

'So your material and presentation went out of date. But you have training and experience. Perhaps if you could work on something different . . . ?'

'I wouldn't want to,' Lynette said. 'Even if I was asked, I'd say no.'

'What's she doing?' cried Monna with horror. 'She mustn't talk like that—'

'Shh,' said everyone else in the room, their attention gripped by the pale tense girl on the screen.

' . . . So one of the things I've learned in the past two or three years is that I don't really want to be a performer. It took me a long time to accept that fact. I'd been brought up to believe the theatre was the *only* career for me.'

'When did it come home to you that you were in the wrong world then? I believe you were on tour and collapsed under the strain—'

'That's not the whole story. The fact is, I developed diabetes four years ago.'

'Diabetes? But Miss Lee, no word about that ever appeared in the newspapers—'

'I kept it secret. I was really silly.' Lynette looked straight at the camera. 'I thought it would look like a weakness, that

550

it would make me seem less important, lacking somehow in ability – I didn't want to own up to myself that I had a health problem which would make a big difference in my life–'

'She shouldn't be telling this!' cried Monna. 'That man is flustering her!'

'Monna, he's only asked her half a dozen questions–'

'Shush,' said the others. 'We want to hear . . .'

'But he's doing her so much harm – she's wrecking her chances–'

Someone crossed the room to turn up the sound on the television set. Monna fell silent as she caught what was now being said in the interview.

'You didn't even tell your *mother*?'

'No, I knew it would upset her dreadfully. I told no one,' said Lynette, with a rise and fall of her shoulders as comment on her own foolishness. 'I thought I could manage everything without letting anyone know, and I did, in fact, except that my sister Corie walked in on me one evening while I was giving myself an insulin injection.'

'Your sister Corie. That's Corie Duggan, the photographer, I believe.'

'Yes, she's been a wonderful friend to me,' Lynette said. 'Though she was against it, I persuaded her to keep the secret, and she did, faithfully . . . Until . . . well, you mentioned it earlier . . . I collapsed on stage . . . I made a spectacle of myself . . . Corie was with me, luckily for me. She'd been worried because touring didn't agree with me, you see, and so she'd travelled with me . . .' Her voice dwindled away as she recalled the misery of that time.

'She had to bring you home?'

'Yes.'

'And after that you told your mother about the diabetes?'

'Corie told her. You see, I was so weak and silly, and in a sort of daze . . . There was a sort of family conference . . . You know how families are . . .' She smiled a little and Borderman smiled back. She went on. 'It was decided . . . well, we kept my illness a secret . . . My mother felt it would harm my career . . . such as it was.'

'Your career. That had developed into a succession of overseas tours, am I right?'

'Only overseas audiences seemed to want me. But you see I got cold feet. I couldn't face them.'

'Because you're a diabetic?'

'No. No, because . . .' Lynette's voice sank lower. 'Because I lost my baby.'

The words took a moment to register. Then Dennis Borderman frowned, taken aback. Clearly this hadn't been in the brief provided for him by William Tranton.

In Mrs Duggan's living-room there was a gasp of disbelief.

Monna leaped to her feet. 'That's not true!' she cried. 'Why is she saying that? It's not true!'

'Monna – please – calm down–' Corie's attention had left the screen, was entirely centred on her mother.

'Why is she telling such a dreadful lie? My little girl never got pregnant! She would have *told* me . . .'

'Please, please – Monna – don't take it like this. I don't know why she's telling these things, but she's only telling the truth–'

'That's not so! I don't believe it! I won't allow this, you must ring and tell them to cancel–'

'Monna, you mustn't take it like this. Now, now . . . Come along . . .' She put an arm around Monna's shaking shoulders and led her protesting from the living-room.

In the dining-room she put her in a chair, found the brandy in the sideboard, and poured a generous measure.

'Drink this . . .'

Her mother pushed the glass away roughly. Brandy splashed over her vivid green velvet dress. Her face was suffused with colour, her eyes were alight with anger.

'Don't speak to me! Don't touch me! How dare you! You – *you* weren't surprised when she said that!'

'I was surprised she said it on the air. But I wasn't surprised by the fact.'

'You knew.'

'Yes.'

'But you never told *me*.'

Corie set down the brandy glass on a nearby table. 'Monna, if Lynette had wanted you to know, she'd have told you.'

'Why didn't she tell me? Why? Why?'

'You'll have to ask her that.'

'I'll never speak to her again! She's humiliated me in front of my friends! How dare she?'

She started to her feet, walked out of the dining-room; Corie followed her for fear of what she might do next. She might walk into the living-room, smash the TV set – anything. But she simply walked across the hall and up the stairs. On a step midway up she paused. She looked down regally, controlling her dismay and anger with all the technique learned through so many years on stage.

'Tell my *friends* that they're welcome to my hospitality for the rest of the evening. But if one of them dares to speak to me of what we witnessed, I shall turn my back.'

'Monna—'

'And as for you, you can tell Lynette that I disown her.'

'You don't mean that—'

'Goodnight, Corie.'

And with that Mrs Duggan went to her room to hide from the disgrace her well-beloved daughter had brought upon her.

When Corie went back into the living-room, Lynette was speaking on screen, the camera concentrating on her haggard face.

'I blamed myself terribly. I lost my baby because I wouldn't be sensible about it. If I'd spoken to my doctor, he would have told you have to be especially careful if you're a diabetic and get pregnant. I was thinking only about myself, not about my baby. Silly dreams, about telling the baby's father when it was too late to change anything, and then we'd have to get married and we'd settle down in domestic bliss. I wouldn't have to go on tour any more because I'd have to stay at home and look after my baby. I wouldn't have to face audiences who found me rather boring. I wouldn't have to hope for engagements that never came. I could be a mother and a housewife. You see how silly and selfish I was?'

'You're very hard on yourself, Miss Lee—'

'No harder than I deserve. It's something I'm going to have to live with for the rest of my life.'

'You've just revealed this tragedy to me and to the viewers tonight. Was it known to the baby's father?'

'No.'

'Who is he? Someone you obviously cared for very much, if you hoped to marry him.'

'I don't want to talk about that. I can talk about my own mistakes, but I don't want to drag in anyone else. It wouldn't be fair.'

'Did your family know about it?'

'Only Corie. Corie was there at the time. She brought me home from Australia after I had the miscarriage. I think I must have been behaving like a zombie. But I made her promise not to tell anyone because – once again, you see – I was thinking about myself, about how people would blame me for how I'd behaved. It's a bad mistake to keep something like that locked up inside you. It eats and eats at you.'

'How did you come to the present state, where you feel you can talk about it?'

'I went into a clinic. I think I really lost my grip on reality to the extent that I couldn't cope. Luckily others who cared for me took me to see this place where you can get help. It's taken a long time, but I think I've put most of the pieces together again.'

'You mean you can face the world again?'

'Yes, I hope so.'

'In fact, you've taken this interview as the opportunity to do it?' he suggested, having gathered his wits together after the shock of her revelation.

'Yes, to wipe the slate clean, to make a new start.'

'But not in show business?' Borderman said with a

sympathetic smile on his broad face.

She shook her head.

'Now here you are. You haven't even reached your late twenties but your life has held a lot of sadness, loss, disappointment. As you've so honestly told your story to me and to the audience out there, you come over as an innocent . . . someone who's been ordered about most of her life. Tell me, whom do you blame?'

Corie held her breath. Monna? Sasha Lenoir? Even, perhaps, the big sister who'd been over-protective towards her?

'I blame myself,' said Lynette. 'I accepted what other people said and felt about me, without ever examining it. I was too eager to have everybody love me. I never argued, never stood up to anyone for my own opinion – because, in fact, I didn't have any opinion. I thought I only existed if I pleased other people. That's childish, isn't it?'

Borderman raised his eyebrows. 'Childlike, perhaps. We all want other people to like us – it's natural.'

'But not when it leads to the feeling that you don't have any reality in yourself. And that's how it worked with me. Of course, I don't claim I've sorted it all out. I had a lot of growing up to do and perhaps it isn't finished yet. But one thing I know for sure – I want to do something more meaningful with the rest of my life. I don't want just to please people – I want to help them. If I can,' she added with some wistfulness, 'because of course I haven't any qualifications except as a singer and dancer.'

'As a singer and dancer who gave very great pleasure to many, many people,' Borderman said encouragingly. 'If they've been watching this evening – and I think they have – they'll add admiration to their feelings about you. Not many women would have been so honest and so direct. Lynette Lee, thank you for telling us your "Background Story" which we hope will help others to work through their own problems. Thank you – and goodnight, everyone.'

The music swelled, the view of the two people in the two armchairs slowly faded.

'Well!' said one of Monna's old friends, heaving himself to his feet. 'That's the kind of thing that makes the licence worth the money!'

Almost at once the phone in the hall was ringing. It was Opal from her home in Surrey. 'My God, Corie! Did you expect any of that?'

'I didn't know what to expect.'

'How did Monna take it?'

'She retreated to her room about half-way through. I missed quite a bit of it, trying to soothe her down.'

'I don't wonder she was upset. It upset *me* – and I was less blinkered about Lynette than Monna.'

'I hope it's done what she hoped – made an end of the past, set her on a new path for the future.'

'And what about Monna? How are we to treat it where she's concerned?'

'We're never to mention it.'

'I'll be happy to fall in with that!'

'And she says she disowns Lynette.'

'Oh, that won't last long. Thank goodness I'm not living in London any more – at least she can't get at me except by phone. Try to calm her down, Corie. She doesn't really want to be on bad terms with Lynette.'

'I'll do what I can,' Corie agreed with a sigh.

By the time she replaced the receiver, Monna's friends had quietly left. The lodgers had dispersed, two to their own rooms, one to make a cup of cocoa.

Corie collected up the dirty glasses from the living-room and the plates with the remains of canapés. She put them in the kitchen, said a brief goodnight to the cocoa-maker, and left.

She was home in good time to greet Lynette when she arrived in the BBC limousine escorted by William.

'What did you think?' she asked in anxiety as she took off her coat and hat.

'It certainly caused a furore at 42 Bayswater Crescent.'

'Was Monna . . . Was she very shocked?'

'Furious is more the word.'

'Oh dear.' Lynette sank into a chair.

'Don't worry about it,' William said. 'You knew it was going to cause a row; you accepted that from the outset.'

'Yes, but – What am I going to say to her now I've done it?'

'You won't be called upon to say anything. She doesn't want anyone to mention the interview to her, and she disowns you.'

'She does?'

'Oh, Lord – what does that mean?' William inquired in bewildered anxiety.

'I can't tell you,' said Corie. 'It's never happened before. A bit like being drummed out of the Army, I suppose.'

'You don't seem to take it very seriously?'

'Compared with real problems, being in my mother's black books isn't serious. Besides, she won't hold to it.'

Within a few days she was proved right. Next morning the newspapers were ringing with praises for the previous evening's 'Background Story'. 'Sweetness, honesty and courage . . .' 'Lynette Lee's Confession – Unsparing Honesty . . .' 'She Shared Her Mistakes and Her Regret: She's Our Lynette Again . . .'

Corie stayed at home with Lynette in the flat, expecting some kind of regretful reaction to last night's talk. The phone never stopped ringing. People who long ago had ceased to think about Lynette wanted to wish her well, to say they admired her.

Editors rang up – from Sunday newspapers wanting all the dirt, from women's magazines wanting the 'great love story'. To Corie's surprise Lynette dealt with them well. 'I'm sorry, I can't do that . . . No . . . No, I'm not prepared to name the man . . .'

That didn't deter the Sundays. It had been well known that Lynette was deeply attached to her agent, Sasha Lenoir. She was on record as saying she wouldn't want to live without him. Although they couldn't name him for fear of a libel action, the journalists hinted. 'Lynette and her agent always had a lover-like look . . .' 'Friends tell us that

Lynette often spoke of marrying her manager . . .'

Mr Lenoir, consulted on that point, replied that he had not seen Miss Lee for a considerable time. As Miss Lee had now left show business, he was no longer her agent and therefore preferred not to comment.

One of the serious Sundays had a piece on the woman's page about the naïvety Lynette had shown. 'She seemed to think that expecting a baby would naturally cause the man to marry her. We took a survey of some well-known entertainers and actresses. Here are their reactions . . .' And on the whole the survey showed that marriage didn't seem to be expected. The newspaper thereupon invited readers to write in with their views.

All in all, it was good business for the press.

What was more important to Monna, it kept Lynette's name in front of the public. On the Tuesday following 'Background Story', she rang Corie at the photographic studio. She couldn't, of course, ring Lynette: Lynette was still in disgrace. But Corie well understood that this was the beginning of forgiveness.

'You've seen the papers?'

'Yes, of course.'

'They've certainly been very *kind* to Lynette.'

'Yes.'

'Did you expect that?'

'I never even thought about it beforehand, Monna.'

'You haven't my experience, of course. A performer always has to look ahead and think of the public image. I must admit . . .'

'You expected it to damage her?'

'Yes, I did, but then the moral climate has changed . . . Did you see that piece in the *Sunday Monitor*? About not getting married?'

'Yes, I saw it.'

Monna made a tutting sound. 'I must say . . . In *my* day it would have been a terrible disgrace . . .'

'Of course, I realise that.'

'How is Lynette?'

'Amazingly well. I thought she might have a bad reaction, but she's coping with all the inquiries—'

'Inquiries? Is anyone offering her a part?'

'As a matter of fact, yes — but she's refused it.'

'She refused a part? Is she out of her mind?' Monna was incredulous.

'It was in a straight play, Monna. She felt she was totally untrained for that kind of thing.'

'Oh, a straight play.' Her mother had no respect for entertainments that consisted entirely of people talking. To her, song and dance were of the essence. 'But if someone offers her something in a Christmas show—'

'She'll refuse.'

'Now look here, Corie, you're not to let her—'

'Monna, didn't you understand what she was doing on "Background Story"? She was declaring her independence. I can't tell her what to do, neither can you, neither can anyone.'

'It's all very well to talk like that, but you must admit, Corie, it's madness to throw away all this wonderful publicity. It makes her valuable to a producer—'

'She knows that. It's not the kind of value she wants any more.'

'But what's she going to *do*?' wailed Monna. To her it was unbelievable — more than twenty years of training being thrown away just when the public's interest had been whetted again.

'As a matter of fact, she's gone to talk about a job this very morning.'

'A job?' Hope soared in the rich voice coming over the phone. 'With whom? Monty — is it Monty? I know he's got a production coming—'

'It's nothing to do with showbiz. She's gone to talk to the chairman of the Trust for Diabetes Research.'

'I beg your pardon? To whom?'

'To the chairman of the Trust—'

'But that's a charity!'

'Yes, they rang and asked her to—'

'Good God, Corie, my talented little girl isn't going to waste her time doing unpaid jobs for a charity?'

'Perhaps it's not unpaid. As far as I could gather, they want her to be assistant to the head of the fund-raising department—'

'To the head cashier? Is that what you're saying? They want her to be an office girl?'

'Monna, I know nothing about it except that they rang to ask if she would meet to discuss the idea. She's there now, they're taking her to lunch—'

'Oh, lunch,' said Monna, hope reviving. 'They want her to open a fête or something, that's what it is.'

'You may be right,' Corie agreed, and the conversation ended.

Lynette arrived at the studio about four o'clock to report on the day's events. She was flushed with eagerness and pleasure.

'The chairman – Mr Tyler – he said I had done a wonderful thing for the cause of diabetics – he said I'd brought the problem out into the open – I told him I was only thinking of myself and he said yes, I had a perfect right to do that, but I had also helped—'

'Slow down, slow down,' Corie begged. 'Mr Tyler is the man who rang you?'

'Yes, he's about sixty, retired from business, came to help the Trust because he has a son with diabetes. It turns out Dr Usborne's on the board.'

'Good gracious.'

'Yes, Mr Tyler passed on a message from him. I must ring him, Corie, it's ages since I've seen him because of course Dr Vantoni was supervising . . . Well, anyhow, he offered me a job. They need to raise funds to finance a research project. They want me to go in as assistant to Mr Wittersborg—'

'But doing what?' Corie put in, perplexed.

'That's what I said. Mr Wittersborg was at the lunch, he explained.' Lynette's brows drew together as she tried to remember the discussion. 'They raise a fair amount, but

560

they feel they're not reaching enough of the public. The public are interested in *me* at the moment so they think if I go around giving talks and attending fund-raising events—'

'What you're saying is they want to cash in on you.'

'Exactly.'

Corie studied her. 'And you wouldn't mind that?'

'Of course not! I told you, I want to *help*. If I can put a few more coppers in collecting boxes, I'm only too willing—'

'But Lynette, wouldn't this be a pretty short-term thing? I mean, is the public going to remember "Background Story" for very long?'

'Maybe not. What does it matter if it's short term? Nothing lasts for ever, Corie.'

'So are they asking you to do this for free?'

'No, no, I shall actually be part of the organisation, they want me to be there in the office if people ring to ask for advice or help, but of course I'll also be out and about quite a bit helping to raise money. One thing will please Monna—' She broke off, laughing.

'What?'

'They're putting on a Christmas Charity Show at the Golders Green Hippodrome and they want me to take part! Almost top billing, it'll be. I couldn't help grinning when they mentioned it. They thought I was pleased about going on stage again and began to say they didn't often run a show, but when I told them I was just thinking about my mother's reaction they relaxed.'

'She'll be in her element! She'll forget she disowned you. Oh, Lynette, I wonder if it won't make her think—'

'Don't worry,' Lynette said with surprising calmness. 'I'll make it clear to her that this is a one-off.'

They went over it again and then paused for the obligatory afternoon tea. Corie had a sitter coming at five. Lynette put on her outdoor coat and prepared to leave.

'I shan't be in this evening, Corie,' she said. 'I'm meeting William to tell him what happened.'

'Of course. That's quite OK.'

'And Corie . . .'

'What?'

'The offices of the Trust for Diabetes Research are in Harrow. It would be too far for me to travel back and forth every day. I think . . . Well, it seems good sense . . .'

'You'll be finding a place of your own in Harrow?'

Lynette paused, her hands up to her head as she adjusted her fur hat. She looked at her sister, then her hands slid down her cheeks until they covered her mouth. Her eyes mirrored her distress.

'I'll be moving out, Corie,' she said at last, from behind the shelter of her hands.

'That's all right.'

'You don't mind?'

'Of course not.'

They hugged each other. Lynette wiped tears from her lashes. 'It seems such a huge step,' she said with a tremulous laugh. 'Just think, Corie – I've never lived on my own before in my entire life.'

'You'll be fine, love!'

'Yes. I shall. I know I shall.'

'Off you go – you'll want to change into something less businesslike for an evening with William,' Corie teased.

'Yes, quite right.' Next moment, with a little wave, Lynette had gone.

Corie looked at the closed door. Her little sister was at last all grown up.

A voice spoke from behind her. 'Hey,' said Bertie, 'you going to put the lights ready for Mrs Decourcy-Smith or do I have to do it?'

She turned with a wry smile. After all, the world had to go on, even though families changed and lives took a different turn.

Chapter Twenty-eight

Corie had expected to miss Lynette's presence in the flat. But after the first day of wondering how her little sister was faring all on her own in the place found for her by the charity in Harrow, she began to enjoy the freedom.

One of the greatest benefits concerned the phone calls from Drew. Drew and Corie had sworn not to let distance make them drift apart again, so they telephoned each other as often as possible. For Drew, the best time was when his long day was eventually over — somewhere between one and two in the morning in Washington.

This meant that Corie's phone often rang at about six o'clock in the morning in London. In the past she'd always worried whether it would disturb Lynette, a light sleeper. But now she need have no concern over that.

She would lie in bed listening to his voice, reaching out to him over the vast distances. There was something very special in those moments: it seemed as if they were alone in the universe, two stars invisibly but unbreakably linked. She learned every nuance of his speech. She knew when he was tired, when he was despondent, when he was frustrated. She even knew when he was filled with the same longing that sometimes seized her as they talked — a desire to touch, to caress, to have some physical reward for the passion that had to be held in check.

In those dark cold hours of the winter morning, she would confide her hopes and fears. Talking to him about Lynette's new start in life helped her get it into perspective. Hearing the problems in Drew's life helped her feel as if she were taking part in his life.

It became clear that he was growing disenchanted about politics.

'You find yourself wondering how this guy ever got where he is,' he confided after a whole day wasted on a recalcitrant Representative. 'He's prejudiced, he's old-fashioned, he couldn't point out Berlin on the map if you asked him. But because he's got influence with German-American societies, the President's got to win him over about his policy for East Germany . . .'

'I think it's the same everywhere, Drew. Getting unpopular things through our Parliament is just as difficult.'

'Maybe. But not everything can be worked out by wheeling and dealing, by profit and loss, dollars and cents. Real people are suffering – I've seen it myself when I've visited the family over there.'

'That reminds me . . . How's Werner?' she asked. This cousin, whom she'd never met, was quite a familiar character to her through frequent mentions in the past.

'We-ell . . .' he said. There was a long hesitation.

'What is it, Drew?'

'Werner's disappeared.'

'Disappeared? In what sense? You've lost touch? He's moved?'

'He's vanished,' Drew said, and she could hear his anxiety. 'None of the old contacts seem able to tell me what's happened. I think there's been a helluva clamp-down behind the Wall.'

'Drew, I'm so sorry. I know you feel close to him.'

'Yeah, he's more like a kid brother than a cousin . . . You understand, of course, Corie. It's how you feel about Lynette.'

'I understand.' Her agreement was wholehearted. 'Have you asked your friends in the government to inquire about him?'

'That's just the point!' he said, and now she heard the anger. 'They've warned me to shut up about it—'

'They won't help?'

'Quite the opposite. I've been told not to be a nuisance. The chief of the White House staff told me to get a sense of proportion.'

'Proportion?'

'Well, you see, if it became known that someone in the President's office was worried about a relative behind the Iron Curtain, that gives the East German security forces a bit of a lever to use against the President—'

'Oh, that's nonsense!'

'That's taking it to its furthest extent. Of course, Jack isn't going to be influenced in any decision just because I happen to have a cousin missing in the East. But you see . . . If I tried to get someone in office to pull weight on Werner's behalf, then Ulbricht can say that the US government is trying to help a criminal . . .'

'Werner isn't a criminal!' Corie protested.

'Sure, we know that and they know that, but they can say what they like. Remember that poor kid who died among the barbed wire – they issued a statement saying he was awaiting sentence for armed assault. It's a complete lie, the kid was an engineering apprentice. But they could say what they liked about Werner, and if my government was taking an interest in him, it could turn out very embarrassing.'

'And that's why you're being given the cold shoulder?'

'That's it.'

'I can see why you're beginning to dislike politics.'

'Honey, I'm sorry to take up our time together groaning about things like this . . .'

'It's all right. I want to share your worries.'

'Worries is an understatement. I can't get the least whisper about Werner from any of the contacts who used to send on messages. I can't help wondering . . .' His words died away.

'You think he's been arrested?'

'I don't know. That's the bad thing – we just don't know. My mom and dad are scared sick about him.'

He sounded exhausted. She guessed he'd had a heavy day and had yet a heavier one ahead.

'Go to bed, darling,' she told him. 'Things will look better after a night's sleep.'

He laughed, agreed, and said goodbye.

Christmas approached and with it came Lynette's appearance in the charity show. The entire Duggan family, including a heavily pregnant Opal escorted by her anxious husband, were present.

To Monna's disappointment, Lynette only appeared twice – once in the former favourite 'Dancing with My Shadow', and once at the beginning of the finale where she led the entire cast in a version of the Twist.

'The Twist!' her mother lamented. 'How any daughter of mine could get involved in a show where she has to dance the Twist!'

'Monna, it was just so that all the cast could be brought on for the finale,' Opal soothed. 'You could see some of them were too old to do more than just a few little wiggles.'

'Little wiggles! It's got no dignity!'

'You're right, and that's one of the reasons it's popular.'

'Opal, you may think that means something, but I don't understand you. But then I don't understand most of what goes on in show business these days. How people can want to watch young men who look as if they should still be in school, cavorting about and singing up in the falsetto range of their voices – give me a good hearty baritone any day!'

They all smiled on her in sympathetic acceptance. She would never change, but she had begun to see that she was out of touch, that it was no good hoping for a return to the great days of music hall, of robust baritones and tenors singing selections from *Show Boat* or soubrettes in chiffon dresses doing soft-shoe dances.

She had even begun to be resigned to the fact that Lynette's stage career was over. Although the critics were pleased with her showing in the Charity Gala, they remarked that the figure who drifted through 'Dancing with My Shadow' had not been the rounded, girlish creature of ten years ago. The lilting voice had lost its fresh, lark-like quality. Lynette Lee had changed, and though they complimented her on her performance, they made it clear they saw no great future ahead for her.

'This would be a good set of reviews to put in the

scrapbook as a closing item,' Corie rather carefully suggested to Monna.

Her mother, the newspapers spread all around her on the sofa and the table and the floor, shook her head in disagreement. 'There'll be others,' she declared. But there was no longer a ringing conviction in her tone.

Corie intended to report this to Drew next time they spoke, but in fact the thought was put out of her head by his first words.

'What do you know, Corie! I've had word from Werner!'

'No! How is he? Is everything all right?'

'Well, that's still not clear. What happened was . . . You know there's a big Trade Fair in Leipzig in the autumn?'

She'd never heard of it but she said, 'Go on.'

'Businessmen from all over the world go there. Someone who knows Werner looked up one of the businessmen in his hotel, on the pretext of bringing him information about some new scientific glassware, and handed the guy a brochure with a postcard tucked inside. The man posted the card on to my mother and father when he got back to Paris, with a note explaining how he got it.'

'And what does the card say?' Corie asked eagerly.

'Not much,' said Drew. 'It's obviously been handed on from one person to another so it's not in good shape. But what you can read simply says he's staying out of sight until he can get out of the country.'

'Staying out of sight where?'

'That's the sixty-four-thousand-dollar question. I imagine he's somewhere in the Leipzig area.'

'His parents – your aunt and uncle – they live there?'

'They have a farm outside the city. But he's not going to go anywhere near them if he's in trouble. And in fact, when we hear from them, they never mention him. Of course that's probably because they're afraid their letters are censored—'

'Censored!'

'Sure, the way I hear it, everybody in East Germany informs on everybody else, and letters and phone calls are under investigation all the time.'

'But that's awful, Drew . . .'

'And that's why I've decided to go and get him out.'

Corie drew in a breath. It took her a long time to ask, 'Go to East Germany? But won't your superiors be against that?'

'I'm not going to tell them, Corie. I've never had a vacation since I began working for Jack before the election, so I'm going to take a month off and do it on my own time.'

'You're not telling anyone?'

'No.'

'Drew . . . Is that wise? Wouldn't it be better to ask them for some help?'

'They wouldn't give it,' he said curtly.

'But . . . Drew . . . Listen, I'm not trying to stop you from doing this, but if anything went wrong in East Germany, if they recognised your name as being on the President's personal staff—'

She heard him begin to speak then stop. 'Yeah,' he said at last, 'that could be bad all round.'

'Think about it, Drew. Before you do anything, give it a lot of thought.'

'I will, sweetheart, don't worry.'

But she did worry. She was afraid the next time the phone rang, he might be speaking from East Germany.

The plan evolved gradually. First of all Drew arranged to take a month's vacation. Then, without much prompting, he came to London. They had a rapturous reunion at Heathrow, then drove in her faithful old camper to her flat. There, for the first few hours, they forgot the world and all its problems, especially any talk about dangerous trips behind the Iron Curtain.

But on the following morning, as they sat in dressing-gowns drinking early-morning coffee in front of the living-room's electric fire, Corie summoned up her courage to lay an idea before Drew.

'Did I ever tell you I got a letter from the Embassy of the

German Democratic Republic inviting me to visit their
country?' she began.

'You did? No, I don't remember you ever mentioning
that.' He thrust out bare feet towards the meagre warmth of
the fire.

'They were hurt because I took those pix of the boy who
died trapped by the wire. You remember I gave them free to
any paper that wanted to use them.'

'I sure do.'

'Well, they wrote and said I'd been misled about the boy,
who was a criminal, and all that rubbish.' Corie took a sip
of her coffee. 'They said they'd always thought of me as a
friend because of the photos I took of President Batistá
scuttling out of Cuba as the rebels marched nearer – I don't
know if you remember that.'

'Of course I do, Corie. I remember all about you,' he said,
leaning forward to kiss her collarbone as her dressing-gown
slipped aside.

'Don't do that. You'll make me spill my coffee,' she said,
attempting to be sensible. 'I'm only talking about those
Batistá pix because it made people like the East German
government think of me as being on the side of "revolutionary democracy".'

'Yeah and so?' he said, still only half attending,
attempting to take her coffee cup away so as to remove her
excuse for sitting up straight in her chair.

'They issued an invitation. I never bothered to reply
because I couldn't think of how to do it politely. But . . .
Drew, behave yourself, listen to what I'm saying!'

'I'm behaving,' he protested, 'although the conditions
make it very difficult and besides, I'm half frozen. Why
don't you get some central heating?'

'Because the landlord wouldn't let me have the work
done, even if I wanted to. Besides, I don't feel the cold. I've
got my love to keep me warm, as the song says.'

This he took as surrender, which in fact it was. For a time
she forgot about her determination to lay her plan before
him. There were kisses and embraces that led on to yet

more delights. It was almost an hour later, and the January sun was at last peeping through the window, when they returned to serious matters.

'To go back to what I was saying . . .'

'What were you saying? Apart from that you love me?'

'No wonder you're getting bored with politics! You won't keep your mind on the matter in hand.'

'Is that a complaint?'

'I've no complaints,' she acknowledged, laughing, 'but now be serious, pay attention. I wrote to the Embassy of the German Democratic—'

'Now look here, I may not have been paying close attention but I distinctly remember you said you didn't write to them.'

'That was then. I'm talking about now – recently. I wrote to the Embassy at the beginning of the month, telling them I'd begun to have qualms of conscience about the way I behaved last August, and wondering whether perhaps I could pay a visit to East Germany to take some pictures.'

Drew, tying his tie, paused to stare at her. 'Wondering whether *you* could pay a visit?'

'Bringing with me my assistant.'

'Corie . . .'

'And I got a reply on Tuesday, the day before you were due to land.' She went to the bureau drawer, took out an envelope, and handed it to him.

He read the letter quickly, and then again with more attention. 'It offers you visas and a letter of permission at twenty-four hours' notice!'

'Yes.'

'Corie, what are you thinking?'

'Let's go back a bit. You intend to go to East Germany and find Werner. And then what?'

'Get him out.'

'How?'

'*I* don't know,' he said angrily. 'False papers, a forged passport—'

'Where were you going to get those?'

He shrugged. 'It's got its advantages, walking around in the corridors of power. I've got a friend in the CIA who's promised to make papers available when I want them.'

Corie considered this. 'The passport for Werner would have to contain his photograph. How were you going to get one?'

'I've got one with me – it's a snapshot taken when he was helping on the farm a couple of years ago.'

'Can I see it?'

He fetched his jacket, took out his wallet, and extracted a small photograph. Corie looked at it in the strong winter light from the window.

'There's no way you could ever make this look like a passport photograph. He's laughing.'

'Well, this friend of mine said they could do something with it—'

She shook her head. 'I'm in the business, Drew. This is never going to look like a passport pic, unless you superimpose someone else's features on Werner's, and then you might as well start with a fake.'

Drew received back the photograph. 'It's the only one I had where he's about the right age,' he said with a sigh. 'All the others in the family album show him at about seventeen or eighteen – and he's changed a lot since then.'

'No doubt. So getting him out with false papers is going to have its problems,' Corie said.

'All the ways of getting him out are going to present problems,' said Drew. 'He's on the run so he's clearly wanted by the Volkspolizei. They'll be watching for him.'

'Exactly.'

He frowned at her. 'You're cooking up something.'

'Yes. I thought about all the problems and it seems to me the best way to get Werner out is not to gamble on forged papers but simply smuggle him out.'

'Smuggle him? I don't get it.'

'Smuggle him the way people used to smuggle brandy and tobacco. Smuggle him the way they smuggle gold or drugs. Conceal him from the border officials.'

'Conceal him in what?' Drew challenged. 'Don't say in the boot of a car — it's the first place they look. They also use mirrors on rollers to inspect the underside of vehicles in case anyone's hanging on below. Concealing a human being is more difficult than concealing gold, Corie. You can't mould a human being to fit under the bumper.'

'No, but you could persuade a human being to lie still inside a cupboard for half an hour while he goes through passport control.'

'In a *cupboard*?'

'Yes. In my mobile camper. It's got cupboards fitted along one side for photographic equipment.'

'What!'

'Here I am, an invited guest,' Corie said, pointing to herself. 'I drive into East Germany with my assistant Drew Richter, we find Werner and drive back. Half an hour's drive from the border patrol, we put him into the equipment cupboard. I don't think the sentries are going to search the vehicle of a photographer who's come to East Germany at the invitation of the government and has the papers to prove it. We drive through. As soon as we're safely on the Western side, we let Werner out and there he is — free.'

For what seemed like an aeon Drew considered it. Then he said, 'No.'

'Why not?'

'I'm not taking you behind the Iron Curtain to look for a man who's in disgrace with the regime. It's too dangerous.'

'Drew, I know it's dangerous! I've thought about nothing else since you said you were going after him. How do you think I feel about letting you go there and perhaps being arrested?'

'That's different . . .'

'How is it different? Because you're a man? You're supposed to do the dangerous things?'

'Well, in the first place Werner's my cousin—'

'It doesn't matter who he is, if you go to get him out, you're in danger. I want to be there with you.'

'No.'

'But Drew, don't you see, if we go together it reduces the risk? They might be looking for a male relative – they might even be looking for *you*, the cousin who used to visit the family in Leipzig. But they're not going to suspect *me*, coming at the invitation of the government, with all the proper papers—'

'No.'

'If we do it my way, there's no need for forged papers for Werner. Werner never needs to show himself. He can be over the border into safety without ever being in danger.'

'Absolutely not.'

'Don't be so blinkered, Drew. You're saying that you'd rather take a risky method and do it on your own—'

'Damn right I would.'

'But you're reducing Werner's chances by doing it that way.'

'Werner's been taking risks all his grown-up life—'

'But even he has had to go into hiding! He knows he's already in danger otherwise he wouldn't have disappeared. They're looking for him, he stays out of sight – but you're saying he has to walk out into the spotlight with a forged passport . . .'

'I'm saying you are not going to be involved. I began this trip with the idea of taking a few risks for myself, but I'm certainly not going to let you—'

'Oh, that's great!' she cried. 'You're going to East Germany, you're probably going to attract the attention of this all-embracing police force you spoke of, and I'm to sit here in London nearly going out of my mind with worry?'

'Ah, sweetheart,' he said, and took her in his arms. 'Don't talk like that. I'm sorry, I know it's going to be tough for you—'

She pushed him away with her fists. 'Don't try to sweet-talk me into agreeing. I won't let you go without me, so you'd better get used to the idea!'

'Now look here, Corie—'

'It's so risky! You're going there with your own name, your own passport – how do you know they're not on the watch for you to do just that? And maybe lead them straight to Werner when you get word of him?'

'That's going to happen anyway, even if I used your scheme.'

'Not at all! You can get a set of false papers from your contact in the CIA – you can get them for yourself, not Werner. Then as Joe Doakes, my assistant, you're not attracting any attention. As Joe Doakes you can move about fairly freely. You find Werner, you arrange a meeting place, we drive up and collect him.'

'And if anyone sees us doing that we're in big trouble . . .'

'Not at all! I'm simply picking up a local to act as a photographic subject – I'm going to photograph the local factory and want a worker in the foreground – easy!'

'Easy? It's putting you right in the middle of it!'

'It's where I want to be, Drew. I don't want to be left behind to wring my hands—'

'You'd rather be in an East German prison?'

'There! You admit you're expecting trouble, yet you expect me to let you go on your own while I'm left at home to worry.'

'If you think I'm taking you you can just think again.'

'Don't you see how much better it is for us to go as a team?' she insisted. 'I have a *reason* for going – I've been invited, I'm going to take pix, I can get commissions from newspapers and magazines to prove it's a bona fide project. And you're my German-speaking assistant, without whom I'd be a bit at a loss.'

'You've got it all worked out . . .'

'I'm trying to use all our advantages, Drew. Two people who are expected have much more chance of success than a man on his own, who arrives as a visitor without any good reason and whose name might well be on some list of people to look out for.'

'I don't want you mixed up in this, Corie.'

'No, and it's because – the way you've been looking at it

574

– it's full of dangers. But if you look at it my way, it's less frightening: we're guests of the state, we'll have travel permits and all that—'

'And we'll also probably have a minder, who'll go with us everywhere and only show us what we're supposed to see,' Drew put in in irritation. 'Be sensible, Corie.'

'So what if we have a minder? He's there to mind *me*, isn't he? To make sure I don't take pictures that would be bad propaganda. All right, I'll let him lead me around wherever they want to. *You're* the one who's got to find Werner, and as my assistant you'll have all sorts of chores to do while I'm off with my official escort – you could be processing some film in my mobile workshop, or buying something I forgot to bring. You could move about without being bothered, you could use the phone, speak to people in cafés, do what you like.'

They were still standing face to face, Corie gazing up into Drew's eyes, her hands resting against his chest to hold him off. She felt him take several slow breaths. She had made him stop and think.

'But . . . if anything went wrong?' he said at last.

'Well, then, if you really feel you must, you could say I knew nothing about it. You'd say you used me as a way to get into East Germany.'

'And you'd agree to that?'

'Yes,' she said, knowing she lied, knowing she would never dissociate herself from Drew if he were in danger.

It took them all day to arrive at agreement. Corie kept insisting that Drew's chances of helping his cousin would be doubled if they went as a team. Drew was determined not to let her walk into danger.

The deadlock was ended by a desperate, almost childish remark of Corie's. 'All right then, if I can't go with you, I'll go without you.'

'Don't be absurd. You've no real reason for going to East Germany.'

'Yes I have! If you get into trouble and end up in jail, I can speak up on your behalf.'

'Corie!'

'After all, I'm going to be there as a guest of the state. If you should need help—'

'I won't need help.'

'Oh, it's absolutely safe, is it? So why can't we go together?'

'I didn't say that.'

'What you're saying is that, if anything goes wrong, you'd be absolutely on your own. You told me yourself the White House didn't want to know.'

'That's true, but you wouldn't be in any position to—'

'I'd be *there*, that's the point. This whole business is risky and you just won't admit the odds are improved if you go as my assistant.'

'I'm not saying it's a bad idea, I just don't want you getting involved.'

'But I am involved! And it comes down to this, Drew. Either we go together and work as a team, or we go separately and I have to keep watching and trying to read the newspapers to see if you'd been picked up.'

'You'd make yourself look very strange . . .'

'Yes, maybe I would, always pestering my official escort to translate the news bulletins. I'd be better off if I was with you, with someone who speaks fluent German and can keep me from putting my foot in it.'

'Corie, this is blackmail!'

'You bet it is,' she agreed.

There seemed to be no way he could prevent her. He gave in, very grudgingly. The decision was made, he telephoned his contact in the CIA, who agreed to meet him the following morning. He put down the receiver, his face grim. He was angry with Corie, and for once she didn't know what to say to him to make things better.

Bedtime came. They said a stiff goodnight before retiring to their rooms: Corie to her own bedroom, Drew to the spare room occupied in the past by Lynette.

Corie couldn't sleep. She was waiting for Drew to relent, to come to her and say everything was all right. But the bedside clock ticked away the hours and still he didn't come.

About two in the morning she could bear it no longer. She got up, pulled on her dressing-gown, and went to Drew's room. The moment she opened the door, he pulled himself up on an elbow.

'Can't sleep either?' he asked.

She crept on bare feet to the bedside, and without speaking laid her cheek alongside his on the pillow.

'Fine pair of fools we are,' he murmured into her ear. 'As if there isn't enough misery in the world without adding to it out of stubbornness.'

'Drew darling, I'm sorry.'

'I am too.' He put his arms about her to pull her under the covers, for her skin was prickling with the cold.

For a long time they simply lay in each other's arms, letting mutual forgiveness and trust lap them about. They talked to each other quietly, confessing fears and anxieties, making promises of constancy, of steadfastness, of eternal love. Only when dawn was approaching did they let passion take them as it had so often in the past.

This time was different. They had had a quarrel, about something serious, not merely a lovers' tiff. They had come to an agreement but without warmth or regard – it was merely an unwilling surrender on Drew's part to the determination of Corie.

Now they had made it up. In doing so they had learned even more about each other. They were in love, this they had always known. But now they knew that besides being lovers, they were friends, held together by a strong, unique bond of understanding and interdependence, of matched reliance and need.

In the morning, Drew went to meet his CIA friend. When he came back he reported that he would be given his false papers in two days' time, but that Johnson – if that was his name – didn't want to know anything about their purpose. If anything went wrong, they were on their own.

Corie spent most of that day on the telephone arranging

bona fide commissions from newspapers and magazines. *Maestro* asked her to take photographs of the Berlin Opera House. *Europe Day* asked for photographs of East German athletes in training, particularly the stars of ice skating. The Features editor of the *Globe*, although not wildly enthusiastic, said he would look at anything she could produce about the general standard of living behind the Iron Curtain. Standards were always said to be low, but he'd like pictorial proof.

After that she telephoned the Embassy to say she would like to travel to East Germany as soon as possible, naming the periodicals who had commissioned her. The Press Officer was enthusiastic – no problem at all, he would start proceedings at once, visas and travel documents for herself and her assistant, of course, if she would just be good enough to call in tomorrow or the day after with the necessary passports he would probably lay an itinerary before her straight away. The Berlin Opera, yes, certainly no problem, and perhaps she would like to see the Leipzig Opera House also, a very famous house, with a world-famous orchestra?

'Of course, I'm happy to go wherever you think I could get interesting pictures,' she said, then turned with some triumph to Drew. 'Leipzig,' she reported, 'they're actually inviting us to Leipzig!'

'And that's where we're likely to get close to Werner,' Drew acknowledged, and threw up his hands in a gesture that admitted she'd been right.

His passport turned out to be for one Emile Gustauvry, born in the French province of Alsace. Alsace had formerly belonged to Germany, had changed hands between France and her neighbour more than once. The inhabitants of the region spoke both languages with equal ease. This would account for the fluency of Drew's German. His occupation was given as 'photographic technician', and date stamps had been provided in the passport to show that he'd lived in England for a little over six years.

'You'd better teach me a bit of jargon about darkroom

processes,' he suggested. 'If anybody gets into conversation with me about my supposed job, I'd better know what to say.'

Corie did better. She took him to the studio, put him in Bertie's charge, and let him have a day's experience of the work.

She, for her part, made flying visits to her family. Opal was surprised when she heard her big sister was going abroad. 'You know Junior's expected at almost any moment, Corie. Can't you put it off?'

'What d'you need me for?' Corie teased. 'You've got a husband, and a doctor, and a hospital all lined up.'

'But I wanted you to arrive at my bedside with a bouquet of roses,' Opal complained.

They laughed and hugged each other.

Lynette was less affected by the news of Corie's trip. She was busy, working on a fund-raising campaign to be launched in the spring. 'Have a lovely time,' she said almost absently as they kissed on parting.

Monna was predictably baffled by the news that her eldest daughter was going behind the Iron Curtain. 'I can't understand why you have to keep gadding about all over the place,' she said. 'Goodness knows you have enough nice people in London wanting portraits taken . . .'

'Yes, but travel broadens the mind, Monna.'

'So they say, but is broadness of mind actually much in evidence in East Germany?'

'Perhaps not,' Corie agreed, and promised to send postcards.

Both Corie and Drew were tense when they went to the Embassy to obtain their travel documents. If there were to be a hitch, now was the time – when Drew presented his forged passport. But all was sweetness and light. Herr Loewenstein summoned a secretary who came with two portfolios. It amused Corie that hers was of better quality than the one for her 'assistant'. She got plastic made to look like pigskin, Drew got stiff card. Inside each were the various passes and permissions needed to travel within the

German Democratic Republic, maps with their routes carefully delineated, vouchers for accommodation and meals, and permits for fuel for Corie's vehicle.

Herr Loewenstein was a little taken aback when he discovered the vehicle was a mobile camper.

'But, Fräulein, you are not expecting to sleep in this vehicle?' he asked in dismay.

'No, no, although I have done so when necessary in the past. No, it's a mobile darkroom. I find it useful to develop and print my work sometimes, just to see what I've captured on the film.'

'I see. Understood. Very sensible. Yes, that is quite in order. I would have been sad if you wanted to live the *Zigeunerleben*,' he said with a smile, 'because I have arranged for you to be accommodated in some very fine hotels.' He looked a little envious. Perhaps he himself wasn't allowed to stay in such places when he was in his homeland.

On 12 February, a cold and blustery Monday, Corie Duggan and her assistant Emile Gustauvry set out in her Volkswagen Caravette for the Continent. They took the ferry from Dover to Ostend, stayed overnight in Hanover, and drove on towards East Germany.

Their route had been planned by the Embassy Press Office so as to avoid West Berlin, the usual crossing point for foreigners entering the East. Drew suggested it was so they wouldn't make unfavourable comparisons when they crossed from the glittering success of West Berlin into East Berlin.

The part of the journey on the West German autobahn was very slow. Traffic was very congested. It was mid-afternoon when they drove into Helmstedt, just before the border with East Germany.

'All Allied travellers will present their documents at Soviet checkpoints fifty metres ahead,' announced a large notice at the roadside.

Corie felt a little shiver of apprehension.

They were in a solid queue of vehicles: buses, lorries,

vans, some private cars. A young man collected papers from the drivers, delivered them to a desk where two girls in semi-uniform outfits – dark, plain skirt, white blouse, red tie – made the necessary checks. Even simply looking in from outside, it was clear to see that the mass of paperwork was too much for them.

'So much for being a guest of the state and getting preferential treatment,' Drew remarked.

'When they get to our documents perhaps they'll get a move-on,' said Corie, pulling up the collar of her camel-hair jacket. It was very cold in the van with the heater virtually ineffective. Outside, frost still lingered, though it was late in the February day.

'We ought to be annoyed, really, oughtn't we? Invited guests of the government, kept hanging about at a frontier checkpoint?' remarked Drew.

She glanced at him. In some ways he was a stranger to her since their last day in London. He had had his brown hair cut by a barber in Soho so as to have the style favoured in France – a rather bushy effect over the temples, with no parting. He had put away his American toothpaste and shaving cream in favour of French products so that when she leaned against him, he even smelled different. His own clothes were in the spare room in Stamford Street. He was wearing trousers and sweater from a shop in Dover which stocked Breton fishermen's gear, and over it he had a raincoat borrowed from a French friend.

The effect was to change him from Drew Richter into a Frenchman who still had the voice of the man she loved yet in other ways was subtly different.

Now, to show his impatience, he opened the door on the passenger side, put his head out, and called in German, 'Hi, what are we waiting for?'

'*Moment, mein Herr, bitte,*' replied one of the girls from inside the frontier office.

Drew shrugged emphatically, to show his impatience. He got out a Gauloise and lit up. Corie hated Gauloises: she nudged him with her elbow. 'That's carrying Frenchness too far, darling!'

Drew grinned, drew deeply on the cigarette, and expelled a cloud of pungent blue smoke into the air. Corie fanned it away with her hand. A moment later, mercifully, the door of the prefab office opened to allow the emergence of a plump overcoated man with a briefcase.

'Fräulein Duggan?' he asked, bowing.

'Yes, I'm Miss Duggan. Good morning.'

'Good morning. Assistant Supervisor of Records Verbermends,' he said, bowing again. He looked with surprise at her transport but went on: 'It is my privilege to be your escort because of my knowledge of photographic records. You are Herr Gustauvry?'

Drew nodded. 'Why are we hanging about?' he demanded.

'My apologies. I meant to be here to greet you,' Verbermends said to Corie, ignoring Drew, 'but unfortunately I had a puncture. All is now in order, however. Your papers, Fräulein. Yours, Herr Gustauvry. If you will just drive forward, Fräulein Duggan, you will be through the barrier and you will see my car up ahead – a black Lada. If you will draw up behind it, I will get in and drive ahead to show you the way. Understood?'

'Thank you,' said Corie, and put her Volkswagen van in motion.

She pulled out of the line of stationary vehicles, crept slowly forward. Envious faces stared out at her from the lorries still stuck in the queue. The barrier rose, fell behind her with a faint metallic sound as it met its fastener, as definite as a door closing.

They were behind the Iron Curtain.

Chapter Twenty-nine

When they at length reached East Berlin, Drew was impressed to discover they were to stay in the Hotel Adlon.

'In the old days this was the best hotel in Germany,' he remarked to Corie as their overnight bags were carried in by a uniformed bellboy. 'Maybe there *is* something in being a guest of the government. But heaven knows what they'll think of a guest who turns up in a mobile caravan!'

The Adlon was unperturbed. With polite competence a porter took the Caravette to the hotel garage.

But the great hotel had fallen on hard times. Wrecked during World War II by air attack and Russian bombardment, it had lost all but the rear wing. This had been restored as a prestige effort, but the place was cold and not too inviting. The furnishings in Corie's room were ancient and heavy, the carpet was worn, the mirror over the huge dressing-table was a little speckled with damp.

Yet when they went out with their escort the next day, she was on the whole pleasantly surprised by East Berlin. Flower beds had replaced the rubble of the immediate post-war era. On the site of the old Chancellery – Hitler's last fortress – a public park had been laid out. Gangs of workmen were busy restoring the imposing old buildings – the museums, the art galleries, the Humboldt University.

Herr Verbermends was pleased when Corie put her cameras to work at once. It didn't occur to him she was photographing the gangs of workmen. She also took little shots of the Russian soldiers who seemed much in evidence, some on duty at intersections, some perhaps on leave.

Lunch was offered to them by members of the Chamber of Commerce. Corie understood only what was translated to her by either Drew or Herr Verbermends, but she smiled and nodded, took everyone's picture, and was clearly regarded as a very cooperative visitor.

After lunch, Drew took the chance to murmur, 'I'd like to get off on my own. Could you send me back to the Adlon for something?'

'Of course.' She gave it a moment's thought then, when Verbermends joined them after prolonged goodbyes to their hosts, she said, 'I think I'm going to need my blue filter. Just pop back and fetch it for me, Emile.'

'Right away,' he agreed, and walked off before their guide could stop him.

The afternoon was spent among the local schools. This was a real pleasure to Corie. The children were neatly dressed and healthy, anxious to try out their English on her. Corie used up all her film, and wished she'd brought her big camera to do some impromptu portraits.

Drew rejoined them with her blue filter in its little case. She put it on the lens simply for the sake of seeming to need it, but the blue of the winter sky was fading now to dusk.

'You use the blue filter often?' Verbermends asked, raising his bushy eyebrows.

'Helps to protect the lens from dust,' Corie said.

'Ah, of course.' But it was clear he hadn't been too pleased at seeing Drew walk off without an escort, on an errand he by no means viewed as necessary.

He drove them back to the hotel, reminded them that he would return to take dinner with them and escort them to the Opera, and bowed himself away.

'Where did you go?' Corie asked over tea made with real English teabags in the hotel lounge.

'I went to leave a message with a friend who used to keep me in touch with Werner. Can't tell whether anything will come of it.'

'When will you know?'

'Oh, soon. This evening, perhaps.'

They parted to bath and change for the evening. With memories of other opera houses, Corie put on black satin trousers and a white silk blouse. Herr Verbermends looked both pleased and put out about it when he joined them for dinner. She realised later, when they reached the Opera House, that she was considerably overdressed.

All the other women seemed to be in afternoon frocks, perhaps their best but certainly lacking the elegance of the clothes she'd seen at the Vienna Opera. The men were in dark suits and silver-grey ties, as uniform almost as a black tie and dinner jacket. Drew's grey slacks and blazer were a little more informal than even the East Germans desired.

However, Verbermends introduced them to the others in their box and on the whole seemed rather proud of Corie's finery. She couldn't imagine how anyone was ever going to get a message to Drew without being noticed by their assiduous escort. He stuck close, translated into Corie's ear, and at one point seemed to be trying to hold her hand.

The opera that evening was *Hansel and Gretel*. There were many children in the audience, Corie noticed. At the interval, people flocked out to the foyer to buy mulled wine, lemonade, and the German equivalent of hot dogs. Herr Verbermends had already ordered wine but there was some slight delay – he hurried off to complain.

Almost at once a young woman in a black dress and a white apron approached. '*Glühwein, mein Herr?*' she asked, offering a tray.

'*Zweimal, danke.*' While Corie took a glass, Drew brought out money and paid for it. The girl seemed to say she didn't have much small change, they spent a few seconds handing money back and forth. Drew took his glass of wine, the waitress departed.

When Verbermends came back to find they'd already been served, he was a little vexed but thought nothing of it. Neither did Corie, at least not until she and Drew were back at the hotel saying goodnight at their room doors.

'After you do your stint behind the scenes of the Opera tomorrow, try to get us to the university,' he murmured after kissing her chastely on the cheek.

'The university?'

'One of Werner's former fellow-students is teaching there. He wants to talk to me.'

'How do you know?'

'The waitress passed me a slip of paper.'

Corie laughed, then shivered. 'Drew . . .'

'Yes, it's scary, isn't it? Nobody can just walk up and talk to us.'

'How did they know where to contact you?'

'That was part of the message I left this afternoon. If I'm to get in touch, I have to let them know where I'm going to be.'

'I see.'

She slept badly that night. The room seemed so vast, the furniture so overpowering, the sense of being far away from all that was safe and familiar was very strong. If she could have been in Drew's arms, she could have found comfort – but that was impossible in the circumstances.

Next morning was spent meeting the singers and management of the Opera. Corie was using available light with black-and-white film, and became so absorbed she almost forgot their target for later in the day. But when Herr Verbermends remarked that after lunch he would like to show her the Museum of German History, a glance from Drew reminded her.

'That sounds wonderful,' she agreed, 'but I wonder if we could fit in a visit to the university? I'd so much like to take pictures of the students – the rising generation of managers and organisers—'

'Certainly! Nothing could be easier! Fräulein Duggan, I shall arrange for you to visit the Students' Union Hall. I believe this evening there is a debate on "The Formation of Public Morals".'

'Thank you, you're very kind, Herr Verbermends, but don't forget I couldn't follow a debate in German,' she replied with a smile.'

'Ach . . . of course . . .'

'Could we just drop in during the afternoon? Just for a few shots—'

'Of course, of course. I will telephone.'

It wasn't clear whether he was telephoning the university to set up the visit or telephoning his superiors to report that the programme was being altered a little. Whichever, he came back beaming. *'Das stimmt!* Now for lunch, the cafeteria for the staff here at the Opera . . .' Herr Verbermends was very interested in his food.

The university stood with other big buildings on Unter den Linden. The courtyards were busy with students hurrying to classes, noticeboards announcing public lectures and debates lined the railings. A second-hand bookstall was doing good business on the pavement outside.

Verbermends led them inside, up a staircase, and into a rather sombre office. A secretary rose to greet them, they were ushered on into another larger office where the head of the Department of Social Studies had been delegated to welcome them.

Coffee was offered, Corie was told she had the freedom of the university. 'Thank you, that's very kind. Now I wonder where I should start?' she mused, looking under her lashes at Drew.

'How about one of the lecture halls?' he prompted.

'That would be quite all right. Let me see . . . Dr Kallern is lecturing on "Modes of Intellectual Expression", Dr Estelmann is giving his "Historical Crises and Instigations", and in the Science Department, Dr Schandosky is demonstrating "Tidal Currents and Continental Drift".'

'Demonstrating?' Drew said. 'With maps? Graphs?'

'Both, I believe.'

'Maps would make good pictorial background,' Corie said, taking her cue. 'Could we drop in on the tidal currents lecture?'

Nothing could be easier.

Dr Schandosky, a short young man with wiry hair and glasses, descended from his podium to be introduced. 'I am honoured to have you in my class,' he said in slow, painful English. He showed no resentment at having his lecture disrupted.

Soon the students were crowded round, eager to practise their English, eager to have their pictures taken. One girl student wanted to know whether Corie's sweater was mohair. 'Nothing here is so smart,' she said wistfully.

It was quite a mêlée, and lasted for over half an hour. With many thanks, Corie withdrew, to be escorted on to the Museum of German History where she took as many pictures as she felt would mollify Herr Verbermends.

Once more she had to wait for the end of the evening before she could ask any questions. This time the place was the darkroom in the mobile camper, where they could be sure of not being overheard. Besides, it kept up the fiction that the van was useful as a workroom. Corie processed film while they talked in low voices.

'Did you meet whoever it was you had to talk to?'

Drew sighed, sounding depressed. 'Werner's nowhere near Leipzig. It seems he tried to get up a petition against the building of the Wall and had to make a run for it, hoping to get out of the country. They think he's in Rostock.'

'Rostock? Where's Rostock?'

'In the north, on the Baltic coast.'

'The Baltic?' Corie's geography wasn't of the best, but she did seem to recall that the Baltic was somewhere around Norway and Sweden. Nothing in the official itinerary took them so far north.

She waited for Drew to speak, but she could sense that he was shaking his head in the dimness of the darkroom.

'We could ask to go to Rostock,' she suggested.

'Why on earth should we? It's a not-very-big seaport in what used to be Mecklenburg-Schwerin. I think its only claim to fame is that it was the home of the Heinkel aeroplane.'

She paused to think. She wished she'd had a better education so that the place names he mentioned might mean something to her. 'Mecklenburg-Schwerin . . . What sort of a province is that? Could I ask to visit a factory, or a shipyard . . . ?'

'Mecklenburg . . . It's mainly agricultural, I think . . . Potatoes, sugar-beet, stuff like that.'

'I could say I'd like to do some landscapes.'

'I don't think that would be very convincing, sweetheart, especially in February. It's flat and swampy, I think. Kind of dismal.'

She was silent. She didn't know how to help.

After a long moment Drew said, 'Collective farms.'

'What did you say?'

'Collective farms! A couple of years ago the government brought in collective farms — they said people could volunteer to join their land into big estates but it was more or less compulsory. Uncle Berne had to put his farm near Leipzig into the scheme. I'm pretty sure Mecklenburg is one of the areas with big collectives. How would you like to go and photograph the workers on a collective farm?'

'I've nothing against it,' she said, eager to fall in with any possible plan. 'It might really interest the *Globe* — the Features editor wanted something about the standard of living.'

'We'll have to go a bit carefully. We don't want to express a lot of interest in the idea and get taken off to some showplace in Saxony. We want to go north, to Mecklenburg or anywhere in the general direction of Rostock.'

'Tell me something about the district that would make it appeal to me as a photographer,' she suggested. She was hanging strips of film up to dry as she spoke.

'Mecklenburg . . . I've never been there . . . Life's a bit hard there, always has been, I think. It's got lakes, with a lot of wild ducks, and there's a cathedral — that's in the provincial capital, Schwerin . . . I don't really know, Corie.'

A sound outside in the hotel garage alarmed them. They fell silent. But it was only a car being driven out at the request of one of the guests. Nevertheless, uneasy, they said goodnight after a hasty kiss, and made a good show of carrying in fresh supplies of film when they went indoors.

In the event, it wasn't the least bit difficult to get Herr

Verbermends to take them to Mecklenburg. He thought it was his own idea.

The weather continued bitterly cold. Verbermends remarked that it made life difficult for the food situation because the root crops – potatoes, turnips – were frozen in the clamps. Corie spoke nostalgically of the warmth and fertility of Cuba. Verbermends smiled and patted Corie's hand. He approved of Cuba, a pro-Communistic country. Corie talked about the sugar cane, about the hardship she'd seen among the cane-cutters and the pictures she'd taken there.

'Ah, here in the GDR we make our sugar from beet. We have always been in the forefront of sugar production. It might interest you to see how it is produced in Europe – a great contrast to the bad things you saw in Cuba before the Revolution, for our beet is grown on cooperative farms.'

'Cooperative farms,' Corie echoed, 'really, how interesting! Those would be very big, very efficient?'

'Of course, of course. Only two years ago, our government put into operation a plan to increase farming efficiency so that now output is increasing all the time.'

That being so, Corie thought privately, why are sugar and butter rationed? And why is there a queue standing outside every butcher's? But aloud she said, 'I'd love to take some photographs of the sugar industry. I did this in Cuba, you know – the Batistá government flew a group of us to–'

'Alas, we could not arrange air transport. But certainly if it would interest you, Fräulein, I could take you to see–'

'How kind you are, Herr Verbermends! Nothing is too much trouble to you.'

'But that is why I am here, Fräulein, to take trouble on your account. Now, where shall we go to see a farm which produces sugar-beet for processing?'

'Where are the factories? Near Berlin?'

'Not at all, Fräulein Duggan,' cried Verbermends, laughing and patting her again for her innocence.

'Near Leipzig? We're going to Leipzig tomorrow, aren't we?'

'No, there is nothing very impressive of that kind near Leipzig. I think one would have to go to the north to see the beet-fields and the factories. Perhaps to Schwerin or Neubrandenburg . . .'

'Schwerin . . . I think I've heard of Schwerin,' Corie said, fluttering her eyelashes at him. 'Isn't there a famous old cathedral?'

'Oh, as to that, there are many cathedrals in the GDR. Our government preserves all historic sites.'

'They do excellent work. But my real interest is in the daily life of the people, how they earn their living. I believe it would be a good idea to follow an industry through from beginning to end – from the growing of the beet to the sugar in the coffee cup. Would that be possible? Or is it too difficult for you to put Mecklenburg into our plan of action?'

'Dear lady, leave it to me,' cried Verbermends, piqued at the idea of anything being too difficult for him. 'I have friends in the Ministry of Agriculture who would be only too delighted . . . I believe there is a large new cooperative north of Schwerin . . . I will arrange it.'

Off he went, a self-satisfied smile on his chubby face.

'Have you ever thought of joining the diplomatic service?' Drew murmured, smothering a grin behind his hand.

It took a couple of days to arrange the trip to the north of the GDR, but in the meantime there was plenty to occupy them. They went to Leipzig, and by means of complicated arrangements through callboxes, Drew was able to speak to his uncle who was waiting at a public phone in his farming village.

'He's got no recent news of Werner. The last he heard, he was lying low near Rostock. I've got the name and telephone number of a guy who might be able to tell me more if we get to Schwerin.'

'All we've been able to manage is to make a trip to the north, probably Schwerin. How are we actually going to get to Rostock?'

'Aha,' said Drew, with a smile of triumph. 'You were asked to get pix of some of the skating stars?'

'Yes.'

'Well, Katja Lunser trains at the ice-rink in Rostock.'

'How did you find that out?' she asked, amazed.

'I got it by chatting to the chambermaid when she came to make my bed this morning. "We might be going north," I said, "does anybody interesting live up near the Baltic?" Her face lit up. She adores Katja Lunser.'

Herr Verbermends announced success in organising the trip to Schwerin. He would be unable to accompany them, unfortunately; he had official correspondence to attend to in Berlin which would take most of the day, but he would travel by train to join them in Schwerin the day after their arrival. All was arranged for them. They had only to present themselves at Der Goldene Hirsch in the city centre and they would find rooms awaiting them. He would take them to the cooperative farm. They would spend two days on the sugar-beet project. Certainly he could arrange for Fräulein Duggan to interview Katja Lunser at some point during the trip.

To drive north out of Leipzig with no watchful escort hovering nearby in a Lada should have been a pleasure. But troops, both East German and Russian, were more in evidence in the sombre, winter-locked landscape. Their presence was quite blatant. They moved about in armed troop-carriers and carried arms. Corie shivered at the thought that Verbermends, whom she'd manipulated with a few feminine wiles, was the representative of this naked power.

Schwerin proved to be on the southern shore of Lake Schwerin, which meant that it was even colder than Berlin because of the bitter wind blowing off the icy water. The city itself was rather plain, grey under a grey sky, but not without charm of a sedate kind. There was less traffic in the streets than in Berlin or Leipzig, and the people seemed rather more workworn. But the welcome at the Golden

Hart was cheerful, there was a log fire burning in the big stone hearth in the lounge and, even though the coffee tasted as if it was made from roasted barley, it was hot and reviving.

Corie unpacked while Drew went out to find a public callbox. When they met for the evening meal his narrow face was tight with frustration. 'I got through and the guy put the phone down on me when I told him what I wanted.'

'Why would he do that?'

'Who knows? Thinks his phone is tapped, maybe, or that I was somebody from the Vopo trying to trap him.'

'Will you ring him again?'

'I don't know whether I ought to. It might be putting him in danger.'

They ate their food with an absent-mindedness that positively hurt the waiter. 'Is anything wrong, sir?' he asked Drew. 'It is very good duck, this district is famous for the wild duck.'

'Thank you, yes, it's very good,' Drew said.

'The wine? Does the wine please you?'

'What's he saying?' Corie asked.

'He's disappointed that we don't take more interest in the meal.'

'Oh, I'm sorry,' she said, smiling up at the waiter, who brightened. 'Tell him we're worried about business, we're here on business.'

When this was conveyed, the waiter inquired what sort of business they were in and on hearing Corie was a photographer asked if they were going to photograph the hotel. 'It's an old building, *mein Herr*, it dates from 1481. The cathedral too – very old, well worth photographing.'

He withdrew, reassured that there was nothing wrong with the roast duck and pickled apple. Corie said, 'He's right. We should get out tomorrow while we're still free of Verbermends and walk about taking pix. We could arrange to be in the street where this phone contact lives, and perhaps get a word with him.'

'But we don't know his address.'

'We know his name and he's on the phone. His address will be in the phone book.'

'Corie, what would I do without you?' Drew asked and, picking up her hand, implanted a kiss in its palm.

Next day was bitterly cold and bright. They set out as soon as it was light, dutifully photographed the hotel, the cathedral, and some of the old merchants' houses in the city centre.

They had made sure they were fairly conspicuous, hung about with cameras and camera bags, Drew carrying the folding tripod over his shoulder. Corie was wearing dark blue cord trousers, a bright blue padded jacket made in Switzerland, and a blue woollen scarf bound around her head to keep her ears warm. Women paused as they walked by to look at her – her clothes, her air of casual elegance, her confidence.

She made a point of talking quite loudly to Drew in English. They attracted attention wherever they chose to stop.

In Pernuckenstrasse, outside the address of Friedrich Ollertrud, a little crowd collected to watch them set up for a photographic session. The street was quite ordinary, with blocks of flats along either side, but there was a view of Lake Schwerin at the end which made it interesting.

They had arranged to be there at about the time when the shops closed and the people of Schwerin headed home for the midday meal. They could only hope that Herr Ollertrud didn't work in a factory with a canteen offering subsidised food.

Luck was with them. At about ten minutes after one, a young man came trudging up the street from the lakeside, his shoulders hunched against the cold in an old sheepskin jacket. He paused on seeing the group watching the photographers at work, shrugged to himself, and opened the outer door of the block of flats.

Drew crossed the pavement, went in after him as if to use the shelter to examine a piece of equipment, and saw him open the mailbox for Ollertrud.

Corie waited, sighting through her view camera at the lake. When Drew emerged, he nodded. She beckoned him. 'Could we get up on the roof of one of the blocks?' she asked loudly in English. 'The view of the lake would be much better there.'

Drew translated this to the little audience of loiterers, explaining they were on a project organised by the Ministry of Agriculture. Someone immediately darted forward: yes, perfectly possible, he lived on the top floor, he had a key to the roof, please allow him to escort the talented lady up to the roof.

Drew picked up the equipment. Corie led the way after their host, who introduced himself as Tchernin. In a few moments she was out on the asphalt roof of the block with her camera, while Drew was supposedly toiling up with the rest of the equipment.

What he did, however, was to ring the bell at Apartment Four.

For ten minutes Corie kept Mr Tchernin busy 'helping' her to take pictures of Lake Schwerin. Drew eventually joined her, explaining in embarrassment to Tchernin that he'd spilled the photographic bag on the staircase. Mr Tchernin invited them into his *Wohnung* for a glass of something warming; they drank a little very strong schnapps and then made their farewells.

'Did it work?' she asked as they made their way back to the shopping centre in search of lunch.

He nodded. 'Ollertrud's a very wary guy. I had to give him my family tree back to Adam before he was sure I really was Werner's cousin.'

'And can he put you in touch with Werner?'

'He's going to try. We'll hear in a day or two.'

Corie sighed. 'Drew . . . It's all so difficult and complex . . .'

'I know, sweetheart.'

They found a plain little café where they got a mushroom omelette and some rather tough rye bread. There was no wine, only local beer. People eyed them with curiosity, but it was clear they were already known to the inhabitants of Schwerin as mad foreign photographers authorised to behave as they liked by the government. So there were faint smiles when they held hands and drank out of each other's beer mugs.

Verbermends walked in.

Corie saw him first and was so startled she gasped. 'Drew!'

Their official minder came to the table. 'Good afternoon, may I join you?'

'Of course,' Corie said faintly.

Verbermends glanced about. Something told the proprietor that here was an important man. He hurried up. Verbermends gave his order after a cursory glance at the hand-written menu. 'Very poor food here,' he said. 'Why did you not eat at the hotel?'

'No reason. We were out and about, this was handy,' said Drew.

'Handy?'

'Convenient.'

'Ah yes. You must excuse me. I am sometimes at a loss with some little English idiom.' He took off his heavy overcoat, handed it to a waiter to hang up. He sat down, shrugged to make his tubby body comfortable, then said after a moment's thoughtful pause, 'I am also at a loss with what I saw as I walked in. I understood that you were employer and employee?'

Why, thought Corie, he's jealous!

'Oh, Emile and I are close friends,' she said. 'Friends and colleagues for years.'

'I see.'

His food came, he sampled a few mouthfuls and looked put out. It was clear he would much rather have been at the Golden Hart, eating roast duck or wild boar.

'So . . . You went out taking pictures of the city, I gather.'

'Yes, we've been at work all morning.'

'Oh, yes, it's quite the talk of the town.' He looked at

Drew. 'That is the right expression – the talk of the town?'

'Yes, very idiomatic.'

'You were in Pernuckenstrasse, I hear.'

'Oh yes. An interesting view of the lake,' Corie said.

'You should ask my advice before choosing your locations. Pernuckenstrasse has some shady characters.' He smiled. 'Shady characters – that means also "black sheep", I believe.'

'Your English is so good,' Corie said. 'But everyone here tries so hard to speak good English—'

'My English isn't so good as Herr Gustauvry's, however,' Verbermends broke in. 'I can tell his is flawless. Where did you study, *mein Herr*?'

'At Strasbourg. And of course I've lived for six years in London.'

'That must be a great help in speaking idiomatically.' He gave his attention to his stew.

Under her lashes Corie looked at Drew. His brows came together in a momentary frown. He too was worried. Verbermends was angry with them – that couldn't be good.

The waiter came to ask if they would take coffee. Verbermends pushed away his plate, and ordered coffee for all of them. Corie began chatting about problems with the light, wondering if she should use flash when they resumed this afternoon. Verbermends played a part in the conversation but showed none of his usual indulgent warmth towards her.

The coffee was poor, but Corie drank it with relief in the hope that it meant they could soon leave the café. There was something strange about sitting in this workaday little place yet feeling they were somehow in danger.

When the waiter came with the bill, Verbermends took charge of it. Corie and Drew went out. They waited on the pavement for him, turned away from the door, busy with camera equipment so that he wouldn't see them speak to each other.

'Is it just that he's annoyed because he thinks we're more

than friends, or is it Pernuckenstrasse that's bothering him?' Drew muttered.

'Jealousy comes into it,' she told him. 'I don't know what he had in mind for later but he's been holding my hand and patting me quite a lot.'

'Fat little toad,' he grunted.

Herr Verbermends joined them. 'What are your plans for this afternoon?'

'I hear they make furniture here. It would be nice to get some shots of that.'

'That would need some prior arrangement, I'm afraid.'

'Of course. Now that you're here, Herr Verbermends, perhaps you'd like to suggest a good location?'

'We will go to the town hall. There are some old documents about the struggle of the peasants against the Margraves . . .'

It wasn't the least bit photogenic, but Corie didn't protest. They fell into step with him.

'What was that you called Herr Gustauvry when I came into the café?' he inquired as he walked at Corie's side.

'What?' said Corie. 'I don't remember.'

'I think you said "Dru". Is it a name?'

Corie was speechless.

'Ah, that . . .' said Drew. 'It's my nickname.'

'Really? And where does it come from?'

'It's from my reputation as a worker,' Drew said. 'I was always reliable when it came to getting the prints made – if I was asked I always replied, "*Druckfertig*", ready for the press. So years ago my colleagues started called me Drucki and then Dru, and it's stuck with me. Of course my English friends have no idea where it sprang from.'

'I see,' said Herr Verbermends.

The afternoon was uncomfortable. Verbermends seemed only partly mollified. They returned to the Golden Hart in time for afternoon tea, which wasn't on a par with the tea served at the Adlon but somehow cheered Corie. At dinner Verbermends laid out the plan for the next day's visit to the cooperative farm. He was brisk, businesslike, with none of the little genialities towards Corie that they'd become accustomed to.

As they parted in the hotel corridor that night, Corie said, 'Do you think anything's really wrong?'

'Who knows? Maybe he had a bad day at the office yesterday. Maybe he's suspicious because we went to Pernuckenstrasse where, it seems, a known undesirable lives. Maybe he's just annoyed because he caught me holding your hand.'

'That was clever about your name, Drew!'

'I hope it satisfied him. He's only got to ask someone to look into your file—'

'My file!'

'Of course they've got a file on you. They wouldn't invite anyone into the country without having background information. And if the file shows you've been friendly with an American called Drew Richter for years . . .'

'Oh, God, what a fool I've been. You were right, Drew – I shouldn't have come. I've put you in danger.'

'No, no.' He almost took her in his arms, but there was always the risk of a passing guest or servant. 'We're not in danger, all that's happened is that our minder's in a bad mood. Let's just be sweet to him tomorrow and hope everything goes back to normal.'

Next morning in the silvery light of the rising winter sun, Corie was out in the courtyard putting her cameras into the Caravette when Drew came out to join her. He put his arms around her, swung her around, and cried boisterously, 'Here we go for another day's work!'

'Drew!' Corie exclaimed in surprise, struggling to be free and trying to protect her precious Leica.

'Isn't it a wonderful day?' carolled Drew. 'Sun's going to shine!' Then into her ear, very softly, he said, 'Take care what you say today while we're travelling. I think they've bugged the camper.'

Chapter Thirty

Her first reaction was a surge of sheer panic.

Almost at once it was washed away in a wave of anger. How dare they! How dare they invade her privacy, eavesdrop on her conversations, oversee her conduct!

Her face burning, she shoved herself free of Drew. She was so angry she wanted to hit someone − but she couldn't hit Drew. She clenched her fist and hit the side panel of the camper.

'Rotten, isn't it?' he murmured, strolling a yard or two away from the van.

'Are you sure about this?' she asked, following his lead.

'Pretty sure. I got hardly any sleep last night, I was hoping some message might come from Ollertrud. Around two I heard someone crossing the courtyard − not a usual thing in a provincial town like this where they roll up the pavements at ten. I looked out of the window and there was this guy with tools opening the door of the camper. He fiddled about inside for a minute or two then closed the door and walked off.'

Now anger had receded, and she was able to think. 'That's serious, isn't it? It means they suspect something.'

'It might mean that. On the other hand it might just be Verbermends using his political pull to snoop on us.'

'I hate him,' Corie said forcefully.

'Don't say that while we're in the van, honey.'

Verbermends himself arrived a few minutes later, overcoated and bearing his briefcase as ever. He looked less resentful than on the previous day, perhaps because he felt he'd gained the upper hand again.

'Ready to go?' he inquired. 'I will lead the way in case you can't follow the map.'

601

'Thank you,' said Corie, and summoned up all her actress training to give him a beaming smile.

He had commandeered an official car from some local government depot. He clambered in, started the engine. Drew opened the door of the Caravette for Corie.

'These things don't have much range,' he murmured. 'He'll have to stay not more than about a mile from us if he's to hear anything.'

'But we've got to stay close or we might miss the way.'

'Right. So mind your p's and q's.'

Verbermends drove sedately out of the hotel courtyard in his Wartburg. Corie drove after him.

The sun was still very low in the sky. Though the shadows were long, the light was extraordinarily clear and silvery. Corie longed to be out on foot with her camera, catching the sheen on the hide of a grazing horse, the glitter of the spokes of a passing bicycle.

'Are we going to do portrait studies of Miss Lunser?' Drew asked. 'Or action shots?'

'Both, I hope. Which reminds me, *Europe Day* asked for transparencies and I've run out of film so we'll have to stop somewhere in the next day or so and buy some.'

'Agfachrome CT 18,' Drew suggested.

'If we can get it so far from civilization,' she said, with a momentary glance around the front of the camper as if looking for the transmitter.

Drew laughed then changed it to a cough. He shook his head at her in reproach. She shrugged. She'd be careful what she said, but not too careful.

A drive of about forty miles brought them to a large signboard in German. Verbermends was waiting at the turning, signalling to go to the right down a minor road.

'What does the board say?' Corie asked.

'Workers' Joy Cooperative Farm.'

Corie laughed. 'Someone has a sense of humour!' she whispered.

The headquarters of Workers' Joy was in the village of Strenghal. The chairman of the cooperative hurried out to greet them. He shook hands with Herr Verbermends, shook hands with Drew, bowed and shook hands with Corie. He had under his arm a brochure about his farm, and a schedule for their visit. 'First of course a cup of coffee. Then at nine-thirty we are expected in the barns so that you can see the beet in store. Then at ten we shall go out into the fields so that you can see some of the crop growing – normally there is no beet still in the fields at this time of year but because of problems with tractor fuel . . .'

It was a truly dreadful day. They trudged around the village to be shown this and that. Corie's cameras were in use all the time, but were not directed at the subjects being pointed out to her. Instead she chose to picture a pretty aproned girl throwing scraps to the pigs, sides of meat being transported in an open flat-bed wagon with no protection, an old lady carrying a bucket of coal into her cottage.

Lunch was taken on the dot of midday, in the kitchen of one of the farms. Corie ate little but – with consent from those sitting at the table – moved about, constantly catching details of the scene.

Everything was scrupulously clean, but there were bent forks and mismatched crockery, workworn hands and frayed jerseys, a joyless air instead of busy chatter.

The afternoon plan had to be abandoned after a short time. Snow began to fall, the light was very poor.

'We might as well go now to the sugar-beet factory,' said Verbermends in a rather peremptory tone. 'I intended to start there tomorrow but since we are hampered here by the weather, we should not waste time. I will telephone.'

He went into the office of the farm chairman. A leader of one of the work teams, known as a brigadier, approached them. 'Have you enjoyed your visit?' he inquired in English.

Corie gave a smile of surprise. 'Oh, you speak English!'

'I was a prisoner-of-war in England for two years. I worked on a farm in Yorkshire. A good life, I was lucky.'

'Why didn't you come up earlier and speak to us—'

'Fräulein, nowadays it's best not to seem talented.'

'I'm sorry,' Corie said, holding out her hand.

He backed off. 'No, someone might report it.'

'Of course.'

He shrugged. 'I'm like a lot of the others, *ein Rettig*.'

'What does that mean?'

Drew laughed. 'A radish?'

'*Ja*, a Red on the outside, white on the inside. But I'm good with the stock so they leave me alone.'

Verbermends appeared, turning up his collar against the insistent snow. '*Das stimmt*,' he said. 'Come along, Fräulein, useless to stand here getting cold.'

He led the way to their vehicles. As they reached his car he paused to say, 'What was *Abteilungsführer* Greinigen saying to make you laugh?'

Corie was too taken aback to reply. Drew said, 'A joke about milk production, *mein Herr* – I didn't really think it was funny, did you, Corie?'

'Hah,' said Verbermends, 'Greinigen is too apt to make jokes about the farm and its methods. He was one of the last to bring his land into the scheme. You should pay no attention to him.'

'Of course,' said Corie rather faintly.

They followed Verbermends in his Wartburg to a larger village some ten miles off. The sugar-making factory was on the outskirts, making itself known by the sweet smell hanging over it. In some ways it was the exact opposite of the cane-processing factory she'd been taken to in Cuba – there everything had been lush and green, here all was sombre: an icy landscape, a sky like gunmetal.

Yet there was a similarity – the same pretence that everyone loved the conditions under which they lived. They were greeted by the factory manager, in a serge suit and a stiff collar, bowing and making large gestures of welcome. He spoke fair English in which he delivered a list of statistics, factory norms, excellence of achievement, social activities for the workers.

Drew brought in the camera bag. As always Corie tried to get her shots using available light, but the sky outside was so dark, the factory so gloomy, that after about a quarter of an hour of wasted time she gave up.

'Go out and get my flashgun, Drew.'

'Right away.'

He went back past the crushing machine and through the big shed where the beet was piled ready to be shovelled into the crusher. The parking lot was a piece of rough ground on which beet had been tipped ready to take inside by wheelbarrow. Men were trudging in and out wheeling loads.

Corie waited, trying to assess what to take. There were both men and women in coarse cotton overalls. The noise from the machine was overpowering, the smell of the glucose nauseating. It seemed a very long time before Drew came back with the flash equipment.

When he handed it to her, he pressed her hand. She shot him a quick glance. He gave her the very slightest of nods.

Something had happened, something helpful. She was buoyed up by this through the rest of the noisy, sticky, depressing visit. Thankfully they accepted yet more bad coffee in the manager's office, offered thanks and goodbyes, and drove away at last into the coming night of the Baltic landscape.

'A long, miserable day,' Drew muttered as they turned into the main road. 'Let's have some music.' He switched on the radio, was rewarded with static, but tuned along the dial until he found an orchestra playing thirties-style dance music.

Under cover of the sound he said, 'Those guys who push the barrows are an interesting lot.'

'Really?'

'Had a few words with one of them. Young fellow, recently moved to the district.'

Corie looked at him. Her lips silently formed the name, 'Werner?'

Drew nodded.

'But that's—' she broke off. She'd been going to say,

'That's wonderful.' Instead she said, 'That's not surprising, men have to go where the work is. Is he going to stay around?'

'Who knows. We didn't talk for long, you were waiting for your flashgun.'

They fell silent. The radio was giving them a foxtrot with a heavy hand on the drums.

'We ought to talk about the cataloguing. You took some shots today that I didn't note down,' said Drew.

'I wrote them in my notebook. We can sort it out this evening after dinner.'

What they were doing was giving a reason for having a talk together. Certainly they needed to talk if Drew had contacted Werner.

They completed the rest of the journey to Schwerin in silence except for the heavy beat of the dance music which, they hoped, had prevented their conversation being clear to Verbermends in his Wartburg.

At dinner their escort was as usual more interested in the food than anything else. The main course was an excellent cutlet of sturgeon which certainly deserved respect. When coffee was being served he said with a faint air of knowingness, 'You didn't enjoy today?'

'What makes you say that?' Corie asked, surprised. Then almost at once she remembered that before he turned on the radio Drew had remarked they'd had a miserable day. So he really was eavesdropping on what they said in the mobile camper. She had to clench her hands on her napkin not to burst out in reproach.

'I think you seem a little low in spirits,' Verbermends said. 'To cheer us up, shall we have a liqueur?'

'No, thank you.'

'In this district they make a very good cherry brandy. I recommend it.'

'No thank you,' said Corie, longing to get up and walk out on him. 'In fact, if you don't mind, I think I'll go upstairs. I've got a headache from the noise at the refinery. Emile, when you've finished your meal, come to my room with the catalogue. I don't want to get in a muddle with the lists.'

'Very well, Corie,' he answered, then turned to their escort. 'I'll take you up on that liqueur, if you don't mind, *mein Herr*.'

'Of course,' Verbermends said sourly. It wasn't Drew's company he wanted.

Half an hour later Drew tapped and came in. Corie had got out the pocket notebook in which she always noted down the date, time of day, and location of her shots. Drew had the loose-leaf binder under his arm. They spread the books out on the dressing-table, sat down on the dressing-stool, kissed each other lightly on the lips, and held hands.

'This is like being on my first date,' Drew said.

'To me it's more like being in a cage. I hate this, Drew. I didn't realise how scary it would be.' She glanced about fearfully. 'Is it all right to talk here?'

'I think so. But just to be on the safe side, let's keep it quiet.' He put his arms around her so that they were cheek to cheek. 'Has its compensations, huh?'

'Oh, Drew . . .' But it was infinitely comforting to be held so close. 'What did Werner say?' she murmured.

'He's in a bad state, poor guy. Friends give him an occasional night's shelter, but he's been sleeping rough for nearly a month now. Ollertrud got a message to him that we were to be at the refinery, so he's been hanging around in the nearby fields. When he saw us drive in he walked in and began pushing a wheelbarrow about—'

'That was dangerous! Suppose someone had challenged him?'

'I don't think they pay too much attention to the loading gangs. He says he'll be in Rostock tomorrow.'

'We could pick him up and—'

'And then what?' Drew said with a sigh. 'Our travel visas give us permission to drive back through Helmstedt via East Berlin in three days' time. We can't take Werner from Rostock to Helmstedt in a camper with a bug in it – he can't lie silent in a cupboard for three days, Corie.'

'Could he get to the Helmstedt border? We could pick him up there.'

'I doubt it. He's pretty beat, and he's got no papers – if anyone gets suspicious of him while he's travelling, he's had it.'

'I see.'

They sat in silence for a while. Drew dropped a kiss on her cheek, and then turned her so that he could kiss her on her lips. 'Oh, honey, it's been such a long time . . .'

'I can't wait to get out of this terrible country . . .'

'First thing we'll do, we'll buy champagne and shut ourselves up in a hotel room for a week.'

They kissed again, more passionately, their longing for each other rising in intensity.

There came a peremptory knock on the door.

They sprang apart.

'What d'you bet?' Drew said and, getting up, went to open the door.

Verbermends was on the threshold.

He peered into the room. What he saw was Corie sitting at her dressing-table with notebooks spread out – perhaps perfectly innocent. But her hair was ruffled, she was flushed – to a suspicious man the signs were clear.

There was about him the hint of a little too much cherry brandy and a slight unsteadiness. All the same, he spoke with perfect enunciation. 'I thought perhaps you might not have aspirin, Fräulein.'

'Aspirin?' Corie said, at a loss.

'For your headache.'

'Oh. Yes. Thank you, Herr Verbermends. You're very considerate.' She came to the door to accept the aspirin tube.

'It grows late,' he said, looking at his watch. 'And Fräulein Corie is not well. She needs rest, Herr Gustauvry.'

'You're right,' said Drew. He turned to kiss Corie lightly on the cheek in goodnight. 'See you in the morning, sweetheart.'

'Yes, Emile.'

It was worrying. Verbermends was becoming too possessive.

Early next morning and before breakfast, Corie went out to the Volkswagen to fetch her cameras for loading. After a few minutes, Drew joined her. They walked with her camera bag away from the camper. There was no knowing if Verbermends took his receiver indoors or left it in his car. Better safe than sorry.

'I know what to do,' Drew said quietly. 'We're not going back to Helmstedt. We've got to leave East Germany via Rostock.'

'Leave it? How?' she said, puzzled.

'By sea.'

'You mean, steal a boat?' She drew away from him in alarm.

'Nothing so dramatic. We'll get our visas altered so that we can take the ferry across to Gjedser.'

'Gjedser? Where's Gjedser?'

'In Denmark.'

'Denmark? We're close to Denmark?' she asked in amazement.

'About thirty miles away across the Baltic.'

'You mean it?' She almost clasped him in her arms in gratitude. Thirty miles away — freedom!

But then her elation died. 'How are we going to get our visas altered? What reason could we give?'

'We aren't going to give a reason. We're going to have a quarrel with Verbermends and demand to go home.'

'Drew!'

'It'll work. He's on the verge of a row half the time — he's full of frustration and jealousy, all we've got to do is make him explode.'

'But . . . But . . . He's got so much power — think of the way he says "I shall have to telephone", the way people run around for him.'

'All the easier for him to get our travel papers altered. If we have to stay with him for another three days, with Werner on our minds, we might slip up. One wrong word might make him check up on you.'

'You really think they've got a file on me?'

'It's likely. But don't worry, any request by Verbermends would get low priority — after all, he's only a petty official. We ought to be able to run rings round him.' He smiled, and she saw that he knew what he was doing. 'Last night really rattled him. He came upstairs on purpose to find us up to no good, and he's furious about it. Believe me, darling, I've handled people ever since I got into the public-relations business, and Verbermends is just spoiling for a fight. So let's give him one.'

'All right,' she said fearfully. 'When?'

'Let's give it a start at breakfast. Just follow my lead.'

They went into the Golden Hart, where breakfast was being served. The smell of the harsh coffee was somewhat ameliorated by the scent of newly baked rolls. Verbermends was nowhere in sight. As they settled in their places, Drew asked the waiter about him and received an answer which made him laugh.

'What did he say?' Corie inquired.

'The waiter says the little fat man is still sleeping it off. Apparently he tied on a load last night.'

True enough, Verbermends was very late putting in an appearance. He clearly had a headache. He said with a stiff politeness, 'I apologise for not being yet ready to set off. Within half an hour, however, we shall be on our way again to the sugar factory.'

'Corie thought we'd cut that out after all,' Drew said. 'It's a dreary sort of a place and it gave her a headache.'

'But . . . but . . . I have made the arrangements.'

'Well, you'll have to un-make them.'

'Un-make . . . ? You mean alter them? But that is not convenient. The manager is expecting us.'

'Ring and tell him it's been cancelled.'

'But he is the son-in-law of a member of the town council . . .'

Drew shrugged and spread cherry jam on the last of his bread roll. Corie buried her nose in her big coffee cup.

There was something comic in the bafflement of their hitherto all-powerful guardian.

'Fräulein Duggan, you do not wish to return to the sugar refinery?' Verbermends said at last.

'Not in the least. The light's still poor, I'd have to use flash: I hate working with flash. You'd better ring and tell the manager it's off.'

Verbermends drank some coffee. For a moment she felt sorry for him. He clearly had a headache and his day was not starting well.

'It would really be better if we went. You could see the rest of the processing – you only saw a part yesterday . . .'

'But what's the use if the pix are dark and muddy?'

'Well . . . that is so, of course . . . I could explain that the conditions are not good for photography, Herr Glaser would perhaps understand. Yes,' Verbermends said, straightening his shoulders, 'after all he has to accept what I tell him because I represent the Press Department of the Ministry of Information.'

'Good for you,' said Drew.

Verbermends looked at him. 'I beg your pardon?'

'I said good for you. It's a term of approval.'

'Thank you.' But he knew the tone belied the words. 'What then shall we do instead? Would you like to do more photography in Schwerin? Go to the cathedral?'

'We did all that a couple of days ago. What d'you think, Corie?'

'I'd like to be indoors,' she said. 'I had enough yesterday of walking around in the freezing cold.'

Herr Verbermends was upset. It was the first time the charming Fräulein Duggan had spoken unkindly about any part of her time in East Germany.

'We could perhaps go again to the town hall. There are some paintings by local artists—'

'I came here to take photographs of people, not look at paintings by amateurs,' Corie broke in.

'Of course. Forgive me, I am a little at a loss.'

'What about Rostock?' Corie said. 'What's Rostock like?'

'Well, that . . . Yes, of course, we planned to go to Rostock this afternoon. Fräulein Lunser and her teacher are expecting us at the ice-rink – or perhaps,' he said with some resentment, 'you would find an ice-rink too cold also?'

'At least it doesn't actually snow at an ice-rink,' Drew said disagreeably. 'Let's settle for Katja Lunser and the ice-rink, and let's hope we can get some decent coffee there.'

Tight-lipped with anger, Verbermends got up and went out to use the telephone.

'Do you think we piled it on too much?' Corie muttered in anxiety.

'He ain't seen nothing yet,' said Drew. 'Just wait till we get to Rostock.'

They drove north-east through Mecklenburg and Moderan on a road surfaced with black ice. Occasional snowflakes drifted against the windscreen. For the first time since knowing of the transmitter hidden in the camper, they talked almost freely. They were affectionate towards each other, talked about friends in London, made plans for when they got home. The intention was to make Verbermends feel shut out and envious.

Clearly it worked, for when they got out at Rostock he was icily polite to them. They were in a sports centre of recent date, somewhat stark architecturally but impressive all the same. The *Eisbahn* had a big rink and capacious seating for the audience. Fräulein Lunser and her teacher Fräu Ralinweit were waiting for them in the café. Coffee and *Kekse* were offered – 'English shortbread,' said Fräu Ralinweit proudly, 'We bring back from Fortum *und* Mossman.'

The session with the skating star was the most enjoyable of all Corie's appointments behind the Iron Curtain. Pretty and vivacious, Katja Lunser prattled on in a manner quite different from the caution she had encountered elsewhere. Herr Verbermends translated unless, at a loss, he turned to Fräu Ralinweit for the English of a skating term.

They spent two hours at the *Eisbahn*. Then, Fräu Ralinweit scolding that now her pupil must do some serious practice, they made their farewells and went to the city centre for a late midday meal.

The hotel was the Gärtner, and clearly its reputation for good food wasn't on a par with the Golden Hart of Schwerin. Verbermends looked glumly at the menu, and was proved right when an *Eintopfgericht* consisting mainly of potato and turnip was placed before them.

He complained to the waiter, the waiter appeared to say it was the best he had to offer, Verbermends demanded something better and the waiter withdrew to speak to the cook.

'Can't understand how they can be short of meat for a stew,' remarked Drew, 'when you think of how marvellous the collective farms are supposed to be.'

'The term for the plan used in the GDR is the cooperative farm,' Verbermends corrected. 'We don't use the words "collective farm".'

'Too reminiscent of Russian failures in that line?'

'The Russians . . . Our friends the Russians . . . It has nothing to do with the Russians,' spluttered Verbermends. 'They have their methods, we have ours.'

'Well, whichever, it doesn't seem to work. Otherwise why are we offered meatless stew?'

'A temporary shortage . . . the extreme cold weather . . .'

'It's certainly cold,' said Corie, who had kept on her padded jacket even though they were in the dining-room. 'Is there no heating in this hotel?'

'A temporary shortage of heating fuel.'

'How temporary? Will the heating come on tonight? Will there be any hot water for a bath?'

'I will inquire after lunch,' Verbermends said snappily.

'If we ever get it,' said Drew. 'We've been waiting twenty minutes now. It would have been better to take that vegetable stew you sent back.'

'Herr Gustauvry, please remember that I have had to alter plans at a moment's notice,' said Verbermends in a tone of venom. 'You will agree that I have done my best—'

'This is your best?' Drew riposted. 'I never saw such a dismal effort as this trip. Hotels that look as if they haven't had a lick of paint since the war, food that's dull and tasteless, everything as cold as the Arctic—'

'I am not responsible for the weather, *mein Herr*,' snapped their escort, 'and as for the hotels and the food, the German Democratic Republic gives priority to the things that matter . . .'

'Such as what?'

'Industry, economic improvement—'

'I didn't see much "improvement" in the factories we visited in Leipzig, and that refinery yesterday was practically prehistoric. Men with barrows carting beet to the crushers—'

'In due course it will be modernised. In any case, what do you know about industry, you spend your life in the decadence of capitalist society, taking portraits of rich, idle women . . .'

'I don't take the pictures, Verbermends, I help the expert do that. And I get around—'

'Oh yes, trotting around like a servant, fetching and carrying—'

'Excuse me,' Corie intervened, 'Emile is not my servant. I told you before, he's a friend – a dear, close friend.'

'Evidently! From what I saw last night when I came to your door with aspirin—'

'Oh, so that's it,' Corie cried, 'you're setting yourself up as a judge of my behaviour! How dare you?'

'Fräulein Corie, we have standards in our society. It is not fitting that you and your employee—'

'It's none of your business!' she exclaimed, getting up. 'I'm going out to find somewhere else to have lunch. Come on, *Drew*!'

He too rose to his feet. 'Listen, my friend,' he said to Verbermends, 'when we get back to Berlin you can be sure we're going to make a complaint about the way you've behaved!'

They stalked out of the hotel together, drawing startled

glances from the other guests. Outside, they stopped to stare at one another.

'Well, how did we do?' Corie asked.

'Poor little guy,' Drew said. 'He's sitting there now wondering what hit him.'

'What happens now?'

'Let him sit and stew, while we find somewhere else to eat.'

They found a restaurant in the same street which provided a stew almost identical to the one in the Gärtner. They took their time, and when in the end they strolled back into the hotel, it was almost four in the afternoon. Verbermends was in the lounge waiting for them.

'I apologise,' he said stiffly. 'I should not have said what I did. I can only say I am not quite myself today.'

'Too much drink last night,' Drew remarked in a neutral tone.

Verbermends went red. 'I did not have too much to drink.'

'Oh no? That looked very much like a hangover when you staggered in to breakfast this morning. What do you do, put it on the expense account and claim we did the drinking?'

'Herr Gustauvry, I must remind you that we still have some days of our tour to go, and we must somehow manage to be on good term—'

'I don't think so,' Corie said.

'I beg your pardon?'

'I don't think I want to go on with this tour. It would be most uncomfortable. You were quite disparaging about my morals – I can't believe I'll be happy finishing this tour with you as my escort.'

'Perhaps,' Drew suggested with apparent innocence, 'we could telephone your superiors in Berlin and ask for a replacement?'

The angry red in Verbermends cheeks paled to an ashen white. 'No, that would not be a good idea,' he croaked.

'I certainly don't want to go on in the company of a man who takes it upon himself—'

'Fräulein Corie, please – one moment – I apologised . . .'

'So you should. And in any case, you needn't pretend to be so shocked because Emile and I were having a kiss or two last night. You know very well you've been nudging and patting me almost ever since we met.'

'Fräulein!'

'And let me tell you, it's shocked me! It happens a lot in London and Paris, but here where women are regarded as equals and comrades, I expected better,' Corie said, giving a performance that would have got her a role at any audition. 'I put up with it because I didn't want to make problems on this tour, but the way I feel now I'd just like to drop the whole thing and go home.'

'Let's throw the stuff in the camper and head back to Berlin,' Drew suggested. 'If anyone asks us why we cut the trip short we can just say we had a disagreement with our guide – you wouldn't say anything about the way he's been pawing you, would you, Corie?'

Verbermends made a great effort. He said in placatory tones, 'If you really feel you wish to cut the tour short, I . . . I . . . I accept that. We can leave in the morning.'

'And drive all the way back on those damned icy roads,' groaned Drew.

'I wish we'd never come so far north. It's a long drive back and the landscape isn't inviting. It's a pity we have to go back via Berlin at all – I got all the shots of Berlin in the first few days.'

They stood in silence in the draughty hotel lobby. The desk-clerk looked at them with curiosity.

'There is another way, Fräulein,' Verbermends said.

'What do you mean?'

'If you really wish to end your tour and go home—'

'I certainly do!'

'You could take the ferry.'

'What ferry?'

'Rostock is a seaport. There is a ferry to Copenhagen.'

She looked at Drew. 'What do you think?' she asked.

'I always get sea-sick.'

'Oh, it's not far, Herr Gustauvry. Only about an hour and a half on the steamer.'

'Well, that's not too long . . .'

'Let's do it, Emile.'

'Whatever you say, Corie.'

'But what about our travel documents?' she wondered, opening her handbag and beginning to rummage for them.

'Leave it to me,' said Verbermends, recovering control of the situation. 'I will telephone.'

When they met again at dinner that evening he was able to tell them that documents permitting them to leave East Germany by the Rostock to Gjedser ferry would be awaiting them at the town hall by ten the next morning. The Gjedser ferry left the docks at two in the afternoon; they would be in Denmark by four-thirty, allowing for the east wind and tide.

Corie sent Drew out later in search of photographic magazines to take home. The real reason was so that he could seek out his cousin at the rendezvous he had arranged during their short talk at the refinery.

Next day, after an early lunch, they set off behind Verbermends's Wartburg to be conducted to the quay. Corie allowed the distance between them to widen to almost quarter of a mile – there was no danger of losing the way because traffic signs advertised '*Hafen*'. When the Wartburg was safely round a curve ahead. Drew reached under the seat, found the bug, and threw it out of the window.

They pulled up in front of a warehouse for agricultural vehicles. From the shelter of a doorway stepped a ragged figure. Drew opened the back of the Caravette, Werner clambered in, the door was closed upon him and they were off again.

On arrival at the ferry wharf they said a very formal farewell to Herr Verbermends. His chubby features were strained into a polite smile. 'Thank you for taking an interest in the GDR,' he said. 'I hope you have taken some good photographs.'

'The photographs are fine,' she said, almost sorry for him. 'I shall write to thank the Press Office.'

'Could you perhaps say the tour was curtailed because of the cold weather?' he ventured.

She could tell his career might suffer if no good reason was given for the curtailment. 'I shall say I wished to get home to my younger sister, whose first baby is expected any day now.'

'Thank you, Fräulein,' he said with fervour. '*Gute Reisen.*'

'Goodbye, *mein Herr.*'

Although her heart beat fast when the customs official examined their documents, it seemed no one dreamed of doubting them or searching the vehicle. A cursory glance through the open back door was all that was given.

Once the ferry was well out on the Baltic, Drew went to help his cousin Werner out of the cupboard in which he'd been lying for just over an hour.

The young man, whom Corie had never even met, scrambled out, stretching and wincing.

'Not a very comfortable method of travel,' he said. 'But effective.'

He and Drew hugged each other, slapped each other on the back.

Then the scarecrow figure turned to Corie.

'Well, Fräulein Corie,' he said, 'I don't normally kiss strangers, but here I make an exception.'

He threw his arms about her, kissed her heartily so that his unshaven chin rasped her face, and danced her about in triumph.

Over his shoulder Corie caught Drew's eye. He was smiling at her with a mixture of relief, admiration and love that turned her heart over.

Chapter Thirty-one

The Danish customs officials were quite unsurprised when Werner presented himself without a passport or travel documents. He was by no means the first refugee they had seen from East Germany.

It had been agreed between them that Werner would say he had stowed away in Corie's camper without her knowledge. Otherwise they would have to explain why they were helping him, which might mean bringing out the fact that Drew and Werner were cousins, and that Drew's passport was a fake. The reverberations for the White House might not have been desirable. It was easier if Werner seemed on his own.

He was led away, uncomplaining, to a detention centre to be held while the Danes looked into his case. It hurt Corie to see him go, but Werner was blowing kisses at her as he went.

'We've got to do something, Drew,' she said as they set off for Copenhagen. 'It's horrible that he's got out to so-called freedom and ends up under detention.'

Drew sighed and shrugged. 'If we'd gone out through Helmstedt we could have handed him straight over to the West Germans who've a committee set up to deal quickly with refugees. But Denmark's different. And I can't do anything through my contacts. Don't forget, the White House told me to stay out of Werner's affairs.'

They discussed it off and on through the drive to Copenhagen. Once settled in their hotel, Corie sat down with the telephone.

The housekeeper at Helen Holstead's home in up-state New York informed her that Mrs Holstead was in New York for the opera. She declined to give her the New York telephone number, but that didn't matter as Drew was able to recall it from memory. The phone at the New York apartment was answered by Donna, the social secretary, who began rather coldly but warmed a little when Corie announced herself. 'Miss Duggan – of course I remember you. How are you?'

'I'm well,' Corie said, 'but I'm calling from Copenhagen so I wonder if I could speak—'

'Copenhagen! Just a moment, Mrs Holstead was just about to go out to a charity committee, but I'll tell her you're on the line.'

A moment later Helen Holstead's cheerful voice came through loud and clear. 'Corie Duggan! What are you doing in Copenhagen? Travel brochure pix again?'

'Nothing like that, Helen. I've just come out of East Germany—'

'East Germany!'

'Yes, and Helen, I brought someone with me. Are you listening, Helen? This person is a relative of a good friend of ours—'

'I'm not following you, Corie.'

'I don't want to say too much on the telephone. You remember our friend who worked on the election campaign and went on to a job among the top men?'

A momentary pause. 'I'm with you so far,' Helen said.

'He has a cousin. You recall hearing about the cousin?'

'Oh, sure – of course. Drew was worried – I mean our friend was worried—' Helen broke off and there was a longer pause. Then she said in something like awe, 'Corie Duggan, you're not saying you've brought the *cousin* out of . . .' Her voice trailed away. 'Jumping Jehosaphat!' she breathed.

'That's what I'm saying, Helen.'

'Yeah,' said Helen. 'So why are you calling me?'

'This young man's in a detention centre now. Of course the Danes are being absolutely kind and nice to him and he's perfectly safe, but somehow . . . It seems wrong . . . If you could have seen him, Helen, he was like a scarecrow, he'd been on the run for about six weeks.' She was forgetting her super caution about tapped telephone lines as she warmed to her subject. 'We're in Copenhagen at the moment but we've got to get home − at least, *I'd* like to, my kid sister's having her first baby and I'd like to—'

'Who's "we"?' Helen interrupted. 'Someone was with you on this rescue trip? Someone *special*?'

'Well, yes ... But he's doing this on his own time, he was warned off by the big boys because they said it might turn out to be embarrassing for them.'

'Huh!' It was a grunt of contempt. 'Typical!'

'What we wondered was, could you do anything for our young man in the detention centre? You've got so many important friends, I thought perhaps you could get someone to put in a word.'

'Aha!' said Helen, and Corie could almost hear the wheels spinning. 'Denmark ... I know someone in last year's trade delegation about farm prices ... Then who else? Well, good heavens, the soprano I'm going to hear tonight is from Copenhagen originally, and considering the donations I make to the Metropolitan Opera ... Leave it with me, honey. I'll see what I can do.'

'Oh, thank you, Helen, thank you!'

'And now let me have a word with your travelling companion.'

Corie handed the phone to Drew. He said, 'Hello, Helen?' and then fell silent as he received a lecture from the other end. All he said was 'Yes, Helen,' and 'Of course, Helen,' until at last he hung up.

'She's annoyed with me.'

'Because you might have embarrassed the government?'

'No, because I didn't let her in on it beforehand.' He laughed. 'With friends like Helen, who needs the CIA?'

Within twenty-four hours, Werner Richter was released from the detention centre under the auspices of the West German ambassador. Drew provided a room in their hotel, a set of new clothes, and funds obtained through a transfer from his bank account in Washington. A West German passport would be issued before the end of the month.

'What will you do after that?' Corie asked him.

'First I have to get word to my parents that I'm safe and sound,' he said. 'Then I go to West Berlin, of course, to work at getting others out. In the meantime, I shall eat. I intend to eat four meals a day for the rest of my life.'

Corie had meanwhile telephoned home, to be greeted with the news that she was now the proud aunt of Robert Clark Davis, seven pounds four ounces, doing well, as was his happy mother.

'I must get back,' Corie said to Drew wistfully. 'I'm dying to see them.'

'No reason why we shouldn't go. Werner doesn't need us — you can see all he needs is a few more days of decent food and rest and he'll be his old self.'

'So we could leave now?'

'Why not?'

'Let's fly home, Drew! Going back by the car ferry would mean at least another day—'

'What will you do with Old Faithful?' He meant the Volkswagen Caravette.

'Let's give him to charity.'

They reached London on a wet, blustery March day. On the way to Stamford Street, Drew stopped the taxi to buy two bottles of champagne. 'You remember our plan?' he inquired with a mischievous grin as he got back in the taxi.

They were still in bed at midday the next day when Corie's doorbell rang. Drowsily she lifted her head.

'Pay no attention and they'll go away,' Drew murmured.

But the caller wasn't to be discouraged. He kept his finger on the buzzer so that in the end she had to drag herself up, struggle into a dressing-gown, and go to the door.

On the doorstep stood Ingram Holstead.

'Why don't you answer your phone?' he demanded, barging past her. 'I've been ringing you for hours!'

'I took the phone off the hook . . .'

'My God, you look as if you've been dragged through a hedge backwards!'

It was very likely true. Her hair was in a tangle, there was sleep-dust under her eyelids, she was barefoot. He surveyed her with cynical black eyes, but then a light gleamed in them, a reawakened interest.

'You like to talk about "hidden beauty",' he grunted. 'There must be something in it. Even in your present state you've got something . . .'

'Ingram, would you please turn around and go?'

'Get yourself dressed and made up, I want you to come straight back with me to the *Globe*.'

'What on earth for?' she protested, trying to gather her wits.

'To dictate a story, of course. I'm putting it on the front page . . .'

'What, with pictures of collective farmers and factory workers?'

'Nonsense! Collective farms? I want the real story.'

'Ingram,' she objected, 'I went to East Germany to get pictures and your Features editor asked for—'

'Never mind the rubbish you fed Mack, I want the truth. *And* I want pix of this man you brought out with you.'

'What are you talking about?' Now she was fully awake. At all costs she must prevent Ingram from splashing the story across the headlines. It could be dangerous for Werner and harmful to Drew's career. She pulled her dressing-gown closer about her as a defence against this aggressive male.

'I got it from Helen on the phone last night. She was full of praise about how you'd helped get some chap out.'

Corie threw up her hands in dismay. For once Helen Holstead had blundered. But perhaps it was her own fault, perhaps she should have warned her that this had to be kept under wraps.

'It's not for publication,' she said.

'The hell it isn't! You've a contract with my Features editor and I want the story.'

'I don't know what you're talking about. I went to East Germany to take pictures and I've *got* pictures, and in a day or two Mack shall have them for his feature.'

'Can we just stop beating around the bush? You got that assignment from Mack as an excuse to get into the country. I'm entitled to—'

'You're entitled to a portfolio of pix. And you'll get them. Now, as I've only just got up I'd like you to go.'

'I'm not going until I get the story,' he said, and sat down uninvited in the living-room, still in his overcoat. 'And I want a picture of the man—'

'Absolutely not!'

'So you admit there was a man?'

'I don't admit anything. You've misunderstood a piece of chit-chat.'

'I'll find out for myself in the end,' he said, leaning back and looking solid and settled, as if he were ready to stay for ever. 'You might as well tell me.'

'I'd like you to go. As you can see, I haven't started the day yet.'

'I'm not going until I hear the story. I'm on to this before anybody else in Fleet Street. Your name attached to a bit of derring-do would make a nice balance to tomorrow's story about Borg Olivier and Malta and all that boring stuff. I'm staying here until I get it.'

She shrugged. 'In that case I'll go and make some coffee. You can sit there till midnight if you like, I have nothing to tell you.'

As she walked towards the kitchen, he sprang up to seize her arm. 'Don't you dare walk out on me!' he cried, and he was genuinely angry. Some spark had been kindled when he looked at her in her dishevelled state, some remembrance of things past. 'I've had this kind of treatment from you before and I'm not going to have it again!'

The bedroom door opened. Drew emerged, tying his dressing-gown cord. 'What the devil's going on?' he asked.

Ingram Holstead gave a great gasp of surprise. He let go Corie's arm.

'Who the hell's that?' he demanded.

'It's absolutely none of your business.'

'None of my business? I walk in here and find—'

'Nobody asked you in. In fact I've asked you to go.'

'I'm not going until I get an explanation.'

'Who *is* this guy?' Drew asked in amazement.

'His name's Ingram Holstead, he owns the *Globe*—'

'Owns the *Globe*. Oh, Helen's husband.' Drew paused. 'Helen's husband? What's Helen's husband doing here, making demands as if he had special rights here?'

'You mind your own business!' Ingram roared. 'Corie and I have a very important relationship.'

'No we have not,' said Corie.

'Corie, you know you and I were more than friends . . .'

She was shaking her head vehemently. 'It was over before it started.'

'Only because you wanted it that way.'

'That ought to tell you something,' Drew put in. 'If Corie didn't want it, there never was a "relationship". So what right have you got to come slamming in here and start a shouting match?'

'You just stay out of this!'

'No, that's not possible. Drew is involved in everything I'm involved in,' Corie said.

Her tone gave him pause. He looked from one to the other and his mind took in nuances he had missed before. He had been angry, indignant — yes, of course, because he'd found another man with the woman he regarded as his own. But that had been simply the reaction of the possessive male. He'd thought he could bully his rival out of the game.

'This isn't just a one-night stand? You're claiming it's serious?' he asked in a tone of derision.

'Ingram, going in fear of your life on the other side of the Iron Curtain teaches you one thing – not to play the fool over what really matters.'

'And he matters?' Ingram pointed an unsteady finger at Drew. He tried to see this man as a rival who might win – superior to him in some way, but how?

'And vice versa,' said Drew, going to put an arm about Corie's shoulders.

She turned her head to smile up at him. Ingram made a movement that might have beeen the beginnings of a grab at her. Drew said quietly, 'Now, now, don't be foolish.' Ingram drew back. Although he was heavier and broader than Drew, he was also older and not half so fit. Perhaps this was a rival to be wary of, after all.

'Corie,' he ventured, 'I understand I've blundered in on something . . . And you feel a special bond because he . . . he's the man you got out of East Germany?'

'Nothing of the kind,' said Drew. 'The name's Drew Richter, I'm from Washington.'

'But Corie just said – she mentioned behind the Iron Curtain—'

'I was there. Let's leave it at that.'

'You mean you were part of this story about the refugee? You helped her, is that it?'

'Ingram,' Corie said, 'if you cast your mind back, you'll remember I told you once you were looking for the man I loved in the wrong place. I said you should have looked in Washington.'

Ingram frowned, trying to sort out his recollections. 'He's the man who invited you to the Inauguration? One of the campaign team? Yes . . . of course . . . Helen's talked about him . . . Drew Richter.' He shrugged and smiled in dismissal. Now he felt on firmer ground. 'But I remember what Helen said . . . I mean he's a fetcher and carrier, a nobody – in some minor job at the White House.'

'Not any more,' Drew said. 'I've decided to give up politics.' At Corie's surprised glance he nodded. 'Yes, honey, what you said about finding out what really matters – that was right. I don't think I'm cut out for the political game. When I get back I'm going to tell them I quit.'

'There you are,' Ingram said in triumph, 'a nobody – he doesn't even have a job! You must be mad to throw yourself away on him, Corie!'

For years Ingram had been able to get his way by the force of his own success, his evident power. He was sure it would win for him now. Compared with his own superior influence and eminence, this man was a nonentity.

'What I do with my life is my business,' Corie began.

'No, it isn't, it concerns me! You know how I feel about you – just seeing you again after all this time makes me realise how I've missed you! Think what I could give you, Corie! I could make you the biggest name in your profession, give you anything you wanted – fame, opportunity—'

'But I'm not running an auction to find the highest bidder, Ingram. I'm planning the rest of my life.'

'And she's going to spend it with me,' Drew said, holding her a little closer.

Ingram stood baffled, staring at them. It seemed incredible. She just didn't want what he had to offer.

After a moment Corie broke free from Drew's embrace. She came to take Ingram by the elbow and lead him into the hall.

'Goodbye, Ingram.'

'Don't . . .' He shrugged himself free. 'I don't want to go . . . Don't you understand, Corie . . . I can't just lose you like this . . . Not to *him*.'

She smiled. 'He's the one, Ingram. He's my future . . .'

'Future? He hasn't *got* a future. He just told you, he's giving up his job.'

'How can you be so silly?' she asked gently. 'I'd go with him, barefoot and in rags. I love him.'

'But what about me?' he said. He was ashamed of his pleading tone. But he couldn't help himself. 'You've always been special to me . . . I don't have anyone . . . I'm so lonely . . .'

Corie felt a pang of pity. To the outward view he had everything – fame, money, power. Yet he was lonely – she could tell it was true. He wasn't a young man any more, his family were far away across the Atlantic.

'Why don't you give Helen a ring?' she suggested.

'Helen?'

'Why not? She once told me that although you almost always ended up having a row, she loved to hear your voice on the phone.'

'Really?' He was surprised, puzzled.

She gave him a little shake. 'Grow up, Ingram. You can't go on for the rest of your life grabbing at a succession of women.'

'I don't want to. I want *you* . . .'

'No you don't. If you hadn't had a reason to come rushing here this morning you'd have got on very well without me. You would have done a hard day's work, gone out to a party or a show with friends—'

'But none of my friends means anything. Really there's no one who cares . . .'

'You've got a wife who cares and two nice children – why don't you—'

'Oh yes, go on, tell me to settle down!'

She laughed. 'I can't imagine either you or Helen ever settling down. Just ring her, Ingram. Tell her what you've just told me – that you're lonely.'

'She'd only laugh and say it served me right.'

'Well, if she does, agree with her.'

'Let her get away with putting me in the wrong?' He was still protesting loudly when she closed the door on him.

When she returned to the living-room, Drew remarked, 'I notice you didn't contradict me when I said you'd be spending the rest of your life with me.'

She went into his arms with a little laugh. 'I know a good thing when I hear it,' she said.

When they'd sealed the bargain with a kiss, he said, 'One problem.'

'What?' She was startled.

'I'm walking out on that twenty-four-hour-a-day tie up with politics. I won't have a job, but I'll get one – that'll be OK.'

'Oh, if that's all – I can get enough work to support the pair of us . . .'

'We might have to go along with that for a bit until I can get started. I thought I might go back to PR – I still have plenty of contacts. But that's not the problem. It's that troublesome family of yours – what are they going to do if I whisk you away to the States?'

'Oh, that.' She shook her head at him. 'They'll manage. Monna's got her theatrical lodgers, Lynette's got William, Opal's got her husband and baby – they'll be all right.'

Drew gave her a teasing glance. 'Seems to me Opal's set us a good example. Let's get married and start a family.'

She knew he was right. She had spent long enough trying to care for her sisters and her mother. Now it was time to think of her own happiness; to think of it not as snatched moments with the man she loved, but as a future that could stretch before her for ever.

Outside the March sky was clearing, the rainclouds were gliding apart to reveal the sun. Springtime – a spring day. Noon of the first day of her new life.

THE FINAL PATTERN

'Tessa Barclay always spins a fine yarn . . .
gripping and entertaining'
Wendy Craig

Jenny Armstrong, mistress of the thriving Corvill and Son
weaving business, returns to her native Scotland
determined to achieve prosperity and comfort for her
reunited family. But the death of her brother Ned brings
disruption and harm . . .

Once again young Heather Armstrong is caught up in her
widowed Aunt Lucy's machinations; Jenny's rekindled love
affair with her husband Ronald is threatened and
strangers lurk in doorways to spy on the Armstrongs and
their friends. Jenny uncovers a terrible secret in Lucy's past
that still demands vengeance, and there is an unknown
enemy to be reckoned with . . .

THE FINAL PATTERN is the compelling sequel to
A WEB OF DREAMS and BROKEN THREADS –
'Just what a historical novel should be' Elizabeth Longford
'Filled with fascinating historical detail and teeming with
human passions' Marie Joseph
– also available from Headline.

FICTION/SAGA   0 7472 3542 2

BROKEN THREADS

'Filled with fascinating
historical detail and
teeming with human
passions' Marie Joseph

Jenny Corvill, mistress of the Waterside Mill in Galashiels
and driving force behind the prosperous weaving concern
of Corvill & Son, is determined to relinquish the reins of
the business to her new husband and enjoy life as a young
bride. But no sooner is the honeymoon over than her plans
are disrupted – and by her own sister-in-law, Lucy.

For the pretty and frivolous Lucy the delights of life in the
Scottish Borders are severely limited and she leaps at the
chance to set up a second home in fashionable London.
Seduced by a smooth-talking playboy and headstrong
under the spell of love she plunges the Corvill family into
disaster. As a result Jenny is forced to undertake a
heartrending journey into the dens of the Victorian
underworld.

'Just what a historical novel ought to be' Elizabeth
Longford

'Tessa Barclay always spins a fine yarn. Her novels are
gripping and entertaining' Wendy Craig

From the bestselling author of the Craigallan and
Champagne series, BROKEN THREADS is a charming and
engrossing companion to A WEB OF DREAMS – also
available from Headline.

FICTION/SAGA 0 7472 3554 6

Wychwood

EVTHOMPSON

His magnificent new saga

Dolly Quilter leaps at the chance to take her son Sebastian out of the festering London slums to the household of Sir Nelson Fettiplace. The baronet's large estate on the edge of the Wychwood Forest, in the Cotswolds, seems the ideal place for Seb to regain his failing health.

But Swinbrook Manor proves a false haven, and – with the help of the Manor's head groom and his daughter, Carrie – the pair eventually find a home with the kindly farmer, Christian Timms. Here Seb grows strong and sturdy, and discovers he has a natural skill with horses. But a fateful encounter with a beautiful woman has already thrown the young man's emotions into turmoil. For Anna is a gypsy and her way of life is completely alien to Seb's own.

Torn between his romantic inclinations and pressure from his mother – who hopes he and Carrie will make a match – Seb finds himself caught up in an upheaval that goes beyond the merely personal: for the ancient forest of Wychwood is as doomed as the way of life of the gypsies who inhabit it, and Seb must take on the might of the Establishment before he can follow the dictates of his heart.

'Well researched and appealingly done...a slice of English history that is of perennial interest' *The Sunday Times*

Praise for E.V. Thompson's previous novels
'A vigorous and fascinating piece of storytelling from the pen of a first-class professional' *Sunday Telegraph*
'Romantic adventure unfolds in masterly style' *Today*
'An engrossing read' *Best*
'Excellent characters enhance a fine tale' *Liverpool Daily Post*

FICTION/SAGA   0 7472 3918 5

A selection of bestsellers from Headline